Library of America, a nonprofit organization,
champions our nation's cultural heritage
by publishing America's greatest writing in
authoritative new editions and providing resources
for readers to explore this rich, living legacy.

JOHN WILLIAMS

JOHN WILLIAMS

COLLECTED NOVELS

Butcher's Crossing
Stoner
Augustus
Related Writings

Daniel Mendelsohn, *editor*

THE LIBRARY OF AMERICA

Published in the United States by Library of America.
Visit our website at www.loa.org.

Stoner copyright © 1965, 1988 by John Williams. *Augustus* copyright ©
1972 by John Williams, copyright © 1995 by Nancy Williams. Published by
arrangement with The University of Arkansas Press.

Butcher's Crossing copyright © 1960, 1988 by John Williams. "The Western:
Definition of the Myth," copyright © 1961 by John Williams. "Fact in Fiction:
Problems for the Historical Novelist," copyright © 1973 by John Williams.
"The Future of the Novel," copyright © 1973 by John Williams. "Remarks
upon Accepting the National Book Award for *Augustus*" © 2021 by Nancy
Williams. Published by arrangement with the Estate of John Williams.

This paper exceeds the requirements of
ANSI/NISO Z39.48–1992 (Permanence of Paper).

Distributed to the trade in the United States
by Penguin Random House Inc.
and in Canada by Penguin Random House Canada Ltd.

Library of Congress Control Number: 2020952615
ISBN 978–1–59853–702–4

First Printing
The Library of America—349

Manufactured in the United States of America

Contents

Contents

BUTCHER'S CROSSING

. . . everything that has life gives sign of satisfaction, and the cattle that lie on the ground seem to have great and tranquil thoughts. These halcyons may be looked for with a little more assurance in that pure October weather which we distinguish by the name of the Indian summer. The day, immeasurably long, sleeps over the broad hills and warm wide fields. To have lived through all its sunny hours, seems longevity enough. The solitary places do not seem quite lonely. At the gates of the forest, the surprised man of the world is forced to leave his city estimates of great and small, wise and foolish. The knapsack of custom falls off his back with the first step he takes into these precincts. Here is sanctity which shames our religions, and reality which discredits our heroes. Here we find Nature to be the circumstance which dwarfs every other circumstance, and judges like a god all men that come to her.

Nature, Ralph Waldo Emerson

Aye, and poets send out the sick spirit to green pastures, like lame horses turned out unshod to the turf to renew their hoofs. A sort of yarb-doctors in their way, poets have it that for sore hearts, as for sore lungs, nature is the grand cure. But who froze to death my teamster on the prairie? And who made an idiot of Peter the Wild Boy?

The Confidence Man, Herman Melville

PART ONE

1.

THE COACH from Ellsworth to Butcher's Crossing was a dougherty that had been converted to carry passengers and small freight. Four mules pulled the cart over the ridged, uneven road that descended slightly from the level prairie into Butcher's Crossing; as the small wheels of the dougherty entered and left the ruts made by heavier wagons, the canvas-covered load lashed in the center of the cart shifted, the rolled-up canvas side curtains thumped against the hickory rods that supported the lath and canvas roof, and the single passenger at the rear of the wagon braced himself by wedging his body against the narrow sideboard; one hand was spread flat against the hard leather-covered bench and the other grasped one of the smooth hickory poles set in iron sockets attached to the sideboards. The driver, separated from his passenger by the freight that had been piled nearly as high as the roof, shouted above the snorting of the mules and the creaking of the wagon:

"Butcher's Crossing, just ahead."

The passenger nodded and leaned his head and shoulders out over the side of the wagon. Beyond the sweating rumps and bobbing ears of the mules he caught a glimpse of a few bare shacks and tents set in a cluster before a taller patch of trees. He had an instantaneous impression of color—of light dun blending into gray set off by a heavy splash of green. Then the bouncing of the wagon forced him to sit upright again. He gazed at the swaying mound of goods in front of him, blinking rapidly. He was a man in his early twenties, slightly built, with a fair skin that was beginning to redden after the day's exposure to the sun. He had removed his hat to wipe the sweat from his forehead and had not replaced it; his light brown hair, the color of Virginia tobacco, was neatly clipped, but it lay now in damp unevenly colored ringlets about his ears and forehead. He wore yellowish-brown nankeen trousers that were nearly new, the creases still faintly visible in the heavy cloth. He had earlier removed his brown sack coat, his vest, and his tie; but even in the breeze made by the dougherty's slow forward progress, his white linen shirt was spotted with sweat and hung limply on him. The blond nap of a two-day-old beard glistened with moisture; occasionally he rubbed his face with a soiled handkerchief, as if the stubble irritated his skin.

As they neared town, the road leveled and the wagon went forward more rapidly, swaying gently from side to side, so that the young man was able to relax his grasp on the hickory pole and slump forward more easily on the hard bench. The clop of the mules' feet became steady and muffled; a cloud of dust like yellow smoke rose about the wagon and billowed behind it. Above the rattle of harness, the mules' heavy breathing, the clop of their hooves, and the uneven creaking of the wagon could be heard now and then the distant shout of a human voice and the nickering of a horse. Along the side of the road bare patches appeared in the long level of prairie grass; here and there the charred, crossed logs of an abandoned campfire were visible; a few hobbled horses grazed on the short yellow grass and raised their heads sharply, their ears pitched forward, at the sound of the wagon passing. A voice rose in anger; someone laughed; a horse snorted and neighed, and a bridle jingled at a sudden movement; the faint odor of manure was locked in the hot air.

Butcher's Crossing could be taken in almost at a glance. A group of six rough frame buildings was bisected by a narrow dirt street; there was a scattering of tents beyond the buildings on either side. The wagon passed first on its left a loosely erected tent of army drab with rolled-up sides, which held from the roof flap a flat board crudely lettered in red, JOE LONG, BARBAR. On the opposite side of the road was a low building, almost square, windowless, with a flap of canvas for a door; across the bare front boards of this building were the more carefully executed letters, in black, BRADLEY DRY GOODS. In front of the next building, a long rectangular structure of two stories, the dougherty stopped. From within this building came a low, continuous murmur of voices, and there could be heard the regular clink of glass on glass. The front was shaded by a long overhang of roof, but there was discernible in the shadow over the entrance-way an ornately lettered sign, in red with black edging, which said: JACKSON'S SALOON. Upon a long bench in front of this place sat several men lethargically staring at the wagon as it came to a halt. The young passenger began to gather from the seat beside him the clothing he had doffed earlier in the heat of the day. He put on his hat and his coat and stuffed the vest and cravat into a carpetbag upon which he had been resting his feet. He lifted the carpetbag over the sideboard into the street and with the same motion lifted a leg over the boards and stepped onto the hanging iron plate that let him descend to the ground. When his boot struck the earth, a round puff of dust flew up, surrounding his foot; it settled on the new black leather and on the bottom of his trouser leg, making their colors nearly the same. He picked up his bag and walked under the projecting roof into the shade; behind him the driver's curses mingled with the clank of iron and the jingling of harness chain as he detached the rear doubletree from the wagon. The driver called plaintively:

"Some of you men give me a hand with this freight."

The young man who had got off the wagon stood on the rough board sidewalk watching the driver struggle with the reins that had tangled with the harness trace. Two of the men who had been sitting on the bench got up, brushed past him, and went slowly into the street; they contemplated the rope that secured the freight and began unhurriedly to tug at the knots. With a final jerk the driver managed to unsnarl the reins; he led the mules in a long diagonal across the street toward the livery stable, a low open building with a split-log roof supported by unpeeled upright logs.

After the driver led his team into the stable, another stillness came upon the street. The two men were methodically loosening the ropes that held the covered freight; the sounds from inside the saloon were muffled as if by layers of dust and heat. The young man stepped forward carefully upon the odd lengths of scrap board set directly on the earth. Facing him was a half-dugout with a sharply slanting roof at the near edge of which was a hinged covering, held upright by two diagonal poles, which let down to cover the wide front opening; inside the dugout, on benches and shelves, were scattered a few saddles and a half dozen or more pairs of boots; long strips of raw leather hung from a peg that jutted out of the sod wall near the opening. To the left of this small dugout was a double-storied structure, newly painted white with red trimmings, nearly as long as Jackson's Saloon and somewhat higher. In the dead center of this building was a wide door, above which was a neatly framed sign that read BUTCHER'S HOTEL. It was toward this that the young man slowly walked, watching the street dust pushed forward in quick, dissipating jets by his moving feet.

He entered the hotel and paused just beyond the open door to let his eyes become accustomed to the dimness. The vague shape of a counter rose in front of him to his right; behind it, unmoving, stood a man in a white shirt. A half dozen straight leather-seated chairs were scattered about the room. Light was given from square windows set regularly in the three walls he could see; the squares were covered with a translucent cloth that billowed slightly inward as if the dimness and comparative coolness were a vacuum. He went across the bare wood floor to the waiting clerk.

"I would like a room." His voice echoed hollowly in the silence.

The clerk pushed forward an opened ledger and handed him a steel-tipped quill. He signed slowly, William Andrews; the ink was thin, a pale blue against the gray page.

"Two dollars," the clerk said, pulling the ledger closer to him and peering at the name. "Two bits extra if you want hot water brought up." He looked up suddenly at Andrews. "Be here long?"

"I'm not sure," Andrews said. "Do you know a J. D. Mc-Donald?"

"McDonald?" The clerk nodded slowly. "The hide man? Sure. Everybody knows McDonald. Friend of yours?"

"Not exactly," Andrews said. "Do you know where I can find him?"

The clerk nodded. "He has an office down by the brining pits. About a ten-minute walk from here."

"I'll see him tomorrow," Andrews said. "I just got in from Ellsworth a few minutes ago and I'm tired."

The clerk closed the ledger, selected a key from a large ring that was attached to his belt, and gave the key to Andrews. "You'll have to carry your own bag up," he said. "I'll bring up the water whenever you want it."

"About an hour," Andrews said.

"Room fifteen," the clerk said. "It's just off the stairs."

Andrews nodded. The stairs were unsided treads without headers that pitched sharply up from the far wall and cut into a small rectangular opening in the center level of the building. Andrews stood at the head of a narrow hall that bisected the long row of rooms. He found his own room and entered through the unlocked door. In the room there was space only for a narrow rope bed with a thin mattress, a roughly hewn table with a lamp and a tin wash basin, a mirror, and a straight chair similar to those he had seen below in the lobby. The room had one window that faced the street; set into it was a light detachable wood frame covered with a gauzelike cloth. He realized that he had seen no glass windows since he had got into town. He set his carpetbag on the bare mattress.

After he had unpacked his belongings, he shoved his bag under the low bed and stretched himself out on the uneven mattress; it rustled and sank beneath his weight; he could feel the taut ropes which supported the mattress against his body. His lower back, his buttocks, and his upper legs throbbed dully; he had not realized before how tiring the journey had been.

But now the journey was done; and as his muscles loosened, his mind went back over the way he had come. For nearly two weeks, by coach and rail, he had let himself be carried across the country. From Boston to Albany, from Albany to New York, from New York— The names of the cities jumbled in his memory, disconnected from the route he had taken. Baltimore, Philadelphia, Cincinnati, St. Louis. He remembered the grinding discomfort of the hard coach chairs, and the inert waiting in grimy depots on slatted wooden benches. All the discomforts of his journey now seeped outward from his bones, brought to consciousness by his knowledge of the journey's end.

He knew he would be sore tomorrow. He smiled, and closed his eyes against the brightness of the covered window that he faced. He dozed.

Some time later the clerk brought up a wooden tub and a bucket of steaming water. Andrews roused himself and scooped up some of the hot water in the tin basin. He soaped his face and shaved; the clerk returned with two more buckets of cold water and poured them in the tub. When he had left the room, Andrews undressed slowly, shaking the dust from his garments as he drew them off; he laid them carefully on the straight chair. He stepped into the tub and sat down, his knees drawn up to his chin. He soaped himself slowly, made drowsy by the warm water and the late afternoon quiet. He sat in the tub until his head began to nod forward; when at last it touched his knees, he straightened himself and got out of the tub. He stood on the bare floor, dripping water, and looked about the room. Finding no towel, he took his shirt off the chair and dried himself.

A dimness had crept into the room; the window was a pale glow in the gathering murk, and a cool breeze made the cloth waver and billow; it appeared to throb like something alive, growing larger and smaller. From the street came the slowly rising mutter of voices and the sounds of boots clumping on the board walks. A woman's voice was raised in laughter, then abruptly cut off.

The bath had relaxed him and eased the increasing throb of his strained back muscles. Still naked, he pushed the folded linsey-woolsey blanket into a shape like a pillow and lay down on the raw mattress. It was rough to his skin. But he was asleep before it was fully dark in his room.

During the night he was awakened several times by sounds not quite identified on the edge of his sleeping mind. During these periods of wakefulness he looked about him and in the total darkness could not perceive the walls, the limits of his room; and he had the sensation that he was blind, suspended in nowhere, unmoving. He felt that the sounds of laughter, the voices, the subdued thumps and gratings, the jinglings of bridle bells and harness chains, all proceeded from his own head, and whirled around there like wind in a hollow sphere. Once he thought he heard the voice, then the laughter, of a woman very near, down the hall, in one of the rooms. He lay awake for several moments, listening intently; but he did not hear her again.

2.

ANDREWS breakfasted at the hotel. In a narrow room at the rear of the first floor was a single long table, around which was scattered a number of the straight chairs that appeared to be the hotel's principal furniture. Three men were at one end of

the table, hunched together in conversation; Andrews sat alone
at the other end. The clerk who had brought his water up the
day before came into the dining room and asked Andrews if he
wanted breakfast; when Andrews nodded, he turned and went
toward the small kitchen behind the three men at the far end
of the table. He walked with a small limp that was visible only
from the rear. He returned with a tray that held a large plate
of beans and hominy grits, and a mug of steaming coffee. He
put the food before Andrews, and reached to the center of the
table for an open dish of salt.

"Where could I find McDonald this time of the morning?"
Andrews asked him.

"In his office," the clerk said. "He's there most of the time,
day and night. Go straight down the road, toward the creek,
and turn off to your left just before you get to the patch of
cottonwoods. It's the little shack just this side of the brining
pits."

"The brining pits?"

"For the hides," the clerk said. "You can't miss it."

Andrews nodded. The clerk turned again and left the room.
Andrews ate slowly; the beans were lukewarm and tasteless
even with salt, and the hominy grits were mushy and barely
warmed through. But the coffee was hot and bitter; it numbed
his tongue and made him pull his lips tight along his even white
teeth. He drank it all, as swiftly as the heat would allow him.

By the time he finished breakfast and went into the street,
the sun had risen high above the few buildings of the town
and was bearing down upon the street with an intensity that
seemed almost material. There were more people about than
there had been the afternoon before, when he first had come
into the town; a few men in dark suits with bowler hats mingled with a larger number more carelessly dressed in faded blue
levis, soiled canvas, or broadcloth. They walked with some purpose, yet without particular hurry, upon the sidewalk and in
the street; amid the drab shades of the men's clothing there was
occasionally visible the colorful glimpse—red, lavender, pure
white—of a woman's skirt or blouse. Andrews pulled the brim
of his slouch hat down to shade his eyes, and walked along the
street toward the clump of trees beyond the town.

He passed the leather goods shop, the livery stable, and a
small open-sided blacksmith shop. The town ended at that

point, and he stepped off the sidewalk onto the road. About two hundred yards from the town was the turnoff that the clerk had described; it was little more than twin ribbons of earth worn bare by passing wheels. At the end of this path, a hundred yards or so from the road, was a small flat-roofed shack, and beyond that a series of pole fences, arranged in a pattern he could not make out at this distance. Near the fences, at odd angles, were several empty wagons, their tongues on the earth in directions away from the fences. A vague stench that Andrews could not identify grew stronger as he came nearer the office and the fences.

The shack door was open. Andrews paused, his clenched hand raised to knock; inside the single room was a great clutter of books, papers, and ledgers scattered upon the bare wood floor and piled unevenly in the corners and spilling out of crates set against the walls. In the center of this, apparently crowded there, a man in his shirt sleeves sat hunched over a rough table, thumbing with intense haste the heavy pages of a ledger; he was cursing softly, monotonously.

"Mr. McDonald?" Andrews said.

The man looked up, his small mouth open and his brows raised over protuberant blue eyes whose whites were of the same shaded whiteness as his shirt. "Come in, come in," he said, thrusting his hand violently up through the thin hair that dangled over his forehead. He pushed his chair back from the table, started to get up, and then sat back wearily, his shoulders slumping.

"Come on in, don't just stand around out there."

Andrews entered and stood just inside the doorway. Mc-Donald waved in the direction of a corner behind Andrews, and said:

"Get a chair, boy, sit down."

Andrews drew a chair from behind a stack of papers and placed it in front of McDonald's desk.

"What do you want—what can I do for you?" McDonald asked.

"I'm Will Andrews. I reckon you don't remember me."

"Andrews?" McDonald frowned, regarding the younger man with some hostility. "Andrews. . . ." His lips tightened; the corners of his mouth went down into the lines that came up from his chin. "Don't waste my time, goddammit; if I'd remembered you I'd have said something when you first came in. Now—"

"I have a letter," Andrews said, reaching into his breast pocket, "from my father. Benjamin Andrews. You knew him in Boston."

McDonald took the letter that Andrews held in front of him. "Andrews? Boston?" His voice was querulous, distracted. His eyes were on Andrews as he opened the letter. "Why, sure. Why didn't you say you were— Sure, that preacher fellow." He read the letter intently, moving it about before his eyes as if that might hasten his perusal. When he had finished, he refolded the letter and let it drop onto a stack of papers on the table. He drummed his fingers on the table. "My God! Boston. It must have been twelve, fourteen years ago. Before the war. I used to drink tea in your front parlor." He shook his head wonderingly. "I must have seen you at one time or another. I don't even remember."

"My father has spoken of you often," Andrews said.

"Me?" McDonald's mouth hung open again; he shook his head slowly; his round eyes seemed to swivel in their sockets. "Why? I only saw him maybe half a dozen times." His gaze went beyond Andrews, and he said without expression: "I wasn't anybody for him to speak of. I was a clerk for some dry goods company. I can't even remember its name."

"I think my father admired you, Mr. McDonald," Andrews said.

"Me?" He laughed shortly, then glowered suspiciously at Andrews. "Listen, boy. I went to your father's church because I thought I might meet somebody that would give me a better job, and I started going to those little meetings your father had for the same reason. I never even knew what they were talking about, half the time." He said bitterly, "I would just nod at anything anybody said. Not that it did a damn bit of good."

"I think he admired you because you were the only man he ever knew who came out here—who came west, and made a life for himself."

McDonald shook his head. "Boston," he half whispered. "My God!"

For another moment he stared beyond Andrews. Then he

lifted his shoulders and took a breath. "How did old Mr. Andrews know where I was?"

"A man from Bates and Durfee was passing through Boston.
He mentioned you worked for the Company in Kansas City. In
Kansas City, they told me you had quit them and come here."

McDonald grinned tightly. "I have my own company now. I
left Bates and Durfee four, five years ago." He scowled, and one
hand went to the ledger he had closed when Andrews entered
the shack. "Do it all myself, now. . . . Well." He straightened
again. "The letter says I should help you any way I can. What
made you come out here, anyway?"

Andrews got up from the chair and walked aimlessly about
the room, looking at the piles of papers.

McDonald grinned; his voice lowered. "Trouble? Did you
get in some kind of trouble back home?"

"No," Andrews said quickly. "Nothing like that."

"Lots of boys do," McDonald said. "That's why they come
out here. Even a preacher's son."

"My father is a lay minister in the Unitarian Church," Andrews said.

"It's the same thing." McDonald waved his hand impatiently.
"Well, you want a job? Hell, you can have a job with me. God
knows I can't keep up. Look at all this stuff." He pointed to
the stacked papers; his finger was trembling. "I'm two months
behind now and getting further behind all the time. Can't find
anybody around here to sit still long enough to—"

"Mr. McDonald," Andrews said. "I know nothing about
your business."

"What? You don't what? Why, it's hides, boy. Buffalo hides.
I buy and sell. I send out parties, they bring in the hides. I sell
them in St. Louis. Do my own curing and tanning right here.
Handled almost a hundred thousand hides last year. This year
—twice, three times that much. Great opportunity, boy. Think
you could handle some of this paper work?"

"Mr. McDonald—"

"This paper work is what gets me down." He ran his fingers
through the thin black strands of hair that fell about his ears.

"I'm grateful, sir," Andrews said. "But I'm not sure—"

"Hell, it's only a start. Look." With a thin hand like a claw
he grasped Andrews's arm above the elbow and pushed him

toward the doorway. "Look out there." They went into the hot sunlight; Andrews squinted and winced against the brightness. McDonald, still clutching at his arm, pointed toward the town. "A year ago when I came here there were three tents and a dugout over there—a saloon, a whorehouse, a dry goods store, and a blacksmith. Look at it now." He pushed his face up to Andrews and said in a hoarse whisper, his breath sweet-sour from tobacco: "Keep this to yourself—but this town's going to be something two, three years from now. I've got a half dozen lots staked out already, and the next time I get to Kansas City, I'm going to stake out that many more. It's wide open!" He shook Andrews's arm as if it were a stick; he lowered his voice, which had grown strident. "Look, boy. It's the railroad. Don't go talking this around; but when the railroad comes through here, this is going to be a *town.* You come in with me; I'll steer you right. Anybody can stake out a claim for the land around here; all you have to do is sign your name to a piece of paper at the State Land Office. Then you sit back and wait. That's all."

"Thank you, sir," Andrews said. "I'll consider it."

"*Consider* it!" McDonald released his arm and stepped back from him in astonishment. He threw up his hands and they fluttered as he walked around once in a tight, angry little circle. "Consider it? Why, boy, it's an opportunity. Listen. What were you doing back in Boston before you came out here?"

"I was in my third year at Harvard College."

"You see?" McDonald said triumphantly. "And what would you have done after your fourth year? You'd have gone to work for somebody, or you'd have been a schoolteacher, like old Mr. Andrews, or— Listen. There ain't many like us out here. Men with vision. Men who can think to tomorrow." He pointed a shaking hand toward the town. "Did you see those people back there? Did you talk to any of them?"

"No, sir," Andrews said. "I only got in from Ellsworth yesterday afternoon."

"Hunters," McDonald said. His dry thin lips went loose and open as if he had tasted something rotten. "All hunters and hard cases. That's what this country would be if it wasn't for men like us. People just living off the land, not knowing what to do with it."

"Are they mostly hunters in town?"

"Hunters, hard cases, a few eastern loafers. This is a hide town, boy. It'll change. Wait till the railroad comes through."

"I think I'd like to talk to some of them," Andrews said.

"Who?" McDonald shouted. "Hunters? Oh, my God! Don't tell me you're like the other younguns that come in here. Three years at Harvard College, and you want to use it that way. I ought to have known it. I ought to have known it when you first came."

"I just want to talk to some of them," Andrews said.

"Sure," McDonald said bitterly. "And the first thing you know, *you'll* be wanting to go out." His voice became earnest. "Listen, boy. Listen to me. You start going out with those men, it'll ruin you. Oh, I've seen it. It gets in you like buffalo lice. You won't care any more. Those men—" Andrews clawed in the air, as if for a word.

"Mr. McDonald," Andrews said quietly, "I appreciate what you're trying to do for me. But I want to try to explain something to you. I came out here—" He paused and let his gaze go past McDonald, away from the town, beyond the ridge of earth that he imagined was the river bank, to the flat yellowish green land that faded into the horizon westward. He tried to shape in his mind what he had to say to McDonald. It was a feeling; it was an urge that he had to speak. But whatever he spoke he knew would be but another name for the wildness that he sought. It was a freedom and a goodness, a hope and a vigor that he perceived to underlie all the familiar things of his life, which were not free or good or hopeful or vigorous. What he sought was the source and preserver of his world, a world which seemed to turn ever in fear away from its source, rather than search it out, as the prairie grass around him sent down its fibered roots into the rich dark dampness, the Wildness, and thereby renewed itself, year after year. Suddenly, in the midst of the great flat prairie, unpeopled and mysterious, there came into his mind the image of a Boston street, crowded with carriages and walking men who toiled sluggishly beneath the arches of evenly spaced elms that had been made to grow, it seemed, out of the flat stone of sidewalk and roadway; there came into his mind the image of tall buildings, packed side by side, the ornately cut stone of which was grimed by smoke and city filth; there came into his mind the image of the river Charles winding among plotted fields and villages and towns, carrying the refuse of man and city out to the great bay.

He became aware that his hands were tightly clenched; the tips of his fingers slipped in the moisture of his palms. He loosened his fists and wiped his palms on his trousers.

"I came out here to see as much of the country as I can," he said quietly. "I want to get to know it. It's something that I have to do."

"Young folks," said McDonald. He spoke softly. Flat lines of sweat ran through the glinting beads of moisture that stood out on his forehead, and ran into his tangled eyebrows, which were lowered over the eyes that regarded Andrews steadily. "They don't know what to do with themselves. My God, if you'd start now—if you had the sense to start now, by the time you're forty, you could be—" He shrugged. "Ahhh. Let's get back out of the sun."

They re-entered the dim little shack. Andrews discovered that he was breathing heavily; his shirt was soaked with perspiration, and it clung to his skin and slid unpleasantly over it as he moved. He removed his coat and sank into the chair before McDonald's table; he felt a curious weakness and lassitude descend from his chest and shoulders to his fingertips. A long silence fell upon the room. McDonald's hand rested on his ledger; one finger moved aimlessly above the page but did not touch it. At last he sighed deeply and said:

"All right. Go and talk to them. But I'll warn you: Most of the men around here hunt for me; you're not going to have an easy time getting into a party without my help. Don't try to hook up with any of the men I send out. You leave my men alone. I won't be responsible. I won't have you on my conscience."

"I'm not even sure I want to go on a hunt," Andrews said sleepily. "I just want to talk to the men that do."

"Trash," McDonald muttered. "You come out here all the way from Boston, Massachusetts, just to get mixed up with trash."

"Who should I talk to, Mr. McDonald?" Andrews asked.

"What?"

"Who should I talk to?" Andrews repeated. "I ought to talk

to someone who knows his business, and you told me to keep away from your men."

McDonald shook his head. "You don't listen to a word a man says, do you? You got it all figured out."

"No, sir," Andrews said. "I don't have anything figured out. I just want to know more about this country."

"All right," McDonald said tiredly. He closed the ledger that he had been fingering and tossed it on a pile of papers. "You talk to Miller. He's a hunter, but he ain't as bad as the rest of them. He's been out here most of his life; at least he ain't as bad as the rebels and the hard Yankees. Maybe he'll talk to you, maybe he won't. You'll have to find out for yourself."

"Miller?" Andrews asked.

"Miller," McDonald said. "He lives in a dugout down by the river, but you'll more likely find him in Jackson's. That's where they all hang out, day and night. Ask anybody; everybody knows Miller."

"Thank you, Mr. McDonald," Andrews said. "I appreciate your help."

"Don't thank me," McDonald said. "I'm doing nothing for you. I'm giving you a man's name."

Andrews rose. The weakness had gone into his legs. It is the heat, he thought, and the strangeness. He stood still for a moment, gathering his strength.

"One thing," McDonald said. "Just one thing I ask you." He appeared to Andrews to recede into the dimness.

"Of course, Mr. McDonald. What is it?"

"Let me know before you go out, if you decide to go. Just come back here and let me know."

"Of course," Andrews said. "I'll be seeing you often, I hope. It's just that I want to have a little more time before I decide anything."

"Sure," McDonald said bitterly. "Take all the time you can. You got plenty."

"Goodbye, Mr. McDonald."

McDonald waved his hand, angrily, and turned his attention abruptly to the papers on his desk. Andrews walked slowly out of the shack, into the yard, and turned on the wagon trail that led to the main road. At the main road, he paused. Across from him and some yards to his left was the clump of cottonwoods;

beyond that, intersecting the road, must be the river; he could not see the water, but he could see the humped banks clustered with low-growing shrub and weed winding off into the distance. He turned and went back toward the town.

It was near noon when he arrived at the hotel; the tiredness that had come upon him in McDonald's shack remained. In the hotel dining room he ate lightly of tough fried meat and boiled beans, and sipped bitter hot coffee. The hotel clerk, who limped in and out of the dining room, asked him if he had found McDonald; he replied that he had; the clerk nodded and said nothing more. Soon Andrews left the dining room, went up to his room, and lay on his bed. He watched the cloth screen at his window billow softly inward until he was asleep.

3.

WHEN he awoke his room was dark; the cloth screen at his window let in a flickering brightness from the street below. He heard distant shouts beneath the querulous murmur of many voices, and the snorting of a horse and the clop of hooves. For a moment he could not remember where he was.

He got up abruptly and sat on the edge of his bed. The mattress rustled beneath him; he relaxed, and ran his fingers through his hair, down over the back of his head and neck, and stretched his head backward, welcoming the soreness that warmed pleasantly up between his shoulder blades. In the darkness he walked across his room to the small table, which was outlined dimly beside the window. He found a match on the table and lit the lamp beside the washbasin. In the mirror his face was a sharp contrast of yellow brightness and dark shadow. He put his hands in the lukewarm water of the basin and rinsed his face. He dried his hands and face on the same shirt he had used the day before. By the flickering light of the lamp, he put on his black string tie and brown sack coat, which was beginning to smell of his own sweat, and stared at himself in the mirror as if he were a stranger. Then he blew the lamp out, and made his way out of the room.

The street lay in long shadows cast by the yellow lights that
came from the open doors and windows of the few buildings of
Butcher's Crossing. A lone light came from the dry goods store
opposite the hotel; bulky figures moved about it, their sizes exaggerated by the shadows. More light, and the sound of laughter and heavily clumping feet came from the saloon next to it.
A few horses were tethered to the roughly hewn hitching rail
set out eight or ten feet from the sidewalk in front of Jackson's;
they were motionless, but the moving lights glinted on their
eyeballs and on the smooth hair of their flanks. Up the street,
beyond the dugout, two lanterns hung on logs in front of the
livery stable; just beyond the livery stable, a dull red glow came
from the blacksmith shop, and there could be heard the heavy
clank of hammer upon iron and the angry hissing as hot metal
was thrust into water. Andrews went in a slow diagonal across
the street toward Jackson's.

The room he entered was long and narrow; its length extended at a right angle from the street, and its width was
such that four men could not stand with comfort shoulder to shoulder across it. Half a dozen lanterns hung from
unpainted, sooty rafters; the light they gave was reflected
sharply downward, so that the surface of everything in the
room glinted with yellow light and everything beneath those
surfaces fell into vague shadows. Andrews walked forward.
To his right a long bar extended nearly the length of the
room; the bar top was two thick-hewn planks placed side
by side, and supported by unfinished split logs set directly
on the unevenly planked floor. He breathed deeply, and the
sharp mingled odor of burning kerosene, sweat, and liquor
gathered in his lungs; he coughed. He went to the bar, which
was only a little higher than his waist; the bartender, a short
bald man with large mustaches and a yellow skin, looked at
him without speaking.

"A beer," Andrews said.

The bartender drew a heavy mug from beneath the bar
and turned to one of several kegs that stood on large wooden
boxes. He turned a spigot and let the beer slide in white bub-
bles down the side of the mug. Setting the mug before Andrews, he said:

"That'll be two bits."

Andrews tasted the beer; it seemed warmer than the room, and its flavor was thin. He laid a coin on the table.

"I'm looking for a Mr. Miller," he said. "I was told I might find him here."

"Miller?" The bartender turned indifferently and looked at the far end of the room where, in the shadows, there were two small tables about which were seated half a dozen men drinking quietly. "Don't seem to be in here. You a friend of his?"

"I've never met him," Andrews said. "I want to see him on a matter of—business. Mr. McDonald said that I would probably find him here."

The bartender nodded. "You might find him in the big room." He indicated with his eyes a point behind Andrews; Andrews turned and saw that there was a closed door that must lead to another room. "He's a big man, clean shaved. Probably be sitting with Charley Hoge—little feller, gray-haired."

Andrews thanked the bartender, finished his beer, and went through the door on the narrow side of the saloon. The room he entered was large and more dimly lighted than the one he had left. Though many lanterns hung from hooks on the smoked rafters, only a few were lighted; the room lay in pools of light and larger irregular spaces of shadow. Rudely shaped tables were arranged so that there was an empty oval space in the center of the room; at the back a straight staircase led up to the second floor. Andrews walked forward, opening his eyes wide against the dimness.

At one of the tables sat five men playing cards; they did not look up at Andrews, nor did they speak among themselves. The slap of cards and the tiny click of poker chips came upon the quietness. At another table sat two girls, their heads close together, murmuring; a man and a woman were seated together nearby; a few other groups were gathered at shadowed tables elsewhere in the large room. There was a quiet, slow fluidity to the scene which was strange to Andrews, and it absorbed him so that for a moment he did not remember why he had come here. At the far end of the room, through the dimness and the smoke, he saw seated at a table two men and a woman. They were somewhat apart from the others, and the larger of the men was looking directly at him. Andrews moved across the open space toward them.

When he stood before their table, all three of them were looking up at him. The four remained for several moments unmoving and silent; Andrews's attention was on the large man directly in front of him, but he was aware of the girl's rather pale plump face and yellow hair that seemed to flow from round bare shoulders, and of the smaller man's long nose and gray stubbled face.

"Mr. Miller?" Andrews asked.

The large man nodded. "I'm Miller," he said. His pupils were black and sharply distinct from the whites, and his brows were set closely above them in a frown that wrinkled the broad bridge of his nose. His skin was slightly yellowed and smooth like cured leather, and at the corners of his wide mouth deep ridges curved up to the thick base of his nose. His hair was heavy and black; it was parted at the side, and lay in thick ropes over half his ears. He said again, "I'm Miller."

"My name is Will Andrews. I—my family are old friends of J. D. McDonald. Mr. McDonald said you might be willing to talk to me."

"McDonald?" Miller's heavy, almost hairless lids came down over his eyes in a slow blink. "Sit down, son."

Andrews sat in the empty chair between the girl and Miller. "I hope I'm not interrupting anything."

"What does McDonald want?" Miller asked.

"I beg your pardon?"

"McDonald sent you over here, didn't he? What does he want?"

"No, sir," Andrews said. "You don't understand. I just wanted to talk with someone who knew this country. Mr. McDonald was kind enough to give me your name."

Miller looked at him steadily for a moment, and then nodded. "McDonald's been trying to get me to head a party for him for two years now. I thought he was trying again."

"No, sir," Andrews said.

"You work for McDonald?"

"No, sir," Andrews said. "He offered me a job, but I turned it down."

"Why?" Miller asked.

Andrews hesitated. "I didn't want to be tied down. I didn't come out here for that."

Miller nodded, and shifted his bulk; Andrews realized that the man beside him had been motionless until this moment. "This here is Charley Hoge," Miller said, moving his head slightly in the direction of the gray man who sat opposite Andrews.

"I'm pleased to meet you, Mr. Hoge," Andrews said, and put his hand across the table. Hoge was grinning at him crookedly, his sharp face sunk down between narrow shoulder blades. He slowly raised his right arm, and suddenly thrust his forearm across the table. The arm ended at the wrist in a white nub that was neatly puckered and scarred. Involuntarily, Andrews drew his own hand back. Hoge laughed; his laughter was an almost soundless wheeze that seemed forced from his thin chest.

"Don't mind Charley, son," Miller said. "He always does that. It's his idea of fun."

"Lost it in the winter of sixty-two," Charley Hoge said, still gasping with his laughter. "It froze, and would have dropped clean off, if—" He shivered suddenly, and continued to shiver as if he felt the cold again.

"You might buy Charley a drink of whisky, Mr. Andrews," Miller said almost gently. "That's another one of his ideas of fun."

"Of course," Andrews said. He half rose from his chair. "Shall I—"

"Never mind," Miller said. "Francine will get the drinks." He nodded at the blonde girl. "This is Francine."

Andrews was still half raised above the table. "How do you do," he said, and bowed slightly. The girl smiled, her pale lips parting over teeth that were very white and slightly irregular.

"Sure," Francine said. "Does anybody else want something?" She spoke slowly and with the trace of a Germanic accent.

Miller shook his head.

"A glass of beer," Andrews said. "And if you would like something?"

"No," Francine said. "I'm not working now."

She got up and moved away from the table; for a few moments Andrews's eyes followed her. She was heavy, but she moved with grace across the room; she wore a dress of some shiny material with broad white and blue stripes. The bodice was tight, and it pushed the fullness of her flesh upward. Andrews turned questioningly toward Miller as he sat down.

"Does she—work here?" Andrews asked.

"Francine?" Miller looked at him without expression. "Francine is a whore. There are nine, ten of them in town; six of them work here, and there are a couple of Indians that work the dugouts down by the river."

"A scarlet woman," Charley Hoge said; he was still shivering. "A woman of sin." He did not smile.

"Charley is a Bible man," Miller said. "He can read it pretty good."

"A—whore," Andrews said, and swallowed. He smiled. "Somehow, she doesn't look like—a—"

The corners of Miller's wide mouth lifted slightly. "Where'd you say you was from, son?"

"Boston," he said. "Boston, Massachusetts."

"Ain't they got whores in Boston, Massachusetts?"

Andrews's face warmed. "I suppose so," he said. "I suppose so," he said again. "Yes."

Miller nodded. "They got whores in Boston. But a whore in Boston, and a whore in Butcher's Crossing; now, there's two different things."

"I see," Andrews said.

"I don't reckon you do," Miller said. "But you will. In Butcher's Crossing, a whore is a necessary part of the economy. A man's got to have something besides liquor and food to spend his money on, and something to bring him back to town after he's been out on the country. In Butcher's Crossing, a whore can pick and choose, and still make a right smart amount of money; and that makes her almost respectable. Some of them even get married; make right good wives, I hear, for them that want wives."

Andrews did not speak.

Miller leaned back in his chair. "Besides, this is a slack time, and Francine ain't working. When a whore ain't working, I guess she looks just about like anybody else."

"Sin and corruption," Charley Hoge said. "She's got the taint within her." With his good hand, he grasped the edge of the table so tightly that the knuckles showed blue-white against the brown of his skin.

Francine returned to the table with their drinks. She leaned over Andrews's shoulder to set Charley Hoge's glass of whisky before him. Andrews was aware of her warmth, her smell; he shifted. She put his beer before him, and smiled; her eyes were pale and large, and her reddish-blond lashes, soft as down, made her eyes appear wide and unblinking. Andrews took some coins from his pocket and put them in her palm.

"Do you want me to leave?" Francine asked Miller.

"Sit down," Miller said. "Mr. Andrews just wants to talk."

The sight of the whisky had calmed Charley Hoge; he took the glass in his hand and drank rapidly, his head thrown back and his Adam's apple running like a small animal beneath the gray fur of his bearded throat. When he finished the drink, he hunched himself back in his chair and remained still, watching the others with cold little gray eyes.

"What did you want to talk about, Mr. Andrews?" Miller asked.

Andrews looked uncomfortably at Francine and Charley Hoge. He smiled. "You put it kind of abruptly," he said.

Miller nodded. "I figured to."

Andrews paused, and said: "I guess I just want to know the country. I've never been out here before; I want to know as much as I can."

"What for?" Miller asked.

Andrews looked at him blankly.

"You talk like you're an educated man, Mr. Andrews."

"Yes, sir," he said. "I was three years at Harvard College."

"Well," Miller said, "three years. That's quite a spell. How long you been away from there?"

"Not long. I left to come out here."

Miller looked at him for a moment. "Harvard College." He shook his head. "I learned myself to read one winter I was snowed in a trapper's shack in Colorado. I can write my name on paper. What do you think you can learn from me?"

Andrews frowned, and suppressed a tone of annoyance he felt creep into his voice. "I don't even know you, Mr. Miller," he said with a little heat. "It's like I said. I want to know something about this country. Mr. McDonald said you were a good man to talk to, that you knew as much about this country as any man around. I had hoped that you would be kind enough to converse with me for an hour or so, to acquaint me with—"

Miller shook his head again, and grinned. "You sure talk easy, son. You do, for a fact. That what you learn to do at Harvard College?"

For a moment, Andrews stared at him stiffly. Then he smiled. "No, sir. I reckon not. At Harvard College, you don't talk; you just listen."

"Sure, now," Miller said. "That's reason enough for any man to leave. A body's got to speak up for his self, once in a while."

"Yes, sir," Andrews said.

"So you came out here. To Butcher's Crossing."

"Yes, sir."

"And when you learn what you want to learn, what'll you do? Go back and brag to your kinfolk? Write something for the papers?"

"No, sir," Andrews said. "It's not for any of those reasons. It's for myself."

Miller did not speak for several moments. Then he said, "You might buy Charley another glass of whisky; and I'll have a glass myself this time."

Francine rose. She spoke to Andrews: "Another beer?"

"Whisky," Andrews said.

After Francine left their table, Andrews was silent for some time; he did not look at either of the two men at the table with him.

Miller said: "So you didn't tie up with McDonald."

"It wasn't what I wanted."

Miller nodded. "This is a hunt town, boy. If you stay around, there ain't much choice about what you do. You can take a job with McDonald and make yourself some money, or you can start yourself some kind of little business and hope that the railroad does come through, or you can tie up with a party and hunt buffalo."

"That's about what Mr. McDonald said."

"And he didn't like the last idea."

Andrews smiled. "No, sir."

"He don't like hunters," Miller said. "And they don't like him either."

"Why?"

Miller shrugged. "They do the work, and he gets all the money. They think he's a crook, and he thinks they're fools. You can't blame either side; they're both right."

Andrews said, "But you're a hunter yourself, aren't you, Mr. Miller?"

Miller shook his head. "Not like these around here, and not for McDonald. He outfits his own parties, and gives them fifty cents a head for raw hides—summer hides, not much more than thin leather. He has thirty or forty parties out all the time; he gets plenty of skins, but the way it's split up, the men are lucky if they make enough to get through the winter. I hunt on my own or I don't hunt at all." Miller paused; Francine had returned with a quarter-filled bottle and fresh glasses and a small glass of beer for herself. Charley Hoge moved quickly toward the glass of whisky she set before him; Miller took his own glass in his large, hairless hand and cupped it; Andrews took a quick sip. The liquor burned his lips and tongue and warmed his throat; he could taste nothing for the burning.

"I come out here four years ago," Miller continued, "the same year McDonald did. My God! You should have seen this country then. In the spring, you could look out from here and see the whole land black with buffalo, solid as grass, for miles. There was only a few of us then, and it was nothing for one party to get a thousand, fifteen hundred head in a couple of weeks hunting. Spring hides, too, pretty good fur. Now it's hunted out. They travel in smaller herds, and a man's lucky to get two or three hundred head a trip. Another year or two, there won't be any hunting left in Kansas."

Andrews took another sip of whisky. "What will you do then?"

Miller shrugged. "I'll go back to trapping, or I'll do some mining, or I'll hunt something else." He frowned at his glass. "Or I'll hunt buffalo. There are still places they can be found, if you know where to look."

"Around here?" Andrews asked.

"No," Miller said. He moved his large, black-suited body restlessly in the chair and pushed his untasted drink precisely to the center of the table. "In the fall of sixty-three, I was

trapping beaver up in Colorado. That was the year after Charley here lost his hand, and he was staying in Denver and wasn't
with me. The beaver was late in furring out that year, so I left
my traps near the river I was working and took my mule up
towards the mountains; I was hoping to get a few bears. Their
skin was good that year, I had heard. I climbed all over the
side of that mountain near three days, I guess, and wasn't able
to even catch sight of a bear. On the fourth day, I was trying
to work my way higher and further north, and I come to a
place where the mountain dropped off sharp into a little gorge.
I thought maybe there might be a side stream down there
where the animals watered, so I worked my way down; took
me the best part of a day. They wasn't no stream down there.
They was a flat bed of bare ground, ten, twelve foot wide,
packed hard as rock, that looked like a road cut right through
the mountain. Soon as I saw it, I knew what it was, but I
couldn't believe what I saw. It was buffalo; they had tromped
the earth down hard, going this way and coming back, for
years. I followed the bed up the mountain the rest of that day,
and near nightfall come out on a valley bed flat as a lake. That
valley wound in and out of the mountains as far as you could
see; and they was buffalo scattered all over it, in little herds,
as far as a man could see. Fall fur, but thicker and better than
winter fur on the plains grazers. From where I stood, I figured
maybe three, four thousand head; and they was more around
the bends of the valley I couldn't see." He took the glass from
the center of the table and gulped quickly, shuddering slightly
as he swallowed. "I had the feeling no man had ever been in
that valley before. Maybe some Indians a long time ago, but
no man. I stayed around two days, and never saw a human
sign, and never saw one coming back out. Back near the river,
the trail curved out against the side of the mountain and was
hid by trees; working up the river, a man would never see it."

Andrews cleared his throat. When he spoke, his voice
sounded strange and hollow to himself: "Did you ever go back
there?"

Miller shook his head. "I never went back. I knew it would
keep. A man couldn't find it unless he knew where it was, or
unless he stumbled on it accidental like I did; and that ain't
very likely."

"Ten years," Andrews said. "Why haven't you gone back?"

Miller shrugged. "Things ain't been right for it. One year Charley was laid up with the fever, another year I was promised to something else, another I didn't have a stake. Mainly I haven't been able to get together the right kind of party."

"What kind do you need?" Andrews asked.

Miller did not look at him. "The kind that'll let it be my hunt. They ain't many places like this left, and I never wanted any of the other hunters along."

Andrews felt an obscure excitement growing within him. "How many men would it take for a party like this?"

"That would depend," Miller said, "on who was getting it up. Five, six, seven men in most parties. Myself, on this hunt, I'd keep it small. One hunter would be enough, because he'd have all the time he needed to make his kill; he could keep the buffalo in the valley all the time he needs. A couple of skinners and a camp man. Four men ought to be able to do the job about right. And the fewer the men, the bigger the take will be."

Andrews did not speak. On the edge of his sight, Francine moved forward and put her elbows on the table. Charley Hoge took a deep, sharp breath, and coughed gently. After a long while, Andrews said:

"Could you get up a party this late in the year?"

Miller nodded, and looked over Andrews's head. "Could be done, I suppose."

There was a silence. Andrews said: "How much money would it take?"

Miller's eyes lowered and met Andrews's; he smiled slightly. "Are you just talking, son, or have you got yourself interested in something?"

"I've got myself interested," Andrews said. "How much money would it take?"

"Well, now," Miller said. "I hadn't thought serious about going out this year." He drummed his heavy pale fingers on the table top. "But I suppose I could think about it, now."

Charley Hoge coughed again, and added an inch of whisky to his half-filled glass.

"My stake's pretty low," Miller said. "Whoever came in would have to put up just about all the money."

"How much?" Andrews said.

"And even so," Miller continued, "he'd have to understand that it would still be my hunt. He'd have to understand that."

"Yes," Andrews said. "How much would it take?"

"How much money you got, son?" Miller asked gently.

"A little over fourteen hundred dollars," Andrews said.

"You'd want to go along, of course."

Andrews hesitated. Then he nodded.

"To work, I mean. To help with the skinning."

Andrews nodded again.

"It would still be my hunt, you understand," Miller said.

Andrews said: "I understand."

"Well, it might be arranged," Miller said, "if you wanted to put up the money for the team and provisions."

"What would we need?" Andrews asked.

"We'd need a wagon and a team," Miller said slowly. "Most often the team is mules, but a mule needs grain. A team of oxen could live off the land, going and coming, and they pull a heavy enough load. They're slow, but we wouldn't be in a great hurry. You got a horse?"

"No," Andrews said.

"We'd need a horse for you, and maybe for the skinner, who-ever he is. You shoot a gun?"

"Do you mean a—pistol?"

Miller smiled tightly. "No man in his right mind has any use for them little things," he said, "unless he wants to get killed. I mean a rifle."

"No," Andrews said.

"We ought to get you a small rifle. I'll need powder and lead —say a ton of lead and five hundred pounds of powder. If we don't use it all, we can get refunds. In the mountains, we can live off the land, but we have to have food going and coming back. Couple of sacks of flour, ten pounds of coffee, twenty of sugar, couple pounds of salt, a few sides of bacon, twenty pounds of beans. We'll need some kettles and a few tools. A little grain for the horses. I'd say five or six hundred dollars would do it easy."

"That's nearly half of all the money I have," Andrews said.

Miller shrugged. "It's a lot of money. But you stand to make a lot more. With a good wagon, we ought to be able to load in close to a thousand skins. They should bring us near twenty-five hundred dollars. If there's a big kill, we can let some of the hides winter over and go back in the spring and get them. I'll take 60 per cent and you get 40; I'm taking a bit more than usual, but it's my hunt, and besides I take care of Charley here. You'll take care of the other skinner. When we get back, you should be able to sell the team and wagon for about what you paid for it; so you'll make out all right."

"I ain't going," Charley Hoge said. "That's a country of the devil."

Miller said pleasantly, "Charley lost that hand up in the Rockies; he ain't liked the country since."

"Hell fire and ice," Charley Hoge said. "It ain't for human man."

"Tell Mr. Andrews about losing your hand, Charley," Miller said.

Charley Hoge grinned through his short, grizzled beard. He put the stump of his hand on the table and inched it toward Andrews as he spoke. "Miller and I was hunting and trapping early one winter in Colorado. We was up on a little rise just before the mountains when a blizzard come up. Miller and I got separated, and I slipped on a rock and hit my head and got knocked clean out of my senses. Don't know how long I laid there. When I come to, the blizzard was still blowing, and I could hear Miller calling."

"I'd been looking for Charley nearly four hours," Miller said.

"I must've knocked a glove off when I fell," Charley Hoge continued, "because my hand was bare and it was froze stiff. But it wasn't cold. It just kind of tingled. I yelled at Miller, and he come over, and he found us a shelter back in some rocks; they was even some dry logs, and we was able to keep a fire going. I looked at that hand, and it was blue, a real bright blue. I never seen anything like it. And then it got warmed up, and then it started to hurt; I couldn't tell whether it hurt like ice or whether it hurt like fire; and then it turned red, like a piece of fancy cloth. We was there two, three days, and the blizzard didn't let up. Then it turned blue again, almost black."

"It got to stinking," Miller said, "so I knew it had to come off."

Charley Hoge laughed with a wheezing, cracking voice. "He kept telling me it had to come off, but I wouldn't listen to him.

We argued almost half a day about it, until he finally wore me down. He never would of talked me into it if I hadn't got so tired. Finally I just laid back and told him to cut away."

"My God," Andrews said, his voice barely a whisper.

"It wasn't as bad as you might think," he said. "By that time the hurt was so bad I could just barely feel the knife. And when he hit bone, I passed out, and it wasn't bad at all then."

"Charley got careless," Miller said. "He shouldn't have slipped on that rock. He ain't been careless since, have you, Charley?"

He laughed. "I been mighty careful since then."

"So you see," Miller said, "why Charley don't like the Colorado country."

"My God, yes!" Andrews said.

"But he'll go with us," Miller continued. "With only one hand, he's a better camp man than most."

"No," Charley Hoge said. "I ain't going. Not this time."

"It'll be all right," Miller said. "This time of year, it's almost warm up there; there won't be no snow till November." He looked at Andrews. "He'll go; all we'll need is a skinner. We'll need a good one, because he'll have to break you in."

"All right," Andrews said. "When will we be leaving?"

"We should hit the mountains about the middle of September; it'll be cool up there then, and the hides should be about right. We should leave here in about two weeks. Then a couple of weeks to get there, a week or ten days on the kill, and a couple of weeks back."

Andrews nodded. "What about the team and the supplies?"

"I'll go into Ellsworth for those," Miller said. "I know a man there who has a sound wagon, and there should be oxen for sale; I'll pick up the supplies there, too, because they'll be cheaper. I should be back in four, five days."

"You'll make all the arrangements," Andrews said.

"Yes. You leave it all to me. I'll get you a good horse and a varmint rifle. And I'll get us a skinner."

"Do you want the money now?" Andrews asked.

The corners of Miller's mouth tightened in a close smile. "You don't lose any time making up your mind, do you, Mr. Andrews?"

"No, sir," Andrews said.

"Francine," Miller said, "we all ought to have another drink on this. Bring us all some more whisky—and bring yourself some too."

Francine looked for a moment at Miller, then at Andrews; her eyes stayed upon Andrews as she rose and went away from the table.

"We can have a drink on it," Miller said, "and then you can give me the money. That will close it."

Andrews nodded. He looked at Charley Hoge, and beyond him; he was drowsy with the heat and with the warm effects of the whisky he had drunk; in his mind were fragments of Miller's talk about the mountain country to which they were going, and those fragments glittered and turned and fell softly in accidental and strange patterns. Like the loose stained bits of glass in a kaleidoscope, they augmented themselves with their turning and found light from irrelevant and accidental sources.

Francine returned with another bottle and placed it in the center of the table; no one spoke. Miller lifted his glass, poised it for a moment where the light from a lantern struck it with a reddish-amber glow. The others silently raised their glasses and drank, not putting the glasses down until they were empty. Andrews's eyes watered at the burning in his throat; through the moisture he saw Francine's face shimmering palely before him. Her own eyes were upon him, and she was smiling slightly. He blinked and looked at Miller.

"You got the money with you?" Miller asked.

Andrews nodded. He opened a lower button of his shirt and withdrew from his money belt a sheaf of bills. He counted six hundred dollars upon the scarred table and returned the other bills to his belt.

"And that's all there is to it," Miller said. "I'll ride into Ellsworth tomorrow and pick up what we need and be back in less than a week." He shuffled through the bills, selected one, and held it out to Charley Hoge. "Here. This will keep you while I'm gone."

"What?" Charley Hoge asked, his voice dazed. "Ain't I coming with you?"

"I'll be busy," Miller said. "This will take care of you for a week."

Charley Hoge nodded slowly, and then whipped the bill out of Miller's hand, crushed it, and thrust it into his shirt pocket.

Andrews pushed his chair back from the table and arose; his limbs felt stiff and reluctant to move. "I believe I'll turn in, if there's nothing else we need to talk about."

Miller shook his head. "Nothing that can't wait. I'll be pulling out early in the morning, so I won't see you till I get back. But Charley'll be around."

"Good night," Andrews said. Charley Hoge grunted and looked at him somberly.

"Good night, ma'am," Andrews said to Francine, and bowed slightly, awkwardly, from the shoulders.

"Good night, Mr. Andrews," Francine said. "Good luck."

Andrews turned from them and walked across the long room. It was nearly deserted, and the pools of light on the rough-planked floor and the hewn tables seemed sharper, and the shadows about those pools deeper and more dense than they had been earlier. He walked through the saloon and out onto the street.

The glow from the blacksmith shop had all but disappeared, and the lanterns hung on the poles in front of the livery stable had burned down so that only rims of yellow light spread from the bottoms of glass bulbs; the few horses that remained tethered in front of the saloon were still, their heads slumped down nearly between their legs. The sound of Andrews's boots upon the board walk was loud and echoing; he went into the street and walked across to his hotel.

4.

FOR THE first few days after Miller left Butcher's Crossing for Ellsworth, Andrews spent much of his time in his hotel room; he lay on the thin mattress of his narrow bed and gazed at the bare walls, the roughly planked floor, the flat low ceiling. He thought of his father's house on Clarendon Street near Beacon and the river Charles. Though he had left there with his portion of an uncle's bequest less than a month before, he felt that the house, in which he had been born and in which he had lived his youth, was very distant in time; he could summon only the dimmest image of the tall elms that surrounded the house, and of the house itself. He remembered more clearly the great dim parlor and the sofa covered with dark red velvet upon which he had lain on summer afternoons, his cheek brushed by the heavy pile, his eyes following, until they were confounded, the intricately entwined floral design carved upon the walnut frame of the sofa. As if it were important, he strained his memory; beside the sofa there had been a large lamp with a round milk-white base encircled by a chain of painted roses, and beyond that, on the wall, neatly framed, was a series of water colors done by a forgotten aunt during her Grand Tour. But the image would not stay with him. Unreal, it thinned like blown fog; and Andrews came back to himself in a raw bare room in a crudely built frame hotel in Butcher's Crossing.

From that room he could see nearly all the town; when he discovered that he could take the gauze-covered frame out of the window, he spent many hours sitting there, his arms folded on the lower frame of the window opening, his chin resting on one forearm, gazing out upon the town. His gaze alternated between the town itself, which seemed to move in a sluggish erratic rhythm like the pulse of some brute existence, and the surrounding country. Always, when his gaze lifted from the town, it went westward toward the river, and beyond. In the clean early morning light, the horizon was a crisp line above which was the blue and cloudless sky; looking at the horizon, sharply defined and with a quality of absoluteness, he thought of the times when, as a boy, he had stood on the rocky coast of Massachusetts Bay, and looked eastward across the gray Atlantic until his mind was choked and dizzied at the immensity he gazed upon. Older now, he looked upon another immensity in another horizon; but his mind was filled with some of the wonder he had known as a child. As if it were an intimation of some knowledge he had long ago lost, he thought now of those early explorers who had set out upon another waste, salt and wide. He remembered hearing of the superstition that told them they would come to a sharp brink, and sail over it, to fall forever from the world in space and darkness. The legends had not kept them back, he knew;

but he wondered how often, in their lonely sailing, they had intimations of depthless plunge, and how often they were repeated in their dreams. Looking at the horizon, he could see the line waver in the rising heat of the day; by late afternoon, with the rising winds, the line became indistinct, merged with the sky, and to the west was a vague country whose limits and extents were undefined. And as night came upon the land, creeping from the brightness sunk like a coal in the western haze, the little town that held him seemed to contract as the dark expanded; and he had, at moments, when his eye lost a point of reference, a sensation like falling, as the sailors must have had in their dreams in their deepest fears. But a light would flicker on the street below him, or a match would flare, or a door would open to let lantern light gleam on a passing boot; and he would again discover himself sitting before an open window in his hotel room, his muscles aching from inactivity and strain. Then he would let himself drop upon his bed and sleep in another darkness that was more familiar and more safe.

Occasionally he would interrupt his wait by the window and go down into the street. There the few buildings in Butcher's Crossing broke up his view of the land, so that it no longer stretched without limit in all directions—though at odd moments he had a feeling as if he were at a great distance above the town, and even above himself, gazing down upon a miniature cluster of buildings, about which crawled a number of tiny figures; and from this small center the land stretched outward endlessly, blotched and made shapeless by the point from which it spread.

But more usually, he wandered upon the street among the people who seemed to flow into and out of Butcher's Crossing as if by the impulse of an erratic but rhythmical tide. He went up and down the street, in and out of stores, paused, and went swiftly again, adjusting his motions to those of the people he moved among. Though he sought nothing in his mingling, he had odd and curious impressions that seemed to him important, perhaps because he did not seek them. He was not aware of these impressions as they occurred to him; but in the evening, as he lay in darkness on his bed, they came back to him with the force of freshness.

He had an image of men moving silently in the streets amidst a clatter of sound that was extraneous to them, that defined rather than dispersed their silence. A few of them wore guns thrust carelessly in their waistbands, though most of them went unarmed. In his image, their faces had a marked similarity; they were brown and ridged, and the eyes, lighter than the skin, had a way of looking slightly upward and beyond whatever they appeared to gaze at. And finally he had the impression that they moved naturally and without strain in a pattern so various and complex that his mind could not grasp it, a pattern whose secret passages could not be forced or opened by the will.

During Miller's absence, he spoke of his own volition to only three persons—Francine, Charley Hoge, and McDonald.

Once he saw Francine on the street; it was at noon, when few people were about; she was walking from Jackson's Saloon toward the dry goods store, and they met at the entrance, which was directly across the street from the hotel. They exchanged greetings, and Francine asked him if he had got used to the country yet. As he replied, he noticed minute beads of sweat that stood out distinctly above her full upper lip and caught the sunlight like tiny crystals. They spoke for some moments, and an awkward silence fell between them; Francine stood solid and unmoving before him, smiling at him, her wide pale eyes blinking slowly. At last he muttered an apology and walked away from her, up the street, as if he had some place to go.

He saw her again early one morning as she descended the long stairway that came from the upper floor of Jackson's Saloon. She wore a plain gray dress with the collar unbuttoned at the throat, and she came down the stairs with great care; the stairs were steep and open, so that she watched her feet as she placed them precisely at the center of the thick boards. Andrews stood on the board sidewalk and watched her come down; she did not wear a hat, and as she came out of the shadow of the building, the morning brightness caught her loose reddish-gold hair and gave warmth to her pale face. Though she had not seen him as she came down, she looked up at him without surprise when she got to the sidewalk.

"Good morning," Andrews said.

She nodded and smiled; she remained facing him with one hand still on the rough wooden bannister of the stair; she did not speak.

"You're up early this morning," he said. "There's hardly anyone on the street."

"When I get up early, I take a walk sometimes."

"All alone?"

She nodded. "Yes. It's good to walk alone in the morning; it's cool then. Soon it'll be winter and too cold to walk, and the hunters will be in town, and I won't be alone at all. So in the summer and fall I walk when I can in the morning."

"This is a beautiful morning," Andrews said.

"Yes," Francine said. "It's very cool."

"Well," Andrews said doubtfully, and started to move away, "I suppose I'll leave you to your walk."

Francine smiled and put her hand on his arm. "No. It's all right. You walk with me for a while. We'll talk."

She took his arm, and they walked slowly up and down the street, speaking quietly, their voices distinct in the morning stillness. Andrews moved stiffly; he did not look often at the girl beside him, and he was conscious of every muscle that moved him with her. Though afterward he thought often about their walk, he could not remember anything they said.

He saw Charley Hoge more frequently. Usually their conversations were brief and perfunctory. But once, casually, in a remote connection, he mentioned that his father was a lay minister in the Unitarian Church. Charley Hoge's eyes widened, his mouth dropped incredulously, and his voice took on a new note of respect. He explained to Andrews that he had been saved by a traveling preacher in Kansas City, and had been given a Bible by that same man. He showed Andrews the Bible; it was a cheap edition, worn, with several pages torn. A deep brownish stain covered the corners of a number of the pages; Charley explained that this was blood, buffalo blood, that he had got on the Bible just a few years ago; he wondered if he had committed, even by accident, a sacrilege; Andrews assured him that he had not. Thereafter Charley Hoge was eager to talk; sometimes he even went to the effort of seeking Andrews out to discuss with him some point of fact or question of interpretation about the Bible. Soon,

almost to his surprise, it occurred to Andrews that he did not
know the Bible well enough to talk about it even on Charley
Hoge's terms—had not, in fact, ever read it with any degree
of thoroughness. His father had encouraged his reading of
Mr. Emerson, but had not, to his recollection, insisted that
he read the Bible. Somewhat reluctantly, he explained this
to Charley Hoge; Charley Hoge's eyes became lidded with
suspicion, and when he spoke to Andrews again it was in the
tone of evangelicism rather than equality.

As he listened to Charley Hoge's exhortations, his mind
wandered away from the impassioned words; he thought of
the times, short months before, when he had been compelled
to be present each morning at eight at King's Chapel in Harvard College, to listen to words much like the words to which
he listened now. It amused him to compare the crude barroom
that smelled of kerosene, liquor, and sweat to the austere dark
length of King's Chapel where hundreds of soberly dressed
young men gathered each morning to hear the mumbled word
of God.

Listening to Charley Hoge, thinking of King's Chapel, he
realized quite suddenly that it was some irony such as this
that had driven him from Harvard College, from Boston, and
thrust him into this strange world where he felt unaccountably
at home. Sometimes after listening to the droning voices in the
chapel and in the classrooms, he had fled the confines of Cambridge to the fields and woods that lay southwestward to it.
There in some small solitude, standing on bare ground, he felt
his head bathed by the clean air and uplifted into infinite space;
the meanness and the constriction he had felt were dissipated
in the wildness about him. A phrase from a lecture by Mr. Emerson that he had attended came to him: I become a transparent eyeball. Gathered in by field and wood, he was nothing; he
saw all; the current of some nameless force circulated through
him. And in a way that he could not feel in King's Chapel, in
the college rooms, or on the Cambridge streets, he was a part
and parcel of God, free and uncontained. Through the trees
and across the rolling landscape, he had been able to see a hint
of the distant horizon to the west; and there, for an instant,
he had beheld something as beautiful as his own undiscovered
nature.

Now, on the flat prairie around Butcher's Crossing, he regularly wandered, as if seeking a chapel more to his liking than King's or Jackson's Saloon. On one such sojourn, on the fifth day after Miller had left Butcher's Crossing, and on the day before he returned, Andrews went for the second time down the narrow rutted road toward the river, and on an impulse turned off the road onto the path that led to McDonald's shack.

Andrews walked through the doorway without knocking. McDonald was seated behind his littered desk; he did not move as Andrews came into the room.

"Well," McDonald said, and cleared his throat angrily, "I see you've come back."

"Yes, sir," Andrews said. "I promised I would tell you if—"

McDonald waved his hand impatiently. "Don't tell me," he said, "I already know. . . . Pull up a chair."

Andrews got a chair from the corner of the room and brought it up beside the desk.

"You know?"

McDonald laughed shortly. "Hell, yes, I know; everybody in town knows. You gave Miller six hundred dollars, and you're off on a big hunt, up in Colorado, they say."

"You even know where we're going," Andrews said.

McDonald laughed again. "You don't think you're the first one that Miller has tried to get in on this deal, do you? He's been trying for four years, maybe more—ever since I've known him, anyway. By this time, I thought he'd have stopped."

Andrews was silent for a moment. Finally, he said: "It doesn't make any difference."

"You'll lose your tail, boy. Miller saw them buffalo, if he saw them at all, ten, eleven years ago. There's been a lot of hunting since then, and the herds have scattered; they don't all go where they used to go. You might find a few old strays, but that's all; you won't get your money back."

Andrews shrugged. "It's a chance. Maybe I won't."

"You could still back out," McDonald said. "Look." He leaned across the table and pointed a stiff index finger at Andrews. "You back out. Miller will be mad, but he won't make trouble; you can get four, five hundred dollars back on the stuff you've laid out for. Hell, I'll buy it from you. And if you really want to go out on a hunt, I'll fix you up; I'll send you out on one of my parties from here. You won't be gone more than three or four days, and you'll make more off of those three or four days than you will off the whole trip with Miller."

Andrews shook his head. "I've given my word. But it's kind of you, Mr. McDonald; I thank you very much."

"Well," McDonald said after a moment. "I didn't think you'd back out. Too stubborn. Knew it when I first saw you. But it's your money. None of my business."

They were silent for a long while. Andrews said at last, "Well, I wanted to see you before I left. Miller will be coming back tomorrow or the next day, and I won't know when we'll take off from here." He got up from the chair and put it back in its corner.

"One thing," McDonald said, not looking at him. "That's rough country you're going up into. You do what Miller tells you. He may be a son-of-a-bitch, but he knows the country; you listen to him, and don't go thinking you know anything at all."

Andrews nodded. "Yes, sir." He went forward until his thighs pressed against McDonald's desk and he was bent a little above McDonald's disheveled face. "I hope you do not think I am ungrateful in this matter. I know that you are a kind man, and that you have my best interests in mind. I am truly indebted to you." McDonald's mouth had slowly opened and now it hung incredulously wide, and his round eyes were watching Andrews. Andrews turned from him and walked out of the little shack into the sunlight.

In the sunlight he paused. He wondered if he wished to go back to the town just now. Unable to decide, he let his feet carry him vaguely along the wagon tracks to the main road; there he hesitated for a moment, to turn first one way and another, as the needle of a compass, slow to settle, discovers its point. He believed—and had believed for a long time—that there was a subtle magnetism in nature, which, if he uncon- sciously yielded to it, would direct him aright, not indifferent to the way he walked. But he felt that only during the few days that he had been in Butcher's Crossing had nature been so purely presented to him that its power of compulsion was sufficiently strong to strike through his will, his habit, and his idea. He turned west, his back toward Butcher's Crossing and the towns and cities that lay eastward beyond it; he walked past the clump of cottonwoods toward the river he had not seen, but which had assumed in his mind the proportions of a vast boundary that lay between himself and the wildness and freedom that his instinct sought.

The mounded banks of the river rose abruptly up, though the road ascended less steeply in a gradual cut. Andrews left the road and went into the prairie grass, which whipped about his ankles and worked beneath his trouser legs and clung to his skin. He paused atop the mound and looked down at the river; it was a thin, muddy trickle over flat rocks where the road crossed it, but above and below the road deeper pools lay flat and greenish brown in the sun. He turned his body a little to the left so that he could no longer see the road that led back to Butcher's Crossing.

Looking out at the flat featureless land into which he seemed to flow and merge, even though he stood without moving, he realized that the hunt that he had arranged with Miller was only a stratagem, a ruse upon himself, a palliative for ingrained custom and use. No business led him where he looked, where he would go; he went there free. He went free upon the plain in the western horizon which seemed to stretch without interruption toward the setting sun, and he could not believe that there were towns and cities in it of enough consequence to disturb him. He felt that wherever he lived, and wherever he would live hereafter, he was leaving the city more and more, withdrawing into the wilderness. He felt that that was the central meaning he could find in all his life, and it seemed to him then that all the events of his childhood and his youth had led him unknowingly to this moment upon which he poised, as if before flight. He looked at the river again. On this side is the city, he thought, and on that the wilderness; and though I must return, even that return is only another means I have of leaving it, more and more.

He turned. Butcher's Crossing lay small and unreal before him. He walked slowly back toward the town, on the road, his feet scuffing in the dust, his eyes watching the puffs of dust that his feet went beyond.

5.

LATE on the sixth day following his departure from Butcher's Crossing, Miller returned.

In his room, Andrews heard shouts on the street below him and heard the thump of heavy feet; above these sounds, muffled by the distance, came the crack of a whip and the deep-throated howl of a driver. Andrews came to his feet and strode to the window; he leaned out over the ledge and looked toward the eastern approach to the town.

A great cloud of dust hung upon the air, moved forward, and dissipated itself in its forward movement; out of the dust plodded a long line of oxen. The heads of the lead team were thrust downward, and the two beasts toed in toward each other, so that occasionally their long curving horns clashed, causing both beasts to shake their heads and snort, and separate for a few moments. Until the team got very near the town —the lead oxen passing Joe Long's barber shop—the wagon was scarcely visible to the townspeople who stood about the sidewalks and to Will Andrews who waited above them.

The wagon was long and shallow, and it curved downward toward the center so that it gave the fleeting appearance of a flat-bottomed boat supported by massive wheels; faded blue paint flecked the sides of the wagon, and the vestiges of red paint could be seen on the slow-turning spokes near the centers of the scarred, massive wheels. A heavy man in a checked shirt sat high and erect on a wagon box seat clipped near the front; in his right hand was a long bull-whip which he cracked above the ears of the lead team. His left hand pulled heavily against an upright hand brake, so that the oxen, which moved forward under his whip, were restrained by the heavy weight of the wagon above its half-locked wheels. Beside the wagon, slouched in his saddle, Miller rode a black horse; he led another, a sorrel, which was saddled but riderless.

The procession passed the hotel and passed Jackson's Saloon. Andrews watched it go beyond the livery stable, beyond the blacksmith's shop, and out of town. He watched until he could see little but the moving cloud of dust made brilliant and impenetrable by the light of the falling sun, and he waited until the dust cloud stopped and thinned away down in the hollow of the river. Then he went back to his bed and lay upon it, his palms folded beneath the back of his head, and stared up at the ceiling.

He was still staring at the ceiling, at the random flickerings of light upon it, an hour later when Charley Hoge knocked at his door and entered without waiting for a reply. He paused just inside the room; his figure was shadowy and vague, enlarged by the dim light that came from the hall.

"What are you laying here in the dark for?" he asked.

"Waiting for you to come up and get me," Andrews said. He lifted his legs over the side of the bed and sat upright on its edge.

"I'll light the lamp," Charley Hoge said. He moved forward in the darkness. "Where is it?"

"On the table near the window."

He pulled a match across the wall beside the window; the match flared yellow. With the hand that held the match, he lifted the smoked chimney from the lamp, set it down on the table, touched the match to the wick, and replaced the chimney. The room brightened as the wick's burning grew steadier, and the flickerings from the out-of-doors were submerged. Charley Hoge dropped the burnt match to the floor.

"I guess you know Miller's back in town."

Andrews nodded. "I saw the wagon as it came past. Who was with him?"

"Fred Schneider," Charley Hoge said. "He's going to be our skinner. Miller's worked with him before."

Andrews nodded again. "I suppose Miller got everything he needed."

"Everything's ready," Charley Hoge said. "Miller and Schneider are at Jackson's. Miller wants you to come over so we can get everything settled."

"All right," Andrews said. "I'll get my coat."

"Your coat?" Charley Hoge asked. "Boy, if you're cold now, what are you going to do when we get up in the mountains?"

Andrews smiled. "I'm not cold. I'm just in the habit of wearing it."

"A man loses lots of habits in time," Charley Hoge said. "Come on, let's go."

The two men left the room and went down the stairs. Charley Hoge went a few steps in front of Andrews, who had to hurry to keep up with him; he walked with quick, nervous strides, and his thin, drawn-in shoulders jerked upward with his steps.

Miller and Schneider were waiting at the long narrow bar of Jackson's. They stood at the bar with glasses of beer in front of them; a light mantle of dust clung about the shoulders of Schneider's red-checked shirt, and the ends of his straight, bristling brown hair visible beneath a flat-brimmed hat were caked white with trail dust. The two men turned as Charley Hoge and Will Andrews came down the room toward them.

Miller's flat thin lips curved upward in a tight smile. A precise swath of black beard shadowed the heavy lower half of his face. "Will," he said softly. "Did you think I wasn't coming back?"

Andrews smiled. "No. I knew you'd be back."

"Will, this is Fred Schneider; he's our skinner."

Andrews extended his hand and Schneider took it. Schneider's handclasp was loose, indifferent; he shook Andrews's hand once with a quick pumping motion. "How do," he said. His face was round, and though the lower part was covered with a light brown stubble, the whole face gave the appearance of being smooth and featureless. His eyes were wide and blue, and they regarded Andrews from beneath heavy, sleepy lids. He was a man of medium height, thickly built; he gave the immediate impression of being at all times watchful, alert, and on his guard. He wore a small pistol in a black leather holster hung high on his waist.

Miller drained the last of his beer from his glass. "Let's go in the big room where we can sit down," he said, wiping a bit of foam from his lips with a forefinger.

The others nodded. Schneider stood aside and waited for them to pass through the side door; then he followed, closing the door carefully behind him. The group of four men, with Miller in the lead, went toward the back of the room. They took a table near the stairs; Schneider sat with his back to the stairs, facing the room; Andrews sat in front of him. Charley Hoge was at Andrews's left, and Miller was at his right.

Miller said, "On my way back from the river, I stopped in

and saw McDonald. He'll buy our hides from us. That'll save us packing to Ellsworth."

"How much will he pay?" asked Schneider.

"Four dollars apiece for prime hides," Miller said. "He's got a buyer for prime hides back east."

Schneider shook his head. "How much for summer hides? You won't find any prime skins for another three months."

Miller turned to Andrews. "I haven't made any arrangements with Schneider, and I haven't told him where we're going. I thought I ought to wait till we all got together."

Andrews nodded. "All right," he said.

"Let's have a drink while we talk," Miller said. "Charley, see if you can find somebody to bring us back a pitcher of beer and some whisky."

Charley Hoge scraped his chair back on the floor, and went swiftly across the room.

"Did you make out all right at Ellsworth?" Andrews asked.

Miller nodded. "Got a good buy on the wagon. Some of the oxen haven't been broken in, and a couple of them need to be shod; but the lead team is a good one, and the rest of them will be broke in after the first few days."

"Did you have enough money?"

Miller nodded again, indifferently. "Got a little left over, even. I found you a nice horse; I rode it all the way back. All we need to pick up here is some whisky for Charley, a few sides of bacon, and— Do you have any rough clothes?"

"I can pick some up tomorrow," Andrews said.

"I'll tell you what you need."

Schneider looked sleepily at the two men. "Where are we going?"

Charley Hoge came across the room; behind him, carrying a large tray with a pitcher, bottle, and glasses upon it, Francine weaved among the tables. Charley Hoge sat down, and Francine put the bottle of whisky and the pitcher of beer in the center of the table and put the glasses in front of the men. She smiled at Andrews, and turned to Miller. "Did you bring me what I asked for from Ellsworth?"

"Yeah," Miller said. "I'll give it to you later. You set at another table for awhile, Francine. We got business to talk over."

Francine nodded, and walked to a table where another girl

and a man were sitting. Andrews watched her until she sat down; when he turned, he saw that Schneider's eyes were still upon her. Schneider blinked slowly once, and turned his eyes to Andrews. Andrews looked away.

All of the men except Charley Hoge filled their glasses with beer; he took the bottle of whisky before him, uncorked it, and let the pale amber liquor gurgle into his glass nearly to the brim.

"Where are we going?" Schneider asked again.

Miller set his glass of beer to his lips and drank in long even swallows. He put the glass on the table and turned it with his heavy fingers.

"We're going to the mountain country," Miller said.

"The mountain country," Schneider said. He put his glass on the table as if the taste of the beer had suddenly become unpleasant. "Up in the Colorado Territory."

"That's right," Miller said. "You know the country."

"I know it," Schneider said. He nodded for several moments without speaking. "Well, I guess I ain't lost much time. I can get a good night's sleep and start back for Ellsworth early tomorrow morning."

Miller did not speak. He took his glass up and finished his beer, and sighed deeply.

"Why in the hell do you figure to go clear across the country?" Schneider asked. "You can find plenty of buffalo thirty, forty mile from here."

"Summer hides," Miller said. "Thin as paper, and just about as strong."

Schneider snorted. "What the hell do you care? You can get good money for them."

"Fred," Miller said, "we've worked together before. I wouldn't lead you into something that wasn't good. I got a herd staked out; nobody knows anything about it except me. We can get back a thousand hides easy, maybe more. You heard McDonald; four dollars apiece for prime hides. That's four thousand dollars, six hundred dollars for your share, maybe more. That's a damn sight better than you'll do anywhere else around here."

Schneider nodded. "If there's buffalo where you say there is. How long has it been since you seen this herd?"

"It's been some time," Miller said. "But that don't worry me."

"It worries me," said Schneider. "I know for a fact you ain't been in the mountain country for eight, nine years; maybe longer."

"Charley's going," Miller said. "And Mr. Andrews here is going; he's even put up the money."

"Charley will do anything you tell him to," Schneider said. "And I don't know Mr. Andrews."

"I won't argue with you, Fred." Miller poured himself another glass of beer. "But it seems like you're letting me down."

"You can find another skinner who ain't got as much sense as I have."

"You're the best there is," Miller said. "And for this trip, I wanted the best."

"Hell," Schneider said. He reached for the pitcher of beer; it was almost empty. He held it up and called to Francine. Francine got up from the table where she was sitting, took the pitcher, and left without speaking. Schneider took the bottle of whisky from in front of Charley Hoge and poured several fingers of it into his beer glass. He drank it in two gulps, grimacing at the burning.

"It's too much of a gamble," he said. "We'd be gone two months, maybe three; and we might have nothing to show for it. It's been a long time since you seen them buffalo; a country can change in eight or nine years."

"We won't be gone more than a month and a half, or two months," Miller said. "I got fresh, young oxen; they should make near thirty miles a day going, and maybe twenty coming back."

"They might make fifteen going and ten coming, if you pushed them right hard."

"The days are long this time of year," Miller said. "The country's nearly level right up to where we're going, and there's water all along the way."

"Hell," Schneider said. Miller did not speak. "All right," Schneider said. "I'll go. But no shares. I'm taking no chances. I'll take sixty dollars a month, straight, starting the day we leave here and ending the day we get back."

"That's fifteen dollars more than usual," Miller said.

"You said I was the best," Schneider said, "and you offered shares. Besides, that's rough country where you intend to go."

Miller looked at Andrews; Andrews nodded.

"Done," Miller said.

"Where's that gal with the beer?" Schneider asked.

Charley Hoge took the bottle of whisky from in front of Schneider and replenished his glass. He sipped the liquor delicately, appreciatively; his small gray eyes darted between Miller and Schneider. He grinned sharply, craftily at Schneider, and said:

"I knowed all along you'd give in. I knowed it from the first."

Schneider nodded. "Miller always gets what he's after."

They were silent. Francine came across the room with their pitcher of beer and set it on the table. She smiled briefly at the group, and spoke again to Miller.

"You about finished with your business?"

"Almost," Miller said. "I left your package in the front room, under the bar. Why don't you run out and see if it's what you wanted. Maybe you can come back a little later and have a drink with us."

Francine said, "All right," and started to move away. As she moved, Schneider put out a hand and laid it on her arm. Andrews stiffened.

"Sprechen sie Deutsch?" he asked. He was grinning.

"Yes," she said.

"Ach," he said. "Ich so glaube. Du arbeitest jetzt, nicht wahr?"

"Nein," Francine said.

"Ja," Schneider said, still grinning. "Du arbeitest mit mir, nicht wahr?"

"All right," Miller said. "We've got things to talk about. Go on now, Francine."

Francine moved away from Schneider's hand and went quickly across the room.

"What was that all about?" asked Andrews. His voice was tight.

"Why, I just asked her if she wanted a little job of work," Schneider said. "I ain't seen a better looking whore since I was in St. Louis."

Andrews looked at him for a moment; his lips tingled with anger, and his hands, beneath the table, were tightly clasped. He turned to Miller. "When do we figure on leaving?"

"Three or four days," Miller said. He looked from Andrews to Schneider with faint amusement. "The wagon needs a little work, and like I said a couple of the oxen need to be shod. Nothing's going to hold us up."

Schneider poured himself a glass of beer. "You said there was water all the way. What route do we take?"

Miller smiled. "Don't worry about that. I have that all figured out. I've thought it over in my mind for a long time."

"All right," Schneider said. "Do I work alone?"

"Mr. Andrews will help you."

"He ever done any skinning before?" He looked at Andrews, grinning again.

"No," Andrews said shortly. His face grew warmer.

"I'd feel better about it if I worked with somebody I knew better," Schneider said. "No offense."

"I think you'll find that Mr. Andrews will be a lot of help, Fred." Miller's voice was gentle, and he did not look at Schneider.

"All right," Schneider said. "You're the boss. But I ain't got any extra knives."

"All of that's taken care of," Miller said. "All we need is to get Will some work clothes; we can do that tomorrow."

"You've got it all figured out, haven't you?" Schneider spoke indifferently; the sleepy look had come back into his pale eyes. Miller nodded.

Andrews finished the last dregs of his warm beer. "I take it, then, that there's nothing else we have to talk about tonight."

"Nothing that won't keep," Miller said.

"Then I think I'll go back to the hotel. I have a few letters I ought to write."

"All right, Will," Miller said. "But we ought to get those clothes tomorrow. Why don't you meet me at the dry goods store just after noon."

Andrews nodded. He said good night to Charley Hoge, and laid a bill on the table. "I'd be obliged if you'd all have another drink on me." He walked across the room, through the door into the smoky bar, and quickly onto the street.

The anger which had risen within him back in the room, listening to Schneider talk to Francine, began to subside. A light breeze came in from the river, and carried with it the odor of manure and the acrid smell of heated impure metal from the blacksmith shop across the street from him. A red glow from the shop filtered through the yellow light of a lantern hung within the doorway; the soft whoosh of bellows working could be heard among the clangs of metal on hot metal. He breathed deeply of the cooling night air, and started off the board sidewalk to cross the street to his hotel.

But he halted, with one foot in the dust of the street and the other still resting on the edge of a thick plank. He had heard, or thought he had heard, his name whispered behind him, somewhere in the darkness. He turned uncertainly, and heard more distinctly the voice that called to him:

"Mr. Andrews! Over here."

The whispered voice seemed to come from one corner of the long saloon building. He went toward it, his way lighted by the irregular glow that came from the half-door and the small high windows of Jackson's Saloon.

It was Francine. Though he had not expected to see her, he looked at her without surprise; she stood on the first step of the long steep stairway that led up the side of the building. Her face was made pale and vague by the darkness, and her body was a dark shadow in the darkness around her. She reached out her hand and laid it on his shoulder; on the step, she stood above him, and looked down at him when she spoke:

"I thought that was you. I've been waiting here for you to come out."

Andrews's voice came with difficulty. "I—I got tired of talking to them. I needed some fresh air."

She smiled and drew back a little, her hand still light on his shoulder; her face fell into shadow, and he could see only her eyes and her teeth revealed by her smiling in the reflection of dim light.

"Come upstairs with me," she said softly. "Come up for a while."

He swallowed, and tried to speak. "I—"

"Come on," she said. "It'll be all right."

She exerted a gentle pressure on his shoulder, and turned

away from him; he heard the rustle of her clothes as she started up the stairs. He followed, groping for the rough handrail on his left, his eyes desperately trying to make out the shape that went softly and slowly above him, pulling him with her invisibly.

They paused at the small square landing at the top of the stairs. She stood in the dark shade of the doorway, fumbling with the latch; for an instant, Andrews looked out over Butcher's Crossing; what he could see of the town was a dark, irregular shadow like a blotch upon the glimmer of the plain. The thin edge of a new moon hung in the west. The door creaked open, Francine whispered something, and he followed her into the darkness of the doorway.

A small dim light burned in the distance; its illumination was thin and local, but he could make out that they were in a narrow hall. The muffled sounds of men's voices and the clump of boots on wood came from below; he realized that they were just above the large hall beside Jackson's saloon, out of which he had walked a few moments before. He groped forward, and his hands touched the smooth stiff material of Francine's dress.

"Here," she whispered. She found his hand, and took it; her hand felt cool and moist to his own. "Down this way."

He went blindly after her, his feet sliding and catching on the rough boards of the floor. They stopped; dimly he made out a doorway. Francine opened the door, saying, "This is my room," and went in. Andrews followed, blinking against the light that came when the door was opened.

Inside the room, he closed the door and leaned against it, his eyes following Francine, who moved across the small room to a table upon which a lamp, its base milk-white and decorated with brightly painted roses, burned dimly. She turned the lamp up so that the room was more brightly illumined; the light revealed the smallness of the room, the neatly made iron bedstead, a small, curving sofa whose wooden frame was carved with twined flowers and upon which were cushions covered with dark red velvet. The walls of the room were newly papered; upon them hung several framed engravings of woodland scenes. Here and there on the walls the brightly flowered wallpaper curled and peeled, revealing naked wood. Though he did not know what he had expected, Andrews was taken aback and made slightly uncomfortable by the familiarity of the room. For a moment he did not move.

Francine, her back to the light, was smiling; again, he was aware of the light glinting from her eyes and teeth. She motioned to the couch. Andrews nodded and went across the floor; when he sat down, he looked at his feet; there was a thin carpet, worn and stained, over the floor. Francine came across the room from the table beside the bed and sat on the couch beside him; she sat a little sideways, so that she was facing him; her back was straight, and she looked almost prim, there in the lamplight, with her hands folded in her lap.

"You—you have a nice place here," Andrews said.

She nodded, pleased. "I have the only carpet in town," she said. "I had it sent in from St. Louis. Pretty soon I'm going to get a glass window. The dust blows in and it's hard to keep a place clean."

Andrews nodded, and smiled. He drummed his fingers on his knees. "Have—you been here long? In Butcher's Crossing?"

"Two years," she said indifferently. "I was in St. Louis before that, but there were too many girls there. I didn't like it." Her eyes were upon him as if she had no interest in what she was saying. "I like it here. I can rest in the summer, and there aren't so many people."

He spoke to her, but he hardly knew what he said; for as he spoke, his heart went out to her in an excess of pity. He saw her as a poor, ignorant victim of her time and place, betrayed by certain artificialities of conduct, thrust from a great mechanical world upon this bare plateau of existence that fronted the wilderness. He thought of Schneider, who had caught her arm and spoken coarsely to her; and he imagined vaguely the humiliations she had schooled herself to endure. A revulsion against the world rose up within him, and he could taste it in his throat. Impulsively he reached across the sofa and took her hand.

"It—must be a terrible life for you," he said suddenly.

"Terrible?" She frowned thoughtfully. "No. It's better than St. Louis. The men are better, and there aren't so many girls."

"You have no family, no one you can go to?"

She laughed. "What would I do with a family?" She squeezed his hand, and raised it, and turned it palm upward. "So soft," she said. She caressed his palm with her thumb, which moved slowly and rhythmically in small circles. "That's the only thing I don't like about the men here. Their hands are so rough."

He was trembling. With his free hand he grasped the armrest of the sofa and held it tightly.

"What do they call you?" Francine asked softly. "Is it William?"

"Will," Andrews said.

"I'll call you William," she said. "It's more like you, I think." She smiled slowly at him. "You're very young, I think."

He removed his hand from the smooth caress of her fingers. "I am twenty-three."

She came closer to him, sliding across the sofa; the rustle of her stiff smooth dress sounded like soft cloth tearing. Her shoulder lightly pressed against his shoulder, and she breathed gently, evenly.

"Don't be angry," she said. "I'm glad you're young. I want you to be young. All of the men here are old and hard. I want you to be soft, while you can be. . . . When will you go with Miller and the others?"

"Three or four days," Andrews said. "But we will be back within the month. And then—"

Francine shook her head, though she continued smiling. "Yes, you'll be back; but you won't be the same. You'll not be so young; you will become like the others."

Andrews looked at her confusedly, and in his confusion cried: "I will only become myself!"

She continued as if he had not interrupted. "The wind and sun will harden your face; your hands will no longer be soft."

Andrews opened his mouth to reply; he had become vaguely angry at her words. But he did not speak his anger; and as he looked at her in the lamplight, his anger died. There was a simplicity and earnestness, a sweet but not profound sorrow in her expression, which disarmed him, and which raised a tenderness with the pity he had felt a moment earlier. At that instant it seemed to him incredible that she could be what her profession termed her. He extended the hand that he had withdrawn, and covered her hand.

"You are—" he began, and hesitated, and began again. "You are—" But he could not finish; he did not know what he wanted to say.

"But for a little while," Francine said, "you will be here; for three or four days you will be young and soft."

"Yes," Andrews said.

"You will stay here for those days?" Francine said softly. She ran her fingertips lightly over the back of his hand. "You will make love to me?"

He did not speak; he was aware of her fingers moving upon his hand, and he concentrated upon that sensation.

"I'm not working now," Francine said quickly. "It's for love; it's because I want you."

He shook his head numbly, not in refusal but in despair. "Francine, I—"

"I know," she said softly, smiling again. "You have not had a woman before, have you?" He did not speak. "Have you?"

He remembered several abortive experiments with a younger cousin of his, a small, petulant girl, some years before; he remembered his urgency, his embarrassment, and his eventual boredom; and he remembered his father's averted face and vague words after the visiting parents of the girl left their home. "No," he said.

"It's all right," Francine said. "I'll show you. Here." She stood up, and extended her hands down to him. He grasped them and stood up before her. She came close to him, almost touching him; he felt her soft stomach come against him; his muscles contracted, and he flinched slightly away.

"It's all right," Francine said, her breath warm against his ear. "Don't think of anything." She laughed softly. "Are you all right?"

"Yes," he said shakily.

She pulled away from him a little and looked at his face; it seemed to him that her lips had grown thicker, and that her eyes had darkened. She moved her body against him. "I wanted you the first time I saw you," she said. "Without you even touching me, or talking to me." She moved away, her eyes still dark upon him; she reached her arms up behind her neck and began unsnapping her dress. He watched her numbly, his arms held awkwardly at his sides. Suddenly, she shook her body and the dress fell in a gray heap at her feet. She was nude; her body gleamed in the lamplight. Delicately she stepped out of the dress, and her flesh quivered with the movement; her heavy breasts swung slowly as she walked toward him.

"Now," she said, and lifted her lips up to him. He kissed her with dry lips, tasting wetness; she whispered against his lips, and her hands fumbled with his shirt front; he felt her hands go inside his shirt, go lightly over the tensed muscles of his chest. "Now," she said again; it was a bruised sound, and it seemed to echo in his head.

He pulled away from her a little to look at her soft heavy body that clung to him like velvet, held there of its own nature; there was a serenity on her face, almost as if it were asleep; and he felt that she was beautiful. But suddenly there came into his mind the words that Schneider had used, back in the saloon —he had said he hadn't seen a better looking whore since he had left St. Louis; and the look of her face changed, though he could not tell in what respect. He was assailed by the knowledge that others had seen this face as he was seeing it now; that others had kissed her on her wet lips, had heard the voice he was hearing, had felt the same breath he was feeling upon his own face, now. They had quickly paid their money, and had gone, and others had come, and others. He had a quick and irrational image of hundreds of men, steadily streaming in and out of a room. He turned, pulled away from her, suddenly dead inside himself.

"What is it?" Francine said sleepily. "Come back."

"No!" he said hoarsely, and flung himself across the room, stumbling on the edge of the rug. "My God! . . . No. I'm— I'm sorry." He looked up. Francine stood dumbly in the center of the room; her arms were held out as if to describe a shape to him; there was a look of bewilderment in her eyes. "I can't," he said to her, as if he were explaining something. "I can't."

He looked at her once more; she did not move, and the look of bewilderment did not leave her face. He pulled open the door and let the knob fly violently from his hand; he ran into the dark hall and stumbled down its length, opened the door to the landing, and stood for a moment on the landing, breathing air in deep, famished gulps. When his legs regained some of their strength, he went down the stairs, feeling his way by the rough bannister.

He stood for a moment on the rough sidewalk, and looked up and down the street. He could not see much of Butcher's Crossing in the darkness. He looked across the street at his hotel; a dim light came from the doorway. He went across the dusty street toward it. He did not think of Francine, or of what had happened in the room above Jackson's Saloon. He thought of the three or four days that he would have to wait in this place before Miller and the others were ready. He thought of how he might spend them, and he wondered how he might press them into one crumpled bit of time that he could toss away.

PART TWO

1.

IN THE early dawn, on the twenty-fifth day of August, the four men met behind the livery stable where their wagon, loaded with six weeks' provisions, waited for them. A sleepy stable man, scratching his matted hair and cursing mechanically under his breath, yoked their oxen to the wagon; the oxen snorted and moved uneasily in the faint light cast by a lantern set on the ground. His task completed, the stable man grunted and turned away from the four men; he shambled back toward the livery stable, swinging the lantern carelessly beside him, and dropped upon a pile of filthy blankets that lay on the open ground outside. Lying on his side, he raised the globe of the lantern and blew out the flame. In the darkness, three of the men mounted their horses; the fourth clambered into the wagon. For a few moments none of them spoke or moved. In the silence and darkness the heavy breathing of the stable man came regular and deep, and the thin squeak of leather upon wood sounded as the oxen moved against their yokes.

From the wagon Charley Hoge cleared his throat and said: "Ready?"

Miller sighed deeply, and answered, his voice muffled and quiet: "Ready."

Upon the silence came the sudden pop of braided leather as Charley Hoge let his bull-whip out above the oxen, and his voice, shrill and explosive, cracked: "Harrup!"

The oxen strained against the weight of the wagon, their hooves pawing and thudding dully in the earth; the wheels groaned against the hickory axles; for a moment there was a jumble of sound—wood strained against its grain, rawhide and leather slapped together and pulled in high thin screeches, and metal jangled against metal; then the sound gave way to an easy rumble as the wheels turned and the wagon slowly began to move behind the oxen.

The three men preceded the wagon around the livery stable and into the wide dirt street of Butcher's Crossing. Miller rode first, slouched in his saddle; behind him, forming a broad-based triangle, rode Schneider and Andrews. Still, no one

61

spoke. Miller looked ahead into the darkness that was gradually beginning to lift; Schneider kept his head down, as if he were asleep in his saddle; and Andrews looked on either side of him at the little town that he was leaving. The town was ghostly and dim in the morning darkness; the fronts of the buildings were gray shapes that rose out of the earth like huge eroded stones, and the half-dugouts appeared to be piles of rubble thrown carelessly about open holes. The procession passed Jackson's Saloon, and soon it was past the town. In the flat country beyond the town, it seemed to be darker; the clopping of the horses' hooves became dull and regular in the ears of the men, and the thin clogging odor of dust clung about their nostrils, and was not blown away in the slowness of their passage.

Beyond the town the procession passed on its left McDonald's small shack and the pole-fenced brining pits; Miller turned his head, grunted something inaudible to himself, and chuckled. A little past the clump of cottonwood trees, where the road began to go upward over the mounded banks of the stream, the three men on horseback came to a pause and the wagon behind them creaked to a halt. They turned and looked back, widening their eyes against the darkness. As they looked at the vague sprawling shape of Butcher's Crossing, a dim yellow light, disembodied and hanging casually in the darkness, came on; from somewhere a horse neighed and snorted. With one accord, they turned again on their horses and began to descend the road that led across the river.

Where they crossed, the river was shallow; its trickling around the flat rocks that had been laid in the soft mud as a bed for crossing had a murmurous sound that was intensified by the darkness; the dim light from the filling moon caught irregularly upon the water as it flowed, and there was visible upon the stream a constant glitter that made it appear wider and deeper than it was. The water barely came above their horses' hooves, and flowed unevenly over the turning rims of the wagon wheels.

A few moments after they crossed the stream, Miller again pulled his horse to a halt. In the dimness, the other men could see him raise himself in the saddle and lean toward the lifting darkness in the west. As if it were heavy, he lifted his arm and pointed in that direction.

"We'll cut across country here," he said, "and hit the Smoky Hill trail about noon."

The first pink streaks of light were beginning to show in the east. The group turned off the road and set across the flat land; in a few minutes, the narrow road was no longer visible to them. Will Andrews turned in his saddle and looked back; he could not be sure of the point where they had left the road, and he could see no mark to guide them in their journey westward. The wagon wheels went easily and smoothly through the thick yellow-green grass; the wagon left narrow parallel lines behind it, which were quickly swallowed up in the level distance.

The sun rose behind them, and they went more quickly forward, as if pushed by the increasing heat. The air was clear, and the sky was without clouds; the sun beat against their backs and brought sweat through their rough clothing.

Once the group passed a small hut with a sod roof. The hut was set on the open plain; behind it a small plot of ground had been cleared once, but now it was going back to the yellow-green grass that covered the land. A broken wagon wheel lay near the front entrance, and a heavy wooden plow was rotting beside it. Through the wide door, at the side of which hung a scrap of weathered canvas, they could see an overturned table and the floor covered with dust and rubble. Miller turned in his saddle and spoke to Andrews:

"Gave it up." His voice had a thin edge of satisfaction. "Lots of them have tried it, but don't many make it. They pull out when it gets a little bad."

Andrews nodded, but he did not speak. As they went past the hut, his head turned; he watched the place until his view of it was cut off by the wagon that came behind them.

By noon the horses' hides were shining with sweat, and white flecks of foam covered their mouths and were sent flying into the air as they shook their heads against the bits. The heat throbbed against Andrews's body, and his head pounded painfully with the beat of his pulse; already the flesh on his upper thighs was tender from rubbing against the saddle flaps, and his buttocks were numb on the hard leather of the seat. Never before had he ridden for more than a few hours at a time; he winced at the thought of the pain he would feel at the end of the day.

Schneider's voice broke upon him: "We ought to be getting to the river about this time. I don't see no sign of it yet."

His voice was directed to no one in particular, but Miller turned and answered him shortly. "It ain't far. The animals can hold out till we get there."

Hardly had he finished speaking when Charley Hoge, behind them in the wagon, perched higher on his wagon seat than they in their saddles, called in his high voice: "Look ahead! You can see the trees from here."

Andrews squinted and strained his eyes against the noon brightness. After a few moments he was able to make out a thin dark line that slashed up through the yellow field.

Miller turned to Schneider. "Shouldn't be more than ten minutes from here," he said, and smiled a little. "Think you can hold out?"

Schneider shrugged. "I ain't in no hurry. I was just wondering if we was going to find it as easy as you thought."

Miller rapped his horse gently across the rump with one hand, and the horse went forward a bit more rapidly. Behind him Andrews heard the sharp crack of Charley Hoge's whip, and heard his wordless cry to the oxen. He turned. The oxen lumbered forward more swiftly, as if they had been awakened from a reverie. A light breeze came toward them, ruffling the grass in a soft sweep. The horses' ears pitched forward; beneath him Andrews felt a sudden stiffening and a surge of movement as his horse went ahead.

Miller pulled back on his reins and called to Andrews: "Hold him hard. They smell water. If you ain't careful, he'll run away with you."

Andrews grasped the reins tightly and pulled hard against the forward movement of the horse; the horse's head came back, the black eyes wide and the coarse black mane flying. He heard behind him the thin squeak of leather straining as Charley Hoge braked against the oxen, and heard the oxen lowing as if in agony at their restraint.

By the time they got to the Smoky Hill, the animals were quieter, but tense and impatient. Andrews's hands were sore from pulling against the reins. He dismounted; hardly had he got his feet on the ground when his horse sprang away from him and tore through the low underbrush that lined the river.

His legs were weak. He took a few steps forward and sat shakily in the shade of a scrub oak; the branches scratched against his back, but he did not have the will to move. He watched dully as Charley Hoge set the brake on the wagon and unyoked the first team of oxen from the heavy singletree. With his one hand pulling hard against the yoke, his body slanted between the oxen, Charley Hoge let himself be pulled toward the stream. He returned in a few moments and led another pair to the stream, while the remaining oxen set up a deep and mindless lowing. Miller dropped upon the ground beside Andrews; Schneider sat across from them, his back to another tree, and looked about indifferently.

"Charley has to lead them down two at a time, yoked together," Miller said. "If he let them all go down together, they might trample each other. They ain't got much more sense than buffalo."

By the time the last oxen were released from the wagon, the horses began to amble back from the river. The men removed the bits from their horses' mouths and let them graze. Charley got some dried fruit and biscuits from the wagon, and the men munched on them.

"Might as well take it easy for a while," Miller said. "The stock will have to graze; we can take it easy for a couple of hours."

Small black flies buzzed about their damp faces, and their hands were busy slapping them away; the slow gurgle of the river, hidden by the dense brush, came to their ears. Schneider lay on his back and placed a dirty red handkerchief over his face and folded his bare hands under his armpits; soon he was asleep, and the center of the red handkerchief rose and fell gently with his breathing. Charley Hoge wandered along the grassy outer bank of the river toward the grazing animals.

"How far have we come this morning?" Andrews asked Miller, who sat erect beside him.

"Pretty near eight miles," Miller answered. "We'll do better when the team is broke in. They ain't working together like they ought to." There was a silence. Miller continued: "A mile or so ahead, we run into the Smoky Hill trail; it follows the river pretty close all the way into the Colorado Territory. It's easy traveling; should take us less than a week."

"And when we get into the Colorado?" Andrews asked.

Miller grinned briefly and shook his head. "No trail there. We'll just travel on the country."

Andrews nodded. The weakness in his body had given way to a lassitude. He stretched his limbs and lay on his stomach, his chin resting on his folded hands. The short grass, green under the trees and moist from the seepage of the river, tickled his nostrils; he smelled the damp earth and the sweet sharp freshness of the grass. He did not sleep, but his eyes drooped and his breath came evenly and deeply. He thought of the short distance they had come, and he tensed muscles that were growing sore. It was only the beginning of the journey; what he had seen this morning—the flatness, the emptiness, the yellow sea of undisturbed grass—was only the presentiment of the wilderness. Another strangeness was waiting for him when they left the trail and went into the Colorado Territory. His half-closed eyes nearly recaptured the sharp engravings he had seen in books, in magazines, when he was at home in Boston; but the thin black lines wavered upon the real grass before him, took on color, then faded. He could not recapture the strange sensations he had had, long ago, when he first saw those depictions of the land he now was seeking. Among the three men who waited beside the river, the silence was not broken until Charley Hoge began leading the oxen back to the wagon to yoke them for the resumption of the afternoon trip.

The trail upon which they went was a narrow strip of earth that had been worn bare by wagon wheels and hooves. Occasionally deep ruts forced the wagon off into the tall grass, where the land was often more level than on the trail. Andrews asked Miller why they stuck to the trail, and Miller explained that the sharp grass, whipping all day against the hooves and fetlocks of an ox, could make him footsore. For the horses, which lifted their hooves higher even in a slow walk, there was less danger.

Once, along the trail, they came upon a wide strip of bare earth that intersected their path. In this strip the earth was packed tightly down, though its surface was curiously pocked with regular indentations. It extended away from the river almost as far as the eye could see, and gradually merged into the prairie grass; on the other side of the men, it led toward the river, gradually increasing in width to the very edge of the river, which at this point was bare of brush and tree.

"Buffalo," Miller said. "This is their watering place. They come across here—" he pointed to the plain, "in a straight line, and spread out at the river. No reason for it. I've seen a thousand buffalo lined up in ruts like this, one behind another, waiting for water."

Along the trail they saw no other signs of the buffalo that day, though Miller remarked that they were getting into buffalo country. The sun whitened the western sky and threw its heat against their movement. Their horses bowed their heads and stumbled on the flat land, their sleek coats shining with sweat; the oxen plodded before the wagon, their breathing heavy and labored. Andrews pulled his hat down to shade his face, and bent his head so that he saw only the horse's curved black mane, the dark brown pommel of his saddle, and the yellow land moving jerkily beneath him. He was soaked with sweat, and the flesh of his thighs and buttocks was raw from its chafing against the saddle. He shifted his position until the shifting offered him no relief, and then he tethered his horse on the tailgate of the wagon and clambered upon the spring seat beside Charley Hoge. But the hard wood of the seat pained him more than the saddle, and the dust from the oxen's hooves choked him and made his eyes burn; he had to sit rigid and tense upon the narrow board to hold himself erect against the slow swaying of the wagon. Soon, with a few words to Charley Hoge, who had not spoken to him, he got off the wagon and once again resumed his shifting position in his saddle. For the rest of the afternoon he rode in a kind of pain that approached numbness but never achieved it.

When the sun descended beyond the vast curve of the horizon, reddening the sky and the land, the animals lifted their heads and went forward more swiftly. Miller, who had ridden all day ahead of the party, turned and shouted to Charley Hoge:

"Whip them up! They can stand it, now the day's turned cool. We need to make another five miles before we set camp."

For the first time since early in the morning, the sharp crack of Charley Hoge's whip sounded above the creaking of the wagon and the thud of the oxen's hooves. The men stirred their horses to a fast walk that occasionally broke into a slow jarring trot.

After the sun went down the darkness came swiftly; and still the group moved forward. The moon rose thinly behind them; it seemed to Andrews that their motion carried them nowhere, that they were agitated painfully upon a small dim plateau that moved beneath them as they had the illusion of going forward. In the near darkness, he grasped the horn of his saddle and raised himself up by pressing his unsteady feet upon the stirrups.

About two hours later, Miller, a vague shape that seemed a part of the animal he rode, halted and shouted back to them in a voice clear and sharp in the darkness:

"Pull her up at that clump of willows, Charley. We camp here."

Andrews went cautiously toward Miller, holding his reins tightly against the movement of his horse. Dark against the lesser darkness, the brush of the river bank sprang up before him. He tried to remove one foot from a stirrup to dismount but his leg was so stiff and numb that he was unable to do so. Finally he reached down and grasped the stirrup by its strap and tugged until he could feel the stirrup swing free. Then he threw the weight of his body to one side and half fell from his horse; he supported himself for a few moments on the ground by holding hard to his saddle.

"Rough day?" The voice was low but close to his ear. He turned; Miller's broad white face hung in the darkness.

Andrews swallowed and nodded, not trusting himself to speak.

"It takes some getting used to," Miller said. "A couple days' riding, then you'll be all right." He untied Andrews's bedroll from behind his saddle and gave the horse a heavy slap on the rump. "We'll bed down in that little draw on the other side of the willows. Think you can manage now?"

Andrews nodded and took the bedroll from him. "Thanks," he said. "I'm all right." He walked unsteadily in the direction that Miller had indicated, though he could see nothing beyond the dark clump of the willow. Dim shapes moved around him, and he realized that Charley Hoge had already unyoked the oxen and they were crashing their way to the river. He heard the sound of a shovel pushing into earth and grating on rock, and saw the glint of moonlight on the blade as it was turned. He went nearer; Charley Hoge was digging a small pit. With his good hand he held the handle of the shovel, while with one foot he thrust the blade into the ground; then, bending over, he cradled the handle in the bend of his other arm and levered the shovel up, spilling the earth beside the pit he was digging. Andrews dropped his bedroll to the ground and sat upon it, his arms thrust between his legs, his fingers curled loosely on the ground.

After a few moments, Charley Hoge stopped his digging and went away into the darkness, returning with a bundle of twigs and small branches. He dropped them into the pit and struck a match, which flamed fretfully in the darkness, and thrust the match among the small twigs. Soon the fire was burning brightly, leaping up into the darkness. Not until then did Andrews notice Schneider lounging across from him on the other side of the fire. Schneider grinned at him once, sardonically, his face flickering in the flame-light; then he lay back on his bedroll and pulled his hat over his face.

For the next hour or two, in his exhaustion, Andrews was only vaguely aware of what happened around him. Charley Hoge came in and out of his sight, feeding the fire; Miller came up near him, spread out his bedroll, and lay upon it, his gaze directed at the fire; Andrews dozed. He came awake with a start at the aroma of brewing coffee, and looked about him with a sudden bewilderment; for a moment all he could see was the small glowing patch of coals in front of him, which sent an intense heat against his face and arms. Then he was aware of the bulky figures of Schneider and Miller standing near the pit; painfully he raised himself from the bedroll and joined them. In silence the men drank their coffee and ate the scalding beans and side pork that Charley Hoge had prepared. Andrews found himself eating wolfishly, in great gulps, though he was not aware of any hunger. The men scraped the large pot clean of the food, and sopped the liquid in their tin plates with crumbs of dried biscuit. They drained the blackened coffeepot to the dregs, and sat on their bedrolls with their hot coffee, sipping slowly, while Charley Hoge carried the utensils down to the river.

Without removing his shoes, Andrews folded his bedroll over him and lay on the ground. Mosquitoes buzzed about his face, but he did not brush them away. Just before he went to sleep, he heard in the distance the sound of horses' hooves and the faint squeal of rapidly turning wagon wheels; the far sound of a man's voice shouting indistinguishable words rose above the other noises. Andrews lifted himself on an elbow.

Miller's voice came to him, very close, out of the darkness. "Buffalo hunters. Probably one of McDonald's outfits." His voice was edged with contempt. "They're going too fast; can't have many hides."

The sounds faded into the distance. For a while, Andrews remained on his elbow, his eyes straining in the direction that the sounds had come from. Then his arm tired and he lay down and slept almost immediately.

2.

THE GREAT plain swayed beneath them as they went steadily westward. The rich buffalo grass, upon which their animals fattened even during the arduous journey, changed its color throughout the day; in the morning, in the pinkish rays of the early sun, it was nearly gray; later, in the yellow light of the midmorning sun, it was a brilliant green; at noon it took on a bluish cast; in the afternoon, in the intensity of the sun, at a distance, the blades lost their individual character and through the green showed a distinct cast of yellow, so that when a light breeze whipped across, a living color seemed to run through the grass, to disappear and reappear from moment to moment. In the evening after the sun had gone down, the grass took on a purplish hue as if it absorbed all the light from the sky and would not give it back.

After their first day's journey, the country lost some of its flatness; it rolled out gently before them, and they traveled from soft hollow to soft rise, as if they were tiny chips blown upon the frozen surface of a great sea.

Upon the surface of this sea, among the slow hollows and crests, Will Andrews found himself less and less conscious of any movement forward. During the first few days of the journey he had been so torn with the raw agony of movement that each forward step his mount took cut itself upon his nerves and upon his mind. But the pain dulled after the first days, and a kind of numbness took its place; he felt no sensation of his buttocks upon the saddle, and his legs might have been of wood, so stiffly and without feeling did they set about the sides of his horse. It was during this numbness that he lost the awareness of any progression forward. The horse beneath him took him from hollow to crest, yet it seemed to him that the land rather than the horse moved beneath him like a great treadmill, revealing in its movement only another part of itself.

Day by day the numbness crept upon him until at last the numbness seemed to be himself. He felt himself to be like the land, without identity or shape; sometimes one of the men would look at him, look through him, as if he did not exist; and he had to shake his head sharply and move an arm or a leg and glance at it to assure himself that he was visible.

And the numbness extended to his perception of the others who rode with him on the empty plain. Sometimes in his weariness he looked at them without recognition, seeing but the crudest shapes of men. At such times he knew them only by the positions they occupied. As at the beginning of the journey, Miller rode ahead and Andrews and Schneider formed the base of a triangle behind him. Often, as the group approached out of a hollow a slight rise of land, Miller, no longer outlined against the horizon, seemed to merge into the earth, a figure that accommodated itself to the color and contour of the land upon which it rode. After the first day's journey, Miller spoke very little, as if hardly aware of the men who rode with him. Like an animal, he sniffed at the land, turning his head this way and that at sounds or scents unperceived by the others; sometimes he lifted his head in the air and did not move for long moments, as if waiting for a sign that did not come.

Beside Andrews, but across from him by thirty feet or more, rode Schneider. His broad hat pulled low over his eyes and his stiff hair bristling beneath his hat like a bundle of weathered straw, he slumped in his saddle. Sometimes his eyes were closed and he swayed in the saddle, dozing; at other times, awake, he stared sullenly at a spot between his horse's ears. Occasionally

he took a chew of tobacco from a square black plug that he kept
in his breast pocket, and spat contemptuously at the ground as
if at something that had offended him. Seldom did he look at
any of the others, and he did not speak unless it was necessary.

Behind the men on horses, Charley Hoge rode high on
the clip seat of the wagon. Covered by the light dust that the
horses and the oxen lifted and through which he passed, Charley Hoge held his head erect, his eyes raised above the oxen
and the men before him. Sometimes he called out to them
in a thin, mocking, cheerful voice; sometimes he hummed
tunelessly to himself, keeping time with the stump of his right
wrist; and sometimes his toneless voice cracked into a quavering hymn that jarred the hearing of all three men, who turned
and looked back upon Charley Hoge's oblivious, contorted
face with the open mouth and squinted eyes that saw none of
them. At night, after the men were fed and the animals hobbled, Charley Hoge would open his worn and filthy Bible and
mouth silently to himself by the dying light of the campfire.

On their fourth day out of Butcher's Crossing, for the second time Andrews saw the sign of buffalo.

It was Miller who made him see it. The group had come
out of one of the interminable hollows that rolled through the
Kansas plains; Miller, on top of the small rise, halted his horse
and beckoned. Andrews rode up beside him.

"Look out yonder," Miller said, and lifted his arm.

Andrews followed the direction that Miller indicated. At
first he could see only the rolling land that he had seen before; then, in the distance, his gaze settled upon a patch of
white that gleamed in the late morning sun. At the distance
from which he regarded it the patch had no shape, and barely
had the substance to make itself visible in the blue-green grass
that surrounded it. He turned back to Miller. "What is it?" he
asked.

Miller grinned. "Let's ride over and get a closer look."

They let their horses go in an easy lope across the ground;
Schneider came more slowly behind them, while Charley Hoge
turned the ox team slightly so that he followed, far behind
them, in the same direction.

As they drew nearer to the spot Miller had indicated, Andrews began to see that it was more than a patch of white;

whatever it was spread over a relatively large area of ground, as if strewn there carelessly by a huge, inhuman hand. Near the area Miller pulled his horse up abruptly and dismounted, winding the reins around the saddle horn so that the horse's neck was arched downward. Andrews did the same, and walked up beside Miller, who stood unmoving, looking out over the scattered area.

"What is it?" Andrews asked again.

"Bones," Miller said, and grinned at him once more. "Buffalo bones."

They walked closer. In the short prairie grass, the bones gleamed whitely, half-submerged in the blue-green grass, which had grown up around them. Andrews walked among the bones, careful not to disturb them, peering curiously as he passed.

"Small kill," Miller said. "Must not have been more than thirty or forty. Fairly recent, too. Look here."

Andrews went to him. Miller stood before a skeleton that was almost intact. From the curving, notched spine, which showed upon its top regular indentations of a grayish color, depended the broad-bowed blades of the rib cage. The rib bones were very broad and sweeping at the front, but nearer the flanks of the animal they sharply decreased in breadth and length; near the flank, the ribs were only nubs of white held to the spinal column by dried cords of sinew and gristle. Two broad flanges of bone at the end of the spine nestled in the grass; trailing behind these flanges, flat in the grass, were the two wide and sharply tapering bones of the rear legs. Andrews walked around the skeleton, which lay upright on what had once been its belly, peering closely at it; but he did not touch it.

"Look here," Miller said again. He pointed to the skull, which lay directly before the open oval front of the rib cage. The skull was narrow and flat, curiously small before the huge skeleton, which at its largest point reached slightly higher than Andrews's waist. Two short horns curved up from the skull, and a wisp of dried fur clung to the flat top of the skull.

"This carcass ain't more than two years old," Miller said. "It's still got a stink to it."

Andrews sniffed; there was the faint rank odor of dried and crumbling flesh. He nodded, and did not speak.

"This here fellow was a big one," Miller said. "Must have been near two thousand pound. You don't see them around here that big very often."

Andrews tried to visualize the animal from the remains that rested stilly on the prairie grass; he called to his memory the engravings that he had seen in books. But that uncertain memory and the real bones would not merge; he could not imagine the animal as it had been.

Miller kicked at one of the broad ribs; it snapped from the spine and fell softly in the grass. He looked at Andrews and moved his arm in a broad gesture to the country around them. "There was a time, in the days of the big kills, when you could look a mile in any direction and see the bones piled up. Five, six years ago, we'd have been riding through bones from Pawnee Fork clean to the end of the Smoky Hill. This is what the Kansas hunt has come to." He kicked again, contemptuously, at another rib. "And these won't be here long. Some dirt farmer will run across these and load them in a wagon and cart them off for fertilizer. Though there ain't enough here to hardly bother with."

"Fertilizer?" Andrews asked.

Miller nodded. "Buffalo's a curious critter; there ain't a part of him you can't use for something." He walked the length of the skeleton, bent, and picked up the broad bone of a hind leg; he swung it in the air as if it were a club. "The Indians used these bones for everything from needles to war clubs—knives so sharp they could split you wide open. They'd glue pieces of the bone together with pieces of horn for their bows, and use another piece, whittled down, for an arrowhead. I've seen necklaces carved so pretty out of little pieces of this, you'd think they was made in St. Louis. Toys for the little ones, combs for the squaws' hair—all out of this here bone. Fertilizer." He shook his head, and swung the bone again, flung it away from him; it sailed high in the air; catching the sun, it fell in the soft grass, bounced once, and was still.

Behind them a horse snorted; Schneider had ridden up near them.

"Let's get going," he said. "We'll see plenty of bones before we're through with this trip—leastways, if there's the kind of herd up in them mountains that there's supposed to be."

"Sure," Miller said. "This is just a little pile anyway."

The wagon came near them; in the hot noon air, Charley Hoge's voice raised quaveringly; he sang that God was his strong salvation, that he feared no foe, nor darkness nor temptation; he stood firm in the fight, with God at his right hand. For a moment the three men listened to the tortured voice urging its message upon the empty land; then they pushed their horses before the wagon and resumed their slow course across the country.

The signs of the buffalo became more frequent; several times they passed over packed trails left by great herds that went down to the river for water, and once they came upon a huge saucerlike depression, nearly six feet in depth at its deepest point and over forty feet across; grass grew to the very edge of this shallow pit, but in the pit itself the earth had been worked to a fine dust. This, Miller explained to Andrews, was a buffalo wallow, where the great beasts found relief from the insects and lice that plagued them by rolling about in the dust. No buffalo had been there for a long time; Miller pointed out that there were no buffalo chips about and that the grass around the pit was green and uncropped.

Once they saw the dead body of a buffalo cow. It lay stiffly on its side in the thick green grass; its belly was distended, and a foul stench of decaying flesh spread from it. At the approach of the men, two vultures that had been tearing at the flesh rose slowly and awkwardly into the air, and circled high above their carrion. Miller and Andrews rode near the carcass and dismounted. Upon the still, awkward shape the fur was a dull umber roughed to black in spots; Andrews started to go nearer, but the stench halted him. His stomach tightened; he pulled back, and circled the beast so that the wind carried the full force of the odor away from him.

Miller grinned at him. "Kind of strong, ain't it?" Still grinning, he went past Andrews and squatted down beside the buffalo, examining it carefully. "Just a little cow," he said. "Whoever shot her, missed the lights; more than likely, this one just plain bled to death. Probably left behind by the main herd." He kicked at the stiff, extended lower leg. The flesh thudded dully, and there was a light ripping sound as if a piece of stiff cloth had been torn. "Ain't been dead more than a week;

it's a wonder there's any meat left." He shook his head, turned, and walked back to his horse, which had shied away from the odor. When Miller approached, the horse's ears flattened and it leaned backward away from him; but Miller spoke soothingly and the horse stilled, though the muscles around its forelegs were tense and trembling. Miller and Andrews mounted and rode past the wagon and past Schneider, who had taken no notice of their stopping. The odor of the rotting buffalo clung in Miller's clothes, and even after he had gone ahead of Andrews, occasionally a light breeze would bring the odor back and cause Andrews to pull his hand across his nostrils and his mouth, as if something unclean had touched them.

Once, also, they saw a small herd; and again it was Miller who pointed it out to Andrews. The herd was little more than clustered specks of blackness in the light green of the prairie; Andrews could make out no shape or movement, though he strained his eyes against the bright afternoon sun and raised himself high in the saddle.

"It's just a little herd," Miller said. "The hunters around here have cut them all up into little herds."

The three of them—Andrews, Miller, and Schneider—were riding abreast. Schneider said impartially, to no one: "A body has sometimes got to be satisfied with a little herd. If that's the way they run, that's the way a body has got to cut them."

Miller, his eyes still straining at the distant herd, said: "I can recollect the day when you never saw a herd less than a thousand head, and even that was just a little bunch." He swept his arm in a wide half-circle. "I've stood at a place like this and looked out, and all I could see was black—fifty, seventy-five, a hundred thousand head of buffalo, moving over the grass. Packed so tight you could walk on their backs, walk all day, and never touch the ground. Now all you see is stragglers, like them out there. And grown men hunt for them." He spat on the ground.

Again Schneider addressed the air: "If all you got is stragglers, then you hunt for stragglers. I ain't got my hopes up any longer for much more."

"Where we're going," Miller said, "you'll see them like we used to in the old days."

"Maybe so," Schneider said. "But I ain't got my hopes up too high."

From the wagon behind them came the high crackle of Charley Hoge's voice. "Just a little bitty herd. You never saw nothing that little in the old days. The Lord giveth and the Lord taketh away."

At the sound of Charley Hoge's voice, the three men had turned; they listened him out; when he finished, they turned again; but they could no longer find the tiny smudge of black in the expanse of the prairie. Miller went on ahead, and Schneider and Andrews dropped back; none of them spoke again of what they had seen.

Such interruptions of their journey were few. Twice on the trail they passed small parties going in their direction. One of these parties consisted of a man, his wife, and three small children. Grimed with dust, their faces drawn and sullen with weariness, the woman and children huddled in a small wagon pulled by four mules and did not speak; the man, eager to talk and almost breathless in his eagerness, informed them that he had driven all the way from Ohio where he had lost his farm, and that he planned to join a brother who had a small business in California; he had begun the journey with a group of other wagons, but the lameness of one of his mules had so slowed his progress that he was now nearly two weeks behind the main party, and he had little hope of ever catching up. Miller examined the lame mule, and advised the man to swing up to Fort Wallace, where he could rest his team, and wait for another wagon train to come through. The man hesitated, and Miller told him curtly that the mule could not make it farther than Fort Wallace, and that he was a fool to continue on the trail alone. The man shook his head stubbornly. Miller said nothing more; he motioned to Andrews and Schneider, and the party pulled around the man and woman and the children and went ahead. Late in the evening the dust from the small mule-drawn wagon could be seen in the distance, far behind them. Miller shook his head.

"They'll never make it. That mule ain't good for two more days." He spat on the ground. "They should of turned off where I told them."

The other party they passed was a larger one of five men on horseback; these men were silent and suspicious. Reluctantly, they informed Miller that they were on their way to Colorado where they had an interest in an undeveloped mining claim, which they intended to work. They refused Charley Hoge's invitation to join them for supper, and they waited in a group for Miller's party to pass. Late that night, after Miller, Andrews, Schneider, and Hoge had bedded down, they heard the muffled clop of hooves circling around and passing them.

Once, where the trail skirted close to the river, they came upon a wide bluff, from the side of which had been excavated a series of crude dugouts. On the flat hard earth in front of the dugouts several brown, naked children were playing; behind the children, near the openings of the dugouts, squatted half a dozen Indians; the women were shapeless in the blankets they held about them despite the heat, and the men were old and wizened. As the group passed, the children ceased their play and looked at them with dark, liquid eyes; Miller waved, but none of the Indians gave any sign of response.

"River Indians," Miller said contemptuously. "They live on catfish and jack rabbits. They ain't worth shooting anymore."

But as their journey progressed such interruptions came to seem more and more unreal to Andrews. The reality of their journey lay in the routine detail of bedding down at night, arising in the morning, drinking black coffee from hot tin cups, packing bedrolls upon gradually wearying horses, the monotonous and numbing movement over the prairie that never changed its aspect, the watering of the horses and oxen at noon, the eating of hard biscuit and dried fruit, the resumption of the journey, the fumbling setting up of camp in the darkness, the tasteless quantities of beans and bacon gulped savagely in the flickering darkness, the coffee again, and the bedding down. This came to be a ritual, more and more meaningless as it was repeated, but a ritual which nevertheless gave his life the only shape it now had. It seemed to him that he moved forward laboriously, inch by inch, over the space of the vast prairie; but it seemed that he did not move through time at all, that rather time moved with him, an invisible cloud that hovered about him and clung to him as he went forward.

The passing of time showed itself in the faces of the three

men who rode with him and in the changes he perceived within himself. Day by day he felt the skin of his face hardening in the weather; the stubble of hair on the lower part of his face became smooth as his skin roughened, and the backs of his hands reddened and then browned and darkened in the sun. He felt a leanness and a hardness creep upon his body; he thought at times that he was moving into a new body, or into a real body that had lain hidden beneath layers of unreal softness and whiteness and smoothness.

The change that he saw in the others was less meaningful to him, and less extreme. Miller's heavy, evenly shaped beard thickened on his face and began to curl at the extreme ends; but the change was more readily apparent in the way he sat his saddle, in his stride upon the ground, and in the look of his eyes that gazed on the opening prairie. An ease, a familiarity, a naturalness began to replace the stiff and formal attitude that Andrews had first encountered in Butcher's Crossing. He sat his saddle as if he were a natural extension of the animal he rode; he walked in such a way that it appeared his very movement was caressing the contours of the ground; and his gaze upon the prairie seemed to Andrews as open and free and limitless as the land that occasioned his regard.

Schneider's face seemed to recede and hide in the slowly growing beard that bristled like straw upon his darkening skin. Day by day Schneider withdrew into himself; he spoke to the others less frequently, and in his riding he appeared to be almost attempting to disassociate himself from them: he looked always in a direction that was away from them, and at night he ate his food silently, turned sideways from the campfire, and bedded down and was asleep long before the others.

Of them all, Charley Hoge showed the least change. His gray beard bristled a bit more fully, and his skin reddened but did not brown in the weather; he looked about him impartially, slyly, and spoke abruptly and without cause to all of them, expecting no answer. When the trail was level, he took out his worn and tattered Bible and thumbed through its pages, his weak gray eyes squinting through the dust. At regular intervals throughout the day he reached beneath the wagon seat and drew out a loosely corked bottle of whisky; he pulled the cork out with his yellowed teeth, dropped it into his lap, and took long noisy swallows. Then, in his high, thin, quavering voice he sang a hymn that floated faintly through the dust and died in the ears of the three men who rode before him.

On the sixth day of their traveling, they came to the end of the Smoky Hill Trail.

3.

THE DARK green line of trees and brush that they had followed all the way from Butcher's Crossing turned in a slow curve to the south. The four men, who came upon the turning in the midmorning of their sixth day of journey, halted and gazed for some moments at the course of the Smoky Hill River. From where they halted, the land dropped off so that in the distance, through the brush and trees of the banks, they could see the slow-moving water. In the distance it lost its muddy green hue; the sunlight silvered its surface, and it appeared to them clear and cool. The three men brought their horses close together; the oxen turned their heads toward the river and moaned softly; Charley Hoge called them to a halt, and set the brake handle of the wagon; he jumped off the spring seat, clambered from the wagon, and walked briskly over to where the others waited. He looked up at Miller.

"Trail turns here with the river," Miller said. "Follows it all the way up to the Arkansas. We could follow it and be sure of plenty of water, but it would put us near a week off getting where we're aiming at."

Schneider looked at Miller and grinned; his teeth were white in his dust-encrusted face.

"I take it you don't aim to go by the trail."

"It'd put us a week off, maybe more," Miller said. "I've gone across this country before." He waved toward the flat country in the west that lay beyond the Smoky Hill Trail. "They's water there, for a body that knows where it is."

Schneider, still grinning, turned to Andrews. "Mr. Andrews, you don't look like you ever been thirsty in your life; real thirsty, I mean. So I guess it won't do much good to ask you what you want to do."

Andrews hesitated; then he shook his head. "I have no right to speak. I don't know the country."

"And Miller does," Schneider said, "or at least that's what he tells us. So we go where Miller says."

Miller smiled and nodded. "Fred, you sound like you want an extra week's pay. You ain't afraid of a little dry stretch, are you?"

"I've had dry stretches before," Schneider said. "But I never have got over feeling put out when I saw horses and bull-oxes being watered and me with a dry throat."

Miller's smile widened. "It takes the grit out of a man," he said. "It's happened to me. But they's water less than a day from here. I don't think it'll come to that."

"Just one thing more," Schneider said. "How long did you say it's been since you went over this bit of land?"

"A few years," Miller said. "But some things don't leave a man." Though the smile remained on his face, his voice stiffened. "You don't have no serious complaints yet, do you, Fred?"

"No," Schneider said. "I just thought there was a few things I ought to say. I said I'd go along with you back at Butcher's Crossing, and I'll go along with you now. It don't matter to me one way or another."

Miller nodded, and turned to Charley Hoge. "Reckon we'd better rest the stock and water them up good before we go on. And we'd better carry along as much water as we can, just in case. You take care of the team, and we'll get what water we can back up to the wagon."

While Charley Hoge led the oxen down to the river, the others went to the wagon and found what containers they could for carrying water. From a broad square of canvas that covered their provisions, Miller fashioned a crude barrel, held open and upright by slender green saplings that he cut at the river bank. Two of the more slender saplings he tied together and bent into a circle, and tied again; this he attached near the four corners of the square canvas with leather thongs. The shorter and stubbier saplings he cut to a length, notched, and attached to the circled saplings, thus forming a receptacle some five feet in diameter and four feet in height. With buckets and kettles that Charley Hoge used for cooking and with one small wooden keg, the three men filled the canvas barrel three-quarters full; it took them the better part of an hour to do so.

"That's enough," Miller said. "If we put any more in, it would just slosh out."

They rested in the shade beside the Smoky Hill, while the hobbled oxen wandered along the banks, grazing on the rich grass that grew in the moisture. Because of the intense heat, and because of the dry country over which they would be traveling, Miller told them, they would begin their second drive somewhat later; so Charley Hoge had time to cook up some soaked beans, sowbelly, and coffee. Until the afternoon sun pushed the shade beyond them, they lay wearily on the grassy bank of the river, listening to the rustle of the water that flowed past them smoothly, coolly, effortlessly, that flowed back through the prairie through which they had worked their way, past Butcher's Crossing, and onward to the east. When the sun touched his face, Andrews sat up. Miller said: "Might as well get started." Charley Hoge gathered his oxen, yoked them in pairs, and put them to the wagon. The party turned to the flat land upon which they could see neither tree nor trail to guide them, and went forward upon it. Soon the line of green that marked the Smoky Hill River was lost to them; and in the flat unbroken land Andrews had to keep his eyes firmly fixed on Miller's back to find any direction to go in.

Twilight came upon them. Had it not been for his tiredness, and the awkward, shambling weariness of the horses beneath the weight they carried forward, Andrews might have thought that the night came on and held them where they started, back at the bend of the Smoky Hill. During the afternoon's drive he had seen no break in the flat country, neither tree, nor gully, nor rise in the land that might serve as a landmark to show Miller the way he went. They camped that night without water.

Few words were exchanged as they broke the packs from their horses and set up the night's camp on the open prairie. Charley Hoge led the oxen one by one to the back of the wagon; Miller held the large canvas receptacle erect while the oxen drank. By the light of a lantern he kept careful watch on the level of water; when an ox had drunk its quota, Miller would say sharply: "That's enough," and kick at the beast as Charley Hoge tugged its head away. When the oxen and the horses had drunk, the tank remained one-fourth full.

Much later, around the campfire, which Charley Hoge had prepared with wood gathered at their noon stop, the men squatted and drank their coffee. Schneider, whose tight impassive face seemed to twitch and change in the flickering firelight, said impersonally:

"I never cared for a dry camp."

No one spoke.

Schneider continued: "I guess there's a drop or two left in the tank."

"It's about a fourth full," Miller said.

Schneider nodded. "We can make one more day on that, I figure. It'll be a mite dry, but we should make one more day."

Miller said, "I figure one more day."

"If we don't come across some water," Schneider said.

"If we don't come across some water," Miller agreed.

Schneider lifted his tin cup and drained the last dreg of coffee from it. In the firelight, his raised chin and throat bristled and quivered. His voice was cool and lazy. "I reckon we'd better hit some water tomorrow."

"We'd better," Miller said. Then: "There's plenty of water; it's just there for the finding." No one answered him. He went on. "I must have missed a mark somewhere. There should have been water right along here. But it's nothing serious. We'll get water tomorrow, for sure."

The three men were watching him intently. In the dying light, Miller returned each of their stares, looking at Schneider at length, coolly. After a moment he sighed and put his cup carefully on the ground in front of Charley Hoge.

"Let's get some sleep," Miller said. "I want to get an early start in the morning, before the heat sets in."

Andrews tried to sleep, but despite his tiredness he did not rest soundly. He kept being awakened by the low moaning of the oxen, which gathered at the end of the wagon, pawed the earth, and butted against the closed tailgate that protected the little store of water in the open canvas tank.

Andrews was shaken from his uneasy sleep by Miller's hand on his shoulder. His eyes opened on darkness, and on the dim hulk of Miller above him. He heard the others moving about, stumbling and cursing in the early morning dark.

"If we can get them going soon enough, they won't miss the watering," Miller said.

By the time the false light shone in the east, the oxen were yoked; the party again moved westward.

"Give your horses their heads," Miller told them. "Let them set their own pace. We'll do better not to push any of them till we get some water."

The animals moved sluggishly through the warming day. As the sun brightened, Miller rode far ahead of the main party; he sat erect in his saddle and moved his head constantly from one side to another. Occasionally he got off his horse and examined the ground closely, as if it concealed some sign that he had missed atop his horse. They continued their journey well into the middle of the day, and past it. When one of the oxen stumbled and in getting to its feet gashed at its fellow with a blunt horn, Miller called the party to a halt.

"Fill your canteens," he said. "We've got to water the stock and there won't be any left."

Silently, the men did as they were told. Schneider was the last to approach the canvas tank; he filled his canteen, drank from it in long, heavy gulps, and refilled it.

Schneider helped Charley Hoge control the oxen as, one by one, they were led to the rear of the wagon and the open tank of water. When the oxen were watered and tethered at some distance from the wagon, the horses were allowed to finish the water. After the horses had got from the tank all that they were able, Miller broke down the saplings that gave the canvas its shape, and with Charley Hoge's help drained the water that remained in the folds of the canvas into a wooden keg.

Charley Hoge untethered the oxen and let them graze on the short yellowish grass. Then he returned to the wagon and broke out a package of dried biscuits.

"Don't eat too many of them," Miller said. "They'll dry you out."

The men squatted in the narrow shade cast by the wagon. Slowly and delicately, Schneider ate one of the biscuits and took a small sip of water after it.

Finally he sighed, and spoke directly to Miller: "What's the story, Miller? Do you know where there's water?"

Miller said: "There was a little pile of rocks a piece back I think I remember. Another half-day, and we ought to hit a stream."

Schneider looked at him quizzically. Then he stiffened, took a deep breath, and asked, his voice soft: "Where are we, Miller?"

"No need to worry," Miller said. "Some of the landmarks have changed since I was here. But another half-day, and I'll get us fixed."

Schneider grinned, and shook his head. He laughed softly and sat down on the ground, shaking his head.

"My God," he said. "We're lost."

"As long as we keep going in that direction," Miller pointed away from their shadows, toward the falling sun, "we're not lost. We're bound to run into water tonight, or early in the morning."

"This is a big country," Schneider said. "We're not bound to do anything."

"No need to worry," Miller said.

Schneider looked at Andrews, still grinning. "How does it feel, Mr. Andrews? Just thinking about it makes you thirsty, don't it?"

Andrews looked away from him quickly, and frowned; but what he said was true. The biscuit in his mouth felt suddenly dry, like sun-beat sand; he had swallowed against the dryness. He noticed that Charley Hoge put his half-eaten biscuit into his shirt pocket.

"We can still cut south," Schneider said. "Another day, at the most a day and a half, we'll run into the Arkansas. The stock might just hold up for a day and a half."

"It would put us a week off," Miller said. "And besides, there's no cause for it; we may get a little dry, but we'll make it all right. I know this country."

"Not so well you don't get lost in it," Schneider said. "I say, we turn to the Arkansas. We'll be sure of water there." He pulled up a tuft of the dry, yellow grass that surrounded them. "Look at this. There's been a drought in this country. How do we know the streams ain't dried up? What if the ponds are empty?"

"There's water in this country," Miller said.

"Seen any sign of buffalo?" Schneider looked at each of them. "Not a sign. And you won't find buffalo where there ain't no water. I say, we ought to head for the Arkansas."

Miller sighed and smiled distantly at Schneider. "We'd never make it, Fred."

"What?"

"We'd never make it. We've been heading at an angle ever since we left the Smoky Hill. With watered stock, it would take us two and a half days—almost as bad as going back to the Smoky Hill. Dry, this stock would never make it."

"God damn it," Schneider said quietly, "you ought to have let us know."

Miller said: "There's nothing to worry about. I'll get you to water, if I have to dig for it."

"God damn it," Schneider said. "You son of a bitch. I'm half a mind to cut out on my own. I might just make it."

"And you might not," Miller said. "Do you know this country, Fred?"

"You know damn well I don't," Schneider said.

"Then you'd better stick with the party."

Schneider looked from one of them to another. "You're pretty sure the party's going to stick with you?"

Miller's tight face relaxed, and the loose ridges came again about the corners of his mouth. "I'm going ahead, just like I've been going. I just have to get the feel of the land again. I've been watching too close, trying too hard to remember. Once I get the feel of the country again, I'll be all right. And the rest of you will be all right, too."

Schneider nodded. "Hoge will stick with you, I guess. That right, Charley?"

Charley Hoge lifted his head abruptly, as if startled. He rubbed the stump of his wrist. "I go where God wills," he said. "He will lead us to where water is when we are athirst."

"Sure," Schneider said. He turned to Andrews. "Well, that leaves us, Mr. Andrews. What do you say? It's your wagon and your team. If you say we go south, Miller would have a hard time going against you."

Andrews looked at the ground; between the dry thin blades of grass the earth was powdery. Though he did not look up, he felt the eyes of the others upon him. "We've come this far," he said. "We might as well keep on with Miller."

"All right," Schneider said. "You're all crazy. But it looks like I've got no choice. Do whatever you want to do."

Miller's thin flat lips lengthened in a slight smile. "You worry too much, Fred. If it gets that bad, we can always get by on Charley's whisky. There must be nine or ten gallons of it left."

"The horses will be glad to hear that," Schneider said. "I can see us walking out of here on ten gallons of whisky."

"You worry too much," Miller said. "You'll live to be a hundred and five."

"I've had my say. I'll go along with you. Now let me get some rest." He lay on his side, rolled under the shade of the wagon, and came to rest with his back to them.

"We all might as well try to get some sleep," Miller said. "It won't do to travel in the heat. We'll rest ourselves, and get the drive started this evening."

Lying on his side, his folded arm supporting his head, Andrews looked out of the shade across the level prairie. As far as he could see, the land was flat and without identity. The blades of grass that stood up stiffly a few inches from his nose blurred and merged into the distance, and the distance came upon him with a rush. He closed his eyes upon what he saw, and his vague fingers pushed at the grass until they parted it, and he could feel the dry powdery earth upon his fingertips. He pressed his body against the ground, and did not look at anything, until the terror that had crept upon him from his dizzying view of the prairie passed, as if through his fingertips, back into the earth whence it had come. His mouth was dry. He started to reach for his canteen, but he did not. He forced thirst away from him, and put thought from his mind. After a while, his body, tense against the earth, relaxed; and before the afternoon was over, he slept.

When the edge of the sun cut into the far horizon they resumed their journey.

Night came on rapidly. In the moonlight, Miller, ahead of them, was a frenzied, hunched figure, whose body swayed this way and that in his saddle. Though Andrews and Schneider let their horses go at their own paces, Miller spurred in an erratic zigzag across the land that seemed to glow out of the night. To no apparent purpose, Miller would cut at a sharp angle from a path they took, and follow the new course for half an hour or so, only to abandon it and cut in another direction.

For the first few hours, Andrews tried to keep their course in his mind; but weariness dulled his attention, and the stars in the clear sky, and the thin moon, whirled about his head; he closed his eyes and slumped forward in the saddle, letting his horse trail Schneider and Miller. Even in the cool of the night, thirst gnawed at him, and occasionally he took a small sip of water from his canteen. Once they paused to let the oxen graze; Andrews remained in his saddle, sleepily aware of what was going on.

They traveled into the next morning, and into the heat of the day. The oxen moved slowly; they moaned almost constantly, and their breaths were dry and rasping. Even Andrews could see that their coats were growing dull, and that the bones were showing sharply along their ribs and flanks.

Schneider rode up beside him and jerked his head back in the direction of the oxen. "They look bad. Their tongues will start swelling next. Then they won't be able to breathe and pull at the same time. We should have headed south. With luck, we might have made it."

Andrews did not answer. His throat felt unbearably dry. Despite himself he reached behind his saddle for his canteen and took two long swallows of water. Schneider grinned and drew his horse away. With an effort of will Andrews closed his canteen and replaced it behind his saddle.

Shortly before noon Miller pulled his horse to a halt, dismounted, and walked back toward the slowly moving wagon. He motioned to Charley Hoge to stop.

"We'll wait the heat out here," he said shortly. He walked into the shade of the wagon; Schneider and Andrews came up to him. "They look bad, Miller," Schneider said. He turned to Charley Hoge: "How do they drive?"

Charley Hoge shook his head.

"Their tongues are beginning to swell. They won't last out the day. And the horses. Look at them."

"Never mind that," Miller said. His voice was low and toneless, almost a growl. The black pupils of his eyes were shining and blank; they were fixed upon the men without appearing to see them. "How much water's left in the canteens?"

"Not much," Schneider said. "Maybe enough to get us through the night."

"Get them," Miller said.

"Now look," Schneider said. "If you think I'm going to use water for anything except myself, you—"

"Get them," Miller said. He turned his eyes to Schneider. Schneider cursed softly, got to his feet, and returned with his own and Andrews's canteens. Miller gathered them, put his with them, and said to Charley Hoge: "Charley, get the keg and bring your canteen down here."

Schneider said: "Now, look, Miller. Those oxen will never make it. No use wasting what little water we got. You can't—"

"Shut up," Miller said. "Arguing about it will just make us drier. Like I said, we still have Charley's whisky."

"My God!" Schneider said. "You were serious."

Charley Hoge returned to the shade beside the wagon and handed Miller a canteen and the wooden keg. Miller set the keg carefully on the ground, rotating it a few times under the pressure of his hands so that it rested level on the stubby grass. He unscrewed the tops of the canteens, one by one, and carefully poured the water into the keg, letting the canteens hang above it for several minutes, until the last globules of water gathered on the mouths, hung, and finally dropped. After the last canteen was emptied, about four inches of water was in the keg.

Schneider picked up his empty canteen, looked at it carefully, and then looked at Miller. With all his strength, he flung the canteen against the side of the wagon, from where it rebounded back toward him, past him, and fell into the grass.

"God damn it!" he shouted; his voice was startling in the hot prairie quiet. "What good do you expect to do with that little bit of water? You're throwing it away!"

Miller did not look at him. He spoke to Charley Hoge: "Charley, unyoke the oxen and lead them around here one at a time."

While the three men waited—Miller and Andrews still, Schneider quivering and turning in an impotent rage—Charley Hoge singly detached the oxen and led them around to Miller. Miller took a rag from his pocket, soaked it in the water, and squeezed it gently, holding it carefully above the keg so that no water was lost.

"Fred, you and Will get a hold of his horns; hold him steady."

While Schneider and Andrews grasped each of the horns, Charley Hoge circled the beast's bony and corded neck with his good arm, digging his heels in the ground and pulling against the forward surge of the ox. With the wet rag, Miller bathed the dry lips of the ox; then he put the rag into the water again and squeezed it so that no water was wasted.

"Pull up on the horns," he said to Schneider and Andrews.

When the ox's head was up, Miller grasped the upper lip of the beast and pulled upward. The tongue, dark and swollen, quivered in its mouth. Again with care, Miller bathed the rough distended flesh; his hand and wrist were thrust out of sight up into the ox's throat. Withdrawing his hand, he squeezed hard on the wet rag, and a few drops of water trickled on the tongue, which absorbed them like a dark dry sponge.

One by one the oxen's mouths were bathed. Sweatless and hot, the three men held the beasts and dug their feet into the earth; Schneider cursed steadily, quietly; Andrews breathed in heavy gasps the dry air that was rough like a burr in his throat, and tried to keep his arms from trembling loose from the smooth hot horns of the oxen. After each ox had been treated, Charley Hoge led it back to its yoke and returned with another. Despite the haste with which they worked, it was the better part of an hour before they finished with the last animal.

Miller leaned against the side of the wagon; his dry, leather-like skin stood out from his black beard with a faint yellowish cast.

"They ain't so bad," he said breathing heavily. "They'll last to nightfall; and we still got a bit of water left." He pointed to the muddy inch or so of water that remained in the keg.

Schneider laughed; it was a dry sound that turned into a cough. "A pint of water for eight oxen and three horses."

"It'll keep the swelling down," Miller said. "It's enough for that."

Charley Hoge returned from the front of the wagon. "Do we unyoke them now and take a rest?"

"No," Miller said. "Their tongues'll swell as bad standing here as they will if we keep on. And we can keep them from grazing better if we're on the move."

"On the move where?" Schneider said. "How long you think them cows can pull this here wagon?"

"Long enough," Miller said. "We'll find water."

Schneider moved suddenly, and whirled to Miller. "I just thought," he said. "How much lead and powder you got in that wagon?"

"Ton and a half, two tons," Miller said, not looking at him.

"Well, my God," Schneider said. "No wonder them animals is dry. We could go twice as far if we'd dump the stuff."

"No," Miller said.

"We can find water, and maybe come back and pick it up. It ain't as if we intended to just leave it here."

"No," Miller said. "We get there like we started out, or we don't get there at all. There ain't no need to get in a panic."

"You crazy son of a bitch," Schneider said. He kicked one of the heavy hickory wheel spokes. "God damn it. Crazier'n hell." He kicked the spoke again, and pounded a fist on the rim of the wheel.

"Besides," Miller said calmly, "it wouldn't make all that difference. On this land, a full wagon can pull almost as easy as an empty one, once the team gets started."

"It's no good talking to him," Schneider said. "No good at all." He strode out of the shade and went to his horse, which had been tethered to the end of the wagon, its head held high so that it could not graze. Andrews and Miller followed him more slowly.

"It does Fred good to blow off now and then," Miller said to Andrews. "He knows if we left the load here we might be a week finding it again, if we found it at all. Looking for it might put us in as bad shape as we are now. We don't leave a heavy enough trail to follow back, and you can't mark a trail very well in land like this."

Andrews looked behind him. It was true. The wheels of the wagon in the short stiff grass, on the baked earth, left hardly an impression; even now the grass over which they had driven was springing erect to hide the evidence of their passage. Andrews tried to swallow, but the contraction of his muscles was stopped by his dry throat.

Their horses moved sluggishly; and beneath Charley Hoge's cracking whip and before his thin sharp voice, the oxen moved weakly against the pull of the wagon. They shambled unsteadily forward, working not as a team but as separate beasts struggling from the whip and the sound of the driving voice behind them. Once in the afternoon the party came near a shallow depression in the earth, the bottom of which was cracked in an intricate pattern of dried mud. They looked sullenly at the dried-up pond and did not speak.

In the middle of the afternoon, Miller forced each of them to take a short swallow of Charley Hoge's whisky.

"Don't take much," he warned. "Just enough to get your throat wet. More than that will make you sick."

Andrews gagged on the liquor. It seared his dry tongue and throat as if a torch had been thrust into his mouth; when he ran his tongue over his cracked dry lips, they burned with a pain that lingered for many minutes later. He closed his eyes and clung to his saddle horn as the horse went forward; but the darkness upon his closed eyelids was shot with spears of light that whirled dizzily; he was forced to open them again and observe the trackless and empty way they went.

By sundown the oxen again were breathing with sharp grunting moans; their tongues were so swollen that they moved with their mouths half open; their heads were down, swinging from side to side. Miller called the wagon to a halt. Again Schneider and Andrews held the horns of the beasts; but even though both men were much weaker than they had been earlier, their task was easier. The oxen dumbly and without resistance let themselves be pulled around, and did not even show interest in the water with which Miller bathed their mouths.

"We won't stop," Miller said. His voice was a heavy flat croak. "Better to keep them moving while they're still on their feet."

He stood the bucket on its edge and sopped up the last of the water with the rag. He bathed the mouths of the horses; when he finished, the rag was almost dry.

After the sun dropped beneath the flat horizon before them, darkness came on quickly. Andrews's hands clung to the saddle horn; they were so weak that again and again they slipped from it, and he hardly had the strength to pull them back. Breathing was an effort of agony; slumped inertly in his saddle, he learned to snuffle a little air through his nostrils and to exhale it quickly, and to wait several seconds before he repeated the process. Sometime during the night he discovered that his mouth was open and that he could not close it. His tongue pushed between his teeth, and when he tried to bring them together a dull dry pain spread in his mouth. He remembered the sight of the oxen's tongues, black and swollen and dry; and he pushed his mind away from that image, away from himself, and tried to push his mind into a place as dark and unbounded as the night in which he traveled. Once, an ox stumbled and would not get back upon its feet; the three men had to dismount and with their little remaining strength pull and tug and prod the beast upright. Then the oxen would not or could not summon strength to get the wagon into motion, so the three pushed against the wagon spokes, while Charley Hoge's whip cracked above the oxen, until the wheels began to move and the beasts took up the forward movement in a slow shamble. Andrews tried to wet his mouth with a little of Charley Hoge's whisky, but most of the liquid ran off his lips down the corners of his mouth. He rode most of the night in a state that alternated between a mild delirium and intense pain. Once he came to his senses and found himself alone in the darkness; he had no sense of place, no knowledge of direction. In a panic he whirled one way and another in his saddle; he looked upward into the immense bowl of the sky, and downward at the earth upon which he rode; and the one seemed as far away as the other. Then he heard faintly the creak of the wagon, and prodded his horse in that direction. In a few moments he was back with the others, who had not noticed his lagging behind. Even with them, he shivered for a long while, the panic he had felt when he thought himself abandoned still upon him; for a long while the panic kept him alert, and he followed Miller's dim movements, not as if those movements might lead him where he wished to go, but as if they might save him from wandering into a nothingness where he would be alone.

Shortly after dawn, they found water.

Afterward Andrews remembered as if from a dream the first sign they had that water was near. In the early light from the east Miller stiffened in his saddle and raised his head like an alert animal. Then, almost imperceptibly, he pulled his horse in a slightly northerly direction, his head still raised and alert. A few moments later he reined his horse more sharply north, so that Charley Hoge had to dismount from the wagon and prod the oxen toward Miller's horse. Then, as the first small edge of the sun came above the flat line in the east, Andrews was aware that his horse had begun to quiver beneath him. He saw that Miller's horse, too, was straining impatiently; its ears were pitched sharply forward, and it was held by Miller's taut reins. Miller twisted in his saddle and faced those behind him. In the soft yellow light that fell upon Miller's face, Andrews could see the cracked lips, raw and slightly bleeding from the distended cracks, parted in a grotesque smile.

"By God," Miller called; his voice was rasping and weak, but it held a deep note of triumph. "By God, we found it. Hold your horses back, and—" Turning still farther around, he raised his voice, "Charley, hold on to them oxen as hard as you can. They'll smell it in a few minutes, and they're like to go crazy."

Andrews's horse bolted suddenly; startled, he pulled back with all his strength on the reins, and the horse reared upward, its front hooves pawing the air. Andrews leaned frantically forward, burrowing his face in the horse's mane, so that he would not topple off.

By the time they came in sight of the stream, which wound in a flat treeless gully cut on the level land, the animals were quivering masses of flesh held back by the tiring muscles of the men. When the sound of the stream came to their ears, Miller called back to them: "Jump off, and let 'em go!"

Andrews lifted one foot from a stirrup; as he did so, the horse, relieved of the pressure of the reins, lunged forward, spilling Andrews to the ground. By the time he got to his feet, the horses were at the stream, on their knees, their heads thrust down into the shallow trickle.

Charley Hoge called from the wagon: "Somebody come here and give me a hand with this brake!" With his hand and with the crook of the elbow of his other arm, he was pulling against the large hand brake at the side of the wagon; the locked wheels of the wagon tore through the short grass, raising dust. Andrews stumbled across the ground and climbed upon the wagon by way of the unmoving wheel spokes. He took the hand brake from Charley Hoge's grasp.

"Got to get them unyoked," Charley Hoge said. "They'll kill theirselves if they go at this much longer."

The brake jerked and trembled under Andrews's grasp; the smell of scorched wood and leather came to his nostrils. Charley Hoge jumped from the wagon and ran to the lead team. With deft movements, he knocked the pins from an oxbow, and jerked the oxbow from the yoke, jumping aside as the ox lunged forward, past him, toward the stream. Miller and Schneider stood on either side of the team, trying to quiet the oxen as Charley Hoge unyoked them. When the last ox was unyoked, the three men went in a stumbling trot across the ground to a spot a few feet upstream from where the animals were lined.

"Take it easy," Miller said, when they had flung themselves down on their stomachs beside the narrow, muddy stream. "Just get your mouths wet at first. Try to drink too much, and you'll make yourselves sick."

They wet their mouths and let a little of the water trickle down their throats, and then lay for a few moments on their backs, letting their hands remain behind their heads, the water trickling softly and coolly over them. Then they drank again, more deeply; and rested again.

They stayed at the stream all that day, letting the animals have their fill of water, and grazing them on the short dry grass. "They've lost a lot of strength," Miller said. "They'll be a full day getting even part of it back."

Shortly before noon, Charley Hoge gathered some drift-wood that he found along the stream, and started a fire. He put some dry beans on to cook, and fried some side meat, which they wolfed immediately with the last of the dried bis-cuits, washing it all down with quantities of coffee. They slept the afternoon through; while they slept, the fire died down beneath the beans, and Charley Hoge had to start it again. Later, in the darkness, they ate the beans, undercooked and hard, and drank more coffee. They listened for a while to the slow, contented movement of the livestock around them; and themselves contented, they lay on their bedrolls around the embers of the campfire and slept, hearing in their sleep the quiet thin gurgle of the stream they had found.

They resumed their journey before dawn the next morning, only a little weak from the ordeal of thirst they had endured. Miller led the party with more confidence, now that water had been found. He spoke of the water as if it were a live thing that attempted to elude him. "I've found it, now," he had said back at the camp beside the stream. "It won't get away from me again."

And it did not get away. They made their way westward in an erratic course over the featureless land, finding water always at their day's end; usually they came upon it in darkness, when to Schneider and Andrews it seemed impossible that it could be found.

On the fourteenth day of their journey, they saw the mountains.

For much of the previous afternoon, they had traveled toward a low bank of clouds that distantly shrouded the western horizon, and they had traveled into the night before they found water. So they rose late that morning.

By the time they awoke, the sky was steel-blue and the sun was burning heavily in the east. Andrews rose from his bedroll with a start; they had not remained so late in camp during all the journey. The other men were still in their bedrolls. He started to call to them; but his eyes were caught by the brilliant clearness of the sky. He let his eyes wander unfocused over the high clear dome; and as they settled to the west, as they always settled, he stiffened and looked more closely. A small low uneven hump of dark blue rose on the farthest extremity of land that he could see. He sprang up and went a few steps forward, as if those few steps would enable him to see more closely. Then he turned back to the sleeping men; he went to Miller and shook his shoulder excitedly.

"Miller!" he said. "Miller, wake up."

Miller stirred and opened his eyes, and came quickly to a sitting position, instantly awake.

"What is it, Will?"

"Look." Andrews pointed to the west. "Look over there."

Not looking where Andrews pointed, Miller grinned. "The mountains. I reckoned we should be in sight of them sometime today."

By this time the others were awake. Schneider looked once at the thin far ridge, shrugged, got his bedroll together and lashed it behind his saddle. Charley Hoge gave the mountains a quick glance and turned away, busying himself with the preparations for the morning meal.

Late in the morning they began again their long trek westward. Now that their goal was visible, Andrews found that the land upon which they traveled took on features that he had not been able to recognize before. Here the land dipped into a shallow gully; there a small cropping of stone stood out from the earth; elsewhere in the distance a scrubby patch of trees smudged the greenish-yellow of the landscape. Before, his eyes had remained for most of the time fixed upon Miller's back; now they strained into the distance, toward the uneven hump of earth, now sharp, now blurred, upon the far horizon. And he found that he hungered after them much as he had thirsted after the water; but he knew the mountains were there, he could see them; and he did not know precisely what hunger or thirst they would assuage.

The journey to the foothills took them four days. Gradually, with their going, the mountains spread and reared upon the land. As they came nearer Miller grew more impatient; when they nooned at a stream (the number of which increased as they traveled), he was hardly able to wait for the stock to water and graze. He urged them on, more and more swiftly, until at last the crack and hiss of Charley Hoge's whip was regular and steady and the oxen's lips were flecked and dripping with white foam. They drove late into each night, and were on the move again before the sun rose.

Andrews felt that the mountains drew them onward, and drew them with increasing intensity as they came nearer, as if they were a giant lodestone whose influence increased to the degree that it was more nearly approached. As they came nearer he had again the feeling that he was being absorbed, included in something with which he had had no relation before; but unlike the feeling of absorption he had experienced on the anonymous prairie, this feeling was one which promised, however vaguely, a richness and a fulfillment for which he had no name.

Once they came upon a broad trail running north and south. Miller paused upon it, got off his horse, and examined the path that had been worn in the grass.

"Cattle trail, looks like. They must have started running cattle up from Texas." He shook his head. "It wasn't here the last time I come through."

Late in the afternoon, just before dark, Andrews saw in the distance the long thin parallel lines of a railroad, which found a level course by winding among the gentle hillocks that were beginning to swell upon the land; but Miller had already seen it.

"My God!" Miller said. "A railroad!"

The men increased the paces of their mounts, and in a few minutes halted beside the humped foundation of the road. The tops of the rails gleamed dully in the last light of the sun. Miller got off his horse and stood unmoving for a moment. He shook his head, knelt, and ran his fingers over the smooth steel of the tracks. Then, his hand still upon the metal, he raised his eyes to the mountains, which now loomed high and jagged in the orange and blue light of the afternoon sky.

"My God!" he said again. "I never thought they'd get a railroad in this country."

"Buffalo," Schneider said. He remained on his horse, and spat at the rails. "Big herd. I never seen big herds yet, where a railroad's been in a few years."

Miller did not look up at him. He shook his head, and then rose to his feet and mounted his horse.

"Come on," he said abruptly. "We got a long way to go before we set up camp."

Though they passed several clear streams, Miller forced them to travel for nearly three hours after dark. The travel was slow, for as they approached the mountains the land was more broken; frequently, they had to skirt large groves of trees that grew near the streams, and had to bypass several sharp hills that rose vaguely out of the darkness. Once, in the distance, they saw the glimmering of a light that might have come from the open door of a house. They continued their drive until they were out of its sight, and for some time afterward.

Early the next morning, they were in the foothills. A few pines were scattered on the sharply rising sides of the hills that cut off their view of the mountains. Miller, riding ahead, guided the wagon along the land that gently rose up to the hills; he pointed to a sharp strip of pines that descended from one of these, and they made in that direction. The hills dropped sharply into a valley; at the bottom of the cut, the land leveled on either side of a small stream. They followed this draw onto a broad flat valley, which stretched to the very base of the mountains.

"We should hit the river by noon," Miller said. "Then we start to climb."

But it was shortly after noon when they came upon the river. The land on the side from which they approached was clear; a few sumacs, already tinged with yellow, and a few clumps of scrub willow straggled along the bank. The bed of the river was wide; it was perhaps two hundred yards from the rise on their side to a steep ledge on the other. But for many yards beyond either bank, and in the bed itself, grass was growing, and even a few small trees and shrubs. Through the years, the river had cut away at earth and solid stone; now it ran thin and shallow at the center of its path in a swath no more than thirty feet in width. It ran smoothly and clearly among rocks, some flat and some thrust sharply up from the bed, here and there breaking into whirling eddies and white-topped riffles.

They nooned at the point at which they had first approached the river. While the other stock was grazing, Miller mounted his horse and rode away in a northeasterly direction, following the river's flow. Andrews wandered away from Charley Hoge and Schneider, who were resting beside the wagon, and sat on the bank. The mountain was a mass of pines. On the far bank the heavy brown trunks raised thirty or forty feet before the boughs spread to hold deep green clusters of pine needles. In the spaces between the huge trunks were only other trunks, and others, on and on, until the few trees that he could see merged into an image of denseness, impenetrable and dark, compounded of tree and shadow and lightless earth, where no human foot had been. He raised his eyes, and followed the surface of the mountain as it jutted steeply upward. The image of the pines was lost, and the image of the denseness, and indeed even the image of the mountain itself. He saw only a deep green mat of needle and bough, which became in his gaze without identity or size, like a dry sea, frozen in a moment of calm, the billows regular and eternally still—upon which he might walk for a moment or so, only to sink as he moved upon it, slowly sink into its green mass, until he was in the very heart of the airless forest, a part of it, darkly alone. He sat for a long time upon the bank of the river, his eyes and his mind caught in the vision he had.

He was still sitting on the bank when Miller returned from his downstream journey.

Miller rode silently up to the resting men, who gathered around him as he drew his horse to a halt and dismounted.

"Well," Schneider said, "you been gone long enough. Did you find what you were looking for?"

Miller grunted. His eyes went past Schneider, and ranged up and down the line of the river that he could see from where he stood.

"I don't know," Miller said. "It seems like the country has changed." His voice was quietly puzzled. "It seems like everything is different from what it was."

Schneider spat on the ground. "Then we still don't know where we are?"

"I didn't say that." Miller's eyes continued to range the line of the river. "I been here before. I been all over this country before. I just can't seem to get things straight."

"If this ain't the damndest chase I ever been on," Schneider said. "I feel like we're looking for a pin in a stack of hay." He walked angrily away from the little group. He sat down at the wagon, his back against the spokes of a rear wheel, and looked sullenly out over the flat valley across which they had traveled.

Miller walked to the bank of the river where Andrews had sat during his absence. For several minutes he stared across the river into the forest of pines that thrust up through the side of the mountain. His legs were slightly spread, and his large shoulders slumped forward; his head drooped, and his arms hung loosely at his sides. Every now and then one of his fingers twitched, and the slight movements turned his hands this way and that. At last he sighed, and straightened.

"Might as well get started," he said, turning to the men. "We ain't going to find nothing as long as we sit here."

Schneider protested that there was no use for them all to join in the search, since only Miller would know the spot he wanted (if even Miller would know it) when he came upon it. Miller did not answer him. He directed Charley Hoge to yoke the oxen; soon the party was making its way in a southwesterly direction, opposite to the way that Miller had taken alone earlier in the afternoon.

All afternoon they made their way upriver. Miller went near the riverbank; sometimes, when the bank became too brushy, he rode his horse into the river itself, where the horse stumbled over the stones that littered the bed nearly to the edge of either bank. Once a thick grove of pines, which grew up to the very bank of the river, deflected the course of the wagon; the men in the main party skirted the grove, while Miller kept to the river bed. Andrews, with Schneider and Charley Hoge, did not see Miller for more than an hour; when finally the wedge-shaped grove was skirted, he saw Miller far ahead of them, upriver, leaning out from his saddle to inspect the far bank.

They made camp early that night, only an hour or so after the sun went down behind the mountains. With darkness, a chill came in the air; Charley Hoge threw more branches on the fire and dragged upon the branches a sizable log, which Schneider, in an excess of energy and anger, had cut from a pine tree whose top had been snapped the winter before by the weight of snow and wind. The fire roared violently in the quiet, driving the men back from it and lighting their faces a deep red. But after the fire died down to large embers the chill came again; Andrews got an extra blanket from the wagon and added it to his thin bedroll.

In the morning, silently, they broke camp. Andrews and Charley Hoge worked together; Schneider and Miller, apart from each other, stood apart from the two who worked. Schneider whittled savagely on a slender bough of pine; the shavings piled up on the ground where he was sitting, between his upraised knees. Miller stood again at the bank of the river, his back to the others, and gazed into the shallow flow of clear water that came from the direction in which they were to travel.

The morning's journey began lethargically. Schneider slumped in his saddle; when he looked up from the ground, his eyes came to rest sullenly upon Miller's back. Charley Hoge snapped the long whip perfunctorily over the ears of the lead oxen, and drank frequently from one of the bottles he kept in the box under his spring seat. Only Miller, who seemed to Andrews to become less and less a part of the group, kept restlessly ahead, now on the bank, now on the edge of the river bed, now in the water itself, which flowed whitely around the fetlocks of his horse. Miller's restlessness began to affect Andrews, and he found himself gazing with an increasing intensity at the anonymous green forest that edged the river and defined the course of their passage.

In the middle of the morning, ahead of them, Miller halted his horse. The horse stood near the center of the river bed; as the others came up close to him, Andrews could see that Miller was gazing thoughtfully, but without real interest, at a spot on the bank opposite them. When the wagon halted, Miller turned to the group and said quietly:

"This is the place. Charley, turn your wagon down here and come straight across."

For a moment, none of them moved. Where Miller pointed was no different from any of the places along the unchanging stretch of mountainside that they had passed that morning or the previous afternoon. Miller said again:

"Come on. Turn your wagon straight across."

Charley Hoge shrugged. He cracked his whip above the left ear of the off-ox, and set the hand brake for the descent down the heavily sloping riverbank. Schneider and Andrews went ahead, following closely behind Miller, who turned his horse straight into the thick forest of pines.

For a moment, as he and Schneider and Miller pressed their horses directly into the face of the forest, Andrews had a sensation of sinking, as if he were being absorbed downward into a softness without boundary or mark. The sound of their horses' breathing, the clop of their hooves, and even the few words the men spoke, all were absorbed in the quiet of the forest, so that all sound came muted and distant and calm, one sound much the same as another, whether it was the snort of a horse or a spoken word; all was reduced to soft thuds which seemed to come, not from themselves, but from the forest, as if there beat within it a giant heart, for anyone to hear.

Schneider's voice, made soft and dull and unconcerned by the forest, came from beside Andrews: "Where the hell are we going? I don't see no sign of buffalo here."

Miller pointed downward. "Look what we're on."

The horses' hooves, Andrews saw, were sliding the smallest bit upon what he had thought was the grayish-green bed of the forest; a closer look showed him that they were riding over a series of long flat stones that grew up from the base of the mountain and wound among the trees.

"They don't leave no track here that a man would notice," Miller said. Then he leaned forward in the saddle. "But look up there."

The stone trail ended abruptly ahead of them, and a natural clearing widened among the trees and wound gradually up the side of the mountain. The bed of this clearing held a broad, regular swath of earth worn bare of grass; raw earth and stones showed the boundaries of the path. Miller kicked his horse up to the point where it began, and dismounted; he squatted in the middle of the path and inspected it carefully.

"This is their road." His hand caressed the hard-packed contours of the earth. "There's been a herd over it not too long ago. Looks like a big one."

"By God!" Schneider said. "By God!"

Miller rose. "It's going to be hard climbing from now on. Better tie your horses to the tail of the wagon; Charley'll be needing our help."

The buffalo trail went up the mountainside at an irregular angle. The wagon made its way up the steeply pitched incline; it went slowly upward, and then dipped sharply down in a hollow, and then went upward again. Andrews, after he had hitched his horse to the tailgate, strode beside the wagon with long, strong steps. The fresh high air filled his lungs, and gave him a strength he was not aware of having felt before. Beside the wagon, he turned to the two men, who were lagging some distance behind.

"Come on," he called in an excess of exuberance and strength; he laughed a little, excitedly. "We'll leave you behind."

Miller shook his head; Schneider grinned at him. Neither man spoke. They shuffled awkwardly over the rough trail; their movements were slow and resigned and deliberate, as if made by old men walking to no purpose and with great reluctance.

Andrews shrugged and turned away from them. He looked ahead at the trail, eagerly, as if each turn would bring him a new surprise. He went in front of the wagon, striding along easily and swiftly; he loped down the small hollows, and climbed the rises with long, heavy thrusts of his legs. At a high rise, he paused; for a moment the wagon was out of his sight;

he stood on a large stone that jutted up between two pines, and looked down; the mountain fell off sharply from the trail, and he could see for miles in either direction the river they had crossed only a few minutes before, and the land stretching level to the foothills that lay behind them. The land looked calm and undisturbed; he wondered idly at the half-submerged fear he had had of it during their crossing. Now that they were over it, it had the appearance of a friend known for a long while —it offered him a sense of security, a sense of comfort, and a knowledge that he could return to it and have that security and comfort whenever he wished. He turned. Above him, before him, the land was shrouded and unknown; he could not see it or know where they went. But his view of the other country, the level country behind him, touched upon what he was to see; and he felt a sense of peace.

He heard his name called. The sound came to him faintly from the trail below where the wagon was making its way upward. He leaped down from the rock, and trotted back to the wagon, which had halted before a sharp rise of the trail. Miller and Schneider were standing at the rear wheels; Charley Hoge sat on the clip seat, holding the hand brake against the backward roll of the wagon.

"Give us a hand here," Miller said. "This pull's a little steep for the oxen."

"All right," Andrews said. He noticed that his breath was coming rapidly, and that there was a slight ringing in his ears. He set his shoulder to the lower rear wheel, as Schneider had to the one pitched at a higher level on the other side of the trail. Miller faced him, and pulled at a large round wheel spoke, as Andrews pushed. Charley Hoge's whip whistled behind them, and then cracked ahead of them, over the oxen's heads, as his voice raised in a long, loud "Harrup!" The oxen inched forward, straining; Charley Hoge released the hand brake, and for an instant the men at the wheels felt a heavy, sickening, backward roll; then the weight of the oxen took hold; and as the men strained at the wheels, the wagon slowly began to move forward and upward on the trail.

The blood pounded in Andrews's head. Dimly, he saw muscles like large ropes coil around Miller's forearms, and saw the veins stand out heavily on his forehead. As the wheel turned, he found another spoke and put his shoulder to it; his breath came in gasps that sent sharp pains in his throat and chest. Bright points lighted the dimness in his eyes, and the points whirled; he closed his eyes. Suddenly he felt air in front of his hands, and then the sharp stones of the trail were digging in his back.

As from a great distance, he heard voices.

Schneider said: "He looks kind of blue, don't he?"

He opened his eyes; the brightness danced before him, and the dark green needles of the pines were very close, then very far away, and a patch of blue sky was revealed above the needles. He heard the rasping sound of his own breath; his arms lay helplessly at his sides, and the heaving of his chest pushed the back of his head against a rock; otherwise he did not move.

"He'll be all right." Miller's voice was slow and measured and easy.

Andrews turned his head. Schneider and Miller were squatting to his left; the wagon was some distance away, atop the rise which had momentarily halted it.

"What happened?" Andrews's voice was thin and weak.

"You passed out," Miller told him. Schneider chuckled. "In these mountains, you got to take it easy," Miller continued. "Air's thinner than what a body's used to."

Schneider shook his head, still chuckling. "Boy, you was sure going great there for a while. Thought you'd get clean over the mountain before it hit you."

Andrews smiled weakly, and raised himself on one elbow; the movement caused his breath, which had quieted somewhat, again to come rapidly and heavily. "Why didn't you slow me down?"

Miller shrugged. "This is something a body's got to find out for his self. It don't do no good to tell him."

Andrews got to his feet, and swayed dizzily for a moment; he caught at Miller's shoulder, and then straightened and stood on his own strength. "I'm all right. Let's get going."

They walked up the rise to the wagon. Andrews was breathing heavily again and his hands were shaking by the time they had gone the short distance.

Miller said: "I'd tell you to ride your horse for a while till you get your strength back, but it wouldn't be a good idea.

Once you get your wind broke, it's better to keep on going afoot. If you rode your horse now, you'd just have it all to do over again."

"I'm all right," Andrews said.

They started off again. This time, Andrews kept behind Miller and Schneider and tried to imitate their awkward, stumbling gait. After a while he discovered that the secret was to keep his limbs loose and let his body fall forward, and to use his legs only to keep his body from the ground. Though his breath still came in shallow gasps, and though after a slightly steep ascent the lights still whirled before his eyes, he found that the peculiar shambling rhythm of the climb prevented him from becoming too tired. Every forty-five minutes Miller called for a halt and the men rested. Andrews noticed that neither Miller nor Schneider sat when they rested. They stood upright, their chests heaving regularly; at the instant the heaving subsided they started off again. After discovering the agony of getting up from a sitting or lying position, Andrews began standing with them; it was much easier and much less tiring to resume the climb from a standing position than from a sitting one.

Throughout the afternoon the men walked beside the wagon; and when the trail narrowed they walked behind it, putting their shoulders to the wheels when a slope caused the hooves of the oxen to slip and slide on the hard trail.

By midafternoon, they had pushed and tugged halfway up the side of the mountain. Andrews's legs were numb, and his shoulder burned from repeated pushings against the wagon wheel. Even when he rested, the sharp thin air, cool and dry, pricked against his throat and caused sharp pains in his chest. He longed to rest, to sit on the ground, or to lie on the soft pine needles just off the trail; but he knew what the pain of rising would be; so he stood with the others when they rested, and looked up the trail to where it disappeared among the thick pines.

Late in the afternoon the trail made a turning so abrupt that Charley Hoge had to back the wagon up several times, angling it more to his right each time, so that finally it could negotiate the angle, its right wheels brushing against the pines, the left coming dangerously close to the brink of a sheer gully that descended three or four hundred feet. Past the turning, the party halted. Miller pointed ahead; the trail went steeply up to a point between two rough peaks, dark and jagged against the bright afternoon sky.

"There it is," Miller said. "Just beyond them peaks."

Charley Hoge cracked his whip above the oxen's ears, and whooped. Startled, the oxen lurched forward and upward; their hooves dug into the earth, and slipped; the men again put their shoulders against the wheels of the wagon.

"Don't push them too hard," Miller called to Charley Hoge. "It's a long pull, all the way to the top."

Foot by foot, they pulled and pushed the wagon up the last steep ascent. Sweat came out on their faces, and was instantly dried by the high, cool air. Andrews heard the groaning sound of air pulled into lungs, and realized that the sound he heard was his own, so loud that it almost drowned out the breathing of the other men, the creak of the wagon as it strained unnaturally upward, and the heavy sounds of the oxen's breathing and plodding and slipping on the trail. He gasped for air, as if he were drowning; his arms, hanging loose as his shoulder ground against the spokes, wanted to flail, as if they might raise him to more air. The numbness of his legs intensified, and suddenly they were numb no longer; he felt that hundreds of needles were pricking into his flesh, and that the needles warmed, became white-hot, and burned outward from his bone to his flesh. He felt that the sockets of his bones—ankle, knee, and hip—were being crushed by the weight they impelled forward. Blood pounded in his head, throbbed against his ears, until even the sound of his own breathing was submerged; and a red film came over his eyes. He could not see before him; he pushed blindly, his will supplanting his strength, becoming his body, until his pain submerged them both. Then he pitched forward, away from the wagon; the sharp stones on the path cut into his hands, but he did not move. He stayed for several moments on his hands and knees, and watched with a detached curiosity the blood from his cut palms seeping out and darkening the earth upon which they rested.

After a few moments, he was aware that the wagon had come to a halt just as he had pitched away from it, and that it was standing level now, no longer at an angle from the trail. On his right the sheer side of a rock thrust upward; to his left, above the wagon, no more than thirty feet away, was another very like it. He tried to get to his feet, but he slipped to his knees and remained there for a moment more. Still on his hands and knees, he saw Charley Hoge sitting erect on the wagon seat, looking out before him, not moving; Miller and Schneider were hanging on the wheels they had pushed; they, too, were looking before them, and they were silent. Andrews crawled a few feet forward, and pushed himself upright; he wiped his bloody hands on his shirt.

Miller turned to him. "There it is," he said quietly. "Take a look."

Andrews walked up to him, and stood looking where he pointed. For perhaps three hundred yards, the trail cut down between the pines; but at that point, abruptly, the land leveled. A long narrow valley, flat as the top of a table, wound among the mountains. Lush grass grew on the bed of the valley, and waved gently in the breeze as far as the eye could see. A quietness seemed to rise from the valley; it was the quietness, the stillness, the absolute calm of a land where no human foot had touched. Andrews found that despite his exhaustion he was holding his breath; he expelled the air from his lungs as gently as he could, so as not to disturb the silence.

Miller tensed, and touched Andrews's arm. "Look!" He pointed to the southwest.

A blackness moved on the valley, below the dark pines that grew on the opposite mountain. Andrews strained his eyes; at the edges of the patch, there was a slight ripple; and then the patch itself throbbed like a great body of water moved by obscure currents. The patch, though it appeared small at this distance, was, Andrews guessed, more than a mile in length and nearly a half mile in width.

"Buffalo," Miller whispered.

"My God!" Andrews said. "How many are there?"

"Two, three thousand maybe. And maybe more. This valley winds in and out of these hills; we can just see a little part of it from here. No telling what you'll find on farther."

For several moments more, Andrews stood beside Miller and watched the herd. He could, at the distance from which he viewed, make out no shape, distinguish no animal from another. From the north a cool wind began to rise; it came through the pass; Andrews shivered. The sun had fallen far below the mountain opposite them, and its shadow darkened the place where they stood.

"Let's get down and set up camp," Miller said. "It'll be dark soon."

Slowly, as if a procession, the group made its way down the incline to the valley. They were at the level ground before dark rolled from the mountain.

4.

THEY set up camp near a small spring. The spring water flashed in the last light as it poured thinly over smooth rock into a pool at the base of the mountain, and thence overflowed into a narrow stream half hidden by the thick grass of the valley.

"There's a little lake a few miles to the south," Miller said. "That's where the buff'll go to water."

Charley Hoge unyoked the oxen and set them to graze on the valley grass. With the help of Andrews, he dragged the large sheet of canvas from the wagon; then he cut several slender boughs from a young pine, and the two men constructed a box frame, over which they stretched the canvas, securing it carefully and tucking it so that the edges made a floor upon the grass. Then, from the wagon, they lugged the boxes of gunpowder and placed them within the small square tent.

"If I got this powder wet," Charley Hoge chuckled, "Miller would kill me."

After he had finished helping Charley Hoge, Andrews got an ax and went with Schneider a little way up the side of the mountain and began cutting a supply of wood for the camp. They let the logs remain where they were felled, hacking off the smaller branches and piling them beside the trees. "We'll get the horses and drag them down later," Schneider said. By dark, they had felled half a dozen fair-sized trees. Each returned to the camp with an armload of branches; and they dragged between them the trunk of a small tree.

Charley Hoge had built a fire against a huge boulder, which was twice the height of any of the men and so deeply creviced at one point that it formed a natural draft for the smoke. Though the fire was blazing high, he already had the coffeepot resting at one edge of the fire, and on another he had set the familiar pot of soaked beans. "Last night we'll have to eat beans," Charley Hoge said. "Tomorrow we'll have buffalo meat; maybe I'll even get a little small game, and we'll have a stew."

Across the trunks of two close-set pines, he had nailed a heavy straight bough; upon this bough, neatly hung, were his utensils—a large skillet, two pans, a ladle, several knives whose handles were discolored and scarred but whose blades gleamed in the leaping flame, a small hatchet, and an ax. Resting on the ground was a large iron kettle, the outside black but the inside gleaming a dull grayish-silver. Beside this, against the trunk of one of the trees, was the large box that contained the other provisions.

After the men finished eating, they hollowed long oval depressions in the loose pine needles; in these depressions they laid crisscross small branches, and upon the branches leveled the pine needles they had scooped out, so that they could put their bedrolls upon a springy mattress that held their bodies lightly and comfortably. They placed their bedrolls close to the fire, near the boulder; thus, they were partially protected from weather coming from the north or west across the valley; the forest would hold off the weather from the east.

By the time their beds were made, the fire had died to gray-coated embers. Miller watched the coals intently, his face a dark red in their glow. Charley Hoge lighted the lantern that hung on the bough beside his cooking utensils; the feeble light was lost in the darkness. He carried the lantern to the fire where the men sat. Miller rose and got the heavy iron kettle from the ground and set it squarely in the bed of coals. Then he took the lantern and handed it to Charley Hoge, who followed him to the large box of provisions beside the tree. From the box Miller removed two large bars of lead and carried them to the fire; he stuck them into the kettle, crossing them so that their weight did not upset it. Then he went to the little square tent that Charley Hoge and Will Andrews had constructed, and took from it a box of powder and a smaller box of caps; he carefully tucked the canvas back around the remaining powder before he left.

At the campfire he knelt beside his saddle, which rested near his bedroll, and took from his saddlebag a large loose sack which was secured at the mouth by a leather thong. He untied the thong, and spread the cloth on the ground; hundreds of dully gleaming brass shell cases descended in a loose mound. Andrews edged closer to the two men.

The lead in the blackened kettle shifted above the heat. Miller inspected the kettle, and moved it so that the heat came through more evenly. Then, with a hatchet, he opened the box of gunpowder and tore open the heavy paper that protected the black grains. Between his thumb and forefinger, he took a pinch and threw it on the fire where it blazed for an instant with a blue-white flame. Satisfied, Miller nodded, and dug again into his saddlebag; he withdrew a bulky flat object, hinged on one side, that opened to disclose a number of shallow depressions evenly spaced and connected to each other by tiny grooves. He carefully cleaned this mold with a greased rag; when Miller closed it, Andrews could see a tiny cuplike mouth at its top.

Again Miller reached into his bag and took out a large ladle. He inserted it in the now-bubbling kettle of lead, and delicately spooned the molten lead into the mouth of the bullet mold. The hot lead crackled on the cool mold; a drop spattered on Miller's hand, which held the mold, but he did not flinch. After the mold was filled, Miller thrust it into a bucket of cold water that Charley Hoge had brought up to him; the mold hissed in the water, which bubbled in white froth. Then Miller withdrew the mold, and spilled the bullets on the cloth beside the cartridge cases.

When the pile of lead bullets was about equal in size to the pile of brass cartridges, Miller put the mold aside to cool. Quickly but carefully he examined the molded bullets; occasionally he smoothed the base of one with a small file; more rarely he tossed a defective one back into the iron kettle, which he had set back from the fire. Before he put the bullets into a new pile beside the empty brass shells, he rubbed the base of each pellet in a square of beeswax. From the square container beside the powder box, he took the tiny caps and thrust them easily into the empty shells, tamping them carefully with a small black tool.

Again from his saddlebag he drew out a narrow spoon and a crumpled wad of newspaper. With the spoon he measured a quantity of gunpowder; over the opened box of gunpowder, he held a shell casing and filled it three-quarters full of the black gunpowder. He tapped the casing sharply on the edge of the box to level the powder, and with his free hand tore a bit from the crumpled newspaper and wadded that into the shell. Finally he picked up one of the lead bullets and jammed it into the loaded shell case with the heel of his palm. Then with his strong white teeth, he crimped the edge of the brass casing where it held the butt of the bullet, and threw the bullet carelessly into yet a third pile.

For several minutes the three men watched Miller reload the shell casings. Charley Hoge watched delightedly, grinning and nodding his head at Miller's skill; Schneider watched sleepily, indifferently, yawning now and then; Andrews watched with intent interest, trying to impress in his memory the precise nature of each of Miller's movements.

After a while Schneider roused himself and spoke to Andrews:

"Mr. Andrews, we got work to do. Get your knives, and let's sharpen them up."

Andrews looked at Miller, who jerked his head in the direction of the large provisions box. In the dim light of the lantern Andrews pawed through the box; at last he found the flat leather case that Miller had got for him back in Butcher's Crossing. He took the case back to the fire, which was now leaping in the flame of a fresh log that Charley Hoge had thrown on. He opened the case. The knives gleamed brightly in the firelight; the bone handles were clean and unscarred.

Schneider had got his knives from his saddlebag; he removed one from its case and tested its edge against his calloused thumb. He shook his head, and spat heartily on a long grayish-brown whetstone, whose center was worn away so that the surface of the stone described a long curve; with the flat of his knife he distributed the spittle evenly on the surface. Then he worked the blade on the stone in a long oval, holding the blade at a careful angle, and managing the oval movement so that the stone bit equally into each part of the blade. Andrews watched him for a few moments; then he selected a knife and tested his own blade on his thumb. The edge pressed into the soft hump of flesh, but it did not bite.

"You'll have to sharpen them all," Schneider said, glancing up at him; "a new knife's got no cutting edge."

Andrews nodded and took from his case a new whetstone; he spat on it, as he had seen Schneider do, and spread the spittle upon the surface.

"You ought to soak your stone in oil for a day or two before you use it," Schneider said. "But I guess it don't make no difference this time."

Andrews began rotating the blade upon the stone; his movements were awkward, and he could not find the rhythm which would allow every part of the blade to be equally whetted.

"Here," Schneider said, dropping his own knife and stone. "You got the blade pitched too high. You might get a sharp edge like that, but it wouldn't last more than one or two skins. Give it to me."

Schneider skillfully ran the blade over the stone, whipping it back and forward so swiftly that Andrews could hardly see it. Schneider turned the blade over and showed Andrews the angle at which he held it to the stone.

"You get a long cutting edge like this," Schneider said. "It'll last you near a full day's skinning without sharpening again. You make your cut too narrow, you'll ruin your knife." He handed the knife butt-first to Andrews. "Try it."

Andrews touched the blade to his thumb; he felt a hot little pain. A thin line of red appeared diagonally across the ball of his thumb; he watched it dumbly as it widened, and as the blood ran irregularly in the tiny whorls of his thumb.

Schneider grinned. "That's the way a knife should cut. You got a good set of knives."

Under Schneider's supervision, Andrews sharpened the other knives. As he sharpened each knife of a different shape or size, Schneider explained its use to him. "This one here's for long work," Schneider said. "You can slit a bull from throat to pecker without taking it out of the skin." And: "This one's for close work, around the hooves. This one's good for dressing your meat down, once the bull's skinned. And this one's for scraping the skin, once she's off."

When at last Schneider was satisfied with the knives, Andrews returned them to their cases. From the new movement to which he had been introduced, his arm was tired; from the tightness with which he had held the knives while sharpening them, his right hand was numb. A chill wind blew from the pass; Andrews shivered, and moved closer to the fire.

Miller's voice came from the darkness behind the three men who sat silently around the campfire. "Everything ready for tomorrow?" The men turned. The firelight caught the buttons on Miller's shirt and the fringes of his opened buckskin jacket, and glinted on his heavy nose and forehead; his dark beard blended into the darkness so that Andrews had the momentary impression of a head floating above the merest suggestion of a body. Then Miller came up to them and sat down.

"Everything's ready," Schneider said.

"Good." Miller drew a bullet from one of the bulging pockets of his jacket. On a flat rock near the fire he marked with the lead tip a long irregular oval that curved nearly into a semicircle.

"Near as I can remember," Miller said, "this is the shape of the valley. We only saw a little bit of it this afternoon. A few miles on, around this first bend, it widens out to maybe four, five miles across; and it goes on twenty or twenty-five miles. It don't look like a lot of ground, but the grass is thick and rich, and it grows back almost as fast as it's cropped; it'll feed a hell of a lot of buffalo."

In the fire, a burned-through log fell and sent into the air a shower of sparks that glowed and died in the darkness.

"Our job is easy," Miller went on. "We start our kill with the little herd we saw this morning, and then we work down the valley. Nothing to worry about; there ain't no way out of this canyon except the way we came through. Leastways, there's no way for buffalo. Mountains steepen around the first bend; lots of places there's nothing up but sheer rock."

"This'll be the main camp?" Schneider asked.

Miller nodded. "As we work down the valley, Charley'll follow us with the wagon to pick up the hides; we'll bale them back here. We might have to make a few camps away from here, but not many; when we get to the end of the valley, if there are any buffalo left, we can herd them back up toward here. In the long run, it'll save us time."

"Just one thing," Schneider said. "Start us off easy. Mr. Andrews, here, is going to need a few days before he'll be much help. And I don't want to have to skin stiff buffalo."

"The way this is set up," Miller said, "there's no hurry. If we had to, we could stay here all winter picking them off."

Charley Hoge threw another log on the already blazing fire. In the intense heat, the log flared instantly into flame. For that moment, the faces of the four men gathered around the fire were lighted fully, and each could see the other as if in daylight. Then the outer bark of the log burned away, and the firelight died to a steady flame. Charley Hoge waited for several minutes; then, with a shovel, he banked the flames with dead ashes, so that in the yellow light of the lantern the men could see only the whitish-yellow smoke struggling upward through the ashes. Without further words, they turned into their bedrolls.

For a long time after he had bedded down, Will Andrews listened to the silence around him. For a while the acrid smell of the smothered pine log's burning warmed his nostrils; then the wind shifted and he could no longer smell the smoke or hear the heavy breaths of the sleeping men around him. He turned so that he faced the side of the mountain over which they had traveled. From the darkness that clung about the earth he lifted his gaze and followed the dim outlines of particular trees as they rose from the darkness and gradually gained distinctness against the deep blue cloudless sky that twinkled with the light of the clear stars. Even with an extra blanket on his bedroll, he was chilled; he could see the gray cloud of his breath as he breathed the sharp night air. His eyes closed upon the image of a tall conical pine tree outlined blackly against the luminous sky, and despite the cold he slept soundly until morning.

5.

WHEN Andrews awoke, Charley Hoge was already up and dressed; he huddled over the fire, adding twigs to the coals that had been kept overnight by the banking. Andrews lay for a moment in the comparative warmth of his bedroll, and watched his breath fog the air. Then he flung the blankets aside, and, shivering, got into his boots, which were stiff and hard from the cold. Without lacing them, he clumped over to the fire. The sun had not yet come over the mountain against which their camp was set; but on the opposite mountain, at the top, a mass of pine trees was lighted by the early sun; a patch of turning aspen flamed a deep gold in the green of the pines.

Miller and Schneider arose before Charley Hoge's coffee began to boil. Miller beckoned to Andrews; the three men trudged out of their cover of trees onto the level valley, where a hundred yards away their hobbled horses were grazing. They led the animals back to the camp and saddled them before the coffee, the side meat, and the fried mush were ready.

"They ain't moved much," Miller said, pointing through the trees. Andrews saw the thin black line of the herd strung out around the bend of the valley. He drank his coffee hurriedly, scalding his mouth. Miller ate his breakfast calmly, slowly. After he finished, he went a little way into the forest and from a low branch selected a forked bough and chopped it off about two feet from the fork; with his knife, he trimmed the fork so that the two small branches protruded from the main branch about six inches; then he sharpened the thick base of the main branch. From his pile of goods beside his bedroll, he got his gun and unwrapped the oilskin which protected it from the night dampness. He inspected the gun carefully, and thrust it into the long holster attached to his saddle. The three men mounted their horses.

In the open valley, Miller pulled his horse up and spoke to the two men on either side of him. "We'll go straight to them. Point your horses behind mine, and don't let them swerve out. As long as we keep straight at them they won't scare."

Andrews rode behind Miller, his horse at a slow walk. His hands ached; he looked at his knuckles; the skin was stretched white across the bones. He relaxed his grip on the reins, and let his shoulders slump; he was breathing heavily.

By the time they had gone halfway across the width of the valley, the herd, slowly grazing, had rounded the bend. Miller led the two men up near the base of the mountain.

"We'll have to go easy from here," he said. "You never know how the wind will be blowing in these mountains. Tie your horses up; we'll go on foot."

Walking one behind the other with Miller in the lead, the men made their way around the blunt rocky base of the mountain. Miller halted suddenly, and held up one hand.

Without turning his head, he spoke to those behind him in the normal tones of conversation: "They're just ahead, not more than three hundred yards away. Go easy, now." He squatted and ripped off a few blades of grass and with his hand held high let them fall to the ground. The wind carried the blades back toward him. He nodded. "Wind's right." He rose and went forward more slowly.

Andrews, carrying over one shoulder the bag containing Miller's ammunition, shifted his burden; and as he shifted it, he saw a movement in the herd in front of him.

Again without turning his head, Miller said: "Just keep walking straight. As long as you don't move out of the line, they won't get scared."

Now Andrews could see the herd clearly. Against the pale yellow-green of the grass, the dark umber of the buffalo stood out sharply, but merged into the deeper color of the pine forest on the steep mountainside behind them. Many of the buffalo were lying at ease upon the soft valley grass; those were mere humps, like dark rocks, without identity or shape. But a few stood at the edges of the herd, like sentinels; some were grazing lightly, and others stood unmoving, their huge furry heads slumped between their forelegs, which were so matted with long dark fur that their shapes could not be seen. One old bull carried thick scars on his sides and flanks that could be seen even at the distance where the three men walked; the bull stood somewhat apart from the other animals; he faced the approaching men, his head lowered, his upward curving ebony horns shining in the sunlight, bright against the dark mop of hair that hung over his head. The bull did not move as they came nearer.

Miller paused again. "No need for all of us to go on. Fred, you wait here; Will, you follow me; we'll have to try to skirt them. Buffalo always face downwind; can't get a good shot from this angle."

Schneider dropped to his knees and let himself down to a prone position; with his chin resting on his folded hands, he regarded the herd. Miller and Andrews cut to their left. They had walked about fifteen yards when Miller raised his hand, palm outward; Andrews halted.

"They're beginning to stir," Miller said. "Go easy."

Many of the buffalo at the outer edges of the herd had got to their feet, raising themselves stiffly on their forelegs, and then upon their hind legs, wobbling for a moment until they had taken a few steps forward. The two men remained still.

"It's the moving that stirs them up," Miller said. "You could stand right in front of them all day and not bother them, if you could get there without moving."

The two men began again their slow movement forward. When the herd showed another sign of restlessness, Miller dropped to his hands and knees; Andrews came up behind him, awkwardly dragging the sack of ammunition at his side.

When they were broadside to the herd and about a hundred and fifty yards away from it, they stopped. Miller stuck into the ground the forked branch he had been carrying, and rested his gun barrel on the fork. Andrews crawled up beside him.

Miller grinned at him. "Watch the way I do it, boy. You aim just a little behind the shoulder blade, and about two-thirds of the way down from the top of the hump; that is, if you're shooting from behind, the way we are. This is the heart shot. It's better to get them a little from the front, through the lights; that way, they don't die so quick, but they don't run so far after they're shot. But with a wind, you take a chance, try-ing to get in front of them. Keep your eye on the big bull, the one with the scars all over him. His hide ain't worth a damn, but he looks like the leader. You always try to pick out the leader of a herd and get him first. They ain't apt to run so far without a leader."

Andrews watched intently as Miller lined his gun upon the old bull. Both of Miller's eyes were open along the sights of his gun barrel. The stock was tight against his cheek. The muscles of his right hand tensed; there was a heavy *crrack* of the rifle; the stock kicked back against Miller's shoulder, and a small cloud of smoke drifted away from the mouth of the gun barrel.

At the sound of the gun, the old bull jumped, as if startled by a sharp blow on his rump; without hurry, he began loping away from the men who lay on their bellies.

"Damn," Miller said.

"You missed him," Andrews said; there was amazement in his voice.

Miller laughed shortly. "I didn't miss him. That's the trouble with heart-shot buffalo. They'll go a hundred yards sometimes."

The other buffalo began to be aroused by the movement of their leader. Slowly at first, a few raised themselves on their thick forelegs; and then suddenly the herd was a dark mass of moving fur as it ran in the direction its leader had taken. In the closely packed herd, the humps of the animals bobbed rhythmically, almost liquidly; and the roar of the hooves came upon the two men who lay watching. Miller shouted something that Andrews could not distinguish in the noise.

The buffalo passed their wounded leader, and ran beyond him some three hundred yards, where their running gradually spent itself, and where they stood, milling uneasily about. The old bull stood alone behind them, his massive head sunk below his hump; his tail twitched once or twice, and he shook his head. He turned around several times, as another animal might have done before sleeping, and finally stood facing the two men who were more than two hundred yards away from him. He took three steps toward them, and paused again. Then, stiffly, he fell on his side, his legs straight out from his belly. The legs jerked, and then he was still.

Miller rose from his prone position and brushed the grass off the front of his clothing. "Well, we got the leader. They won't run so far the next time." He picked up his gun, his shooting stick, and a long wire-handled cleaning patch that he had laid beside him. "Want to go over and take a look?"

"Won't we scare the rest of them?"

Miller shook his head. "They had their scare. They won't be so spooky now."

They walked across the grass to where the dead buffalo lay. Miller glanced at it casually and scuffed its fur with the toe of his boot.

"Ain't worth skinning," he said. "But you have to get the leader out of the way, if you're going to do any good with the rest of them."

Andrews regarded the felled buffalo with some mixture of feeling. On the ground, unmoving, it no longer had that kind of wild dignity and power that he had imputed to it only a few minutes before. And though the body made a huge dark mound on the earth, its size seemed somehow diminished.

The shaggy black head was cocked a little to one side, held so by one horn that had fallen upon an unevenness of the ground; the other horn was broken at the tip. The small eyes, half-closed, but still brightly shining in the sun, stared gently ahead. The hooves were surprisingly small, almost delicate, cloven neatly like those of a calf; the thin ankles seemed incapable of having supported the weight of the great animal. The broad swelling side was covered with scars; some were so old that the fur had nearly covered them, but others were new, and shone flat and dark blue on the flesh. From one nostril, a drop of blood thickened in the sun, and dropped upon the grass.

"He wasn't good for much longer anyway," Miller said. "In another year he would have weakened, and been picked off by the wolves." He spat on the grass beside the animal. "Buffalo never dies of old age. He's either killed by a man or dragged down by a wolf."

Andrews glanced across the body of the buffalo and saw the herd beyond. It had settled; a few of the animals were still milling about; but more of them were grazing or resting on the grass.

"We'll give them a few minutes," Miller said. "They're still a mite skittish."

They walked around the buffalo that Miller had killed and made their way in the direction of the herd. They walked slowly but with less caution than they had during their first approach. When they came within two hundred and fifty yards, Miller stopped and tore off a small handful of grass-blades; he held them up and let them fall. They fell slowly downward, scattering this way and that. Miller nodded in satisfaction.

"Wind's died," he said. "We can get on the other side, and run them back toward camp; less hauling of the skins that way."

They made a wide circle, approached, and stopped a little more than a hundred yards away from the closely bunched herd. Andrews lay on his stomach beside Miller, who adjusted his Sharps rifle in the crotch of his shooting stick.

"Should get two or three this time, before they run," he said.

He examined the disposition of the herd with some care for several minutes. More of the buffalo lowered themselves to the grass. Miller confined his attention to the buffalo milling around the edges of the herd. He leveled his rifle toward a large bull that seemed more active than the others, and squeezed gently on the trigger. At the noise of his shot, a few of the buffalo got to their feet; they all turned their heads in the direction from which the shot came; they seemed to stare at the little cloud of smoke that rose from the barrel of the gun and thinned in the still air. The bull gave a start forward and ran for a few steps, stopped, and turned to face the two men who lay on the ground. Blood dropped slowly from both nostrils, and then dropped more swiftly, until it came in two crimson streams. The buffalo that had begun to move away at the sound of the shot, seeing their new leader hesitate, stopped in wait for him.

"Got him through the lights," Miller said. "Watch." He reloaded his rifle as he spoke, and swung it around in search of the most active of the remaining buffalo.

As he spoke, the wounded bull swayed unsteadily, staggered, and with a heavy lurch fell sideways. Three smaller animals came up curiously to the fallen bull; for a few seconds they stared, and sniffed at the warm blood. One of them lifted its head and bawled, and started to trot away. Immediately, beside Andrews, another shot sounded; and the younger bull jumped, startled, ran a few feet, and paused, the blood streaming from its nostrils.

In quick succession, Miller shot three more buffalo. By the time he had shot the third, the entire herd was on its feet, milling about; but the animals did not run. They wandered about in a loose circle, bawling, looking for a leader to take them away.

"I've got them," Miller whispered fiercely. "By God, they're buffaloed!" He upended his sack of ammunition so that several dozen shells were quickly available to him. When he could reach them, Andrews collected the empty cartridges. After he had downed his sixth buffalo, Miller opened the breech of his rifle and swabbed out the powder-caked barrel with the cleaning patch tied on the end of the long stiff wire.

"Run back to the camp and get me a fresh rifle and some more cartridges," he said to Andrews. "And bring a bucket of water."

Andrews crawled on his hands and knees in a straight line away from Miller. After several minutes, he looked back over his shoulder; he got to his feet and trotted in a wide circle around the herd. When he turned around the bend in the valley, he saw Schneider sitting with his back propped against a rock, his hat pulled low over his eyes. At the sound of Andrews's approach, Schneider pushed his hat back and looked up at him.

"Miller has them buffaloed," Andrews said, panting. "They just stand there and let him shoot them. They don't even run."

"God damn it," Schneider said quietly. "He's got a stand. I was afraid of it. Sounded like the shots was coming too regular and close."

From the distance, they heard the sound of a shot; it was faint and inoffensive where they heard it.

"They just stand there," Andrews said again.

Schneider pulled his hat over his eyes and leaned against his rock. "You better hope they run pretty soon. Else we'll be working all night."

Andrews went toward the horses, which were standing close together, their heads erect and their ears pitched forward at the sound of Miller's gunfire. He got on his own horse, and set it at a gallop across the valley to their camp.

At his approach, Charley Hoge looked up from his work; he had spent the morning of the other men's absence felling a number of slender aspens and dragging them to the scattered trees at the edge of their camp.

"Give me a hand with some of these poles," Charley called to him as he dismounted. "Trying to set up a corral for the livestock."

"Miller's got a stand of buffalo," Andrews said. "He wants a fresh rifle and some cartridges. And some water."

"'I God," Charley Hoge said. "His name be praised." He dropped the aspen pole that with the crook of his bad arm he had half lifted up across the trunk of a pine, and scurried toward the canvas-covered store of goods near the rock chimney. "How many head?"

"Two hundred fifty, three hundred. Maybe more."

"'I God," Charley Hoge said. "If they don't scatter, it'll be as big a stand as he ever had." From the covered framework of pine boughs, Charley Hoge pulled an ancient rifle whose stock was nicked and stained and split at one point, the split being closed by tightly wound wire. "This here's just an old Ballard —nothing like the Sharps—but it's a Fifty, and he can use it enough to cool his good gun off. And here's some shells, two boxes—all we got. With what he filled last night, ought to be enough."

Andrews took the gun and the shells, in his haste and nervousness dropping a box of the latter. "And some water," Andrews said, stopping to retrieve the box of shells.

Charley Hoge nodded and went across the spring, where he filled a small wooden keg. Handing it to Andrews, he said: "Get a little of this warm before you use it on a rifle barrel; or don't let the barrel get too hot. Cold water on a real hot barrel can ruin it mighty quick."

Andrews, mounted on his horse, nodded. He clasped the keg to his chest with one arm, and reined the horse away from the camp. He pointed his horse toward the sound of the gunfire, which still came faintly across the long flat valley, and let the horse have its head; his arms tightly clasped the water keg and the spare rifle, and he held the reins loosely in one hand. He pulled his horse to a halt near the bend of the valley where Schneider was still dozing, and dismounted awkwardly, nearly dropping the keg of water in his descent. He wrapped the reins about a small tree and made his way in a wide half-circle around the valley bend to where Miller, enveloped now in a light gray haze of gunsmoke, lay on the ground and fired every two or three minutes into the milling herd of buffalo. Andrews crawled up beside him, carrying the water keg with one arm and sliding the rifle over the slick grass with his other hand, which supported him.

"How many of them have you got?" Andrews asked.

Miller did not answer; he turned upon him wide, black-rimmed eyes that stared at, through him, blankly, as if he did not exist. Miller grabbed the extra rifle, and thrust the Sharps into Andrews's hands; Andrews took it by the stock and the barrel, and immediately dropped it. The barrel was painfully hot.

"Clean her out," Miller said in a flat, grating voice. He thrust the cleaning rod toward him. "She's getting caked inside."

Careful not to touch the metal of the barrel, Andrews broke the rifle and inserted the cleaning patch into the mouth of the barrel.

"Not that way," Miller told him in a flat voice. "You'll foul the firing pin. Sop your patch in water, and go through the breech."

Andrews opened the keg of water and got the tufted end of the cleaning rod wet. When he inserted the rod into the breech of the barrel the hot metal hissed, and the drops of water that got on the outside of the barrel danced for a moment on the blued metal and disappeared. He waited for a few moments, and reinserted the patch. Drops of smoke-blackened water dripped from the end of the barrel. After cleaning the fouled gun, he took a handkerchief from his pocket, dipped it into the still-cool spring water, and ran it over the outside of the barrel until the gun was cool. Then he handed it back to Miller.

Miller shot, and reloaded, and shot, and loaded again. The acrid haze of gunsmoke thickened around them; Andrews coughed and breathed heavily and put his face near the ground where the smoke was thinner. When he lifted his head he could see the ground in front of him littered with the mounded corpses of buffalo, and the remaining herd—apparently little diminished—circling almost mechanically now, in a kind of dumb rhythm, as if impelled by the regular explosions of Miller's guns. The sound of the guns firing deafened him; between shots, his ears throbbed dully, and he waited, tense in the pounding silence, almost dreading the next shot which would shatter his deafness with a quick burst of sound nearly like pain.

Gradually the herd, in its milling, moved away from them; as it moved, the two men crawled toward it, a few yards at a time, maintaining their relative position to the circling buffalo. For a few minutes, beyond the heavy cloud of gunsmoke, they could breathe easily; but soon another haze formed and they were breathing heavily and coughing again.

After a while Andrews began to perceive a rhythm in Miller's slaughter. First, with a deliberate slow movement that was a tightening of the arm muscles, a steadying of his head, and a slow squeeze of his hand, Miller would fire his rifle; then quickly he would eject the still-smoking cartridge and reload; he would study the animal he had shot, and if he saw that it was cleanly hit, his eyes would search among the circling herd for a buffalo that seemed particularly restless; after a few seconds, the wounded animal would stagger and crash to the ground; and then he would shoot again. The whole business seemed to Andrews like a dance, a thunderous minuet created by the wildness that surrounded it.

Once during the stand, several hours after Miller had felled the first of the buffalo, Schneider crawled up behind them and called Miller's name. Miller gave no sign that he heard. Schneider called again, more loudly, and Miller jerked his head slightly toward him; but still he did not answer.

"Give it up," Schneider said. "You got seventy or eighty of them already. That's more than enough to keep Mr. Andrews and me busy half the night."

"No," Miller said.

"You got a good stand already," Schneider said. "All right. You don't have to—"

Miller's hand tightened, and a shot boomed over Schneider's words.

"Mr. Andrews here won't be much help; you know that," Schneider said, after the echoes of the gunshot had drifted away. "No need to keep on shooting more than we'll be able to skin."

"We'll skin all we shoot, Fred," Miller said. "No matter if I shoot from now till tomorrow."

"God damn it!" Schneider said. "I ain't going to skin no stiff buff."

Miller reloaded his gun, and swung it around restlessly on the shooting stick. "I'll help you with the skinning, if need be. But help you or not, you'll skin them, Fred. You'll skin them hot or cold, loose or hard. You'll skin them if they're bloated, or you'll skin them if they're froze. You'll skin them if you have to pry the hides loose with a crowbar. Now shut up, and get away from here; you'll make me miss a shot."

"God *damn* it!" Schneider said. He pounded the earth with his fist. "All right," he said, raising himself up to a crouching position. "Keep them as long as you can. But I ain't going to—"

"Fred," Miller said quietly, "when you crawl away from here, crawl away quiet. If these buffalo spook, I'll shoot you."

For a moment Schneider remained in his low crouch. Then he shook his head, dropped to his knees, and crawled away from the two men in a straight line, muttering to himself. Miller's hand tightened, his finger squeezed, and a shot cracked in the thudding quietness.

It was the middle of the afternoon before the stand was broken.

The original herd had been diminished by two-thirds or more. In a long irregular swath that extended beyond the herd for nearly a mile, the ground was littered with the dark mounds of dead buffalo. Andrews's knees were raw from crawling after Miller, as they made their way yard by yard in slow pursuit of the southward list of the circling herd. His eyes burned from blinking against the gunsmoke, and his lungs pained him from breathing it; his head throbbed from the sound of gunfire, and upon the palm of one hand blisters were beginning to form from his handling of the hot barrels. For the last hour he had clenched his teeth against any expression of the pain his body felt.

But as the pain of his body increased, his mind seemed to detach itself from the pain, to rise above it, so that he could see himself and Miller more clearly than he had before. During the last hour of the stand he came to see Miller as a mechanism, an automaton, moved by the moving herd; and he came to see Miller's destruction of the buffalo, not as a lust for blood or a lust for the hides or a lust for what the hides would bring, or even at last the blind lust of fury that toiled darkly within him—he came to see the destruction as a cold, mindless response to the life in which Miller had immersed himself. And he looked upon himself, crawling dumbly after Miller upon the flat bed of the valley, picking up the empty cartridges that he spent, tugging the water keg, husbanding the rifle, cleaning it, offering it to Miller when he needed it—he looked upon himself, and did not know who he was, or where he went.

Miller's rifle cracked; a young cow, hardly more than a calf, stumbled, got to its feet, and ran erratically out of the circling herd.

"Damn it," Miller said without emotion. "A leg shot. That will do it."

While he was speaking, he was reloading; he got another shot off at the wounded buffalo; but it was too late. On the second shot, the cow wheeled and ran into the milling herd. The circle broken, the herd halted and was still for a moment. Then a young bull broke away, and the herd followed, the mass of animals pouring out of their own wide circle like water from a spout, until Miller and Andrews could see only a thin dark stream of bobbing humps thudding away from them down the winding bed of the valley.

The two men stood erect. Andrews stretched his cramped muscles, and almost cried aloud in pain as he straightened his back.

"I thought about it," Miller said, speaking away from Andrews toward the dwindling herd. "I thought about what would happen if I didn't get a clean shot. So I didn't get a clean shot. I broke a leg. If I hadn't thought about it, I could have got the whole herd." He turned to Andrews; his eyes were wide and blank, the pupils unfocused and swimming in the whites. The unbearded skin of his face was black with the ash of gunpowder, and his beard was caked with it. "The whole herd," he said again; and his eyes focused upon Andrews and he smiled a little with the corners of his mouth.

"Was it a big stand?" Will Andrews asked.

"I never had a bigger," Miller said. "Let's count them down."

The two men began to walk back down the valley, following the loose, spread-out trail of felled buffalo. Andrews was able to keep the numbers straight in his mind until he had counted nearly thirty; but his attention was dissipated by the sheer quantity of the dead beasts, and the numbers he repeated to himself spread in his mind and whirled as in a pool; and he gave up his effort to count. Dazedly he walked beside Miller as they threaded their way among the buffalo, some of which had fallen so close together that their bodies touched. One bull had dropped so that its huge head rested upon the side of another buffalo; the head seemed to watch them as they approached, the dark blank shining eyes regarding them disinterestedly, then staring beyond them as they passed. The hot cloudless sun beat down upon them as they plodded over the thick spongy grass, and the heat raised from the dead animals a rank odor of must and wildness; the smooth swishing sound that their boots made in the tall grass intensified the silence around them; the dull pulsations in Andrews's head began to subside, and after the acrid smell of gunpowder, the strong odor of the buffalo was almost welcome. He hitched the empty water keg to a more comfortable position on his shoulder, and strode erect beside Miller.

Schneider was waiting for them where the long swath of buffalo ended. He sat on the mounded side of a large bull; his feet barely reached the ground. Behind him, their horses grazed quietly, their reins knotted loosely together and trailing.

"How many?" Schneider asked sadly.

"A hundred and thirty-five," Miller said.

Schneider nodded somberly. "About what I figured." He slid off the side of the buffalo and picked up his case of skinning knives, which he had put on the ground beside the felled bull. "Might as well get started," he said to Andrews; "we got a long afternoon and a long night ahead of us." He turned to Miller. "You going to help?"

For a moment, Miller did not answer. His arms hung long at his sides, his shoulders drooped, and there was on his face an expression of emptiness; his mouth hung slightly open, and his head swung from side to side as he gazed upon the receding field of dead buffalo. He swung his body around to Schneider.

"What?" he asked dully.

"You going to help?"

Miller brought his hands up, chest-high, and opened them. The forefinger of his right hand was puffed and swollen and curved inward toward his palm; slowly he straightened it. Across the palm of his left hand a long narrow blister, pale against the grained blackness of the surrounding flesh, extended diagonally from the base of the forefinger to the heel of the palm near the wrist. Miller flexed his hands and grinned, standing erect.

"Let's get started," he said.

Schneider beckoned to Andrews. "Get your knives, and come with me."

Andrews followed him to a young bull; the two men knelt together before it.

"You just watch me," Schneider said.

He selected a long curving blade and grasped it firmly in his right hand. With his left hand he pushed back the heavy collar of fur around the buffalo's neck; with his other hand he made a small slit in the hide, and drew his knife swiftly from the throat across the belly. The hide parted neatly with a faint ripping sound. With a stubbier knife, he cut around the bag that held the testicles, cut through the cords that held them and the limp penis to the flesh; he separated the testicles, which were the size of small crab-apples, from the other parts of the bag, and tossed them to one side; then he slit the few remaining inches of hide to the anal opening.

"I always save the balls," he said. "They make mighty good eating, and they put starch in your pecker. Unless they come off an old bull. Then you better just stay away from them."

With still another knife, Schneider cut around the neck of the animal, beginning at that point where he had made the belly slit and lifting the huge head up and supporting it on one knee so that he could cut completely around the throat. Then he slit around each of the ankles, and ripped down the inside of each leg until his knife met the first cut down the belly. He loosened the skin around each ankle until he could get a hand-hold on the hide, and then he shucked the hide off the leg until it lay in loose folds upon the side of the buffalo. After he had laid the skin back on each leg, he loosened the hide just above the hump until he could gather a loose handful of it. Upon this, he knotted a thin rope that he got from his saddlebag; the other end he tied to his saddle horn. He got in the saddle, and backed his horse up. The hide peeled off the buffalo as the horse backed; the heavy muscles of the bull quivered and jerked as the hide was shucked off.

"And that's all there is to it," Schneider said, getting down from his horse. He untied the rope from the bullhide. "Then you spread it out flat on the ground to dry. Fur side up, so it won't dry out too fast."

Andrews estimated that it had taken Schneider a little over five minutes to complete the job of skinning. He looked at the buffalo. Without its hide, it seemed much smaller; yellowish white layers of fat thinned upon the smooth blue twists of muscle; here and there, where flesh had come off with the skin, dark clots of blood lay on the flesh. The head, with its ruff of fur and its long beard beneath the chin, appeared monstrously large. Andrews looked away.

"Think you can do it?" Schneider asked.

Andrews nodded.

"Don't try to hurry it," Schneider said. "And don't pick an old bull; stick to the young light ones at first."

Andrews selected a bull about the same size as the one Schneider had skinned. As he approached it, it seemed to him that he shrank inside his clothes, which were suddenly stiff upon him. Gingerly he pulled from his case a knife similar to the one Schneider had used, and forced his hands to go through the motions he had seen a few moments before. The hide, apparently so soft on the belly, offered a surprising resistance to his knife; he forced it, and felt it sink into the hide and deeper into the flesh of the animal. Unable to draw the knife in the smooth easy sweep that he had observed Schneider use, he hacked an irregular cut across the belly. He could not make his hands touch the testicles of the buffalo; instead he cut carefully around the bag on both sides.

By the time he had slit the hide on the legs and around the throat, he was sweating. He pulled at the hide on one of the legs, but his hands slipped; with his knife, he loosened the flesh from the hide and pulled again. The hide came from the leg with large chunks of flesh hanging upon it. He managed to get enough hide gathered at the hump to take the knot of his rope, but when he backed his horse up to pull it loose, the knot slipped, and the horse almost sat back on its haunches. He pulled a bit more of the hide loose and knotted the rope more firmly. The horse pulled again. The hide ripped from the flesh, half spinning the buffalo around; he backed his horse up, and the hide split, coming off the side of the buffalo and carrying with it huge hunks of meat.

Andrews looked helplessly at the ruined hide. After a moment, he turned to seek out Schneider, who was busily engaged some hundred feet away ripping at the belly of a large bull. Andrews counted six carcasses that Schneider had stripped during the time of his own work with a single one. Schneider looked in his direction, but he did not pause in his work. He knotted his rope about the hide, backed his horse up, and spread the shucked skin on the grass. Then he walked over to where Andrews waited. He looked at the ruined hide that still was attached to the rump of the buffalo.

"You didn't get a clean pull," he said. "And you didn't cut even around the neck. If you cut too deep, you get into the meat, and that part pulls loose too easy. Might as well give this one up."

Andrews nodded, loosened the knot around the hide, and approached another buffalo. He made his cuts more carefully this time; but when he tried to shuck the hide, again the hide split away as it had done before. Tears of rage came to his eyes.

Schneider came up to him again.

"Look," he said, not unkindly, "I don't have time to fool with you today. If Miller and I don't get these hides off in a few hours, these buffs will be stiff as boards. Why don't you drag a calf back to camp and dress it down? We need some meat, anyhow; and you can work on the carcass, get the feel of it. I'll help you fix up a rig."

Not trusting himself to speak, Andrews nodded; he felt a hot, irrational hatred for Schneider welling up in his throat.

Schneider selected a young cow, hardly more than a calf, and looped a rope around its chin and neck; he pulled the rope short, and knotted it around Andrews's saddle horn, so that with the pull of the horse the head of the buffalo did not drag on the ground.

"You'll have to walk your horse back," Schneider said. "He'll have enough to do dragging this cow."

Andrews nodded again, not looking at Schneider. He pulled the reins, and the horse leaned forward, its hooves slipping in the turf; but the carcass of the young buffalo slid a little, and the horse gained its footing and began to strain its way across the valley. Andrews plodded tiredly before the horse, loosely pulling it forward by the reins.

By the time he got back to the camp, the sun had gone behind the western range of mountains; there was a chill in the air that went through his clothing and touched his sweaty skin. Charley Hoge trotted out from the camp to meet him.

"How many?" Charley Hoge called.

"Miller counted a hundred and thirty-five," Andrews said.

"'I God," Charley Hoge said. "A big one."

Near the camp, Andrews halted his horse and untied the rope from the saddle horn.

"Nice little calf you got," Charley Hoge said. "Make good eating. You going to dress her down, or you want me to?"

"I'll dress her," Andrews said. But he made no movement.

He stood looking at the calf, whose open transparent eyes were filmed over blankly with a layer of dust.

After a moment, Charley Hoge said: "I'll help you fix up a scaffold."

The two men went to the area where earlier Charley Hoge had been working on the corral for the livestock. The corral, roughly hexagonal in shape, had been completed; but there were still a few long aspen poles lying about. Charley Hoge pointed out three of equal length and they dragged them back to where the buffalo calf lay. They pounded the ends of the poles into the ground, and arranged them in the form of a tripod. Andrews mounted his horse, and lashed the poles together at the top. Charley Hoge threw the rope, which was still attached to the calf's head, over the top of the tripod, and Andrews tied the loose end to his saddle horn. He backed his horse up until the calf was suspended, its hooves barely brushing the short grass. Charley Hoge held the rope until Andrews returned to the tripod and secured the rope firmly to the top, so that the buffalo would not drop.

The buffalo hung; they surveyed it for a moment without speaking. Charley Hoge went back to his campfire; Andrews stood before the hung calf. In the distance, across the valley, he saw a movement; it was Schneider and Miller returning. Their horses went in a swift walk across the valley bed. Andrews took a deep breath, and put his knife carefully to the exposed belly of the calf.

He worked more slowly this time. After he had made the cuts in the belly, around the throat, and around the ankles, he carefully peeled the hide back so that it hung loosely down the sides of the animal. Then, reaching high above the hump, he ripped the hide from the back. It came off smoothly, with only a few small chunks of the flesh adhering to it. With his knife he scraped the largest of these chunks off, and spread the skin on the grass, flesh side downward, as he had seen Schneider do. While he stood back, looking down at his hide, Miller and Schneider rode up beside him and dismounted.

Miller, his face streaked with the black residue of powder smoke and smears of brownish-red blood, looked at him dully for a moment, and then looked at the hide spread on the ground. He turned and shambled unsteadily toward the campsite.

"Looks like a clean job," Schneider said, walking around the hide. "You won't have no trouble. Course, it's easier when your carcass is hanging."

"How did you and Miller do?" Andrews asked.

"We didn't get halfway through. We'll be working most of the night."

"I wish I could help," Andrews said.

Schneider walked over to the skinned calf and slapped the naked rump of it. "Nice fat little calf. She'll make good eating."

Andrews went to the calf and knelt; he fumbled among the knives in his case. He raised his head to Schneider, but he did not look at him.

"What do I do?" he asked.

"What?"

"What do I do first? I've never dressed an animal before."

"My God," Schneider said quietly. "I keep forgetting. Well, first you better de-gut her. Then I'll tell you how to cut her up."

Charley Hoge and Miller came around the tall chimney rock and leaned against it, watching. Andrews hesitated for a moment, then stood up. He pushed the point of his knife against the breastbone of the calf, and poked until he found the softness of the stomach. He clenched his teeth, and pushed the knife in the flesh, and drew the knife downward. The heavy, coiled blue-and-white guts, thicker than his forearm, spilled out from the clean edge of the cut. Andrews closed his eyes, and pulled the knife downward as quickly as he could. As he straightened up, he felt something warm on his shirtfront; a gush of dark, half-clotted blood had dropped from the opened cavity. It spilled upon his shirt and dripped down upon the front of his trousers. He jumped backward. His quick movement sent the calf rocking slowly on the rope, and made the thick entrails slowly emerge from the widening cut. With a heavy, liquid, sliding thud they spilled upon the ground; like something alive, the edge of the mass slid toward Andrews and covered the tops of his shoes.

Schneider laughed loudly, slapping his leg. "Cut her loose!" he shouted. "Cut her loose before she crawls all over you!"

Andrews swallowed the heavy saliva that spurted in his mouth. With his left hand he followed the thick slimy main gut up through the body cavity; he watched his forearm disappear into the wet warmth of the body. When his left hand came upon the end of the gut, he reached his other hand with the knife up beside it, and sliced blindly, awkwardly at the tough tube. The rotten smell of the buffalo's half-digested food billowed out; he held his breath, and hacked more desperately with his knife. The tube parted, and the entrails spilled down, gathering in the lower part of the body. With both arms, he scooped the guts out of the cavity until he could find the other attachment; he cut it away and tore the insides from the calf with desperate scooping motions, until they spread in a heavy mass on the ground around his feet. He stepped back, pale, breathing heavily through his opened mouth; his arms and hands, held out from his body, dripping with blood, were trembling.

Miller, still leaning against the chimney rock, called to Schneider: "Let's have some of that liver, Fred."

Schneider nodded, and took a few steps to the swinging carcass. With one hand he steadied it, and with the other reached into the open cavity. He jerked his arm; his hand came out carrying a large piece of brownish purple meat. With a few quick strokes of his knife, he sliced it in two, and tossed the larger of the pieces across to Miller. He caught the liver in the scoop of his two hands, and clutched it to his chest so that it would not slide out of his grasp. Then he lifted it to his mouth, and took a large bite from it; the dark blood oozed from the meat, ran down the sides of his chin, and dropped to the ground. Schneider grinned and took a bite from his piece. Still grinning, chewing slowly, his lips dark red from the meat, he extended the meat toward Andrews.

"Want a chew?" he asked, and laughed.

Andrews felt the bitterness rise in his throat; his stomach contracted in a sudden spasm, and the muscles of his throat pulled together, choking him. He turned and ran a few paces from the men, leaned against a tree, doubled over, and retched. After a few moments, he turned to them.

"You finish it up," he called to them. "I've had enough."

Without waiting for a reply, he turned again and walked toward the spring that trickled down some seventy-five yards beyond their camp. At the spring he removed his shirt; the blood from the buffalo was beginning to stiffen on his undershirt. As quickly as he could, he removed the rest of his

clothing and stood in the late afternoon shadow, shivering in
the cool air. From his chest to below his navel was the brownish red stain of buffalo blood; and in removing his clothing,
his arms and hands had brushed against other parts of his
body so that he was blotched with stains hued from a pale
vermilion to a deep brownish crimson. He thrust his hands
into the icy pool formed by the spring. The cold water clotted the blood, and for a moment he feared that he could not
remove it from his skin. Then it floated away in solid tendrils;
and he splashed water on his arms, his chest, and his stomach,
gasping at the cold, straining his lungs to gather air against the
repeated shocks of it.

When he had removed from his naked body the last flecks of
blood he could see, he knelt on the ground and wrapped his
arms around his body; he was shivering violently, and his skin
had a faintly bluish cast. He took his clothing, article by article,
and immersed it in the tiny pool; he scrubbed it as hard as he
could, wringing each article out thoroughly and resubmerging
it several times, until the water was muddied and tinged with
a dirty red. Finally, with bits of fine gravel and soil gathered
from the thin banks of the pool, he scrubbed at his blood-
stained boots; but the blood and slime from the buffalo had
entered into the pores of the leather and he could not scrub
the stain away. He put the wet and wrinkled clothing back on
and walked back to the camp. By this time it was nearly dark;
and his clothing was stiff with the cold by the time he got to
the campfire.

The buffalo had been dressed; the innards, the head, the
hooves, and the lean bony sides had been dragged away from
the campsite and scattered. On a spit over the fire, which was
smoking and flaming higher than it should have been, was im-
paled a large chunk of the hump meat; beside the fire on a
square of dirty canvas, in a dark irregular pile, was the rest
of the meat. Andrews went up to the fire, and put his body
against the heat; from the wrinkles of his clothing rose little
wisps of steam. None of the men spoke to him; he did not look
directly at them.

After a few moments, Charley Hoge took a small box from
the canvas-covered cache and examined it by the light of
the fire; Andrews saw that it contained a fine white powder.

Charley Hoge went around the chimney rock toward the scattered remains of the buffalo, muttering to himself as he went.

"Charley's out wolfing," Miller said to no one. "I swear, he thinks a wolf is the devil himself."

"Wolfing?" Andrews spoke without turning.

"You sprinkle strychnine over raw meat," Miller said. "You keep it up a few days around a camp, you won't have any trouble with wolves for a long time."

Andrews turned so that his back received the heat of the campfire; when he turned, the front of his clothing immediately cooled and the still-wet cloth was icy on his skin.

"But that ain't the reason Charley does it," Miller said. "He looks at a dead wolf like it was the devil his self, killed."

Schneider, squatting on his haunches, rose and stood beside Andrews, sniffing hungrily at the meat, which was beginning to blacken around the edges.

"Too big a piece," Schneider said. "Won't be done for an hour. A body gets a hunger, skinning all day; and he needs food if he's going to skin all night."

"It won't be so bad, Fred," Miller said. "There's a moon, and we'll get a little rest before the meat's done."

"It gets any colder," Schneider said, "and we'll be prying loose stiff hides."

Charley Hoge came into sight around the chimney rock, which now loomed dark against the light sky. He carefully placed the box of strychnine back in its cache, dusted his hands off on his trouser legs, and inspected the buffalo roast. He nodded, and set the coffeepot on the edge of the fire, where some coals were beginning to glow dully. Soon the coffee was boiling; the aroma of the coffee and the rich odor of the meat dripping and falling into the fire blended and came across to the men who waited for their food. Miller smiled, Schneider cursed lazily, and Charley Hoge cackled to himself.

Instinctively, remembering his revulsion earlier at the sight and odor of the buffalo, Andrews turned away from the rich smells; but he realized suddenly that they struck him pleasantly. He hungered for the food that was being prepared. For the first time since he had returned from his cold bath at the spring, he turned and looked at the other men.

He said sheepishly: "I guess I didn't do so good, dressing the buffalo."

Schneider laughed. "You tossed everything you had, Mr. Andrews."

"It's happened before," Miller said. "I've seen people do worse."

The moon, nearly full, edged over the eastern range; as the fire died, its pale bluish light spread through the trees and touched the surfaces of their clothing, so that the deep red glow cast by the coals was touched by the cold pale light where the two colors met on their bodies. They sat in silence until the moon was wholly visible through the trees. Miller measured the angle of the moon, and told Charley Hoge to take the meat, done or not, off the spit. Charley Hoge sliced great chunks of the half-done roast onto their plates. Miller and Schneider picked the meat up in their hands and tore at it with their teeth, holding it sometimes in their mouths while they snapped their fingers from the heat. Andrews sliced his meat with one of his skinning knives; the meat was tough but juicy, and it had the flavor of strong, undercooked beef. The men washed it down with gulps of scalding bitter coffee.

Andrews ate only a part of the meat that Charley Hoge had given him. He put his plate and cup down beside the fire, and lay back on his bedroll, which he pulled up near the fire, and watched the other men wordlessly gorge themselves on the meat and coffee. They finished what Charley Hoge had given them, and ate more. Charley Hoge, himself, ate almost delicately from a thin slice of the roast which he cut into very small pieces. He washed down the small bites he took with frequent sips of coffee that he had strongly laced with whisky. After Miller and Schneider had finished the last bit of the hump roast, Miller reached for Charley Hoge's jug, took a long swallow, and passed the jug to Schneider, who turned the jug up and let the liquor gurgle long in his throat; he swallowed several times before he handed the jug to Andrews, who held the mouth of the jug against his closed lips for several seconds before taking a small, cautious swallow.

Schneider sighed, stretched, and lay on his back before the fire. He spoke from deep in his throat, his voice a soft, slow growl: "A belly full of buffalo meat, and a good drink of whisky. All a body would need now is a woman."

"There ain't no sin in buffalo meat nor corn whisky," said Charley Hoge. "But a woman, now. That's a temptation of the flesh."

Schneider yawned, and stretched again on the ground. "Remember that little whore back in Butcher's Crossing?" He looked at Andrews. "What was her name?"

"Francine," Andrews said.

"Yeah, Francine. My God, that was a pretty whore. Wasn't she kind of heated up for you, Mr. Andrews?"

Andrews swallowed, and looked into the fire. "I didn't notice that she was."

Schneider laughed. "Don't tell me you didn't get into that. My God, the way she kept looking at you, you could have had it for damn near nothing—or nothing, come to think of it. She said she wasn't working. . . . How was it, Mr. Andrews? Was it pretty good?"

"Leave it be, Fred," Miller said quietly.

"I want to know how it was," Schneider said. He raised himself on one elbow; his round face, red in the dull glow of the coals, peered at Andrews; there was a fixed, tight smile on his face. "All soft and white," he said hoarsely, and licked his lips. "What did you do? Tell me what—"

"That's enough, Fred," Miller said sharply.

Schneider looked at Miller angrily. "What's the matter? I got a right to talk, ain't I?"

"You know it's no good thinking about women out here," Miller said. "Thinking about what you can't have will drive you off your feed."

"Jezebels," Charley Hoge said, pouring another cup of whisky, which he warmed with a bit of coffee. "The work of the devil."

"What you don't think about," Miller said, "you don't miss. Come on. Let's get after those hides while we have some good light."

Schneider got up and shook himself as an animal might after having been immersed in water. He laughed, clearing his throat. "Hell," he said, "I was just having me some fun with Mr. Andrews. I know how to handle myself."

"Sure," Miller said. "Let's get going."

The two men walked away from the campfire to where their horses were tethered at a tree. Just before they went beyond the dim circle of light cast by the campfire, Schneider turned and grinned at Andrews.

"But the first thing I'm going to do when we get back to Butcher's Crossing is hire myself a little German girl for a couple of days. If you get in too much of a hurry, Mr. Andrews, you might just have to pull me off."

Andrews waited until he heard the two men ride away, and watched as they loped across the pale bed of the valley, until their dark bobbing shapes merged into the darker rise of the western range of mountains. Then he slid into his bedroll and closed his eyes; he listened for a long while as Charley Hoge cleaned the utensils he had used for cooking, and tidied the camp. After a while there was silence. In the darkness Andrews ran his hand over his face; it was rough and strange to his touch; the beard, which he was constantly surprised to feel upon his face, distracted his hands and made his features unfamiliar to him; he wondered how he looked; he wondered if Francine would recognize him if she could see him now.

Since the night when he had gone up to her room in Butcher's Crossing, he had not let himself think of her. But with Schneider's mention of her name earlier in the evening, thoughts of her flooded upon him; he was not able to keep her image away. He saw her as he had seen her in those last moments in her room before he had turned and fled; seeing her in his mind, he turned restlessly upon his rough bed.

Why had he run away? From where had come that deadness inside him that made him know he must run away? He remembered the sickness in the pit of his stomach, the revulsion which had followed hard upon the vital rush of his blood as he had seen her stand naked and swaying slowly, as if suspended by his own desire, before him.

In the moment before sleep came upon him, he made a tenuous connection between his turning away from Francine that night in Butcher's Crossing, and his turning away from the gutted buffalo earlier in the day, here in the Rocky Mountains of Colorado. It came to him that he had turned away from the buffalo not because of a womanish nausea at blood and

stench and spilling gut; it came to him that he had sickened
and turned away because of his shock at seeing the buffalo, a
few moments before proud and noble and full of the dignity of
life, now stark and helpless, a length of inert meat, divested of
itself, or his notion of its self, swinging grotesquely, mockingly,
before him. It was not itself; or it was not that self that he had
imagined it to be. That self was murdered; and in that murder
he had felt the destruction of something within him, and he
had not been able to face it. So he had turned away.

Once again, in the darkness, his hand came from beneath
the covers and moved across his face, sought out the cold,
rough bulge of his forehead, followed the nose, went across
the chapped lips, and rubbed against the thick beard, searching
for his features. When sleep came upon him his hand was still
resting on his face.

6.

THE DAYS grew shorter; and the green grass of the flat mountain park began to yellow in the cool nights. After the first
day the men spent in the valley, it rained nearly every afternoon, so that they soon got in the habit of leaving their work
at about three and lying about the camp under a tarpaulin
stretched from the high sides of the wagon and pegged into
the ground. They talked little during these moments of rest;
they listened to the light irregular patter of the rain, broken
by the sheltering pines, as it dropped on the canvas tarpaulin;
and they watched beneath the high belly of the wagon the
small rain. Sometimes it was misty and gray like a heavy fog
that nearly obscured the opposite rise of tree-grown mountain; and sometimes it was bright and silvery, as the drops,
caught by the sun, flashed like tiny needles from the sky into
the soft earth. After the rain, which seldom lasted for an hour,
they would resume their chase and slaughter of the buffalo,
working usually until late in the evening.

Deeper and deeper into the valley the herd was pushed, until Andrews, Miller, and Schneider were rising in the morning
before the sun appeared so that they could get in a good day;

by the middle of the first week they had to ride more than an hour to get to the main herd.

"We'll chase them once clean to the end of the valley," Miller said when Schneider complained of their long rides. "And then we'll chase them back up this way. If we keep them going back and forth, they'll break up in little herds, and we won't be able to get at them so easy."

Every two or three days Charley Hoge hitched the oxen to the wagon and followed the trail of the slaughter, which was marked by a bunched irregular line of stretched skins. Andrews and Schneider, and sometimes Miller, went with him; and as the wagon moved slowly along, the three men flung the stiff flintskins into the wagon. When all the skins were picked up, the wagon returned them to the main camp, where they were again tossed from the wagon upon the ground. Then the men stacked them one upon another, as high as they could reach. When a stack was between seven and eight feet in height, green thongs, stripped from the skin of a freshly killed buffalo, were passed through the cuts on the leg-skins of the top and bottom hides, and pulled tight and tied. Each stack contained between seventy-five and ninety hides, and each was so heavy that it took the combined strength of the four to boost it under the shelter of the trees.

At the skinning, Will Andrews's skill slowly increased. His hands toughened and became sure; his knives lost their new brightness, and with use they cut more surely so that soon he was able to skin one buffalo to Schneider's two. The stench of the buffalo, the feel of the warm meat on his hands, and the sight of clotted blood came to have less and less impact upon his senses. Shortly he came to the task of skinning almost like an automaton, hardly aware of what he did as he shucked the hide from an inert beast and pegged it to the ground. He was able to ride through a mass of skinned buffalo covered black with feeding insects, and hardly be aware of the stench that rose in the heat from the rotting flesh.

Occasionally he accompanied Miller in his stalking, though Schneider habitually stayed behind and rested, waiting for enough animals to be slaughtered for the skinning to begin. As he went with him, Andrews came to be less and less concerned with Miller's slaughter of the beasts as such; he came to notice the strategy that Miller employed at keeping the buffalo confined to a reasonable area, and at keeping the felled animals in such a pattern that they might be easily and economically skinned.

Once Miller allowed Andrews to take his rifle and attempt a stand. Lying on the ground on his stomach, as he had so often seen Miller do, Andrews chose his buffalo and caught him cleanly through the lungs. He killed three more before he shot badly and the small herd dispersed. When it was over he let Miller go ahead while he remained on his stomach, toying with the empty cartridges he had used, trying to fix the feelings he had had at the kill. He looked at the four buffalo that lay nearly two hundred yards away from him; his shoulder tingled from the heavy recoil of the Sharps rifle. He could feel nothing else. Some grass-blades worked their way into his shirt front and tickled his skin. He got up, brushed the grass away, and walked slowly away from where he had lain, away from Miller, and went to where Schneider lay on the grass, near where their horses were tethered to one of the pines that stood down from the mountainside, slightly into the valley. He sat down beside Schneider; he did not speak; the two men waited until the sound of Miller's rifle became faint. Then they followed the trail of dead buffalo, skinning as they went.

At night the men were so exhausted that they hardly spoke. They wolfed the food that Charley Hoge prepared for them, drained the great smoked coffeepot, and fell exhausted upon their bedrolls. In their increasing exhaustion, to which Miller drove them with his inexorable pursuit, their food and their sleep came to be the only things that had much meaning for them. Once Schneider, desiring a change of food, went into the woods and managed to shoot a small doe; another time Charley Hoge rode across the valley to the small lake where the buffalo watered and returned with a dozen fat foot-long trout. But they ate only a small part of the venison, and the taste of the trout was flat and unsatisfying; they returned to their steady diet of rich, strong buffalo meat.

Every day Schneider cut the liver from one of the slain buffalo; at the evening meal, almost ritually, the liver was divided into roughly equal portions and passed among them. Andrews learned that the taking of the raw liver was not an ostentation on the part of the three older men. Miller explained to him that unless one did so, one got what he called the "buff sickness," which was a breaking out of the skin in large, ulcerous sores, often accompanied by fever and general weakness. After learning this, Andrews forced himself to take a bit of the liver every evening; he did not find the taste of it pleasant, but in his tiredness the faintly warm and rotten taste and the slick fiberless texture did not seem to matter much.

After a week in the valley, there were ten thonged stacks of hides set close together in a small grove of pines, and still Andrews could see no real diminution of the herds that grazed placidly on the flat bed of the valley.

The days slid one into another, marked by evening exhaustion and morning soreness; as it had earlier, on their overland voyage when they searched for water, time again seemed to Andrews to hold itself apart from the passing of the days. Alone in the great valley high in the mountains the four men, rather than being brought close together by their isolation, were thrust apart, so that each of them tended more and more to go his own way and fall upon his own resources. Seldom did they talk at night; and when they did, their words were directed to some specific business concerned with the hunt.

In Miller especially Andrews perceived this withdrawal. Always a man whose words were few and direct, he became increasingly silent. At evening, in the camp, he was by turns restless, his eyes going frequently from the camp to across the valley, as if he were trying to fix the buffalo herd and command it even though he could not see it; and indifferent, almost sullen, staring lethargically into the campfire, often not answering for minutes after his name was spoken or a question was asked of him. Only during the hunt, or when he was helping Andrews and Schneider with the skinning, was he alert; and even that alertness seemed to Andrews somehow unnaturally intense. He came to have an image of Miller that persisted even when Miller was not in his sight; he saw Miller's face, black and dull with powder smoke, his white teeth clenched behind his stretched-out leathery lips, and his eyes, black and shining in their whites, surrounded by a flaming red line of irritated lids. Sometimes this image of Miller came into his mind at night, in his dreams; and more than once he came awake with a start and thrust himself upward out of his bedroll, and found that he was breathing quickly, shallowly, as if in fright, as the sharp image of those eyes upon him dulled and faded and died in the darkness around him. Once he dreamed that he was some kind of animal who was being pursued; he felt a relentless presence that chased him from cover to cover, and at last penned him in a corner of blackness from which there was no retreat; before he awoke in fear, or at a dreamed explosion of violence, he thought he caught a glimpse of those eyes burning at him from the darkness.

A week passed, and another; the stacks of hides beside their camp grew in number. Both Schneider and Charley Hoge became increasingly restless, though the latter did not give direct voice to his restlessness. But Andrews saw it in the looks that Charley Hoge gave to the sky in the afternoon when it clouded for the rain that Andrews and Schneider had grown to expect and welcome; he saw it in Charley Hoge's increased drinking—the empty whisky crocks grew in number almost as fast as did the ricks of buffalo hides; and he saw it also at night when, against the growing cold, Charley Hoge built the fire to a roaring furnace that drove the rest of them away and covered himself when he bedded down with a pressing number of buffalo hides that he had managed to soften by soaking them in a thick soup of water and wood ash.

One evening, near the end of their second week, while they were taking their late evening meal, Schneider took from his plate a half-eaten buffalo steak and threw it in the fire, where it sizzled and curled and threw up a quantity of dark smoke.

"I'm getting damned sick of buffalo meat," he said, and for a long moment afterward was silent, brooding at the fire until the steak was a black, twisted ash that dulled the red coals upon which it lay. "Damn sick of it," he said again.

Charley Hoge sloshed his coffee and whisky in his tin cup, inspected it for a second, and drank it, his thin gray-fur-covered neck twisting as he swallowed. Miller looked at Schneider dully and then returned his gaze to the fire.

"God damn it, didn't you hear me?" Schneider shouted, to any or all of them.

Miller turned slowly. "You said you were getting tired of

buffalo meat," he said. "Charley will cook up a batch of beans tomorrow."

"I don't want no more beans, and I don't want no sow-belly, and I don't want no more sour biscuits," Schneider said. "I want some greens, and some potatoes; and I want me a woman."

No one spoke. In the fire a green knot exploded and sent a shower of sparks in the air; they floated in the darkness and the men brushed them off their clothes as they settled.

Schneider said more quietly: "We been here two weeks now; that's four days longer than we was supposed to be. And the hunting's been good. We got more hides now than we can load back. What say let's pack out of here tomorrow?"

Miller looked at him as if he were a stranger. "You ain't serious, are you, Fred?"

"You're damn right I am," Schneider said. "Look. Charley's ready to go back; ain't you, Charley?" Charley Hoge did not look at him; he quickly poured some more coffee into his cup, and filled it to the brim with whisky. "It's getting on into fall," Schneider continued, his eyes still on Charley Hoge. "Nights are getting cold. You can't tell what kind of weather you're going to get, this time of year."

Miller shifted, and brought his intense gaze directly upon Schneider. "Leave Charley alone," he said quietly.

"All right," Schneider said. "But just tell me. Even if we do stay around here, how are we going to load all the hides back?"

"The hides?" Miller said, his face for a moment blank. "The hides? . . . We'll load what we can, leave the others; we can come back in the spring and pack them out. That's what we said we'd do, back in Butcher's Crossing."

"You mean we're going to stay here till you've wiped out this whole herd?"

Miller nodded. "We're going to stay."

"You're crazy," Schneider said.

"It'll take another ten days," Miller said. "Two more weeks at the outside. We'll have plenty of time before the weather turns."

"The whole god damned herd," Schneider said, and shook his head wonderingly. "You're crazy. What are you trying to do? You can't kill every god damned buffalo in the whole god damned country."

Miller's eyes glazed over for a moment, and he stared toward Schneider as if he were not there. Then the film slid from his eyes, he blinked, and turned his face toward the fire.

"It won't do no good to talk about it, Fred. This is my party, and my mind's made up."

"All right, god damn it," Schneider said. "It's on your head. Just remember that."

Miller nodded distantly, as if he were no longer interested in anything that Schneider might want to say.

Angrily Schneider gathered his bedroll and started to walk away from the campfire. Then he dropped it and came back.

"Just one more thing," he said sullenly.

Miller looked up absently. "Yes?"

"We been gone from Butcher's Crossing now just a little over a month."

Miller waited. "Yes?" he said again.

"A little over a month," Schneider said again. "I want my pay."

"What?" Miller said. His face was puzzled for a moment.

"My pay," Schneider said. "Sixty dollars."

Miller frowned, and then he grinned. "You thinking of spending it right soon?"

"Never mind that," Schneider said. "You just give me my pay, like we agreed."

"All right," Miller said. He turned to Andrews. "Mr. Andrews, will you give Mr. Schneider his sixty dollars?"

Andrews opened his shirt front and took some bills from his money belt. He counted out sixty dollars, and handed the money to Schneider. Schneider took the money, and went to the fire, knelt, and carefully counted it. Then he thrust the bills into a pocket and went to where he had dropped his bedroll. He picked it up and went out of sight into the darkness. The three men around the fire heard the snapping of branches and the rustle of pine needles and cloth as Schneider put his bedroll down. They listened until they heard the regular sound of his breath, and then his angry snoring. They did not speak. Soon they, too, bedded down for the night. When they woke in the morning a thin rind of frost crusted the grass that lay on the valley bed.

In the morning light Miller looked at the frosted valley and said:

"Their grass is playing out. They'll be trying to get through the pass and down to the flat country. We'll have to keep pushing them back."

And they did. Each morning they met the buffalo in a frontal attack, and pushed them slowly back toward the sheer rise of mountains to the south. But their frontal assault was little more than a delaying tactic; during the night the buffalo grazed far beyond the point they had been turned back from the day before. On each succeeding day the main herd came closer and closer to the pass over which it had originally entered the high park.

And as the buffalo pressed dumbly, instinctively, out of the valley, the slaughter grew more and more intense. Already withdrawn and spare with words, Miller became with the passing days almost totally intent upon his kill; and even at night, in the camp, he no longer gave voice to his simplest needs—he gestured toward the coffeepot, he grunted when his name was spoken, and his directions to the rest of them became curt motions of hands and arms, jerks of the head, and guttural growlings deep in his throat. Each day he went after the buffalo with two guns; during the kill, he heated the barrels to that point just shy of burning them out.

Schneider and Andrews had to work more and more swiftly to skin the animals Miller left strewn upon the ground; almost never were they able to finish their skinning before sundown, so that nearly every morning they were up before dawn hacking tough skins from stiff buffalo. And during the day, as they sweated and hacked and pulled in a desperate effort to keep up with Miller, they could hear the sound of his rifle steadily and monotonously and insistently pounding at the silence, and pounding at their nerves until they were raw and bruised. At night, when the two of them rode wearily out of the valley to the small red-orange glow that marked their camp in the darkness, they found Miller slouched darkly and inertly before the fire; except for his eyes he was as still and lifeless as one of

the buffalo he had killed. Miller had even stopped washing off
his face the black powder that collected there during his firing;
now the powder smoke seemed a permanent part of his skin,
ingrained there, a black mask that defined the hot, glaring brilliance of his eyes.

Gradually the herd was worn down. Everywhere he looked
Andrews saw the ground littered with naked corpses of buffalo, which sent up a rancid stench to which he had become
so used that he hardly was aware of it; and the remaining herd
wandered placidly among the ruins of their fellows, nibbling at
grass flecked with their dry brown blood. With his awareness
of the diminishing size of the herd, there came to Andrews
the realization that he had not contemplated the day when
the herd was finally reduced to nothing, when not a buffalo
remained standing—for unlike Schneider he had known, without questioning or without knowing how he knew, that Miller
would not willingly leave the valley so long as a single buffalo
remained alive. He had measured time, and had reckoned the
moment and place of their leaving, by the size of the herd,
and not—as had Schneider—by numbered days that rolled
meaninglessly one after another. He thought of packing the
hides into the wagon, yoking the oxen, which were beginning
to grow fat on inactivity and the rich mountain grass, to the
wagon, and making their way back down the mountain, and
across the wide plains, back to Butcher's Crossing. He could
not imagine what he thought of. With a mild shock, he realized that the world outside the wide flat winding park hemmed
on all sides by sheer mountain, had faded away from him; he
could not remember the mountain up which they had labored,
or the expanse of plain over which they sweated and thirsted,
or Butcher's Crossing, which he had come into and left only
a few weeks before. That world came to him fitfully and un-
clearly, as if hidden in a dream. He had been here in the high
valley for all of that part of his life that mattered; and when he
looked out upon it—its flatness, and its yellow-greenness, its
high walls of mountain wooded with the deep green of pine
in which ran the flaming red-gold of turning aspen, its jutting
rock and hillock, all roofed with the intense blue of the airless
sky—it seemed to him that the contours of the place flowed
beneath his eyes, that his very gaze shaped what he saw, and

in turn gave his own existence form and place. He could not think of himself outside of where he was.

On their twenty-fifth day in the mountains they arose late. For the last several days, the slaughter had been going more slowly; the great herd, after more than three weeks, seemed to have begun to realize the presence of their killers and to have started dumbly to prepare against them; they began to break up into a number of very small herds; seldom was Miller able to get more than twelve or fourteen buffalo at a stand, and much time was wasted in traveling from one herd to another. But the earlier sense of urgency was gone; the herd of some five thousand animals was now less than three hundred. Upon these remaining three hundred, Miller closed in—slowly, inexorably —as if more intensely savoring the slaughter of each animal as the size of the herd diminished. On the twenty-fifth day they arose without hurry; and after they had taken breakfast they even sat around the fire for several moments letting their coffee cool in their tin cups. Though they could not see it through the thick forest of pines behind them, the sun rose over the eastern range of mountains; through the trees it sent diffused mists of light that gathered on their cups, softening their hard outlines and making them glow in the semishade. The sky was a deep thin blue, cloudless and intense; crevices and hollows on the broad plain and in the sides of the mountain sent up nearly invisible mists which could be seen only as they softened the edges of rock and tree they surrounded. The day warmed, and promised heat.

After finishing their coffee, they loitered around the camp while Charley Hoge led the oxen out of the aspen-pole corral and yoked them to the empty wagon. For several days hides had been drying where Andrews and Schneider had pegged them; it was time for them to be gathered and stacked.

Schneider scratched his beard, which was tangled and matted like wet straw, and stretched his arms lazily. "Going to be a hot day," he said, pointing to the clear sky. "Probably won't even get a rain." He turned to Miller. "How many of the buff do you think's left? Couple of hundred?"

Miller nodded, and cleared his throat.

Schneider continued: "Think we'll be able to clean them up in three or four more days?"

Miller turned to him, as if only then aware that he had spoken. He said gruffly: "Three or four more days should do it, Fred."

"God damn," Schneider said happily. "I don't know whether I can last that long." He punched Andrews on the arm. "What about you, boy? Think you can wait?"

Andrews grinned. "Sure," he said.

"A pocketful of money, and all the eats and women you can hold," Schneider said. "By God, that's living."

Miller moved impatiently. "Come on," he said. "Charley's got the team yoked. Let's get moving."

The four men moved slowly from the camp area. Miller rode ahead of the wagon; Andrews and Schneider wound their reins about their saddle horns and let their horses amble easily behind it. The oxen, made lazy and irritable by their inactivity, did not pull well together; the morning silence was broken by Charley Hoge's half-articulated, shouted curses.

Within half an hour the little procession had arrived at where the first buffalo had been killed and skinned more than three weeks before. The meat on the corpses had dried to a flintlike hardness; here and there the flesh had been torn away by the wolves before they had been killed or driven away by Charley Hoge's strychnine; where the flesh was torn, the bones were white and shining, as if they had been polished. Andrews looked ahead of him into the valley; everywhere he looked he saw the mounded bodies. By next summer, he knew, the flesh would be eaten away by vultures or rotted away by the elements; he tried to imagine what the valley would look like, spread about with the white bones. He shivered a little, though the sun was hot.

Soon the wagon was so thickly surrounded by corpses that Charley Hoge was unable to point it in a straight direction; he had to walk beside the lead team, guiding it among the bodies. Even so, the huge wooden wheels now and then passed over an outthrust leg of a buffalo, causing the wagon to sway. The increasing heat of the day intensified the always present stench of rotting flesh; the oxen shied away from it, lowing discontentedly and tossing their heads so wildly that Charley Hoge had to stand many feet away from them.

When they had made their slow way to where a wide space

was covered with pegged-out skins and fresh corpses, Andrews and Schneider got down from their horses. They tied large handkerchiefs about the lower parts of their faces, so that they could work without being disturbed by the horde of small black flies that buzzed about the rank meat.

"It's going to be hot working," Schneider said. "Look at that sun."

Above the eastern trees, the sun was a fiery mass at which Andrews could not look directly; unhindered by mist or cloud, it burned upon them, instantly drying the sweat that it pulled from their faces and hands. Andrews let his eyes wander about the sky; the cool blueness soothed them from the burning they had from his brief glance toward the sun. To the south, a small white cloud had formed; it hung quiet and tiny just above the rise of the mountains.

"Let's get going," Andrews said, kicking at a small peg that held a skin flat against the earth. "It doesn't look like it'll get any cooler."

A little more than a mile away, a slight dark movement was visible among the low mounds of corpses; a small herd was grazing quietly and moving slowly toward them. Miller abruptly reined his horse away from the three men who were busy loading the hides, and galloped toward the herd.

As the men worked, Charley Hoge led the oxen between them, so that neither would have to take more than a few steps to fling his hides upon the wagon bed. Shortly after Miller rode off, Andrews and Schneider heard the distant boom of his rifle; they lifted their heads and stood for a few moments listening. Then they resumed their work, unpegging and tossing the hides into the moving wagon more slowly, in rhythm with the booming sound of Miller's rifle. When the sound ceased, they paused in their work and sat on the ground, breathing heavily.

"Don't sound like we're going to have to do much skinning today," Schneider panted, pointing in the direction of Miller's firing. "Sounds like he only got twelve or fourteen so far."

Andrews nodded and lay back in a half-reclining position, resting his body on his elbows and forearms; he removed the large red bandana from his lower face so that his flesh might have the coolness of a faint breeze that had come up during their rest. The throbbing of his head gradually subsided as the breeze became stronger and cooled him. After about fifteen minutes, Miller's rifle sounded again.

"He found another little herd," Schneider said, rising to his feet. "We might as well try to keep up with him."

But as they worked, they noticed that the rifle shots no longer came with the same regularity, marking a rhythm by which they could kick the stakes, raise the hides, and sail them onto the wagon. Several shots came briefly spaced, in a sharp flurry; there was a silence of several minutes; then another brief flurry of shots. Andrews and Schneider looked at each other in puzzlement.

"It don't sound right," Schneider said. "Maybe they're getting skittish."

The closely-spaced shots were followed by the brief sharp thunder of pounding hooves; in the distance could be seen a light cloud of dust raised by the running buffalo. The men heard another burst of rifle fire, and they saw the cloud of dust turn and go away from them, back into the depths of the valley. A few minutes later they heard another faint rumbling of hooves, and saw another cloud of dust rise at a different spot some distance east of the earlier stampede. And again they heard the brief, close explosions of Miller's rifle, and saw the dust cloud veer and go back beyond the point from which it had begun.

"Miller's got himself some trouble," Schneider said. "Something's got into them buff."

In the minutes that the men had been standing still, listening to the gunshots and watching the dust trails, the burning heat had lessened perceptibly. A thin haze had come between them and the sun, and the breeze from the south had grown stronger.

"Come on," Andrews said. "Let's get these hides loaded while we've got a breeze."

Schneider lifted his hand. "Wait." Charley Hoge had left the oxen, and now stood near Schneider and Andrews. The rapid drumming of a running horse came to them; among the scattered flayed bodies of the buffalo Miller appeared, galloping toward them. When he came near the standing men, he pulled his horse so abruptly to a halt that it reared, its forehooves for a moment pawing the air.

"They're trying to get out of the valley," Miller's voice came in a croaking rasp. "They've broke up in ten or twelve little herds, and I can't turn them back fast enough; I need some help."

Schneider blew his nose contemptuously. "Hell," he said wearily, "let them go. There are only a couple of hundred of them left."

Miller did not look at Schneider. "Will, you get on your horse and wait over there." He pointed west to a spot two or three hundred yards from the side of the mountain. "Fred, you ride over there—" He pointed in the opposite direction, to the east. "I'll stay in the middle." He spoke to both Andrews and Schneider. "If a herd comes in your direction, head it off; all you have to do is shoot into it two or three times. It'll turn."

Schneider shook his head. "It's no good. If they're broke up in little herds, we can't turn them all back."

"They won't all come at once," Miller said. "They'll come two or three at a time. We can turn them back."

"But what's the use?" said Schneider, his voice almost a wail. "What the hell's the use? It ain't going to kill you to let a few of them get away."

"Hurry it up," said Miller. "They're liable to start any minute."

Schneider raised his hands to the air, shrugged his shoulders, and went to his horse; Miller spurred toward the middle of the valley. Andrews mounted his horse, started to ride in the direction that Miller had pointed to him, and then rode up to the wagon to which Charley Hoge had returned.

"You got a rifle, Charley?" Andrews asked.

Charley Hoge turned nervously. He nodded and drew a small rifle from beneath the clip seat. "It's just your little varmint rifle," he said as he handed it to him, "but it'll turn them."

Andrews took the rifle and rode toward the side of the mountain. He pointed his horse in the direction that the buffalo would come from, and waited. He looked across the valley; Miller had stationed himself in the center, and he leaned forward on his horse toward the herds that none of them could see. Beyond Miller, small in the distance, Schneider slouched on his horse as if he were asleep. Andrews turned again to the south and listened for the pounding of hooves which would mark the run of a herd.

He heard nothing save the soft whistling of the wind around his ears, which were beginning to tingle from the coolness. The southern reaches of the valley were softening in a faint mist that was coming down from the mountains; the small cloud that had earlier hovered quietly above the southern peaks now extended over the boxed end of the valley; the underside of the cloud was a dirty gray, above which the sunlit white vapor twisted and coiled upon itself before a thrusting wind that was not felt on the ground here in the valley.

A heavy rumble shook the earth; Andrews's horse started backward, its ears flattened about the sides of its head. For an instant Andrews searched the upper air about the southern mountains, thinking that he had heard the sound of thunder; but the rumbling persisted beneath him. Directly in front of him, in the distance, a faint cloud of dust arose, and blew away as soon as it had arisen. Then suddenly, out of the shadow, onto that part of the valley still flooded in sunlight, the buffalo emerged. They ran with incredible swiftness, not in a straight line toward him, but in swift swerves and turns, as if they evaded invisible obstacles suddenly thrust before them; and they swerved and turned as if the entire herd of thirty or forty buffalo were one animal with one mind, a single will—no animal straggled or turned in a direction that was counter to the movement of the others.

For several moments Andrews sat motionless and stiff on his horse; he had an impulse to turn, to flee the oncoming herd. He could not believe that a few shots from the small varmint rifle that he cradled in his right arm could be heard or even felt by a force that came onward with such speed and strength and will; he could not believe they could be turned. He twisted in the saddle, moving his neck stiffly so that he could see Miller. Miller sat still, watching him; after a moment Miller shouted something that was drowned in the deepening rumble of the buffalo's stampede, and pointed toward them, motioning with his hand and arm as if he were throwing stones at them.

Andrews dug his heels into his horse's sides; the horse went forward a few steps and then halted, drawing back on its haunches. In a kind of desperation and fear, Andrews dug his heels again into the heaving sides of his mount, and beat with his rifle butt upon the quivering haunches. The horse leaped forward, almost upsetting him; it galloped for a moment wildly, throwing its head against the bit that Andrews held too tightly; then, soothed by its own motion, it steadied and ran easily forward toward the herd. The wind slapped into Andrews's face and swept tears from his eyes. For an instant he could not see where he was going.

Then his vision cleared. The buffalo were less than three hundred yards away from him, swerving and turning erratically, but heading toward him. He pulled his horse to a halt and flung his rifle to his shoulder; the stock was cold against his cheek. He fired once into the midst of the rushing herd; he barely heard the rifle shot above the thunder of hooves. He fired again. A buffalo stumbled and fell, but the others came around it, flowed over it like tumbling water. He fired again, and again. Suddenly, the herd swerved to his left, cutting across the valley toward Miller. Andrews heeled his horse and ran alongside the fleeing herd, firing into its rushing mass. Gradually the herd turned, until it was running with unabated speed back in the direction from which it had come.

Andrews pulled his horse to a stop; panting, he looked after the running herd and listened to the diminishing roar of pounding hooves. Then, upon that sound, faintly, came another similar to it. He looked across the valley. Another herd, slightly smaller than the first, sped across the flat land toward Schneider. He watched as Schneider fired into it, followed it as it swerved, and turned it back.

In all, the three of them turned back six rushes of the buffalo. When at last no sound of running hooves broke the silence, and after they had waited for many minutes in anticipation of another rush, Miller beckoned them to ride toward him in the center of the valley.

Andrews and Schneider rode up to Miller quietly, letting their horses walk so that they could hear a warning if the buffalo decided to charge again. Miller was looking across the valley, squinting at where the buffalo had run.

"We got them," Miller said. "They won't try to break out again like that."

A tremor of elation that he could not understand went through Andrews. "I never thought anything like that was possible," he said to Miller. "It was almost as if they were doing it together, as if they'd planned it." It seemed to him that he had not really thought of the buffalo before. He had skinned them by the hundreds, he had killed a few; he had eaten of their flesh, he had smelled their stench, he had been immersed in their blood; but he had not thought of them before as he was thinking of them now. "Do they do things like that very often?"

Miller shook his head. "You might as well not try to figure them out; you can't tell what they might do. I've been hunting them for twenty years and I don't know. I've seen them run clean over a bluff, and pile up a hundred deep in a canyon— thousands of them, for no reason at all that a man could see. I've seen them spooked by a crow, and I've seen men walk right in the middle of a herd without them moving an inch. You think about what they're going to do, and you get yourself in trouble; all a man can do is not think about them, just plow into them, kill them when he can, and not try to figure anything out." As he spoke, Miller did not look at Andrews; his eyes were on the valley, which was still now, and empty, save for the trampled bodies of the buffalo they had killed. He took a deep breath and turned to Schneider. "Well, Fred, we got us some cool weather anyhow. It won't be so bad working, now."

"Wait a minute," Schneider said. His eyes were fixed on nothing; he held his head as if he were listening.

"You hear them again?" Miller asked.

Schneider motioned with his hand for quiet; he sat in his saddle for a few minutes more, still listening; he sniffed twice at the air.

"What is it?" Miller asked.

Schneider turned to him slowly. "Let's get out of here." His voice was quiet.

Miller frowned, and blinked. "What's wrong?"

"I don't know," Schneider said. "But something is. Something don't feel right to me."

Miller snorted. "You're spooked easier than a buffalo. Come on. We got half a day in front of us. They'll quiet down in a while and I can get a good number before it's dark."

"Listen," Schneider said.

The three men sat in their saddles, quiet, listening for something they did not know. The wind had died, but a slight chill remained in the air. They heard only silence; no breeze rustled through the pines, no bird called. One of their horses snorted; someone moved in the saddle, and there came the thin sound of leather creaking. To break the silence, Miller slapped his leg; he turned to Schneider and said loudly:

"What the hell—"

But he did not continue. He was silenced by Schneider's outstretched arm and hand and finger, which seemed to point at nothing. Puzzled, Andrews looked from one of them to another; and then his gaze halted in the air between them. Out of the air, large and soft and slow, like a falling feather, drifted a single snowflake. As he watched, he saw another, and another.

A grin broke out on his face, and a nervous bubble of laughter came up in his throat.

"Why, it's snowing," he said, laughing, looking again from one of them to the other. "Did you ever think this morning that—"

His voice died in his throat. Neither Miller nor Schneider looked at him, and neither gave any sign that they knew he had spoken. Their faces were tense and strained at the thickening sky from which the snow was falling more and more rapidly. Andrews looked quickly at Charley Hoge, who was sitting motionless some yards from the others on his high wagon seat. Charley Hoge's face was raised upward, and his arms were clasped together over his chest; his eyes rolled wildly, but he did not move his head or unclasp his arms.

"Let's go," Miller said quietly, still looking at the sky. "We might just make it before it gets too bad."

He pulled his horse around and rode a few steps up to Charley Hoge. He leaned from the saddle and shook Charley Hoge roughly by the shoulder.

"Let's haul, Charley."

For a moment, Charley Hoge did not seem to know Miller's presence; and when he turned to face him, he did not appear to recognize the large black-bearded face, which was beginning to glisten from the melting snowflakes. Then his eyes focused, and he spoke in a trembling voice:

"You said it would be all right." His voice gained strength, became accusing: "You said we'd make it out before the snows came."

"It's all right, Charley," Miller said. "We got plenty of time."

Charley Hoge's voice rose: "I said I didn't want to come. I told you—"

"Charley!" Miller's voice cracked. And then he said more softly: "We're just wasting time. Get your team headed back to camp."

Charley Hoge looked at Miller, his mouth working, but moving upon words that did not become sound. Then he reached behind him and took from its clip the long bull-whip, the braided leather of which trailed from the heavy butt. He whistled it over the ears of the lead team, in his fright letting the tip come too low, and drawing blood from the ear of the right lead ox. The ox threw his head around wildly and jumped forward, pulling the surprised weight of the other animals; for a moment the team floundered, each member pulling in a different direction. Then they settled together and pulled steadily. Charley Hoge cracked his whip again and the team broke into a lumbering run; he made no effort to guide the animals among the corpses of the buffalo. The wagon wheels, passing over the bodies, pitched the wagon wildly about. Stiff hides slithered off and fell to the ground; no one paused to retrieve them.

The three men on horseback rode close to the wagon; they had to pull back on their reins to keep the animals from bolting and running ahead. Within a few minutes the air was white with snow; dimly, on either side, they could see the veiled green of the mountainside; but they could not see ahead to their camp. The shadowy pine trees on either side of them guided their movement upon the flat bed of the valley. Andrews squinted ahead toward their camp, but all he could see was snow, the flakes circling and slowly falling, one against another and another and another; in his riding, they came at him, and if he looked at them, his head whirled as they did and he became dizzy. He fixed his eyes upon the moving wagon and saw the snow unfocused, a general haze that surrounded him and isolated him from the others, though he could see them dimly as they rode. His bare hands, holding the reins and clutching his saddle horn as his horse trotted and loped unevenly among the corpses of the buffalo, reddened in the cold; he tried to thrust one of them in a pocket of his trousers, but the rough stiff cloth was so painful that he removed his hand and kept it in the open.

After the first few minutes the ground was covered white with snow; the wagon wheels, cutting easily through it, left thin parallel ribbons of darkness behind them. Andrews glanced back; within seconds after the wheels cut the snow, the shallow ruts began to fill and only a few feet behind them were whitened so that he could not tell where they had been; despite their movement and the pitching of the wagon, he had the feeling that they were going nowhere, that they were caught on a vast treadmill that heaved them up but did not carry them forward.

The breeze that had died when the first snowflakes began to fall came up again; it swirled the snow about them, whipping it into their faces, causing them to squint their eyes against its force. Andrews's jaws began to ache; he realized that for some moments he had been clenching his teeth together with all the strength he had; his lips, drawn back over his teeth in an aimless snarl, smarted and pained him as the cold pushed against the tiny cracks and rawness there. He relaxed his jaws and dropped his head, hunching his shoulders against the cold which drove through the thin clothing upon his flesh. He looped the reins about his saddle horn and grasped it with both hands, letting his horse find its own way.

The wind grew stronger and the snow came in thick flurries. For an instant Andrews lost sight of the wagon and of the other men; a numb, vague panic made him lift his head; somewhere to his left he heard, above the whistle of the wind, the creak and thump of the wagon wheels. He pulled his horse in the direction of the sound, and after a moment saw the heavy shape of the wagon careening over the littered ground and dimly saw the hunched figure of Charley Hoge swaying on the high clip seat, lashing the thick air with his bull-whip; softly, muffled by the snow and drowned by the wind, its wet crack sounded.

And still the wind increased. It howled over the mountains and blew the snow into stinging pellets; in great sheets, it lifted the snow off the ground and spread it again; it thrust the fine white freezing powder into the crevices of their clothing where

it melted from their bodies' warmth; and it hardened the moisture so that their clothing hung heavy and stiff upon them and
gathered the cold to their flesh. Andrews clutched his saddle
horn more firmly; there was no sensation in his hands. He removed one hand stiffly from the horn and flexed it, and beat
it against the side of his leg until it began to throb painfully;
then he did the same with the other hand. By then the first had
grown numb again. A small pile of snow gathered in his saddle
in the sharp V formed by his legs.

Above the wind he heard a faint shout; the wagon loomed up
suddenly before him; his horse halted, pitching him forward.
He heard the shout again and thought it was his name that
was called. He guided his horse along the side of the wagon,
hunching himself against the wind and peering out of his half-
closed eyes every second or so, trying to see who had called
him. Miller and Schneider, their horses close together facing
the wind, waited for him at the front of the wagon. When he
came up to them, he saw Charley Hoge huddled between the
two horses, his back hunched to the wind.

Stiffly, leaning against the wind, their faces turned down
so that the brims of their hats were blown against their cheeks,
the men dismounted from their horses, and, crouching against
the wind, thrusting themselves at an angle through it, came
toward Andrews; Miller beckoned him to get down. As he
dismounted, the force of the wind pushed his unsupported
body forward and he stumbled, one foot for a moment caught
in the stirrup.

Miller staggered up to him, grasped him by the shoulders,
and put his bearded face—which was now stiff and icy in spots,
where snow had melted and frozen—to Andrews's ear. He
shouted: "We're going to leave the wagon here; it slows us up
too much. You hold on to the horses while Fred and I unyoke
the team."

Andrews nodded and pulled the reins with him as he went
toward the horses. His own horse pulled back, almost dis-
lodging the reins from his numb hand; he jerked heavily on
the reins and the horse followed him. Still holding the reins in
one hand, he stooped and fumbled in the snow, which lifted
and swirled about his feet as if disturbed by a long explosion,
until he found the knotted reins of the other horses. As he

straightened, Charley Hoge, whose back had been toward him, turned; the stump of his forearm was thrust inside his light coat, and his good arm pressed it close to his body as his body hunched over it. For a moment Charley Hoge looked at Andrews without seeing him; his pale eyes were open and unblinking against the stinging wind and snow, and they focused on nothing. His mouth was moving rapidly and his lips twitched one way and another, causing the beard about his mouth to jerk unevenly. Andrews shouted his name but the wind tore the word from his lips; Charley Hoge's eyes did not move. Andrews came a little closer; shifting all three reins to one hand, he reached out his other to touch Charley Hoge on the shoulder. At his touch, Charley Hoge jerked back away and cowered, his eyes still glazed and his lips still working. Andrews shouted again:

"It'll be all right, Charley. It'll be all right."

He was barely able to hear what Charley Hoge repeated over and over, to the wind, the snow, and the cold:

"God help me. Lord Jesus Christ help me. God help me."

At a thump behind him, Andrews turned; a dim dark bulk loomed out of the whiteness and lumbered past him. The first of the oxen had been unyoked by Miller and Schneider. As the shape lumbered into the whiteness and disappeared, the horses which Andrews held bolted. Their quick movement caught him by surprise, and before he could throw his weight against the reins, one of the horses' bellies had brushed heavily against Charley Hoge, knocking him to the ground. Andrews started involuntarily toward him, and as he did so the three horses moved together, pulling him around and forward, so that he was off balance; his feet flew into the air behind him, and he landed heavily on his stomach and chest in the snow. Somehow he managed to hold on to the reins. Flat on the snow, he grinned foolishly at his blue-red hands that clutched the thin strips of leather. Snow flew around him, and he was aware of the heavy lift and fall of hooves on either side of his head; he realized slowly and almost without surprise that he was being dragged along the ground on his stomach.

He pulled his weight against the moving reins and managed to get his knees under his body; then he pulled harder, so that his knees went before him as he leaned backward and sawed on the reins. The rear leg of one of the horses brushed against his shoulder, and he nearly lost his balance; but he regained it and lifted himself upward again, thrusting his legs down in a desperate leap, stumbling to his feet, and running along with the horses for several yards. Then he dug his heels into the snow and sawed again on the reins; he felt himself being carried along, but less swiftly. His heels went beneath the snow, caught on the grass, and plowed shallowly into the earth. The horses slowed, and halted. He stood for a moment panting; he was still smiling foolishly, though his legs were trembling and his arms were without strength, as he turned and looked behind him.

Whiteness met his eyes. He could not see the wagon, or the oxen, or the men who stood near them. He listened, trying to hear a sound to guide him; nothing came above the increasing moan of the wind. He knelt and looked behind him at the path he had scraped in the snow; a narrow, rough depression showed shallowly. He pulled the horses with him as he followed the path, stooping close to the ground and brushing at the snow with his free hand. After a few yards the trail began to fill, and soon it disappeared before the gusts of wind and blown snow. As nearly as he could guess, he continued to walk in the direction from which he had been pulled. He hoped that he had been carried away from the wagon in a straight line, but he could not be sure. Every now and then he shouted; his voice was whipped from his mouth and carried behind him by the wind. He hurried, and stumbled in the snow; from his feet and hands, numbness crept toward his body. He looked about him wildly. He tried to walk forward slowly and steadily, conserving his strength; but his legs jerked beneath him and carried him forward in an uneven gait that was half trot, half run. The horses, whose reins he carried, seemed an intolerable burden, though they moved docilely behind him; he had to use all his will to keep from dropping the reins and running blindly in the snow. He sobbed, and fell to his knees. Awkwardly, with the reins still clutched in his right hand, he crawled forward.

Distantly, he heard a shout; he paused and lifted his head. To his right, a little closer, the sound came again. He got to his feet and ran toward it, his sobbing breath becoming a rasping laugh. Suddenly, out of the white and gray of the driving snow, the blurred shape of the wagon loomed; and he saw three figures huddled beside it. One of them detached itself and walked toward him. It was Miller. He shouted something that Andrews did not understand, and took the reins that Andrews still held. When he lifted the reins, Andrews's hand was lifted stiffly to chest level; he looked at it and tried to loose the fingers. He could not make them move. Miller took his hand and pried the fingers back from the leather. His hand empty, Andrews worked his fingers, opening and closing his hand until the cramp was gone.

Miller came near him and shouted in his ear: "You all right?"

Andrews nodded.

"Let's get going," Miller shouted. Bending against the wind, the two men struggled toward the wagon and Charley Hoge and Schneider. Miller drew Schneider's and Andrews's heads together and shouted again: "I'll put Charley on with me. You two stay close."

Beside the wagon the men mounted their horses. Miller pulled Charley Hoge up behind him; he tightly grasped Miller around the stomach and buried his head against Miller's back; his eyes were screwed shut, and his mouth still worked upon the words that none of them could hear. Miller moved his horse away from the wagon; Andrews and Schneider followed. In a few moments the wagon was blotted from their sight by a solid wall of falling snow.

Shortly they passed beyond the ground that was curved by the white mounds of buffalo carcasses; Miller pushed his horse to a gallop, and the others followed. The gaits of their horses were awkward, jolting them in their saddles so that they had to hang on to their saddle horns with both hands. Now and then they came upon stretches of ground where the snow lay in heavy drifts; there the horses slowed to a walk and plowed through the snow which covered their forelegs halfway up to their knees.

Andrews's sense of direction had become numbed by the swirling white vortex of snow. The faint gray-green of the pine trees that blanketed the opposing mountainsides, which had earlier guided them in the general direction of the valley's mouth, had long been shrouded from the views of all of them; beyond the horses and the figures huddled upon them,

Andrews could not see any mark that showed him where they went. The same whiteness met his eyes wherever he looked; he had the sensation that, dizzily, they were circling around and around in a circle that gradually decreased, until they were spinning furiously upon a single point.

And still Miller spurred his horse, and beat its flanks, which glistened with sweat even in the driving, bitter cold. The three horses were grouped closely together; with a kind of vague horror that he could not understand, Andrews saw that Miller had closed his eyes against the stinging gale, and kept them closed, his head turned downward and to the side so that it was visible to Andrews even in their heavy gallop. Miller kept a tight hold on the reins, guiding the horse in a direction that he did not see. The others followed him blindly, trusting his blindness.

Suddenly, out of the storm, a dark wall reared up before them; it was the mountainside of trees, upon which the snow, driven by the fierce wind, could not settle. The ghostly shape of the large chimney rock where they had built their fires loomed vaguely, a dirty yellow-gray against the white snow. Miller slowed his horse to a walk, and led the others to the aspen-pole corral that Charley Hoge had built. Trying to keep their backs to the wind, they dismounted and led their horses into the corral, tethering them close together in the farthest corner. They left their saddles on, hooking the stirrups over the horns so that in the wind they would not beat against the horses' sides. Miller motioned for them to follow him; bent almost double in the face of the wind, they made their way out of the corral toward the spot where they had stacked and baled the buffalo hides. The stacks of hides were drifted high with snow; some of them had blown over, and rested lengthwise on the ground; others swayed sharply before the strong gusts of wind; the corners of two or three loose hides, scattered over the ground, protruded from the snow; Andrews realized that this was what remained of an unthonged pile of hides, half as high as the completed ricks. Most of them had been blown away by the powerful wind. For a few moments, the men stood still, huddled close together beside a stack of hides.

Half leaning against it, a great weariness came over Andrews; despite the cold, his limbs loosened and his eyelids dropped.

Dimly he remembered something that he had been told, or
that he had read, about death by freezing. With a shiver of
fright he stood up away from the hides. He flailed his arms,
beating them against his sides until he could feel the blood run
through them more swiftly; and he began to jog around in a
small circle, lifting his knees as he ran.

Miller pushed himself away from the rick of hides where he
had been resting and stood in his path; he put both hands on
Andrews's shoulders, and said, his face close and his voice loud:
"Be still. You want to get yourself froze to death, just keep
moving around; that'll do it right quick."

Andrews looked at him dully.

"You work up a sweat," Miller continued, "and it'll freeze
around you as soon as you're still for a minute. You just do
what I tell you and you'll be all right." He returned to Schneider. "Fred, cut some of them hides loose."

Schneider fumbled in one of the pockets of his canvas coat
and brought out a small pocketknife. He sawed at the frozen
thongs until they parted and spilled the compressed hides out
of their confines. Immediately, the wind caught half a dozen of
them, lifted them high, and sailed them in various directions;
some of them landed high in the branches of the pines, and
others scudded along the snow toward the open valley and
disappeared.

"Grab yourselves three or four of them," Miller shouted; and
he fell upon a small pile that slid from the larger stack. Quickly
Andrews and Schneider did the same; but Charley Hoge did
not move. He remained huddled, half crouching. Miller, on his
stomach, carrying the hides with him, crawled across the snow
to where a few of the skins remained in the unbound pile. He
pulled at the stiff thong that Schneider had hacked and managed to extricate a length of it from the bottom hide, where it
was fastened to the small hole in the skin of what had been a
buffalo leg. He cut this length into a number of pieces of equal
length. Schneider and Andrews crawled across the snow and
watched him as he worked.

With his short knife, Miller punched holes in each of the
legs of the hides which he secured beneath him. Then, turning
two of the skins against each other, so that fur touched fur,
he thonged the legs together. The two other furs he turned

so that the fur of each was to the weather, and placed them crosswise, one above and one beneath the crude open-ended and open-sided sack he had fashioned. When he had thonged the legs of the last two skins, there lay on the ground a rough but fairly effective protection against the weather, a bag whose ends were open but whose sides were loosely closed, into which two men could crawl and protect themselves against the main fury of the wind and hurtling snow. Miller dragged the heavy bag across the snow, pulled it among some of the fallen ricks, and jammed one open end against a bank of snow that was collecting against the fallen pile. Then he helped Charley Hoge crawl into the bag, and returned to Andrews and Schneider. Andrews lifted himself a little off the ground, and Miller pulled two of the hides from beneath him and began thonging the legs together.

"This will keep you from freezing," he shouted above the wind. "Just keep close together in this, and don't let yourselves get wet. You won't be warm, but you'll live." Andrews got to his knees and tried to grasp the edges of the hides, to pick them up and carry them to Miller, who had almost finished the first part of the shelter; but his fingers were so numb that he could not make them move with any precision; they hung at the ends of his hands and moved feebly and erratically over the frozen fur, without strength or sensation. Bending his hands from the wrists, shoving them through the snow under the hides, he staggered to his feet; pressing the hides against his lower body, he started to walk with them to Miller; but a gust of wind caught him, thrusting the hides heavily against him, and nearly lifted him off his feet. He fell to the ground again, near Miller, and pushed the hides through the snow to him.

Schneider had not moved. He lay on his stomach, on his small stack of hides, and looked at Miller and Andrews; through the snow and ice that glittered and stiffened his tangled hair and beard, his eyes gleamed.

After Miller had crossed the hides and as he was tying the last thong to hold them together, he shouted to Schneider: "Come on! Let's drag this over to where Charley and me are laying."

For a moment, through the ice and snow white on his face, Schneider's bluish lips retracted in what looked like a grin. Then slowly, from side to side, he shook his head.

"Come on!" Miller shouted again. "You'll freeze your ass off if you lay out here much longer."

Strongly through the howling wind came Schneider's voice: "No!"

Dragging the shelter between them, Andrews and Miller came closer to Schneider. Miller said:

"You gone crazy, Fred? Come on, now. Get inside this with Will, here. You're going to get froze stiff."

Schneider grinned again, and looked from one of them to another.

"You sons-of-bitches can go to hell." He closed his mouth and worked his jaws back and forth, trying to draw spittle; bits of ice and flakes of snow worked loose from his beard and were whipped away by the wind. He spat meagerly on the snow in front of him. "Up to now, I've done what you said. I went with you when I didn't want to go, I turned away from water when I knew they was water behind me, I stayed up here with you when I knew I hadn't ought to stay. Well, from now on in, I don't want to have nothing to do with you. You sons-of-bitches. I'm sick of the sight of you; I'm sick of the smell of you. From here on in, I take care of myself. That's all I give a damn about." He reached one hand forward to Miller; the fingers clawed upward, and trembled from his anger. "Now give me some of them thongs, and leave me be. I'll manage for myself."

Miller's face twisted in a fury that surpassed even Schneider's; he pounded a fist into the snow, where it sank deep to the solid ground.

"You're crazy!" he shouted. "Use your head. You'll get yourself froze. You never been through one of these blizzards."

"I know what to do," Schneider said. "I been thinking about it ever since this started. Now give me them thongs, and leave me be."

The two men stared at each other for several moments. The tiny snowflakes, thick and sharp as blowing sand, streamed between them. Finally Miller shook his head and handed the remaining thongs to Schneider. His voice became quieter. "Do what you have to do, Fred. It don't matter a damn to me." He turned a little to Andrews and jerked his head back toward the fallen bales. "Come on, let's get out of this." They crawled across the snow away from Schneider, pulling Andrews's shelter with them. Once Andrews looked back; Schneider had begun to lash his hides together. He worked alone and furiously in the open space of storm, and did not look in their direction.

Miller and Andrews placed the shelter beside the one which was humped with Charley Hoge's body, and shoved its open end against the bale of hides. Miller held the other end open and shouted to Andrews:

"Get in and lay down. Lay as quiet as you can. The more you move around, the more likely you are to get froze. Get some sleep if you can. This is liable to last for some time."

Andrews went into the bag feet first. Before his head was fully inside, he turned and looked at Miller.

Miller said: "You'll be all right. Just do what I said." Then Andrews put his head inside, and Miller closed the flap, stamping it into the snow so that it would stay closed. Andrews blinked against the darkness; the rancid smell of the buffalo came into his nostrils. He thrust his numb hands between his thighs, and waited for them to warm. They were numb for a long time and he wondered if they were frozen; when they finally began to tingle and then to pain him with their slowly growing warmth, he sighed and relaxed a little.

The wind outside found its way through the small openings of the bag and blew snow in upon him; the sides of the bag were thrust against him by the wind as it came in heavy gusts. As it lessened, the sides of the bag moved away from him. He felt movement in the shelter next to his own, and over the wind he thought he heard Charley Hoge cry out in fear. As his face warmed, the rough hair of the buffalo hide irritated his skin; he felt something crawl over it, and tried to brush it away; but the movement opened the sides of his shelter and a stream of snow sifted in upon him. He lay still and did not attempt to move again, though he realized that what he had felt on his cheek was one of the insects parasitic upon the buffalo—a louse, or a flea, or a tick. He waited for the bite into his flesh, and when it came he forced himself not to move.

After a time, the stiff hide shelter pressed upon him with an increasing weight. The wind seemed to have lessened, for no longer did he hear the angry snarl and moan about his ears. He raised the flap of his shelter, and felt the weight of the snow above him; in the darkness he saw only the faintest suggestion of light. He moved his hand toward it; it met the dry, crumbling cold of solidly banked snow.

Under the snow, between the skins that had only a few days before held together the flesh of the buffalo, his body rested. Slowly its sluggish blood generated warmth, and sent the warmth to his body's skin, and out to the close hide of the buffalo; thence his body gathered its own small warmth, and loosened within it. The shrill drone of the wind above him lulled his hearing, and he slept.

For two days and three nights the storm roared about the high valley where the men were trapped; they lay hidden under drifts of snow and did not move beneath them, except to emerge to relieve themselves, or to poke holes in the drifted banks to allow fresh air into their close dark caves of skin. Once Andrews had to come out into the weather to release water that he had held inside him until his groin and upper thighs throbbed with pain. Weakly he pushed the snow aside from his head-flap, and crawled into the bitter cold, blinking his eyes; he emerged into a darkness that was absolute. He felt the snow sting against his cheeks and forehead; he winced at the cold air that cut into his lungs; but he could see nothing. Afraid to move, he crouched where he had emerged and made water into the night. Then he fumbled back through the snow and squirmed into his close shelter, which still held a bit of the body warmth that he had left.

Much of the time he slept; when he did not sleep, he lay motionless on his side, knees drawn up on his chest, so that his body would give warmth to itself. Awake, his mind was torpid and unsure, and it moved as sluggishly as his blood. Thoughts, unoccasioned and faint, drifted vaguely into his mind and out. He half remembered the comforts of his home in Boston; but that seemed unreal and far away, and of those thoughts there remained in his mind only thin ghosts of remembered sensation—the feel of a feather bed at night, the dim comfortable closeness of a front parlor, the sleepy hum of unhurried conversation below him after he had gone to bed.

He thought of Francine. He could not bring her image to his mind, and he did not try; he thought of her as flesh, as softness, as warmth. Though he did not know why (and though it did not occur to him to wonder why), he thought of her as a part of himself that could not quite make another part of himself warm. Somehow he had pushed that part away from him once. He felt himself sinking toward that warmth; and cold, before he met it, he slept again.

7.

ON THE morning of the third day, Andrews turned weakly under the weight of the snow and burrowed through the long drift that had gathered at his head. Though he had grown somewhat used to the cold, which even in sleep enveloped the thin edge of warmth his body managed to maintain, he flinched and closed his eyes, hunching his neck into his shoulders as his flesh came against the packed coldness of the snow.

When he came from under the snow, his eyes were still closed; he opened them upon a brilliance that seared them over for an instant with a white hotness. Though melting snow clung in patches to his hands, he clapped them over his eyes and rubbed them until the pain subsided. Gradually, by squinting his eyelids open a little at a time, he accustomed his eyes to daylight. When at last he was able to look around him, he viewed a world that he had not seen before.

Under a cloudless sky, and glittering coldly beneath a high sun, whiteness spread as far as he could see. It lay thickly drifted about the site of their camp and lay like movement frozen, in waves and hillocks over the broad sweep of the valley. The mountainside, which had defined the valley's winding course, now was softened and changed; in a gentle curve the snow lay in drifts about the dark pines that straggled from the mountain into the flat valley, so that only the tips of the trees showed dark against the whiteness of the snow. The snow was gathered high upon the mountainside, so that no longer did his eyes meet a solid sheet of green; now he saw each tree sharply defined against the snow which surrounded it. For a long time he stood where he had come out of his shelter and looked about him wonderingly, and did not move, reluctant to push through the snow which bore no mark of anything save itself.

Then he stooped and poked one finger through the thin crust in front of him. He made his hand into a fist and enlarged the hole his finger had made. He scooped a handful of the snow, and let it trickle through his fingers in a small white pile beside the hole from which he had scooped it. Then, weak from lack of food and dizzy from his days and nights of lying in darkness, he stumbled forward a few steps through the waist-high drift; he turned around and around, looking at the land which had become so familiar to him that he had got out of the habit of noticing it, and which now was suddenly strange to him, so strange that he could hardly believe that he had looked upon it before. A clear and profound silence rose from the valley, above the mountains, and into the sky; the sound of his breathing came loudly to him; he held his breath to gather the quality of the silence. He heard the slither and drop of the snow as it fell from his trouser legs into the harder snow packed around his feet; in the distance there came the soft echoing snap of a branch that gave beneath its weight of snow; across the camp, from the drifted corral, came the sharp snort of a horse, so loud that Andrews imagined for a moment that it was only a few feet away. He turned toward the corral, expelling his clouded breath; beyond the drifted snow he saw the horses move.

Gathering air into his lungs, he shouted as loudly as he could; and after he had shouted, he remained with his mouth open, listening to the sound of his own voice that boomed as it grew fainter, and after what seemed to him a long time, trailed into the silence, dispersed by distances and absorbed by the snow. He turned to the mounds of snow, under one of which he had lain for two days; under the other Miller and Charley Hoge still lay. He saw no movement; a sudden fear caught him, and he took a few steps through the snow. Then he saw a tremor, saw the snow break from above the mound, and saw the break lengthen toward him. Miller's head—black and rough against the smooth whiteness from which it emerged— came into sight; the heavy arms, like those of a swimmer, flailed the snow aside and Miller stood upright, blinking furiously. After a moment he squinted at Andrews and said hoarsely, his voice wavering and unsure: "You all right, boy?"

"Yes," Andrews said. "You and Charley?"

Miller nodded. He looked across the expanse of their camp-site. "I wonder how Fred made out. Likely as not he froze to death."

"The last I saw, before we settled in, he was over there," Andrews said, and pointed toward the chimney rock around which they had earlier arranged their camp. They walked toward it, their going uncertain; they sometimes plowed through drifted snow that came above their waists, and some-times easily in snow that barely reached the middle of their calves. They went around the high rock, poking cautiously into the snow with their boots.

"No telling where he is now," Miller said. "We might not find him till the spring thaw."

But as he spoke, Andrews saw the snow move and break very close to him, beside the chimney rock.

"Here he is!" he shouted.

Between Miller and Andrews a rough shape came up through the snow. Great chunks of white ice clung to the matted hair of the buffalo hide and fell away, revealing the flat umber color; for an instant, Andrews drew back in fear, thinking irrationally that somehow a buffalo was rearing itself upward to confront them. But in the next instant, Schneider had thrown aside the skins in which he had wrapped himself like a mummy, and was standing blindly between them, his eyes screwed shut, an ex-pression of pain furrowing the flesh between his eyebrows and pulling his mouth to one side.

"Jesus Christ, it's bright," Schneider said, his voice an un-clear croak. "I can't see a thing."

"Are you all right?" Andrews asked.

Schneider opened his eyes to a slit, recognized Andrews, and nodded. "I think my fingers got a little frostbit, and my feet are damn near froze off; but I managed all right. If I ever get thawed out, I'll know for sure."

As well as they could—with their hands, their feet, and the folded buffalo hides that Schneider had discarded—the three men scraped away a large area of snow from around the chim-ney rock; upon the frozen ground, and over the charred, ice-coated remains of an old campfire, they piled what dry twigs they could strip from the snow-weighted lower branches of the pine trees. Miller dug into their cache of goods and found an old tinderbox, some crumpled paper that had not been wetted by the snow, and several unused cartridges. He laid the paper under the dry branches, worked the lead bullets loose from the cartridges, and poured the gunpowder upon the paper, crumpling more paper on the powder. He struck the tinderbox and ignited the powder, which flared powerfully, igniting the paper. Soon a small fire blazed, melting the snow that clung to the inward side of the rock.

"We'll have to keep this going," Miller said. "It's mighty hard to start a fire in a blowing wind with wet wood."

As the fire grew stronger, the men dug into the snow for logs and piled them, wet, upon the fire. They huddled about the warmth, so close that steam rose from their damp clothing; Schneider sat on his buffalo skins and thrust his boots close to the fire, almost into it. The smell of scorching leather mixed with the heavier smell of the burning logs.

After he had warmed himself, Miller walked across the campsite, following the irregular path that he and Andrews had made earlier, toward the place between the bales where Charley Hoge still lay. Andrews watched him go, following his progress with eyes that moved in a head that did not turn. The heat from the fire bit into his skin and pained him, and still he had the urge to get closer, to hover over the fire, to take the fire inside himself. He bit his lips with the pain of the heat, but he did not move away. He remained before the fire until his hands were a bright red, and until his face burned and throbbed. Then he backed away and instantly he was cold again.

Miller led Charley Hoge back across the snow toward the fire. Charley Hoge went before Miller, shambling loosely in the broken path, his head down, stumbling to his knees now and then. Once, when the path turned, he plowed into the unbroken snow, and halted and turned only when Miller caught at him and turned him gently back. When the two men came up before the fire, Charley Hoge stood inertly before it, his head still down, his face hidden from the others.

"He don't quite know where he is yet," Miller said. "He'll be all right in a little while."

As the fire warmed him, Charley Hoge began to stir. He looked dully at Andrews, at Schneider, and back at Miller; then he returned his gaze to the flames, and moved closer to them; he thrust the stump of his wrist close to the heat, and held it there for a long time. Finally he sat before the fire and rested his chin on his knees, which he cradled close to his chest with arms folded tightly around them; he gazed steadily into the flames, and blinked slowly, unseeingly, every now and then.

Miller went to the corral and inspected the horses; he returned leading his own horse, and reported to the men around the fire that the others seemed to be in good shape, considering the weather they had gone through. Digging again into the cache of their goods, he found the half-filled sack of grain that they had brought along to supplement the grass diet of the horses; he measured out a small quantity and fed it slowly to his horse. He told Schneider to feed the others after a while. He let his own horse wander about the area for a few moments until its muscles were loosened and it had gained strength from its food. Then, scraping the ice and snow off the saddle and tightening the cinch around its belly, he mounted.

"I'm going to ride up toward the pass and see how bad it is," he said. He rode slowly away from them. His horse walked with head down, delicately lifting its fore-hooves out of the neat holes they made, and more delicately placing them on the thin crust and letting them sink, as if only by their own weight, through the snow.

After several minutes, when Miller was out of hearing, Schneider said to the fire: "It ain't no use for him to go look. He knows how bad it is."

Andrews swallowed. "How bad is it?"

"We'll be here for a while," Schneider said, and chuckled without humor; "we'll be here for a spell."

Charley Hoge raised his head and shook it, as if to clear his mind. He looked at Schneider, and blinked. "No," he said loudly, hoarsely. "No."

Schneider looked at Charley Hoge and grinned. "You come alive, old man? How did you like your little rest?"

"No," Charley Hoge said. "Where's the wagon? We got to get hitched up. We got to get out of here."

Charley Hoge got to his feet and swayed, looking wildly about him. "Where is it?" He took a step away from the fire. "We can't lose too much time. We can't—"

Schneider rose and put a hand on Charley Hoge's arm. "Take it easy," he said, gruffly and soothingly. "It's all right. Miller'll be back in a minute. He'll take care of everything."

As suddenly as he had arisen, Charley Hoge sat back on the ground. He nodded at the fire and mumbled: "Miller. He'll get us out of here. You wait. He'll get us out."

A heavy log, thawed to wetness by the heat, fell into the bed of coals; it hissed and cracked, sending up heavy plumes of blue-gray smoke. The three men squatted in the little circle of bare ground, which was soggy from the snow that had turned to water and seeped from the closely surrounding drifts. Waiting for Miller to return, they did not speak; torpid from the heat of the fire and weak from the two-day lack of food, they did not think of moving or feeding themselves. Every now and then Andrews reached over to the thinning bank beside him and lethargically took a handful of snow, stuffed it into his mouth, and let it melt on his tongue and trickle down his throat. Though he did not look beyond the campfire, the whiteness of the snow over the valley, caught and intensified by the brilliant sun, burned into his averted face, causing his eyes to smart and his head to throb.

Miller was gone from the camp nearly two hours. When he returned, he rode past the campsite without looking at anyone. He left his trembling and winded horse in the snow-banked corral and slogged wearily through the snow up to where they waited around the fire. He warmed his hands—blue-black from the cold and ingrained powder smoke that remained on them—and turned around several times to warm himself thoroughly before he spoke.

After a minute of silence, Schneider said harshly: "Well? How does it look?"

"We're snowed in good," Miller said. "I couldn't get within half a mile of the pass. Where I turned back, the snow was maybe twelve foot deep in places; and it looked like it was worse farther on."

Schneider, squatting, slapped his knees, and rose upright. He kicked at a charred log that had fallen from the fire and was sizzling on the wet ground.

"I knowed it," Schneider said dully. "By God, I knowed it before you told me." He looked from Miller to Andrews and back again. "I told you sons-of-bitches we ought to get out of here, and you wouldn't listen to me. Now look what you got yourselves into. What are you going to do now?"

"Wait," Miller said. "We get ourselves fixed up against another blow, and we wait."

"Not this feller," Schneider said. "This feller's going to get his self out of here."

Miller nodded. "If you can figure any way, Fred, you go to it."

Andrews rose, and said to Miller: "Is the pass we came over the only way out?"

"Unless you want to walk up over the mountain," Miller said, "and take your chances that way."

Schneider spread his arms out. "Well, what's wrong with that?"

"Nothing," Miller said, "if you're fool enough to try it. Even if you rigged up some snowshoes, you couldn't carry anything with you. You'd sink down in the first soft snow you came to. And you can't live off the land in the high country in the winter."

"A man with belly could do it," Schneider said.

"And even if you was fool enough to try that, you take a chance on another blow. Did you ever try to wait out a blizzard on the side of a mountain? You wouldn't last an hour."

"It's a chance," Schneider said, "that could be took."

"And even if you was fool enough to take that chance, without knowing the country you came out in, you might walk around for a week or two before you saw somebody to set you straight. There ain't nothing between here and Denver, to speak of; and Denver's a long way off."

"You know the country," Schneider said. "You could point us the way to go."

"And besides," Miller said. "We'd have to leave the goods here."

For a moment Schneider was silent. Then he nodded, and kicked at the wet log again. "That's it," he said in a tight voice. "I might of knowed. It's the goddamned hides you won't let go of."

"It's more than the hides," Miller said. "We couldn't take anything with us. The horses would run wild, and the cattle

would go off with the buffalo that's still here. We'd have nothing to show for the whole try."

"That's it," Schneider said again, his voice rising. "That's
what's behind it. Well, the goods don't mean that much to me.
I'll go over by myself if need be. You just point out a route
to me and give me a few landmarks, and I'll chance it on my
own."

"No," Miller said.

"What?"

"I need you here," Miller said. "Three—" He glanced at
Charley Hoge, who was rocking himself before the fire, hum-
ming tunelessly under his breath. "Two men can't manage the
wagon and the hides down the mountain. We'll need you to
help."

Schneider stared at him for a long moment. "You son-of-a-
bitch," he said. "You won't even give me a chance."

"I'm giving you your chance," Miller said quietly. "And
that's to stay here with us. Even if I told you a route and some
signs, you'd never make it. Your chance to stay alive is here
with the rest of us."

Again Schneider was silent for several moments. At last he
said: "All right. I should have knowed better than to ask. I'll sit
here on my ass all winter and draw my sixty a month, and you
sons-of-bitches can go to hell." He turned his back to Miller
and Andrews, and thrust his hands angrily toward the fire.

Miller looked at Charley Hoge for a moment, as if to speak
to him. Then he abruptly turned to Andrews. "Dig around in
our goods and see if you can find a sack of beans. And find one
of Charley's pots. We got to get some food in us."

Andrews nodded, and did as he was ordered. As he was poking through the snow, Miller left the campsite and returned a
few minutes later dragging several stiff buffalo hides. He made
three trips back and forth between the campsite and the place
where the hides rested, returning each time with more. After
he had made a pile of about a dozen, he poked in the snow
until he found the ax. Then, with the ax on his shoulder, he
trudged away from the camp, up the mountain, among the
great forest of pine trees, the lower branches of which curved
downward under the weight of the snow. The tips of many of
them touched the whitened earth, so that the snow that held

them down and the snow upon which they rested appeared to be the same, eccentric and bizarre curves to which the trees conformed. Under the arches thus formed Miller walked, until it appeared, as he went into the distance, that he was walking into a cave of dark green and blinding crystal.

In his absence Andrews threw several handfuls of dried beans into the iron kettle he had dug out of the snow. After the beans he scooped in several masses of snow, and placed the pot at the back of the fire, so that the kettle rested against one side of the rock. He had not been able to find the bag of salt in the snow, but he had found a small rind of salt pork wrapped in oilskin and a can of coffee. He dropped the rind into the kettle and searched again until he found the coffeepot. By the time Miller returned from the forest, the kettle of beans was bubbling and the faint aroma of coffee was beginning to rise from the pot.

On his shoulders Miller balanced several pine boughs, thick and heavy at the raw yellow butts where they had been chopped, narrowing behind him where the smaller branches and pine needles swept a heavy trail in the snow, roughing it and covering the tracks he made as he stumbled down the side of the mountain. Bent beneath the weight of the boughs, Miller staggered the last few steps up to the fire and let the boughs crash to the snow on either side of him; a fine cloud like white dust exploded up from the ground and whirled for several minutes in the air.

Beneath the grime and dirt Miller's face was blue-gray from cold and exhaustion. He swayed for several minutes where he had dropped the logs and then he walked with unsteady straightness to the fire and, still standing, warmed himself. He stood so, without speaking, until the coffee bubbled up over the sides of the pot and hissed on the coals.

His voice weak and empty, he said to Andrews: "Find the cups?"

Andrews moved the pot to the edge of the fire; his hand burned on the hot handle, but he did not flinch. He nodded. "I found two of them. The others must have blown away."

Into the two cups he poured the coffee that he had brewed. Schneider walked up. Andrews handed one of the cups to Miller, and one to Schneider. The coffee was thin and weak, but the men gulped at the scalding liquid without comment. Andrews threw another small handful of coffee into the steaming pot.

"Go easy on that," Miller said, holding the tin cup in both his hands, juggling it to prevent his hands from burning and cupping it to gather its heat. "We ain't got enough coffee now to last us; just let it boil longer."

With his second cup of coffee Miller seemed to regain some of his strength. He sipped from a third cup and passed it along to Charley Hoge, who sat still before the fire and did not look at any of the men. After his second cup, Schneider returned to the edge of the circle, beyond Charley Hoge, and stared gloomily into the coals, which glowed faintly and grayly against the blinding whiteness that filtered through the trees, intensifying the shadow in which they sat.

"We'll build a lean-to here," Miller said.

Andrews, his mouth loose and tingling from the hot coffee, said indistinctly: "Wouldn't it be better out in the open, in the sun?"

Miller shook his head. "In the daytime, maybe; not at night. And if another blow came up, no lean-to we could build would last more than a minute on open ground. We build here."

Andrews nodded and drank the last of his coffee, tilting the cup up and throwing his head back so that the warm rim of the cup touched the bridge of his nose. The beans, softening in the boiling water, sent up a thin aroma. Though he was not aware of hunger, Andrews's stomach contracted at the odor and he bent over at the sudden pain.

Miller said: "Might as well get to work. Beans won't be ready to eat for two or three hours, and we have to get this up before night."

"Mr. Miller," Andrews said; and Miller, who had started to rise, paused and looked at him, crouched on one knee.

"Yes, boy?"

"How long will we have to be here?"

Miller stood up, and bent to brush off the black peat mud and wet pine needles that clung to his knees. From his bent head and under his black, tangled brows, he raised his eyes and looked directly at Andrews.

"I won't try to fool you, boy." He jerked his head toward
Schneider, who had turned in their direction. "Or Fred either.
We'll be here till that pass we come over thaws out."

"How long will that take?" Andrews asked.

"Three, four weeks of good warm weather would do it,"
Miller said. "But we ain't going to have three or four weeks before winter sets in hard. We're here till spring, boy. You might
as well set your mind to it."

"Till spring?" Andrews said.

"Six months at the least, eight months at the most. So we
might as well dig in good, and get ourselves set for a long
wait."

Andrews tried to realize how long six months would be, but
his mind refused to move upon the figure. How long had they
been here now? A month? a month and a half? Whatever it
was, it had been so filled with newness and work and exhaustion, that it seemed like no period that could be measured,
thought about, or put up against anything else. Six months.
He spoke the words, as if they would mean more coming aloud
from his lips. "Six months."

"Or seven, or eight," Miller said. "It won't do no good
thinking about them. Let's get to work before this coffee wears
off."

The rest of the day Andrews, Miller, and Schneider spent in
constructing the lean-to. They stripped the smaller branches
from the slender pine logs and piled them in a neat bundle near
the fire. As Miller and Andrews worked on the logs, Schneider
hacked from a stiff hide, the smallest and youngest he could
find, a number of uneven but relatively slender thongs. His
knives blunted quickly on the stonelike hides, and he had to
sharpen a knife several times before it would peel off a single thong. After he had hacked a large number of thongs, he
bent them so that they would fit into a huge kettle that he
found among Charley Hoge's things buried in the snow. From
around the fire he raked what dead ashes he could and put
them in the kettle with the thongs. Then he called Miller and
Andrews over to where he stood and told them to urinate in
the kettle.

"What?" Andrews said.

"Piss in it," Schneider said, grinning. "You know how to piss, don't you?"

Andrews looked at Miller. Miller said: "He's right. That's the way the Indians do it. It helps draw the stiffness out of the hide."

"Woman piss is best," Schneider said. "But we'll have to make do with what we got."

Solemnly the three men made water into the iron kettle. Schneider inspected the level to which the ashes had risen; shaking his head regretfully, he threw several handfuls of snow into the kettle to bring the sooty mixture up to a level that would cover the thongs. He set the kettle on the fire, and joined Andrews and Miller in their work.

They cut the stripped logs to lengths, and set four of them —two short and two long—in a rectangle before the fire. To secure the logs, they dug into the soggy ground, cutting through the spreading roots of the trees and breaking through scattered subterranean rock, to a depth of nearly two feet. Into these holes they set the logs, so that the taller ones were facing the fire. The more slender and longer boughs they notched so that they would fit firmly, and lashed them to the thick uprights set into the ground, thus forming a sturdy boxlike frame that slanted from the foot-high stubs at the rear to the height of a man's shoulders at the front. They lashed the branches with the urine-and-ash-soaked thongs that were still so stiff they were barely workable. By that time it was midafternoon, and they paused, nearly exhausted, to eat the hard beans that had been boiling in the iron kettle. The four men ate out of a common pot, using whatever utensils they could salvage out of the snow, beneath which they lay scattered. The beans, without salt, were tasteless and lay heavy on their stomachs; but they worked them down and cleaned the heavy pot of its last morsel. When Miller, Schneider, and Andrews returned to their frame, the buffalo-hide thongs had hardened and contracted, and held the logs together like bands of iron. They spent the rest of the afternoon stringing buffalo hides to the frame, using the thongs which had softened in their bath of urine and wood ash. All around the frame they dug a shallow trench, into which they stuffed the ends of the hides, and covered them over with moist earth and peat, so that no air or moisture could run inside the shelter.

Before darkness came, the shelter was finished. It was a sturdy structure, walled and floored with buffalo skins, which were thonged and overlaid so that from the back and sides, at least, it was virtually water- and wind-proof. From the broad front, several hides were suspended loosely and arranged so that in a wind they could be secured by long pegs thrust into the ground. The men dug what remained of their bedrolls out of the snow, divided the remaining blankets equally, and spread them before the fire to dry. In the last light of the sun, which threw the snow-wrapped land into a glittering cold blue and a brilliant orange, Andrews looked at the shelter of log and buffalo hide that they had spent the day constructing. He thought: this will be my home for the next six or eight months. He wondered what it would be like, living there. He dreaded boredom; but that expectation was not fulfilled.

Their days were occupied with work. They cut narrow strips of softened hide in two-foot lengths, scraped the fur from them, made four-inch slits in the center of each, and wore these like masks over their eyes to cut down the blinding glare of the snow. From the pile of small branches of pine they selected lengths which they soaked and bent in oval shapes, and tied upon them a latticework of hide strips, using them as crude snowshoes to walk upon the thin hard crust of the snow without sinking down into it. From the softened hide they fashioned clumsy stockinglike boots, which they secured to the calves of their legs with thongs, and which kept their feet from freezing. They cured several hides to supplement the blankets that had blown away during the blizzard, and they even made for themselves loosely fitting robes which served in lieu of greatcoats. They cut wood for the fire, dragging the huge logs through the snow until the area around the camp was packed and hard, and they could slide them along the iced surface with little effort. They kept the fire going night and day, taking turns during the night getting up and walking into the sharp cold to thrust logs beneath the banked ashes. Once, during a heavy wind that lasted half the night, Andrews watched the campfire consume a dozen thick logs without once breaking into flame, the embers kept at a glowing intense heat by the wind.

On the fourth day after the blizzard, as Schneider and Andrews took axes and started into the woods to increase the stockpile of logs that grew beside the chimney rock, Miller announced that he would ride into the valley and shoot a buffalo; their meat was low, and the day promised to be fair. Miller mounted the lone horse in the corral—the other two had been turned loose to live with the oxen as best they could on what grass might be found in the valley—and rode slowly away from the campsite. He returned nearly six hours later, and slid wearily off his horse. He tramped through the snow to the three men who waited for him around the campfire.

"No buffalo," he said. "They must have got out during the blow, before the pass was snowed in."

"We ain't got much meat left," Schneider said. "The flour's ruined, and we only got one more sack of beans."

"This ain't so high that game will be hard to find," Miller said. "I'll go out again tomorrow and maybe get us a deer. If the worst comes, we can live on fish; the lake's froze over, but not so thick a body can't chop through."

"Did you see the stock?" Schneider asked.

Miller nodded. "The oxen came through. The snow's blowed away enough in spots so they'll manage. The horses are looking poorly, but with luck they'll get through."

"With luck," Schneider said.

Miller leaned back from the fire, stretched, and grinned at him.

"Fred, I swear you ain't got a cheerful bone in your body. Why, this ain't bad; we're set now. I recollect one winter I got snowed in up in Wyoming, all by myself. Clean above timber line, and no way to get down. So high they was no game; I lived all winter off my horse and one mountain goat, and the only shelter I had was what I made out of that horseskin. This is good living. You got no call to complain."

"I got call," Schneider said, "and you know it."

But as the days passed, Schneider's complaining became more and more perfunctory, and at last ceased altogether. Though he slept at night in the hide shelter with the other men, he spent more and more time alone, speaking to the others only when he was directly addressed, and then as briefly and noncommittally as he could. Often when Miller was off hunting for meat, Schneider would leave the campsite and remain away until late in the afternoon, returning with nothing to show for his absence. Through his apparent resolve to have little to do with the others of the party, he got into the habit of talking to himself; once Andrews came upon him and heard him speaking softly, crooningly, as if to a woman. Embarrassed and half-afraid, Andrews backed away from him; but Schneider heard him, and turned to face him. For a moment, the two men looked at each other; but it was as if Schneider saw nothing. His eyes were glazed and empty, and after a moment they turned dully away. Puzzled and concerned, Andrews mentioned Schneider's new habit to Miller.

"Nothing to worry about," Miller said. "A man by his self gets to doing that. I've done it myself. You got to talk, and for four men cooped together like we are, it ain't good to talk too much among their selves."

Thus, much of the time, Andrews and Charley Hoge were left to themselves at the camp while Miller hunted and Schneider wandered alone, speaking to whatever image floated before his mind.

Charley Hoge, after the first numb shock that came with his emergence from the snow, began slowly to recognize his surroundings and even to accept them. Among the debris of the camp that remained after the fury of the blizzard had spent itself, Miller had managed to find two gallon crocks of whisky that were unbroken; day by day he doled this out to Charley Hoge, who drank it with the weak thin bitter coffee made by boiling over and over the grounds used the previous day. Warmed and loosened by repeated doses of the coffee and whisky, Charley Hoge began to stir a little about the campsite—though at first he would not go beyond the wide circle between their shelter and the campfire which had been melted of the snow by the heat and their tramping upon it. One day, however, he stood bolt upright before the campfire, so suddenly that he sloshed and spilled a bit of his coffee-and-whisky. He looked around him wildly; dropping his cup to the ground, he slapped his hand about his chest, and thrust it into

his jacket. Then he ran into the snow. Falling to his knees near
the large tree where he had kept his goods, he began scrabbling in the snow, poking his hand downward and throwing
the snow aside in small furious flurries. When Andrews went
up to him and asked him what the matter was, Charley Hoge
croaked only, over and over: "The book! The book!," and dug
more furiously into the snow.

For nearly an hour he dug, every few minutes running back
to the campfire to warm his hand and the blue puckered stump
at his wrist, whimpering like a frightened animal. Realizing
what he was after, Andrews joined him in his search, though
he had no way of knowing where he ought to look. Finally,
Andrews's numbed fingers, pushing aside a cake of snow, encountered a soft mass. It was Charley Hoge's Bible, opened
and soaked, in a bed of snow and ice. He called to Charley
Hoge and lifted the Bible, holding it like a delicate plate in his
hands, so that the soaked pages would not tear. Charley Hoge
took it from him, his hand trembling; the rest of the afternoon
and part of the next morning he spent drying the book page
by page, before the campfire. In the days thereafter, he filled
his idleness by sipping a weak mixture of coffee and whisky and
leafing through the blurred, soiled pages. Once Andrews, tense
and near anger because of his inactivity and the silence that
came upon the camp in Miller's absence, asked Charley Hoge
to read him something. Charley Hoge looked at him angrily
and did not answer; he returned to his Bible and thumbed
through it dully, his forefinger laboriously tracing the lines and
his brows drawn together in concentration.

Miller was most at ease in his isolation. Away from the camp
in search of food during the day, he always returned shortly
before twilight, appearing sometimes behind the men who
waited for him, sometimes in front of them—but always appearing suddenly, as if he had thrust himself up out of the landscape. He would walk toward them silently, his dark bearded
face often shagged and glittering with snow and ice, and drop
whatever he had killed upon the snow near the campfire. Once
he killed a bear and butchered it where it fell. When he appeared with the huge hindquarters of the bear balanced on
each shoulder, staggering beneath their weight, it seemed to

Andrews for an instant that Miller himself was some great animal, grotesquely shaped, its small head hunched between tremendous shoulders, bearing down upon them.

As the others weakened on their steady diet of wild meat,
Miller's strength and endurance increased. After a full day of
hunting, he still dressed his own kill and prepared the evening
meal, taking over most of the duties that Charley Hoge seemed
no longer capable of performing. And sometimes, late, on clear
nights, he went into the woods with an ax, and the men who
stayed by the warmth of the campfire could hear the sharp hard
ring of cold metal biting into cold pine.

He spoke infrequently to the others; but his silence was
not of that intentness and desperation that Andrews had seen
during the hunt and slaughter of the buffalo. In the evenings,
hunched before the fire that reflected upon the shelter behind
them and returned the warmth to their backs, Miller stared
into the yellow flames whose light flickered over his dark,
composed features; upon his flat lips there was habitually a
smile that might have been of contentment. But the pleasure
he took was not in the company, even silent, of the other men;
he looked at the fire and beyond it into the darkness that was
here and there lightened by the pale glow of moon or stars
upon the drifted snow. And in the mornings before he set out
for his hunting, as he fixed breakfast for the men and himself,
he performed his tasks with neither pleasure nor annoyance
but as if they were only a necessary prelude for his leaving.
When he left the camp his movements seemed to flow into the
landscape; and on his snowshoes of young pine and buffalo
thongs, he glided without effort and merged into the dark
forest upon the snow.

Andrews watched the men around him, and waited. Sometimes at night, crowded with the others in the close warm
shelter of buffalo hide, he heard the wind, that often suddenly
sprang up, whistle and moan around the corners of the shelter;
at such moments the heavy breathing and snoring of his companions, the touch of their bodies against his own, and their
body stench gathered in the closeness of the shelter seemed
almost unreal. At such times he felt a part of himself go outward into the dark, among the wind and the snow and the featureless sky where he was whirled blindly through the world.

Sometimes when he was near sleep he thought of Francine, as he had thought of her when he had been alone beneath the great storm; but he thought of her more precisely now; he could almost bring her image before his closed eyes. Gradually he let the remembrance of that last night with her come to him; and at last he came to think of it without shame or embarrassment. He saw himself pushing away from him her warm white flesh, and he wondered at what he had done, as if wondering at the actions of a stranger.

He came to accept the silence he lived in, and tried to find a meaning in it. One by one he viewed the men who shared that silence with him. He saw Charley Hoge sipping his hot thin mixture of coffee and watered whisky, warding off the bitter edge of cold that pressed against him at all times, even as he hunched over a blazing fire, and saw his blurred, rheumy eyes fixed upon the ruined pages of his Bible, as if desperately to keep those eyes from looking beyond into the white waste of snow that diminished him. He saw Fred Schneider withdraw into himself, away from his fellows, as if his lone sullen presence were the only defense he had against the great cold whiteness all around. Schneider tramped brutally through the snow, throwing as wide and rough a swath as his feet could make; through the thin slits in the narrow buffaloskin that he wore almost constantly tied over his eyes, he looked at the snow, Andrews thought, as if it were something alive, as if it were something against which he was waiting to spring, biding his time. He had taken to wearing again the small pistol that Andrews had first noticed back at Butcher's Crossing; sometimes when he muttered and mumbled to himself, his hand would creep up to his waistband, and gently caress the stock of the pistol. As for Miller—Andrews always paused when he thought of the shape that he wished Miller to take. He saw Miller rough and dark and shaggy against the whiteness of the snow; like a distant fir tree, he was distinct from the landscape, and yet an inevitable part of it. In the mornings he watched Miller go into the deep forest; and he always had the feeling that Miller did not so much go out of his sight as merge and become so intrinsic to the landscape that he could no longer be seen.

He was unable to view himself. Again, as if he were a

stranger, he thought of himself as he had been a few months before at Butcher's Crossing, looking westward from the river at the land he was now in. What had he thought then? What had he been? How had he felt? He thought of himself now as a vague shape that did nothing, that had no identity. Once, on a bright cloudless day that threw blindingly dark shadows over himself and Charley Hoge and Schneider as they sat around the pale campfire, he had a restless urge, a necessity to get away from the two silent hulks on either side of him. Without a word to either, he strapped his seldom-used snowshoes to his feet and trudged away from the camp into the valley. For a long time he walked, his eyes upon his feet that shuffled sibilantly through the crusted snow. Though his feet were cold to numbness above the snow, the back of his neck burned beneath the unshadowed sun. When his legs began to ache from the constant awkward shuffling forward, he stopped and raised his head. All around him was whiteness which glittered with needlelike points of fire. He gasped at the immensity of what he saw. He raised his eyes a little more, and saw in the distance the wavering dark points of pine trees that lifted up the mountainside toward the pure blue sky; but as he looked at the dark-and-bright rim of the mountain that cut into the blue of the sky, the whole mountainside shimmered and the edge of the horizon blurred; and suddenly all was whiteness—above, below, all around him—and he took an awkward backward step as a sharp burning pain started in his eyes. He blinked and cupped his hands over his eyes; but even upon his closed lids he saw only whiteness. A small inarticulate cry came from his lips; he felt that he had no weight in the whiteness, and for a moment he did not know whether he remained upright or whether he had gone down into the snow. He moved his hands upon air, and then bent his knees and moved his hands downward. They touched the crusted softness of the snow. He dug his fingers into the snow, gathering small handfuls, and thrust his hands against his eyes. It was not until then that he realized that he had come away from the camp without his snow-blinders, and that the sun, reflected against the unbroken snow, had seared his eyes so that he could not see. For a long while he knelt in the snow, massaging his closed lids with the snow he scraped under his fingers. Finally, through barely-spread fingers that he kept over his eyes, he was able to make out what he thought was the dark mass of tree and rock that marked the campsite. With his eyes closed, he trudged toward it; in his blindness, he sometimes lost his balance and tumbled into the snow; when he did so, he risked quick glimpses through his fingers so that he could correct the direction in which he traveled. When he finally arrived at the camp, his eyes were so burned that he could see nothing, not even in brief glimpses. Schneider came out to meet him and guided him into the shelter, where he lay in darkness for the better part of three days, while his eyes healed. Thereafter, he did not look upon the snow again without his rawhide blinders to protect him; and he did not go again into the great white valley.

Week by week, and at last month by month, the men endured the changing weather. Some days were hot and bright and summery, so still that no breeze dislodged a flake of snow hanging on the tip of a pine bough; some days a cold gray wind whistled through the valley, funneled by the long reach of mountain on either side. Snow fell, and on quiet days it made the air a solid mass that moved gently downward from a graywhite sky; and sometimes it was driven hard by various winds, which piled it in thick banks about their shelter, so that from the outside it appeared that they lived in a hollowed cave of snow. The nights were desperately, bitterly cold; no matter how closely they put their bodies together, and no matter how heavily they weighted themselves down with buffalo hides, they slept in a tense discomfort. Day slipped into indistinguishable day, and week into week; Andrews had no sensation of passing time, nothing against which to measure the coming thaw of spring. Every now and then he looked at the notches in a stripped pine branch that Schneider had made to keep track of the days; dully, mechanically, he counted them, but the number had no meaning for him. He was made aware of the passing of the months by the fact that at regular intervals Schneider came up to him and asked him for his month's pay. At such times, he solemnly counted from his money belt the money Schneider demanded, wondering vaguely where he kept it after he got it. But even this gave him no consciousness of passing time; it was a duty he performed when Schneider asked him; it had nothing to do with the time that did not pass, but which held him unmoving where he was.

8.

LATE in March and early in April, the weather settled; and day by day, with an agonizing slowness, Andrews watched the snow melt in the valley. It melted first where it had drifted most thinly, so that the once level valley became a patchwork of bleached grass and humped banks of dirtying snow. The days became weeks; and from the moisture that seeped into the earth from the melting snow, and from the steadying heat of the season, new growth poked up among the matted winter grass. A light film of green overlaid the grayish yellow of last year's growth.

As the snow melted and seeped into the quickening soil, game became more plentiful; deer wandered into the valley and cropped the fresh young blades of grass, and grew so bold that often they grazed within a few hundred yards of the camp; at a sound they would raise their heads, and their small conical ears would pitch upward as their bodies lowered and tensed, ready for flight; then, if the sound were not repeated, they would resume their grazing, their tawny necks bent in a delicate curve toward the earth. Mountain quail whistled among the treetops above them and lighted beside the deer, and fed with them, their mottled gray-and-white-and-buff bodies blending into the earth upon which they moved. With game so close and available, Miller no longer wandered in the forest; almost contemptuously, cradling Andrews's small repeater in the crook of his elbow, he walked a few steps away from the camp, and throwing the rifle butt casually to his shoulder brought down as much game as they needed. The men were replete with venison, quail, and elk; what dressed game they could not eat spoiled in the growing warmth. Every day, Schneider trudged through the melting snow toward the pass to inspect the snow mass slowly melting between them and the outside world. Miller looked at the sun and calculated with his somber glances the widening patches of bare earth that were beginning to eat toward the mountainside, and did not speak. Charley Hoge kept to his worn Bible; but every now and then, as if with surprise, he lifted his head and gazed upon the changing land. They gave less care to the fire they had attended all winter long;

several times they let it go out, and had to start it again with the tinderbox that Miller carried in his shirt pocket.

Even though the valley was almost cleared, the snow still lay in heavy drifts where the flat land rose upward into tree and mountain. Miller let out to graze the horse they had kept corralled all winter; gaunt from its meager supply of grain and what little forage it had been able to find, the horse cropped the new grass to the bare earth around the area that fronted their campsite. When it had regained some of its lost strength, Miller saddled it and rode away from the camp into the valley, and returned after several hours with the two horses that had run loose during the winter. After their long freedom, they were nearly wild; when Miller and Schneider tried to hobble them, so that they would not stray from the camp, they reared and turned their heads, manes flying and eyes rolling upward so that the whites were visible. After a few days of grazing on the young grass their coats began to take on a faint shine and their wildness decreased. At last the men were able to saddle them; the cinches they passed under their bellies could not be tightened, so gaunt had they become during their lean winter.

"A few more days of bad weather," Miller said bleakly, "and we wouldn't have had any horses. We'd of had to walk back to Butcher's Crossing."

The horses saddled and tamed, Miller, Andrews, and Schneider rode into the valley. They paused at the wagon, which had endured on the open plain the fury of the winter; a few of the floor boards had warped and the metal fittings showed thin layers of rust.

"It'll be all right," Miller said. "Needs a little grease here and there, but she'll do the job we need her to do." He leaned from his horse and touched with his forefinger the heavy metal band that encircled the wagon wheel; he looked at the bright rust on his fingertip and wiped his finger on his dirt-stiffened trousers.

From where the wagon rested, the men rode off in search of the oxen that had been loosed during the storm.

They found them all alive. Not so gaunt and bony as the horses had been, they were much wilder. When the men approached them, they broke into motion and pounded away in clumsy fright. The three men spent four days rounding up the eight oxen and leading them back to the camp, where they were hobbled and set to graze. As their bellies filled on the rapidly growing grass, they too lost some of their wildness; and before the week was out, the men were able to yoke them to the wagon and work them for a few hours aimlessly about the valley, among the wasted corpses of the buffalo killed in the fall. In the growing warmth, these corpses began to give off a heavy stench, and around them the grass grew thick and green.

As the weather warmed, the chill that had been in his bones all winter began to leave Andrews. His muscles loosened as he worked with the stock; his sight sharpened upon the greening earth; and his hearing, accustomed winter-long to noises absorbed in heavy layers of snow, began to take in the myriad sounds of the valley—the rustling of breezes through stiff pine boughs, the slither of his feet through the growing grass, the creak of the leather as his saddle moved on his horse, and the sound of the men's voices carrying across distances and diminishing into space.

As the stock fattened and became once again used to working under human hands, Schneider spent more and more time moving between the camp and the snow-packed pass that would let them out of the high valley and down the mountain into the flat country. On some days he returned, excited and eager, going up to each of them and speaking in a rapid, hoarsely whispering voice.

"It's going fast," he would say. "Underneath the rind, it's all hollow and mushy. Just a few days, now, and we can get through."

At other times he came back glumly.

"The god damned crust keeps the cold in. If we could just have a warm night or two, it might loosen up."

And Miller would look at him with a cool, not unfriendly amusement, and say nothing.

One day Schneider rode back from an inspection of the snow pack with more excitement than was usual.

"We can get through, men!" he said, his words running upon each other. "I went clean through, to the other side of the pack."

"On horseback?" Miller asked, not rising from the buffalo skin on which he lay.

"On foot," Schneider said. "Not more than forty or fifty yards of deep snow, and it's clean as a whistle from there on."

"How deep?" Miller asked.

"Not deep," Schneider said. "And it's soft as meal mush."

"How deep?" Miller asked.

Schneider raised his hand, palm downward, a few inches over his head. "Just a mite over a body's head. We could go through it easy."

"And you walked through it, you say?"

"Easy," Schneider said. "Clean to the other side."

"You god damned fool," Miller said quietly. "Did you stop to think what would happen if that wet snow caved in on you?"

"Not Fred Schneider," he said, and pounded himself on the chest with a closed fist. "Fred Schneider knows how to take care of his self. He takes no chances."

Miller grinned. "Fred, you're so hot for some soft living and easy tail, you'd burn your ass through hell if it would get you to it quick."

Schneider waved his fist impatiently. "Never mind about that. Ain't we going to get loaded?"

Miller stretched himself more comfortably on the buffalo hide. "No hurry," he said lazily. "If it's as deep as you say it is —and I know it ain't any less—we still got a few days."

"But we can get through *now!*" Schneider said.

"Sure," Miller said. "And take a chance on a cave-in. Get those oxen buried under a couple of ton of wet snow, not to say anything about ourselves, and then where would we be?"

"Ain't you even going to look?" Schneider wailed.

"No need to," said Miller. "Like I said, if it's anywhere near as deep as you say, we still got a few days. We'll just wait for a while."

So they waited. Charley Hoge, coming slowly out of his long dream during the winter, worked the oxen with the wagon for an hour or so every day, until they pulled, without a load at least, as easily as they had the previous fall. Under Charley Hoge's direction, Andrews smoked quantities of foot-long trout and great strips of venison to sustain them on their journey down the mountain and across the plain. Miller took to wandering again upon the mountainside, which was still drifted heavily in softening snow, with two rifles—his own Sharps and Andrews's varmint rifle—cradled in the crook of his arm. Frequently the men who remained at camp heard the booming of the Sharps or the smart crack of the small rifle; sometimes Miller brought his kill back to camp with him; more often he let it lie where it had dropped. At camp, his eyes constantly roved over the long valley and about the rising contours of surrounding mountainside; when he had to look away for one reason or another, he seemed to do so with reluctance.

Schneider's sullenness, which followed upon Miller's first refusal to leave the valley, turned into a kind of silent ferocity, of which Miller was the apparently unaware object. Schneider spoke to Miller only to insist that he accompany him to the pass, virtually every day, to inspect the snow pack that remained. When Schneider asked, Miller complied, neither good-naturedly nor bad-naturedly. He rode impassively away with Schneider, and returned impassively, his face set in calm untroubled lines beside Schneider's anger-reddened features. And to Schneider's half-articulate insistence, he replied only:

"Not yet."

To Andrews, though he said nothing, the last few days were the most difficult to endure. Again and again, at the imminent prospect of leaving, he found his hands clenched into fists, his palms sweaty; yet he could not have said where his eagerness to be gone came from. He could understand Schneider's impatience—he knew of Schneider's simple desire to fill his belly with civilized food, to surround his body with the softness of a clean bed, and to empty his gathered lust into the body of any waiting woman. But his own desire, though it may have included in some way all of those, was at once more intense and more vague. To what did he wish to return? From where did he wish to go? And yet the desire remained, for all its vagueness, sharp and painful within him. Several times he followed the trampled path in the snow that Miller and Schneider took to the pass, and stood where the snow lay thickly drifted in the narrow cut between the twin peaks that marked the entrance to the valley. Above the drifts, the raw brown-red rock of the peaks cut into the blue sky. He peered down the narrow open trench that Schneider had worn in the snow, but it twisted so that he could not see through it to the open country beyond.

Helpless before Miller's calm, they waited. They waited even when the snow, gathered in the solid shadow of the forest, began to melt and run in narrow rivulets past their campsite. They waited until late in April. Then one night before the campfire, suddenly Miller spoke:

"Get a good night's sleep. We load up and pull out tomorrow."

After he spoke, there was a long silence. Then Schneider rose to his feet, jumped in the air, and let out a loud whoop. He slapped Miller on the back. He turned around two or three times, laughing wordlessly. He slapped Miller on the back again.

"By God, it's about time! By God, Miller! You really ain't a bad feller, are you?" He walked in a tight circle for several minutes, laughing to himself, and speaking senselessly to the other men.

After an instant of elation at Miller's announcement, Andrews felt a curious sadness like a presentiment of nostalgia come over him. He looked at the small campfire burning cheerily against the darkness, and looked beyond the campfire into the darkness. There was the valley that he had come to know as well as the palm of his own hand; he could not see it, but he knew it was there; and there were the wasting corpses of the buffalo for whose hides they had traded their sweat and their time and a part of their strength. The ricks of those hides lay also in the darkness, hidden from his sight; in the morning they would load them on the wagon and leave this place, and he felt that he would never return, though he knew he would have to come back with the others for the hides they could not carry with them. He felt vaguely that he would be leaving something behind, something that might have been precious to him, had he been able to know what it was. That night, after the fire died, he lay in darkness, alone, outside the shelter, and let the spring chill creep through his clothing into his flesh; he slept at last, but in the night he awoke several times, and blinked into the starless dark.

In the first clear light of morning, Schneider roused them from their sleep. As celebration of their last day, they decided to drink what remained of the coffee, which they had been hoarding for several weeks. Charley Hoge made the coffee strong and black; after the weak brew made from reused grounds, the fresh bitter fragrance went to their heads and gave a new strength to their bodies. They yoked the oxen to the wagon, and drew the wagon up to the open area where the hides lay in their tall bales.

While Andrews, Schneider, and Miller boosted the great bales onto the wagon bed, Charley Hoge cleaned their camp area and packed the smoked fish and meat with the other trail goods into the large crate that had stood covered in canvas beside their campsite all winter. Weakened by their long diet of game meat and fish, the three men struggled against the weight of the bales. Six of the huge bales, laid in pairs, covered the bed of the wagon; upon these, the men managed to boost six more, so that the bound hides rose to the height of a man above the sideboards of the wagon. And though they were gasping and half faint from their labor, Miller urged them to pile six more bales upon the twelve, so that at last the hides balanced precariously ten or twelve feet above the spring clip seat which Charley Hoge was to occupy.

"Too many," Schneider gasped, after the last bale had been shoved in place. Breathing hoarsely, his face beneath its grime and smoke paler than his light hair and beard, he moved away from the wagon and looked at its towering load. "It'll never make it down the mountain. It'll tip over the first time it gets off level."

From the pile of goods that Charley Hoge had been sorting beside the wagon, Miller gathered what pieces of rope he could find. He did not answer Schneider. He knotted odd pieces of rope together, and began securing rope to the gussets and eyes along the top of the sideboard. Schneider said:

"Tying them down will just make it worse. And this wagon wasn't meant to carry this heavy a load. Break an axle, and then where'll you be?"

Miller threw a rope over the top of the bales. "We'll steady her as we go down," he said. "And if we take it careful, the axles will hold up." He paused for a moment. "I want us to go back into Butcher's Crossing with a real load. And watch their eyes bug out."

They lashed the hides to the wagon as tightly as they could, straining against the ropes, pulling them so heavily that the hides, flattened, pushed against the sideboards of the wagon and made them bulge outward. When the load was secure they stood away and looked at it, and then looked at the baled hides that remained. Andrews estimated that there were nearly forty of them on the ground.

"Two more wagon loads," Miller said. "We can come back for these later this spring. We're carrying around fifteen hundred hides—and there's better than three thousand here. Say forty-six, forty-seven hundred hides in all. If the price holds up, that's better than eighteen thousand dollars." He grinned flatly at Andrews. "Your share will come to better than seven thousand dollars. That ain't bad for a winter of doing nothing, is it?"

"Come on," Schneider said. "You can count your money when you get it in your hand. Let's finish loading and get out of here."

"You ought to of held out for shares, Fred," Miller said. "You'd of made a lot more money. Let's see—"

"All right," Schneider said. "I ain't complained. I took my chance. And you ain't got your load back to town yet, either."

"Let's see," Miller said. "If you'd held out for a sixth, you'd—"

"All right," Andrews said; his own voice surprised him. He felt a faint anger at Miller rise in him. "I said I'd take care of Schneider. And I'll give him a share above and beyond his salary."

Miller looked at Andrews slowly. He nodded very slightly, as if he recognized something. "Sure, Will. It's yours to do with."

Schneider, his face reddening, looked angrily at Andrews. "No, I thank you. I asked for sixty a month, and I been getting it. Fred Schneider takes care of his self; he don't ask nothing of nobody."

"All right," Andrews said; he grinned a little foolishly. "I'll buy you one big drunk back in Butcher's Crossing."

"I thank you," Schneider said gravely. "I'll be obliged to you for that."

They stowed their camp goods and their smoked food under the high wagon seat, and looked around them to see if anything had been left. Through the trees, the shelter in which they had spent their winter looked small and insufficient for the task it had performed. It would be here, Andrews knew, when they returned later in the spring or summer for the other hides; but in the following seasons, dried by the heat of the sun and cracked in the bitter cold of snow and ice, it would begin to disintegrate, crumble into patches and shreds; until at last it would be no more, and only the stumps of the logs they had set in the ground would remain to show their long winter. He wondered if another man would see it before it rotted in the weather and trickled down into the deep bed of pine needles upon which it stood.

They left the other bales of hides where they were, not bothering to push them back out of sight among the trees. Using the last of his strychnine, Charley Hoge sprinkled the hides to discourage vermin from nesting in the bales. Miller, Andrews, and Schneider saddled their horses, wrapped their blankets and small goods in softened buffalo hides, and strapped these behind their saddles. Charley Hoge clambered atop the high clip seat; at a signal from Miller, he leaned far to one side of the piled bales of hides, unfurled his long bull-whip behind him, and brought it smartly alongside the team of oxen. The splayed leather at the tip cracked loudly, and the crack was followed immediately by Charley Hoge's thin howling shout: "Harrup!" The startled oxen strained against the weight of the wagon, and dug their cloven hooves deep into the earth. The wooden yokes cut into their shoulder flesh, and the wood, strained in the pulling, gave sounds like deep groans. The freshly greased wheels turned on their axles and the wagon inched forward, gaining speed as the oxen found their balance against the weight they pulled. Under the weight of the hides, the wheels sank past their rims in the softened earth and left deep parallel ruts that were dark and heavy in the light yellow-green. Behind them, the men could see the ruts as far as they extended.

At the pass the snow was still fetlock deep; but it was soft, and the oxen made their way through it with comparative ease, though the wagon wheels sank in the wet earth halfway up to their hubs. At the highest point of the pass, precisely between the two peaks that were like the gigantic posts of a ruined gate that let them in and out of the valley, they paused. Schneider and Miller inspected the wagon brake that would keep the wagon from spilling too rapidly down as they descended the

mountainside. As they did so, Andrews looked back upon the
valley which in a few moments would be gone from his sight.
At this distance, the new growth of grass was like a faint green
mist that clung to the surface of the earth and glistened in the
early morning sun. Andrews could not believe that this same
valley had been the one he had seen pounding and furious
with the threshings of a thousand dying buffalo; he could not
believe that the grass had once been stained and matted with
blood; he could not believe that this was the same stretch of
land that had been torn by the fury of winter blizzards; he
could not believe that a few weeks ago it had been stark and
featureless under a blinding cover of white. He looked up and
down its length, as far as he could see. Even from this distance,
if he strained his eyes, he could see the expanse dotted with
the dark carcasses of the buffalo. He turned away from it and
pushed his horse over the pass, away from the other men and
the wagon which remained immobile at the summit. After a
few moments he heard behind him the slow thud of the horses'
hooves and the slow creak of the wagon. The party began its
long descent.

A few yards beyond the pass, the three men on horseback
dismounted and tied their horses loosely together, letting them
trail behind them as they made their way down the mountain.
The buffalo path, which they had followed up the mountain in
the fall, was soft, though not so muddy as the earth had been
back in the valley. Because of the softness, the wheels of the
wagon had a tendency to slip sideways off the trail whenever it
pitched from a level and followed the slope of the mountain;
Miller found three lengths of rope in Charley Hoge's goods
crate, and secured these lengths high upon the load. As the
wagon descended, the three men walked beside it and above
it, level with the top of the load, and pulled steadily against
the ropes, so that the wagon did not topple over as it angled
broadly away from the mountain. Sometimes, when the trail
turned sharply, the tottering weight of the high-piled wagon
nearly pulled them off their feet; they slid downward on the
slick grass, their heels digging for a hold in the earth, their
hands burning on the ropes they pulled.

They went down the mountain more slowly than they had
come up. Charley Hoge, dwarfed by the hides piled behind

him, sat erect upon his wagon seat, angling as the wagon angled, regulating its speed by a judicious mixture of cracking
whip and applied hand brake. They stopped frequently; animal
and man, weakened by the long winter, were unable to go for
long without rest.

Before midday they found a level plateau that extended a
short way out from the mountain. They took the bits from
their horses' mouths and unyoked the oxen and let them graze
on the thick grass that grew among the small rocks that littered the plateau. On a broad flat rock, Charley Hoge cut into
equal portions a long strip of smoked venison, and passed the
portions among the men. Andrews's hand received the meat
limply, and put it to his mouth; but for several minutes he did
not eat. Exhaustion pulled at his stomach muscles, sickening
him; tiny points darkened and brightened before his eyes, and
he lay back on the cool grass. After a while he was able to tear
at the tough leatherlike meat. His gums, inflamed by the long
diet of game, throbbed at the toughness; he let the meat soften
on his tongue before he chewed it. After he had forced most
of it down his throat, he stood, despite the tiredness that still
pulsed in his legs, and looked about him. The mountainside
was a riot of varied shade and hue. The dark green of the pine
boughs was lightened to a greenish yellow at the tips, where
new growth was starting; scarlet and white buds were beginning to open on the wild-berry bushes; and the pale green
of new growth on slender aspens shimmered above the silver-
white bark of their trunks. All about the ground the pale new
grass reflected the light of the sun into the shadowed recesses
beneath the great pines, and the dark trunks glowed in that
light, faintly, as if the light came from the hidden centers of
the trees themselves. He thought that if he listened he could
hear the sound of growth. A light breeze rustled among the
boughs, and the pine needles whispered as they were rubbed
together; from the grass came a mumble of sound as innumerable insects rustled secretly and performed their invisible
tasks; deep in the forest a twig snapped beneath the pad of an
unseen animal. Andrews breathed deeply of the fragrant air,
spiced with the odor of crushed pine needles and musky from
the slow decay that worked upward from the earth in the shadows of the great trees.

Just before noon the men resumed their slow journey downward; Andrews turned back and looked up the mountain they had descended. The trail had wound so erratically that he was no longer sure where he ought to look to find where they had come from. He looked upward, toward where he thought the summit of the mountain might be; but he could not see it. The trees that surrounded their trail cut off his view, and he could not see where they had been, or gauge how far they had come. He turned again. The trail twisted below him, out of sight. He took his place between Schneider and Miller, and again the group began its torturous descent of the mountain.

The sun beat upon him, and released the stench of his own body and that of the two men on either side of him. Sickened, he turned his head one way and another, trying to get the odor of a fresh breeze. He realized suddenly that he had not bathed since that first afternoon, months before, when he had been soaked by the blood of the buffalo; nor had his clothing been washed, or even removed. All at once his shirt and his trousers were stiff and heavy on his body, and the thought of them unpleasant in his mind. He felt his skin contract from the touch of his own clothing. He shuddered, as if caught in a chill wind, and let his breath come in and out of his opened mouth. And as they more steeply descended the mountain and came nearer to the flat country, the consciousness of his own filth grew within him. At last he was in a kind of nervous agony of which he could give no evidence. When the group rested, Andrews sat apart from the others and held himself rigid so that he could not feel his flesh move against his clothing.

In the middle of the afternoon there came to their ears a low faint roar, as of wind rushing through a tunnel. Andrews paused to listen; on his right, Schneider, who kept his eyes straight ahead on the swaying wagon, bumped into him. Schneider grunted a curse, but did not take his eyes from the wagon, as Andrews moved ahead to an equal distance between Schneider and Miller. Gradually the sound of the roaring became louder; the steadiness and intensity of it made Andrews revise his first impression that it was a wind sweeping upon the edge of the mountain, where the flat land came up to meet it.

Miller turned and grinned at Andrews and Schneider. "Hear that? We ain't got much further to go."

Then Andrews realized that the sound he heard must be the river, swollen with the spring run-off.

The thought of the end of their descent, and of cool water, quickened their steps and gave them a new strength. Charley Hoge cracked his whip and released his hand brake a few inches. The wagon swayed perilously on the uneven trail; at one point, the wheels on the side facing the three men lifted several inches off the ground; and as Charley Hoge whooped and set his brake, and as the three men pulled desperately on their ropes, the wagon shuddered for an instant before it was pulled back on all four wheels, rocking from one side to another beneath the unbalanced weight of the hides. After that they proceeded somewhat more slowly; but still the imminence of rest conserved their strength, and they did not stop again until they reached the flat moss-covered rock that gently sloped into the river bank.

On the flat bed of rock, they dropped their ropes and sprawled in rest. The rock was cool and moist from the spray flung by the river that ran alongside it, and the sound of the water rushing was so heavy that they had to shout above it.

"High for this time of year," Schneider yelled.

Miller nodded. Andrews squinted against the fine spray. The water flowed from bank to bank, broken at places into whirling ripples by unseen rock deep in the river bed. Here and there, the flowing stream broke into white foam; the foam and stray bits of bark and green leaves rushing upon the surface of the water were the only indications of the speed and thrust that the water gained in its long drop from the mountains. In the early fall, when they had crossed it last, the river had been a thin trickle that barely covered the bed of rock; now it stretched from bank to bank and cut away the earth opposite where they rested. Andrews looked up and down the river; on either side of him, the narrowest part stretched to at least a hundred yards.

Charley Hoge unyoked the oxen and let them join the horses at the edge of the bank. The animals touched their muzzles delicately upon the surface of the rushing water and flung their heads upward as the spray hit their eyes and nostrils.

On the rock, Schneider half crawled and half slid past Andrews and Miller. He knelt beside the river, cupped his hands into the water, and drank noisily from the streaming bowl of his hands. Andrews went across the rock and sat beside him. After Schneider had finished drinking, Andrews let his legs slide over the rock into the river; the force of the water caught him unprepared, and swung his lower body halfway around before he could stiffen his legs against the cold sharp thrust. The water broke in swirls and white riffles around his legs, just below the knees; the cold was like needles, but he did not move his legs. Little by little, holding to the rock behind him, he let his body into the stream; his breath came in gasps from the shock of the cold. Finally, his feet found the rocky bottom of the stream, and he leaned away from the bank toward the water that rushed at him, so that he stood free of the bank, balanced against the force of the river. He found a knobby protuberance on the rock to his right; he grasped the knob, and let his body fully down into the water. He squatted, submerging himself to his shoulders, holding his breath at the intense cold; but after a moment the cold left him and the feel of the water flowing about his body, washing at the accumulated filth of a winter, was pleasant and soothing, and almost warm. Still tightly grasping the rock with his right hand, he let his body be carried with the rushing of the stream, until at last it lay loose and straight in the course of the water, held near the foaming surface by the river's flow. Nearly weightless, holding to the knob of rock, he lay for several moments in the water, his head turned to one side and his eyes closed.

Above the roar of the water, he heard a noise. He opened his eyes. Schneider squatted on the rock above and to one side of him, grinning widely. His hand cupped, and went into the water; it came up suddenly, and pushed water into Andrews's face. Andrews gasped and drew himself out, bringing his free hand up quickly as he did so, splashing water at Schneider. For several moments, the two men, laughing and sputtering, dashed water toward each other as if they were playing children. Finally Andrews shook his head and sat panting on the rock beside Schneider. A light breeze chilled his skin but there was sunlight to warm him. Later, he knew, his clothes would stiffen on his body; but now they were loose and comfortable to his skin, and he felt almost clean.

"Jesus God," Schneider said, and stretched to lie on the sloping rock. "It's good to be down off that mountain." He turned to Miller. "How long you think we'll be, getting back to Butcher's Crossing?"

"Couple of weeks at the most," Miller said. "We'll go back quicker than we came."

"I ain't hardly going to stop," said Schneider, "except to get my belly full of greens and wash it around with some liquor, and then see that little German girl for a bit. I'm going straight on to St. Louis."

"High living," Miller said. "St. Louis. I didn't know you liked it that high, Fred."

"I didn't either," Schneider said, "until just a minute ago. Man, it takes a winter away from it to give you a taste for living."

Miller got up from the rock and stretched his arms out and up from his sides. "We'd better find our way across this river before it starts getting dark."

While Miller gathered their horses from around the banks where they were cropping at the lush grass, Andrews and Schneider helped Charley Hoge round up the oxen and yoke them to the wagon. By the time they finished, Miller had brought their horses up near them, and, mounted on his own, had found what looked like a crossing. The other men stood side by side on the bank and watched silently as Miller guided his horse into the swift water.

The horse was reluctant to go in; it advanced a few steps into the graveled bed of a shallow eddy and halted, lifting its feet, one by one, and shaking them delicately just above the surface. Miller patted the animal on its shoulder, and ran his fingers through its mane, leaning forward to speak soothingly in its ear. The horse went forward; the water flowed and parted whitely around its fetlocks, and as it advanced the water rose upward, until it flowed around the shanks and then around the knees. Miller led the horse in a zigzag path across the river; when it slipped on the smooth underwater rocks, Miller let it stand still for a moment and soothed it with small pats, speaking softly. In the middle of the river, the water rose above Miller's stirruped feet and submerged belly of the horse, parting on its shoulder and thigh. Very slowly, Miller zigzagged to shallower water; in a few minutes, he was across the river and on dry land. He waved, and then pushed his horse back into the water, zigzagging again so that the lines of his return intersected the lines of his going.

Back on the bank where the others waited, Miller got down from his horse and walked over to them; his water-filled boots squished with each step, and water streamed behind him, darkening the rock.

"It's a good crossing," Miller said. "Nearly flat all the way, and straight across. It's a little deep right in the middle, but the oxen can make it all right; and the wagon's heavy enough to weight itself down."

"All right," Schneider said. "Let's get going."

"Just a minute," Miller said. "Fred, I want you to ride alongside the lead team and guide them across. I'll go in front, you just follow along behind me."

Schneider squinted at him for a few moments, and then shook his head.

"No," he said, "I think maybe I'd better not do it. I never have liked oxen, and they ain't too fond of me. Now if it was mules, I'd say all right. But not oxen."

"There's nothing to it," Miller said. "You just ride a little downstream from them; they'll go right straight across."

Schneider shook his head again. "Besides," he said, "I don't figure it's my job."

Miller nodded. "No," he agreed, "I guess it ain't, rightly speaking. But Charley ain't got a horse."

"You could let him have yours," Schneider said, "and you could double up with Will, here."

"Hell," Miller said, "there ain't no use making a fuss over it. I'll lead them across myself."

"No," Charley Hoge said. The three men turned to him in surprise. Charley Hoge cleared his throat. "No," he said again. "It's my job. And I don't need no horse." He pointed with his good hand to the off-ox in the lead team. "I'll ride that one acrost. That's the best way to do it, anyhow."

Miller looked at him narrowly for a moment. "You feel up to it, Charley?" he asked.

"Sure," Charley Hoge said. He reached into his shirt and pulled out the warped and stained Bible. "The Lord will provide. He'll turn my steps in the right path." He contracted his stomach and thrust the Bible inside his shirt under his belt.

Miller looked at him for another moment, and then abruptly nodded. "All right. You follow straight along behind me, hear?" He turned to Andrews. "Will, you take your horse across now. Go just like I did, only you go straight across. If you find any big rocks, or any big holes, stop your horse and yell out so we can see where they are. It won't take a very big jolt to turn this wagon over."

"All right," Andrews said. "I'll wait for you on the other side."

"Now be careful," Miller said. "Take it slow. Let your horse set her own speed. That water's mighty fast."

"I'll be all right," Andrews said. "You and Charley just take care of the hides."

Andrews walked to his horse and mounted. As he turned toward the river, he saw Charley Hoge pull himself up on one of the oxen. The beast moaned and pulled away from the strange weight, and Charley Hoge patted it on the shoulder. Schneider and Miller watched Andrews as he set his horse into the first shallow.

The horse shuddered beneath him as the water climbed above its fetlocks and swirled about its knees. Andrews set his eyes upon the wet and trampled earth across the river where Miller had emerged, and kept his horse pointed straight toward it. Beneath him he felt the uncertainty of the horse's footing; he tried to make himself loose and passive in the saddle, and slackened the reins. In the middle of the river, the water, sharply cold, came midway between his ankle and his knee; the heavy thrust pressed his leg against the horse's side. As the animal stepped slowly forward, Andrews felt for brief instants the sickening sensation of weightlessness as he and the horse were buoyed and pushed aside by the swift current. The roaring was intense and hollow in his ears; he looked down from the point of land that dipped and swayed in his sight, and saw the water. It was a deep but transparent greenish brown, and it flowed past him in thick ropes and sheeted wedges, in shapes that changed with an incredible complexity before his gaze. The sight dizzied him, and he raised his eyes to look again at the point of earth toward which he aimed.

He reached the shallows without coming across a hole or rock that was likely to cause difficulty for the wagon. When his horse clambered upon dry land, Andrews dismounted and waved to the men who waited on the opposite bank.

Miller, small in the distance that was intensified by the water rushing across it, raised his arm in a stiff response and then let it drop to his side. His horse started forward. After he had gone fifteen or twenty feet into the river, he turned and beckoned to Charley Hoge, who waited astride one of the lead oxen, his oxgoad held high in his good left hand. He let the goad down lightly upon the shoulder of the lead ox, and the team lumbered forward into the shallows. The load of skins swayed as the wagon wheels came off the tiny drop of the bank into the river.

On the bank upstream from the wagon, Schneider waited on his horse, watching intently the progress of the wagon as it went deeper in the swirling river. After a minute, he too turned his horse and followed the wagon, eight or ten yards upstream from it.

When the lead oxen sank to their bellies in the heavy stream, the oxen farthest back, next to the wagon, still had not gone above their knees. Andrews then understood the safety of the crossing; by the time the farthest oxen were insecure and had the struggle to maintain their footing, the other oxen would be in the shallows and could pull the main weight of the wagon; and when the wagon was sunk to its bed, and the sides would receive the full force of the river, all the oxen would be in shallower water, and could maintain a steady pull upon it. He smiled a little at the fear he had not known he had until the instant he lost it, and watched Miller, who had pulled many yards ahead of the lead oxen, hurry his horse through the shallows and up on dry land. Miller dismounted, nodded curtly to Andrews, and stood on the riverbank, guiding Charley Hoge toward him with quick beckoning gestures of both hands.

When the lead oxen were in the shallows within ten feet of the bank, Charley Hoge slipped off the bull he had ridden across and sloshed in the knee-deep water beside them, looking back at the wagon, which was nearing the deepest part of the river. He slowed the oxen and spoke soothingly to the lead team.

Miller said: "Easy, now. Bring them in easy."

Andrews watched the wagon dip toward the hollow in the center of the river. He turned his head a little, and saw that Schneider, still upstream, had pulled up even with the wagon. Water curled about the belly of his horse; Schneider's eyes intently watched the water before him, between the ears of his slowly moving horse. Andrews looked away from Schneider, swinging his gaze upriver, following the dense line of trees that in some spots grew so close to the bank that their trunks were darkened halfway up by the flung spray. But suddenly his gaze fixed itself upon the river. For an instant paralyzed, he raised himself as tall as he could and looked intently at that point that had caught his eye.

A log, splintered at the downstream end, nearly as thick as a man's body and twice as long, bobbed like a matchstick and hurtled forward, half in and half out of the swirling water. Andrews ran to the edge of the bank and shouted, pointing upstream:

"Schneider! Look out! Look out!"

Schneider looked up and cupped his ear toward the faint voice that came across the roaring of the water. Andrews called again, and Schneider leaned forward a little in his saddle, trying to hear.

The splintered end of the log thrust into the side of Schneider's horse with a ripe splitting thud that was clearly audible above the roar of the water. For an instant the horse struggled to keep upright; then the log tore away, and the horse gave a short high scream of agony and fear, and fell sideways toward the wagon; Schneider went into the water as the horse fell. The horse turned completely over, above Schneider, and for an instant the great gaping hole that had been its belly reddened the water around it. Schneider came up between the fore and hind legs of the horse, facing the men who stood on the bank. For an instant, the men could see his face quite clearly; he was frowning a little, as if vaguely puzzled, and his lips were twisted in a slight grimace of annoyance and contempt. He put out his left hand, as if to push the horse away from him; the horse turned again and one of its hind hooves thudded heavily high on Schneider's head. Schneider stiffened to his full length and quivered as if in a chill; his expression did not change. Then the blood came down solidly over his face like a red mask, and he toppled slowly and stiffly into the water beside his horse.

The horse and the log hit the wagon broadside at almost the same instant. The wagon was pushed sideways over the rocks; the high load swayed, and pulled the wagon; water gathered over the feebly threshing horse, and piled upon the bottom of the wagon bed. With a great groan, the wagon toppled on its side.

As it toppled, Charley Hoge jumped out of the way of the oxen, which were being pulled back into the river by the weight of the overturned wagon. For a moment, the wagon drifted lazily at the middle of the river, held to some stability by the weight of the near oxen, which threshed against their yokes and beat the water to a froth; then, caught more firmly, the wagon scraped against the rock bottom of the river, and swung lazily around, dragging the oxen with it. As the oxen's footholds on the river bed were loosened, the wagon drifted more swiftly away and began to break up on the heavier rocks downstream. The lashing that held the load broke, and buffalo hides exploded in all directions upon the water, and were rapidly borne out of sight. For perhaps a minute, the men who stood on the bank could see the oxen struggling head over heels in the water, and could see the smashed wagon turning and drifting into the distance. Then they could see nothing, though they stood for several minutes more looking downstream where the wagon had disappeared.

Andrews dropped to his hands and knees and swung his head from side to side like a wounded animal. "My God!" he said thickly. "My God, my God!"

"A whole winter's work," Miller said in a flat dead voice. "It took just about two minutes."

Andrews raised his head wildly, and got to his feet. "Schneider," he said. "Schneider. We've got to—"

Miller put his hand on his shoulder. "Take it easy, boy. Won't do no good to worry about Schneider."

Andrews wrung his hands; his voice broke. "But we've got to—"

"Easy," Miller said. "We can't do anything for him. He was dead when he hit the water. And it would be foolish to try to look for him. You saw how fast them oxen was carried down."

Andrews shook his head numbly. He felt his body go loose, and felt his legs shamble away from Miller. "Schneider," he whispered. "Schneider, Schneider."

"He was a blasphemer," Charley Hoge's voice cracked high and thin. Andrews stumbled over to him, and looked blearily down at his face.

Charley Hoge looked unseeingly down the river; his eyes blinked rapidly, and the muscles of his face twitched uncontrolled, as if his face were falling apart. "He was a blasphemer," Charley Hoge said again, and nodded rapidly. He closed his eyes, and clutched at his belly, where his Bible was still strapped. He said in a high thin singsong voice: "He lay with scarlet women and he fornicated and he blasphemed and he took the name of the Lord in vain." He opened his eyes and turned his unseeing face toward Andrews. "It's God's will. God's will be done."

Andrews backed away from him, shaking his head as Charley Hoge nodded his.

"Come on," Miller said. "Let's get out of here. Nothing we can do."

Miller led Charley Hoge up to his horse and helped him to mount behind the saddle. Then he swung himself up and called back to Andrews: "Come on, Will. The sooner we get away from here, the better it'll be."

Andrews nodded, and stumbled toward his horse. But before he mounted he turned and looked again at the river. His eye was caught by something on the opposite bank. It was Schneider's hat, black and sodden and shapeless, caught and held by the water between two rocks that jutted out from the bank.

"There's Schneider's hat," Andrews said. "We ought not to leave it there."

"Come on," Miller said. "It's going to get dark soon."

Andrews mounted his horse and followed Miller and Charley Hoge as they rode slowly away from the river.

PART THREE

1.

O N A bleak afternoon late in May, three men rode in an easterly direction along the Smoky Hill Trail; a northern wind slanted a fine, cold rain upon them so that they huddled together, their faces turned down and away. For ten days they had come in nearly a straight line across the great plains, and the two horses that carried them were tired; their heads drooped downward, and their bony sides heaved at the exertion of walking on level ground.

Shortly past midafternoon, the sun broke through the slate-like clouds, and the wind died. Steam rose from the mud through which their horses stumbled, and the wet heat stifled the men who sat lethargically on their saddles. On their right were still visible the low-lying trees and bushes that lined the banks of the Smoky Hill River. For several miles they had been off the trail, cutting across the flat country toward Butcher's Crossing.

"Just a few more miles," Miller said. "We'll be there before dark."

Charley Hoge, sitting behind Miller, eased his buttocks on the bony rump of the horse; his good hand was hooked into Miller's belt, and the stump of his right wrist hung loosely at his side. He looked across at Andrews, who rode abreast of Miller; but there was no recognition in his eyes. His lips moved silently, and every now and then his head bobbed quickly, nervously, as if he responded to something that the others did not hear.

A little more than an hour later they were in sight of the humped bank of the narrow stream that cut across the road to Butcher's Crossing. Miller dug his heels into his horse's sides; the horse jumped forward, trotted for a few moments, and then settled into its usual slow gait. Andrews raised himself in his saddle, but he could not see the town above the high banks of the stream. Where they rode now, the rain had not fallen; and the dust of the road, stirred by the slow shuffle of their horses' hooves, rose about them and clung to their damp clothing, and streaked their faces where the sweat ran.

They came up the road over the hump of river bank, and Andrews got a quick glimpse of Butcher's Crossing before they descended into the narrow gulley where the shallow stream ran. It was little fuller than it had been last fall; the water that trickled along its bed was a thick, muddy brown. The men let their horses halt in the middle and drink of the muddy water before they urged them on.

They passed on their left the clump of cottonwoods, scrawny and bare in new leafage; again, Andrews strained his eyes eastward toward Butcher's Crossing. In the late afternoon sun the buildings were ruddy where they were not sharply cast in shadow. A lone horse grazed between themselves and the town; though several hundred yards distant, it raised its head at their approach and trotted away in a short burst of speed.

"Let's turn in here for a minute," Miller said, and jerked his head in the direction of the wagon-track road to their right. "We got things to talk over with McDonald."

"What?" Andrews said. "What do we need to talk to him about?"

"The hides, boy, the hides," Miller said impatiently. "We still got better'n three thousand hides waiting for us where we left them."

"Of course," Andrews said. "For a minute I forgot."

He turned his horse and rode beside Miller upon the twin tracks of earth worn bare by passing wagons. Here and there in the wagon tracks, small tufts of new grass sprouted and spread to the level stretch of grass that covered the prairie.

"Looks like McDonald had a good winter," Miller said. "Look at them hides."

Andrews looked up. Bales of buffalo hides were piled about the tiny shack that served McDonald as an office, so that as the men rode up they could see only a small section of the warped roof. The bales spread out from the immediate area of the shack and lay irregularly about the edges of the fenced brining pits. Scattered among the bales were a dozen or more wagons; some, upright, blistered and warped in the heat; their wheels were sunk in the earth and grass grew green and strong above their rims. Others were overturned, the metal bands about the spoked wheels showing brilliant spots of rust in the afternoon sun.

Andrews turned to Miller and started to speak, but the expression on Miller's face stayed him. Beneath the black curly beard, Miller's mouth was loose with puzzlement; his large eyes narrowed as they surveyed the scene.

"Something's wrong here," he said, and dismounted from his horse, leaving Charley Hoge seated slackly behind the saddle.

Andrews got off his horse and followed Miller as he threaded his way among the bales of hides toward McDonald's shack.

The door of the shack was loose on its rusted hinges. Miller pushed it open and the two men went inside. Papers lay scattered on the floor, opened ledgers had spilled from untidy piles, and the chair behind McDonald's desk was overturned. Andrews stooped and picked up a sheet of paper from the floor; the writing had been washed away, but the print of a heel mark still showed upon it. He picked up another, and another; all showed the ravages of neglect and weather.

"Looks like Mr. McDonald hasn't been here for some time," Andrews said.

For several moments Miller looked somberly about the room. "Come on," he said abruptly, and turned and clumped across the floor, his feet grinding into the scattered papers. Andrews followed him outside. The men mounted their horses and rode away from the shack toward Butcher's Crossing.

The single street that bisected the group of shacks and buildings that made up the town was nearly deserted. From the blacksmith shop on their right came the slow light clank of metal striking metal; in the light shadows of the open shelter there was the vague slow movement of a man's body. On the left, set back from the road, was the large sleeping house that lodged many of the hunters during their brief stays in town; the muslin covering of one of the high windows was torn, and it sagged outward and moved sluggishly in the light hot breeze. Andrews turned his head. In the dimness of the livery stable two horses drowsed, standing upright over empty feed troughs. As they passed Jackson's Saloon, two men, who had been sitting on the long bench beside the doorway of the saloon, got slowly up and walked to the edge of the board walk and watched the three men on their two horses. Miller looked closely at the men and then shook his head at Andrews.

"Looks like everybody's asleep or dead," he said. "I don't even recognize them two."

They stopped their horses in front of Butcher's Hotel, and wrapped their reins loosely around the hitching post set several yards away from the walk in front of the building. Before they went inside, they loosened the cinches under the bellies of their horses and untied their bedrolls from behind their saddles. During all this Charley Hoge sat motionless on the rump of Miller's horse. Miller tapped him on the knee and Charley Hoge turned dully.

"Get down, Charley," Miller said. "We're here."

Charley Hoge did not move; Miller grasped his arm and, gently, half pulled him down to the ground. With Charley Hoge walking unsteadily between them, Andrews and Miller went into the hotel.

The wide lobby was almost completely bare; two straight chairs, one of them with a splintered back, stood together against a far wall; a fine patina of dust covered the floor, the walls, and the ceiling. As they walked across to the counter of the desk clerk, their steps left distinct prints on the wood floor.

In the dimness of the enclosing counter an aging man dressed in rough work clothing dozed in a straight chair tilted back against a bare desk. Miller slapped his palm hard on the surface of the counter. The man's rasping breath caught sharply, his mouth closed, and the chair came forward; for an instant he glowered sightlessly; then he blinked. He got up and came unsteadily to the counter, yawning and scratching at the gray stubble around his chin.

"What can I do for you?" he mumbled, and yawned again.

"We want two rooms," Miller said evenly, and threw his bedroll across the counter; dust exploded silently upward, and hung in the dim air.

"Two rooms?" the old man said, his eyes focusing upon them. "You want two rooms?"

"How much?" Miller asked. Andrews threw his bedroll down beside Miller's.

"How much?" The man scratched his chin again; a faint rasping came to Andrews's ears. The old man, still looking at them, fumbled beneath the counter and brought up a closed ledger. "I dunno. Dollar apiece sound all right?"

Miller nodded and shoved the ledger, which the old man had opened in front of him, to Andrews. Miller said: "We'll want some tubs and some hot water, and some soap and razors. How much will that be?"

The old man scratched his chin. "Well, now. What're you fellows used to paying for such a chore?"

"I paid two bits last year," Andrews said.

"That sounds reasonable," the old man said. "Two bits apiece. I think I'll be able to heat up some water for you."

"What's the matter with this damn town?" Miller said loudly, and again slapped his palm upon the counter. "Did everybody die?"

The old man shrugged nervously. "I don't know, mister. I only been here a few days, myself. On my way to Denver, and ran out of money. Man said, you take care of this place good, and you keep what you make. That's all I know."

"Then I don't suppose you've heard of a man named McDonald. J. D. McDonald."

"Nope. Like I said, I only been here—"

"All right," Miller said. "Where are our rooms?"

The old man handed them two keys. "Right up the stairs," he said. "The numbers are on the keys."

"Lead the horses over to the livery stable," Miller said. "They need taking care of bad."

"The horses over to the livery stable," the old man repeated. "Yes, sir."

Miller and Andrews picked up their bedrolls and went to the stairs. The dust lay smooth and unbroken on the steps.

"Looks like we're the first customers in a long time," Andrews said.

"Something's wrong," Miller said. With Charley Hoge between them, the three men bumped together going up the stairs. "I don't like the way things feel."

Their rooms were side by side, just off the stairs; the number on Andrews's key was seventeen. As Miller and Charley Hoge started into their room, Andrews said: "If I get through before you do, I'll be outside. I want to look around a little."

Miller nodded, and pushed Charley Hoge before him.

When Will Andrews turned his key in the lock and pushed the door inward, a billow of musty air came from the unused room. He left the door half open and went to the muslin-covered window; the cloth in its wooden frame was clogged with dust. He detached the frame from the window, and set it on the floor beside a wooden rain shutter which showed no sign of having been used against the weather. A warm breeze moved sluggishly through the room.

Andrews unrolled the mattress on the narrow rope bed, and sat on the bare ticking. He removed his shoes, fumbling with the strips of buffalo hide that months before had replaced the original thongs; the soles were worn thin, and the leather of the uppers had cracked through. He held one shoe in his hands and gazed at it for several moments; curiously, he pulled against the leather; it ripped like heavy paper. Quickly, he removed the rest of his clothing, and heaped it in a pile beside the bed; he unstrapped his stained and crumpled money belt and dropped it on the mattress. Naked, he rose from the bed and stood in the center of the room in the amber light that came through the window. He looked down at his bare flesh; it was a dirty, grayish white, like the underbelly of a fish. He pushed his fore-finger along the hairless skin of his belly; dirt came off in long thin rolls and revealed more dirt beneath. He shuddered, and went to the washstand near the window. He took a dusty towel from the rack, shook it out, and wrapped it around his loins; he went back to the bed and sat, and waited for the old man to come up with his tub and water.

The old man, breathing heavily, came up shortly with two tubs, depositing one in Miller's and Charley Hoge's room and the other in Andrews's room.

Shoving the tub to the center of the floor, the old man looked curiously at Andrews, who remained sitting on the bed.

"By God," he said. "You men sure got a powerful stink to you. How long since you had a bath?"

Andrews thought for a moment. "Not since last August."

"Where you been?"

"Colorado Territory."

"Oh. Prospecting?"

"Hunting."

"For what?"

Andrews looked at him in tired surprise. "Buffalo."

"Buffalo," the old man said, and nodded vaguely. "I think I heared once they used to be buffalo up there."

Andrews did not speak. After a moment the old man sighed and backed toward the door. "Water'll be hot in a few minutes. Anything else you need, just let me know."

Andrews pointed to the heap of clothing on the floor beside the bed. "You might take these out with you, and get me some new ones."

The old man picked up the clothing, holding it in one hand, away from him. Andrews got a bill from his money belt and put it in the man's other hand.

"What'll I do with these?" the old man asked, moving the clothing slightly.

"Burn them," Andrews said.

"Burn them," the man repeated. "Any special kind of clothes you want from the dry goods store?"

"Clean ones," Andrews said.

The old man cackled, and went out of the room; Andrews did not move from the bed until he returned with two buckets of water. He watched as the old man poured them into the tub. From his pockets the old man withdrew a razor, a pair of scissors, and a large bar of yellow soap.

"I had to buy the razor," he said, "but the scissors is mine. I'll bring your clothes up directly."

"Thanks," Andrews said. "And you might as well be heating up some more water."

The old man nodded. "I reckoned this wouldn't get you clean. I've already got some started."

Andrews waited for a few moments after the old man had left the room. Then, holding the soap, he stepped into the lukewarm water and lowered himself. He sloshed water over his upper body and soaped himself vigorously, watching with a kind of ecstasy the dirt fall away in long strips beneath the gritty soap. His body, covered with tiny unhealed insect bites, stung from the strong soap; nevertheless he raked his finger-nails roughly across his flesh, working the soap in, and leaving long red welts in crisscrosses on his body. He soaped his hair and beard and watched the black streams of water run back into the tub. His own stench, released by the cleansing he gave himself, rose from the water, and made him hold his breath.

When the old man came back in his room with fresh water, Andrews, naked and dripping grayish water on the bare floor, helped him lug the tub to the open window. They emptied it on the sidewalk below. The water splashed into the street and was immediately absorbed into the dust.

"Whew," the old man said. "That's mighty powerful water." He had brought Andrews's new clothes with him and had tossed them upon the bed before they emptied the water; now he pointed to them. "Hope they fit; it was the nearest I could get to what you throwed away."

"They'll be all right," Andrews said.

He bathed more leisurely, building suds over his body and watching them float on the surface of the water. At last he stepped from the tub and toweled himself dry, marveling at the whiteness of his skin, and slapping it to see the rosy welts appear there. Then he went to the washbasin, where the old man had left the razor and scissors. He raised his eyes to the mirror that was hung crookedly above the basin.

Though he had seen his face dimly and darkly in the pools and streams where they had watered, from the mountains across the great plain, and though he had grown used to the feel upon his face and beneath his fingers of the long tangled beard and hair, he was not prepared for what he saw in the mirror. His beard, still damp from the bath, lay twisted in light brown cords on the lower half of his face, so that it seemed he peered at himself in a mask that made his face like that of anyone he might imagine. The upper half of his face was a bloodless brown, darker than his beard or hair; it had hardened in the weather, so that he could see no expression and no identity where he looked. His hair grew over his ears, and hung nearly to his shoulders. For a long time he stared at himself, turning his head from side to side; then he slowly took up the scissors from the table and started cutting away at his beard.

The scissors were dull, and the strands of hair that he caught and lifted in one hand slipped between the blades so that he had to angle the scissor blades to his face, half cutting and half hacking at the tough, fine hair. When he had reduced the beard to a long stubble, he soaped his face with the yellow soap he had bathed in and drew the razor in short careful strokes over his skin. When he finished, he rinsed the soap from his face and looked at himself again in the mirror. Where the beard had been his flesh was a dead white, startling against the brown of his forehead and cheeks. He flexed the muscles of his face, retracting the mouth in a mirthless grin, and took the skin along his jaw between a thumb and forefinger; it felt numb and lifeless. His whole face was diminished, and it stared palely at him from its tangle of hair. He took the scissors up again, and began hacking away at the hair that lay in thick ropes about his face.

After several minutes, he stood back from the mirror and surveyed his work. His hair was awkwardly and unevenly cut, but it no longer made his face appear that of a child. He brushed together the tufts of hair that had settled on the table, crushed them in his hands, and dropped them out of his window, where they dispersed in the air and floated slowly to the ground, catching the late sunlight in flashing glints and then disappearing as they settled on the sidewalk and the earth below him.

The clothes that the old man had got for him were rough and ill-fitting, but the coarse clean feel of them gave his body a vitality and a sensation of delicacy that it had not had in many months. He turned the bottoms of the sharply creased black broadcloth trousers up over the tops of his stiff new shoes, and opened the top button of the heavy blue shirt. He went out of his room, and in the hall paused before Miller's and Charley Hoge's door. He heard from within the sounds of splashing water. He went down the stairs, through the lobby, and stood on the board sidewalk outside the hotel in the heat and stillness of the late afternoon.

The odd lengths of scrap wood that constituted the sidewalk had warped during the winter, and many of them curved upward from their width, so that Andrews in his new shoes had to walk carefully upon them. He looked up and down the street. To the left of the hotel, east of town, a broad square of packed grassless earth shone in the late rays of the sun. After a moment of thought, Andrews recalled that this was the site of the large army tent that had been the establishment of Joe Long, Barbar. Andrews turned, and walked slowly in the other direction, past the hotel. He walked past a half-dugout that was deserted and crumbling in upon itself, and did not pause until he reached the livery stable. In the dimness of the large stable, the two horses that had brought them into Butcher's Crossing munched slowly over a trough of grain. He started to go into the stable, but he did not. He turned slowly and walked back toward the hotel. He leaned against the doorframe and surveyed that part of the town he could see, and waited for Miller and Charley Hoge to come down to join him.

The sun had gone down, and the diffused tremendous light from the west caught the dusty haze that hung over the town, softening the hard outlines of the buildings, when Miller and Charley Hoge came out of the hotel and joined Andrews where he stood waiting on the sidewalk. Miller's face, shorn of its black beard, was heavy and white on his massive shoulders; Andrews looked at him with some surprise; except for his torn and filthy clothing, he looked precisely as he had months before, when Andrews had first walked up to him at the table in Jackson's Saloon. It was Charley Hoge who had undergone the most marked change in appearance. His long beard had been clipped as closely as possible with the scissors, though evidently Miller had not risked using a razor; beneath the gray stubble, Charley Hoge's face had lost its lean craftiness; now it was gaunt and vague and drawn; the cheeks were sunken deeply, the eyes were cavernous and wasted, and the mouth had gone slack and loose; the lips moved unevenly over the broken, yellow teeth, but no sound came. Charley Hoge stood inertly beside Miller, his arms hanging at his sides, the stump of his right wrist protruding from his sleeve.

"Come on," Miller said. "We've got to find McDonald."

Andrews nodded, and the three men went off the board sidewalk into the dust of the street, angling across it toward the low long front of Jackson's Saloon. One by one, Miller first and Andrews last, they went into the narrow, low-ceilinged barroom. It was deserted. Only one of the half-dozen or so lanterns that hung from the sooty rafters was lighted, and its dim glow met the light from outside that came through the front door and cast the room into great flat shadows. On the planked bar stood a bottle of whisky, half empty; beside it was an empty glass.

Miller strode to the bar and slapped his hand heavily upon it, causing the empty glass to jump and teeter on its edge. "Hey!" Miller called, and called again: "Hey, bartender!" No one answered his call.

Miller shrugged, took the bottle of whisky by its neck, and poured the glass nearly full. "Here," he said to Charley Hoge, and pushed the glass toward him. "It's on the house."

Charley Hoge, standing beside Andrews, looked for a moment without moving at the drink of whisky. His eyes turned to Miller, and back to the drink again. Then he seemed to fall forward toward the bar, his feet moving just quickly enough to keep the balance of his body. He took the drink unsteadily, sloshing it over his hand and wrist, and put it thirstily to his lips, leaning his head back and taking it in long noisy gulps.

"Take it slow," Miller said, grasping his crippled arm and shaking it. "You ain't had any in a long time."

Charley Hoge shook his arm as if Miller's hand were a fly upon bare skin. He set the glass down empty; his eyes were streaming and he gasped as if he had been running a long distance. Then his face tightened, and paled; he held his breath for an instant; almost nonchalantly, he leaned across the bar and retched upon the floor behind it.

"Too fast," Miller said. "I told you." He poured only an inch of whisky into the glass. "Try her again."

Charley Hoge drank it in a single gulp. He waited for a moment, and then nodded to Miller. Miller filled the glass again. The bottle was almost empty. He waited until Charley Hoge had drunk some more of the whisky; then he emptied the bottle into his glass, and tossed the bottle behind the bar.

"Let's see if there's anybody in the other room," he said.

Again one by one, with Miller in the lead, the three men went through the door that led into the large room next to the bar. The room was dim, lighted only by the flowing dusk that seeped through the narrow windows set high in the walls. Only two of the many tables were occupied; at one of them, across the room, sat two women, who glanced up as the three men walked through the door. Andrews took a step toward them, peering at them through the dimness; they returned his stare dully; he looked away. At the other table were two men, who glanced at them and then returned to a low-voiced conversation. One of the men wore a white shirt and an apron; he was very small and fat with large moustaches and a perfectly round face that glistened in the dimness. Miller clumped across the rough floor and stood beside the table.

"You the bartender?" he asked the small man.

"That's right," the man said.

"I'm looking for McDonald," Miller said. "Where's he staying?"

"Never heard of no McDonald," the bartender said, and turned back to his companion.

"Used to be the hide buyer around here," Miller said. "His place is just out of town, by the creek. Name of J. D. McDonald."

The bartender had not turned again while he was speaking. Miller let his hand fall on the man's shoulder. He squeezed and pulled the man around to face him.

"You pay attention when I'm talking to you," Miller said quietly.

"Yes, sir," the bartender said. He did not move beneath Miller's grasp. Miller loosened his hand.

"Now, did you hear what I said?"

"Yes, sir," the bartender said. He licked his lips, and put one hand to his shoulder and rubbed it. "I heard you. But I never heard of him. I only been here a month or maybe a little more. I don't know anything about any McDonald or any hide buyer."

"All right," Miller said. He stepped back from the man. "You go in the bar and bring us back a bottle of whisky and some eats. My friend here—" he pointed to Charley Hoge—"threw up behind your counter. You'd better clean it up."

"Yes, sir," the bartender said. "All I'll be able to get for you is some fried side meat and warmed-up beans. That be all right?"

Miller nodded and went to a table several feet away from that of the two men. Andrews and Charley Hoge followed behind him.

"That son-of-a-bitch McDonald," Miller said. "He's run out on us. Now we probably won't be able to get any money for those hides we left until we can deliver them."

Andrews said, "Mr. McDonald probably just got tired of the paper work, and took off for a while. There are too many hides back at his place for him just to leave them."

"I don't know," Miller said. "I never trusted him."

"Don't worry," Andrews said, and looked restlessly about him. One of the two women whispered something to her companion, and got up from the table; she fixed a smile on her face and walked loosely across the floor toward them. Her face was swarthy and thin, and her sparse black hair was fluffed in wisps about it.

"Honey," she said in a thin voice, looking at all of them, her lips pulled back over her teeth, "can I get anything for you? Do you want anything?"

Miller leaned back in his chair, and looked at her with no expression on his face. He blinked twice, slowly, and said: "Sit down. You can have a drink when the man brings the bottle."

The woman sighed and seated herself between Andrews and Miller. Quickly, expertly, she looked them over with small black eyes that moved stiffly behind puffed eyelids. She let the smile loosen on her face.

"Looks like you boys ain't been in town for a long time. Hunters?"

"Yeah," Miller said. "What's wrong around here? This town die?"

The bartender came in with a bottle of whisky and three glasses.

"Honey," the woman said to him, "I left my glass on the other table, and these gentlemen have asked me to have a drink with them. Get it for me, will you?"

The bartender grunted, and got her glass from the other table.

"Do you want my friend to join us?" the woman said, jerking her thumb in the direction of the table where the other woman waited torpidly. "We could make up a little party."

"No," Miller said. "This is all right. Now, what's happened to this town?"

"It's been pretty dead the last few months," the woman said. "No hunters at all. But you wait. Wait till fall. It'll pick up again."

Miller grunted. "Hunting go bad?"

She laughed. "Lord, don't ask me. I don't know anything about that." She winked. "I don't do much talking with the men; that ain't my line."

"You been here long?" Miller asked.

"Over a year," she said, and nodded sadly. "This little town's been good to me; I hate to see it slow down."

Andrews cleared his throat. "Are—many of the same girls still here?"

When she did not smile, the skin hung in loose folds on her face. She nodded. "Some. Lots of them have pulled out, though. Not me. This town's been good to me; I aim to stay around for awhile." She drank deeply from the glass of whisky she had poured.

"If you've been around a year," Miller said, "you must have heard of McDonald. The hide buyer. Is he still around?"

The woman coughed and nodded. "Last I heard, he still was."

"Where's he staying?" Miller asked.

"He was at the hotel for a while," she said. "Last I heard, he was staying in the old bunkhouse, out back."

Miller pushed his barely tasted glass of whisky in front of Charley Hoge. "Drink it," he said, "and let's get out of here."

"Ah, come on," the woman said. "I thought we was going to have a little party."

"You take what's left of this bottle," Miller said, "and you and your friend can have a party. We got business."

"Ah, come on, honey," the woman said, and put her hand on Miller's arm. Miller looked at her hand for a moment, and then casually, with a flick of his fingers, brushed it off, as if it were an insect that had dropped there.

"Well," the woman said, and smiled fixedly, "thanks for the bottle." She took its neck in her bony fingers and got up from the table.

"Wait," Andrews said as she started to move away. "There was a girl here last year—her name was Francine. I was wondering if she was still around."

"Francine? Sure. She's still around. But not for long. She's been packing the last few days. You want me to go up and get her?"

"No," Andrews said. "No, thank you. I'll see her later." He leaned back in his chair, and did not look at Miller.

"For God's sake," Miller said. "Schneider was right. You have had that little whore on your mind. I'd almost forgot about her. Well, you can do what you want about her; but right now we got more important things."

"Don't you want to wait for our food?" Andrews said.

"You can eat later if you want," Miller said. "Right now, we get this McDonald business settled."

They roused Charley Hoge from his contemplation of the empty glass, and went out of the saloon into the dusk. No lights cut through the growing dark. The men stumbled over the board sidewalks as they went up the street. Beyond Jackson's Saloon they turned to their right and made their way past the outdoor staircase that led to the upper floor of Jackson's. As they walked, Andrews looked up at the dark landing and the darker rectangle of the door, and continued looking upward as they passed the building. At the back he saw through a window the faint glow of a lamp; but he could see no movement in the room from which the light came. He stumbled in the thick grass that grew in the open field over which they walked; thereafter he looked before him and guided Charley Hoge beside him.

Some two hundred yards from the rear of Jackson's Saloon, across the field in a westerly angle, the low flat-roofed sleeping house rose vaguely in the dark.

"There's somebody in there," Miller said. "I can see a light."

A weak glow came from the half-opened door. Miller went a few steps ahead of the others, and kicked it open. The three men crowded in; Andrews saw a single huge room, low-raftered and perfectly square. Twenty or thirty beds were scattered about the room; some were overturned, and others were placed at random angles to each other. None of these held mattresses, and none was occupied. At the far end of the room, in a corner, a dim lantern burned, throwing into shadow the shape of a man who sat on the edge of a bed, hunched over a low table. At the sound of the men entering, he lifted his head.

"McDonald!" Miller called.

The figure rose from the bed, and backed out of the light. "Who's that?" he asked in a vague, querulous voice.

The three men advanced toward him, moving through the scattered bed frames. "It's us, Mr. McDonald," Andrews said.

"Who?" McDonald lowered his head and peered out of the light. "Who's that talking?"

The men came into the dim mass of light cast by the lantern hung from a hook in one of the corner rafters. McDonald came close to them, and peered from one of their faces to another, blinking slowly as his protuberant blue eyes took them in.

"My God!" he said. "Miller. Will Andrews. My God! I'd given you up for dead." He came to Andrews, and grasped both his arms with thin, tight hands. "Will Andrews." His hands trembled on Andrews's arms, and then his whole body began trembling.

"Here," Andrews said. "Sit down, Mr. McDonald. I didn't mean to give you a shock."

"My God!" McDonald said again, and sank upon the edge of the bed; he stared at the three men and shook his head from side to side. "Give me a minute to get over it." After a moment, he straightened. "Wasn't there another one of you? Where's your skinner?"

"Schneider," Miller said. "Schneider's dead."

McDonald nodded. "What happened?"

"Drowned," Miller said. "When we were crossing a river on our way back."

McDonald nodded again, vacantly. "You found your buffalo, then."

"We found them," Miller said. "Just like I told you we would."

"Big kill," McDonald said.

"A big one," Miller said.

"How many hides did you bring back?"

Miller breathed deeply, and sat on the edge of a bed facing McDonald. "None," he said. "We lost them in the river, same time Schneider was killed."

McDonald nodded. "The wagon, too, I guess."

"Everything," Miller said.

McDonald turned to Andrews. "Got cleaned out?"

Andrews said, "Yes. But it doesn't matter."

"No," McDonald said. "I guess not."

"Mr. McDonald," Andrews said. "What's the matter here? Why are you staying in this place? We stopped by your office on the way in. What's happened?"

"What?" McDonald said. He looked at Andrews and blinked. Then he laughed dryly. "It takes a lot of telling. Yes, sir. A lot of telling." He turned to Miller. "So you got nothing to show for your trip. You got snowed in the mountains, I guess. And you got nothing to show for a whole winter."

"We got three thousand hides, winter prime, cached away up in the mountains. They're just waiting. We got something to show." Miller looked at him grimly.

McDonald laughed again. "They'll be a comfort to you in your old age," he said. "And that's all they'll be."

"We got three thousand prime hides," Miller said. "That's better than ten thousand dollars, even after our expense of bringing them back down."

McDonald laughed, and his laughter choked in a fit of coughing. "My God, man. Ain't you got eyes? Ain't you looked around you? Ain't you talked to anyone in this town?"

"We had an agreement," Miller said. "You and me. Four dollars apiece for prime hides. Ain't that right?"

"That's right," McDonald said. "That's dead right. Nobody would argue with that."

"And I aim to hold you to it," Miller said.

"You aim to hold me to it," McDonald said. "By God, I wish you could." He got up from the bed and looked down at the three men who sat opposite him. He turned completely around, and, facing them again, lifted his hands and ran his bony fingers through his thinning hair. Then he held his hands, palms up, out toward the three men. "You can't hold me to nothing. Can't you see that? Because I got nothing. Thirty, forty thousand hides down at the pits that I bought and paid for this last fall. All the money I had. You want them? You can have them for ten cents apiece. You might be able to make a little profit on them—next year, or the year after."

Miller lowered his head and swung it before him, slowly, from side to side.

"You're lying," he said. "I can go to Ellsworth."

"Go on," McDonald shouted. "Go on to Ellsworth. They'll laugh at you. Can't you look at it straight? The bottom's dropped out of the whole market; the hide business is finished. For good." He lowered his head and thrust it close to Miller's. "Just like you're finished, Miller. And your kind."

"You're a liar!" Miller said loudly, and moved back away from him. "We had an agreement, man to man. We worked our guts out for them hides, and you ain't going to back out now."

McDonald moved back and looked at him levelly. His voice was cool; "I don't rightly see how I can keep from it. You can't squeeze juice out of a rock." He nodded. "Funny thing. You're just about seven months too late. If you had got back when you was supposed to, you would have got your money. I had it then. You could have helped ruin me."

"You're lying to me," Miller said, more quietly. "It's some trick of yours. Why, just last year, prime hides—prime hides—"

"That was last year," McDonald said.

"Well, what could go wrong in one year? In just one year?"

"You remember what happened to beaver?" McDonald asked. "You trapped beaver once, didn't you? When they stopped wearing beaver hats you couldn't give the skins away. Well, it looks like everybody that wants one has a buffalo robe; and nobody wants any more. Why they wanted them in the first place, I don't know; you never can really get the stink out of them."

"But in just a year," Miller said.

McDonald shrugged. "It was coming. If I'd been back east, I would have knowed it. . . . If you can wait four or five years, maybe they'll find some way to use the leather. Then your prime hides will be just about as good as easy summer skins. You might get thirty, forty cents apiece for them."

Miller shook his head, as if he had been dazed by a blow. "What about the land you own around here?" he asked. "By God, you can sell off some of that and pay us."

"You don't listen to me, do you?" McDonald said. Then his hands started shaking again. "You want the land? You can have that too." He turned and began scrabbling in a box that lay under his bed. He drew out a sheet of paper and laid it on the table and started scribbling on it with the stub of a pen. "Here. I turn it over to you. You can have it all. But you better set yourself to be a dry-land farmer; because you'll have to keep it; or give it away, like I'm giving it to you."

"The railroad," Miller said. "You used to say when the railroad came through, the land would be like gold."

"Ah, yes," McDonald said. "The railroad. Well, it's coming through. They're laying the tracks now. It'll come through about fifty miles north of here." McDonald laughed again. "You want to hear a funny thing? The hunters are selling buffalo meat to the railroad company—and they're letting the hides lay where they skin them, to rot in the sun. Think of all the buffalo you killed. You could have got maybe five cents a pound for all that meat you let lay for the flies and the timber wolves."

There was a silence.

"I killed the timber wolves," Charley Hoge said. "I killed them with strychnine poison."

As if drugged, Miller looked at McDonald, and then at Andrews, and back to McDonald again.

"So you've got nothing now," Miller said.

"Nothing," McDonald said. "I can see it gives you some satisfaction."

"By God, it does," Miller said. "Except that when you ruin yourself, you ruin us too. You sit back here, and we work our guts out, and you say you'll give us money, like that means anything. And then you ruin yourself and take us down with you. But by God, it's almost worth it. Almost."

"Me ruin you?" McDonald laughed. "You ruin yourself, you and your kind. Every day of your life, everything you do. Nobody can tell *you* what to do. No. You go your own way, stinking the land up with what you kill. You flood the market with hides and ruin the market, and then you come crying to me that I've ruined you." McDonald's voice became anguished. "If you'd just listened—all of you. You're no better than the things you kill."

"Go back," Miller said. "Get out of this country. It doesn't want you."

Breathing heavily, McDonald stood slouched tiredly beneath the lantern; his face was cast in a deep shadow. Miller got up from the bed and pulled Charley Hoge up with him. He walked a few steps away from McDonald, pulling Charley Hoge beside him.

"I'm not through with you yet," he said to McDonald. "I'll see you again."

"All right," McDonald said wearily, "if you think it'll do any good."

Andrews cleared his throat. He said to Miller, "I think I'll stay here and talk to Mr. McDonald for a while."

Miller looked at him impassively for a moment; his black hair blended into the darkness behind him, and his heavy pale face was thrust broodingly out of it.

"Do whatever you want," he said. "It makes no difference to me. Our business is finished." And he turned and walked into the darkness, out the door.

After Miller and Charley Hoge had gone, there were several minutes of silence. McDonald reached up to the lantern and raised the wick so that the light about the two men sharpened and made their features more distinct. Andrews moved the bed on which he had been sitting a little closer to the one upon which McDonald slumped.

"Well," McDonald said, "you had your hunt."

"Yes, sir."

"And you lost your tail, just like I said you would."

Andrews did not speak.

"That was what you wanted, wasn't it?" McDonald asked.

"Maybe it was, in the beginning," Andrews said. "Part of it, at least."

"Young people," McDonald said. "Always wanting to start from scratch. I know. You never figured that someone else knew what you was trying to do, did you?"

"I never thought about it," Andrews said. "Maybe because I didn't know what I was trying to do myself."

"Do you know now?"

Andrews moved restlessly.

"Young people," McDonald said contemptuously. "You always think there's something to find out."

"Yes, sir," Andrews said.

"Well, there's nothing," McDonald said. "You get born, and you nurse on lies, and you get weaned on lies, and you learn fancier lies in school. You live all your life on lies, and then maybe when you're ready to die, it comes to you—that there's nothing, nothing but yourself and what you could have done. Only you ain't done it, because the lies told you there was something else. Then you know you could of had the world, because you're the only one that knows the secret; only then it's too late. You're too old."

"No," Andrews said. A vague terror crept from the darkness that surrounded them, and tightened his voice. "That's not the way it is."

"You ain't learned, then," McDonald said. "You ain't learned yet. . . . Look. You spend nearly a year of your life and sweat, because you have faith in the dream of a fool. And what have you got? Nothing. You kill three, four thousand buffalo, and stack their skins neat; and the buffalo will rot wherever you left them, and the rats will nest in the skins. What have you got to show? A year gone out of your life, a busted wagon that a beaver might use to make a dam with, some calluses on your hands, and the memory of a dead man."

"No," Andrews said. "That's not all. That's not all I have."

"Then what? What have you got?"

Andrews was silent.

"You can't answer. Look at Miller. Knows the country he was in as well as any man alive, and had faith in what he believed was true. What good did it do him? And Charley Hoge with his Bible and his whisky. Did that make your winter any easier, or save your hides? And Schneider. What about Schneider? Was that his name?"

"That was his name," Andrews said.

"And that's all that's left of him," McDonald said. "His name. And he didn't even come out of it with that for himself." McDonald nodded, not looking at Andrews. "Sure, I know. I came out of it with nothing, too. Because I forgot what I learned a long time ago. I let the lies come back. I had a dream, too, and because it was different from yours and Miller's, I let myself think it wasn't a dream. But now I know, boy. And you don't. And that makes all the difference."

"What will you do now, Mr. McDonald?" Andrews asked; his voice was soft.

"Do?" McDonald straightened on the bed. "Why, I'm going to do what Miller said I should do; I'm going to get out of this country. I'm going back to St. Louis, maybe back to Boston, maybe even to New York. You can't deal with this country as long as you're in it; it's too big, and empty, and it lets the lies come into you. You have to get away from it before you can handle it. And no more dreams; I take what I can get when I can get it, and worry about nothing else."

"I wish you good luck," Andrews said. "I'm sorry it turned out for you the way it did."

"And you?" McDonald asked. "What about you?"

"I don't know yet," Andrews said. "I still don't know."

"You don't have to," McDonald said. "You come back with

me. We could do all right together; we both know the country now; away from it, we could do something with it."

Andrews smiled. "Mr. McDonald, you talk like you're putting your faith in me, now."

"No," McDonald said. "It's not that at all. It's just that I hate paper work, and you could take some of it off my hands."

Andrews got up from the bed. "I'll let you know when I've had a little more time," he said. "But thanks for asking me." He gave his hand to McDonald; McDonald shook it limply. "I'll be staying at the hotel; don't leave without looking me up."

"All right, boy." McDonald looked up at him; the lids came down slowly over his bulging eyes, and raised. "I'm pleased you came through it alive."

Andrews turned quickly away from him, and went away from the thinning circle of light into the darkness of the room and into the wide darkness that waited outside. A thin new moon hung high in the west, giving the dry grass that rustled under his feet a faint, almost invisible glow. He walked slowly over the uneven ground toward the low dark bulk of Jackson's Saloon; the yellow blob of a lighted lamp still showed in a high window near the center of the building.

He had walked past the long upward angling sweep of the stairs, had stepped upon the board sidewalk, had turned, had even made a few steps down the sidewalk beyond the opening of the stairs, before he knew that he was going to walk up them. He stopped on the sidewalk and turned slowly to walk back to where the stairs began. A weakness came into his legs and rose to his upper body, so that his arms hung loosely at his sides. For several moments he did not move. Then, as if beyond his volition, one of his feet rose to find the first step. Slowly, his hands not touching the bannister on his left nor the wall on his right, he went up the stairs. Again, at the landing at the top of the stairs, he paused. He breathed deeply of the warm, smoky air that hung about the town, until the weakness of his body was gathered into his lungs and breathed out upon the air. He fumbled for the door latch, lifted it, and pushed the door inward. He walked through the doorway and closed the door behind him. A hot still air enclosed him and pressed upon his flesh; he blinked his eyes and breathed more heavily. It was several moments before he realized the depth of the darkness in which he stood; he could see nothing; he took a blind step forward to keep his balance.

He found the wall on his left, and let his hand slide lightly over it as he groped his way forward. His hand went over the recesses of two doorways before he came to a door beneath the sill of which a thin line of yellow light seeped. He stood for a moment close to the door, listening; he heard a rustle of movement from within the room, and then silence. He waited for a moment more, and then stood back from the door and closed his loose hand into a fist and rapped upon it, twice. He heard another rustle of clothing and the light bare pad of feet. The door opened a few inches; he could see nothing but the yellow light, which he felt upon his face. Very slowly, the door opened wider, and he saw Francine, a shape against the glow of the lamp behind her, one hand upon the edge of the door and the other clasped at the collar of a loose wrapper that hung nearly to her ankles. He stood stiff and unmoving and waited for her to speak.

"Is it you?" she asked after a long moment. "Is it Will Andrews?"

"Yes," he said, still stiff and unmoving.

"I thought you were dead," she whispered. "Everybody thought you were dead." Still she did not move from the doorway. Andrews stood awkwardly before her and shifted his weight. "Come in," she said. "I didn't mean to keep you standing outside."

He walked into the room, past Francine, and stood near the edge of the thin carpet; he heard the door close behind him. He turned but he did not look directly at her.

"I hope I didn't disturb you," he said. "I know it's late, but we only got in a few hours ago and I wanted to see you."

"You're all right?" Francine asked, coming closer and looking at him in the light. "What happened to you?"

"I'm all right," he said. "We got snowed in; we had to stay in the mountains all winter."

"And the others?" Francine asked.

"Yes," Andrews said. "All except Schneider. He got killed on the way back, while we were crossing a river."

Almost reluctantly, he raised his eyes and looked at her. Her long yellow hair was pulled in a tight braid so that it lay flat against her head; a few thin lines of tiredness ran from the corners of her eyes; her pale lips were parted over her rather large teeth.

"Schneider," she said. "He was the big man that spoke German to me."

"Yes," Andrews said. "That was Schneider."

Francine shivered in the heat of the room. "I didn't like him," she said. "But it's not good to think that he's dead."

"No," Andrews said.

She moved about the room, her fingers trailing along the carved wood that framed the back of the sofa and restlessly rearranging the knickknacks on the table beside it. Every now and then she looked up at Andrews and gave him a quick, puzzled smile. Andrews watched her movements closely, not speaking, hardly breathing.

She laughed low in her throat, and came across the room to him, where he stood near the door. She touched his sleeve.

"Come over in the light so I can see you better," she said, and pulled gently on the cloth of his shirt sleeve.

Andrews let himself be led near to the table beside the red couch. Francine looked at him closely.

"You haven't changed much," she said. "Your face is browner. You're older." She caught his forearms in both her hands, and lifted them, turning his palms upward. "Your hands," she said sadly, and ran her fingers lightly over one of his palms. "They're hard now. I remember, they were so soft."

Andrews swallowed. "You said they would be hard when I got back. Do you remember?"

"Yes," she said. "I remember."

"That was a long time ago."

"Yes," Francine said. "All winter I've thought you were dead."

"I'm sorry," he said. "Francine—" He paused, and looked down at her face. Her pale blue eyes, wide and transparent, waited for whatever he had to say. He closed his fingers around her hand. "I've wanted to tell you— All winter, while we were snowed in, I thought about it."

She did not speak.

"The way I left you that night," he continued. "I wanted you to know—it wasn't you, it was me. I wanted you to understand about it."

"I know," Francine said. "You were ashamed. But you shouldn't have been. It wasn't as important as you thought. It is—" She shrugged. "It is the way some men are with love, at first."

"Young men," Andrews said. "You said I was very young."

"Yes," Francine said, "and you became angry. It is the way young men are with love. . . . But you should have come back. It would have been all right."

"I know," Andrews said. "But I thought I couldn't. And then I was too far away."

She looked at him closely; she nodded. "You are older," she said again; there was a trace of sadness in her voice. "And I was wrong: you have changed. You have changed so that you can come back."

"Yes," he said. "I have changed that much, at least."

She moved away from him, and turned so that her back was to him, her body outlined sharply by the lamplight. For a long moment there was silence between them.

"Well," Andrews said. "I wanted to see you again, to tell you—" He paused, and did not finish. He started to turn away from her, toward the door.

"Don't go," Francine said. She did not move. "Don't go away again."

"No," Andrews said; he stood still where he had turned. "I won't go away again. I'm sorry. I wasn't trying to make you ask me. I want to stay. I should have—"

"It doesn't matter. I want you to stay. When I thought you were dead, I—" She paused, and shook her head sharply. "You will stay with me for a while." She turned, and shook her head sharply; and the reddish-gold light from the lamp trembled about her hair. "You will stay with me for a while. And you must understand. It's not like it is with the others."

"I know," Andrews said. "Don't talk about it."

They looked at each other without speaking for several moments, making no move toward each other. Then Andrews said: "I'm sorry. It's not the same as it was, is it?"

"No," Francine said. "But it's all right. I'm glad you came back."

She turned away from him and leaned over the lamp. She lowered the wick; still leaning, she looked back over her shoulder at Andrews, and for a long moment studied his face; she did not smile. Then she blew sharply into the lamp chimney and darkness cut across the room. He heard the rustle of Francine's clothing and caught a glimpse of her dim shape as she walked before the window. He heard the rustle of bedclothing being turned back and heard the heavier sound of a body sliding upon sheets. For a while he did not move. Then he fumbled at the buttons of his shirt as he moved across the room to where Francine waited in the darkness.

2.

HE TURNED in the darkness, and felt beneath him the bed sheets dampened by his own sweat. He had awakened suddenly from a deep sleep, and for a moment he did not know where he was. A slow, regular rasp of breath came from beside him; he reached out his hand; it touched warm flesh, and rested there, and moved slightly as the flesh was moved by its breathing.

For five days and nights Will Andrews had stayed in the small close room with Francine, emerging from it only when he took food or drink or purchased some articles of clothing from the depleted stock of Bradley's Dry Goods store. After the first night with Francine he lost all consciousness of time, much as he had lost it back in the mountains, during the storm, under his shelter of snow and buffalo hide. In the dim room, with its single window that remained always curtained, morning became indistinguishable from afternoon; and so long as the lamp was kept burning, it was difficult for him to tell day from night.

In this close half-world of perpetual twilight he immersed himself. He spoke to Francine infrequently; he clasped her to him and heard themselves speak only in their heavy breathing and wordless cries, until at last he thought he found his only existence there. Beyond the four walls that surrounded him he could imagine only a nothingness which was a brightness and a noise that pressed threateningly against him. If he looked too long and too intently, the walls themselves seemed to press upon him, and the objects in his sight—the red couch, the carpet, the knickknacks scattered upon the tables—seemed obscurely to threaten the comfort he found in the half-darkness where he lived. Naked in the dark beside the passive body of Francine, with his eyes closed, he seemed to float weightlessly within himself; and even in waking he partook of some of the quality of the deep sleep he found in the moments after his love-making with Francine.

Gradually he came to look upon his frequent and desperate unions with Francine as if they were performed by someone else. As if from a distance, sightlessly, he observed himself and his sensations as he fulfilled his needs upon a body to which, meaninglessly, he attached a name. Sometimes, lying beside Francine, he looked down the pale length of his own body as if it had nothing to do with himself; he touched his chest, where fine hair like down curled sparsely on the white flesh, and wondered at the sensation of his hand brushing lightly above his skin. Beside him, at these moments, Francine seemed hardly to have any relation to him; she was a presence which assuaged a need in him that he barely knew he had, until the need was met. Sometimes, heavy upon her and lost in the darkness of his passion, he was surprised to find within himself qualities of sensation of which he had been unaware; and when he opened his eyes, meeting the eyes of Francine open and wide and unfathomable below him, again he was almost surprised that she was there. Afterward, he remembered the look in her eyes and wondered what she was thinking, what she was feeling, in the close moments of their passion.

And finally this wondering drew his mind and his eye away from the center of his self and focused them upon Francine. Covertly he watched her as she walked about the dim room, clothed loosely in her thin gray wrapper, or as she lay naked on the bed beside him. Not touching her, he let his eyes go over her body, over her round untroubled face framed loosely by the yellow hair that in the dimness was dark upon the bed sheets; over her full breasts that were laced delicately with an intricate network of blue veins; over her gently mounded belly, which flowed beneath the fine light maidenhair caught in the faint gleams of light that seeped into the room; and down the large firm legs that tapered to her small feet. Sometimes he fell quietly asleep gazing at her, and awoke as quietly, his eyes again upon her, but upon her without recognition, so that he searched again her face and her form as if he had not seen them before.

Near the end of the week a restlessness came upon him. No longer content to lie torpidly in the warm dark room, he more and more frequently left it to wander about the single street of Butcher's Crossing. Seldom did he speak to anyone; never did he linger for more than a few minutes at any place he stopped. He was content to let the sunlight seep into him, as he blinked his eyes upon the brightness. He went once to Butcher's Hotel to pick up his bedroll, to pay for his brief lodging there, and to inform the clerk that he would not be back; once he wandered down the road west of town and rested beneath the grove of cottonwood trees, gazing across the area piled with baled hides that had been McDonald's place of business; several times he went into the bar of Jackson's Saloon and took a glass of luke-warm beer. Once, in the bar, he saw Charley Hoge seated at a rear table, alone except for a bottle of whisky and a half-filled glass. Though Andrews stood for several minutes at the bar, sipping his beer, and though Charley Hoge's glance passed him several times, Charley Hoge gave no sign that he saw him.

Andrews walked the length of the bar and sat down at the table; he nodded to Charley Hoge, and spoke in greeting.

Charley Hoge looked at him blankly and did not answer.

"Where's Miller?" Andrews asked.

"Miller?" Charley Hoge shook his head. "Where he always is, down at our dugout by the river."

"Is he taking it pretty bad?"

"What?" Charley Hoge asked.

"About the hides," Andrews said. He put his nearly empty glass before him on the table and turned it idly between his hands. "It must have been a blow to him. I guess I never realized how much this all meant to him."

"Hides?" Charley Hoge said vaguely, and blinked his eyes. "Miller's all right. He's down at the dugout, resting. He'll be along directly."

Andrews started to speak, and then looked closely into the wide blank eyes that stared at him. "Charley," he said, "are you all right?"

A small perplexed frown crossed Charley Hoge's face; then

his expression was clear and empty. "Sure. I'm all right." He nodded rapidly. "Let's see, now. You're Will Andrews, ain't you?"

Andrews could not look away from the eyes that seemed to grow larger as they stared at him.

"Miller's looking for you," Charley Hoge went on in a high monotonous voice. "Miller says we're all going somewhere, to kill the buffalo. He knows a place in Colorado. I think he wants to see you."

"Charley," Andrews said; his voice trembled, and he clutched his hands hard around the glass to keep them from shaking. "Charley, get hold of yourself."

"We're going on a hunt," Charley Hoge continued in his singsong voice. "You, and me, and Miller. Miller knows a skinner he can get in Ellsworth. It'll be all right. I'm not afraid to go up there any more. The Lord will provide." He smiled and nodded, and continued nodding toward Andrews, though his eyes had turned downward to his glass of whisky.

"Don't you remember, Charley?" Andrews's voice was hollow. "Don't you remember anything about it?"

"Remember?" Charley Hoge asked.

"The mountains—the hunt—Schneider—"

"That's his name," Charley Hoge said. "Schneider. That's the skinner in Ellsworth that Miller's going to get."

"Don't you remember?" Andrews's voice cracked. "Schneider's dead."

Charley Hoge looked at Andrews, shook his head, and smiled; a drop of spittle gathered on his lower lip, swelled, and coursed into the gray stubble around his chin. "Nobody dies," he said softly. "The Lord will provide."

For another moment Andrews looked deep into Charley Hoge's eyes; dull and blue, they were like bits of empty sky reflected in a dirty pool; there was nothing behind them, nothing to stop Andrews's gaze from going on and on. With a sense almost of horror, Andrews drew back and shook his head with a sharp movement. He got up from the table and backed away; Charley Hoge did not change his empty stare or give any sign that he saw Andrews's movement. Andrews turned and walked quickly out of the bar. On the sidewalk, in the bright sunlight, the sense lingered; his legs were weak and his hands were trembling. Swiftly, unsteadily, he went up the street, turned, and took the stairs that led up the side of Jackson's Saloon to Francine's room.

He opened his eyes wide to the dimness of the room; he was still breathing heavily. Francine, lying on the bed, raised herself on an elbow and looked at him; with that movement, her loose gray wrapper parted and one breast drooped toward her forearm, pale against the gray material. Andrews went quickly to the bed; almost roughly, he pulled the wrapper away from her body and let his hands run swiftly, desperately, over her. A small smile came upon Francine's face; her lids dropped; her hands came to Andrews, fumbled with his clothing, and pulled him down upon her.

Later, as he lay beside her, the tumult within him quieted; he tried to tell her of his meeting with Charley Hoge, and of that sense of horror that the meeting had released in him. It was not, he tried to make her understand, so much a result of his recognition that what Charley Hoge showed him in a blind and enveloping stare was something that each of them—Miller, Charley Hoge, Schneider, and even himself—that each of them had had inside them, all along. It was something—he tried to tell her—that McDonald had spoken of by the flickering light of a lantern in the great empty sleeping house the night they had returned to Butcher's Crossing. It was something that he had seen on Schneider's face as he stood stiff and upright in the middle of the river, just after the horse's hoof had split his skull. It was something—

The faint afterlift of a smile hung on Francine's full, pale lips; she nodded; her hand moved softly, soothingly, over his bare chest.

It was something, he continued, speaking in broken phrases that did not say what he intended, it was something that he had felt even in himself, from moment to moment, during the long trek across the plains, and in the kill of the buffalo at the instant the great animal shuddered and crashed to the ground, and in the hot smothering stench that came with the skinning, and in the vision of whiteness during the snowstorm, and in the trackless view in the aftermath of the storm. Was it in everyone? he asked, without using the words. Did it lurk hidden in everyone, waiting to spring out, waiting to devour and rend, until there was left only the blankness he had seen in the blue stare that Charley Hoge now had to give the world? Or did it wait without, crouched like a timber wolf behind a rock, to spring suddenly and horribly without reason upon anyone who passed it by? Or beyond one's knowledge, did one seek it out, this shape of terror, and pass it by in an obscure, perverse hope that it might spring? At that swift moment in the river, did the splintered log seek the belly of Schneider's horse, and the hoof Schneider's skull? Or was it the other way around, Schneider passing by precisely in search of the gray shape, and finding it? What did it mean? he wanted to know. Where had he been?

He turned on the bed; beside him, Francine had dropped into a light sleep; her breath came gently from her parted lips, and her hands lay loosely curled at her sides. He got up quietly, went across the room, turned the wick of the lamp down, and blew into the chimney, extinguishing the light. Through the single curtained window across from him, a last gray light filtered; outside it was growing dark. He returned to the bed and lay carefully next to Francine, on his side, looking at her.

What did it mean? he asked himself again. Even this, his —he hesitated to call it love—his hunger after Francine, what did it mean? He thought again of Schneider; and suddenly he imagined Schneider in his place, alive, lying beside Francine. Without anger or resentment he saw him lying there, and saw him reach across and fondle Francine's breast. He smiled; for he knew that Schneider would not have questioned, as he was questioning; would not have wondered; would not have let a look from Charley Hoge loose within him these doubts and these fears. With a kind of rough and sour friendliness, he would have taken his pleasure from Francine, and would have gone his way, and would not in any particular manner have thought of her again.

As Francine would not have thought again of him. And, he added suddenly, as Francine probably would not think again of him, Will Andrews, who lay now beside her.

In her sleep, in a whisper, Francine mouthed a word that he could not understand; she smiled, her breath caught, she breathed deeply, and moved a little beside him.

Though he did not want the thought to come to him, he knew that he, too, like Schneider, would leave her, would go his own way; though, unlike Schneider, he would think of her, remember her, in a way that he could not yet predict. He would leave her and he would not know her; he would never know her. Now the darkness was nearly complete in the room; he could barely see her face. With his eyes open in the darkness, he slid his hand down her arm until he found her hand, and lay quietly beside her. He thought of the men who had known her appetite and flesh, as he had known them, and had known nothing else; he thought of those men without resentment. In the dark they were faceless, and they did not speak, and they lay still in their breathing like himself. After a long while, his hand still loosely clasping Francine's hand, he slept.

He woke suddenly, and did not know what caused him to awake. He blinked his eyes in the darkness. Across the room a dim glow flickered at the curtained window, died, and flickered again. A shout, thickened by distance, came into the room; the hooves of a horse thudded in the street outside. Andrews eased himself out of bed and stood for a moment, shaking his head sharply. Another burst of excited voices came up from the street; the wooden sidewalks clattered beneath heavy boots. He found his clothes in the darkness and pulled them on hastily; he listened for other sounds; he heard Francine's regular, undisturbed breathing. He went quickly from the room, easing the door shut behind him, and tiptoed down the dark corridor toward the landing outside the building.

To the west, in the direction of the river, clearly visible above the low buildings of Butcher's Crossing, a flame billowed up out of the darkness. For a moment Andrews clutched the handrail of the stairway in disbelief. The fire came from McDonald's shack. Fanned by a heavy breeze from the west, it lighted the tall grove of cottonwoods across the road from it, so that the light gray trunks and deep green leafage were shown clearly against the darkness around them. The fire illumined its own smoke, which coiled upward in thick black ropes, and were dispersed and carried back toward the town on the breeze; a rank, acrid odor bit into Andrews's nostrils. The clatter of running below him broke into his stillness; he went swiftly down the stairs, stumbled on the board sidewalk, and ran up the dusty road toward the fire.

Even at the point where the wagon-wheel trail turned off

the road just above the grove of cottonwoods, he felt the great heat of the fire push against him. He paused there at the twin swaths of worn earth, which were clearly visible in the yellow-red glare of the fire; he was breathing sharply from his running, yet the heavy dregs of sleep were not yet cleared from his mind. Scattered in a wide, irregular semicircle about the flaming shack, fifteen or twenty persons stood, still and small and distinctly outlined against the billowing glare. Singly or in small clusters of two or three, they watched, and did not call out or move; only the dense heavy crackling of the flames came upon the night stillness, and only the great pulsations of the flame moved the men's shadows behind them. Andrews rubbed his hands over his eyes, which were smarting from the haze that settled from the twisting coils of smoke, and ran toward the clusters of people. As he approached them, the intense heat made him turn his face away from the direction he was running, so that he collided with one of the small groups, knocking one of the onlookers aside. The man he bumped against did not look at him; his mouth was open, and his eyes were fixed on the huge blaze, the light of which played upon his face, casting it in deep and changing hues of red.

"What happened?" Andrews gasped.

The man's eyes did not move; he did not speak; he shook his head.

Andrews looked from one face to another and saw no one that he recognized. He went from one person to another, peering into faces that were like distorted masks in the throbbing light.

When he came upon Charley Hoge, cringing before the heat and light and yet crouched as if to spring, he almost did not recognize him. Charley Hoge's mouth was pulled open and awry, as if caught in a cry of terror or ecstasy; and his eyes, streaming from the smoke, were opened wide and unblinking. Andrews could see in them the reduced reflection of the fire, and it seemed almost that the fire was burning there, deep in the vision of Charley Hoge.

Andrews grasped him by the shoulders, and shook him.

"Charley! What happened? How did it start?"

Charley Hoge slid from under his grasp, and darted a few steps away.

"Leave me be," he croaked, his eyes still fixed before him. "Leave me be."

"What happened?" Andrews asked again.

For an instant Charley Hoge turned to him, away from the fire; in the shadow of his brows, his eyes were dull and empty. "The fire," he said. "The fire, the fire."

Andrews started to shake him again; but he paused, his hands lightly resting on Charley Hoge's shoulders. From the crowd came a murmur, low but intense, rising in concert above the hiss and crackle of the flames; he felt more than saw a slight surging forward of the people around him.

He turned in the direction of the movement. For a moment he was blinded by the intensity of the flame—blue and white and yellow-orange, cut through with streaks of black—and his eyes narrowed against the brilliance. Then, among the scattered bales of buffalo hides, high above which the flames turned massively, he saw a dark furious movement. It was Miller, on a horse which reared and screamed in terror at the flames, but which was held under control by the sheer force of Miller's strength. With furious jerks of the reins, which cut the bit deep into the horse's bleeding mouth, and with heavy strokes of his heels against its sides, Miller forced his horse to dart among the scattered bales. For several moments Andrews gaped uncomprehendingly; senselessly, Miller darted up to the very mouth of the flame, and then let his horse pull away, and darted close again.

Andrews turned to Charley Hoge. "What's he doing? He'll kill himself. He—"

Charley Hoge's mouth lifted in a vacant grin. "Watch," he said. "Watch him."

Then Andrews saw, and could not comprehend, and then realized what Miller was doing. Forcing his horse up to the bales piled close to the burning shack, he was pushing the piled bales so that they fell into the open mouth of the flame. Against those bales which lay singly upon the ground, he forced the breast of his horse, and raked the flanks relentlessly, so that the bale was pushed along the ground into the edge of the holocaust.

A cry came from Andrews's dry throat. "The fool!" he

shouted. "He's crazy! He'll kill himself!" And he started to move forward.

"Leave him be," Charley Hoge said. His voice was high and clear and suddenly sharp. "Leave him be," he said again. "It's his fire. Leave him be."

Andrews halted and turned upon Charley Hoge. "You mean— Did he set it?"

Charley Hoge nodded. "It's Miller's fire. You leave him be."

After the first involuntary surge forward, the townspeople had not moved. Now they stood still, and watched Miller gallop recklessly among the smoking bales. Andrews slumped forward, weak and helpless. Like the others, he watched Miller in his wild riding.

After he had tumbled the hides nearest the shack into the fire, Miller rode somewhat away from the flames, leaped off his horse, and tied the reins to the tongue of one of the abandoned wagons that littered the area. A dark figure, shapeless in the outer edges of the firelight, he scuttled to one of the bales that lay on its side near the wagon. He stooped, and in the shadow became indistinguishable from the bale. He straightened, and the shapes became distinct, the bale moving upward as he straightened, seeming to the men who watched a huge appendage of his shoulders. For an instant, he swayed beneath the gigantic shape; then he lurched forward, and ran, halting abruptly at the side of the wagon, so that his burden toppled forward off his shoulders and crashed into the bed of the wagon, which swayed for a moment beneath the impact. Again and again, Miller ranged about the wagon, gathering the bales, swaying beneath their weight, lurching, and running with bent knees to the wagon.

"My God!" one of the townspeople behind Andrews said. "Them bales must weigh three, four hundred pounds."

No one else spoke.

After Miller had boosted the fourth bale upon the wagon, he returned to his horse, unwound a length of rope from his saddle horn, and looped it around the apex of the oaken triangle that secured the wagon tongue to the frame. With the loose end of the rope in his hand, he returned to his horse, mounted it, and wound the end of the rope twice around his saddle horn. He shouted to the horse and dug his heels sharply into its sides; the horse strained forward; the rope tautened, and the wagon tongue lifted beneath the tension. Miller shouted again and slapped his palm on the horse's rump; the sound of the slap cracked above the hiss and rumble of the fire. The wheels moved slowly, screeching on the rusted axles. Again Miller shouted, and dug his heels into the horse; the wagon moved more swiftly; the horse's breath came in heavy groans and its hooves cut the dry earth. Then wagon and horse, as if released from a catapult, careened across the flat earth. Miller yelled once more, and guided horse and wagon straight toward the flame that grew from the shack and the piled hides. At the instant before it seemed that man and horse would plunge into the yellow-hot heart of the fire, Miller swerved his horse suddenly aside, unwinding in a rapid motion the rope from his saddle horn, so that the wagon, unloosed, plunged in its own momentum into the heart of the fire, spewing sparks over an area a hundred feet in diameter. For several moments after the wagon with its load of hides crashed into it, the fire darkened, as if the fury of the assault had extinguished it; then as the wagon caught, it flamed more furiously; and the townspeople drew back several steps before the intensity of the heat.

Behind him Andrews heard the sound of running feet and a shout that was almost a scream, high and animal in its intensity. Dully, he turned. McDonald, his black frock coat flared out at the sides, his arms flailing at random in the air, his sparse hair disheveled, was running toward the knotted bunches of townspeople around the fire—but his eyes looked beyond them wildly, fixed upon his burning office and his smoldering hides. He broke through the group of men, and would have continued running beyond them, had not Andrews caught him and held him back.

"My God!" McDonald said. "It's burning!" He looked wildly around him, at the still and silent men. "Why doesn't somebody do something?"

"There's nothing they can do," Andrews said. "Just stand easy here. You'll get hurt."

Then McDonald saw Miller dragging another wagonload of hides into the widening circle of flames. He turned questioningly to Andrews.

"That's Miller," he said. "What's he doing?" And then, still looking at Andrews, his jaw went slack and his eyes, beneath their tangled brows, widened. "No," McDonald said hoarsely, and shook his head like a wounded beast, from side to side. "No, no. Miller. Did he—"

Andrews nodded.

Another cry, almost of agony, came from McDonald's throat. He twisted away from Andrews, and with hands clenched into fists held like clubs above his head, he ran across the smoldering field toward Miller. On his horse, Miller turned to meet him; his smoke-blackened face broke in a wide and mirthless grin. He waited until McDonald was almost upon him, his fists raised impotently to strike out; then Miller dug his heels into the horse's flanks, dodging away, so that McDonald struck at air. He drew his horse to a halt several yards away from where he had waited; McDonald turned and ran toward him again. Laughing now, Miller spurred away; and again McDonald beat his fists upon emptiness. For perhaps three minutes the two men moved jerkily like marionettes in the open space before the great fire, McDonald, almost sobbing between his clenched yellow teeth, chasing stubbornly and futilely after Miller, and Miller, his lips drawn back in a humorless grimace, always a few feet out of his reach.

Then, suddenly, McDonald stood still; his arms dropped loosely at his sides and he gave Miller a quiet, almost contemplative look, and shook his head. His shoulders slumped; with his knees sagging, he turned away and walked across to where Andrews and Charley Hoge stood. His face was streaked with soot and one eyebrow was singed where a flying ember had caught.

Andrews said: "He doesn't know what he's doing, Mr. McDonald. It looks like he has gone crazy."

McDonald nodded. "Looks like it."

"And besides," Andrews went on, "you said yourself the hides weren't worth anything."

"It's not that," McDonald said quietly. "It's not that they were worth anything. But they were mine."

The three men stood, silent and almost unconcerned, and watched Miller lug the bales and hides and pull the wagons up to stoke the fire. They did not look at each other; they did

not speak. With an interest that appeared nearly detached, Mc-
Donald watched Miller drag the wagons and send them crashing into the ruins of other wagons that stood in stark skeletal
shapes within the fire. Bale after bale, wagon after wagon went
upon the flaming heap, until the fire was more than twice its
original size. It took Miller nearly an hour to complete his task.
When the last wagon with its load of bales went smashing into
the fire, Miller turned and rode slowly up to the three men
who stood together, watching him.

He pulled his horse to a halt; the beast stopped suddenly in
its tracks, its sides heaving so violently that Miller's legs moved
perceptibly above their stirrups; from its mouth, wrenched and
torn by the bit between its teeth, blood dropped and gathered
in the dust. The horse is blown, thought Andrews distantly; it
won't live till daylight.

Miller's face was blacked by the smoke; his eyebrows were
almost completely burned away, and his hair was crisped and
scorched; a long red welt that was beginning to form into a blister lay across his forehead. For a long while Miller looked over
his horse's bowed head, his eyes somberly upon McDonald.
Then his lips drew back over his white teeth, and he laughed
gratingly, deep in his throat. He looked from McDonald to
Charley Hoge to Andrews, and then back to McDonald again.
The grin slowly came off his face. The four men looked at one
another, moving their eyes slowly and searchingly across the
faces about them. They did not move, and they did not speak.

We have something to say to each other, Andrews thought
dimly, but we don't know what it is; we have something we
ought to say.

He opened his mouth, and put his hand out, and moved
toward Miller, as if to speak. Miller glanced down at him;
his glance was casual and distant and empty, without recognition. He loosened himself in his saddle, dug his heels into
the horse's flanks; the horse leaped forward. The movement
caught Andrews unprepared; he stood, his arm still held out,
upraised. The horse's chest caught him on his left shoulder
and spun him around; he stumbled but he did not go to the
ground. When his vision cleared, he saw Miller, hunched over
the horse, riding unsteadily into the distance and the darkness.
As Miller went away, Charley Hoge moved from the two men

and shambled after him. For several moments after they had
gone into the darkness, and after the pounding of hooves had
died in the distance, Andrews stood and looked in the direction they had gone. He turned to McDonald; they looked at
each other in silence. After a while McDonald shook his head,
and he, too, walked away.

3.

NEAR dawn a chill came into the air and pressed lightly against
the backs of the few people who remained to watch the smoldering remains of the fire. They moved forward a few steps to
the edge of the great scorched circle. Small flames licked about
the charred timbers of the shack, blue upon the black-and-
gray ash, and tipped with light yellow; dozens of smoldering
heaps that had been baled hides and that had collapsed upon
themselves, glowed a dull, uneven red, and sent thick twists of
smoke up into the darkness. The uneven flames illumined the
site faintly so that each man who remained stood apart, anonymous in his little portion of shadow. The acrid and rotten smell
of the burned hides grew more intense as the eastward breeze
lessened. One by one, the men who had waited out the fire
turned and made their ways back to Butcher's Crossing with a
quietness that seemed almost deliberate.

At last only Will Andrews remained. He moved toward one
of the charred bales; it appeared to have been blackened but
not consumed by the fire. He kicked it idly and it collapsed,
falling upon itself in a soft explosion of ash. Near the center of
the scorched circle, in which he now stood, one of the timbers
burned through with a faint snap; for an instant, the flames
rose as if their extinguished fury were renewing itself. Until
the brief rekindling spent itself, Andrews stood and gazed with
an absent fixity upon the fire. He thought of Miller, and of the
sudden blankness that had come upon his face in the instant
before he had spurred his horse away from the holocaust he
had started; he remembered the sharpness of Miller's image,
limned and defined and starkly identified against the furious
blaze that he had labored to feed; and he remembered the

merging into darkness of that same stiff figure, as Miller rode away from them on his dying horse. He remembered Charley Hoge, and the image of the fire burning like a vision of hell in his empty eyes; and he remembered the quick, awkward shift of Charley Hoge's body as he turned to follow Miller, as he turned away from the fire, from the townspeople, from the town itself, to follow all that remained to him of the world. And he remembered McDonald, and his flailing against a dark animal shape that would not remain still to receive his fury, a shape that had betrayed a faith that McDonald would not acknowledge; he remembered the sudden slump of McDonald's body when he ceased his vain pursuit and the distant, almost quizzical, look upon his face as he stared before him, as if to search the meaning of his fury.

In the east, above the horizon, the first faint gray of dawn dulled the sky. Andrews moved, his limbs stiff from his long vigil at the fire, turning away from the fire to walk in the lifting darkness back to his room in Butcher's Crossing.

Francine was still asleep. During the night she had thrown aside her covers, and lay now in her nakedness sprawled awkwardly upon the bed, a pale shape that seemed to glow out of the dark. Andrews went very quietly to the window and drew back the curtains. The out-of-doors stretched vast and colorless before him, thickened and unreal in the gray haze that had begun to take on the faintest tinge of pink from the light in the east. He turned from the window and walked back to the bed where Francine lay; he stood above her.

Her hair, lusterless in the morning light, lay in tangles about her face; her mouth was half open, and she breathed heavily in sleep; tiny wrinkles that spread from her eyes were barely visible in the light; an oily film of sweat covered the flesh that sagged in its repose. He had not seen her before as he saw her now, caught in the ugliness of sleep; or if he had, he had not let his eyes stay upon her. But seeing her now, defenseless in sleep and in the innocence of sleep, a friendly and unguarded pity came over him. It seemed to him that he had never looked at her before, had never seen a part of her that he was seeing now; he remembered the first night he had come to her room, months before, and his rush of pity for her in the humiliations, the coarsenesses she had schooled herself to endure. Now that pity seemed to him contemptible and mean.

No, he had not seen her before. Again he turned to the open window. The flat land beyond Butcher's Crossing lay open and clear in the crisp gray light that swelled from the east. Already, on the eastern coast, the sun was up, glinting on the rocks that lined the northern bays, and catching the wings of gulls that wheeled in the high salt air; already it lighted the empty streets of Boston, and shone upon the steeples of the empty churches along Boylston Street and St. James Avenue, on Arlington and Berkeley and Clarendon; it shone through the high windows of his father's house, lighting rooms in which no one moved.

A sense of sorrow that was like a foretaste of grief spread upon his mind; he thought of his father, a thin austere figure that moved before the eye of his mind like a stranger, and then faded impalpably into a gray mist. He closed his eyes in a spasm of regret and pity, and perceived sharply the darkness he brought on by that small motion of his lids. He knew that he would not go back. He would not return with McDonald to his home, to the country that had given him birth, had raised him in the shape he occupied and the condition that he had only begun to recognize, and that had relinquished him to a wilderness in which he had thought to find a truer shape of himself. No, he would never return.

As if balancing himself finely at the edge of an abyss, he turned from the window and looked again at the sleeping figure of Francine. He could hardly recall, now, the passion that had drawn him to this room and this flesh, as if by a subtle magnetism; nor could he recall the force of that other passion which had impelled him halfway across a continent into a wilderness where he had dreamed he could find, as in a vision, his unalterable self. Almost without regret, he could admit now the vanity from which those passions had sprung.

It was that nothingness of which McDonald had spoken back in the sleeping house as he stood beneath the lantern that flickered weakly against the darkness; it was the bright blue emptiness of Charley Hoge's stare, into which he had glimpsed and of which he had tried to tell Francine; it was the contemptuous look that Schneider had given the river just before the hoof had blanked his face; it was the blind enduring set of Miller's face before the white drive of storm in the mountains; it was the hollow glint in Charley Hoge's eyes, when Charley Hoge turned from the dying fire to follow Miller into the night; it was the open despair that ripped McDonald's face into a livid mask during his frenzied pursuit of Miller in the holocaust of the hides; it was what he saw now in Francine's sleeping face that sagged inertly on her pillow.

He looked once more at Francine, and wished to reach out gently and touch her young, aging face. But he did not do so, for fear that he would awaken her. Very quietly he went to the corner of the room and took his bedroll up. From the money belt that lay upon it, he took out two bills, and stuffed them in his pocket; the rest of the bills he neatly piled on the table beside the couch. Wherever Francine went, she would need the money; she would need it to buy a new rug, and curtains for her windows. Once again he looked at her; across the room, in the large bed, she seemed very small. He went quietly across to the door, and did not look back.

Streaks of red lay in soft banks in the east. In the stillness of the deserted street he walked across to the livery stable and got his horse, awakening the stableman to give him one of the bills he had kept. He saddled his horse quickly in the dim light of the stable, mounted, and turned to wave to the stableman; but he had gone back to sleep. He rode out of the stable and down the dusty street of Butcher's Crossing; the clop of his horse's hooves was muffled in the thick dust. He looked on either side of him at what remained of Butcher's Crossing. Soon there would be nothing here; the timbered buildings would be torn down for what material could be salvaged, the sod huts would wash away in the weather, and the prairie grass would slowly creep upon the roadway. Even now, in the light of the early sun, the town was like a small ruin; the light caught upon the edges of the buildings and intensified a bareness that was already there.

He rode past the still smoldering ruins of McDonald's shack and past the cottonwood grove that stood on the right. He crossed the narrow river and brought his horse to a halt. He turned. A thin edge of sun flamed above the eastern horizon. He turned again and looked at the flat country before him, where his shadow lay long and level, broken at the edges by the crisp new prairie grass. His horse's reins were tough and slick in his hands; he was acutely aware of the rocklike smoothness of the saddle he sat in, of the gentle swelling movement of the horse's sides as it took in air and expelled it. He breathed deeply of the fragrant air that rose from the new grass and mingled with the musty sweat of his horse. He gathered the reins firmly in one hand, touched his horse's flanks with his heels, and rode into the open country.

Except for the general direction he took, he did not know where he was going; but he knew that it would come to him later in the day. He rode forward without hurry, and felt behind him the sun slowly rise and harden the air.

STONER

This book is dedicated to my friends and former colleagues in the Department of English at the University of Missouri. They will recognize at once that it is a work of fiction—that no character portrayed in it is based upon any person, living or dead, and that no event has its counterpart in the reality we knew at the University of Missouri. They will also realize that I have taken certain liberties, both physical and historical, with the University of Missouri, so that in effect it, too, is a fictional place.

I

WILLIAM STONER entered the University of Missouri as a freshman in the year 1910, at the age of nineteen. Eight years later, during the height of World War I, he received his Doctor of Philosophy degree and accepted an instructorship at the same University, where he taught until his death in 1956. He did not rise above the rank of assistant professor, and few students remembered him with any sharpness after they had taken his courses. When he died his colleagues made a memorial contribution of a medieval manuscript to the University library. This manuscript may still be found in the Rare Books Collection, bearing the inscription: "Presented to the Library of the University of Missouri, in memory of William Stoner, Department of English. By his colleagues."

An occasional student who comes upon the name may wonder idly who William Stoner was, but he seldom pursues his curiosity beyond a casual question. Stoner's colleagues, who held him in no particular esteem when he was alive, speak of him rarely now; to the older ones, his name is a reminder of the end that awaits them all, and to the younger ones it is merely a sound which evokes no sense of the past and no identity with which they can associate themselves or their careers.

He was born in 1891 on a small farm in central Missouri near the village of Booneville, some forty miles from Columbia, the home of the University. Though his parents were young at the time of his birth—his father twenty-five, his mother barely twenty—Stoner thought of them, even when he was a boy, as old. At thirty his father looked fifty; stooped by labor, he gazed without hope at the arid patch of land that sustained the family from one year to the next. His mother regarded her life patiently, as if it were a long moment that she had to endure. Her eyes were pale and blurred, and the tiny wrinkles around them were enhanced by thin graying hair worn straight over her head and caught in a bun at the back.

From the earliest time he could remember, William Stoner had his duties. At the age of six he milked the bony cows, slopped the pigs in the sty a few yards from the house, and gathered small eggs from a flock of spindly chickens. And even when he started attending the rural school eight miles from the farm, his day, from before dawn until after dark, was filled with work of one sort or another. At seventeen his shoulders were already beginning to stoop beneath the weight of his occupation.

It was a lonely household, of which he was an only child, and it was bound together by the necessity of its toil. In the evenings the three of them sat in the small kitchen lighted by a single kerosene lamp, staring into the yellow flame; often during the hour or so between supper and bed, the only sound that could be heard was the weary movement of a body in a straight chair and the soft creak of a timber giving a little beneath the age of the house.

The house was built in a crude square, and the unpainted timbers sagged around the porch and doors. It had with the years taken on the colors of the dry land—gray and brown, streaked with white. On one side of the house was a long parlor, sparsely furnished with straight chairs and a few hewn tables, and a kitchen, where the family spent most of its little time together. On the other side were two bedrooms, each furnished with an iron bedstead enameled white, a single straight chair, and a table, with a lamp and a wash basin on it. The floors were of unpainted plank, unevenly spaced and cracking with age, up through which dust steadily seeped and was swept back each day by Stoner's mother.

At school he did his lessons as if they were chores only somewhat less exhausting than those around the farm. When he finished high school in the spring of 1910, he expected to take over more of the work in the fields; it seemed to him that his father grew slower and more weary with the passing months.

But one evening in late spring, after the two men had spent a full day hoeing corn, his father spoke to him in the kitchen, after the supper dishes had been cleared away.

"County agent come by last week."

William looked up from the red-and-white-checked oilcloth spread smoothly over the round kitchen table. He did not speak.

"Says they have a new school at the University in Columbia. They call it a College of Agriculture. Says he thinks you ought to go. It takes four years."

"Four years," William said. "Does it cost money?"

"You could work your room and board," his father said. "Your ma has a first cousin owns a place just outside Columbia. There would be books and things. I could send you two or three dollars a month."

William spread his hands on the tablecloth, which gleamed dully under the lamplight. He had never been farther from home than Booneville, fifteen miles away. He swallowed to steady his voice.

"Think you could manage the place all by yourself?" he asked.

"Your ma and me could manage. I'd plant the upper twenty in wheat; that would cut down the hand work."

William looked at his mother. "Ma?" he asked.

She said tonelessly, "You do what your pa says."

"You really want me to go?" he asked, as if he half hoped for a denial. "You really want me to?"

His father shifted his weight on the chair. He looked at his thick, callused fingers, into the cracks of which soil had penetrated so deeply that it could not be washed away. He laced his fingers together and held them up from the table, almost in an attitude of prayer.

"I never had no schooling to speak of," he said, looking at his hands. "I started working a farm when I finished sixth grade. Never held with schooling when I was a young 'un. But now I don't know. Seems like the land gets drier and harder to work every year; it ain't rich like it was when I was a boy. County agent says they got new ideas, ways of doing things they teach you at the University. Maybe he's right. Sometimes when I'm working the field I get to thinking." He paused. His fingers tightened upon themselves, and his clasped hands dropped to the table. "I get to thinking—" He scowled at his hands and shook his head. "You go on to the University come fall. Your ma and me will manage."

It was the longest speech he had ever heard his father make. That fall he went to Columbia and enrolled in the University as a freshman in the College of Agriculture.

*

He came to Columbia with a new black broadcloth suit ordered from the catalogue of Sears & Roebuck and paid for with
his mother's egg money, a worn greatcoat that had belonged
to his father, a pair of blue serge trousers that once a month
he had worn to the Methodist church in Booneville, two white
shirts, two changes of work clothing, and twenty-five dollars in
cash, which his father had borrowed from a neighbor against
the fall wheat. He started walking from Booneville, where in
the early morning his father and mother brought him on the
farm's flat-bed, mule-drawn wagon.

It was a hot fall day, and the road from Booneville to Columbia was dusty; he had been walking for nearly an hour before a goods wagon came up beside him and the driver asked
him if he wanted a ride. He nodded and got up on the wagon
seat. His serge trousers were red with dust to his knees, and his
sun- and wind-browned face was caked with dirt, where the
road dust had mingled with his sweat. During the long ride he
kept brushing at his trousers with awkward hands and running
his fingers through his straight sandy hair, which would not lie
flat on his head.

They got to Columbia in the late afternoon. The driver let
Stoner off at the outskirts of town and pointed to a group of
buildings shaded by tall elms. "That's your University," he said.
"That's where you'll be going to school."

For several minutes after the man had driven off, Stoner
stood unmoving, staring at the complex of buildings. He had
never before seen anything so imposing. The red brick buildings stretched upward from a broad field of green that was
broken by stone walks and small patches of garden. Beneath
his awe, he had a sudden sense of security and serenity he had
never felt before. Though it was late, he walked for many minutes about the edges of the campus, only looking, as if he had
no right to enter.

It was nearly dark when he asked a passer-by directions to
Ashland Gravel, the road that would lead him to the farm
owned by Jim Foote, the first cousin of his mother for whom
he was to work; and it was after dark when he got to the white
two-storied frame house where he was to live. He had not seen
the Footes before, and he felt strange going to them so late.

They greeted him with a nod, inspecting him closely. After a moment, during which Stoner stood awkwardly in the doorway, Jim Foote motioned him into a small dim parlor crowded with overstuffed furniture and bric-a-brac on dully gleaming tables. He did not sit.

"Et supper?" Foote asked.

"No, sir," Stoner answered.

Mrs. Foote crooked an index finger at him and padded away. Stoner followed her through several rooms into a kitchen, where she motioned him to sit at a table. She put a pitcher of milk and several squares of cold cornbread before him. He sipped the milk, but his mouth, dry from excitement, would not take the bread.

Foote came into the room and stood beside his wife. He was a small man, not more than five feet three inches, with a lean face and a sharp nose. His wife was four inches taller, and heavy; rimless spectacles hid her eyes, and her thin lips were tight. The two of them watched hungrily as he sipped his milk.

"Feed and water the livestock, slop the pigs in the morning," Foote said rapidly.

Stoner looked at him blankly. "What?"

"That's what you do in the morning," Foote said, "before you leave for your school. Then in the evening you feed and slop again, gather the eggs, milk the cows. Chop firewood when you find time. Weekends, you help me with whatever I'm doing."

"Yes, sir," Stoner said.

Foote studied him for a moment. "College," he said and shook his head.

So for nine months' room and board he fed and watered the livestock, slopped pigs, gathered eggs, milked cows, and chopped firewood. He also plowed and harrowed fields, dug stumps (in the winter breaking through three inches of frozen soil), and churned butter for Mrs. Foote, who watched him with her head bobbing in grim approval as the wooden churner splashed up and down through the milk.

He was quartered on an upper floor that had once been a storeroom; his only furniture was a black iron bedstead with sagging frames that supported a thin feather mattress, a broken table that held a kerosene lamp, a straight chair that sat unevenly on the floor, and a large box that he used as a desk. In the winter the only heat he got seeped up through the floor from the rooms below; he wrapped himself in the tattered quilts and blankets allowed him and blew on his hands so that they could turn the pages of his books without tearing them.

He did his work at the University as he did his work on the farm—thoroughly, conscientiously, with neither pleasure nor distress. At the end of his first year his grade average was slightly below a B; he was pleased that it was no lower and not concerned that it was no higher. He was aware that he had learned things that he had not known before, but this meant to him only that he might do as well in his second year as he had done in his first.

The summer after his first year of college he returned to his father's farm and helped with the crops. Once his father asked him how he liked school, and he replied that he liked it fine. His father nodded and did not mention the matter again.

It was not until he returned for his second year that William Stoner learned why he had come to college.

By his second year he was a familiar figure on the campus. In every season he wore the same black broadcloth suit, white shirt, and string tie; his wrists protruded from the sleeves of the jacket, and the trousers rode awkwardly about his legs, as if it were a uniform that had once belonged to someone else.

His hours of work increased with his employers' growing indolence, and he spent the long evenings in his room methodically doing his class assignments; he had begun the sequence that would lead him to a Bachelor of Science degree in the College of Agriculture, and during this first semester of his second year he had two basic sciences, a course from the school of Agriculture in soil chemistry, and a course that was rather perfunctorily required of all University students—a semester survey of English literature.

After the first few weeks he had little difficulty with the science courses; there was so much work to be done, so many things to be remembered. The course in soil chemistry caught his interest in a general way; it had not occurred to him that the brownish clods with which he had worked for most of his life were anything other than what they appeared to be, and he began vaguely to see that his growing knowledge of them might be useful when he returned to his father's farm. But the required survey of English literature troubled and disquieted him in a way nothing had ever done before.

The instructor was a man of middle age, in his early fifties; his name was Archer Sloane, and he came to his task of teaching with a seeming disdain and contempt, as if he perceived between his knowledge and what he could say a gulf so profound that he would make no effort to close it. He was feared and disliked by most of his students, and he responded with a detached, ironic amusement. He was a man of middle height, with a long, deeply lined face, cleanly shaven; he had an impatient gesture of running his fingers through the shock of his gray curling hair. His voice was flat and dry, and it came through barely moving lips without expression or intonation; but his long thin fingers moved with grace and persuasion, as if giving to the words a shape that his voice could not.

Away from the classroom, doing his chores about the farm or blinking against the dim lamplight as he studied in his windowless attic room, Stoner was often aware that the image of this man had risen up before the eye of his mind. He had difficulty summoning up the face of any other of his instructors or remembering anything very specific about any other of his classes; but always on the threshold of his awareness waited the figure of Archer Sloane, and his dry voice, and his contemptuously offhand words about some passage from Beowulf, or some couplet of Chaucer's.

He found that he could not handle the survey as he did his other courses. Though he remembered the authors and their works and their dates and their influences, he nearly failed his first examination; and he did little better on his second. He read and reread his literature assignments so frequently that his work in other courses began to suffer; and still the words he read were words on pages, and he could not see the use of what he did.

And he pondered the words that Archer Sloane spoke in class, as if beneath their flat, dry meaning he might discover a clue that would lead him where he was intended to go; he hunched forward over the desk-top of a chair too small to hold him comfortably, grasping the edges of the desk-top so tightly that his knuckles showed white against his brown hard skin; he frowned intently and gnawed at his underlip. But as Stoner's and his classmates' attention grew more desperate, Archer Sloane's contempt grew more compelling. And once that contempt erupted into anger and was directed at William Stoner alone.

The class had read two plays by Shakespeare and was ending the week with a study of the sonnets. The students were edgy and puzzled, half frightened at the tension growing between themselves and the slouching figure that regarded them from behind the lectern. Sloane had read aloud to them the seventy-third sonnet; his eyes roved about the room and his lips tightened in a humorless smile.

"What does the sonnet mean?" he asked abruptly, and paused, his eyes searching the room with a grim and almost pleased hopelessness. "Mr. Wilbur?" There was no answer. "Mr. Schmidt?" Someone coughed. Sloane turned his dark bright eyes upon Stoner. "Mr. Stoner, what does the sonnet mean?"

Stoner swallowed and tried to open his mouth.

"It is a sonnet, Mr. Stoner," Sloane said dryly, "a poetical composition of fourteen lines, with a certain pattern I am sure you have memorized. It is written in the English language, which I believe you have been speaking for some years. Its author is William Shakespeare, a poet who is dead, but who nevertheless occupies a position of some importance in the minds of a few." He looked at Stoner for a moment more, and then his eyes went blank as they fixed unseeingly beyond the class. Without looking at his book he spoke the poem again; and his voice deepened and softened, as if the words and sounds and rhythms had for a moment become himself:

"That time of year thou mayst in me behold
When yellow leaves, or none, or few, do hang
Upon those boughs which shake against the cold,
Bare ruin'd choirs where late the sweet birds sang.
In me thou see'st the twilight of such day
As after sunset fadeth in the west;
Which by and by black night doth take away,
Death's second self, that seals up all in rest.

In me thou see'st the glowing of such fire,
That on the ashes of his youth doth lie,
As the death-bed whereon it must expire,
Consumed with that which it was nourisht by.
    This thou perceivest, which makes thy love more strong,
    To love that well which thou must leave ere long."

In a moment of silence, someone cleared his throat. Sloane repeated the lines, his voice becoming flat, his own again.

"This thou perceivest, which makes thy love more strong,
To love that well which thou must leave ere long."

Sloane's eyes came back to William Stoner, and he said dryly, "Mr. Shakespeare speaks to you across three hundred years, Mr. Stoner; do you hear him?"

William Stoner realized that for several moments he had been holding his breath. He expelled it gently, minutely aware of his clothing moving upon his body as his breath went out of his lungs. He looked away from Sloane about the room. Light slanted from the windows and settled upon the faces of his fellow students, so that the illumination seemed to come from within them and go out against a dimness; a student blinked, and a thin shadow fell upon a cheek whose down had caught the sunlight. Stoner became aware that his fingers were unclenching their hard grip on his desk-top. He turned his hands about under his gaze, marveling at their brownness, at the intricate way the nails fit into his blunt finger-ends; he thought he could feel the blood flowing invisibly through the tiny veins and arteries, throbbing delicately and precariously from his fingertips through his body.

Sloane was speaking again. "What does he say to you, Mr. Stoner? What does his sonnet mean?"

Stoner's eyes lifted slowly and reluctantly. "It means," he said, and with a small movement raised his hands up toward the air; he felt his eyes glaze over as they sought the figure of Archer Sloane. "It means," he said again, and could not finish what he had begun to say.

Sloane looked at him curiously. Then he nodded abruptly and said, "Class is dismissed." Without looking at anyone he turned and walked out of the room.

William Stoner was hardly aware of the students about him who rose grumbling and muttering from their seats and shuffled out of the room. For several minutes after they left he sat unmoving, staring out before him at the narrow planked flooring that had been worn bare of varnish by the restless feet of students he would never see or know. He slid his own feet across the floor, hearing the dry rasp of wood on his soles, and feeling the roughness through the leather. Then he too got up and went slowly out of the room.

The thin chill of the late fall day cut through his clothing. He looked around him, at the bare gnarled branches of the trees that curled and twisted against the pale sky. Students, hurrying across the campus to their classes, brushed against him; he heard the mutter of their voices and the click of their heels upon the stone paths, and saw their faces, flushed by the cold, bent downward against a slight breeze. He looked at them curiously, as if he had not seen them before, and felt very distant from them and very close to them. He held the feeling to him as he hurried to his next class, and held it through the lecture by his professor in soil chemistry, against the droning voice that recited things to be written in notebooks and remembered by a process of drudgery that even now was becoming unfamiliar to him.

In the second semester of that school year William Stoner dropped his basic science courses and interrupted his Ag School sequence; he took introductory courses in philosophy and ancient history and two courses in English literature. In the summer he returned again to his parents' farm and helped his father with the crops and did not mention his work at the University.

When he was much older, he was to look back upon his last two undergraduate years as if they were an unreal time that belonged to someone else, a time that passed, not in the regular flow to which he was used, but in fits and starts. One moment was juxtaposed against another, yet isolated from it, and he had the feeling that he was removed from time, watching as it passed before him like a great unevenly turned diorama.

He became conscious of himself in a way that he had not done before. Sometimes he looked at himself in a mirror, at the long face with its thatch of dry brown hair, and touched his sharp cheekbones; he saw the thin wrists that protruded inches out of his coat sleeves; and he wondered if he appeared as ludicrous to others as he did to himself.

He had no plans for the future, and he spoke to no one of his uncertainty. He continued to work at the Footes' for his room and board, but he no longer worked the long hours of his first two years at the University. For three hours every afternoon and for half a day on the weekends he allowed himself to be used as Jim and Serena Foote desired; the rest of the time he claimed as his own.

Some of this time he spent in his little attic room atop the Foote house; but as often as he could, after his classes were over and his work at the Footes' done, he returned to the University. Sometimes, in the evenings, he wandered in the long open quadrangle, among couples who strolled together and murmured softly; though he did not know any of them, and though he did not speak to them, he felt a kinship with them. Sometimes he stood in the center of the quad, looking at the five huge columns in front of Jesse Hall that thrust upward into the night out of the cool grass; he had learned that these columns were the remains of the original main building of the University, destroyed many years ago by fire. Grayish silver in the moonlight, bare and pure, they seemed to him to represent the way of life he had embraced, as a temple represents a god.

In the University library he wandered through the stacks, among the thousands of books, inhaling the musty odor of leather, cloth, and drying page as if it were an exotic incense. Sometimes he would pause, remove a volume from the shelves, and hold it for a moment in his large hands, which tingled at the still unfamiliar feel of spine and board and unresisting page. Then he would leaf through the book, reading a paragraph here and there, his stiff fingers careful as they turned the pages, as if in their clumsiness they might tear and destroy what they took such pains to uncover.

He had no friends, and for the first time in his life he became aware of loneliness. Sometimes, in his attic room at night, he would look up from a book he was reading and gaze in the dark corners of his room, where the lamplight flickered against the shadows. If he stared long and intently, the darkness gathered into a light, which took the insubstantial shape of what he had been reading. And he would feel that he was out of time, as he had felt that day in class when Archer Sloane had spoken to him. The past gathered out of the darkness where it stayed, and the dead raised themselves to live before him; and the past and the dead flowed into the present among the alive, so that he had for an intense instant a vision of denseness into which he was compacted and from which he could not escape, and had no wish to escape. Tristan, Iseult the fair, walked before him; Paolo and Francesca whirled in the glowing dark; Helen and bright Paris, their faces bitter with consequence, rose from the gloom. And he was with them in a way that he could never be with his fellows who went from class to class, who found a local habitation in a large university in Columbia, Missouri, and who walked unheeding in a midwestern air.

In a year he learned Greek and Latin well enough to read simple texts; often his eyes were red and burning from strain and lack of sleep. Sometimes he thought of himself as he had been a few years before and was astonished by the memory of that strange figure, brown and passive as the earth from which it had emerged. He thought of his parents, and they were nearly as strange as the child they had borne; he felt a mixed pity for them and a distant love.

Near the middle of his fourth year at the University, Archer Sloane stopped him one day after class and asked him to drop by his office for a chat.

It was winter, and a low damp midwestern mist floated over the campus. Even at midmorning the thin branches of the dogwood trees glistened with hoarfrost, and the black vines that trailed up the great columns before Jesse Hall were rimmed with iridescent crystals that winked against the grayness. Stoner's greatcoat was so shabby and worn that he had decided not to wear it to see Sloane even though the weather was freezing. He was shivering as he hurried up the walk and up the wide stone steps that led into Jesse Hall.

After the cold, the heat inside the building was intense. The grayness outside trickled through the windows and glassed doors on either side of the hall, so that the yellow tiled floors glowed brighter than the gray light upon them, and the great oaken columns and the rubbed walls gleamed from their dark. Shuffling footsteps hissed upon the floors, and a murmur of voices was muted by the great expanse of the hall; dim figures moved slowly, mingling and parting; and the oppressive air gathered the smell of the oiled walls and the wet odor of woolen clothing. Stoner went up the smooth marble stairs to Archer Sloane's second-floor office. He knocked on the closed door, heard a voice, and went in.

The office was long and narrow, lighted by a single window at the far end. Shelves crowded with books rose to the high ceiling. Near the window a desk was wedged, and before this desk, half turned and outlined darkly against the light, sat Archer Sloane.

"Mr. Stoner," Sloane said dryly, half rising and indicating a leather-covered chair facing him. Stoner sat down.

"I have been looking through your records." Sloane paused and lifted a folder from his desk, regarding it with detached irony. "I hope you do not mind my inquisitiveness."

Stoner wet his lips and shifted on the chair. He tried to fold his large hands together so that they would be invisible. "No, sir," he said in a husky voice.

Sloane nodded. "Good. I note that you began your course of studies here as an agriculture student and that sometime during your sophomore year you switched your program to literature. Is that correct?"

"Yes, sir," Stoner said.

Sloane leaned back in his chair and gazed up at the square of light that came in from the high small window. He tapped his fingertips together and turned back to the young man who sat stiffly in front of him.

"The official purpose of this conference is to inform you that you will have to make a formal change of study program, declaring your intention to abandon your initial course of study and declare your final one. It's a matter of five minutes or so at the registrar's office. You will take care of that, won't you?"

"Yes, sir," Stoner said.

"But as you may have guessed, that is not the reason I asked you to drop by. Do you mind if I inquire a little about your future plans?"

"No, sir," Stoner said. He looked at his hands, which were twisted tightly together.

Sloane touched the folder of papers that he had dropped on his desk. "I gather that you were a bit older than the ordinary student when you first entered the University. Nearly twenty, I believe?"

"Yes, sir," Stoner said.

"And at that time your plans were to undertake the sequence offered by the school of Agriculture?"

"Yes, sir."

Sloane leaned back in his chair and regarded the high dim ceiling. He asked abruptly, "And what are your plans now?"

Stoner was silent. This was something he had not thought about, had not wanted to think about. He said at last, with a touch of resentment, "I don't know. I haven't given it much thought."

Sloane said, "Are you looking forward to the day when you emerge from these cloistered walls into what some call the world?"

Stoner grinned through his embarrassment. "No, sir."

Sloane tapped the folder of papers on his desk. "I am informed by these records that you come from a farming community. I take it that your parents are farm people?"

Stoner nodded.

"And do you intend to return to the farm after you receive your degree here?"

"No, sir," Stoner said, and the decisiveness of his voice surprised him. He thought with some wonder of the decision he had suddenly made.

Sloane nodded. "I should imagine a serious student of literature *might* find his skills not precisely suited to the persuasion of the soil."

"I won't go back," Stoner said as if Sloane had not spoken. "I don't know what I'll do exactly." He looked at his hands and said to them, "I can't quite realize that I'll be through so soon, that I'll be leaving the University at the end of the year."

Sloane said casually, "There is, of course, no absolute need for you to leave. I take it that you have no independent means?"

Stoner shook his head.

"You have an excellent undergraduate record. Except for

your"— he lifted his eyebrows and smiled—"except for your sophomore survey of English literature, you have all A's in your English courses; nothing below a B elsewhere. If you could maintain yourself for a year or so beyond graduation, you could, I'm sure, successfully complete the work for your Master of Arts; after which you would probably be able to teach while you worked toward your doctorate. If that sort of thing would interest you at all."

Stoner drew back. "What do you mean?" he asked and heard something like fear in his voice.

Sloane leaned forward until his face was close; Stoner saw the lines on the long thin face soften, and he heard the dry mocking voice become gentle and unprotected.

"But don't you know, Mr. Stoner?" Sloane asked. "Don't you understand about yourself yet? You're going to be a teacher."

Suddenly Sloane seemed very distant, and the walls of the office receded. Stoner felt himself suspended in the wide air, and he heard his voice ask, "Are you sure?"

"I'm sure," Sloane said softly.

"How can you tell? How can you be sure?"

"It's love, Mr. Stoner," Sloane said cheerfully. "You are in love. It's as simple as that."

It was as simple as that. He was aware that he nodded to Sloane and said something inconsequential. Then he was walking out of the office. His lips were tingling and his fingertips were numb; he walked as if he were asleep, yet he was intensely aware of his surroundings. He brushed against the polished wooden walls in the corridor, and he thought he could feel the warmth and age of the wood; he went slowly down the stairs and wondered at the veined cold marble that seemed to slip a little beneath his feet. In the halls the voices of the students became distinct and individual out of the hushed murmur, and their faces were close and strange and familiar. He went out of Jesse Hall into the morning, and the grayness no longer seemed to oppress the campus; it led his eyes outward and upward into the sky, where he looked as if toward a possibility for which he had no name.

In the first week of June, in the year 1914, William Stoner, with sixty other young men and a few young ladies, received his Bachelor of Arts degree from the University of Missouri.

To attend the ceremony, his parents—in a borrowed buggy drawn by their old dun mare—had started the day before, driving overnight the forty-odd miles from the farm, so that they arrived at the Footes' shortly after dawn, stiff from their sleepless journey. Stoner went down into the yard to meet them. They stood side by side in the crisp morning light and awaited his approach.

Stoner and his father shook hands with a single quick pumping action, not looking at each other.

"How do," his father said.

His mother nodded. "Your pa and me come down to see you graduate."

For a moment he did not speak. Then he said, "You'd better come in and get some breakfast."

They were alone in the kitchen; since Stoner had come to the farm the Footes had got in the habit of sleeping late. But neither then nor after his parents had finished breakfast could he bring himself to tell them of his change of plans, of his decision not to return to the farm. Once or twice he started to speak; then he looked at the brown faces that rose nakedly out of their new clothing, and thought of the long journey they had made and of the years they had awaited his return. He sat stiffly with them until they finished the last of their coffee, and until the Footes roused themselves and came into the kitchen. Then he told them that he had to go early to the University and that he would see them there later in the day, at the exercises.

He wandered about the campus, carrying the black robe and cap that he had hired; they were heavy and troublesome, but he could find no place to leave them. He thought of what he would have to tell his parents, and for the first time realized the finality of his decision, and almost wished that he could recall it. He felt his inadequacy to the goal he had so recklessly chosen and felt the attraction of the world he had abandoned. He grieved for his own loss and for that of his parents, and even in his grief felt himself drawing away from them.

He carried this feeling of loss with him throughout the graduation exercises; when his name was spoken and he walked across the platform to receive a scroll from a man faceless behind a soft gray beard, he could not believe his own presence, and the roll of parchment in his hand had no meaning. He could only think of his mother and father sitting stiffly and uneasily in the great crowd.

When the ceremonies were over he drove with them back to the Footes', where they were to stay overnight and start the journey home the following dawn.

They sat late in the Footes' parlor. Jim and Serena Foote stayed up with them for a while. Every now and then Jim and Stoner's mother would exchange the name of a relative and lapse into silence. His father sat on a straight chair, his legs spread apart, leaning a little forward, his broad hands clasping his kneecaps. Finally the Footes looked at each other and yawned and announced that it was late. They went to their bedroom, and the three were left alone.

There was another silence. His parents, who looked straight ahead in the shadows cast by their own bodies, every now and then glanced sideways at their son, as if they did not wish to disturb him in his new estate.

After several minutes William Stoner leaned forward and spoke, his voice louder and more forceful than he had intended. "I ought to have told you sooner. I ought to have told you last summer, or this morning."

His parents' faces were dull and expressionless in the lamplight.

"What I'm trying to say is, I'm not coming back with you to the farm."

No one moved. His father said, "You got some things to finish up here, we can go back in the morning and you can come on home in a few days."

Stoner rubbed his face with his open palm. "That's—not what I meant. I'm trying to tell you I won't be coming back to the farm at all."

His father's hands tightened on his kneecaps and he drew back in the chair. He said, "You get yourself in some kind of trouble?"

Stoner smiled. "It's nothing like that. I'm going on to school for another year, maybe two or three."

His father shook his head. "I seen you get through this evening. And the county agent said the farm school took four years."

Stoner tried to explain to his father what he intended to do, tried to evoke in him his own sense of significance and purpose. He listened to his words fall as if from the mouth of another, and watched his father's face, which received those words as a stone receives the repeated blows of a fist. When he had finished he sat with his hands clasped between his knees and his head bowed. He listened to the silence of the room.

Finally his father moved in his chair. Stoner looked up. His parents' faces confronted him; he almost cried out to them.

"I don't know," his father said. His voice was husky and tired. "I didn't figure it would turn out like this. I thought I was doing the best for you I could, sending you here. Your ma and me has always done the best we could for you."

"I know," Stoner said. He could not look at them longer. "Will you be all right? I could come back for a while this summer and help. I could—"

"If you think you ought to stay here and study your books, then that's what you ought to do. Your ma and me can manage."

His mother was facing him, but she did not see him. Her eyes were squeezed shut; she was breathing heavily, her face twisted as if in pain, and her closed fists were pressed against her cheeks. With wonder Stoner realized that she was crying, deeply and silently, with the shame and awkwardness of one who seldom weeps. He watched her for a moment more; then he got heavily to his feet and walked out of the parlor. He found his way up the narrow stairs that led to his attic room; for a long time he lay on his bed and stared with open eyes into the darkness above him.

II

T̲WO WEEKS̲ after Stoner received his Bachelor of Arts degree, Archduke Francis Ferdinand was assassinated at Sarajevo by a Serbian nationalist; and before autumn war was general all over Europe. It was a topic of continuing interest among the older students; they wondered about the part America would eventually play, and they were pleasantly unsure of their own futures.

But before William Stoner the future lay bright and certain and unchanging. He saw it, not as a flux of event and change and potentiality, but as a territory ahead that awaited his exploration. He saw it as the great University library, to which new wings might be built, to which new books might be added and from which old ones might be withdrawn, while its true nature remained essentially unchanged. He saw the future in the institution to which he had committed himself and which he so imperfectly understood; he conceived himself changing in that future, but he saw the future itself as the instrument of change rather than its object.

Near the end of that summer, just before the beginning of the autumn semester, he visited his parents. He had intended to help with the summer crop; but he found that his father had hired a Negro field hand who worked with a quiet, fierce intensity, accomplishing by himself in a day nearly as much as William and his father together had once done in the same time. His parents were happy to see him, and they seemed not to resent his decision. But he found that he had nothing to say to them; already, he realized, he and his parents were becoming strangers; and he felt his love increased by its loss. He returned to Columbia a week earlier than he had intended.

He began to resent the time he had to spend at work on the Foote farm. Having come to his studies late, he felt the urgency of study. Sometimes, immersed in his books, there would come to him the awareness of all that he did not know, of all that he had not read; and the serenity for which he labored was shattered as he realized the little time he had in life to read so much, to learn what he had to know.

He finished his course work for the Master of Arts degree in the spring of 1915 and spent the summer completing his thesis, a prosodic study of one of Chaucer's *Canterbury Tales*. Before the summer was out the Footes told him that they would not need him any longer on the farm.

He had expected his dismissal and in some ways he welcomed it; but for a moment after it happened he had a twinge of panic. It was as if the last tie between himself and the old life had been cut. He spent the last weeks of the summer at his father's farm, putting the finishing touches on his thesis. By that time Archer Sloane had arranged for him to teach two classes of beginning English to incoming freshmen, while he started to work toward his Ph.D. For this he received four hundred dollars a year. He removed his belongings from the Footes' tiny attic room, which he had occupied for five years, and took an even smaller room near the University.

Though he was to teach only the fundamentals of grammar and composition to a group of unselected freshmen, he looked forward to his task with enthusiasm and with a strong sense of its significance. He planned the course during the week before the opening of the autumn semester, and saw the kinds of possibility that one sees as one struggles with the materials and subjects of an endeavor; he felt the logic of grammar, and he thought he perceived how it spread out from itself, permeating the language and supporting human thought. In the simple compositional exercises he made for his students he saw the potentialities of prose and its beauties, and he looked forward to animating his students with the sense of what he perceived.

But in the first classes he met, after the opening routines of rolls and study plans, when he began to address himself to his subject and his students, he found that his sense of wonder remained hidden within him. Sometimes, as he spoke to his students, it was as if he stood outside himself and observed a stranger speaking to a group assembled unwillingly; he heard his own flat voice reciting the materials he had prepared, and nothing of his own excitement came through that recitation.

He found his release and fulfillment in the classes in which he himself was a student. There he was able to recapture the sense of discovery he had felt on that first day, when Archer

Sloane had spoken to him in class and he had, in an instant, become someone other than who he had been. As his mind engaged itself with its subject, as it grappled with the power of the literature he studied and tried to understand its nature, he was aware of a constant change within himself; and as he was aware of that, he moved outward from himself into the world which contained him, so that he knew that the poem of Milton's that he read or the essay of Bacon's or the drama of Ben Jonson's changed the world which was its subject, and changed it because of its dependence upon it. He seldom spoke in class, and his papers rarely satisfied him. Like his lectures to his young students, they did not betray what he most profoundly knew.

He began to be on familiar terms with a few of his fellow students who were also acting instructors in the department. Among those were two with whom he became friendly, David Masters and Gordon Finch.

Masters was a slight dark youth with a sharp tongue and gentle eyes. Like Stoner, he was just beginning his doctoral program, though he was a year or so younger than Stoner. Among the faculty and the graduate students he had a reputation for arrogance and impertinence, and it was generally conceded that he would have some difficulty in finally obtaining his degree. Stoner thought him the most brilliant man he had ever known and deferred to him without envy or resentment.

Gordon Finch was large and blond, and already, at the age of twenty-three, beginning to run to fat. He had taken an undergraduate degree from a commercial college in St. Louis, and at the University had made various stabs at advanced degrees in the departments of economics, history, and engineering. He had begun work on his degree in literature largely because he had been able, at the last minute, to get a small instructing job in the English Department. He quickly showed himself to be the most nearly indifferent student in the department. But he was popular with the freshmen, and he got along well with the older faculty members and with the officers of the administration.

The three of them—Stoner, Masters, and Finch—got in the habit of meeting on Friday afternoons at a small saloon in downtown Columbia, drinking large schooners of beer and talking late into the night. Though he found the only social pleasure he knew in these evenings, Stoner often wondered at their relationship. Though they got along well enough together, they had not become close friends; they had no confidences and seldom saw each other outside their weekly gatherings.

None of them ever raised the question of that relationship. Stoner knew that it had not occurred to Gordon Finch, but he suspected that it had to David Masters. Once, late in the evening, as they sat at a rear table in the dimness of the saloon, Stoner and Masters talked of their teaching and study with the awkward facetiousness of the very serious. Masters, holding aloft a hard-boiled egg from the free lunch as if it were a crystal ball, said, "Have you gentlemen ever considered the question of the true nature of the University? Mr. Stoner? Mr. Finch?"

Smiling, they shook their heads.

"I'll bet you haven't. Stoner, here, I imagine, sees it as a great repository, like a library or a whorehouse, where men come of their free will and select that which will complete them, where all work together like little bees in a common hive. The True, the Good, the Beautiful. They're just around the corner, in the next corridor; they're in the next book, the one you haven't read, or in the next stack, the one you haven't got to. But you'll get to it someday. And when you do—when you do—" He looked at the egg for a moment more, then took a large bite of it and turned to Stoner, his jaws working and his dark eyes bright.

Stoner smiled uncomfortably, and Finch laughed aloud and slapped the table. "He's got you, Bill. He's got you good."

Masters chewed for a moment more, swallowed, and turned his gaze to Finch. "And you, Finch. What's your idea?" He held up his hand. "You'll protest you haven't thought of it. But you have. Beneath that bluff and hearty exterior there works a simple mind. To you, the institution is an instrument of good —to the world at large, of course, and just incidentally to yourself. You see it as a kind of spiritual sulphur-and-molasses that you administer every fall to get the little bastards through another winter; and you're the kindly old doctor who benignly pats their heads and pockets their fees."

Finch laughed again and shook his head. "I swear, Dave, when you get going—"

Masters put the rest of the egg in his mouth, chewed contentedly for a moment, and took a long swallow of beer. "But you're both wrong," he said. "It is an asylum or—what do they call them now?—a rest home, for the infirm, the aged, the discontent, and the otherwise incompetent. Look at the three of us—*we* are the University. The stranger would not know that we have so much in common, but *we* know, don't we? We know well."

Finch was laughing. "What's that, Dave?"

Interested now in what he was saying, Masters leaned intently across the table. "Let's take you first, Finch. Being as kind as I can, I would say that you are the incompetent. As you yourself know, you're not really very bright—though that doesn't have everything to do with it."

"Here, now," Finch said, still laughing.

"But you're bright enough—and *just* bright enough—to realize what would happen to you in the world. You're cut out for failure, and you know it. Though you're capable of being a son-of-a-bitch, you're not quite ruthless enough to be so consistently. Though you're not precisely the most honest man I've ever known, neither are you heroically dishonest. On the one hand, you're capable of work, but you're just lazy enough so that you can't work as hard as the world would want you to. On the other hand, you're not quite so lazy that you can impress upon the world a sense of your importance. And you're not lucky—not really. No aura rises from you, and you wear a puzzled expression. In the world you would always be on the fringe of success, and you would be destroyed by your failure. So you are chosen, elected; providence, whose sense of humor has always amused me, has snatched you from the jaws of the world and placed you safely here, among your brothers."

Still smiling and ironically malevolent, he turned to Stoner. "Nor do you escape, my friend. No indeed. Who are you? A simple son of the soil, as you pretend to yourself? Oh, no. You, too, are among the infirm—you are the dreamer, the madman in a madder world, our own midwestern Don Quixote without his Sancho, gamboling under the blue sky. You're bright enough—brighter anyhow than our mutual friend. But you have the taint, the old infirmity. You think there's something *here*, something to find. Well, in the world you'd learn soon enough. You, too, are cut out for failure; not that you'd fight the world. You'd let it chew you up and spit you out, and you'd lie there wondering what was wrong. Because you'd always expect the world to be something it wasn't, something it had no wish to be. The weevil in the cotton, the worm in the beanstalk, the borer in the corn. You couldn't face them, and you couldn't fight them; because you're too weak, and you're too strong. And you have no place to go in the world."

"What about you?" Finch asked. "What about yourself?"

"Oh," Masters said, leaning back, "I'm one of you. Worse, in fact. I'm too bright for the world, and I won't keep my mouth shut about it; it's a disease for which there is no cure. So I must be locked up, where I can be safely irresponsible, where I can do no harm." He leaned forward again and smiled at them. "We're all poor Toms, and we're a-cold."

"King Lear," Stoner said seriously.

"Act Three, Scene Four," said Masters. "And so providence, or society, or fate, or whatever name you want to give it, has created this hovel for us, so that we can go in out of the storm. It's for us that the University exists, for the dispossessed of the world; not for the students, not for the selfless pursuit of knowledge, not for any of the reasons that you hear. We give out the reasons, and we let a few of the ordinary ones in, those that would do in the world; but that's just protective coloration. Like the church in the Middle Ages, which didn't give a damn about the laity or even about God, we have our pretenses in order to survive. And we shall survive—because we have to."

Finch shook his head admiringly. "You sure make us sound bad, Dave."

"Maybe I do," Masters said. "But bad as we are, we're better than those on the outside, in the muck, the poor bastards of the world. We do no harm, we say what we want, and we get paid for it; and that's a triumph of natural virtue, or pretty damn close to it."

Masters leaned back from the table, indifferent, no longer concerned with what he had said.

Gordon Finch cleared his throat. "Well, now," he said earnestly. "You may have something in what you say, Dave. But I think you go too far. I really do."

Stoner and Masters smiled at each other, and they spoke no more of the question that evening. But for years afterward, at odd moments, Stoner remembered what Masters had said; and though it brought him no vision of the University to which he had committed himself, it did reveal to him something about his relationship to the two men, and it gave him a glimpse of the corrosive and unspoiled bitterness of youth.

On May 7, 1915, a German submarine sank the British liner *Lusitania*, with a hundred and fourteen American passengers on board; by the end of 1916 submarine warfare by the Germans was unrestricted, and relations between the United States and Germany steadily worsened. In February 1917 President Wilson broke off diplomatic relations. On April 6 a state of war was declared by Congress to exist between Germany and the United States.

With that declaration, thousands of young men across the nation, as if relieved that the tension of uncertainty had finally been broken, besieged the recruiting stations that had been hastily set up some weeks before. Indeed, hundreds of young men had not been able to wait for America's intervention and had as early as 1915 signed up for duty with the Royal Canadian forces or as ambulance drivers for one of the European allied armies. A few of the older students at the University had done so; and although William Stoner had not known any of these, he heard their legendary names with increasing frequency as the months and weeks drew on to the moment that they all knew must eventually come.

War was declared on a Friday, and although classes remained scheduled the following week, few students or professors made a pretense of meeting them. They milled about in the halls and gathered in small groups, murmuring in hushed voices. Occasionally the tense quietness erupted into near violence; twice there were general anti-German demonstrations, in which students shouted incoherently and waved American flags. Once there was a brief-lived demonstration against one of the professors, an old and bearded teacher of Germanic languages, who had been born in Munich and who as a youth had attended the University of Berlin. But when the professor met the angry and flushed little group of students, blinked in bewilderment, and held out his thin, shaking hands to them, they disbanded in sullen confusion.

During those first days after the declaration of war Stoner also suffered a confusion, but it was profoundly different from that which gripped most of the others on the campus. Though he had talked about the war in Europe with the older students and instructors, he had never quite believed in it; and now that it was upon him, upon them all, he discovered within himself a vast reserve of indifference. He resented the disruption which the war forced upon the University; but he could find in himself no very strong feelings of patriotism, and he could not bring himself to hate the Germans.

But the Germans were there to be hated. Once Stoner came upon Gordon Finch talking to a group of older faculty members; Finch's face was twisted, and he was speaking of the "Huns" as if he were spitting on the floor. Later, when he approached Stoner in the large office which half a dozen of the younger instructors shared, Finch's mood had shifted; feverishly jovial, he clapped Stoner on the shoulder.

"Can't let them get away with it, Bill," he said rapidly. A film of sweat like oil glistened on his round face, and his thin blond hair lay in lank strands over his skull. "No, sir. I'm going to join up. I've already talked to old Sloane about it, and he said to go ahead. I'm going down to St. Louis tomorrow and sign up." For an instant he managed to compose his features into a semblance of gravity. "We've all got to do our part." Then he grinned and clapped Stoner's shoulder again. "You better come along with me."

"Me?" Stoner said, and said again, incredulously, "Me?"

Finch laughed. "Sure. Everybody's signing up. I just talked to Dave—he's coming with me."

Stoner shook his head as if dazed. "Dave Masters?"

"Sure. Old Dave talks kind of funny sometimes, but when the chips are down he's no different from anybody else; he'll do his part. Just like you'll do yours, Bill." Finch punched him on the arm. "Just like you'll do yours."

Stoner was silent for a moment. "I hadn't thought about it," he said. "It all seems to have happened so quickly. I'll have to talk to Sloane. I'll let you know."

"Sure," Finch said. "You'll do your part." His voice thickened with feeling. "We're all in this together now, Bill; we're all in it together."

Stoner left Finch then, but he did not go to see Archer Sloane. Instead he looked about the campus and inquired after David Masters. He found him in one of the library carrels, alone, puffing on a pipe and staring at a shelf of books.

Stoner sat across from him at the carrel desk. When he questioned him about his decision to join the Army, Masters said, "Sure. Why not?"

And when Stoner asked him why, Masters said, "You know me pretty well, Bill. I don't give a damn about the Germans. When it comes down to it, I don't really give a damn about the Americans either, I guess." He knocked his pipe ashes out on the floor and swept them around with his foot. "I suppose I'm doing it because it doesn't matter whether I do it or not. And it might be amusing to pass through the world once more before I return to the cloistered and slow extinction that awaits us all."

Though he did not understand, Stoner nodded, accepting what Masters told him. He said, "Gordon wants me to enlist with you."

Masters smiled. "Gordon feels the first strength of virtue he's ever been allowed to feel; and he naturally wants to include the rest of the world in it, so that he can keep on believing. Sure. Why not? Join up with us. It might do you good to see what the world's like." He paused and looked intently at Stoner. "But if you do, for Christ's sake don't do it for God, country, and the dear old U. of M. Do it for yourself."

Stoner waited several moments. Then he said, "I'll talk to Sloane and let you know."

He did not know what he expected Archer Sloane's response to be; nevertheless he was surprised when he confronted him in his narrow book-lined office and told him of what was not quite yet his decision.

Sloane, who had always maintained toward him an attitude of detached and courtly irony, lost his temper. His long thin face went red, and the lines on either side of his mouth deepened in anger; he half rose from his chair toward Stoner, his fists clenched. Then he settled back and deliberately loosened his fists and spread his hands upon his desk; the fingers were trembling, but his voice was steady and harsh.

"I ask you to forgive my sudden display. But in the last few days I have lost nearly a third of the members of the department, and I see no hope of replacing them. It is not you at whom I am angry, but—" He turned away from Stoner and looked up at the high window at the far end of his office. The light struck his face sharply, accentuating the lines and deepening the shadows under his eyes, so that for a moment he seemed old and sick. "I was born in 1860, just before the War of the Rebellion. I don't remember it, of course; I was too young. I don't remember my father either; he was killed in the first year of the war, at the Battle of Shiloh." He looked quickly at Stoner. "But I can see what has ensued. A war doesn't merely kill off a few thousand or a few hundred thousand young men. It kills off something in a people that can never be brought back. And if a people goes through enough wars, pretty soon all that's left is the brute, the creature that we—you and I and others like us—have brought up from the slime." He paused for a long moment; then he smiled slightly. "The scholar should not be asked to destroy what he has aimed his life to build."

Stoner cleared his throat and said diffidently, "Everything seems to have happened so quickly. Somehow it had never occurred to me, until I talked to Finch and Masters. It still doesn't seem quite real."

"It's not, of course," Sloane said. Then he moved restlessly, turning away from Stoner. "I'm not going to tell you what to do. I'll simply say this: it's your choice to make. There'll be a conscription; but you can be excepted, if you want to be. You're not afraid to go, are you?"

"No, sir," Stoner said. "I don't believe so."

"Then you do have a choice, and you'll have to make it for yourself. It goes without saying that if you decide to join you will upon your return be reinstated in your present position. If you decide not to join you can stay on here, but of course you will have no particular advantage; it is possible that you will have a disadvantage, either now or in the future."

"I understand," Stoner said.

There was a long silence, and Stoner decided at last that

Sloane had finished with him. But just as he got up to leave the office Sloane spoke again.

He said slowly, "You must remember what you are and what you have chosen to become, and the significance of what you are doing. There are wars and defeats and victories of the human race that are not military and that are not recorded in the annals of history. Remember that while you're trying to decide what to do."

For two days Stoner did not meet his classes and did not speak to anyone he knew. He stayed in his small room, struggling with his decision. His books and the quiet of his room surrounded him; only rarely was he aware of the world outside his room, of the far murmur of shouting students, of the swift clatter of a buggy on the brick streets, and the flat chug of one of the dozen or so automobiles in town. He had never got in the habit of introspection, and he found the task of searching his motives a difficult and slightly distasteful one; he felt that he had little to offer to himself and that there was little within him which he could find.

When at last he came to his decision, it seemed to him that he had known all along what it would be. He met Masters and Finch on Friday and told them that he would not join them to fight the Germans.

Gordon Finch, sustained still by his accession to virtue, stiffened and allowed an expression of reproachful sorrow to settle on his features. "You're letting us down, Bill," he said thickly. "You're letting us all down."

"Be quiet," Masters said. He looked keenly at Stoner. "I thought you might decide not to. You've always had that lean, dedicated look about you. It doesn't matter, of course; but what made you finally decide?"

Stoner did not speak for a moment. He thought of the last two days, of the silent struggle that seemed toward no end and no meaning; he thought of his life at the University for the past seven years; he thought of the years before, the distant years with his parents on the farm, and of the deadness from which he had been miraculously revived.

"I don't know," he said at last. "Everything, I guess. I can't say."

"It's going to be hard," Masters said, "staying here."

"I know," Stoner said.

"But it's worth it, you think?"

Stoner nodded.

Masters grinned and said with his old irony, "You have the lean and hungry look, sure enough. You're doomed."

Finch's sorrowful reproach had turned into a kind of tentative contempt. "You'll live to regret this, Bill," he said hoarsely, and his voice hesitated between threat and pity.

Stoner nodded. "It may be," he said.

He told them good-by then, and turned away. They were to go to St. Louis the next day to enlist, and Stoner had classes to prepare for the following week.

He felt no guilt for his decision, and when conscription became general he applied for his deferment with no particular feeling of remorse; but he was aware of the looks that he received from his older colleagues and of the thin edge of disrespect that showed through his students' conventional behavior toward him. He even suspected that Archer Sloane, who had at one time expressed a warm approval of his decision to continue at the University, grew colder and more distant as the months of the war wore on.

He finished the requirements for his doctorate in the spring of 1918 and took his degree in June of that year. A month before he received his degree he got a letter from Gordon Finch, who had gone through Officer's Training School and had been assigned to a training camp just outside New York City. The letter informed him that Finch had been allowed, in his spare time, to attend Columbia University, where he, too, had managed to fulfill the requirements necessary for a doctorate, which he would take in the summer from Teachers College there.

It also told him that Dave Masters had been sent to France and that almost exactly a year after his enlistment, with the first American troops to see action, he had been killed at Château-Thierry.

III

A WEEK BEFORE commencement, at which Stoner was to receive his doctorate, Archer Sloane offered him a full-time instructorship at the University. Sloane explained that it was not the policy of the University to employ its own graduates, but because of the wartime shortage of trained and experienced college teachers he had been able to persuade the administration to make an exception.

Somewhat reluctantly Stoner had written a few letters of application to universities and colleges in the general area, abruptly setting forth his qualifications; when nothing came from any of them, he felt curiously relieved. He half understood his relief; he had known at the University at Columbia the kind of security and warmth that he should have been able to feel as a child in his home, and had not been able to, and he was unsure of his ability to find those elsewhere. He accepted Sloane's offer with gratitude.

And as he did so it occurred to him that Sloane had aged greatly during the year of the war. In his late fifties, he looked ten years older; his hair, which had once curled in an unruly iron-gray shock, now was white and lay flat and lifeless about his bony skull. His black eyes had gone dull, as if filmed over with layers of moisture; his long, lined face, which had once been tough as thin leather, now had the fragility of ancient, drying paper; and his flat, ironical voice had begun to develop a tremor. Looking at him, Stoner thought: He is going to die —in a year, or two years, or ten, he will die. A premature sense of loss gripped him, and he turned away.

His thoughts were much upon death that summer of 1918. The death of Masters had shocked him more than he wished to admit; and the first American casualty lists from Europe were beginning to be released. When he had thought of death before, he had thought of it either as a literary event or as the slow, quiet attrition of time against imperfect flesh. He had not thought of it as the explosion of violence upon a battlefield, as the gush of blood from the ruptured throat. He wondered at the difference between the two kinds of dying, and what the difference meant; and he found growing in him some of that bitterness he had glimpsed once in the living heart of his friend David Masters.

His dissertation topic had been "The Influence of the Classical Tradition upon the Medieval Lyric." He spent much of the summer rereading the classical and medieval Latin poets, and especially their poems upon death. He wondered again at the easy, graceful manner in which the Roman lyricists accepted the fact of death, as if the nothingness they faced were a tribute to the richness of the years they had enjoyed; and he marveled at the bitterness, the terror, the barely concealed hatred he found in some of the later Christian poets of the Latin tradition when they looked to that death which promised, however vaguely, a rich and ecstatic eternity of life, as if that death and promise were a mockery that soured the days of their living. When he thought of Masters, he thought of him as a Catullus or a more gentle and lyrical Juvenal, an exile in his own country, and thought of his death as another exile, more strange and lasting than he had known before.

When the semester opened in the autumn of 1918 it was clear to everyone that the war in Europe could not go on much longer. The last, desperate German counteroffensive had been stopped short of Paris, and Marshal Foch had ordered a general allied counterattack that quickly pushed the Germans back to their original line. The British advanced to the north and the Americans went through the Argonne, at a cost that was widely ignored in the general elation. The newspapers were predicting a collapse of the Germans before Christmas.

So the semester began in an atmosphere of tense geniality and well-being. The students and instructors found themselves smiling at each other and nodding vigorously in the halls; outbursts of exuberance and small violence among the students were ignored by the faculty and administration; and an unidentified student, who immediately became a kind of local folk hero, shinnied up one of the huge columns in front of Jesse Hall and hung from its top a straw-stuffed effigy of the Kaiser.

The only person in the University who seemed untouched by the general excitement was Archer Sloane. Since the day of America's entrance into the war he had begun to withdraw into himself, and the withdrawal became more pronounced as the war neared its end. He did not speak to his colleagues unless departmental business forced him to do so, and it was whispered that his teaching had become so eccentric that his students attended his classes in dread; he read dully and mechanically from his notes, never meeting his students' eyes; frequently his voice trailed off as he stared at his notes, and there would be one, two, and sometimes as many as five minutes of silence, during which he neither moved nor responded to embarrassed questions from the class.

William Stoner saw the last vestige of the bright, ironic man he had known as a student when Archer Sloane gave him his teaching assignment for the academic year. Sloane gave Stoner two sections of freshman composition and an upper division survey of Middle English literature; and then he said, with a flash of his old irony, "You, as well as many of our colleagues and not a few of our students, will be pleased to know that I am giving up a number of my classes. Among these is one that has been my rather unfashionable favorite, the sophomore survey of English literature. You may recall the course?"

Stoner nodded, smiling.

"Yes," Sloane continued, "I rather thought you would. I am asking you to take it over for me. Not that it's a great gift; but I thought it might amuse you to begin your formal career as a teacher where you started as a student." Sloane looked at him for a moment, his eyes bright and intent as they had been before the war. Then the film of indifference settled over them, and he turned away from Stoner and shuffled some papers on his desk.

So Stoner began where he had started, a tall, thin, stooped man in the same room in which he had sat as a tall, thin, stooped boy listening to the words that had led him to where he had come. He never went into that room that he did not glance at the seat he had once occupied, and he was always slightly surprised to discover that he was not there.

On November 11 of that year, two months after the semester began, the Armistice was signed. The news came on a class day, and immediately the classes broke up; students ran aimlessly about the campus and started small parades that gathered, dispersed, and gathered again, winding through halls, classrooms, and offices. Half against his will, Stoner was caught up in one of these which went into Jesse Hall, through corridors, up stairs, and through corridors again. Swept along in a small mass of students and teachers, he passed the open door of Archer Sloane's office; and he had a glimpse of Sloane sitting in his chair before his desk, his face uncovered and twisted, weeping bitterly, the tears streaming down the deep lines of the flesh.

For a moment more, as if in shock, Stoner allowed himself to be carried along by the crowd. Then he broke away and went to his room near the campus. He sat in the dimness of his room and heard outside the shouts of joy and release, and thought of Archer Sloane who wept at a defeat that only he saw, or thought he saw; and he knew that Sloane was a broken man and would never again be what he had been.

Late in November many of those who had gone away to war began to return to Columbia, and the campus at the University was dotted with the olive drab of army uniforms. Among those who returned on extended leaves was Gordon Finch. He had put on weight during his year and a half away from the University, and the broad, open face that had been amiably acquiescent now held an expression of friendly but portentous gravity; he wore the bars of a captain and spoke often with a paternal fondness of "my men." He was distantly friendly to William Stoner, and he took exaggerated care to behave with deference toward the older members of the department. It was too late in the fall semester to assign him any classes, so for the rest of the academic year he was given what was understood to be a temporary sinecure as administrative assistant to the dean of Arts and Sciences. He was sensitive enough to be aware of the ambiguity of his new position and shrewd enough to see its possibilities; his relations with his colleagues were tentative and courteously noncommittal.

The dean of Arts and Sciences, Josiah Claremont, was a small bearded man of advanced age, several years beyond the point of compulsory retirement; he had been with the University ever since its transition, in the early seventies of the preceding century, from a normal college to a full University, and his father had been one of its early presidents. He was so firmly entrenched and so much a part of the history of the

University that no one quite had the courage to insist upon his retirement, despite the increasing incompetence with which he managed his office. His memory was nearly gone; sometimes he became lost in the corridors of Jesse Hall, where his office was located, and had to be led like a child to his desk.

So vague had he become about University affairs that when an announcement came from his office that a reception in honor of the returning veterans on the faculty and administrative staff would be held at his home, most of those who received invitations felt that an elaborate joke was being played or that a mistake had been made. But it was not a joke, and it was not a mistake. Gordon Finch confirmed the invitations; and it was widely hinted that it was he who had instigated the reception and who had carried through the plans.

Josiah Claremont, widowed many years before, lived alone, with three colored servants nearly as old as himself, in one of the large pre–Civil War homes that had once been common around Columbia but were fast disappearing before the coming of the small, independent farmer and the real-estate developer. The architecture of the place was pleasant but unidentifiable; though "Southern" in its general shape and expansiveness, it had none of the neo-classic rigidity of the Virginia home. Its boards were painted white, and green trim framed the windows and the balustrades of the small balconies that projected here and there from the upper story. The grounds extended into a wood that surrounded the place, and tall poplars, leafless in the December afternoon, lined the drive and the walks. It was the grandest house that William Stoner had ever been near; and on that Friday afternoon he walked with some dread up the driveway and joined a group of faculty whom he did not know, who were waiting at the front door to be admitted.

Gordon Finch, still wearing his army uniform, opened the door to let them in; the group stepped into a small square foyer, at the end of which a steep staircase with polished oaken banisters led upward to the second story. A small French tapestry, its blues and golds so faded that the pattern was hardly visible in the dim yellow light given by the small bulbs, hung on the staircase wall directly in front of the men who had entered. Stoner stood gazing up at it while those who had come in with him milled about the small foyer.

"Give me your coat, Bill." The voice, close to his ear, startled him. He turned. Finch was smiling and holding his hand out to receive the coat which Stoner had not removed.

"You haven't been here before, have you?" Finch asked almost in a whisper. Stoner shook his head.

Finch turned to the other men and without raising his voice managed to call out to them. "You gentlemen go on into the main living room." He pointed to a door at the right of the foyer. "Everybody's in there."

He returned his attention to Stoner. "It's a fine old house," he said, hanging Stoner's coat in a large closet beneath the staircase. "It's one of the real showplaces around here."

"Yes," Stoner said. "I've heard people talk about it."

"And Dean Claremont's a fine old man. He asked me to kind of look out for things for him this evening."

Stoner nodded.

Finch took his arm and guided him toward the door to which he had pointed earlier. "We'll have to get together for a talk later on this evening. You go on in now. I'll be there in a minute. There are some people I want you to meet."

Stoner started to speak, but Finch had turned away to greet another group that had come in the front door. Stoner took a deep breath and opened the door to the main living room.

When he came into the room from the cold foyer the warmth pushed against him, as if to force him back; the slow murmur of the people inside, released by his opening the door, swelled for a moment before his ears accustomed themselves to it.

Perhaps two dozen people milled about the room, and for an instant he recognized none of them; he saw the sober black and gray and brown of men's suits, the olive drab of army uniforms, and here and there the delicate pink or blue of a woman's dress. The people moved sluggishly through the warmth, and he moved with them, conscious of his height among the seated figures, nodding to the faces he now recognized.

At the far end another door led into a sitting parlor, which was adjacent to the long, narrow dining hall. The double doors of the hall were open, revealing a massive walnut dining table covered with yellow damask and laden with white dishes and bowls of gleaming silver. Several people were gathered around the table, at the head of which a young woman, tall and slender and fair, dressed in a gown of blue watered silk, stood pouring tea into gold-rimmed china cups. Stoner paused in the doorway, caught by his vision of the young woman. Her long, delicately featured face smiled at those around her, and her slender, almost fragile fingers deftly manipulated urn and cup; looking at her, Stoner was assailed by a consciousness of his own heavy clumsiness.

For several moments he did not move from the doorway; he heard the girl's soft, thin voice rise above the murmur of the assembled guests she served. She raised her head, and suddenly he met her eyes; they were pale and large and seemed to shine with a light within themselves. In some confusion he backed from the doorway and turned into the sitting room; he found an empty chair in a space by the wall, and he sat there looking at the carpet beneath his feet. He did not look in the direction of the dining room, but every now and then he thought he felt the gaze of the young woman brush warmly across his face.

The guests moved around him, exchanged seats, altered their inflections as they found new partners for conversation. Stoner saw them through a haze, as if he were an audience. After a while Gordon Finch came into the room, and Stoner got up from his chair and walked across the room to him. Almost rudely he interrupted Finch's conversation with an older man. Drawing him aside but not lowering his voice, he asked to be introduced to the young woman pouring tea.

Finch looked at him for a moment, the annoyed frown that had begun to pucker his forehead smoothing as his eyes widened. "You what?" Finch said. Though he was shorter than Stoner, he seemed to be looking down on him.

"I want you to introduce me," Stoner said. He felt his face warm. "Do you know her?"

"Sure," Finch said. The start of a grin began to tug at his mouth. "She's some kind of cousin of the dean's, down from St. Louis, visiting an aunt." The grin widened. "Old Bill. What do you know. Sure, I'll introduce you. Come on."

Her name was Edith Elaine Bostwick, and she lived with her parents in St. Louis, where the previous spring she had finished a two-year course of study at a private seminary for young ladies; she was visiting her mother's older sister in Columbia for a few weeks, and in the spring they were to make the Grand

Tour of Europe—an event once again possible, now that the war was over. Her father, the president of one of the smaller St. Louis banks, was a transplanted New Englander; he had come west in the seventies and married the oldest daughter of a well-to-do central Missouri family. Edith had lived all her life in St. Louis; a few years before she had gone east with her parents to Boston for the season; she had been to the opera in New York and had visited the museums. She was twenty years of age, she played the piano, and had artistic leanings which her mother encouraged.

Later, William Stoner could not remember how he learned these things, that first afternoon and early evening at Josiah Claremont's house; for the time of his meeting was blurred and formal, like the figured tapestry on the stair wall off the foyer. He remembered that he spoke to her that she might look at him, remain near him, and give him the pleasure of hearing her soft, thin voice answering his questions and making perfunctory questions in return.

The guests began to leave. Voices called good-bys, doors slammed, and the rooms emptied. Stoner remained behind after most of the other guests had departed; and when Edith's carriage came he followed her into the foyer and helped her with her coat. Just before she started outside he asked her if he might call on her the following evening.

As if she had not heard him she opened the door and stood for several moments without moving: the cold air swept through the doorway and touched Stoner's hot face. She turned and looked at him and blinked several times; her pale eyes were speculative, almost bold. At last she nodded and said, "Yes. You may call." She did not smile.

And so he called, walking across town to her aunt's house on an intensely cold midwestern winter night. No cloud was overhead; the half-moon shone upon a light snow that had fallen earlier in the afternoon. The streets were deserted, and the muffled silence was broken by the dry snow crunching underfoot as he walked. He stood for a long while outside the large house to which he had come, listening to the silence. The cold numbed his feet, but he did not move. From the curtained windows a dim light fell upon the blue-white snow like a yellow smudge; he thought he saw movement inside, but he could not be sure. Deliberately, as if committing himself to something, he stepped forward and walked down the path to the porch and knocked on the front door.

Edith's aunt (her name, Stoner had learned earlier, was Emma Darley, and she had been widowed for a number of years) met him at the door and asked him to come in. She was a short, plump woman with fine white hair that floated about her face; her dark eyes twinkled moistly, and she spoke softly and breathlessly as if she were telling secrets. Stoner followed her into the parlor and sat, facing her, on a long walnut sofa, the seat and back of which were covered with thick blue velvet. Snow had clung to his shoes; he watched it melt and form damp patches on the thick floral rug under his feet.

"Edith tells me you teach at the University, Mr. Stoner," Mrs. Darley said.

"Yes, ma'am," he said and cleared his throat.

"It's so *nice* to be able to talk to one of the young professors there again," Mrs. Darley said brightly. "My late husband, Mr. Darley, was on the board of trustees at the University for a number of years—but I guess you know that."

"No, ma'am," Stoner said.

"Oh," Mrs. Darley said. "Well, we used to have some of the younger professors over for tea in the afternoons. But that was quite a few years ago, before the war. You were in the war, Professor Stoner?"

"No, ma'am," Stoner said. "I was at the University."

"Yes," Mrs. Darley said. She nodded brightly. "And you teach—?"

"English," Stoner said. "And I'm not a professor. I'm just an instructor." He knew his voice was harsh; he could not control it. He tried to smile.

"Ah, yes," she said. "Shakespeare . . . Browning . . ."

A silence came between them. Stoner twisted his hands together and looked at the floor.

Mrs. Darley said, "I'll see if Edith is ready. If you'll excuse me?"

Stoner nodded and got to his feet as she went out. He heard fierce whispers in a back room. He stood for several minutes more.

Suddenly Edith was standing in the wide doorway, pale and unsmiling. They looked at each other without recognition. Edith took a backward step and then came forward, her lips thin and tense. They shook hands gravely and sat together on the sofa. They had not spoken.

She was even taller than he remembered, and more fragile. Her face was long and slender, and she kept her lips closed over rather strong teeth. Her skin had the kind of transparency that shows a hint of color and warmth upon any provocation. Her hair was a light reddish-brown, and she wore it piled in thick tresses upon her head. But it was her eyes that caught and held him, as they had done the day before. They were very large and of the palest blue that he could imagine. When he looked at them he seemed drawn out of himself, into a mystery that he could not apprehend. He thought her the most beautiful woman he had ever seen, and he said impulsively, "I—I want to know about you." She drew back from him a little. He said hastily, "I mean—yesterday, at the reception, we didn't really have a chance to talk. I wanted to talk to you, but there were so many people. People sometimes get in your way."

"It was a very nice reception," Edith said faintly. "I thought everyone was very nice."

"Oh, yes, of course," Stoner said. "I meant . . ." He did not go on. Edith was silent.

He said, "I understand you and your aunt will be going to Europe in a little while."

"Yes," she said.

"Europe . . ." He shook his head. "You must be very excited."

She nodded reluctantly.

"Where will you go? I mean—what places?"

"England," she said. "France. Italy."

"And you'll be going—in the spring?"

"April," she said.

"Five months," he said. "It isn't very long. I hope that in that time we can—"

"I'm only here for three more weeks," she said quickly. "Then I go back to St. Louis. For Christmas."

"That *is* a short time." He smiled and said awkwardly, "Then

I'll have to see you as often as I can, so that we can get to know each other."

She looked at him almost with horror. "I didn't mean that," she said. "Please . . ."

Stoner was silent for a moment. "I'm sorry, I— But I do want to call on you again, as often as you'll let me. May I?"

"Oh," she said. "Well." Her thin fingers were laced together in her lap, and her knuckles were white where the skin was stretched. She had very pale freckles on the backs of her hands.

Stoner said, "This is going badly, isn't it? You must forgive me. I haven't known anyone like you before, and I say clumsy things. You must forgive me if I've embarrassed you."

"Oh, no," she said. She turned to him and pulled her lips in what he knew must be a smile. "Not at all. I'm having a lovely time. Really."

He did not know what to say. He mentioned the weather outside and apologized for having tracked snow upon the rug; she murmured something. He spoke of the classes he had to teach at the University, and she nodded, puzzled. At last they sat in silence. Stoner got to his feet; he moved slowly and heavily, as if he were tired. Edith looked up at him expressionlessly.

"Well," he said and cleared his throat. "It's getting late, and I— Look. I'm sorry. May I call on you again in a few days? Perhaps . . ."

It was as if he had not spoken to her. He nodded, said, "Good night," and turned to go.

Edith Bostwick said in a high shrill voice without inflection, "When I was a little girl about six years old I could play the piano and I liked to paint and I was very shy so my mother sent me to Miss Thorndyke's School for Girls in St. Louis. I was the youngest one there, but that was all right because Daddy was a member of the board and he arranged it. I didn't like it at first but finally I just loved it. They were all very nice girls and well-to-do and I made some lifelong friends there, and—"

Stoner had turned back when she began to speak, and he looked at her with an amazement that did not show on his face. Her eyes were fixed straight before her, her face was blank, and her lips moved as if, without understanding, she read from an invisible book. He walked slowly across the room and sat down beside her. She did not seem to notice him; her eyes remained fixed straight ahead, and she continued to tell him about herself, as he had asked her to do. He wanted to tell her to stop, to comfort her, to touch her. He did not move or speak.

She continued to talk, and after a while he began to hear what she was saying. Years later it was to occur to him that in that hour and a half on that December evening of their first extended time together, she told him more about herself than she ever told him again. And when it was over, he felt that they were strangers in a way that he had not thought they would be, and he knew that he was in love.

Edith Elaine Bostwick was probably not aware of what she said to William Stoner that evening, and if she had been she could not have realized its significance. But Stoner knew what she said, and he never forgot it; what he heard was a kind of confession, and what he thought he understood was a plea for help.

As he got to know her better, he learned more of her childhood; and he came to realize that it was typical of that of most girls of her time and circumstance. She was educated upon the premise that she would be protected from the gross events that life might thrust in her way, and upon the premise that she had no other duty than to be a graceful and accomplished accessory to that protection, since she belonged to a social and economic class to which protection was an almost sacred obligation. She attended private schools for girls where she learned to read, to write, and to do simple arithmetic; in her leisure she was encouraged to do needlepoint, to play the piano, to paint water colors, and to discuss some of the more gentle works of literature. She was also instructed in matters of dress, carriage, ladylike diction, and morality.

Her moral training, both at the schools she attended and at home, was negative in nature, prohibitive in intent, and almost entirely sexual. The sexuality, however, was indirect and unacknowledged; therefore it suffused every other part of her education, which received most of its energy from that recessive and unspoken moral force. She learned that she would have duties toward her husband and family and that she must fulfill them.

Her childhood was an exceedingly formal one, even in the most ordinary moments of family life. Her parents behaved toward each other with a distant courtesy; Edith never saw pass between them the spontaneous warmth of either anger or love. Anger was days of courteous silence, and love was a word of courteous endearment. She was an only child, and loneliness was one of the earliest conditions of her life.

So she grew up with a frail talent in the more genteel arts, and no knowledge of the necessity of living from day to day. Her needlepoint was delicate and useless, she painted misty landscapes of thin water-color washes, and she played the piano with a forceless but precise hand; yet she was ignorant of her own bodily functions, she had never been alone to care for her own self one day of her life, nor could it ever have occurred to her that she might become responsible for the well-being of another. Her life was invariable, like a low hum; and it was watched over by her mother, who, when Edith was a child, would sit for hours watching her paint her pictures or play her piano, as if no other occupation were possible for either of them.

At the age of thirteen Edith went through the usual sexual transformation; she also went through a physical transformation that was more uncommon. In the space of a few months she grew almost a foot, so that her height was near that of a grown man. And the association between the ungainliness of her body and her awkward new sexual estate was one from which she never fully recovered. These changes intensified a natural shyness—she was distant from her classmates at school, she had no one at home to whom she could talk, and she turned more and more inward upon herself.

Upon that inner privacy William Stoner now intruded. And something unsuspected within her, some instinct, made her call him back when he started to go out the door, made her speak quickly and desperately, as she had never spoken before, and as she would never speak again.

During the next two weeks he saw her nearly every evening. They went to a concert sponsored by the new music department at the University; on evenings when it was not too cold they took slow, solemn walks through the streets of Columbia;

but more often they sat in Mrs. Darley's parlor. Sometimes they talked, and Edith played for him, while he listened and watched her hands move lifelessly over the keys. After that first evening together their conversation was curiously impersonal; he was unable to draw her out of her reserve, and when he saw that his efforts to do so embarrassed her, he stopped trying. Yet there was a kind of ease between them, and he imagined that they had an understanding. Less than a week before she was to return to St. Louis he declared his love to her and proposed marriage.

Though he did not know exactly how she would take the declaration and proposal, he was surprised at her equanimity. After he spoke she gave him a long look that was deliberative and curiously bold; and he was reminded of the first afternoon, after he had asked permission to call on her, when she had looked at him from the doorway where a cold wind was blowing upon them. Then she dropped her glance; and the surprise that came upon her face seemed to him unreal. She said she had never thought of him that way, that she had never imagined, that she did not know.

"You must have known I loved you," he said. "I don't see how I could have hidden it."

She said with some hint of animation, "I didn't. I don't know anything about that."

"Then I must tell you again," he said gently. "And you must get used to it. I love you, and I cannot imagine living without you."

She shook her head, as if confused. "My trip to Europe," she said faintly. "Aunt Emma . . ."

He felt a laugh come up in his throat, and he said in happy confidence, "Ah, Europe. I'll take you to Europe. We'll see it together someday."

She pulled away from him and put her fingertips upon her forehead. "You must give me time to think. And I would have to talk to Mother and Daddy before I could even consider . . ."

And she would not commit herself further than that. She was not to see him again before she left for St. Louis in a few days, and she would write him from there after she talked to her parents and had things settled in her mind. When he left that evening he stooped to kiss her; she turned her head, and his lips brushed her cheek. She gave his hand a little squeeze and let him out the front door without looking at him again.

Ten days later he got his letter from her. It was a curiously formal note, and it mentioned nothing that had passed between them; it said that she would like him to meet her parents and that they were all looking forward to seeing him when he came to St. Louis, the following weekend if that was possible.

Edith's parents met him with the cool formality he had expected, and they tried at once to destroy any sense of ease he might have had. Mrs. Bostwick would ask him a question, and upon his answer would say, "Y-e-es," in a most doubtful manner, and look at him curiously, as if his face were smudged or his nose were bleeding. She was tall and thin like Edith, and at first Stoner was startled by a resemblance he had not anticipated; but Mrs. Bostwick's face was heavy and lethargic, without any strength or delicacy, and it bore the deep marks of what must have been a habitual dissatisfaction.

Horace Bostwick was also tall, but he was curiously and unsubstantially heavy, almost corpulent; a fringe of gray hair curled about an otherwise bald skull, and folds of skin hung loosely around his jaws. When he spoke to Stoner he looked directly above his head as if he saw something behind him, and when Stoner answered he drummed his thick fingers upon the center piping of his vest.

Edith greeted Stoner as if he were a casual visitor and then drifted away unconcernedly, busying herself with inconsequential tasks. His eyes followed her, but he could not make her look at him.

It was the largest and most elegant house that Stoner had ever been in. The rooms were very high and dark, and they were crowded with vases of all sizes and shapes, dully gleaming silverwork upon marble-topped tables and commodes and chests, and richly tapestried furniture with most delicate lines. They drifted through several rooms to a large parlor, where, Mrs. Bostwick murmured, she and her husband were in the habit of sitting and chatting informally with friends. Stoner sat in a chair so fragile that he was afraid to move upon it; he felt it shift beneath his weight.

Edith had disappeared; Stoner looked around for her almost frantically. But she did not come back down to the parlor for nearly two hours, until after Stoner and her parents had had their "talk."

The "talk" was indirect and allusive and slow, interrupted by long silences. Horace Bostwick talked about himself in brief speeches directed several inches over Stoner's head. Stoner learned that Bostwick was a Bostonian whose father, late in his life, had ruined his banking career and his son's future in New England by a series of unwise investments that had closed his bank. ("Betrayed," Bostwick announced to the ceiling, "by false friends.") Thus the son had come to Missouri shortly after the Civil War, intending to move west; but he had never got farther than Kansas City, where he went occasionally on business trips. Remembering his father's failure, or betrayal, he stayed with his first job in a small St. Louis bank; and in his late thirties, secure in a minor vice-presidency, he married a local girl of good family. From the marriage had come only one child; he had wanted a son and had got a girl, and that was another disappointment he hardly bothered to conceal. Like many men who consider their success incomplete, he was extraordinarily vain and consumed with a sense of his own importance. Every ten or fifteen minutes he removed a large gold watch from his vest pocket, looked at it, and nodded to himself.

Mrs. Bostwick spoke less frequently and less directly of herself, but Stoner quickly had an understanding of her. She was a Southern lady of a certain type. Of an old and discreetly impoverished family, she had grown up with the presumption that the circumstances of need under which the family existed were inappropriate to its quality. She had been taught to look forward to some betterment of that condition, but the betterment had never been very precisely specified. She had gone into her marriage to Horace Bostwick with that dissatisfaction so habitual within her that it was a part of her person; and as the years went on, the dissatisfaction and bitterness increased, so general and pervasive that no specific remedy might assuage them. Her voice was thin and high, and it held a note of hopelessness that gave a special value to every word she said.

It was late in the afternoon before either of them mentioned the matter that had brought them together.

They told him how dear Edith was to them, how concerned they were for her future happiness, of the advantages she had had. Stoner sat in an agony of embarrassment and tried to make responses he hoped were appropriate.

"An extraordinary girl," Mrs. Bostwick said. "So sensitive." The lines in her face deepened, and she said with old bitterness, "No man—no one can fully understand the delicacy of—of—"

"Yes," Horace Bostwick said shortly. And he began to inquire into what he called Stoner's "prospects." Stoner answered as best he could; he had never thought of his "prospects" before, and he was surprised at how meager they sounded.

Bostwick said, "And you have no—means—beyond your profession?"

"No, sir," Stoner said.

Mr. Bostwick shook his head unhappily. "Edith has had —advantages—you know. A fine home, servants, the best schools. I'm wondering—I find myself afraid, with the reduced standard which would be inevitable with your—ah, condition —that . . ." His voice trailed away.

Stoner felt a sickness rise within him, and an anger. He waited a few moments before he replied, and he made his voice as flat and expressionless as he could.

"I must tell you, sir, that I had not considered these material matters before. Edith's happiness is, of course, my— If you believe that Edith would be unhappy, then I must . . ." He paused, searching for words. He wanted to tell Edith's father of his love for his daughter, of his certainty of their happiness together, of the kind of life they could have. But he did not go on. He caught on Horace Bostwick's face such an expression of concern, dismay, and something like fear that he was surprised into silence.

"No," Horace Bostwick said hastily, and his expression cleared. "You misunderstand me. I was merely attempting to lay before you certain—difficulties—that might arise in the future. I'm sure you young people have talked these things over, and I'm sure you know your own minds. I respect your judgment and . . ."

And it was settled. A few more words were said, and Mrs.

Bostwick wondered aloud where Edith could have been keeping herself all this time. She called out the name in her high, thin voice, and in a few moments Edith came into the room where they all waited. She did not look at Stoner.

Horace Bostwick told her that he and her "young man" had had a nice talk and that they had his blessing. Edith nodded.

"Well," her mother said, "we must make plans. A spring wedding. June, perhaps."

"No," Edith said.

"What, my dear?" her mother asked pleasantly.

"If it's to be done," Edith said, "I want it done quickly."

"The impatience of youth," Mr. Bostwick said and cleared his throat. "But perhaps your mother is right, my dear. There are plans to be made; time is required."

"No," Edith said again, and there was a firmness in her voice that made them all look at her. "It must be soon."

There was a silence. Then her father said in a surprisingly mild voice, "Very well, my dear. As you say. You young people make your plans."

Edith nodded, murmured something about a task she had to do, and slipped out of the room. Stoner did not see her again until dinner that night, which was presided over in regal silence by Horace Bostwick. After dinner Edith played the piano for them, but she played stiffly and badly, with many mistakes. She announced that she was feeling unwell and went to her room.

In the guest room that night, William Stoner could not sleep. He stared up into the dark and wondered at the strangeness that had come over his life, and for the first time questioned the wisdom of what he was about to do. He thought of Edith and felt some reassurance. He supposed that all men were as uncertain as he suddenly had become, and had the same doubts.

He had to catch an early train back to Columbia the next morning, so that he had little time after breakfast. He wanted to take a trolley to the station, but Mr. Bostwick insisted that one of the servants drive him in the landau. Edith was to write him in a few days about the wedding plans. He thanked the Bostwicks and bade them good-by; they walked with him and Edith to the front door. He had almost reached the front gate when he heard footsteps running behind him. He turned. It was Edith. She stood very stiff and tall, her face was pale, and she was looking straight at him.

"I'll try to be a good wife to you, William," she said. "I'll try."

He realized that it was the first time anyone had spoken his name since he had come there.

IV

FOR REASONS she would not explain, Edith did not want to be married in St. Louis, so the wedding was held in Columbia, in the large drawing room of Emma Darley, where they had spent their first hours together. It was the first week in February, just after classes were dismissed for the semester break. The Bostwicks took the train from St. Louis, and William's parents, who had not met Edith, drove down from the farm, arriving on Saturday afternoon, the day before the wedding.

Stoner wanted to put them up at a hotel, but they preferred to stay with the Footes, even though the Footes had grown cold and distant since William had left their employ.

"Wouldn't know how to do in a hotel," his father said seriously. "And the Footes can put up with us for one night."

That evening William rented a gig and drove his parents into town to Emma Darley's house so that they could meet Edith.

They were met at the door by Mrs. Darley, who gave William's parents a brief, embarrassed glance and asked them into the parlor. His mother and father sat carefully, as if afraid to move in their stiff new clothes.

"I don't know what can be keeping Edith," Mrs. Darley murmured after a while. "If you'll excuse me." She went out of the room to get her niece.

After a long time Edith came down; she entered the parlor slowly, reluctantly, with a kind of frightened defiance.

They rose to their feet, and for several moments the four of them stood awkwardly, not knowing what to say. Then Edith came forward stiffly and gave her hand first to William's mother and then to his father.

"How do," his father said formally and released her hand, as if afraid it would break.

Edith glanced at him, tried to smile, and backed away. "Sit down," she said. "Please sit down."

They sat. William said something. His voice sounded strained to him.

In a silence, quietly and wonderingly, as if she spoke her

thoughts aloud, his mother said, "My, she's a pretty thing, isn't she?"

William laughed a little and said gently, "Yes, ma'am, she is."

They were able to speak more easily then, though they darted glances at each other and then looked away into the distances of the room. Edith murmured that she was glad to meet them, that she was sorry they hadn't met before.

"And when we get settled—" She paused, and William wondered if she was going to continue. "When we get settled you must come to visit us."

"Thank you kindly," his mother said.

The talk went on, but it was interrupted by long silences. Edith's nervousness increased, became more apparent, and once or twice she did not respond to a question someone asked her. William got to his feet, and his mother, with a nervous look around her, stood also. But his father did not move. He looked directly at Edith and kept his eyes on her for a long time.

Finally he said, "William was always a good boy. I'm glad he's getting himself a fine woman. A man needs himself a woman, to do for him and give him comfort. Now you be good to William. He ought to have someone who can be good to him."

Edith's head came back in a kind of reflex of shock; her eyes were wide, and for a moment William thought she was angry. But she was not. His father and Edith looked at each other for a long time, and their eyes did not waver.

"I'll try, Mr. Stoner," Edith said. "I'll try."

Then his father got to his feet and bowed clumsily and said, "It's getting late. We'd best be getting along." And he walked with his wife, shapeless and dark and small beside him, to the door, leaving Edith and his son together.

Edith did not speak to him. But when he turned to bid her good night William saw that tears were swimming in her eyes. He bent to kiss her, and he felt the frail strength of her slender fingers on his arms.

The cold clear sunlight of the February afternoon slanted through the front windows of the Darley house and was broken by the figures that moved about in the large parlor. His parents stood curiously alone in a corner of the room; the Bostwicks, who had come in only an hour before on the morning train, stood near them, not looking at them; Gordon Finch walked heavily and anxiously around, as if he were in charge of something; there were a few people, friends of Edith or her parents, whom he did not know. He heard himself speaking to those about him, felt his lips smiling, and heard voices come to him as if muffled by layers of thick cloth.

Gordon Finch was beside him; his face was sweaty, and it glowed above his dark suit. He grinned nervously. "You about ready, Bill?"

Stoner felt his head nod.

Finch said, "Does the doomed man have any last requests?"

Stoner smiled and shook his head.

Finch clapped him on the shoulder. "You just stick by me; do what I tell you; everything's under control. Edith will be down in a few minutes."

He wondered if he would remember this after it was over; everything seemed a blur, as if he saw through a haze. He heard himself ask Finch, "The minister—I haven't seen him. Is he here?"

Finch laughed and shook his head and said something. Then a murmur came over the room. Edith was walking down the stairs.

In her white dress she was like a cold light coming into the room. Stoner started involuntarily toward her and felt Finch's hand on his arm, restraining him. Edith was pale, but she gave him a small smile. Then she was beside him, and they were walking together. A stranger with a round collar stood before them; he was short and fat and he had a vague face. He was mumbling words and looking at a white book in his hands. William heard himself responding to silences. He felt Edith trembling beside him.

Then there was a long silence, and another murmur, and the sound of laughter. Someone said, "Kiss the bride!" He felt himself turned; Finch was grinning at him. He smiled down at Edith, whose face swam before him, and kissed her; her lips were as dry as his own.

He felt his hand being pumped; people were clapping him on the back and laughing; the room was milling. New people came in the door. A large cut-glass bowl of punch seemed to have appeared on a long table at one end of the parlor. There was a cake. Someone held his and Edith's hands together; there was a knife; he understood that he was supposed to guide her hand as she cut the cake.

Then he was separated from Edith and couldn't see her in the throng of people. He was talking and laughing, nodding, and looking around the room to see if he could find Edith. He saw his mother and father standing in the same corner of the room, from which they had not moved. His mother was smiling, and his father had his hand awkwardly on her shoulder. He started to go to them, but he could not break away from whoever was talking to him.

Then he saw Edith. She was with her father and mother and her aunt; her father, with a slight frown on his face, was surveying the room as if impatient with it; and her mother was weeping, her eyes red and puffed above her heavy cheekbones and her mouth pursed downward like a child's. Mrs. Darley and Edith had their arms about her; Mrs. Darley was talking to her, rapidly, as if trying to explain something. But even across the room William could see that Edith was silent; her face was like a mask, expressionless and white. After a moment they led Mrs. Bostwick from the room, and William did not see Edith again until the reception was over, until Gordon Finch whispered something in his ear, led him to a side door that opened onto a little garden, and pushed him outside. Edith was waiting there, bundled against the cold, her collar turned up about her face so that he could not see it. Gordon Finch, laughing and saying words that William could not understand, hustled them down a path to the street, where a covered buggy was waiting to carry them to the station. It was not until they were on the train, which would take them to St. Louis for their week's honeymoon, that William Stoner realized that it was all over and that he had a wife.

They went into marriage innocent, but innocent in profoundly different ways. They were both virginal, and they were conscious of their inexperience; but whereas William, having been raised on a farm, took as unremarkable the natural processes of life, they were to Edith profoundly mysterious and unexpected. She knew nothing of them, and there was something within her which did not wish to know of them.

And so, like many others, their honeymoon was a failure; yet they would not admit this to themselves, and they did not realize the significance of the failure until long afterward.

They arrived in St. Louis late Sunday night. On the train, surrounded by strangers who looked curiously and approvingly at them, Edith had been animated and almost gay. They laughed and held hands and spoke of the days to come. Once in the city, and by the time William had found a carriage to take them to their hotel, Edith's gaiety had become faintly hysterical.

He half carried her, laughing, through the entrance of the Ambassador Hotel, a massive structure of brown cut stone. The lobby was nearly deserted, dark and heavy like a cavern; when they got inside, Edith abruptly quieted and swayed uncertainly beside him as they walked across the immense floor to the desk. By the time they got to their room she was nearly physically ill; she trembled as if in a fever, and her lips were blue against her chalk-like skin. William wanted to find her a doctor, but she insisted that she was only tired, that she needed rest. They spoke gravely of the strain of the day, and Edith hinted at some delicacy that troubled her from time to time. She murmured, but without looking at him and without intonation in her voice, that she wanted their first hours together to be perfect.

And William said, "They are—they will be. You must rest. Our marriage will begin tomorrow."

And like other new husbands of whom he had heard and at whose expense he had at one time or another made jokes, he spent his wedding night apart from his wife, his long body curled stiffly and sleeplessly on a small sofa, his eyes open to the passing night.

He awoke early. Their suite, arranged and paid for by Edith's parents, as a wedding gift, was on the tenth floor, and it commanded a view of the city. He called softly to Edith, and in a few minutes she came out of the bedroom, tying the sash of her dressing gown, yawning sleepily, smiling a little. William felt his love for her grip his throat; he took her by the hand, and they stood before the window in their sitting room, looking down. Automobiles, pedestrians, and carriages crept on the narrow streets below them; they seemed to themselves far removed from the run of humanity and its pursuits. In the distance, visible beyond the square buildings of red brick and stone, the Mississippi River wound its bluish-brown length in the morning sun; the riverboats and tugs that crawled up and down its stiff bends were like toys, though their stacks gave off great quantities of gray smoke to the winter air. A sense of calm came over him; he put his arm around his wife and held her lightly, and they both gazed down upon a world that seemed full of promise and quiet adventure.

They breakfasted early. Edith seemed refreshed, fully recovered from her indisposition of the night before; she was almost gay again, and she looked at William with an intimacy and warmth that he thought were from gratitude and love. They did not speak of the night before; every now and then Edith looked at her new ring and adjusted it on her finger.

They wrapped themselves against the cold and walked the St. Louis streets, which were just beginning to crowd with people; they looked at goods in windows, they spoke of the future and gravely thought of how they would fill it. William began to regain the ease and fluency he had discovered during his early courtship of this woman who had become his wife; Edith clung to his arm and seemed to attend to what he said as she had never done before. They had midmorning coffee in a small warm shop and watched the passers-by scurry through the cold. They found a carriage and drove to the Art Museum. Arm in arm they walked through the high rooms, through the rich glow of light reflected from the paintings. In the quietness, in the warmth, in the air that took on a timelessness from the old paintings and statuary, William Stoner felt an outrush of affection for the tall, delicate girl who walked beside him, and he felt a quiet passion rise within him, warm and formally sensuous, like the colors that came out from the walls around him.

When they left there late in the afternoon the sky had clouded and a thin drizzle had started; but William Stoner carried within him the warmth he had gathered in the museum.

They got back to the hotel shortly after sunset; Edith went into the bedroom to rest, and William called downstairs to have a light dinner sent to their rooms; and on a sudden inspiration, he went downstairs himself into the saloon and asked for a bottle of champagne to be iced and sent up within the hour. The bartender nodded glumly and told him that it would not be a good champagne. By the first of July, Prohibition would be national; already it was illegal to brew or distill liquors; and there were no more than fifty bottles of champagne of any sort in the cellars of the hotel. And he would have to charge more than the champagne was worth. Stoner smiled and told him that would be all right.

Although on special occasions of celebration in her parents' home Edith had taken a little wine, she had never before tasted champagne. As they ate their dinner, set up on a small square table in their sitting room, she glanced nervously at the strange bottle in its bucket of ice. Two white candles in dull brass holders glowed unevenly against the darkness; William had turned out the other lights. The candles flickered between them as they talked, and the light caught the curves of the smooth dark bottle and glittered upon the ice that surrounded it. They were nervous and cautiously gay.

Inexpertly he withdrew the cork from the champagne; Edith jumped at the loud report; white froth spurted from the bottle neck and drenched his hand. They laughed at his clumsiness. They drank a glass of the wine, and Edith pretended tipsiness. They drank another glass. William thought he saw a languor come over her, a quietness fall upon her face, a pensiveness darken her eyes. He rose and went behind her, where she sat at the little table; he put his hands upon her shoulders, marveling at the thickness and heaviness of his fingers upon the delicacy of her flesh and bone. She stiffened beneath his touch, and he made his hands go gently to the sides of her thin neck and let them brush into the fine reddish hair; her neck was rigid, the cords vibrant in their tensity. He put his hands on her arms and lifted gently, so that she rose from the chair; he turned her to face him. Her eyes, wide and pale and nearly transparent in the candlelight, looked upon him blankly. He felt a distant closeness to her, and a pity for her helplessness; desire thickened in his throat so that he could not speak. He pulled her a little toward the bedroom, feeling a quick hard resistance in her body, and feeling at the same moment a willed putting away of the resistance.

He left the door to the unlighted bedroom open; the candle-light glowed feebly in the darkness. He murmured as if to comfort and assure her, but his words were smothered and he could not hear what he said. He put his hands upon her body and fumbled for the buttons that would open her to him. She pushed him away impersonally; in the dimness her eyes were closed and her lips tight. She turned away from him and with a quick movement loosened her dress so that it fell crumpled about her feet. Her arms and shoulders were bare; she shuddered as if from cold and said in a flat voice, "Go in the other room. I'll be ready in a minute." He touched her arms and put his lips to her shoulder, but she would not turn to him.

In the sitting room he stared at the candles that flickered over the remains of their dinner, in the midst of which rested the bottle of champagne, still more than half full. He poured a little of the wine into a glass and tasted it; it had grown warm and sweetish.

When he returned, Edith was in bed with the covers pulled to her chin, her face turned upward, her eyes closed, a thin frown creasing her forehead. Silently, as if she were asleep, Stoner undressed and got into bed beside her. For several moments he lay with his desire, which had become an impersonal thing, belonging to himself alone. He spoke to Edith, as if to find a haven for what he felt; she did not answer. He put his hand upon her and felt beneath the thin cloth of her nightgown the flesh he had longed for. He moved his hand upon her; she did not stir; her frown deepened. Again he spoke, saying her name to silence; then he moved his body upon her, gentle in his clumsiness. When he touched the softness of her thighs she turned her head sharply away and lifted her arm to cover her eyes. She made no sound.

Afterward he lay beside her and spoke to her in the quietness of his love. Her eyes were open then, and they stared at him out of the shadow; there was no expression on her face. Suddenly she flung the covers from her and crossed swiftly to the bathroom. He saw the light go on and heard her retch loudly and agonizingly. He called to her and went across the room;

the door to the bathroom was locked. He called to her again; she did not answer. He went back to the bed and waited for her. After several minutes of silence the light in the bathroom went off and the door opened. Edith came out and walked stiffly to the bed.

"It was the champagne," she said. "I shouldn't have had the second glass."

She pulled the covers over her and turned away from him; in a few moments her breathing was regular and heavy in sleep.

V

THEY RETURNED to Columbia two days earlier than they had planned; restless and strained by their isolation, it was as if they walked together in a prison. Edith said that they really ought to get back to Columbia so that William could prepare for his classes and so that she could begin to get them settled in their new apartment. Stoner agreed at once—and told himself that things would be better once they were in a place of their own, among people they knew and in surroundings that were familiar. They packed their belongings that afternoon and were on the train to Columbia the same evening.

In the hurried, vague days before their marriage Stoner had found a vacant second-floor apartment in an old barnlike house five blocks from the University. It was dark and bare, with a small bedroom, a tiny kitchen, and a huge living room with high windows; it had at one time been occupied by an artist, a teacher at the University, who had been none too tidy; the dark, wide-planked floors were splotched with brilliant yellows and blues and reds, and the walls were smudged with paint and dirt. Stoner thought the place romantic and commodious, and he judged it to be a good place to start a new life.

Edith moved into the apartment as if it were an enemy to be conquered. Though unused to physical labor, she scraped away most of the paint from the floors and walls and scrubbed at the dirt she imagined secreted everywhere; her hands blistered and her face became strained, with dark hollows beneath the eyes. When Stoner tried to help her she became stubborn, her lips tightened, and she shook her head; he needed the time for his studies, she said; this was *her* job. When he forced his help upon her, she became almost sullen, thinking herself to be humiliated. Puzzled and helpless, he withdrew his aid and watched as, grimly, Edith continued awkwardly to scrub the gleaming floors and walls, to sew curtains and hang them unevenly from the high windows, to repair and paint and repaint the used furniture they had begun to accumulate. Though inept, she worked with a silent and intense ferocity, so that by the time William got home from the University in the afternoon

317

she was exhausted. She would drag herself to prepare the evening meal, eat a few bites, and then with a murmur vanish into
the bedroom to sleep like one drugged until after William had
left for his classes the next morning.

Within a month he knew that his marriage was a failure;
within a year he stopped hoping that it would improve. He
learned silence and did not insist upon his love. If he spoke to
her or touched her in tenderness, she turned away from him
within herself and became wordless, enduring, and for days
afterward drove herself to new limits of exhaustion. Out of an
unspoken stubbornness they both had, they shared the same
bed; sometimes at night, in her sleep, she unknowingly moved
against him. And sometimes, then, his resolve and knowledge
crumbled before his love, and he moved upon her. If she was
sufficiently roused from her sleep she tensed and stiffened, turning her head sideways in a familiar gesture and burying it in her
pillow, enduring violation; at such times Stoner performed his
love as quickly as he could, hating himself for his haste and re-
gretting his passion. Less frequently she remained half numbed
by sleep; then she was passive, and she murmured drowsily,
whether in protest or surprise he did not know. He came to
look forward to these rare and unpredictable moments, for in
that sleep-drugged acquiescence he could pretend to himself
that he found a kind of response.

And he could not speak to her of what he took to be her
unhappiness. When he attempted to do so, she accepted what
he said as a reflection upon her adequacy and her self, and she
became as morosely withdrawn from him as she did when he
made love to her. He blamed his clumsiness for her withdrawal
and took upon himself the responsibility for what she felt.

With a quiet ruthlessness that came from his desperation, he
experimented with small ways of pleasing her. He brought her
gifts, which she accepted indifferently, sometimes commenting
mildly upon their expense; he took her on walks and picnics
in the wooded countryside around Columbia, but she tired
easily and sometimes became ill; he talked to her of his work,
as he had done in their courtship, but her interest had become
perfunctory and indulgent.

At last, though he knew her to be shy, he insisted as gently
as he could that they begin to entertain. They had an informal tea to which a few of the younger instructors and assistant

professors in the department were invited, and they gave several small dinner parties. In no way did Edith show whether she was pleased or displeased; but her preparations for the events were so frenzied and obsessive that by the time the guests arrived she was half hysterical from strain and weariness, though no one except William was really aware of this.

She was a good hostess. She talked to her guests with an animation and ease that made her seem a stranger to William, and she spoke to him in their presence with an intimacy and fondness that always surprised him. She called him Willy, which touched him oddly, and sometimes she laid a soft hand upon his shoulder.

But when the guests left, the façade fell upon itself and revealed her collapse. She spoke bitterly of the departed guests, imagining obscure insults and slights; she quietly and desperately recounted what she thought to be unforgivable failures of her own; she sat still and brooding in the litter the guests had left and would not be roused by William and would answer him briefly and distraughtly in a flat, monotonous voice.

Only once had the façade cracked when guests were present.

Several months after Stoner's and Edith's marriage, Gordon Finch had become engaged to a girl whom he had met casually while he was stationed in New York and whose parents lived in Columbia. Finch had been given a permanent post as assistant dean, and it was tacitly understood that when Josiah Claremont died Finch would be among the first to be considered for the deanship of the College. Somewhat belatedly, in celebration of both Finch's new position and the announcement of his engagement, Stoner asked him and his fiancée to dinner.

They came just before dusk on a warm evening in late May, in a shining black new touring car which gave off a series of explosions as Finch expertly brought it to a halt on the brick road in front of Stoner's house. He honked the horn and waved gaily until William and Edith came downstairs. A small dark girl with a round, smiling face sat beside him.

He introduced her as Caroline Wingate, and the four of them talked for a moment while Finch helped her descend from the car.

"Well, how do you like it?" Finch asked, thumping the front fender of the car with his closed fist. "A beauty, isn't it? Belongs to Caroline's father. I'm thinking of getting one just like it, so . . ." His voice trailed away and his eyes narrowed; he regarded the automobile speculatively and coolly, as if it were the future.

Then he became lively and jocular again. With mock secrecy he put his forefinger to his lips, looked furtively around, and took a large brown paper bag from the front seat of the car. "Hooch," he whispered. "Just off the boat. Cover me, pal; maybe we can make it to the house."

The dinner went well. Finch was more affable than Stoner had seen him in years; Stoner thought of himself and Finch and Dave Masters sitting together on those distant Friday afternoons after class, drinking beer and talking. The fiancée, Caroline, said little; she smiled happily as Finch joked and winked. It came to Stoner as an almost envious shock to realize that Finch was genuinely fond of this dark pretty girl, and that her silence came from a rapt affection for him.

Even Edith lost some of her strain and tenseness; she smiled easily, and her laughter was spontaneous. Finch was playful and familiar with Edith in a way, Stoner realized, that he, her own husband, could never be; and Edith seemed happier than she had been in months.

After dinner Finch removed the brown paper bag from the icebox, where he had placed it earlier to cool, and took from it a number of dark brown bottles. It was a home brew that he made with great secrecy and ceremony in the closet of his bachelor apartment.

"No room for my clothes," he said, "but a man's got to keep his sense of values."

Carefully, with his eyes squinted, with the light glistening upon his fair skin and thinning blond hair, like a chemist measuring a rare substance, he poured the beer from the bottles into glasses.

"Got to be careful with this stuff," he said. "You get a lot of sediment at the bottom, and if you pour it off too quick, you get it in the glass."

They each drank a glass of the beer, complimenting Finch upon its taste. It was, indeed, surprisingly good, dry and light and of a good color. Even Edith finished her glass and took another.

They became a little drunk; they laughed vaguely and senti-
mentally; they saw each other anew.

Holding his glass up to the light, Stoner said, "I wonder
how Dave would have liked this beer."

"Dave?" Finch asked.

"Dave Masters. Remember how he used to love beer?"

"Dave Masters," Finch said. "Good old Dave. It's a damned
shame."

"Masters," Edith said. She was smiling fuzzily. "Wasn't he
that friend of yours that was killed in the war?"

"Yes," Stoner said. "That's the one." The old sadness came
over him, but he smiled at Edith.

"Good old Dave," Finch said. "Edie, your husband and I
and Dave used to really lap it up—long before he knew of you,
of course. Good old Dave . . ."

They smiled at the memory of David Masters.

"He was a good friend of yours?" Edith asked.

Stoner nodded. "He was a good friend."

"Château-Thierry." Finch drained his glass. "War's a hell of
a thing." He shook his head. "But old Dave. He's probably
somewhere laughing at us right now. He wouldn't be feeling
sorry for himself. I wonder if he ever really got to see any of
France?"

"I don't know," Stoner said. "He was killed so soon after he
got over."

"Be a shame if he didn't. I always thought that was one of
the main reasons he joined up. To see some of Europe."

"Europe," Edith said distinctly.

"Yeah," Finch said. "Old Dave didn't want too many things,
but he did want to see Europe before he died."

"I was going to Europe once," Edith said. She was smiling,
and her eyes glittered helplessly. "Do you remember, Willy? I
was going with my Aunt Emma just before we got married. Do
you remember?"

"I remember," Stoner said.

Edith laughed gratingly and shook her head as if she were
puzzled. "It seems like a long time ago, but it wasn't. How
long has it been, Willy?"

"Edith—" Stoner said.

"Let's see, we were going in April. And then a year. And now it's May. I would have been . . ." Suddenly her eyes filled with tears, though she was still smiling with a fixed brightness. "I'll never get there now, I guess. Aunt Emma is going to die pretty soon, and I'll never have a chance to . . ."

Then, with the smile still tightening her lips and her eyes streaming with tears, she began to sob. Stoner and Finch rose from their chairs.

"Edith," Stoner said helplessly.

"Oh, leave me alone!" With a curious twisting motion she stood erect before them, her eyes shut tight and her hands clenched at her sides. "All of you! Just leave me alone!" And she turned and stumbled into the bedroom, slamming the door behind her.

For a moment no one spoke; they listened to the muffled sound of Edith's sobbing. Then Stoner said, "You'll have to excuse her. She has been tired and not too well. The strain—"

"Sure, I know how it is, Bill." Finch laughed hollowly. "Women and all. Guess I'll be getting used to it pretty soon myself." He looked at Caroline, laughed again, and lowered his voice. "Well, we won't disturb Edie right now. You just thank her for us, tell her it was a fine meal, and you folks'll have to come over to our place after we get settled in."

"Thanks, Gordon," Stoner said. "I'll tell her."

"And don't *worry*," Finch said. He punched Stoner on the arm. "These things happen."

After Gordon and Caroline had left, after he heard the new car roar and sputter away into the night, William Stoner stood in the middle of the living room and listened to Edith's dry and regular sobbing. It was a sound curiously flat and without emotion, and it went on as if it would never stop. He wanted to comfort her; he wanted to soothe her; but he did not know what to say. So he stood and listened; and after a while he realized that he had never before heard Edith cry.

After the disastrous party with Gordon Finch and Caroline Wingate, Edith seemed almost contented, calmer than she had been at any time during their marriage. But she did not want to have anyone in, and she showed a reluctance to go outside the apartment. Stoner did most of their shopping from lists that Edith made for him in a curiously laborious and childlike handwriting on little sheets of blue notepaper. She seemed happiest when she was alone; she would sit for hours working needlepoint or embroidering tablecloths and napkins, with a tiny indrawn smile on her lips. Her aunt Emma Darley began more and more frequently to visit her; when William came from the University in the afternoon he often found the two of them together, drinking tea and conversing in tones so low that they might have been whispers. They always greeted him politely, but William knew that they saw him with regret; Mrs. Darley seldom stayed for more than a few minutes after he arrived. He learned to maintain an unobtrusive and delicate regard for the world in which Edith had begun to live.

In the summer of 1920 he spent a week with his parents while Edith visited her relatives in St. Louis; he had not seen his mother and father since the wedding.

He worked in the fields for a day or two, helping his father and the Negro hired hand; but the give of the warm moist clods beneath his feet and the smell of the new-turned earth in his nostrils evoked in him no feeling of return or familiarity. He came back to Columbia and spent the rest of the summer preparing for a new class that he was to teach the following academic year. He spent most of each day in the library, sometimes returning to Edith and the apartment late in the evening, through the heavy sweet scent of honeysuckle that moved in the warm air and among the delicate leaves of dogwood trees that rustled and turned, ghost-like in the darkness. His eyes burned from their concentration upon dim texts, his mind was heavy with what it observed, and his fingers tingled numbly from the retained feel of old leather and board and paper; but he was open to the world through which for a moment he walked, and he found some joy in it.

A few new faces appeared at departmental meetings; some familiar ones were not there; and Archer Sloane continued the slow decline which Stoner had begun to notice during the war. His hands shook, and he was unable to keep his attention upon what he said. The department went on with the momentum it had gathered through its tradition and the mere fact of its being.

Stoner went about his teaching with an intensity and ferocity that awed some of the newer members of the department and that caused a small concern among the colleagues who had known him for a longer time. His face grew haggard, he lost weight, and the stoop of his shoulders increased. In the second semester of that year he had a chance to take a teaching over-load for extra pay, and he took it; also for extra pay, he taught in the new summer school that year. He had a vague notion of saving enough money to go abroad, so that he could show Edith the Europe she had given up for his sake.

In the summer of 1921, searching for a reference to a Latin poem that he had forgotten, he glanced at his dissertation for the first time since he had submitted it for approval three years earlier; he read it through and judged it to be sound. A little frightened at his presumption, he considered reworking it into a book. Though he was again teaching the full summer session, he reread most of the texts he had used and began to extend his research. Late in January he decided that a book was possi-ble; by early spring he was far enough along to be able to write the first tentative pages.

It was in the spring of the same year that, calmly and almost indifferently, Edith told him that she had decided she wanted a child.

The decision came suddenly and without apparent source, so that when she made the announcement one morning at break-fast, only a few minutes before William had to leave for his first class, she spoke almost with surprise, as if she had made a discovery.

"What?" William said. "What did you say?"

"I want a baby," Edith said. "I think I want to have a baby."

She was nibbling a piece of toast. She wiped her lips with the corner of a napkin and smiled fixedly.

"Don't you think we ought to have one?" she asked. "We've been married for nearly three years."

"Of course," William said. He set his cup down in its saucer with great care. He did not look at her. "Are you sure? We've never talked about it. I wouldn't want you to—"

"Oh, yes," she said. "I'm quite sure. I think we ought to have a child."

William looked at his watch. "I'm late. I wish we had more time to talk. I want you to be sure."

A small frown came between her eyes. "I told you I was sure. Don't *you* want one? Why do you keep asking me? I don't want to talk about it any more."

"All right," William said. He sat looking at her for a moment. "I've got to go." But he did not move. Then awkwardly he put his hand over her long fingers that rested on the tablecloth and kept it there until she moved her hand away. He got up from the table and edged around her, almost shyly, and gathered his books and papers. As she always did, Edith came into the living room to wait for him to leave. He kissed her on the cheek—something he had not done for a long while.

At the door he turned and said, "I'm—I'm glad you want a child, Edith. I know that in some ways our marriage has been a disappointment to you. I hope this will make a difference between us."

"Yes," Edith said. "You'll be late for your class. You'd better hurry."

After he had gone Edith remained for some minutes in the center of the room, staring at the closed door, as if trying to remember something. Then she moved restlessly across the floor, walking from one place to another, moving within her clothing as if she could not endure its rustling and shifting upon her flesh. She unbuttoned her stiff gray taffeta morning robe and let it drop to the floor. She crossed her arms over her breasts and hugged herself, kneading the flesh of her upper arms through her thin flannel nightgown. Again she paused in her moving and walked purposefully into the tiny bedroom and opened a closet door, upon the inside of which hung a full-length mirror. She adjusted the mirror to the light and stood back from it, inspecting the long thin figure in the straight blue nightgown that it reflected. Without removing her eyes from the mirror she unbuttoned the top of her gown and pulled it up from her body and over her head, so that she stood naked in the morning light. She wadded the nightgown and threw it in the closet. Then she turned about before the mirror, inspecting the body as if it belonged to someone else. She passed her hands over her small drooping breasts and let her hands go lightly down her long waist and over her flat belly.

She moved away from the mirror and went to the bed, which was still unmade. She pulled the covers off, folded them carelessly, and put them in the closet. She smoothed the sheet on the bed and lay there on her back, her legs straight and her arms at her side. Unblinking and motionless, she stared up at the ceiling and waited through the morning and the long afternoon.

When William Stoner got home that evening it was nearly dark, but no light came from the second-floor windows. Vaguely apprehensive, he went up the stairs and flipped the living-room light on. The room was empty. He called, "Edith?"

There was no reply. He called again.

He looked in the kitchen; the dishes from breakfast were still on the tiny table. He went swiftly across the living room and opened the door to the bedroom.

Edith lay naked on the bare bed. When the door opened and the light from the living room fell upon her, she turned her head to him; but she did not get up. Her eyes were wide and staring, and little sounds came from her parted mouth.

"Edith!" he said and went to where she lay, kneeling beside her. "Are you all right? What's the matter?"

She did not answer, but the sounds she had been making became louder and her body moved beside him. Suddenly her hands came out at him like claws, and he almost jerked away; but they went to his clothing, clutching and tearing at it, pulling him upon the bed beside her. Her mouth came up to him, gaping and hot; her hands were going over him, pulling at his clothes, seeking him; and all the time her eyes were wide and staring and untroubled, as if they belonged to somebody else and saw nothing.

It was a new knowledge he had of Edith, this desire that was like a hunger so intense that it seemed to have nothing to do with her self; and no sooner was it sated than it began at once to grow again within her, so that they both lived in the tense expectation of its presence.

Although the next two months were the only time of passion William and Edith Stoner ever had together, their relationship did not really change. Very soon Stoner realized that the force which drew their bodies together had little to do with love; they coupled with a fierce yet detached determination, drew apart, and coupled again, without the strength to surfeit their need.

Sometimes during the day, while William was at the University, the need came so strongly upon Edith that she could not remain still; she would leave the apartment and walk swiftly up and down the streets, going aimlessly from one place to another. And then she would return, draw closed the curtains of the windows, undress herself, and wait, crouched in the semi-darkness, for William to get home. And when he opened the door she was upon him, her hands wild and demanding, as if they had a life of their own, pulling him toward the bedroom, upon the bed which was still rumpled from their use of it the night or the morning before.

Edith became pregnant in June and immediately fell into an illness from which she did not wholly recover during the full time of her waiting. Nearly at the moment she became pregnant, even before the fact was confirmed by her calendar and her physician, the hunger for William that had raged within her for the better part of two months ceased. She made it clear to her husband that she could not endure the touch of his hand upon her, and it began to seem to him that even his looking at her was a kind of violation. The hunger of their passion became a memory, and at last Stoner looked upon it as if it were a dream that had nothing to do with either of them.

So the bed that had been the arena of their passion became the support of her illness. She kept to it most of the day, rising only to relieve her nausea in the morning and to walk unsteadily about the living room for a few minutes in the afternoon. In the afternoon and evening, after he had hurried from his work at the University, William cleaned the rooms, washed the dishes, and made the evening meal; he carried Edith's dinner to her on a tray. Though she did not want him to eat with her, she did seem to enjoy sharing a cup of weak tea with him after dinner. For a few moments in the evening, then, they talked quietly and casually, as if they were old friends or exhausted enemies. Edith would fall asleep soon afterward; and William would return to the kitchen, complete the housework, and then set up a table before the living-room sofa, where he would grade papers or prepare lectures. Then, past midnight, he would cover himself with a blanket he kept neatly folded behind the couch; and with his length curled up on the couch he would sleep fitfully until morning.

*

The child, a girl, was born after a three-day period of labor in the middle of March in the year 1923. They named her Grace, after one of Edith's aunts who had died many years before.

Even at birth Grace was a beautiful child, with distinct features and a light down of golden hair. Within a few days the first redness of her skin turned into a glowing golden pink. She seldom cried, and she seemed almost aware of her surroundings. William fell instantly in love with her; the affection he could not show to Edith he could show to his daughter, and he found a pleasure in caring for her that he had not anticipated.

For nearly a year after the birth of Grace, Edith remained partly bedridden; there was some fear that she might become a permanent invalid, though the doctor could find no specific trouble. William hired a woman to come in during the morning to care for Edith, and he arranged his classes so that he would be at home early in the afternoon.

Thus for more than a year William kept the house and cared for two helpless people. He was up before dawn, grading papers and preparing lectures; before going to the University he fed Grace, prepared breakfast for himself and Edith, and fixed a lunch for himself, which he took to school in his briefcase. After his classes he came back to the apartment, which he swept, dusted, and cleaned.

And he was more nearly a mother than a father to his daughter. He changed her diapers and washed them; he chose her clothing and mended it when it was torn; he fed her and bathed her and rocked her in his arms when she was distressed. Every now and then Edith would call querulously for her baby; William would bring Grace to her, and Edith, propped up in bed, would hold her for a few moments, silently and uncomfortably, as if the child belonged to someone else who was a stranger. Then she would tire and with a sigh hand the baby back to William. Moved by some obscure emotion, she would weep a little, dab at her eyes, and turn away from him.

So for the first year of her life, Grace Stoner knew only her father's touch, and his voice, and his love.

VI

E ARLY IN the summer of 1924, on a Friday afternoon, Archer Sloane was seen by several students going into his office. He was discovered shortly after dawn the following Monday by a janitor who made the rounds of the offices in Jesse Hall to empty the wastebaskets. Sloane was sitting rigidly slumped in his chair before his desk, his head at an odd angle, his eyes open and fixed in a terrible stare. The janitor spoke to him and then ran shouting through the empty halls. There was some delay in the removal of the body from the office, and a few early students were milling in the corridors when the curiously humped and sheeted figure was carried on a stretcher down the steps to the waiting ambulance. It was later determined that Sloane had died sometime late Friday night or early Saturday morning, of causes that were obviously natural but never precisely determined, and had remained the whole weekend at the desk staring endlessly before him. The coroner announced heart failure as the cause of death, but William Stoner always felt that in a moment of anger and despair Sloane had willed his heart to cease, as if in a last mute gesture of love and contempt for a world that had betrayed him so profoundly that he could not endure in it.

Stoner was one of the pallbearers at the funeral. At the services he could not keep his mind on the words the minister said, but he knew that they were empty. He remembered Sloane as he had first seen him in the classroom; he remembered their first talks together; and he thought of the slow decline of this man who had been his distant friend. Later, after the services were over, when he lifted his handle of the gray casket and helped to carry it out to the hearse, what he carried seemed so light that he could not believe there was anything inside the narrow box.

Sloane had no family; only his colleagues and a few people from town gathered around the narrow pit and listened in awe, embarrassment, and respect as the minister said his words. And because he had no family or loved ones to mourn his passing, it was Stoner who wept when the casket was lowered, as if that weeping might reduce the loneliness of the last descent. Whether he wept for himself, for the part of his history and youth that went down to the earth, or whether for the poor thin figure that once kept the man he had loved, he did not know.

Gordon Finch drove him back to town, and for most of the ride they did not speak. Then, when they neared town, Gordon asked about Edith; William said something and inquired after Caroline. Gordon replied, and there was a long silence. Just before they drove up to William's apartment Gordon Finch spoke again.

"I don't know. All during the service I kept thinking about Dave Masters. About Dave dying in France, and about old Sloane sitting there at his desk, dead two days; like they were the same kinds of dying. I never knew Sloane very well, but I guess he was a good man; at least I hear he used to be. And now we'll have to bring somebody else in and find a new chairman for the department. It's like it all just goes around and around and keeps on going. It makes you wonder."

"Yes," William said and did not speak further. But he was for a moment very fond of Gordon Finch; and when he got out of the car and watched Gordon drive away, he felt the keen knowledge that another part of himself, of his past, was drawing slowly, almost imperceptibly away from him, into the darkness.

In addition to his duties as assistant dean, Gordon Finch was given the interim chairmanship of the English Department; and it became his immediate duty to find a replacement for Archer Sloane.

It was July before the matter was settled. Then Finch called those members of the department who had remained in Columbia over the summer and announced the replacement. It was, Finch told the little group, a nineteenth-century specialist, Hollis N. Lomax, who had recently received his Ph.D. from Harvard University but who had nevertheless taught for several years at a small downstate New York liberal-arts college. He came with high recommendations, he had already started publishing, and he was being hired at the assistant professor level. There were, Finch emphasized, no present plans about the departmental chairmanship; Finch was to remain interim chairman for at least one more year.

For the rest of the summer Lomax remained a figure of mystery and the object of speculation by the permanent members of the faculty. The essays that he had published in the journals were dug out, read, and passed around with judicious nods. Lomax did not make his appearance during New Student Week, nor was he present at the general faculty meeting on the Friday before Monday student registration. And at registration the members of the department, sitting in a line behind the long desks, wearily helping students choose their classes and assisting them in the deadly routine of filling out forms, looked surreptitiously around for a new face. Still Lomax did not make an appearance.

He was not seen until the departmental meeting late Tuesday afternoon, after registration had been completed. By that time, numbed by the monotony of the last two days and yet tense with the excitement that begins a new school year, the English faculty had nearly forgotten about Lomax. They sprawled in desk-top chairs in a large lecture room in the east wing of Jesse Hall and looked up with contemptuous yet eager expectancy at the podium where Gordon Finch stood surveying them with massive benevolence. A low hum of voices filled the room; chairs scraped on the floor; now and then someone laughed deliberately, raucously. Gordon Finch raised his right hand and held it palm outward to his audience; the hum quieted a little.

It quieted enough for everyone in the room to hear the door at the rear of the hall creak open and to hear a distinctive, slow shuffle of feet on the bare wood floor. They turned; and the hum of their conversation died. Someone whispered, "It's Lomax," and the sound was sharp and audible through the room.

He had come through the door, closed it, and had advanced a few steps beyond the threshold, where he now stood. He was a man barely over five feet in height, and his body was grotesquely misshapen. A small hump raised his left shoulder to his neck, and his left arm hung laxly at his side. His upper body was heavy and curved, so that he appeared to be always struggling for balance; his legs were thin, and he walked with a hitch in his stiff right leg. For several moments he stood with his blond head bent downward, as if he were inspecting his highly polished black shoes and the sharp crease of his black trousers. Then he lifted his head and shot his right arm out, exposing a stiff white length of cuff with gold links; there was a cigarette in his long pale fingers. He took a deep drag, inhaled, and expelled the smoke in a thin stream. And then they could see his face.

It was the face of a matinee idol. Long and thin and mobile, it was nevertheless strongly featured; his forehead was high and narrow, with heavy veins, and his thick waving hair, the color of ripe wheat, swept back from it in a somewhat theatrical pompadour. He dropped his cigarette on the floor, ground it beneath his sole, and spoke.

"I am Lomax." He paused; his voice, rich and deep, articulated his words precisely, with a dramatic resonance. "I hope I have not disrupted your meeting."

The meeting went on, but no one paid much attention to what Gordon Finch said. Lomax sat alone in the back of the room, smoking and looking at the high ceiling, apparently oblivious of the heads that turned now and then to look at him. After the meeting was over he remained in his chair and let his colleagues come up to him, introduce themselves, and say what they had to say. He greeted each of them briefly, with a courtesy that was oddly mocking.

During the next few weeks it became evident that Lomax did not intend to fit himself into the social, cultural, and academic routine of Columbia, Missouri. Though he was ironically pleasant to his colleagues, he neither accepted nor extended any social invitations; he did not even attend the annual open house at Dean Claremont's, though the event was so traditional that attendance was almost obligatory; he was seen at none of the University concerts or lectures; it was said that his classes were lively and that his classroom behavior was eccentric. He was a popular teacher; students clustered around his desk during his off-hours, and they followed him in the halls. It was known that he occasionally invited groups of students to his rooms, where he entertained them with conversation and recordings of string quartets.

William Stoner wished to know him better, but he did not know how to do so. He spoke to him when he had something to say, and he invited him to dinner. When Lomax answered him as he did everyone else—ironically polite and impersonal —and when he refused the invitation to dinner, Stoner could think of nothing else to do.

It was some time before Stoner recognized the source of his attraction to Hollis Lomax. In Lomax's arrogance, his fluency, and his cheerful bitterness, Stoner saw, distorted but recognizable, an image of his friend David Masters. He wished to talk to him as he had talked to Dave; but he could not, even after he admitted his wish to himself. The awkwardness of his youth had not left him, but the eagerness and straightforwardness that might have made the friendship possible had. He knew what he wished was impossible, and the knowledge saddened him.

In the evenings, after he had cleaned the apartment, washed the dinner dishes, and put Grace to bed in a crib set in a corner of the living room, he worked on the revision of his book. By the end of the year it was finished; and though he was not altogether pleased with it he sent it to a publisher. To his surprise the study was accepted and scheduled for publication in the fall of 1925. On the strength of the unpublished book he was promoted to assistant professor and granted permanent tenure.

The assurance of his promotion came a few weeks after his book was accepted; upon that assurance, Edith announced that she and the baby would spend a week in St. Louis visiting her parents.

She returned to Columbia in less than a week, harried and tired but quietly triumphant. She had cut her visit short because the strain of caring for an infant had been too much for her mother, and the trip had so tired her that she was unable to care for Grace herself. But she had accomplished something. She drew from her bag a sheaf of papers and handed a small slip to William.

It was a check for six thousand dollars, made out to Mr. and Mrs. William Stoner and signed with the bold, nearly illegible scrawl of Horace Bostwick. "What's this?" Stoner asked.

She handed him the other papers. "It's a loan," she said. "All you have to do is sign these. I already have."

"But six thousand dollars! What's it for?"

"A house," Edith said. "A *real* house of our own."

William Stoner looked again at the papers, shuffled through them quickly, and said, "Edith, we can't. I'm sorry, but—look, I'll only be making sixteen hundred next year. The payments on this will be more than sixty dollars a month—that's almost half my salary. And there will be taxes and insurance and—I just don't see how we can do it. I wish you had talked to me."

Her face became sorrowful; she turned away from him. "I wanted to surprise you. I'm able to do so little. And I *could* do this."

He protested that he was grateful, but Edith would not be consoled.

"I was thinking of you and the baby," she said. "You could have a study, and Grace could have a yard to play in."

"I know," William said. "Maybe in a few years."

"In a few years," Edith repeated. There was a silence. Then she said dully, "I can't live like this. Not any longer. In an apartment. No matter where I go I can hear you, and hear the baby, and—the smell. I—can't—stand—the—smell! Day after day, the smell of diapers, and—I can't stand it, and I can't get away from it. Don't you know? Don't you *know*?"

In the end they accepted the money. Stoner decided that he could give up to teaching the summers he had promised himself for study and writing, at least for a few years.

Edith took it upon herself to look for the house. Throughout the late spring and early summer she was tireless in her search, which seemed to work an immediate cure of her illness. As soon as William came home from his classes she went out and often did not return until dusk. Sometimes she walked and sometimes she drove around with Caroline Finch, with whom she had become casually friendly. Late in June she discovered the house she wanted; she signed an option to buy and agreed to take possession by the middle of August.

It was an old two-storied house only a few blocks from the campus; its previous owners had allowed it to run down, the dark green paint was peeling from the boards, and the lawn was brown and infested with weeds. But the yard was large and the house was roomy; it had a bedraggled grandeur that Edith could imagine renewed.

She borrowed another five hundred dollars from her father for furniture, and in the time between the summer session and the beginning of the fall semester William repainted the house; Edith wanted it white, and he had to put three coats on so that the dark green would not show through. Suddenly, in the first week of September, Edith decided that she wanted a party—a housewarming, she called it. She made the announcement with some resolution, as if it were a new beginning.

They invited all those members of the department who had returned from their summer vacations as well as a few town acquaintances of Edith; Hollis Lomax surprised everyone by accepting the invitation, the first he had accepted since his arrival in Columbia a year earlier. Stoner found a bootlegger and bought several bottles of gin; Gordon Finch promised to bring some beer; and Edith's Aunt Emma contributed two bottles of old sherry for those who would not drink hard liquor. Edith was reluctant to serve liquor at all; it was technically illegal to do so. But Caroline Finch intimated that no one at the University would think it really improper, and so she was persuaded.

Fall came early that year. A light snow fell on the tenth of September, the day before registration; during the night a hard freeze gripped the land. By the end of the week, the time of the party, the cold weather had lifted, so that there was only a chill in the air; but the trees were leafless, the grass was beginning to brown, and there was a general bareness that presaged a hard winter. By the chill weather outside, by the stripped poplars and elms that stood starkly in their yard, and by the warmth and the ranked implements of the impending party inside, William Stoner was reminded of another day. For some time he could not decide what he was trying to remember—then he realized that it was on such a day, almost seven years before, that he had gone to Josiah Claremont's house and had seen Edith for the first time. It seemed far away to him, and long ago; he could not reckon the changes that these few years had wrought.

For nearly the whole week before the party Edith lost herself in a frenzy of preparation; she hired a Negro girl for a week to help with the preparations and to serve, and the two of them scrubbed the floors and the walls, waxed the wood, dusted and cleaned the furniture, arranged it and rearranged it—so that on the night of the party Edith was in a state of near exhaustion. There were dark hollows under her eyes, and her voice was on

the quiet edge of hysteria. At six o'clock—the guests were supposed to arrive at seven—she counted the glasses once again
and discovered that she did not have enough for the guests
expected. She broke into tears, rushed upstairs, sobbing that
she didn't care what happened, she wasn't coming back down.
Stoner tried to reassure her, but she would not answer him.
He told her not to worry, that he would get the glasses. He
told the maid that he would return soon and hurried out of
the house. For nearly an hour he searched for a store still open
where he could purchase glasses; by the time he found one,
selected the glasses, and returned to the house it was well after
seven, and the first guests had arrived. Edith was among them
in the living room, smiling and chatting as if she had no care
or apprehension; she greeted William casually and told him to
take the package into the kitchen.

The party was like many another. Conversation began desul-
torily, gathered a swift but feeble energy, and trailed irrelevantly
into other conversations; laughter was quick and nervous, and
it burst like tiny explosives in a continuous but unrelated barrage all over the room; and the members of the party flowed
casually from one place to another, as if quietly occupying
shifting positions of strategy. A few of them, like spies, wandered through the house, led by either Edith or William, and
commented upon the superiority of such older houses as this
over the new, flimsier structures going up here and there on
the outskirts of town.

By ten o'clock most of the guests had taken plates piled with
sliced cold ham and turkey, pickled apricots, and the varied
garniture of tiny tomatoes, celery stalks, olives, pickles, crisp
radishes, and little raw cauliflower ears; a few were drunk and
would not eat. By eleven most of the guests had gone; among
those who remained were Gordon and Caroline Finch, a few
members of the department whom Stoner had known for several years, and Hollis Lomax. Lomax was quite drunk, though
not ostentatiously so; he walked carefully, as if he carried a burden over uneven terrain, and his thin pale face shone through
a film of sweat. The liquor loosened his tongue; and though he
spoke precisely, his voice lost its edge of irony, and he appeared
without defenses.

He spoke of the loneliness of his childhood in Ohio, where his father had been a fairly successful small businessman; he told, as if of another person, of the isolation that his deformity had forced upon him, of the early shame which had no source that he could understand and no defense that he could muster. And when he told of the long days and evenings he had spent alone in his room, reading to escape the limitations that his twisted body imposed upon him and finding gradually a sense of freedom that grew more intense as he came to understand the nature of that freedom—when he told of this, William Stoner felt a kinship that he had not suspected; he knew that Lomax had gone through a kind of conversion, an epiphany of knowing something through words that could not be put in words, as Stoner himself had once done, in the class taught by Archer Sloane. Lomax had come to it early, and alone, so that the knowledge was more nearly a part of himself than it was a part of Stoner; but in the way that was finally most important, the two men were alike, though neither of them might wish to admit it to the other, or even to himself.

They talked till nearly four in the morning; and though they drank more, their talk grew quieter and quieter, until at last no one spoke at all. They sat close together amid the debris of the party, as if on an island, huddling together for warmth and assurance. After a while Gordon and Caroline Finch got up and offered to drive Lomax to his rooms. Lomax shook Stoner's hand, asked him about his book, and wished him success with it; he walked over to Edith, who was sitting erect on a straight chair, and took her hand; he thanked her for the party. Then, as if on a quiet impulse, he bent a little and touched his lips to hers; Edith's hand came up lightly to his hair, and they remained so for several moments while the others looked on. It was the chastest kiss Stoner had ever seen, and it seemed perfectly natural.

Stoner saw his guests out the front door and lingered a few moments, watching them descend the steps and walk out of the light from the porch. The cold air settled around him and clung; he breathed deeply, and the sharp coldness invigorated him. He closed the door reluctantly and turned; the living room was empty; Edith had already gone upstairs. He turned the lights off and made his way across the cluttered room to the stairs. Already the house was becoming familiar to him; he grasped a balustrade he could not see and let himself be guided upward. When he got to the top of the stairs he could see his way, for the hall was illumined by the light from the half-opened door of the bedroom. The boards creaked as he walked down the hall and went into the bedroom.

Edith's clothes were flung in disarray on the floor beside the bed, the covers of which had been thrown back carelessly; she lay naked and glistening under the light on the white unwrinkled sheet. Her body was lax and wanton in its naked sprawl, and it shone like pale gold. William came nearer the bed. She was fast asleep, but in a trick of the light her slightly opened mouth seemed to shape the soundless words of passion and love. He stood looking at her for a long time. He felt a distant pity and reluctant friendship and familiar respect; and he felt also a weary sadness, for he knew that no longer could the sight of her bring upon him the agony of desire that he had once known, and knew that he would never again be moved as he had once been moved by her presence. The sadness lessened, and he covered her gently, turned out the light, and got in bed beside her.

The next morning Edith was ill and tired, and she spent the day in her room. William cleaned the house and attended to his daughter. On Monday he saw Lomax and spoke to him with a warmth that trailed from the night of the party; Lomax answered him with an irony that was like cold anger, and did not speak of the party that day or thereafter. It was as if he had discovered an enmity to hold him apart from Stoner, and he would not let it go.

As William had feared, the house soon proved to be an almost destructive financial burden. Though he allocated his salary with some care, the end of the month found him always without funds, and each month he reduced the steadily dwindling reserve made by his summer teaching. The first year they owned the house he missed two payments to Edith's father, and he received a frosty and principled letter of advice upon sound financial planning.

Nevertheless he began to feel a joy in property and to know a comfort that he had not anticipated. His study was on the first floor off the living room, with a high north window; in the daytime the room was softly illuminated, and the wood paneling glowed with the richness of age. He found in the cellar a quantity of boards which, beneath the ravages of dirt and mold, matched the paneling of the room. He refinished these boards and constructed bookcases, so that he might be surrounded by his books; at a used furniture store he found some dilapidated chairs, a couch, and an ancient desk for which he paid a few dollars and which he spent many weeks repairing.

As he worked on the room, and as it began slowly to take a shape, he realized that for many years, unknown to himself, he had had an image locked somewhere within him like a shamed secret, an image that was ostensibly of a place but which was actually of himself. So it was himself that he was attempting to define as he worked on his study. As he sanded the old boards for his bookcases, and saw the surface roughnesses disappear, the gray weathering flake away to the essential wood and finally to a rich purity of grain and texture—as he repaired his furniture and arranged it in the room, it was himself that he was slowly shaping, it was himself that he was putting into a kind of order, it was himself that he was making possible.

Thus, despite the regularly recurring pressures of debt and need, the next few years were happy, and he lived much as he had dreamed that he might live when he was a young student in graduate school and when he had first married. Edith did not partake of so large a part of his life as he had once hoped; indeed, it seemed that they had entered into a long truce that was like a stalemate. They spent most of their lives apart; Edith kept the house, which seldom had visitors, in spotless condition. When she was not sweeping or dusting or washing or polishing, she stayed in her room and seemed content to do so. She never entered William's study; it was as if it did not exist to her.

William still had most of the care of their daughter. In the afternoons when he came home from the University, he took Grace from the upstairs bedroom that he had converted into a nursery and let her play in the study while he worked.

She played quietly and contentedly on the floor, satisfied to be alone. Every now and then William spoke to her, and she paused to look at him in solemn and slow delight.

Sometimes he asked students to drop by for conferences and chats. He brewed tea for them on a little hotplate that he kept beside his desk, and felt an awkward fondness for them as they sat self-consciously on the chairs, remarked upon his library, and complimented him on the beauty of his daughter. He apologized for the absence of his wife and explained her illness, until at last he realized that his repetitions of apology were stressing her absence rather than accounting for it; he said no more and hoped that his silence was less compromising than were his explanations.

Except for Edith's absence from it, his life was nearly what he wanted it to be. He studied and wrote when he was not pre-paring for class, or grading papers, or reading theses. He hoped in time to make a reputation for himself as both a scholar and a teacher. His expectations for his first book had been both cautious and modest, and they had been appropriate; one reviewer had called it "pedestrian" and another had called it "a competent survey." At first he had been very proud of the book; he had held it in his hands and caressed its plain wrapper and turned its pages. It seemed delicate and alive, like a child. He had reread it in print, mildly surprised that it was neither better nor worse than he had thought it would be. After a while he tired of seeing it; but he never thought of it, and his authorship, without a sense of wonder and disbelief at his own temerity and at the responsibility he had assumed.

VII

O NE EVENING in the spring of 1927 William Stoner came home late. The scent of budding flowers mingled and hung in the moist warm air; crickets hummed in the shadows; in the distance a lone automobile raised dust and sent into the stillness a loud, defiant clatter. He walked slowly, caught in the somnolence of a new season, bemused by the tiny green buds that glowed out of the shade of bush and tree.

When he went into the house Edith was at the far end of the living room, holding the telephone receiver to her ear and looking at him.

"You're late," she said.

"Yes," he said pleasantly. "We had doctor's orals."

She handed him the receiver. "It's for you, long distance. Someone's been trying to get you all afternoon. I told them you were at the University, but they've been calling back here every hour."

William took the receiver and spoke into the mouthpiece. No one answered. "Hello," he said again.

The thin strange voice of a man answered him.

"This Bill Stoner?"

"Yes, who is this?"

"You don't know me. I was passing by, and your ma asked me to call. I been trying all afternoon."

"Yes," Stoner said. His hand holding the mouthpiece was shaking. "What's wrong?"

"It's your pa," the voice said. "I don't rightly know how to start."

The dry, laconic, frightened voice went on, and William Stoner listened to it dully, as if it had no existence beyond the receiver that he held to his ear. What he heard concerned his father. He had been (the voice said) feeling poorly for nearly a week; and because his field hand by himself had not been able to keep up with the furrowing and planting, and even though he had a high fever, he had started out early in the morning to get some planting done. His field hand had found him at mid-morning, lying face down on the broken field, unconscious.

He had carried him to the house, put him in bed, and gone to fetch a doctor; but by noon he was dead.

"Thank you for calling," Stoner said mechanically. "Tell my mother that I'll be there tomorrow."

He put the receiver back on its hook and stared for a long time at the bell-shaped mouthpiece attached to the narrow black cylinder. He turned around and looked at the room. Edith was regarding him expectantly.

"Well? What is it?" she asked.

"It's my father," Stoner said. "He's dead."

"Oh, Willy!" Edith said. Then she nodded. "You'll probably be gone for the rest of the week then."

"Yes," Stoner said.

"Then I'll get Aunt Emma to come over and help with Grace."

"Yes," Stoner said mechanically. "Yes."

He got someone to take his classes for the rest of the week and early the next morning caught the bus for Booneville. The highway from Columbia to Kansas City, which cut through Booneville, was the one that he had traveled seventeen years before, when he had first come to the University; now it was wide and paved, and neat straight fences enclosed fields of wheat and corn that flashed by him outside the bus window.

Booneville had changed little during the years he had not seen it. A few new buildings had gone up, a few old ones had been torn down; but the town retained its bareness and flimsiness, and looked still as if it were only a temporary arrangement that could be dispensed with at any moment. Though most of the streets had been paved in the last few years, a thin haze of dust hung about the town, and a few horse-drawn, steel-tired wagons were still around, the wheels sometimes giving off sparks as they scraped against the concrete paving of street and curb.

Nor had the house changed substantially. It was perhaps drier and grayer than it had been; not even a fleck of paint remained on the clapboards, and the unpainted timber of the porch sagged a bit nearer to the bare earth.

There were some people in the house—neighbors—whom Stoner did not remember; a tall gaunt man in a black suit, white shirt, and string tie was bending over his mother, who sat in a straight chair beside the narrow wooden box that held the body of his father. Stoner started across the room. The tall man saw him and walked to meet him; the man's eyes were gray and flat like pieces of glazed crockery. A deep and unctuous baritone voice, hushed and thick, uttered some words; the man called Stoner "brother" and spoke of "bereavement," and "God, who hath taken away," and wanted to know if Stoner wished to pray with him. Stoner brushed past the man and stood in front of his mother; her face swam before him. Through a blur he saw her nod to him and get up from the chair. She took his arm and said, "You'll want to see your pa."

With a touch that was so frail that he could hardly feel it, she led him beside the open coffin. He looked down. He looked until his eyes cleared, and then he started back in shock. The body that he saw seemed that of a stranger; it was shrunken and tiny, and its face was like a thin brown-paper mask, with black deep depressions where the eyes should have been. The dark blue suit which enfolded the body was grotesquely large, and the hands that folded out of the sleeves over the chest were like the dried claws of an animal. Stoner turned to his mother, and he knew that the horror he felt was in his eyes.

"Your pa lost a lot of weight the last week or two," she said. "I asked him not to go out in the field, but he got up before I was awake and was gone. He was out of his head. He was just so sick he was out of his head and didn't know what he was doing. The doctor said he must have been, or he couldn't have managed it."

As she spoke Stoner saw her clearly; it was as if she too were dead as she spoke, a part of her gone irretrievably into that box with her husband, not to emerge again. He saw her now; her face was thin and shrunken; even in repose it was so drawn that the tips of her teeth were disclosed beneath her thin lips. She walked as if she had no weight or strength. He muttered a word and left the parlor; he went to the room in which he had grown up and stood in its bareness. His eyes were hot and dry, and he could not weep.

He made the arrangements that had to be made for the funeral and signed the papers that needed to be signed. Like all country folk, his parents had burial policies, toward which for most of their lives they had set aside a few pennies each week, even during the times of most desperate need. There was something pitiful about the policies that his mother got from an old trunk in her bedroom; the gilt from the elaborate printing was beginning to fleck away, and the cheap paper was brittle with age. He talked to his mother about the future; he wanted her to return with him to Columbia. There was plenty of room, he said, and (he twinged at the lie) Edith would welcome her company.

But his mother would not return with him. "I wouldn't feel right," she said. "Your pa and I—I've lived here nearly all my life. I just don't think I could settle anywhere else and feel right about it. And besides, Tobe"—Stoner remembered that Tobe was the Negro field hand his father had hired many years ago —"Tobe has said he'd stay on here as long as I need him. He's got him a nice room fixed up in the cellar. We'll be all right."

Stoner argued with her, but she would not be moved. At last he realized that she wished only to die, and wished to do so where she had lived; and he knew that she deserved the little dignity she could find in doing as she wanted to do.

They buried his father in a small plot on the outskirts of Booneville, and William returned to the farm with his mother. That night he could not sleep. He dressed and walked into the field that his father had worked year after year, to the end that he now had found. He tried to remember his father, but the face that he had known in his youth would not come to him. He knelt in the field and took a dry clod of earth in his hand. He broke it and watched the grains, dark in the moonlight, crumble and flow through his fingers. He brushed his hand on his trouser leg and got up and went back to the house. He did not sleep; he lay on the bed and looked out the single window until the dawn came, until there were no shadows upon the land, until it stretched gray and barren and infinite before him.

After the death of his father Stoner made weekend trips to the farm as often as he could; and each time he saw his mother, he saw her grown thinner and paler and stiller, until at last it seemed that only her sunken, bright eyes were alive. During her last days she did not speak to him at all; her eyes flickered faintly as she stared up from her bed, and occasionally a small sigh came from her lips.

He buried her beside her husband. After the services were over and the few mourners had gone, he stood alone in a cold November wind and looked at the two graves, one open to its burden and the other mounded and covered by a thin fuzz of grass. He turned on the bare, treeless little plot that held others like his mother and father and looked across the flat land in the direction of the farm where he had been born, where his mother and father had spent their years. He thought of the cost exacted, year after year, by the soil; and it remained as it had been—a little more barren, perhaps, a little more frugal of increase. Nothing had changed. Their lives had been expended in cheerless labor, their wills broken, their intelligences numbed. Now they were in the earth to which they had given their lives; and slowly, year by year, the earth would take them. Slowly the damp and rot would infest the pine boxes which held their bodies, and slowly it would touch their flesh, and finally it would consume the last vestiges of their substances. And they would become a meaningless part of that stubborn earth to which they had long ago given themselves.

He let Tobe stay on at the farm through the winter; in the spring of 1928 he put the farm up for sale. The understanding was that Tobe was to remain on the farm until it was sold, and whatever he raised would belong to him. Tobe fixed the place up as best he could, repairing the house and repainting the small barn. Even so, it was not until early in the spring of 1929 that Stoner found a suitable buyer. He accepted the first offer he received, of a little over two thousand dollars; he gave Tobe a few hundred dollars, and in late August sent the rest of it to his father-in-law, to reduce the amount owed on the house in Columbia.

In October of that year the stock market failed, and local newspapers carried stories about Wall Street, about fortunes ruined and great lives altered. Few people in Columbia were touched; it was a conservative community, and almost none of the townspeople had money in stocks or bonds. But news began to come in of bank failures across the country, and the beginnings of uncertainty touched some of the townspeople; a few farmers withdrew their savings, and a few more (urged by the local bankers) increased their deposits. But no one was really apprehensive until word came of the failure of a small private bank, the Merchant's Trust, in St. Louis.

Stoner was at lunch in the University cafeteria when the news came, and he immediately went home to tell Edith. The Merchant's Trust was the bank that held the mortgage on their home, and the bank of which Edith's father was president. Edith called St. Louis that afternoon and talked to her mother; her mother was cheerful, and she told Edith that Mr. Bostwick had assured her that there was nothing to worry about, that everything would be all right in a few weeks.

Three days after that Horace Bostwick was dead, a suicide. He went to his office at the bank one morning in an unusually cheerful mood; he greeted several of the bank employees who still worked behind the closed doors of the bank, went into his office after telling his secretary that he would receive no calls, and locked his door. At about ten o'clock in the morning he shot himself in the head with a revolver he had purchased the day before and brought with him in his briefcase. He left no note behind him; but the papers neatly arranged on his desk told all that he had to tell. And what he had to tell was simply financial ruin. Like his Bostonian father, he had invested unwisely, not only his own money but also the bank's; and his ruin was so complete that he could imagine no relief. As it turned out, the ruin was not so nearly total as he thought at the moment of his suicide. After the estate was settled, the family house remained intact, and some minor real estate on the outskirts of St. Louis was sufficient to furnish his wife with a small income for the rest of her life.

But this was not known immediately. William Stoner received the telephone call that informed him of Horace Bostwick's ruin and suicide, and he broke the news to Edith as gently as his estrangement from her would allow him.

Edith took the news calmly, almost as if she had been expecting it. She looked at Stoner for several moments without speaking; then she shook her head and said absently, "Poor mother. What will she do? There has always been someone to take care of her. How will she live?"

Stoner said, "Tell her"—he paused awkwardly—"tell her that, if she wants to, she can come live with us. She will be welcome."

Edith smiled at him with a curious mixture of fondness and contempt. "Oh, Willy. She'd rather die herself. Don't you know that?"

Stoner nodded. "I suppose I do," he said.

So on the evening of the day that Stoner received the call, Edith left Columbia to go to St. Louis for the funeral and to stay there as long as she was needed. When she had been gone a week Stoner received a brief note informing him that she would remain with her mother for another two weeks, perhaps longer. She was gone for nearly two months, and William was alone in the big house with his daughter.

For the first few days the emptiness of the house was strangely and unexpectedly disquieting. But he got used to the emptiness and began to enjoy it; within a week he knew himself to be as happy as he had been in years, and when he thought of Edith's inevitable return, it was with a quiet regret that he no longer needed to hide from himself.

Grace had had her sixth birthday in the spring of that year, and she started her first year of school that fall. Every morning Stoner got her ready for school, and he was back from the University in the afternoon in time to greet her when she came home.

At the age of six Grace was a tall, slender child with hair that was more blond than red; her skin was perfectly fair, and her eyes were dark blue, almost violet. She was quiet and cheerful, and she had a delight in things that gave her father a feeling that was like nostalgic reverence.

Sometimes Grace played with neighbor children, but more often she sat with her father in his large study and watched him as he graded papers, or read, or wrote. She spoke to him, and they conversed—so quietly and seriously that William Stoner was moved by a tenderness that he never foresaw. Grace drew awkward and charming pictures on sheets of yellow paper and presented them solemnly to her father, or she read aloud to him from her first-grade reader. At night, when Stoner put her to bed and returned to his study, he was aware of her absence from his room and was comforted by the knowledge that she slept securely above him. In ways of which he was barely conscious he started her education, and he watched with amazement and love as she grew before him and as her face began to show the intelligence that worked within her.

Edith did not return to Columbia until after the first of the year, so William Stoner and his daughter spent Christmas by themselves. On Christmas morning they exchanged gifts; for her father, who did not smoke, Grace had modeled, at the cautiously progressive school attached to the University, a crude ashtray. William gave her a new dress that he had selected himself at a downtown store, several books, and a coloring set. They sat most of the day before the small tree, talked, and watched the lights twinkle on the ornaments and the tinsel wink from the dark green fir like buried fire.

During the Christmas holiday, that curious, suspended pause in the rushing semester, William Stoner began to realize two things: he began to know how centrally important Grace had become to his existence, and he began to understand that it might be possible for him to become a good teacher.

He was ready to admit to himself that he had not been a good teacher. Always, from the time he had fumbled through his first classes of freshman English, he had been aware of the gulf that lay between what he felt for his subject and what he delivered in the classroom. He had hoped that time and experience would repair the gulf; but they had not done so. Those things that he held most deeply were most profoundly betrayed when he spoke of them to his classes; what was most alive withered in his words; and what moved him most became cold in its utterance. And the consciousness of his inadequacy distressed him so greatly that the sense of it grew habitual, as much a part of him as the stoop of his shoulders.

But during the weeks that Edith was in St. Louis, when he lectured, he now and then found himself so lost in his subject that he became forgetful of his inadequacy, of himself, and even of the students before him. Now and then he became so caught by his enthusiasm that he stuttered, gesticulated, and ignored the lecture notes that usually guided his talks. At first he was disturbed by his outbursts, as if he presumed too familiarly upon his subject, and he apologized to his students; but when they began coming up to him after class, and when in their papers they began to show hints of imagination and the revelation of a tentative love, he was encouraged to do what he had never been taught to do. The love of literature, of language, of the mystery of the mind and heart showing themselves in the minute, strange, and unexpected combinations of letters and words, in the blackest and coldest print—the love which he had hidden as if it were illicit and dangerous, he began to display, tentatively at first, and then boldly, and then proudly.

He was both saddened and heartened by his discovery of what he might do; beyond his intention, he felt he had cheated both his students and himself. The students who had been able theretofore to plod through his courses by the repetition of mechanical steps began to look at him with puzzlement and resentment; those who had not taken courses from him began to sit in on his lectures and nod to him in the halls. He spoke more confidently and felt a warm hard severity gather within him. He suspected that he was beginning, ten years late, to discover who he was; and the figure he saw was both more and less than he had once imagined it to be. He felt himself at last beginning to be a teacher, which was simply a man to whom his book is true, to whom is given a dignity of art that has little to do with his foolishness or weakness or inadequacy as a man. It was a knowledge of which he could not speak, but one which changed him, once he had it, so that no one could mistake its presence.

Thus, when Edith came back from St. Louis, she found him changed in a way that she could not understand but of which she was instantly aware. She returned without warning on an afternoon train and walked through the living room into the study where her husband and her daughter quietly sat. She had meant to shock them both by her sudden presence and by her changed appearance; but when William looked up at her, and she saw the surprise in his eyes, she knew at once that the real change had come over him, and that it was so deep that the effect of her appearance was lost; and she thought to herself, a little distantly and yet with some surprise, I know him better than I ever realized.

William was surprised at her presence and her altered appearance, but neither could move him now as they might once have done. He looked at her for several moments and then got up from his desk, went across the room, and greeted her gravely.

Edith had bobbed her hair and wore over it one of those hats that hugged her head so tightly that the cropped hair lay close to her face like an irregular frame; her lips were painted a bright orange-red, and two small spots of rouge sharpened her cheekbones. She wore one of those short dresses that had become fashionable among the younger women during the past few years; it hung straight down from her shoulders and ended just above her knees. She smiled self-consciously at her husband and walked across the room to her daughter, who sat on the floor and looked up at her quietly and studiously. She knelt awkwardly, her new dress tight around her legs.

"Gracie, honey," she said in a voice that seemed to William to be strained and brittle, "did you miss your mommy? Did you think she was never coming back?"

Grace kissed her mother on the cheek and looked at her solemnly. "You look different," she said.

Edith laughed and got up from the floor; she whirled around, holding her hands above her head. "I have a new dress and new shoes and a new hair-do. Do you like them?"

Grace nodded dubiously. "You look different," she said again.

Edith's smile widened; there was a pale smear of lipstick on one of her teeth. She turned to William and asked, "Do I look different?"

"Yes," William said. "Very charming. Very pretty."

She laughed at him and shook her head. "Poor Willy," she said. Then she turned again to her daughter. "I am different, I believe," she said to her. "I really believe I am."

But William Stoner knew that she was speaking to him. And at that moment, somehow, he also knew that beyond her intention or understanding, unknown to herself, Edith was trying to announce to him a new declaration of war.

VIII

THE DECLARATION was a part of the change that Edith had started bringing about during the weeks she had spent at "home" in St. Louis after her father's death. And it was intensified, and finally given point and savagery, by that other change that came and slowly grew upon William Stoner after he discovered that he might become a good teacher.

Edith had been curiously unmoved at her father's funeral. During the elaborate ceremonies she sat erect and hard-faced, and her expression did not alter when she had to go past her father's body, resplendent and plump, in the ornate coffin. But at the cemetery, when the coffin was lowered into the narrow hole masked by mats of artificial grass, she lowered her expressionless face into her hands and did not raise it until someone touched her shoulder.

After the funeral she spent several days in her old room, the room in which she had grown up; she saw her mother only at breakfast and at dinner. It was thought by callers that she was secluded in her grief. "They were very close," Edith's mother said mysteriously. "Much closer than they seemed."

But in that room Edith walked about as if for the first time, freely, touching the walls and windows, testing their solidity. She had a trunk full of her childhood belongings brought down from the attic; she went through her bureau drawers, which had remained undisturbed for more than a decade. With a bemused air of leisure, as if she had all the time in the world, she went through her things, fondling them, turning them this way and that, examining them with an almost ritualistic care. When she came upon a letter she had received as a child, she read it through from beginning to end as if for the first time; when she came upon a forgotten doll, she smiled at it and caressed the painted bisque of its cheek as if she were a child again who had received a gift.

Finally she arranged all of her childhood belongings neatly in two piles. One of these consisted of toys and trinkets she had acquired for herself, of secret photographs and letters from school friends, of gifts she had at one time received from

distant relatives; the other pile consisted of those things that
her father had given her and of things with which he had been
directly or indirectly connected. It was to this pile that she
gave her attention. Methodically, expressionlessly, with neither
anger nor joy, she took the objects there, one by one, and destroyed them. The letters and clothes, the stuffing from the
dolls, the pincushions and pictures, she burned in the fireplace;
the clay and porcelain heads, the hands and arms and feet of
the dolls she pounded to a fine powder on the hearth; and
what remained after the burning and pounding she swept into
a small pile and flushed down the toilet in the bathroom that
adjoined her room.

When the job was done—the room cleared of smoke, the
hearth swept, the few remaining belongings returned to the
chest of drawers—Edith Bostwick Stoner sat at her small dressing table and looked at herself in the mirror, the silver backing
of which was thinning and flecking away, so that here and there
her image was imperfectly reflected, or not reflected at all, giving her face a curiously incomplete look. She was thirty years
old. The youthful gloss was beginning to fall from her hair,
tiny lines were starting out from around her eyes, and the skin
of her face was beginning to tighten around her sharp cheekbones. She nodded to the image in the mirror, got up abruptly,
and went downstairs, where for the first time in days she talked
cheerfully and almost intimately to her mother.

She wanted (she said) a change in herself. She had too long
been what she was; she spoke of her childhood, of her marriage. And from sources that she could speak of but vaguely
and uncertainly, she fixed an image that she wished to fulfill;
and for nearly the whole of the two months that she stayed in
St. Louis with her mother, she devoted herself to that fulfillment.

She asked to borrow a sum of money from her mother, who
made her an impetuous gift of it. She bought a new wardrobe,
burning all the clothes she had brought with her from Columbia; she had her hair cut short and fashioned in the mode of
the day; she bought cosmetics and perfumes, the use of which
she practiced daily in her room. She learned to smoke, and she
cultivated a new way of speaking which was brittle, vaguely
English, and a little shrill. She returned to Columbia with this

outward change well under control, and with another change secret and potential within her.

During the first few months after her return to Columbia, she was furious with activity; no longer did it seem necessary to pretend to herself that she was ill or weak. She joined a little theater group and devoted herself to the work that was given her; she designed and painted sets, raised money for the group, and even had a few small parts in the productions. When Stoner came home in the afternoons he found the living room filled with her friends, strangers who looked at him as if he were an intruder, to whom he nodded politely and retreated to his study, where he could hear their voices, muted and declamatory, beyond his walls.

Edith purchased a used upright piano and had it put in the living room, against the wall which separated that room from William's study; she had given up the practice of music shortly before her marriage, and she now started almost anew, practicing scales, laboring through exercises that were too difficult for her, playing sometimes two or three hours a day, often in the evening, after Grace had been put to bed.

The groups of students whom Stoner invited to his study for conversation grew larger and the meetings more frequent; and no longer was Edith content to remain upstairs, away from the gatherings. She insisted upon serving them tea or coffee; and when she did she seated herself in the room. She talked loudly and gaily, managing to turn the conversation toward her work in the little theater, or her music, or her painting and sculpture, which (she announced) she was planning to take up again, as soon as she found time. The students, mystified and embarrassed, gradually stopped coming, and Stoner began meeting them for coffee in the University cafeteria or in one of the small cafés scattered around the campus.

He did not speak to Edith about her new behavior; her activities caused him only minor annoyance, and she seemed happy, though perhaps a bit desperately so. It was, finally, himself that he held responsible for the new direction her life had taken; he had been unable to discover for her any meaning in their life together, in their marriage. Thus it was right for her to take what meaning she could find in areas that had nothing to do with him and go ways he could not follow.

Emboldened by his new success as a teacher and by his growing popularity among the better graduate students, he started a new book in the summer of 1930. He now spent nearly all of his free time in his study. He and Edith kept up between themselves the pretense of sharing the same bedroom, but he seldom entered that room, and never at night. He slept on his studio couch and even kept his clothes in a small closet he constructed in one corner of the room.

He was able to be with Grace. As had become her habit during her mother's first long absence, she spent much of her time with her father in his study; Stoner even found a small desk and chair for her, so that she had a place to read and do her homework. They had their meals more often than not alone; Edith was away from the house a great deal, and when she was not away she frequently entertained her theater friends at little parties which did not admit the presence of a child.

Then, abruptly, Edith began staying home. The three of them started taking their meals together again, and Edith even made a few movements toward caring for the house. The house was quiet; even the piano was unused, so that dust gathered on the keyboard.

They had come to that point in their life together when they seldom spoke of themselves or each other, lest the delicate balance that made their living together possible be broken. So it was only after long hesitation and deliberation about consequences that Stoner finally asked her if anything was wrong.

They were at the dinner table; Grace had been excused and had taken a book into Stoner's study.

"What do you mean?" Edith asked.

"Your friends," William said. "They haven't been around for some time, and you don't seem to be so involved with your theater work any more. I was just wondering if there was anything wrong."

With an almost masculine gesture, Edith shook a cigarette from the package beside her plate, stuck it between her lips, and lighted it with the stub of another that she had half finished. She inhaled deeply without taking the cigarette from her lips and tilted her head back, so that when she looked at William her eyes were narrowed and quizzical and calculating.

"Nothing's wrong," she said. "I just got bored with them and the work. Does there always have to be something wrong?"

"No," William said. "I just thought maybe you weren't feeling well or something."

He thought no more about the conversation and shortly thereafter he left the table and went into the study, where Grace was sitting at her desk, immersed in her book. The desk light gleamed in her hair and threw her small, serious face into sharp outline. She has grown during the past year, William thought; and a small, not unpleasant sadness caught briefly at his throat. He smiled and went quietly to his desk.

Within a few moments he was immersed in his work. The evening before, he had caught up with the routine of his classwork; papers had been graded and lectures prepared for the whole week that was to follow. He saw the evening before him, and several evenings more, in which he would be free to work on his book. What he wanted to do in this new book was not yet precisely clear to him; in general, he wished to extend himself beyond his first study, in both time and scope. He wanted to work in the period of the English Renaissance and to extend his study of classical and medieval Latin influences into that area. He was in the stage of planning his study, and it was that stage which gave him the most pleasure—the selection among alternative approaches, the rejection of certain strategies, the mysteries and uncertainties that lay in unexplored possibilities, the consequences of choice. . . . The possibilities he could see so exhilarated him that he could not keep still. He got up from his desk, paced a little, and in a kind of frustrated joy spoke to his daughter, who looked up from her book and answered him.

She caught his mood, and something he said caused her to laugh. Then the two of them were laughing together, senselessly, as if they both were children. Suddenly the door to the study came open, and the hard light from the living room streamed into the shadowed recesses of the study. Edith stood outlined in that light.

"Grace," she said distinctly and slowly, "your father is trying to work. You mustn't disturb him."

For several moments William and his daughter were so stunned by this sudden intrusion that neither of them moved or spoke. Then William managed to say, "It's all right, Edith. She doesn't bother me."

As if he had not spoken, Edith said, "Grace, did you hear me? Come out of there this instant."

Bewildered, Grace got down from her chair and walked across the room. In the center she paused, looking first at her father and then at her mother. Edith started to speak again, but William managed to cut her off.

"It's all right, Grace," he said as gently as he could. "It's all right. Go with your mother."

As Grace went through the study door to the living room, Edith said to her husband, "The child has had entirely too much freedom. It isn't natural for her to be so quiet, so withdrawn. She's been too much alone. She should be more active, play with children her own age. Don't you realize how unhappy she has been?"

And she shut the door before he could answer.

He did not move for a long while. He looked at his desk, littered with notes and open books; he walked slowly across the room and aimlessly rearranged the sheets of paper, the books. He stood there, frowning, for several minutes more, as if he were trying to remember something. Then he turned again and walked to Grace's small desk; he stood there for some time, as he had stood at his own desk. He turned off the lamp there, so that the desk top was gray and lifeless, and went across to the couch, where he lay with his eyes open, staring at the ceiling.

The enormity came upon him gradually, so that it was several weeks before he could admit to himself what Edith was doing; and when he was able at last to make that admission, he made it almost without surprise. Edith's was a campaign waged with such cleverness and skill that he could find no rational grounds for complaint. After her abrupt and almost brutal entrance into his study that night, an entrance which in retrospect seemed to him a surprise attack, Edith's strategy became more indirect, more quiet and contained. It was a strategy that disguised itself as love and concern, and thus one against which he was helpless.

Edith was at home nearly all the time now. During the morning and early afternoon, while Grace was at school, she occupied herself with redecorating Grace's bedroom. She removed the small desk from Stoner's study, refinished and repainted it a pale pink, attaching around the top a broad ribbon of matching ruffled satin, so that it bore no resemblance to the desk Grace had grown used to; one afternoon, with Grace standing mutely beside her, she went through all the clothing William had bought for her, discarded most of it, and promised Grace that they would, this weekend, go downtown and replace the discarded items with things more fitting, something "girlish." And they did. Late in the afternoon, weary but triumphant, Edith returned with a load of packages and an exhausted daughter desperately uncomfortable in a new dress stiff with starch and a myriad of ruffles, from beneath the ballooning hem of which her thin legs stuck out like pathetic sticks.

Edith bought her daughter dolls and toys and hovered about her while she played with them, as if it were a duty; she started her on piano lessons and sat beside her on the bench as she practiced; upon the slightest occasion she gave little parties for her, which neighborhood children attended, vindictive and sullen in their stiff, formal clothing; and she strictly supervised her daughter's reading and homework, not allowing her to work beyond the time she had allotted.

Now Edith's visitors were neighborhood mothers. They came in the mornings and drank coffee and talked while their children were in school; in the afternoons they brought their children with them and watched them playing games in the large living room and talked aimlessly above the noise of games and running.

On these afternoons Stoner was usually in his study and could hear what the mothers said as they spoke loudly across the room, above their children's voices.

Once, when there was a lull in the noise, he heard Edith say, "Poor Grace. She's so fond of her father, but he has so little time to devote to her. His work, you know; and he has started a new book . . ."

Curiously, almost detachedly, he watched his hands, which had been holding a book, begin to shake. They shook for several moments before he brought them under control by

jamming them deep in his pockets, clenching them, and holding them there.

He saw his daughter seldom now. The three of them took
their meals together, but on these occasions he hardly dared to
speak to her, for when he did, and when Grace answered him,
Edith soon found something wanting in Grace's table manners, or in the way she sat in her chair, and she spoke so sharply
that her daughter remained silent and downcast through the
rest of the meal.

Grace's already slender body was becoming thinner; Edith
laughed gently about her "growing up but not out." Her eyes
were becoming watchful, almost wary; the expression that had
once been quietly serene was now either faintly sullen at one
extreme or gleeful and animated on the thin edge of hysteria at
the other; she seldom smiled any more, although she laughed
a great deal. And when she did smile, it was as if a ghost flitted across her face. Once, while Edith was upstairs, William
and his daughter passed each other in the living room. Grace
smiled shyly at him, and involuntarily he knelt on the floor and
embraced her. He felt her body stiffen, and he saw her face go
bewildered and afraid. He raised himself gently away from her,
said something inconsequential, and retreated to his study.

The morning after this he stayed at the breakfast table until
Grace left for school, even though he knew he would be late
for his nine o'clock class. After seeing Grace out the front door,
Edith did not return to the dining room, and he knew that
she was avoiding him. He went into the living room, where
his wife sat at one end of the sofa with a cup of coffee and a
cigarette.

Without preliminaries he said, "Edith, I don't like what's
happening to Grace."

Instantly, as if she were picking up a cue, she said, "What do
you mean?"

He let himself down on the other end of the sofa, away from
Edith. A feeling of helplessness came over him. "You know
what I mean," he said wearily. "Let up on her. Don't drive her
so hard."

Edith ground her cigarette out in her saucer. "Grace has
never been happier. She has friends now, things to occupy her.
I know you're too busy to notice these things, but—surely you

must realize how much more outgoing she's been recently. And she laughs. She never used to laugh. Almost never."

William looked at her in quiet amazement. "You believe that, don't you?"

"Of course I do," Edith said. "I'm her mother."

And she did believe it, Stoner realized. He shook his head.

"I've never wanted to admit it to myself," he said with something like tranquillity, "but you really do hate me, don't you, Edith?"

"What?" The amazement in her voice was genuine. "Oh, Willy!" She laughed clearly and unrestrainedly. "Don't be foolish. Of course not. You're my husband."

"Don't use the child." He could not keep his voice from trembling. "You don't have to any longer; you know that. Anything else. But if you keep on using Grace, I'll—" He did not finish.

After a moment Edith said, "You'll what?" She spoke quietly and without challenge. "All you could do is leave me, and you'd never do that. We both know it."

He nodded. "I suppose you're right." He got up blindly and went into his study. He got his coat from the closet and picked up his briefcase from beside his desk. As he crossed the living room Edith spoke to him again.

"Willy, I wouldn't hurt Grace. You ought to know that. I love her. She's my very own daughter."

And he knew that it was true; she did love her. The truth of the knowledge almost made him cry out. He shook his head and went out into the weather.

When he got home that evening he found that during the day Edith had, with the help of a local handyman, moved all of his belongings out of his study. Jammed together in one corner of the living room were his desk and couch, and surrounding them in a careless jumble were his clothes, his papers, and all of his books.

Since she would be home more now, she had (she told him) decided to take up her painting and her sculpting again; and his study, with its north light, would give her the only really decent illumination the house had. She knew he wouldn't mind a move; he could use the glassed-in sun porch at the back of the house; it was farther away from the living room than his study had been, and he would have more quiet in which to do his work.

But the sun porch was so small that he could not keep his books in any order, and there was no room for either the desk or the couch that he had had in the study, so he stored both of them in the cellar. It was difficult to warm the sun porch in the winter, and in the summer, he knew, the sun would beat through the glass panes that enclosed the porch, so that it would be nearly uninhabitable. Yet he worked there for several months. He got a small table and used it as a desk, and he purchased a portable radiant heater to mitigate a little the cold that in the evenings seeped through the thin clapboard sidings. At night he slept wrapped in a blanket on the sofa in the living room.

After a few months of relative though uncomfortable peace, he began finding, when he returned in the afternoon from the University, odds and ends of discarded household goods— broken lamps, scatter rugs, small chests, and boxes of bric-a-brac —left carelessly in the room that now served as his study.

"It's so damp in the cellar," Edith said, "they'd be ruined. You don't mind if I keep them in here for a while, do you?"

One spring afternoon he returned home during a driving rainstorm and discovered that somehow one of the panes had got broken and that the rain had damaged several of his books and had rendered many of his notes illegible; a few weeks later he came in to find that Grace and a few of her friends had been allowed to play in the room and that more of his notes and the first pages of the manuscript of his new book had been torn and mutilated. "I only let them go in there a few minutes," Edith said. "They have to have someplace to play. But I had no idea. You ought to speak to Grace. I've told her how important your work is to you."

He gave up then. He moved as many of his books as he could to his office at the University, which he shared with three younger instructors; thereafter he spent much of the time that he had formerly spent at home at the University, coming home early only when his loneliness for a brief glimpse of his daughter, or a word with her, made it impossible for him to stay away.

But he had room in his office for only a few of his books, and his work on his manuscript was often interrupted because he did not have the necessary texts; moreover one of his office mates, an earnest young man, had the habit of scheduling student conferences in the evenings, and the sibilant, labored conversations carried on across the room distracted him, so that he found it difficult to concentrate. He lost interest in his book; his work slowed and came to a halt. Finally he realized that it had become a refuge, a haven, an excuse to come to the office at night. He read and studied, and at last came to find some comfort, some pleasure, and even a ghost of the old joy in that which he did, a learning toward no particular end.

And Edith had relaxed her pursuit and obsessive concern for Grace, so that the child was beginning occasionally to smile and even to speak to him with some ease. Thus he found it possible to live, and even to be happy, now and then.

IX

THE INTERIM chairmanship of the English Department, which Gordon Finch had assumed after the death of Archer Sloane, was renewed year after year, until all the members of the department grew used to a casual anarchy in which somehow classes got scheduled and taught, in which new appointments to the staff were made, in which the trivial departmental details somehow got taken care of, and in which year somehow succeeded year. It was generally understood that a permanent chairman would be appointed as soon as it became possible to make Finch the dean of Arts and Sciences, a position that he held in fact if not in office; Josiah Claremont threatened never to die, though he was seldom seen any longer wandering through the halls.

The members of the department went their ways, taught the classes they had taught the year before, and visited one another's offices in the hours between classes. They met together formally only at the beginning of each semester when Gordon Finch called a perfunctory departmental meeting, and on those occasions when the dean of the Graduate College sent them memos requesting that they give oral and thesis examinations to graduate students who were nearing completion of their work.

Such examinations took up an increasing amount of Stoner's time. To his surprise he began to enjoy a modest popularity as a teacher; he had to turn away students who wanted to get into his graduate seminar on the Latin Tradition and Renaissance Literature, and his undergraduate survey classes were always filled. Several graduate students asked him to direct their theses, and several more asked him to be on their thesis committees.

In the fall of 1931 the seminar was nearly filled even before registration; many students had made arrangements with Stoner at the end of the preceding year or during the summer. A week after the semester started, and after the seminar had held one meeting, a student came to Stoner's office and asked to be let in the class.

Stoner was at his desk with a list of the seminar students before him; he was attempting to decide upon seminar tasks for them, and it was particularly difficult since many were new to him. It was a September afternoon, and he had the window next to his desk open; the front of the great building lay in shadow, so that the green lawn before it showed the precise shape of the building, with its semicircular dome and irregular roofline darkening the green and creeping imperceptibly outward over the campus and beyond. A cool breeze flowed through the window, bringing the crisp redolence of fall.

A knock came; he turned to his opened doorway and said, "Come in."

A figure shuffled out of the darkness of the hall into the light of the room. Stoner blinked sleepily against the dimness, recognizing a student whom he had noticed in the halls but did not know. The young man's left arm hung stiffly at his side, and his left foot dragged as he walked. His face was pale and round, his horn-rimmed eyeglasses were round, and his black thin hair was parted precisely on the side and lay close to the round skull.

"Dr. Stoner?" he asked; his voice was reedy and clipped, and he spoke distinctly.

"Yes," Stoner said. "Won't you have a chair?"

The young man lowered himself into the straight wooden chair beside Stoner's desk; his leg was extended in a straight line, and his left hand, which was permanently twisted into a half-closed fist, rested upon it. He smiled, bobbed his head, and said with a curious air of self-depreciation, "You may not know me, sir; I'm Charles Walker. I'm a second-year Ph.D. candidate; I assist Dr. Lomax."

"Yes, Mr. Walker," Stoner said. "What can I do for you?"

"Well, I'm here to ask a favor, sir." Walker smiled again. "I know your seminar is filled, but I want very much to get in it." He paused and said pointedly, "Dr. Lomax suggested that I talk to you."

"I see," Stoner said. "What's your specialty, Mr. Walker?"

"The Romantic poets," Walker said. "Dr. Lomax will be the director of my dissertation."

Stoner nodded. "How far along are you in your course work?"

"I hope to finish within two years," Walker said.

"Well, that makes it easier," Stoner said. "I offer the seminar every year. It's really so full now that it's hardly a seminar any longer, and one more person would just about finish the job. Why can't you wait until next year if you really want the course?"

Walker's eyes shifted away from him. "Well, frankly," he said and flashed his smile again, "I'm the victim of a misunderstanding. All my own fault, of course. I didn't realize that each Ph.D. student has to have at least four graduate seminars to get his degree, and I didn't take any at all last year. And as you know, they don't allow you to take more than one each semester. So if I'm to graduate in two years, I have to have one this semester."

Stoner sighed. "I see. So you don't really have a very special interest in the influence of the Latin tradition?"

"Oh, indeed I do, sir. Indeed I do. It will be most helpful in my dissertation."

"Mr. Walker, you should know this is a rather specialized class, and I don't encourage people to enter it unless they have a particular interest."

"Yes, sir," Walker said. "I assure you that I *do* have a particular interest."

Stoner nodded. "How is your Latin?"

Walker bobbed his head. "Oh, it's fine, sir. I haven't taken my Latin exam yet, but I read it very well."

"Do you have French or German?"

"Oh, yes, sir. Again, I haven't taken the exams yet; I thought I'd get them all out of the way at the same time, at the end of this year. But I read them both very well." Walker paused, then added, "Dr. Lomax said he thought I would surely be able to do the work in the seminar."

Stoner sighed. "Very well," he said. "Much of the reading will be in Latin, a little in French and German, though you might be able to get by without those. I'll give you a reading list, and we'll talk about your seminar topic next Wednesday afternoon."

Walker thanked him effusively and arose from his chair with some difficulty. "I'll get right on to the reading," he said. "I'm sure you won't regret letting me in your class, sir."

Stoner looked at him with faint surprise. "The question had not occurred to me, Mr. Walker," he said dryly. "I'll see you on Wednesday."

The seminar was held in a small basement room in the south wing of Jesse Hall. A dank but not unpleasant odor seeped from the cement walls, and feet shuffled in hollow whispers upon the bare cement floor. A single light hung from the ceiling in the center of the room and shone downward, so that those seated at desk-top chairs in the center of the room rested in a splash of brightness; but the walls were a dim gray and the corners were almost black, as if the smooth unpainted cement sucked in the light that streamed from the ceiling.

On that second Wednesday of the seminar William Stoner came into the room a few minutes late; he spoke to the students and began to arrange his books and papers on the small stained-oak desk that stood squatly before the center of a blackboard wall. He glanced at the small group scattered about the room. Some of them he knew; two of the men were Ph.D. candidates whose work he was directing; four others were M.A. students in the department who had done undergraduate work with him; of the remaining students, three were candidates for advanced degrees in modern language, one was a philosophy student doing his dissertation on the Scholastics, one was a woman of advanced middle age, a high-school teacher trying to get an M.A. during her sabbatical, and the last was a dark-haired young woman, a new instructor in the department, who had taken a job for two years while she completed a dissertation she had begun after finishing her course work at an eastern university. She had asked Stoner if she might audit the seminar, and he had agreed that she might. Charles Walker was not among the group. Stoner waited a few moments more, shuffling his papers; then he cleared his throat and began the class.

"During our first meeting we discussed the scope of this seminar, and we decided that we should limit our study of the medieval Latin tradition to the first three of the seven liberal arts—that is, to grammar, rhetoric, and dialectic." He paused and watched the faces—tentative, curious, and masklike—focus upon him and what he said.

"Such a limiting may seem foolishly rigorous to some of

you; but I have no doubt that we shall find enough to keep us occupied even if we trace only superficially the course of the trivium upward into the sixteenth century. It is important that we realize that these arts of rhetoric, grammar, and dialectic meant something to a late medieval and early Renaissance man that we, today, can only dimly sense without an exercise of the historical imagination. To such a scholar, the art of grammar, for example, was not merely a mechanical disposition of the parts of speech. From late Hellenistic times through the Middle Ages, the study and practice of grammar included not only the 'skill of letters' mentioned by Plato and Aristotle; it included also, and this became very important, a study of poetry in its technical felicities, an exegesis of poetry both in form and substance, and nicety of style, insofar as that can be distinguished from rhetoric."

He felt himself warming to his subject, and he was aware that several of the students had leaned forward and had stopped taking notes. He continued: "Moreover, if we in the twentieth century are asked which of these three arts is the most important, we might choose dialectic, or rhetoric—but we would be most unlikely to choose grammar. Yet the Roman and medieval scholar—and poet—would almost certainly consider grammar the most significant. We must remember—"

A loud noise interrupted him. The door had opened and Charles Walker entered the room; as he closed the door the books he carried under his crippled arm slipped and crashed to the floor. He bent awkwardly, his bad leg extended behind him, and slowly gathered his books and papers. Then he drew himself erect and shuffled across the room, the scrape of his foot across the bare cement raising a loud and grating hiss that sounded sibilantly hollow in the room. He found a chair in the front row and sat down.

After Walker had settled himself and got his papers and books in order around his desk chair, Stoner continued: "We must remember that the medieval conception of grammar was even more general than the late Hellenistic or Roman. Not only did it include the science of correct speech and the art of exegesis, it included as well the modern conceptions of analogy, etymology, methods of presentation, construction, the condition of poetic license and the exceptions to that condition—and even metaphorical language or figures of speech."

As he continued, elaborating upon the categories of grammar he had named, Stoner's eyes flitted over the class; he realized that he had lost them during Walker's entrance and knew that it would be some time before he could once more persuade them out of themselves. Again and again his glance fell curiously upon Walker, who, after having taken notes furiously for a few moments, gradually let his pencil rest on his notebook, while he gazed at Stoner with a puzzled frown. Finally Walker's hand shot up; Stoner finished the sentence he had begun and nodded to him.

"Sir," Walker said, "pardon me, but I don't understand. What can"—he paused and let his mouth curl around the word—"*grammar* have to do with poetry? Fundamentally I mean. *Real* poetry."

Stoner said gently, "As I was explaining before you came in, Mr. Walker, the term 'grammar' to both the Roman and medieval rhetoricians was a great deal more comprehensive than it is today. To them, it meant—" He paused, realizing that he was about to repeat the early part of his lecture; he sensed the students stirring restlessly. "I think this relationship will become clearer to you as we go on, as we see the extent to which the poets and dramatists even of the middle and late Renaissance were indebted to the Latin rhetoricians."

"All of them, sir?" Walker smiled and leaned back in his chair. "Wasn't it Samuel Johnson who said of Shakespeare himself that he had little Latin and less Greek?"

As the repressed laughter stirred in the room Stoner felt a kind of pity come over him. "You mean Ben Jonson, of course."

Walker took off his glasses and polished them, blinking helplessly. "Of course," he said. "A slip of the tongue."

Though Walker interrupted him several times, Stoner managed to get through his lecture without serious difficulty, and he was able to make assignments for the first reports. He let the seminar out nearly half an hour early, and hurried away from the classroom when he saw Walker shuffling toward him with a fixed grin on his face. He clattered up the wooden stairs from the basement and took two at a time the smooth marble stairs that led to the second floor; he had the curious feeling that Walker was doggedly shuffling behind him, trying to over-take him in his flight. A hasty wash of shame and guilt came over him.

On the third floor he went directly to Lomax's office. Lomax was in conference with a student. Stoner stuck his head in the door and said, "Holly, can I see you for a minute after you're through?"

Lomax waved genially. "Come on in. We're just breaking up."

Stoner came in and pretended to examine the rows of books in their cases as Lomax and the student said their last words. When the student left, Stoner sat in the chair that he had vacated. Lomax looked at him inquiringly.

"It's about a student," Stoner said. "Charles Walker. He said you sent him around to me."

Lomax placed the tips of his fingers together and contemplated them as he nodded. "Yes. I believe I did suggest that he might profit from your seminar—what is it?—in the Latin tradition."

"Can you tell me something about him?"

Lomax looked up from his hands and gazed at the ceiling, his lower lip thrust out judiciously. "A good student. A superior student, I might say. He is doing his dissertation on Shelley and the Hellenistic Ideal. It promises to be brilliant, really brilliant. It will not be what some would call"—he hesitated delicately over the word—"*sound*, but it is most imaginative. Did you have a particular reason for asking?"

"Yes," Stoner said. "He behaved rather foolishly in the seminar today. I was just wondering if I should attach any special significance to it."

Lomax's early geniality had disappeared, and the more familiar mask of irony had slipped over him. "Ah, yes," he said with a frosty smile. "The gaucherie and foolishness of the young. Walker is, for reasons you may understand, rather awkwardly shy and therefore at times defensive and rather too assertive. As do we all, he has his problems; but his scholarly and critical abilities are not, I hope, to be judged in the light of his rather understandable psychic disturbances." He looked directly at Stoner and said with cheerful malevolence, "As you may have noticed, he is a cripple."

"It may be that," Stoner said thoughtfully. He sighed and got up from the chair. "I suppose it's really too soon for me to be concerned. I just wanted to check with you."

Suddenly Lomax's voice was tight and near trembling with suppressed anger. "You will find him to be a superior student. I assure you, you will find him to be an *excellent* student."

Stoner looked at him for a moment, frowning perplexedly. Then he nodded and went out of the room.

The seminar met weekly. For the first several meetings Walker interrupted the class with questions and comments that were so bewilderingly far off the mark that Stoner was at a loss as to how to meet them. Soon Walker's questions and statements were greeted with laughter or pointedly disregarded by the students themselves; and after a few weeks he spoke not at all but sat with a stony indignation and an air of outraged integrity as the seminar surged around him. It would, Stoner thought, have been amusing had there not been something so naked in Walker's outrage and resentment.

But despite Walker it was a successful seminar, one of the best classes Stoner had ever taught. Almost from the first, the implications of the subject caught the students, and they all had that sense of discovery that comes when one feels that the subject at hand lies at the center of a much larger subject, and when one feels intensely that a pursuit of the subject is likely to lead—where, one does not know. The seminar organized itself, and the students so involved themselves that Stoner himself became simply one of them, searching as diligently as they. Even the auditor—the young instructor who was stopping over at Columbia while finishing her dissertation—asked if she might report on a seminar topic; she thought that she had come upon something that might be of value to the others. Her name was Katherine Driscoll, and she was in her late twenties. Stoner had never really noticed her until she talked to him after class about the report and asked him if he would be willing to read her dissertation when she got it finished. He told her that he welcomed the report and that he would be glad to read her dissertation.

The seminar reports were scheduled for the second half of the semester, after the Christmas vacation. Walker's report on

"Hellenism and the Medieval Latin Tradition" was due early in the term, but he kept delaying it, explaining to Stoner his difficulty in obtaining books he needed, which were not available in the University library.

It had been understood that Miss Driscoll, being an auditor, would give her report after the credit students had given theirs; but on the last day Stoner had allowed for the seminar reports, two weeks before the end of the semester, Walker again begged that he be allowed one more week; he had been ill, his eyes had been troubling him, and a crucial book had not arrived from inter-library loan. So Miss Driscoll gave her paper on the day vacated by Walker's defection.

Her paper was entitled "Donatus and Renaissance Tragedy." Her concentration was upon Shakespeare's use of the Donatan tradition, a tradition that had persisted in the grammars and handbooks of the Middle Ages. A few moments after she began, Stoner knew that the paper would be good, and he listened with an excitement that he had not felt for a long time. After she had finished the paper, and the class had discussed it, he detained her for a few moments while the other students went out of the room.

"Miss Driscoll, I just want to say—" He paused, and for an instant a wave of awkwardness and self-consciousness came over him. She was looking at him inquiringly with large dark eyes; her face was very white against the severe black frame of her hair, drawn tight and caught in a small bun at the back. He continued, "I just want to say that your paper was the best discussion I know of the subject, and I'm grateful that you volunteered to give it."

She did not reply. Her expression did not change, but Stoner thought for a moment that she was angry; something fierce glinted behind her eyes. Then she blushed furiously and ducked her head, whether in anger or acknowledgment Stoner did not know, and hurried away from him. Stoner walked slowly out of the room, disquieted and puzzled, fearful that in his clumsiness he might somehow have offended her.

He had warned Walker as gently as he could that it would be necessary for him to deliver his paper the next Wednesday if he was to receive credit for the course; as he half expected, Walker became coldly and respectfully angry at the warning, repeated the various conditions and difficulties that had delayed him, and assured Stoner that there was no need to worry, that his paper was nearly completed.

On that last Wednesday, Stoner was delayed several minutes in his office by a desperate undergraduate who wished to be assured that he would receive a C in the sophomore survey course, so that he would not be kicked out of his fraternity. Stoner hurried downstairs and entered the basement seminar room a little out of breath; he found Charles Walker seated at his desk, looking imperiously and somberly at the small group of students. It was apparent that he was engaged in some private fantasy. He turned to Stoner and gazed at him haughtily, as if he were a professor putting down a rowdy freshman. Then Walker's expression broke and he said, "We were just about to start without you"—he paused at the last minute, let a smile through his lips, bobbed his head, and added, so that Stoner would know a joke was being made—"sir."

Stoner looked at him for a moment and then turned to the class. "I'm sorry I'm late. As you know, Mr. Walker is to deliver his seminar paper today upon the topic of 'Hellenism and the Medieval Latin Tradition.'" And he found a seat in the first row, next to Katherine Driscoll.

Charles Walker fiddled for a moment with the sheaf of papers on the desk before him and allowed the remoteness to creep back into his face. He tapped the forefinger of his right hand on his manuscript and looked toward the corner of the room away from where Stoner and Katherine Driscoll sat, as if he were waiting for something. Then, glancing every now and then at the sheaf of papers on the desk, he began.

"Confronted as we are by the mystery of literature, and by its inenarrable power, we are behooved to discover the source of the power and mystery. And yet, finally, what can avail? The work of literature throws before us a profound veil which we cannot plumb. And we are but votaries before it, helpless in its sway. Who would have the temerity to lift that veil aside, to discover the undiscoverable, to reach the unreachable? The strongest of us are but the puniest weaklings, are but tinkling cymbals and sounding brass, before the eternal mystery."

His voice rose and fell, his right hand went out with its fingers curled supplicatingly upward, and his body swayed to the rhythm of his words; his eyes rolled slightly upward, as if he were making an invocation. There was something grotesquely familiar in what he said and did. And suddenly Stoner knew what it was. This was Hollis Lomax—or, rather, a broad caricature of him, which came unsuspected from the caricaturer, a gesture not of contempt or dislike, but of respect and love.

Walker's voice dropped to a conversational level, and he addressed the back wall of the room in a tone that was calm and equable with reason. "Recently we have heard a paper that, to the mind of academe, must be accounted most excellent. These remarks that follow are remarks that are not personal. I wish to exemplify a point. We have heard, in this paper, an account that purports to be an explanation of the mystery and soaring lyricism of Shakespeare's art. Well, I say to you"—and he thrust a forefinger at his audience as if he would impale them—"I say to you, it is not true." He leaned back in his chair and consulted the papers on the desk. "We are asked to believe that one Donatus—an obscure Roman *grammarian* of the fourth century A.D.—we are asked to believe that such a man, a pedant, had sufficient power to determine the work of one of the greatest geniuses in all of the history of art. May we not suspect, on the face of it, such a theory? *Must* we not suspect it?"

Anger, simple and dull, rose within Stoner, overwhelming the complexity of feeling he had had at the beginning of the paper. His immediate impulse was to rise, to cut short the farce that was developing; he knew that if he did not stop Walker at once he would have to let him go on for as long as he wanted to talk. His head turned slightly so that he could see Katherine Driscoll's face; it was serene and without any expression, save one of polite and detached interest; the dark eyes regarded Walker with an unconcern that was like boredom. Covertly, Stoner looked at her for several moments; he found himself wondering what she was feeling and what she wished him to do. When he finally shifted his gaze away from her he had to realize that his decision was made. He had waited too long to interrupt, and Walker was rushing impetuously through what he had to say.

". . . the monumental edifice that is Renaissance literature, that edifice which is the cornerstone of the great poetry of the nineteenth century. The question of proof, endemic to the dull course of scholarship as distinguished from criticism, is also sadly at lack. What *proof* is offered that Shakespeare even read this obscure Roman grammarian? We must remember it was Ben Jonson"—he hesitated for a brief moment—"it was Ben Jonson himself, Shakespeare's friend and contemporary, who said he had little Latin and less Greek. And certainly Jonson, who idolized Shakespeare this side of idolatry, did not impute to his great friend any lack. On the contrary, he wished to suggest, as do I, that the soaring lyricism of Shakespeare was not attributable to the burning of the midnight oil, but to a genius natural and supreme to rule and mundane law. Unlike lesser poets, Shakespeare was not born to blush unseen and waste his sweetness on the desert air; partaking of that mysterious source to whence all poets go for their sustenance, what need had the immortal bard of such stultifying rules as are to be found in a mere grammar? What would Donatus be to him, even if he had read him? Genius, unique and a law unto itself, needs not the support of such a 'tradition' as has been described to us, whether it be generically Latin or Donatan or whatever. Genius, soaring and free, must . . ."

After he became used to his anger Stoner found a reluctant and perverse admiration stealing over him. However florid and imprecise, the man's powers of rhetoric and invention were dismayingly impressive; and however grotesque, his presence was real. There was something cold and calculating and watchful in his eyes, something needlessly reckless and yet desperately cautious. Stoner became aware that he was in the presence of a bluff so colossal and bold that he had no ready means of dealing with it.

For it was clear even to the most inattentive students in the class that Walker was engaged in a performance that was entirely impromptu. Stoner doubted that he had had any very clear idea of what he was going to say until he had sat at the desk before the class and looked at the students in his cold, imperious way. It became clear that the sheaf of papers on the desk before him was only a sheaf of papers; as he became heated, he did not even glance at them in pretense, and toward the end of his talk, in his excitement and urgency he shoved them away from him.

He talked for nearly an hour. Toward the end the other students in the seminar were glancing worriedly at one another, almost as if they were in some danger, as if they were contemplating escape; they carefully avoided looking at either Stoner or the young woman who sat impassively beside him. Abruptly, as if sensing the unrest, Walker brought his talk to a close, leaned back in the chair behind the desk, and smiled triumphantly.

The moment Walker stopped talking Stoner got to his feet and dismissed the class; though he did not realize it at the time, he did so out of a vague consideration for Walker, so that none of them might have the chance to discuss what he had said. Then Stoner went to the desk where Walker remained and asked him if he would stay for a few moments. As if his mind were somewhere else, Walker nodded distantly. Stoner then turned and followed a few straggling students out of the room into the hall. He saw Katherine Driscoll starting away, walking alone down the hall. He called her name, and when she stopped he walked up and stood in front of her. And as he spoke to her he felt again the awkwardness that had come over him when, last week, he had complimented her on her paper.

"Miss Driscoll, I—I'm sorry. It was really most unfair. I feel that somehow I am responsible. Perhaps I should have stopped it."

Still she did not reply, nor did any expression come on her face; she looked up at him as she had looked across the room at Walker.

"Anyhow," he continued, still more awkwardly, "I'm sorry he attacked you."

And then she smiled. It was a slow smile that started in her eyes and pulled at her lips until her face was wreathed in radiant, secret, and intimate delight. Stoner almost pulled back from the sudden and involuntary warmth.

"Oh, it wasn't me," she said, a tiny tremor of suppressed laughter giving timbre to her low voice. "It wasn't me at all. It was *you* he was attacking. I was hardly even involved."

Stoner felt lifted from him a burden of regret and worry that he had not known he carried; the relief was almost physical, and he felt light on his feet and a little giddy. He laughed.

"Of course," he said. "Of course that's true."

The smile eased itself off her face, and she looked at him gravely for a moment more. Then she bobbed her head, turned away from him, and walked swiftly down the hall. Her body was slim and straight, and she carried herself unobtrusively. Stoner stood looking down the hall for several moments after she disappeared. Then he sighed and went back into the room where Walker waited.

Walker had not moved from the desk. He gazed at Stoner and smiled, upon his face an odd mixture of obsequiousness and arrogance. Stoner sat in the chair he had vacated a few minutes before and looked curiously at Walker.

"Yes, sir?" Walker said.

"Do you have an explanation?" Stoner asked quietly.

A look of hurt surprise came upon Walker's round face. "What do you mean, sir?"

"Mr. Walker, please," Stoner said wearily. "It has been a long day, and we're both tired. Do you have an explanation for your performance this afternoon?"

"I'm sure, sir, I intended no offense." He removed his glasses and polished them rapidly; again Stoner was struck by the naked vulnerability of his face. "I said my remarks were not intended personally. If feelings have been hurt, I shall be most happy to explain to the young lady—"

"Mr. Walker," Stoner said. "You know that isn't the point."

"Has the young lady been complaining to you?" Walker asked. His fingers were trembling as he put his glasses back on. With them on, his face managed a frown of anger. "Really, sir, the complaints of a student whose feelings have been hurt should not—"

"Mr. Walker!" Stoner heard his voice go a little out of control. He took a deep breath. "This has nothing to do with the young lady, or with myself, or with anything except your performance. And I still await any explanation you have to offer."

"Then I'm afraid I don't understand at all, sir. Unless . . ."

"Unless what, Mr. Walker?"

"Unless it is simply a matter of disagreement," Walker said. "I realize that my ideas do not coincide with yours, but I have always thought that disagreement was healthy. I assumed that you were big enough to—"

"I will not allow you to evade the issue," Stoner said. His voice was cold and level. "Now. What was the seminar topic assigned to you?"

"You're angry," Walker said.

"Yes, I am angry. What was the seminar topic assigned to you?"

Walker became stiffly formal and polite. "My topic was 'Hellenism and the Medieval Latin Tradition,' sir."

"And when did you complete that paper, Mr. Walker?"

"Two days ago. As I told you, it was nearly complete a couple of weeks ago, but a book I had to get through inter-library loan didn't come in until—"

"Mr. Walker, if your paper was *nearly* finished two weeks ago, how could you have based it, in its entirety, upon Miss Driscoll's report, which was given only last week?"

"I made a number of changes, sir, at the last minute." His voice became heavy with irony. "I assumed that that was permissible. And I did depart from the text now and then. I noticed that other students did the same, and I thought the privilege would be allowed me also."

Stoner fought down a near-hysterical impulse to laugh. "Mr. Walker, will you explain to me what your attack on Miss Driscoll's paper has to do with the survival of Hellenism in the medieval Latin tradition?"

"I approached my subject indirectly, sir," Walker said. "I thought we were allowed a certain latitude in developing our concepts."

Stoner was silent for a moment. Then he said wearily, "Mr. Walker, I dislike having to flunk a graduate student. Especially I dislike having to flunk one who simply has got in over his head."

"Sir!" Walker said indignantly.

"But you're making it very difficult for me not to. Now, it seems to me that there are only a few alternatives. I can give you an incomplete in the course, with the understanding that you will do a satisfactory paper on the assigned topic within the next three weeks."

"But, sir," Walker said. "I have already done my paper. If I agree to do another one I will be admitting—I will admit—"

"All right," Stoner said. "Then if you will give me the manuscript from which you—deviated this afternoon, I shall see if something can be salvaged."

"Sir," Walker cried. "I would hesitate to let it out of my possession just now. The draft is *very* rough."

With a grim and restless shame, Stoner continued, "That's all right. I shall be able to find out what I want to know."

Walker looked at him craftily. "Tell me, sir, have you asked anyone else to hand his manuscript in to you?"

"I have not," Stoner said.

"Then," Walker said triumphantly, almost happily, "I must refuse also to hand *my* manuscript in to you on principle. Unless you require everyone else to hand theirs in."

Stoner looked at him steadily for a moment. "Very well, Mr. Walker. You have made your decision. That will be all."

Walker said, "What am I to understand then, sir? What may I expect from this course?"

Stoner laughed shortly. "Mr. Walker, you amaze me. You will, of course, receive an F."

Walker tried to make his round face long. With the patient bitterness of a martyr he said, "I see. Very well, sir. One must be prepared to suffer for one's beliefs."

"And for one's laziness and dishonesty and ignorance," Stoner said. "Mr. Walker, it seems almost superfluous to say this, but I would most strongly advise you to re-examine your position here. I seriously question whether you have a place in a graduate program."

For the first time Walker's emotion appeared genuine; his anger gave him something that was close to dignity. "Mr. Stoner, you're going too far! You can't mean that."

"I most certainly mean it," Stoner said.

For a moment Walker was quiet; he looked thoughtfully at Stoner. Then he said, "I was willing to accept the grade you gave me. But you must realize that I cannot accept this. You are questioning my competence!"

"Yes, Mr. Walker," Stoner said wearily. He raised himself from the chair. "Now, if you will excuse me . . ." He started for the door.

But the sound of his shouted name halted him. He turned.

Walker's face was a deep red; the skin was puffed so that the eyes behind their thick glasses were like tiny dots. "Mr. Stoner!" he shouted again. "You have not heard the last of this. Believe me, you have not heard the last of this!"

Stoner looked at him dully, incuriously. He nodded distractedly, turned, and went out into the hall. His feet were heavy, and they dragged on the bare cement floor. He was drained of feeling, and he felt very old and tired.

X

A ND HE had not heard the last of it.
He turned his grades in on the Monday following the
Friday closing of the semester. It was the part of teaching he
most disliked, and he always got it out of the way as soon as
he could. He gave Walker his F and thought no more about
the matter. He spent most of the week between semesters
reading the first drafts of two theses due for final presentation
in the spring. They were awkwardly done, and they needed
much of his attention. The Walker incident was crowded from
his mind.

But two weeks after the second semester started he was
again reminded of it. He found one morning in his mailbox a
note from Gordon Finch asking him to drop by the office at his
convenience for a chat.

The friendship between Gordon Finch and William Stoner
had reached a point that all such relationships, carried on long
enough, come to; it was casual, deep, and so guardedly intimate that it was almost impersonal. They seldom saw each
other socially, although occasionally Caroline Finch made a
perfunctory call on Edith. While they talked they remembered
the years of their youth, and each thought of the other as he
had been at another time.

In his early middle age Finch had the erect soft bearing of
one who tries vigorously to keep his weight under control; his
face was heavy and as yet unlined, though his jowls were beginning to sag and the flesh was gathering in rolls on the back of
his neck. His hair was very thin, and he had begun to comb it
so that the baldness would not be readily apparent.

On the afternoon that Stoner stopped by his office, they
spoke for a few moments casually about their families; Finch
maintained the easy convention of pretending that Stoner's
marriage was a normal one, and Stoner professed his conventional disbelief that Gordon and Caroline could be the parents
of two children, the younger of which was already in kinder-
garten.

After they had made their automatic gestures toward their casual intimacy, Finch looked out his window distractedly and said, "Now, what was it I wanted to talk to you about? Oh, yes. The dean of the Graduate College—he thought, since we were friends, I ought to mention it to you. Nothing of any importance." He looked at a note on his memo book. "Just an irate graduate student who thinks he got screwed in one of your classes last semester."

"Walker," Stoner said. "Charles Walker."

Finch nodded. "That's the one. What's the story on him?"

Stoner shrugged. "As far as I could tell, he didn't do any of the reading assigned—it was my seminar in the Latin Tradition. He tried to fake his seminar report, and when I gave him the chance either to do another one or produce a copy of his paper, he refused. I had no alternative but to flunk him."

Finch nodded again. "I figured it was something like that. God knows, I wish they wouldn't waste my time with stuff like this; but it has to be checked out, as much for your protection as anything else."

Stoner asked, "Is there some—special difficulty here?"

"No, no," Finch said. "Not at all. Just a complaint. You know how these things go. As a matter of fact, Walker received a C in the first course he took here as a graduate student; he could be kicked out of the program right now if we wanted to do it. But I think we've about decided to let him take his preliminary orals next month, and let that tell the story. I'm sorry I even had to bother you about it."

They talked for a few moments about other things. Then, just as Stoner was about to leave, Finch detained him casually.

"Oh, there was something else I wanted to mention to you. The president and the board have finally decided that something's going to have to be done about Claremont. So I guess, beginning next year, I'll be dean of Arts and Sciences—officially."

"I'm glad, Gordon," Stoner said. "It's about time."

"So that means we're going to have to get a new chairman of the department. Do you have any thoughts on it?"

"No," Stoner said, "I really haven't thought of it at all."

"We can either go outside the department and bring in somebody new, or we can make one of the present men chairman. What I'm trying to find out is, if we *did* choose someone from the department— Well, do *you* have your eyes on the job?"

Stoner thought for a moment. "I hadn't thought about it, but—no. No, I don't think I'd want it."

Finch's relief was so obvious that Stoner smiled. "Good. I didn't think you would. It means a lot of horse-shit. Entertaining and socializing and—" He looked away from Stoner. "I know you don't go in for that sort of thing. But since old Sloane died, and since Huggins and what's-his-name, Cooper, retired last year, you're the senior member of the department. But if you haven't been casting covetous eyes, then—"

"No," Stoner said definitely. "I'd probably be a rotten chairman. I neither expect nor want the appointment."

"Good," Finch said. "Good. That simplifies things a great deal."

They said their good-bys, and Stoner did not think of the conversation again for some time.

Charles Walker's preliminary oral comprehensives were scheduled for the middle of March; somewhat to Stoner's surprise, he received a note from Finch informing him that he would be a member of the three-man committee who would examine him. He reminded Finch that he had flunked Walker, that Walker had taken the flunk personally, and he asked to be relieved of this particular duty.

"Regulations," Finch answered with a sigh. "You know how it is. The committee is made up of the candidate's adviser, one professor who has had him in a graduate seminar, and one outside his field of specialization. Lomax is the adviser, you're the only one he's had a graduate seminar from, and I've picked the new man, Jim Holland, for the one outside his specialty. Dean Rutherford of the Graduate College and I will be sitting in ex-officio. I'll try to make it as painless as possible."

But it was an ordeal that could not be made painless. Though Stoner wished to ask as few questions as possible, the rules that governed the preliminary oral were inflexible; each professor was allowed forty-five minutes to ask the candidate any questions that he wished, though other professors habitually joined in.

On the afternoon set for the examination Stoner came deliberately late to the seminar room on the third floor of Jesse Hall. Walker was seated at the end of a long, highly polished table; the four examiners already present—Finch, Lomax, the new man, Holland, and Henry Rutherford—were ranged down the table from him. Stoner slipped in the door and took a chair at the end of the table opposite Walker. Finch and Holland nodded to him; Lomax, slumped in his chair, stared straight ahead, tapping his long white fingers on the mirrorlike surface of the table. Walker stared down the length of the table, his head held stiff and high in cold disdain.

Rutherford cleared his throat. "Ah, Mr."—he consulted a sheet of paper in front of him—"Mr. Stoner." Rutherford was a slight thin gray man with round shoulders; his eyes and brows dropped at the outer corners, so that his expression was always one of gentle hopelessness. Though he had known Stoner for many years, he never remembered his name. He cleared his throat again. "We were just about to begin."

Stoner nodded, rested his forearms on the table, clasped his fingers, and contemplated them as Rutherford's voice droned through the formal preliminaries of the oral examination.

Mr. Walker was being examined (Rutherford's voice dropped to a steady, uninflected hum) to determine his ability to continue in the doctoral program in the Department of English at the University of Missouri. This was an examination which all doctoral candidates underwent, and it was designed not only to judge the candidate's general fitness, but also to determine strengths and weaknesses, so that his future course of study could be profitably guided. Three results were possible: a pass, a conditional pass, and a failure. Rutherford described the terms of these eventualities, and without looking up performed the ritualistic introduction of the examiners and the candidate. Then he pushed the sheet of paper away from him and looked hopelessly at those around him.

"The custom is," he said softly, "for the candidate's thesis adviser to begin the questioning. Mr."—he glanced at the paper —"Mr. Lomax is, I believe, Mr. Walker's adviser. So . . ."

Lomax's head jerked back as if he had been suddenly awakened from a doze. He glanced around the table, blinking, a little smile on his lips; but his eyes were shrewd and alert.

"Mr. Walker, you are planning a dissertation on Shelley and the Hellenistic Ideal. It is unlikely that you have thought through your subject yet, but would you begin by giving us some of the background, your reason for choosing it, and so forth."

Walker nodded and began swiftly to speak. "I intend to trace Shelley's first rejection of Godwinian necessitarianism for a more or less Platonic ideal, in the 'Hymn to Intellectual Beauty,' through the mature use of that ideal, in *Prometheus Unbound*, as a comprehensive synthesis of his earlier atheism, radicalism, Christianity, and scientific necessitarianism, and ultimately to account for the decay of the ideal in such a late work as *Hellas*. It is to my mind an important topic for three reasons: First, it shows the quality of Shelley's mind, and hence leads us into a better understanding of his poetry. Second, it demonstrates the leading philosophical and literary conflicts of the early nineteenth century, and hence enlarges our understanding and appreciation of Romantic poetry. And third, it is a subject that might have a peculiar relevance to our own time, a time in which we face many of the same conflicts that confronted Shelley and his contemporaries."

Stoner listened, and as he listened his astonishment grew. He could not believe that this was the same man who had taken his seminar, whom he thought he knew. Walker's presentation was lucid, forthright, and intelligent; at times it was almost brilliant. Lomax was right; if the dissertation fulfilled its promise, it would be brilliant. Hope, warm and exhilarating, rushed upon him, and he leaned forward attentively.

Walker talked upon the subject of his dissertation for perhaps ten minutes and then abruptly stopped. Quickly Lomax asked another question, and Walker responded at once. Gordon Finch caught Stoner's eye and gave him a look of mild inquiry; Stoner smiled slightly, self-deprecatingly, and gave a small shrug of his shoulders.

When Walker stopped again, Jim Holland spoke immediately. He was a thin young man, intense and pale, with slightly protuberant blue eyes; he spoke with a deliberate slowness, with a voice that seemed always to tremble before a forced restraint. "Mr. Walker, you mentioned a bit earlier Godwin's necessitarianism. I wonder if you could make a connection

between that and the phenomenalism of John Locke?" Stoner
remembered that Holland was an eighteenth-century man.

There was a moment of silence. Walker turned to Holland,
removed the round glasses, and polished them; his eyes blinked
and stared, at random. He put them back on and blinked again.
"Would you repeat the question, please."

Holland started to speak, but Lomax interrupted. "Jim,"
he said affably, "do you mind if I extend the question a bit?"
He turned quickly to Walker before Holland could answer.
"Mr. Walker, proceeding from the implications of Professor
Holland's question—namely, that Godwin accepted Locke's
theory of the sensational nature of knowledge—the *tabula
rasa*, and all that—and that Godwin believed with Locke that
judgment and knowledge falsified by the accidents of passion and the inevitability of ignorance could be rectified by
education—given these implications, would you comment on
Shelley's principle of knowledge—specifically, the principle of
beauty—enunciated in the final stanzas of 'Adonais'?"

Holland leaned back in his chair, a puzzled frown on his
face. Walker nodded and said rapidly, "Though the opening
stanzas of 'Adonais,' Shelley's tribute to his friend and peer,
John Keats, are conventionally classical, what with their allusions to the Mother, the Hours, to Urania and so forth, and
with their repetitive invocations—the really classical moment
does not appear until the final stanzas, which are, in effect,
a sublime hymn to the eternal Principle of Beauty. If, for a
moment, we may focus our attention upon these famous lines:

> Life, like a dome of many-colored glass,
> Stains the white radiance of eternity,
> Until Death tramples it to fragments.

"The symbolism implicit in these lines is not clear until we take
the lines in their context. 'The One remains,' Shelley writes a
few lines earlier, 'the many change and pass.' And we are reminded of Keat's equally famous lines,

> 'Beauty is truth, truth Beauty,'—that is all
> Ye know on earth, and all ye need to know.

The principle, then, is Beauty; but beauty is also knowledge.
And it is a conception that has its roots . . ."

Walker's voice continued, fluent and sure of itself, the words emerging from his rapidly moving mouth almost as if— Stoner started, and the hope that had begun in him died as abruptly as it had been born. For a moment he felt almost physically ill. He looked down at the table and saw between his arms the image of his face reflected in the high polish of the walnut top. The image was dark, and he could not make out its features; it was as if he saw a ghost glimmering unsubstantially out of a hardness, coming to meet him.

Lomax finished his questioning, and Holland began. It was, Stoner admitted, a masterful performance; unobtrusively, with great charm and good humor, Lomax managed it all. Sometimes, when Holland asked a question, Lomax pretended a good-natured puzzlement and asked for a clarification. At other times, apologizing for his own enthusiasm, he followed up one of Holland's questions with a speculation of his own, drawing Walker into the discussion, so that it seemed that he was an actual participant. He rephrased questions (always apologetically), changing them so that the original intent was lost in the elucidation. He engaged Walker in what seemed to be elaborately theoretical arguments, although he did most of the talking. And finally, still apologizing, he cut into Holland's questions with questions of his own that led Walker where he wanted him to go.

During this time Stoner did not speak. He listened to the talk that swirled around him; he gazed at Finch's face, which had become a heavy mask; he looked at Rutherford, who sat with his eyes closed, his head nodding; and he looked at Holland's bewilderment, at Walker's courteous disdain, and at Lomax's feverish animation. He was waiting to do what he knew he had to do, and he was waiting with a dread and an anger and a sorrow that grew more intense with every minute that passed. He was glad that none of their eyes met his own as he gazed at them.

Finally Holland's period of questioning was over. As if he somehow participated in the dread that Stoner felt, Finch glanced at his watch and nodded. He did not speak.

Stoner took a deep breath. Still looking at the ghost of his face in the mirrorlike finish of the tabletop, he said expressionlessly, "Mr. Walker, I'm going to ask you a few questions about English literature. They will be simple questions, and they will not require elaborate answers. I shall start early and I shall proceed chronologically, so far as time will allow me. Will you begin by describing to me the principles of Anglo-Saxon versification?"

"Yes, sir," Walker said. His face was frozen. "To begin with, the Anglo-Saxon poets, existing as they did in the Dark Ages, did not have the advantages of sensibility as did later poets in the English tradition. Indeed, I should say that their poetry was characterized by primitivism. Nevertheless, within this primitivism there is potential, though perhaps hidden to some eyes, there is potential that subtlety of feeling that is to characterize—"

"Mr. Walker," Stoner said, "I asked for the principles of versification. Can you give them to me?"

"Well, sir," Walker said, "it is very rough and irregular. The versification, I mean."

"Is that all you can tell me about it?"

"Mr. Walker," Lomax said quickly—a little wildly, Stoner thought—"this roughness you speak of—could you account for this, give the—"

"No," Stoner said firmly, looking at no one. "I want my question answered. Is that all you can tell me about Anglo-Saxon versification?"

"Well, sir," Walker said; he smiled, and the smile became a nervous giggle. "Frankly, I haven't had my required course in Anglo-Saxon yet, and I hesitate to discuss such matters without that authority."

"Very well," Stoner said. "Let's skip Anglo-Saxon literature. Can you name for me a medieval drama that had any influence in the development of Renaissance drama?"

Walker nodded. "Of course, all medieval dramas, in their own way, led into the high accomplishment of the Renaissance. It is difficult to realize that out of the barren soil of the Middle Ages the drama of Shakespeare was, only a few years later, to flower and—"

"Mr. Walker, I am asking simple questions. I must insist upon simple answers. I shall make the question even simpler. Name three medieval dramas."

"Early or late, sir?" He had taken his glasses off and was polishing them furiously.

"*Any* three, Mr. Walker."

"There are so many," Walker said. "It's difficult to— There's *Everyman* . . ."

"Can you name any more?"

"No, sir," Walker said. "I must confess to a weakness in the areas that you—"

"Can you name any other titles—just the titles—of any of the literary works of the Middle Ages?"

Walker's hands were trembling. "As I have said, sir, I must confess to a weakness in—"

"Then we shall go on to the Renaissance. What genre do you feel most confident of in this period, Mr. Walker?"

"The"—Walker hesitated and despite himself looked supplicatingly at Lomax—"the poem, sir. Or—the drama. The drama, perhaps."

"The drama then. What is the first blank verse tragedy in English, Mr. Walker?"

"The first?" Walker licked his lips. "Scholarship is divided on the question, sir. I should hesitate to—"

"Can you name any drama of significance before Shakespeare?"

"Certainly, sir," Walker said. "There's Marlowe—the mighty line—"

"Name some plays of Marlowe."

With an effort Walker pulled himself together. "There is, of course, the justly famous *Dr. Faust.* And—and the—*The Jew of Malfi.*"

"*Faustus* and *The Jew of Malta.* Can you name any more?"

"Frankly, sir, those are the only two plays that I have had a chance to reread in the last year or so. So I would prefer not to—"

"All right. Tell me something about *The Jew of Malta.*"

"Mr. Walker," Lomax cried out. "If I may broaden the question a bit. If you will—"

"No!" Stoner said grimly, not looking at Lomax. "I want answers to my questions. Mr. Walker?"

Walker said desperately, "Marlowe's mighty line—"

"Let's forget about the 'mighty line,'" Stoner said wearily. "What happens in the play?"

"Well," Walker said a little wildly, "Marlowe is attacking the problem of anti-Semitism as it manifested itself in the early sixteenth century. The sympathy, I might even say, the profound sympathy—"

"Never mind, Mr. Walker. Let's go on to—"

Lomax shouted, "Let the candidate answer the question! Give him time to answer at least."

"Very well," Stoner said mildly. "Do you wish to continue with your answer, Mr. Walker?"

Walker hesitated for a moment. "No, sir," he said.

Relentlessly Stoner continued his questioning. What had been an anger and outrage that included both Walker and Lomax became a kind of pity and sick regret that included them too. After a while it seemed to Stoner that he had gone outside himself, and it was as if he heard a voice going on and on, impersonal and deadly.

At last he heard the voice say, "All right, Mr. Walker. Your period of specialization is the nineteenth century. You seem to know little about the literature of earlier centuries; perhaps you will feel more at ease among the Romantic poets."

He tried not to look at Walker's face, but he could not prevent his eyes from rising now and then to see the round, staring mask that faced him with a cold, pale malevolence. Walker nodded curtly.

"You are familiar with Lord Byron's more important poems, are you not?"

"Of course," Walker said.

"Then would you care to comment upon 'English Bards and Scottish Reviewers?'"

Walker looked at him suspiciously for a moment. Then he smiled triumphantly. "Ah, sir," he said and nodded his head vigorously. "I see. *Now* I see. You're trying to trick me. Of course. 'English Bards and Scottish Reviewers' is not by Byron at all. It is John Keats's famous reply to the journalists who attempted to smirch his reputation as a poet, after the publication of his first poems. Very good, sir. Very—"

"All right, Mr. Walker," Stoner said wearily. "I have no more questions."

For several moments silence lay upon the group. Then Rutherford cleared his throat, shuffled the papers on the table before him, and said, "Thank you, Mr. Walker. If you will step outside for a few moments and wait, the committee will discuss your examination and let you know its decision."

In the few moments that it took Rutherford to say what he had to say, Walker recomposed himself. He rose and rested his crippled hand upon the tabletop. He smiled at the group almost condescendingly. "Thank you, gentlemen," he said. "It has been a most rewarding experience." He limped out of the room and shut the door behind him.

Rutherford sighed. "Well, gentlemen, is there any discussion?"

Another silence came over the room.

Lomax said, "I thought he did *quite* well on my part of the examination. And he did rather well on Holland's portion. I must confess that I was somewhat disappointed by the way the latter part of the exam went, but I imagine he was rather tired by that time. He *is* a good student, but he doesn't show up as well as he might under pressure." He flashed an empty, pained smile at Stoner. "And you did press him a bit, Bill. You must admit that. I vote pass."

Rutherford said, "Mr.—Holland?"

Holland looked from Lomax to Stoner; he was frowning in puzzlement, and his eyes blinked. "But—well, he seemed awfully weak to me. I don't know exactly how to figure it." He swallowed uncomfortably. "This is the first orals I've sat in on here. I really don't know what the standards are, but—well, he seemed awfully weak. Let me think about it for a minute."

Rutherford nodded. "Mr.—Stoner?"

"Fail," Stoner said. "It's a clear failure."

"Oh, come now, Bill," Lomax cried. "You're being a bit hard on the boy, aren't you?"

"No," Stoner said levelly, his eyes straight before him. "You know I'm not, Holly."

"What do you mean by that?" Lomax asked; it was as if he were trying to generate feeling in his voice by raising it. "Just what do you mean?"

"Come off it, Holly," Stoner said tiredly. "The man's incompetent. There can be no question of that. The questions

I asked him were those that should have been asked a fair undergraduate; and he was unable to answer a single one of them satisfactorily. And he's both lazy and dishonest. In my seminar last semester—"

"Your seminar!" Lomax laughed curtly. "Well, I've heard about that. And besides, that's another matter. The question is, how he did today. And it's clear"—his eyes narrowed—"it's clear that he did quite well today until you started in on him."

"I asked him questions," Stoner said. "The simplest questions I could imagine. I was prepared to give him every chance." He paused and said carefully, "You are his thesis adviser, and it is natural that you two should have talked over his thesis subject. So when you questioned him on his thesis he did very well. But when we got beyond that—"

"What do you mean!" Lomax shouted. "Are you suggesting that I—that there was any—"

"I am suggesting nothing, except that in my opinion the candidate did not do an adequate job. I cannot consent to his passing."

"Look," Lomax said. His voice had quieted, and he tried to smile. "I can see how I would have a higher opinion of his work than you would. He has been in several of my classes, and—no matter. I'm willing to compromise. Though I think it's too severe, I'm willing to offer him a conditional pass. That would mean he could review for a couple of semesters, and then he—"

"Well," Holland said with some relief, "that would seem to be better than giving him a clear pass. I don't know the man, but it's obvious that he isn't ready to—"

"Good," Lomax said, smiling vigorously at Holland. "Then that's settled. Well—"

"No," Stoner said. "I must vote for failure."

"God *damn* it," Lomax shouted. "Do you realize what you're doing, Stoner? Do you realize what you're doing to the boy?"

"Yes," Stoner said quietly, "and I'm sorry for him. I am preventing him from getting his degree, and I'm preventing him from teaching in a college or university. Which is precisely what I want to do. For him to be a teacher would be a—disaster."

Lomax was very still. "That is your final word?" he asked icily.

"Yes," Stoner said.

Lomax nodded. "Well, let me warn you, Professor Stoner, I do not intend to let the matter drop here. You have made —you have implied certain accusations here today—you have shown a prejudice that—that—"

"Gentlemen, please," Rutherford said. He looked as if he were going to weep. "Let us keep our perspective. As you know, for the candidate to pass, there must be unanimous consent. Is there no way that we can resolve this difference?"

No one spoke.

Rutherford sighed. "Very well, then, I have no alternative but to declare that—"

"Just a minute." It was Gordon Finch; during the entire examination he had been so still that the others had nearly forgotten his presence. Now he raised himself a little in his chair and addressed the top of the table in a tired but determined voice. "As acting chairman of the department I am going to make a recommendation. I trust it will be followed. I recommend that we defer the decision until the day after tomorrow. That will give us time to cool off and talk it over."

"There's nothing to talk over," Lomax said hotly. "If Stoner wants to—"

"I have made my recommendation," Finch said softly, "and it will be followed. Dean Rutherford, I suggest that we inform the candidate of our resolution of this matter."

They found Walker sitting in perfect ease in the corridor outside the conference room. He held a cigarette negligently in his right hand, and he was looking boredly at the ceiling.

"Mr. Walker," Lomax called and limped toward him.

Walker stood up; he was several inches taller than Lomax, so that he had to look down at him.

"Mr. Walker, I have been directed to inform you that the committee has been unable to reach agreement concerning your examination; you will be informed the day after tomorrow. But I assure you"—his voice rose—"I assure you that you have nothing to worry about. Nothing at all."

Walker stood for a moment looking coolly from one of them to another. "I thank you again, gentlemen, for your consideration." He caught Stoner's eye, and the flicker of a smile went across his lips.

Gordon Finch hurried away without speaking to any of them; Stoner, Rutherford, and Holland wandered down the hall together; Lomax remained behind, talking earnestly to Walker.

"Well," Rutherford said, walking between Stoner and Holland, "it's an unpleasant business. No matter how you look at it, it's an unpleasant business."

"Yes, it is," Stoner said and turned away from them. He walked down the marble steps, his steps becoming more rapid as he neared the first floor, and went outside. He breathed deeply the smoky fragrance of the afternoon air, and breathed again, as if he were a swimmer emerging from water. Then he walked slowly toward his house.

Early the next afternoon, before he had a chance to get lunch, he received a call from Gordon Finch's secretary, asking him to come down to the office at once.

Finch was waiting impatiently when Stoner came into the room. He rose and motioned for Stoner to sit in the chair he had drawn beside his desk.

"Is this about the Walker business?" Stoner asked.

"In a way," Finch replied. "Lomax has asked me for a meeting to try to settle this thing. It's likely to be unpleasant. I wanted to talk to you for a few minutes alone, before Lomax gets here." He sat again and for several minutes rocked back and forth in the swivel chair, looking contemplatively at Stoner. He said abruptly, "Lomax is a good man."

"I know he is," Stoner said. "In some ways he's probably the best man in the department."

As if Stoner had not spoken Finch went on, "He has his problems, but they don't crop up very often; and when they do he's usually able to handle them. It's unfortunate that this business should have come up just now; the timing is awkward as hell. A split in the department right now—" Finch shook his head.

"Gordon," Stoner said uncomfortably, "I hope you're not—"

Finch held up his hand. "Wait," he said. "I wish I had told you this before. But then it wasn't supposed to be let out, and it wasn't really official. It's still supposed to be confidential, but —do you remember a few weeks back our talking about the chairmanship?"

Stoner nodded.

"Well, it's Lomax. He's the new head. It's finished, settled. The suggestion came from upstairs, but I ought to tell you that I went along with it." He laughed shortly. "Not that I was in a position to do anything else. But even if I had been I would have gone along with it—then. Now I'm not so sure."

"I see," Stoner said thoughtfully. After a few moments he continued, "I'm glad you didn't tell me. I don't think it would have made any difference, but at least it wasn't there to cloud the issue."

"God damn it, Bill," Finch said. "You've got to understand. I don't give a damn about Walker, or Lomax, or—but you're an old friend. Look. I think you're right in this. Damn it, I know you're right. But let's be practical. Lomax is taking this very seriously, and he's not going to let it drop. And if it comes to a fight it's going to be awkward as hell. Lomax can be vindictive; you know that as well as I do. He can't fire you, but he can do damn near everything else. And to a certain extent I'll have to go along with him." He laughed again, bitterly. "Hell, to a *large* extent I'll have to go along with him. If a dean starts reversing the decisions of a department head he has to fire him from his chairmanship. Now, if Lomax got out of line, I could remove him from the chairmanship; or at least I could try. I might even get away with it, or I might not. But even if I did, there would be a fight that would split the department, maybe even the college, wide open. And, God damn it—" Finch was suddenly embarrassed; he mumbled, "God damn it, I've got to think of the college." He looked directly at Stoner. "Do you see what I'm trying to say?"

A warmth of feeling, of love and fond respect for his old friend, came over Stoner. He said, "Of course I do, Gordon. Did you think I wouldn't understand?"

"All right," Finch said. "And there's one more thing. Somehow Lomax has got his finger in the president's nose, and he leads him around like a cut bull. So it may be even rougher than you think. Look, all you'd have to do is say you'd reconsidered. You could even blame it on me—say I made you do it."

"It isn't a matter of my saving face, Gordon."

"I know that," Finch said. "I said it wrong. Look at it this way. What does it matter about Walker? Sure, I know; it's the principle of the thing; but there's another principle you ought to think of."

"It's not the principle," Stoner said. "It's Walker. It would be a disaster to let him loose in a classroom."

"Hell," Finch said wearily. "If he doesn't make it here, he can go somewhere else and get his degree; and despite everything he might even make it here. You could lose this, you know, no matter what you do. We can't keep the Walkers out."

"Maybe not," Stoner said. "But we can try."

Finch was silent for several moments. He sighed. "All right. There's no use keeping Lomax waiting any longer. We might as well get it over with." He got up from his desk and started for the door that led to the small anteroom. But as he passed Stoner, Stoner put his hand on his arm, delaying him for a moment.

"Gordon, do you remember something Dave Masters said once?"

Finch raised his brows in puzzlement. "Why do you bring Dave Masters up?"

Stoner looked across the room, out of the window, trying to remember. "The three of us were together, and he said—something about the University being an asylum, a refuge from the world, for the dispossessed, the crippled. But he didn't mean Walker. Dave would have thought of Walker as—as the world. And we can't let him in. For if we do, we become like the world, just as unreal, just as . . . The only hope we have is to keep him out."

Finch looked at him for several moments. Then he grinned. "You son-of-a-bitch," he said cheerfully. "We'd better see Lomax now." He opened the door, beckoned, and Lomax came into the room.

He came into the room so stiffly and formally that the slight hitch in his right leg was barely noticeable; his thin handsome face was set and cold, and he held his head high, so that his rather long and wavy hair nearly touched the hump that disfigured his back beneath his left shoulder. He did not look at either of the two men in the room with him; he took a chair opposite Finch's desk and sat as erect as he could, staring at the space between Finch and Stoner. He turned his head slightly toward Finch.

"I asked for the three of us to meet for a simple purpose. I wish to know whether Professor Stoner has reconsidered his ill-advised vote yesterday."

"Mr. Stoner and I have been discussing the matter," Finch said. "I'm afraid that we've been unable to resolve it."

Lomax turned to Stoner and stared at him; his light blue eyes were dull, as if a translucent film had dropped over them. "Then I'm afraid I'm going to have to bring some rather serious charges out in the open."

"Charges?" Finch's voice was surprised, a little angry. "You never mentioned anything about—"

"I'm sorry," Lomax said. "But this is necessary." He said to Stoner, "The first time you spoke to Charles Walker was when he asked you for admittance to your graduate seminar. Is that right?"

"That's right," Stoner said.

"You were reluctant to admit him, were you not?"

"Yes," Stoner said. "The class already had twelve students."

Lomax glanced at some notes he held in his right hand. "And when the student told you he *had* to get in, you reluctantly admitted him, at the same time saying that his admission would virtually ruin the seminar. Is that right?"

"Not exactly," Stoner said. "As I remember, I said one *more* in the class would—"

Lomax waved his hand. "It doesn't matter. I'm just trying to establish a context. Now, during this first conversation, did you not question his competence to do the work in the seminar?"

Gordon Finch said tiredly, "Holly, where's all this getting us? What good do you—"

"Please," Lomax said. "I have said that I have charges to bring. You must allow me to develop them. Now. Did you not question his competence?"

Stoner said calmly, "I asked him a few questions, yes, to see whether he was capable of doing the work."

"And did you satisfy yourself that he was?"

"I was unsure, I believe," Stoner said. "It's difficult to re-member."

Lomax turned to Finch. "We have established, then, first that Professor Stoner was reluctant to admit Walker to his seminar; second, that his reluctance was so intense that he threatened Walker with the fact that his admission would ruin the seminar; third, that he was at least doubtful that Walker was competent to do the work; and fourth, that despite this doubt and these strong feelings of resentment, he allowed him in the class anyway."

Finch shook his head hopelessly. "Holly, this is all pointless."

"Wait," Lomax said. He glanced hastily at his notes and then looked up shrewdly at Finch. "I have a number of other points to make. I could develop them by 'cross examination'"—he gave the words an ironic inflection—"but I am no attorney. But I assure you I am prepared to specify these charges, if it becomes necessary." He paused, as if gathering his strength. "I am prepared to demonstrate, first, that Professor Stoner allowed Mr. Walker into his seminar while holding incipiently prejudiced feelings against him; I am prepared to demonstrate that this prejudicial feeling was intensified by the fact that certain conflicts of temperament and feeling came out during the course of this seminar, that the conflict was aided and intensified by Mr. Stoner himself, who allowed, and indeed at times encouraged, other members of the class to ridicule and laugh at Mr. Walker. I am prepared to demonstrate that on more than one occasion this prejudice was manifested by statements by Professor Stoner, to students and others; that he accused Mr. Walker of 'attacking' a member of the class, when Mr. Walker was merely expressing a contrary opinion, that he admitted anger about this so-called 'attack' and that he moreover indulged in loose talk about Mr. Walker's 'behaving foolishly.' I am prepared to demonstrate, too, that without provocation Professor Stoner, out of this prejudice, accused Mr. Walker of laziness, of ignorance, and of dishonesty. And, finally, that of all the thirteen members of the class, Mr. Walker was the only one —the *only* one—that Professor Stoner singled out for suspicion, asking him *alone* to hand in the text of his seminar report.

Now I call upon Professor Stoner to deny these charges, either singly or categorically."

Stoner shook his head, almost in admiration. "My God," he said. "How you make it sound! Sure, everything you say is a fact, but none of it is true. Not the way you say it."

Lomax nodded, as if he had expected the answer. "I am prepared to demonstrate the truth of everything I have said. It would be a simple matter, if necessary, to call the members of that seminar, individually, and question them."

"No!" Stoner said sharply. "That is in some ways the most outrageous thing you've said all afternoon. I will not have the students dragged into this mess."

"You may have no choice, Stoner," Lomax said softly. "You may have no choice at all."

Gordon Finch looked at Lomax and said quietly, "What are you getting at?"

Lomax ignored him. He said to Stoner, "Mr. Walker has told me that, although he is against doing so in principle, he is now willing to deliver over to you the seminar paper that you cast so many ugly doubts about; he is willing to abide by any decision that you and any other two qualified members of the department may make. If it receives a passing grade from a majority of the three, he will receive a passing grade in the seminar, and he will be allowed to remain in graduate school."

Stoner shook his head; he was ashamed to look at Lomax. "You know I can't do that."

"Very well. I dislike doing this, but—if you do not change your vote of yesterday I shall be compelled to bring formal charges against you."

Gordon Finch's voice rose. "You'll be compelled to do *what*?"

Lomax said coolly, "The constitution of the University of Missouri allows any faculty member with tenure to bring charges against any other faculty member with tenure, if there is compelling reason to believe that the charged faculty member is incompetent, unethical, or not performing his duties in accord with the ethical standards laid out in Article Six, Section Three of the Constitution. These charges, and the evidence to support them, will be heard by the entire faculty, and at the end of the trial the faculty will either uphold the charges by a two-thirds vote or dismiss them with a lesser vote."

Gordon Finch sat back in his chair, his mouth open; he shook his head unbelievingly. He said, "Now, look. This thing is getting out of hand. You can't be serious, Holly."

"I assure you that I am," Lomax said. "This is a serious matter. It's a matter of principle; and—and my integrity has been questioned. It is my right to bring charges if I see fit."

Finch said, "You could never make them stick."

"It is my right, nevertheless, to bring charges."

For a moment Finch gazed at Lomax. Then he said quietly, almost affably, "There will be no charges. I don't know how this thing is going to resolve itself, and I don't particularly care. But there will be no charges. We're all going to walk out of here in a few minutes, and we're going to try to forget most of what has been said this afternoon. Or at least we're going to pretend to. I'm not going to have the department or the college dragged into a mess. There will be no charges. Because," he added pleasantly, "if there are, I promise you that I will do my damnedest to see that you are ruined. I will stop at nothing. I will use every ounce of influence I have; I will lie if necessary; I will frame you if I have to. I am now going to report to Dean Rutherford that the vote on Mr. Walker stands. If you still want to carry through on this, you can take it up with him, with the president, or with God. But this office is through with the matter. I want to hear no more about it."

During Finch's speech, Lomax's expression had gone thoughtful and cool. When Finch finished, Lomax nodded almost casually and got up from his chair. He looked once at Stoner, and then he limped across the room and went out. For several moments Finch and Stoner sat in silence. Finally Finch said, "I wonder what it is between him and Walker."

Stoner shook his head. "It isn't what you're thinking," he said. "I don't know what it is. I don't believe I want to know."

Ten days later Hollis Lomax's appointment as chairman of the Department of English was announced; and two weeks after that the schedule of classes for the following year was distributed among the members of the department. Without surprise Stoner discovered that for each of the two semesters that made up the academic year he had been assigned three classes of freshman composition and one sophomore survey course; his upper-class Readings in Medieval Literature and his graduate seminar had been dropped from the program. It was, Stoner realized, the kind of schedule that a beginning instructor might expect. It was worse in some ways; for the schedule was so arranged that he taught at odd, widely separated hours, six days a week. He made no protest about his schedule and resolved to teach the following year as if nothing were amiss.

But for the first time since he had started teaching it began to seem to him that it was possible that he might leave the University, that he might teach elsewhere. He spoke to Edith of the possibility, and she looked at him as if he had struck her.

"I couldn't," she said. "Oh, I couldn't." And then, aware that she had betrayed herself by showing her fear, she became angry. "What are you thinking of?" she asked. "Our home— our lovely home. And our friends. And Grace's school. It isn't good for a child to be shifted around from school to school."

"It may be necessary," he said. He had not told her about the incident of Charles Walker and of Lomax's involvement; but it became quickly evident that she knew all about it.

"Thoughtless," she said. "Absolutely thoughtless." But her anger was oddly distracted, almost perfunctory; her pale blue eyes wandered from their regard of him and rested casually upon odd objects in the living room, as if she were reassuring herself of their continued presence; her thin, lightly freckled fingers moved restlessly. "Oh, I know all about your trouble. I've never interfered with your work, but—really, you're very stubborn. I mean, *Grace* and I are involved in this. And certainly we can't be expected to pick up and move just because you've put yourself in an awkward position."

"But it's for you and Grace, partly, at least, that I'm thinking about it. It isn't likely that I'll—go much farther in the department if I stay here."

"Oh," Edith said distantly, summoning bitterness to her voice. "That isn't important. We've been poor so far; there's no reason we can't go on like this. You should have thought of this before, of what it might lead to. A cripple." Suddenly her voice changed, and she laughed indulgently, almost fondly.

"Honestly, things are so important to you. What *difference* could it make?"

And she would not consider leaving Columbia. If it came to that, she said, she and Grace could always move in with Aunt Emma; she was getting very feeble and would welcome the company.

So he dropped the possibility almost as soon as he broached it. He was to teach that summer, and two of his classes were ones in which he had a particular interest; they had been scheduled before Lomax became chairman. He resolved to give them all of his attention, for he knew that it might be some time before he had a chance to teach them again.

XI

A FEW WEEKS after the fall semester of 1932 began, it was clear to William Stoner that he had been unsuccessful in his battle to keep Charles Walker out of the graduate English program. After the summer holidays Walker returned to the campus as if triumphantly entering an arena; and when he saw Stoner in the corridors of Jesse Hall he inclined his head in an ironic bow and grinned at him maliciously. Stoner learned from Jim Holland that Dean Rutherford had delayed making the vote of last year official and that finally it had been decided that Walker would be allowed to take his oral preliminaries again, his examiners to be selected by the chairman of the department.

The battle was over then, and Stoner was willing to concede his defeat; but the fighting did not end. When Stoner met Lomax in the corridors or at a department meeting, or at a college function, he spoke to him as he had spoken before, as if nothing had happened between them. But Lomax would not respond to his greeting; he stared coldly and turned his eyes away, as if to say that he would not be appeased.

One day in late fall Stoner walked casually into Lomax's office and stood beside his desk for several minutes until, reluctantly, Lomax looked up at him, his lips tight and his eyes hard.

When he realized that Lomax was not going to speak Stoner said awkwardly, "Look, Holly, it's over and done with. Can't we just drop it?"

Lomax looked at him steadily.

Stoner continued, "We've had a disagreement, but that isn't unusual. We've been friends before, and I see no reason—"

"We have never been friends," Lomax said distinctly.

"All right," Stoner said. "But we've got along at least. We can keep whatever differences we have, but for God's sake, there's no need to display them. Even the students are beginning to notice."

"And well the students might," Lomax said bitterly, "since one of their own number nearly had his career ruined. A brilliant student, whose only crimes were his imagination, an enthusiasm and integrity that forced him into conflict with you—and, yes, I might as well say it—an unfortunate physical affliction that would have called forth sympathy in a normal human being." With his good right hand Lomax held a pencil, and it trembled before him; almost with horror Stoner realized that Lomax was dreadfully and irrevocably sincere. "No," Lomax went on passionately, "for that I cannot forgive you."

Stoner tried to keep his voice from becoming stiff. "It isn't a question of forgiving. It's simply a question of our behaving toward each other so that not too much discomfort is made for the students and the other members of the department."

"I'm going to be very frank with you, Stoner," Lomax said. His anger had quieted, and his voice was calm, matter of fact. "I don't think you're fit to be a teacher; no man is, whose prejudices override his talents and his learning. I should probably fire you if I had the power; but I don't have the power, as we both know. We are—you are protected by the tenure system. I must accept that. But I don't have to play the hypocrite. I want to have nothing to do with you. Nothing at all. And I will not pretend otherwise."

Stoner looked at him steadily for several moments. Then he shook his head. "All right, Holly," he said tiredly. He started to go.

"Just a minute," Lomax called.

Stoner turned. Lomax was gazing intently at some papers on his desk; his face was red, and he seemed to be struggling with himself. Stoner realized that what he saw was not anger but shame.

Lomax said, "Hereafter, if you want to see me—on department business—you will make an appointment with the secretary." And although Stoner stood looking at him for several moments more, Lomax did not raise his head. A brief writhing went across his face; then it was still. Stoner went out of the room.

And for more than twenty years neither man was to speak again directly to the other.

It was, Stoner realized later, inevitable that the students be affected; even if he had been successful in persuading Lomax to put on an appearance, he could not in the long run have protected them from a consciousness of the battle.

Former students of his, even students he had known rather well, began nodding and speaking to him self-consciously, even furtively. A few were ostentatiously friendly, going out of their way to speak to him or to be seen walking with him in the halls. But he no longer had the rapport with them that he once had had; he was a special figure, and one was seen with him, or not seen with him, for special reasons.

He came to feel that his presence was an embarrassment both to his friends and his enemies, and so he kept more and more to himself.

A kind of lethargy descended upon him. He taught his classes as well as he could, though the steady routine of required freshman and sophomore classes drained him of enthusiasm and left him at the end of the day exhausted and numb. As well as he could, he filled the hours between his widely separated classes with student conferences, painstakingly going over the students' work, keeping them until they became restless and impatient.

Time dragged slowly around him. He tried to spend more of that time at home with his wife and child; but because of his odd schedule the hours he could spend there were unusual and not accounted for by Edith's tight disposition of each day; he discovered (not to his surprise) that his regular presence was so upsetting to his wife that she became nervous and silent and sometimes physically ill. And he was able to see Grace infrequently in all the time he spent at home. Edith had scheduled her daughter's days carefully; her only "free" time was in the evening, and Stoner was scheduled to teach a late class four evenings a week. By the time the class was over Grace was usually in bed.

So he continued to see Grace only briefly in the mornings, at breakfast; and he was alone with her for only the few minutes it took Edith to clear the breakfast dishes from the table and put them to soak in the kitchen sink. He watched her body lengthen, an awkward grace come into her limbs, and an intelligence grow in her quiet eyes and watchful face. And at times he felt that some closeness remained between them, a closeness which neither of them could afford to admit.

At last he went back to his old habit of spending most of his time at his office in Jesse Hall. He told himself that he should be grateful for the chance of reading on his own, free from the pressures of preparing for particular classes, free from the pre-determined directions of his learning. He tried to read at random, for his own pleasure and indulgence, many of the things that he had been waiting for years to read. But his mind would not be led where he wished it to go; his attention wandered from the pages he held before him, and more and more often he found himself staring dully in front of him, at nothing; it was as if from moment to moment his mind were emptied of all it knew and as if his will were drained of its strength. He felt at times that he was a kind of vegetable, and he longed for something—even pain—to pierce him, to bring him alive.

He had come to that moment in his age when there occurred to him, with increasing intensity, a question of such overwhelming simplicity that he had no means to face it. He found himself wondering if his life were worth the living; if it had ever been. It was a question, he suspected, that came to all men at one time or another; he wondered if it came to them with such impersonal force as it came to him. The question brought with it a sadness, but it was a general sadness which (he thought) had little to do with himself or with his particular fate; he was not even sure that the question sprang from the most immediate and obvious causes, from what his own life had become. It came, he believed, from the accretion of his years, from the density of accident and circumstance, and from what he had come to understand of them. He took a grim and ironic pleasure from the possibility that what little learning he had managed to acquire had led him to this knowledge: that in the long run all things, even the learning that let him know this, were futile and empty, and at last diminished into a nothingness they did not alter.

Once, late, after his evening class, he returned to his office and sat at his desk, trying to read. It was winter, and a snow had fallen during the day, so that the out-of-doors was covered with a white softness. The office was overheated; he opened a window beside the desk so that the cool air might come into the close room. He breathed deeply, and let his eyes wander over the white floor of the campus. On an impulse he switched out the light on his desk and sat in the hot darkness of his office; the cold air filled his lungs, and he leaned toward the open window. He heard the silence of the winter night, and it seemed to him that he somehow felt the sounds that were absorbed by the delicate and intricately cellular being of the snow. Nothing moved upon the whiteness; it was a dead scene, which seemed to pull at him, to suck at his consciousness just as it pulled the sound from the air and buried it within a cold white softness. He felt himself pulled outward toward the whiteness, which spread as far as he could see, and which was a part of the darkness from which it glowed, of the clear and cloudless sky without height or depth. For an instant he felt himself go out of the body that sat motionless before the window; and as he felt himself slip away, everything—the flat whiteness, the trees, the tall columns, the night, the far stars—seemed incredibly tiny and far away, as if they were dwindling to a nothingness. Then, behind him, a radiator clanked. He moved, and the scene became itself. With a curiously reluctant relief he again snapped on his desk lamp. He gathered a book and a few papers, went out of the office, walked through the darkened corridors, and let himself out of the wide double doors at the back of Jesse Hall. He walked slowly home, aware of each footstep crunching with muffled loudness in the dry snow.

XII

D URING THAT year, and especially in the winter months, he found himself returning more and more frequently to such a state of unreality; at will, he seemed able to remove his consciousness from the body that contained it, and he observed himself as if he were an oddly familiar stranger doing the oddly familiar things that he had to do. It was a dissociation that he had never felt before; he knew that he ought to be troubled by it, but he was numb, and he could not convince himself that it mattered. He was forty-two years old, and he could see nothing before him that he wished to enjoy and little behind him that he cared to remember.

In its forty-third year William Stoner's body was nearly as lean as it had been when he was a youth, when he had first walked in dazed awe upon the campus that had never wholly lost its effect upon him. Year by year the stoop of his shoulders had increased, and he had learned to slow his movements so that his farmer's clumsiness of hand and foot seemed a deliberation rather than an awkwardness bred in the bone. His long face had softened with time; and although the flesh was still like tanned leather, it no longer stretched so tautly over the sharp cheekbones; it was loosened by thin lines around his eyes and mouth. Still sharp and clear, his gray eyes were sunk more deeply in his face, the shrewd watchfulness there half hidden; his hair, once light brown, had darkened, although a few touches of gray were beginning around his temples. He did not think often of the years, or regret their passing; but when he saw his face in a mirror, or when he approached his reflection in one of the glass doors that led into Jesse Hall, he recognized the changes that had come over him with a mild shock.

Late one afternoon in the early spring he sat alone in his office. A pile of freshman themes lay on his desk; he held one of the papers in his hand, but he was not looking at it. As he had been doing frequently of late, he gazed out the window upon that part of the campus he could see from his office. The day was bright, and the shadow cast by Jesse Hall had crept, while he watched, nearly up to the base of the five columns that stood in powerful, isolate grace in the center of the rectangular quad. The portion of the quad in shadow was a deep brownish-gray; beyond the edge of the shadow the winter grass was a light tan, overlaid with a shimmering film of the palest green. Against the spidery black tracings of vine stems that curled around them, the marble columns were brilliantly white; soon the shadow would creep upon them, Stoner thought, and the bases would darken, and the darkness would creep up, slowly and then more rapidly, until . . . He became aware that someone was standing behind him.

He turned in his chair and looked up. It was Katherine Driscoll, the young instructor who last year had sat in on his seminar. Since that time, though they sometimes met in the corridors and nodded, they had not really spoken to each other. Stoner was aware that he was dimly annoyed by this confrontation; he did not wish to be reminded of the seminar and of what had ensued from it. He pushed his chair back and got awkwardly to his feet.

"Miss Driscoll," he said soberly and motioned to the chair beside his desk. She gazed at him for a moment; her eyes were large and dark, and he thought that her face was extraordinarily pale. With a slight ducking motion of the head she moved away from him and took the chair to which he vaguely motioned.

Stoner seated himself again and stared at her for a moment without really seeing her. Then, aware that his regard of her might be taken as rudeness, he tried to smile, and he murmured an inane, automatic question about her classes.

She spoke abruptly. "You—you said once that you would be willing to look over my dissertation whenever I had a good start on it."

"Yes," Stoner said and nodded. "I believe I did. Of course." Then, for the first time, he noticed that she clutched a folder of papers in her lap.

"Of course, if you're busy," she said tentatively.

"Not at all," Stoner said, trying to put some enthusiasm in his voice. "I'm sorry. I didn't intend to sound distracted."

She hesitantly lifted the folder toward him. He took it, hefted it, and smiled at her. "I thought you would be further along than this," he said.

"I was," she said. "But I started over. I'm taking a new tack, and—and I'll be grateful if you'll tell me what you think."

He smiled at her again and nodded; he did not know what to say. They sat in awkward silence for a moment.

Finally he said, "When do you need this back?"

She shook her head. "Any time. Whenever you can get around to it."

"I don't want to hold you up," he said. "How about this coming Friday? That should give me plenty of time. About three o'clock?"

She rose as abruptly as she had sat down. "Thank you," she said. "I don't want to be a bother. Thank you." And she turned and walked, slim and erect, out of his office.

He held the folder in his hands for a few moments, staring at it. Then he put it on his desk and got back to his freshman themes.

That was on a Tuesday, and for the next two days the manuscript lay untouched on his desk. For reasons that he did not fully understand, he could not bring himself to open the folder, to begin the reading which a few months before would have been a duty of pleasure. He watched it warily, as if it were an enemy that was trying to entice him again into a war that he had renounced.

And then it was Friday, and he still had not read it. He saw it lying accusingly on his desk in the morning when he gathered his books and papers for his eight o'clock class; when he returned at a little after nine he nearly decided to leave a note in Miss Driscoll's mailbox in the main office, begging off for another week; but he resolved to look at it hurriedly before his eleven o'clock class and say a few perfunctory words to her when she came by that afternoon. But he could not make himself get to it; and just before he had to leave for the class, his last of the day, he grabbed the folder from his desk, stuck it among his other papers, and hurried across campus to his classroom.

After the class was over at noon he was delayed by several students who needed to talk to him, so that it was after one o'clock when he was able to break away. He headed, with a kind of grim determination, toward the library; he intended to find an empty carrel and give the manuscript a hasty hour's reading before his three o'clock appointment with Miss Driscoll.

But even in the dim, familiar quiet of the library, in an empty carrel that he found hidden in the lower depths of the stacks, he had a hard time making himself look at the pages he carried with him. He opened other books and read paragraphs at random; he sat still, inhaling the musty odor that came from the old books. Finally he sighed; unable to put it off longer, he opened the folder and glanced hastily at the first pages.

At first only a nervous edge of his mind touched what he read; but gradually the words forced themselves upon him. He frowned and read more carefully. And then he was caught; he turned back to where he had begun, and his attention flowed upon the page. Yes, he said to himself, of course. Much of the material that she had given in her seminar report was contained here, but rearranged, reorganized, pointing in directions that he himself had only dimly glimpsed. My God, he said to himself in a kind of wonder; and his fingers trembled with excitement as he turned the pages.

When he came to the last sheet of typescript he leaned back in happy exhaustion and stared at the gray cement wall before him. Although it seemed only a few minutes had elapsed since he started reading, he glanced at his watch. It was nearly four-thirty. He scrambled to his feet, gathered the manuscript hastily, and hurried out of the library; and though he knew it was too late for it to make any difference, he half ran across the campus to Jesse Hall.

As he passed the open door of the main office on his way to his own, he heard his name called. He halted and stuck his head in the doorway. The secretary—a new girl that Lomax had recently hired—said to him accusingly, almost insolently, "Miss Driscoll was here to see you at three o'clock. She waited nearly an hour."

He nodded, thanked her, and proceeded more slowly to his office. He told himself that it didn't matter, that he could return the manuscript to her on Monday and make his apologies then. But the excitement he had felt when he finished the manuscript would not subside, and he paced restlessly around his office; every now and then he paused and nodded to himself. Finally he went to his bookcase, searched for a moment, and withdrew a slender pamphlet with smeared black lettering on the cover: *Faculty and Staff Directory, University of Missouri.*

He found Katherine Driscoll's name; she did not have a telephone. He noted her address, gathered her manuscript from his desk, and went out of his office.

About three blocks from the campus, toward town, a cluster of large old houses had, some years before, been converted into apartments; these were filled by older students, younger faculty, staff members of the University, and a scattering of townspeople. The house in which Katherine Driscoll lived stood in the midst of these. It was a huge three-storied building of gray stone, with a bewildering variety of entrances and exits, with turrets and bay windows and balconies projecting outward and upward on all sides. Stoner finally found Katherine Driscoll's name on a mailbox at the side of the building, where a short flight of cement steps led down to a basement door. He hesitated for a moment, then knocked.

When Katherine Driscoll opened the door for him William Stoner almost did not recognize her; she had swept her hair up and caught it carelessly high in the back, so that her small pink-white ears were bare; she wore dark-rimmed glasses, behind which her dark eyes were wide and startled; she had on a mannish shirt, open at the neck; and she was wearing dark slacks that made her appear slimmer and more graceful than he remembered her.

"I'm—I'm sorry I missed our appointment," Stoner said awkwardly. He thrust the folder toward her. "I thought you might need this over the weekend."

For several moments she did not speak. She looked at him expressionlessly and bit her lower lip. She moved back from the door. "Won't you come in?"

He followed her through a very short, narrow hall into a tiny room, low-ceilinged and dim, with a low three-quarter bed that served as a couch, a long, low table before it, a single upholstered chair, a small desk and chair, and a bookcase filled with books on one wall. Several books were lying open on the floor and on the couch, and papers were scattered on the desk.

"It's very small," Katherine Driscoll said, stooping to pick up one of the books on the floor, "but I don't need much room."

He sat in the upholstered chair across from the couch. She asked him if he would like some coffee, and he said he would. She went into the little kitchen off the living room, and he relaxed and gazed around him, listening to the quiet sounds of her moving around in the kitchen.

She brought the coffee, in delicate white china cups, on a black lacquered tray, which she set on the table before the couch. They sipped the coffee and talked strainedly for a few moments. Then Stoner spoke of the part of the manuscript he had read, and the excitement he had felt earlier, in the library, came over him; he leaned forward, speaking intensely.

For many minutes the two of them were able to talk together unselfconsciously, hiding themselves under the cover of their discourse. Katherine Driscoll sat on the edge of the couch, her eyes flashing, her slender fingers clasping and unclasping above the coffee table. William Stoner hitched his chair forward and leaned intently toward her; they were so close that he could have extended his hand and touched her.

They spoke of the problems raised by the early chapters of her work, of where the inquiry might lead, of the importance of the subject.

"You mustn't give it up," he said, and his voice took on an urgency that he could not understand. "No matter how hard it will seem sometimes, you mustn't give it up. It's too good for you to give it up. Oh, it's good, there's no doubt of it."

She was silent, and for a moment the animation left her face. She leaned back, looked away from him, and said, as if absently, "The seminar—some of the things you said—it was very helpful."

He smiled and shook his head. "You didn't need the seminar. But I am glad you were able to sit in on it. It was a good one, I think."

"Oh, it's shameful!" she burst out. "It's shameful. The seminar—you were—I *had* to start it over, after the seminar. It's shameful that they should—" She paused in bitter, furious confusion, got up from the couch, and walked restlessly to the desk.

Stoner, taken aback by her outburst, for a moment did not speak. Then he said, "You shouldn't concern yourself. These things happen. It will all work out in time. It really isn't important."

And suddenly, after he said the words, it was not important. For an instant he felt the truth of what he said, and for the first time in months he felt lift away from him the weight of a despair whose heaviness he had not fully realized. Nearly giddy, almost laughing, he said again, "It *really* isn't important."

But an awkwardness had come between them, and they could not speak as freely as they had a few moments before. Soon Stoner got up, thanked her for the coffee, and took his leave. She walked with him to the door and seemed almost curt when she told him good night.

It was dark outside, and a spring chill was in the evening air. He breathed deeply and felt his body tingle in the coolness. Beyond the jagged outline of the apartment houses the town lights glowed upon a thin mist that hung in the air. At the corner a street light pushed feebly against the darkness that closed around it; from the darkness beyond it the sound of laughter broke abruptly into the silence, lingered and died. The smell of smoke from trash burning in back yards was held by the mist; and as he walked slowly through the evening, breathing the fragrance and tasting upon his tongue the sharp night-time air, it seemed to him that the moment he walked in was enough and that he might not need a great deal more.

And so he had his love affair.

The knowledge of his feeling for Katherine Driscoll came upon him slowly. He found himself discovering pretexts for going to her apartment in the afternoons; the title of a book or article would occur to him, he would note it, and deliberately avoid seeing her in the corridors of Jesse Hall so that he might drop by her place in the afternoon to give her the title, have a cup of coffee, and talk. Once he spent half a day in the library pursuing a reference that might reinforce a point that he thought dubious in her second chapter; another time he laboriously transcribed a portion of a little-known Latin manuscript of which the library owned a photostat, and was thus able to spend several afternoons helping her with the translation.

During the afternoons they spent together Katherine Driscoll was courteous, friendly, and reserved; she was quietly grateful for the time and interest he expended upon her work, and she hoped she was not keeping him from more important things. It did not occur to him that she might think of him other than as an interested professor whom she admired and whose aid, though friendly, was little beyond the call of his duty. He thought of himself as a faintly ludicrous figure, one in whom no one could take an interest other than impersonal; and after he admitted to himself his feeling for Katherine Driscoll, he was desperately careful that he not show this feeling in any way that could be easily discerned.

For more than a month he dropped by her apartment two or three times a week, staying no more than two hours at any one time; he was fearful that she would become annoyed at his continued reappearances, so he was careful to come only when he was sure that he could be genuinely helpful to her work. With a kind of grim amusement he realized that he was preparing for his visits to her with the same diligence that he prepared for lectures; and he told himself that this would be enough, that he would be contented only to see her and talk to her for as long as she might endure his presence.

But despite his care and effort the afternoons they spent together became more and more strained. For long moments they found themselves with nothing to say; they sipped their coffee and looked away from each other, they said, "Well . . . ," in tentative and guarded voices, and they found reasons for moving restlessly around the room, away from each other. With a sadness the intensity of which he had not expected, Stoner told himself that his visits were becoming a burden to her and that her courtesy forbade her to let him be aware of that. As he had known he would have to do, he came to his decision; he would withdraw from her, gradually, so that she would not realize he had noticed her restlessness, as if he had given her all the help that he could.

He dropped by her apartment only once the next week, and the following week he did not visit her at all. He had not anticipated the struggle that he would have with himself; in the afternoons, as he sat in his office, he had almost physically to restrain himself from rising from his desk, hurrying outside, and walking to her apartment. Once or twice he saw her at a distance, in the halls, as she was hurrying to or from class; he turned away and walked in another direction, so that they would not have to meet.

After a while a kind of numbness came upon him, and he told himself that it would be all right, that in a few days he would be able to see her in the halls, nod to her and smile, perhaps even detain her for a moment and ask her how her work was going.

Then, one afternoon in the main office, as he was removing some mail from his box, he overheard a young instructor mention to another that Katherine Driscoll was ill, that she hadn't met her classes for the past two days. And the numbness left him; he felt a sharp pain in his chest, and his resolve and the strength of his will went out of him. He walked jerkily to his own office and looked with a kind of desperation at his bookcase, selected a book, and went out. By the time he got to Katherine Driscoll's apartment he was out of breath, so that he had to wait several moments in front of her door. He put a smile on his face that he hoped was casual, fixed it there, and knocked at her door.

She was even paler than usual, and there were dark smudges around her eyes; she wore a plain dark blue dressing gown, and her hair was drawn back severely from her face.

Stoner was aware that he spoke nervously and foolishly, yet he was unable to stop the flow of his words. "Hello," he said brightly, "I heard you were ill, I thought I would drop over to see how you were, I have a book that might be helpful to you, are you all right? I don't want to—" He listened to the sounds tumble from his stiff smile and could not keep his eyes from searching her face.

When at last he was silent she moved back from the door and said quietly, "Come in."

Once inside the little sitting-bedroom, his nervous inanity dropped away. He sat in the chair opposite the bed and felt the beginnings of a familiar ease come over him when Katherine Driscoll sat across from him. For several moments neither of them spoke.

Finally she asked, "Do you want some coffee?"

"You mustn't bother," Stoner said.

"It's no bother." Her voice was brusque and had that undertone of anger that he had heard before. "I'll just heat it up."

She went into the kitchen. Stoner, alone in the little room, stared glumly at the coffee table and told himself that he should not have come. He wondered at the foolishness that drove men to do the things they did.

Katherine Driscoll came back with the coffee pot and two cups; she poured their coffee, and they sat watching the steam rise from the black liquid. She took a cigarette from a crumpled package, lit it, and puffed nervously for a moment. Stoner became aware of the book he had carried with him and that he still clutched in his hands. He put it on the coffee table between them.

"Perhaps you aren't feeling up to it," he said, "but I ran across something that might be helpful to you, and I thought—"

"I haven't seen you in nearly two weeks," she said and stubbed her cigarette out, twisting it fiercely in the ashtray.

He was taken aback; he said distractedly, "I've been rather busy—so many things—"

"It doesn't matter," she said. "Really, it doesn't. I shouldn't have . . ." She rubbed the palm of her hand across her forehead.

He looked at her with concern; he thought she must be feverish. "I'm sorry you're ill. If there's anything I can—"

"I am not ill," she said. And she added in a voice that was calm, speculative, and almost uninterested, "I am desperately, desperately unhappy."

And still he did not understand. The bare sharp utterance went into him like a blade; he turned a little away from her; he said confusedly, "I'm sorry. Could you tell me about it? If there's anything I can do . . ."

She lifted her head. Her features were stiff, but her eyes were brilliant in pools of tears. "I didn't intend to embarrass you. I'm sorry. You must think me very foolish."

"No," he said. He looked at her for a moment more, at the pale face that seemed held expressionless by an effort of will. Then he gazed at his large bony hands that were clasped together on one knee; the fingers were blunt and heavy, and the knuckles were like white knobs upon the brown flesh.

He said at last, heavily and slowly, "In many ways I am an ignorant man; it is I who am foolish, not you. I have not come to see you because I thought—I felt that I was becoming a nuisance. Maybe that was not true."

"No," she said. "No, it wasn't true."

Still not looking at her, he continued, "And I didn't want to cause you the discomfort of having to deal with—with my feelings for you, which, I knew, sooner or later, would become obvious if I kept seeing you."

She did not move; two tears welled over her lashes and ran down her cheeks; she did not brush them away.

"I was perhaps selfish. I felt that nothing could come of this except awkwardness for you and unhappiness for me. You know my—circumstances. It seemed to me impossible that you could—that you could feel for me anything but—"

"Shut up," she said softly, fiercely. "Oh, my dear, shut up and come over here."

He found himself trembling; as awkwardly as a boy he went around the coffee table and sat beside her. Tentatively, clumsily, their hands went out to each other; they clasped each other in an awkward, strained embrace; and for a long time they sat together without moving, as if any movement might let escape from them the strange and terrible thing that they held between them in a single grasp.

Her eyes, that he had thought to be a dark brown or black, were a deep violet. Sometimes they caught the dim light of a lamp in the room and glittered moistly; he could turn his head one way and another, and the eyes beneath his gaze would change color as he moved, so that it seemed, even in repose, they were never still. Her flesh, that had at a distance seemed so cool and pale, had beneath it a warm ruddy undertone like light flowing beneath a milky translucence. And like the translucent flesh, the calm and poise and reserve which he had thought were herself, masked a warmth and playfulness and humor whose intensity was made possible by the appearance that disguised them.

In his forty-third year William Stoner learned what others, much younger, had learned before him: that the person one loves at first is not the person one loves at last, and that love is not an end but a process through which one person attempts to know another.

They were both very shy, and they knew each other slowly, tentatively; they came close and drew apart, they touched and withdrew, neither wishing to impose upon the other more than might be welcomed. Day by day the layers of reserve that protected them dropped away, so that at last they were like many

who are extraordinarily shy, each open to the other, unprotected, perfectly and unselfconsciously at ease.

Nearly every afternoon, when his classes were over, he came
to her apartment. They made love, and talked, and made love
again, like children who did not think of tiring at their play.
The spring days lengthened, and they looked forward to the
summer.

XIII

IN HIS extreme youth Stoner had thought of love as an absolute state of being to which, if one were lucky, one might find access; in his maturity he had decided it was the heaven of a false religion, toward which one ought to gaze with an amused disbelief, a gently familiar contempt, and an embarrassed nostalgia. Now in his middle age he began to know that it was neither a state of grace nor an illusion; he saw it as a human act of becoming, a condition that was invented and modified moment by moment and day by day, by the will and the intelligence and the heart.

The hours that he once had spent in his office gazing out of the window upon a landscape that shimmered and emptied before his blank regard, he now spent with Katherine. Every morning, early, he went to his office and sat restlessly for ten or fifteen minutes; then, unable to achieve repose, he wandered out of Jesse Hall and across campus to the library, where he browsed in the stacks for ten or fifteen minutes more. And at last, as if it were a game he played with himself, he delivered himself from his self-imposed suspense, slipped out a side door of the library, and made his way to the house where Katherine lived.

She often worked late into the night, and some mornings when he came to her apartment he found her just awakened, warm and sensual with sleep, naked beneath the dark blue robe she had thrown on to come to the door. On such mornings they often made love almost before they spoke, going to the narrow bed that was still rumpled and hot from Katherine's sleeping.

Her body was long and delicate and softly fierce; and when he touched it his awkward hand seemed to come alive above that flesh. Sometimes he looked at her body as if it were a sturdy treasure put in his keeping; he let his blunt fingers play upon the moist, faintly pink skin of thigh and belly and marveled at the intricately simple delicacy of her small firm breasts. It occurred to him that he had never before known the body of another; and it occurred to him further that that was the reason he had always somehow separated the self of another from the body that carried that self around. And it occurred to him at last, with the finality of knowledge, that he had never known another human being with any intimacy or trust or with the human warmth of commitment.

Like all lovers, they spoke much of themselves, as if they might thereby understand the world which made them possible.

"My God, how I used to lust after you," Katherine said once. "I used to see you standing there in front of the class, so big and lovely and awkward, and I used to lust after you something fierce. You never knew, did you?"

"No," William said. "I thought you were a very proper young lady."

She laughed delightedly. "Proper, indeed!" She sobered a little and smiled reminiscently. "I suppose I thought I was too. Oh, how proper we seem to ourselves when we have no reason to be improper! It takes being in love to know something about yourself. Sometimes, with you, I feel like the slut of the world, the eager, faithful slut of the world. Does that seem proper to you?"

"No," William said, smiling, and reached out for her. "Come here."

She had had one lover, William learned; it had been during her senior year in college, and it had ended badly, with tears and recriminations and betrayals.

"Most affairs end badly," she said, and for a moment both were somber.

William was shocked to discover his surprise when he learned that she had had a lover before him; he realized that he had started to think of themselves as never really having existed before they came together.

"He was such a shy boy," she said. "Like you, I suppose, in some ways; only he was bitter and afraid, and I could never learn what about. He used to wait for me at the end of the dorm walk, under a big tree, because he was too shy to come up where there were so many people. We used to walk miles, out in the country, where there wasn't a chance of our seeing anybody. But we were never really—together. Even when we made love."

Stoner could almost see this shadowy figure who had no face and no name; his shock turned to sadness, and he felt a generous pity for an unknown boy who, out of an obscure lost bitterness, had thrust away from him what Stoner now possessed.

Sometimes, in the sleepy laziness that followed their love-making, he lay in what seemed to him a slow and gentle flux of sensation and unhurried thought; and in that flux he hardly knew whether he spoke aloud or whether he merely recognized the words that sensation and thought finally came to.

He dreamed of perfections, of worlds in which they could always be together, and half believed in the possibility of what he dreamed. "What," he said, "would it be like if," and went on to construct a possibility hardly more attractive than the one in which they existed. It was an unspoken knowledge they both had, that the possibilities they imagined and elaborated were gestures of love and a celebration of the life they had together now.

The life they had together was one that neither of them had really imagined. They grew from passion to lust to a deep sensuality that renewed itself from moment to moment.

"Lust and learning," Katherine once said. "That's really all there is, isn't it?"

And it seemed to Stoner that that was exactly true, that that was one of the things he had learned.

For their life together that summer was not all love-making and talk. They learned to be together without speaking, and they got the habit of repose; Stoner brought books to Katherine's apartment and left them, until finally they had to install an extra bookcase for them. In the days they spent together Stoner found himself returning to the studies he had all but abandoned; and Katherine continued to work on the book that was to be her dissertation. For hours at a time she would sit at the tiny desk against the wall, her head bent down in intense concentration over books and papers, her slender pale neck curving and flowing out of the dark blue robe she habitually wore; Stoner sprawled in the chair or lay on the bed in like concentration.

Sometimes they would lift their eyes from their studies, smile at each other, and return to their reading; sometimes Stoner would look up from his book and let his gaze rest upon the graceful curve of Katherine's back and upon the slender neck where a tendril of hair always fell. Then a slow, easy desire would come over him like a calm, and he would rise and stand behind her and let his arms rest lightly on her shoulders. She would straighten and let her head go back against his chest, and his hands would go forward into the loose robe and gently touch her breasts. Then they would make love, and lie quietly for a while, and return to their studies, as if their love and learning were one process.

That was one of the oddities of what they called "given opinion" that they learned that summer. They had been brought up in a tradition that told them in one way or another that the life of the mind and the life of the senses were separate and, indeed, inimical; they had believed, without ever having really thought about it, that one had to be chosen at some expense of the other. That the one could intensify the other had never occurred to them; and since the embodiment came before the recognition of the truth, it seemed a discovery that belonged to them alone. They began to collect these oddities of "given opinion," and they hoarded them as if they were treasures; it helped to isolate them from the world that would give them these opinions, and it helped draw them together in a small but moving way.

But there was another oddity of which Stoner became aware and of which he did not speak to Katherine. That was one that had to do with his relationship with his wife and daughter.

It was a relationship that, according to "given opinion," ought to have worsened steadily as what given opinion would describe as his "affair" went on. But it did no such thing. On the contrary, it seemed steadily to improve. His lengthening absences away from what he still had to call his "home" seemed to bring him closer to both Edith and Grace than he had been in years. He began to have for Edith a curious friendliness that was close to affection, and they even talked together, now and then, of nothing in particular. During that summer she even cleaned the glassed-in sun porch, had repaired the damage done by the weather, and put a day bed there, so that he no longer had to sleep on the living-room couch.

And sometimes on weekends she made calls upon neighbors and left Grace alone with her father. Occasionally Edith was away long enough for him to take walks in the country with his daughter. Away from the house Grace's hard, watchful reserve dropped away, and at times she smiled with a quietness and charm that Stoner had almost forgotten. She had grown rapidly in the last year and was very thin.

Only by an effort of the will could he remind himself that he was deceiving Edith. The two parts of his life were as separate as the two parts of a life can be; and though he knew that his powers of introspection were weak and that he was capable of self-deception, he could not make himself believe that he was doing harm to anyone for whom he felt responsibility.

He had no talent for dissimulation, nor did it occur to him to dissemble his affair with Katherine Driscoll; neither did it occur to him to display it for anyone to see. It did not seem possible to him that anyone on the outside might be aware of their affair, or even be interested in it.

It was, therefore, a deep yet impersonal shock when he discovered, at the end of the summer, that Edith knew something of the affair and that she had known of it almost from the beginning.

She spoke of it casually one morning while he lingered over his breakfast coffee, chatting with Grace. Edith spoke a little sharply, told Grace to stop dawdling over her breakfast, that she had an hour of piano practice before she could waste any time. William watched the thin, erect figure of his daughter walk out of the dining room and waited absently until he heard the first resonant tones coming from the old piano.

"Well," Edith said with some of the sharpness still in her voice, "you're a little late this morning, aren't you?"

William turned to her questioningly; the absent expression remained on his face.

Edith said, "Won't your little co-ed be angry if you keep her waiting?"

He felt a numbness come to his lips. "What?" he asked. "What's that?"

"Oh, Willy," Edith said and laughed indulgently. "Did you think I didn't know about your—little flirtation? Why, I've known it all along. What's her name? I heard it, but I've forgotten what it is."

In its shock and confusion his mind grasped but one word; and when he spoke his voice sounded to him petulantly annoyed. "You don't understand," he said. "There's no—flirtation, as you call it. It's—"

"Oh, Willy," she said and laughed again. "You look so flustered. Oh, I know all about these things. A man your age and all. It's natural, I suppose. At least they say it is."

For a moment he was silent. Then reluctantly he said, "Edith, if you want to talk about this—"

"No!" she said; there was an edge of fear in her voice. "There's nothing to talk about. Nothing at all."

And they did not then or thereafter talk about it. Most of the time Edith maintained the convention that it was his work that kept him away from home; but occasionally, and almost absently, she spoke the knowledge that was always somewhere within her. Sometimes she spoke playfully, with something like a teasing affection; sometimes she spoke with no feeling at all, as if it were the most casual topic of conversation she could imagine; sometimes she spoke petulantly, as if some triviality had annoyed her.

She said, "Oh, I know. Once a man gets in his forties. But really, Willy, you're old enough to be her father, aren't you?"

It had not occurred to him how he must appear to an outsider, to the world. For a moment he saw himself as he must thus appear; and what Edith said was part of what he saw. He had a glimpse of a figure that flitted through smoking-room anecdotes, and through the pages of cheap fiction—a pitiable fellow going into his middle age, misunderstood by his wife, seeking to renew his youth, taking up with a girl years younger than himself, awkwardly and apishly reaching for the youth he could not have, a fatuous, garishly got-up clown at whom the world laughed out of discomfort, pity, and contempt. He looked at this figure as closely as he could; but the longer he looked, the less familiar it became. It was not himself that he saw, and he knew suddenly that it was no one.

But he knew that the world was creeping up on him, up on Katherine, and up on the little niche of it that they had thought was their own; and he watched the approach with a sadness of which he could not speak, even to Katherine.

*

The fall semester began that September in an intensely colorful Indian summer that came after an early frost. Stoner returned to his classes with an eagerness that he had not felt for a long time; even the prospect of facing a hundred freshman faces did not dim the renewal of his energy.

His life with Katherine continued much as it had been before, except that with the return of the students and many of the faculty he began to find it necessary to practice circumspection. During the summer the old house where Katherine lived had been almost deserted; they had been able thus to be together in almost complete isolation, with no fear that they might be noticed. Now William had to exercise caution when he came to her place in the afternoon; he found himself looking up and down the street before he approached the house, and going furtively down the stairs to the little well that opened into her apartment.

They thought of gestures and talked of rebellion; they told each other that they were tempted to do something outrageous, to make a display. But they did not, and they had no real desire to do so. They wanted only to be left alone, to be themselves; and, wanting this, they knew they would not be left alone and they suspected that they could not be themselves. They imagined themselves to be discreet, and it hardly occurred to them that their affair would be suspected. They made a point of not encountering each other at the University, and when they could not avoid meeting publicly, they greeted each other with a formality whose irony they did not believe to be evident.

But the affair was known, and known very quickly after the fall semester began. It was likely that the discovery came out of the peculiar clairvoyance that people have about such matters; for neither of them had given an outward sign of their private lives. Or perhaps someone had made an idle speculation that had a ring of truth to someone else, which caused a closer regard of them both, which in turn . . . Their speculations were, they knew, to no end; but they continued to make them.

There were signs by which both knew that they were discovered. Once, walking behind two male graduate students,

Stoner heard one say, half in admiration and half in contempt, "Old Stoner. By God, who would have believed it?"—and saw them shake their heads in mockery and puzzlement over the human condition. Acquaintances of Katherine made oblique references to Stoner and offered her confidences about their own love-lives that she had not invited.

What surprised them both was that it did not seem to matter. No one refused to speak to them; no one gave them black looks; they were not made to suffer by the world they had feared. They began to believe that they could live in the place they had thought to be inimical to their love, and live there with some dignity and ease.

Over the Christmas holiday Edith decided to take Grace for a visit with her mother in St. Louis; and for the only time during their life together William and Katherine were able to be with each other for an extended period.

Separately and casually, both let it be known that they would be away from the University during the Christmas holiday; Katherine was to visit relatives in the East, and William was to work at the bibliographical center and museum in Kansas City. At different hours they took separate buses, and met at Lake Ozark, a resort village in the outlying mountains of the great Ozark range.

They were the only guests of the only lodge in the village that remained open the year around; and they had ten days together.

There had been a heavy snow three days before their arrival, and during their stay it snowed again, so that the gently rolling hills remained white all the time they were there.

They had a cabin with a bedroom, a sitting room, and a small kitchen; it was somewhat removed from the other cabins, and it overlooked a lake that remained frozen during the winter months. In the morning they awoke to find themselves twined together, their bodies warm and luxuriant beneath the heavy blankets. They poked their heads out of the blankets and watched their breath condense in great clouds in the cold air; they laughed like children and pulled the covers back over their heads and pressed themselves more closely together. Sometimes they made love and stayed in bed all morning and talked, until the sun came through an east window; sometimes Stoner sprang out of bed as soon as they were awake and pulled the covers from Katherine's naked body and laughed at her screams as he kindled a fire in the great fireplace. Then they huddled together before the fireplace, with only a blanket around them, and waited to be warmed by the growing fire and the natural warmth of their own bodies.

Despite the cold, they walked nearly every day in the woods. The great pines, greenish-black against the snow, reared up massively toward the pale-blue cloudless sky; the occasional slither and plop of a mass of snow from one of the branches intensified the silence around them, as the occasional chatter of a lone bird intensified the isolation in which they walked. Once they saw a deer that had come down from the higher mountains in search of food. It was a doe, brilliantly yellow-tan against the starkness of dark pine and white snow. Now fifty yards away it faced them, one forepaw lifted delicately above the snow, the small ears pitched forward, the brown eyes perfectly round and incredibly soft. No one moved. The doe's delicate face tilted, as if regarding them with polite inquiry; then, unhurriedly, it turned and walked away from them, lifting its feet daintily out of the snow and placing them precisely, with a tiny sound of crunching.

In the afternoon they went to the main office of the lodge, which also served as the village's general store and restaurant. They had coffee there and talked to whoever had dropped in and perhaps picked up a few things for their evening meal, which they always took in their cabin.

In the evening they sometimes lighted the oil lamp and read; but more often they sat on folded blankets in front of the fireplace and talked and were silent and watched the flames play intricately upon the logs and watched the play of firelight upon each other's faces.

One evening, near the end of the time they had together, Katherine said quietly, almost absently, "Bill, if we never have anything else, we will have had this week. Does that sound like a girlish thing to say?"

"It doesn't matter what it sounds like," Stoner said. He nodded. "It's true."

"Then I'll say it," Katherine said. "We will have had this week."

On their last morning Katherine straightened the furniture and cleaned the place with slow care. She took off the wedding band she had worn and wedged it in a crevice between the wall and the fireplace. She smiled self-consciously. "I wanted," she said, "to leave something of our own here; something I knew would stay here, as long as this place stays. Maybe it's silly."

Stoner could not answer her. He took her arm and they walked out of the cabin and trudged through the snow to the lodge office, where the bus would pick them up and take them back to Columbia.

On an afternoon late in February, a few days after the second semester had begun, Stoner received a call from Gordon Finch's secretary; she told him that the dean would like to talk with him and asked if he would drop by that afternoon or the next morning. Stoner told her that he would—and sat for several minutes with one hand on the phone after having hung up. Then he sighed and nodded to himself and went downstairs to Finch's office.

Gordon Finch was in his shirt sleeves, his tie was loosened, and he was leaning back in his swivel chair with his hands clasped behind his head. When Stoner came into the room he nodded genially and waved toward the leather-covered easy chair set at an angle beside his desk.

"Take a load off, Bill. How have you been?"

Stoner nodded. "All right."

"Classes keeping you busy?"

Stoner said dryly, "Reasonably so. I have a full schedule."

"I know," Finch said and shook his head. "I can't interfere there, you know. But it's a damned shame."

"It's all right," Stoner said a bit impatiently.

"Well." Finch straightened in his chair and clasped his hands on the desk in front of him. "There's nothing official about this visit, Bill. I just wanted to chat with you for a while."

There was a long silence. Stoner said gently, "What is it, Gordon?"

Finch sighed, and then said abruptly, "Okay. I'm talking to you right now as a friend. There's been talk. It isn't anything that, as a dean, I have to pay any attention to yet, but—well, sometime I might have to pay attention to it, and I thought

I ought to speak to you—as a friend, mind you—before anything serious develops."

Stoner nodded. "What kind of talk?"

"Oh, hell, Bill. You and the Driscoll girl. You know."

"Yes," Stoner said. "I know. I just wanted to know how far
it has gone."

"Not far yet. Innuendos, remarks, things like that."

"I see," Stoner said. "I don't know what I can do about it."

Finch creased a sheet of paper carefully. "Is it serious, Bill?"

Stoner nodded and looked out the window. "It's serious,
I'm afraid."

"What are you going to do?"

"I don't know."

With sudden violence Finch crumpled the paper that he had
so carefully folded and threw it at a wastebasket. He said, "In
theory, your life is your own to lead. In theory, you ought to
be able to screw anybody you want to, do anything you want
to, and it shouldn't matter so long as it doesn't interfere with
your teaching. But damn it, your life *isn't* your own to lead.
It's—oh, hell. You know what I mean."

Stoner smiled. "I'm afraid I do."

"It's a bad business. What about Edith?"

"Apparently," Stoner said, "she takes the whole thing a good
deal less seriously than anyone else. And it's a funny thing,
Gordon; I don't believe we've ever got along any better than
we have the last year."

Finch laughed shortly. "You never can tell, can you? But
what I meant was, will there be a divorce? Anything like that?"

"I don't know. Possibly. But Edith would fight it. It would
be a mess."

"What about Grace?"

A sudden pain caught at Stoner's throat, and he knew that
his expression showed what he felt. "That's—something else. I
don't know, Gordon."

Finch said impersonally, as if they were discussing someone
else, "You might survive a divorce—if it weren't too messy.
It would be rough, but you'd probably survive it. And if this
—thing with the Driscoll girl weren't serious, if you were just
screwing around, well, that could be handled too. But you're
sticking your neck out, Bill; you're asking for it."

"I suppose I am," Stoner said.

There was a pause. "This is a hell of a job I have," Finch said heavily. "Sometimes I think I'm not the man for it at all."

Stoner smiled. "Dave Masters once said you weren't a big enough son-of-a-bitch to be really successful."

"Maybe he was right," Finch said. "But I feel like one often enough."

"Don't worry about it, Gordon," Stoner said. "I understand your position. And if I could make it easier for you I—" He paused and shook his head sharply. "But I can't do anything right now. It will have to wait. Somehow . . ."

Finch nodded and did not look at Stoner; he stared at his desk top as if it were a doom that approached him with slow inevitability. Stoner waited for a few moments, and when Finch did not speak he got up quietly and went out of the office.

Because of his conversation with Gordon Finch, Stoner was late that afternoon getting to Katherine's apartment. Without bothering to look up or down the street he went down the walk and let himself in. Katherine was waiting for him; she had not changed clothes, and she waited almost formally, sitting erect and alert upon the couch.

"You're late," she said flatly.

"Sorry," he said. "I got held up."

Katherine lit a cigarette; her hand was trembling slightly. She surveyed the match for a moment, and blew it out with a puff of smoke. She said, "One of my fellow instructors made rather a point of telling me that Dean Finch called you in this afternoon."

"Yes," Stoner said. "That's what held me up."

"Was it about us?"

Stoner nodded. "He had heard a few things."

"I imagined that was it," Katherine said. "My instructor friend seemed to know something that she didn't want to tell. Oh, Christ, Bill!"

"It's not like that at all," Stoner said. "Gordon is an old friend. I actually believe he wants to protect us. I believe he will if he can."

Katherine did not speak for several moments. She kicked off her shoes and lay back on the couch, staring at the ceiling. She said calmly, "Now it begins. I suppose it was too much, hoping that they would leave us alone. I suppose we never really seriously thought they would."

"If it gets too bad," Stoner said, "we can go away. We can do something."

"Oh, Bill!" Katherine was laughing a little, throatily and softly. She sat up on the couch. "You are the dearest love, the dearest, dearest anyone could imagine. And I will not let them bother us. I will not!"

And for the next several weeks they lived much as they had before. With a strategy that they would not have been able to manage a year earlier, with a strength they would not have known they had, they practiced evasions and withdrawals, deploying their powers like skillful generals who must survive with meager forces. They became genuinely circumspect and cautious, and got a grim pleasure from their maneuverings. Stoner came to her apartment only after dark, when no one could see him enter; in the daytime, between classes, Katherine allowed herself to be seen at coffee shops with younger male instructors; and the hours they spent together were intensified by their common determination. They told themselves and each other that they were closer than they ever had been; and to their surprise, they realized that it was true, that the words they spoke to comfort themselves were more than consolatory. They made a closeness possible and a commitment inevitable.

It was a world of half-light in which they lived and to which they brought the better parts of themselves—so that, after a while, the outer world where people walked and spoke, where there was change and continual movement, seemed to them false and unreal. Their lives were sharply divided between the two worlds, and it seemed to them natural that they should live so divided.

During the late winter and early spring months they found together a quietness they had not had before. As the outer world closed upon them they became less aware of its presence; and their happiness was such that they had no need to speak of it to each other, or even to think of it. In Katherine's small, dim apartment, hidden like a cave beneath the massive old house, they seemed to themselves to move outside of time, in a timeless universe of their own discovery.

Then, one day in late April, Gordon Finch again called Stoner into his office; and Stoner went down with a numbness that came from a knowledge he would not admit.

What had happened was classically simple, something that Stoner should have foreseen yet had not.

"It's Lomax," Finch said. "Somehow the son-of-a-bitch has got hold of it and he's not about to let go."

Stoner nodded. "I should have thought of that. I should have expected it. Do you think it would do any good if I talked to him?"

Finch shook his head, walked across his office, and stood before the window. Early afternoon sunlight streamed upon his face, which gleamed with sweat. He said tiredly, "You don't understand, Bill. Lomax isn't playing it that way. Your name hasn't even come up. He's working through the Driscoll girl."

"He's what?" Stoner asked blankly.

"You almost have to admire him," Finch said. "Somehow he knew damn well I knew all about it. So he came in yesterday, off-hand, you know, and told me he was going to have to fire the Driscoll girl and warned me there might be a stink."

"No," Stoner said. His hands ached where they gripped the leather arms of the easy chair.

Finch continued, "According to Lomax, there have been complaints, from students mostly, and a few townspeople. It seems that men have been seen going in and out of her apartment at all hours—flagrant misbehavior—that sort of thing. Oh, he did it beautifully; he has no personal objection—he rather admires the girl, as a matter of fact—but he has the reputation of the department and the University to think of. We commiserated upon the necessities of bowing to the dictates of middle-class morality, agreed that the community of scholars ought to be a haven for the rebel against the Protestant ethic, and concluded that practically speaking we were helpless. He said he hoped he could let it ride until the end of the semester but doubted if he could. And all the time the son-of-a-bitch knew we understood each other perfectly."

A tightness in his throat made it impossible for Stoner to speak. He swallowed twice and tested his voice; it was steady and flat. "What he wants is perfectly clear, of course."

"I'm afraid it is," Finch said.

"I knew he hated me," Stoner said distantly. "But I never realized—I never dreamed he would—"

"Neither did I," Finch said. He walked back to his desk and sat down heavily. "And I can't do a thing, Bill. I'm helpless. If Lomax wants complainers, they'll appear; if he wants witnesses, they will appear. He has quite a following, you know. And if word ever gets to the president—" He shook his head.

"What do you imagine will happen if I refuse to resign? If we just refuse to be scared?"

"He'll crucify the girl," Finch said flatly. "And as if by accident you'll be dragged into it. It's very neat."

"Then," Stoner said, "it appears there is nothing to be done."

"Bill," Finch said, and then was silent. He rested his head on his closed fists. He said dully, "There is a chance. There is just one. I think I can hold him off if you—if the Driscoll girl will just—"

"No," Stoner said. "I don't think I can do it. Literally, I don't think I can do it."

"God damn it!" Finch's voice was anguished. "He's counting on that! Think for a minute. What would you do? It's April; almost May; what kind of job could you get this time of year —if you could get one at all?"

"I don't know," Stoner said. "Something . . ."

"And what about Edith? Do you think she's going to give in, give you a divorce without a fight? And Grace? What would it do to her, in this town, if you just took off? And Katherine? What kind of life would you have? What would it do to both of you?"

Stoner did not speak. An emptiness was beginning somewhere within him; he felt a withering, a falling away. He said at last, "Can you give me a week?—I've got to think. A week?"

Finch nodded. "I can hold him off that long at least. But not much longer. I'm sorry, Bill. You know that."

"Yes." He got up from the chair and stood for a moment, testing the heavy numbness of his legs. "I'll let you know. I'll let you know when I can."

He went out of the office into the darkness of the long corridor and walked heavily into the sunlight, into the open world that was like a prison wherever he turned.

*

Years afterward, at odd moments, he would look back upon those days that followed his conversation with Gordon Finch and would be unable to recall them with any clarity at all. It was as if he were a dead man animated by nothing more than a habit of stubborn will. Yet he was oddly aware of himself and of the places, persons, and events which moved past him in these few days; and he knew that he presented to the public regard an appearance which belied his condition. He taught his classes, he greeted his colleagues, he attended the meetings he had to attend—and no one of the people he met from day to day knew that anything was wrong.

But from the moment he walked out of Gordon Finch's office, he knew, somewhere within the numbness that grew from a small center of his being, that a part of his life was over, that a part of him was so near death that he could watch the approach almost with calm. He was vaguely conscious that he walked across the campus in the bright crisp heat of an early spring afternoon; the dogwood trees along the sidewalks and in the front yards were in full bloom, and they trembled like soft clouds, translucent and tenuous, before his gaze; the sweet scent of dying lilac blossoms drenched the air.

And when he got to Katherine's apartment he was feverishly and callously gay. He brushed aside her questions about his latest encounter with the dean; he forced her to laugh; and he watched with an immeasurable sadness their last effort of gaiety, which was like a dance that life makes upon the body of death.

But finally they had to talk, he knew; though the words they said were like a performance of something they had rehearsed again and again in the privacies of their knowledge. They revealed that knowledge by grammatical usage: they progressed from the perfect—"We have been happy, haven't we?"—to the past—"We *were* happy—happier than anyone, I think"—and at last came to the necessity of discourse.

Several days after the conversation with Finch, in a moment of quiet that interrupted the half-hysterical gaiety they had chosen as that convention most appropriate to see them through their last days together, Katherine said, "We don't have much time, do we?"

"No," Stoner said quietly.

"How much longer?" Katherine asked.

"A few days, two or three."

Katherine nodded. "I used to think I wouldn't be able to endure it. But I'm just numb. I don't feel anything."

"I know," Stoner said. They were silent for a moment. "You know if there were anything—*anything* I could do, I'd—"

"Don't," she said. "Of course I know."

He leaned back on the couch and looked at the low, dim ceiling that had been the sky of their world. He said calmly, "If I threw it all away—if I gave it up, just walked out—you would go with me, wouldn't you?"

"Yes," she said.

"But you know I won't do that, don't you?"

"Yes, I know."

"Because then," Stoner explained to himself, "none of it would mean anything—nothing we have done, nothing we have been. I almost certainly wouldn't be able to teach, and you—you would become something else. We both would become something else, something other than ourselves. We would be—nothing."

"Nothing," she said.

"And we have come out of this, at least, with ourselves. We know that we are—what we are."

"Yes," Katherine said.

"Because in the long run," Stoner said, "it isn't Edith or even Grace, or the certainty of losing Grace, that keeps me here; it isn't the scandal or the hurt to you or me; it isn't the hardship we would have to go through, or even the loss of love we might have to face. It's simply the destruction of ourselves, of what we do."

"I know," Katherine said.

"So we are of the world, after all; we should have known that. We did know it, I believe; but we had to withdraw a little, pretend a little, so that we could—"

"I know," Katherine said. "I've known it all along, I guess. Even with the pretending, I've known that sometime, sometime, we would . . . I've known." She halted and looked at him steadily. Her eyes became suddenly bright with tears. "But damn it all, Bill! Damn it all!"

They said no more. They embraced so that neither might see the other's face, and made love so that they would not speak. They coupled with the old tender sensuality of knowing each other well and with the new intense passion of loss. Afterward, in the black night of the little room, they lay still unspeaking, their bodies touching lightly. After a long while Katherine's breath came steadily, as if in sleep. Stoner got up quietly, dressed in the dark, and went out of the room without awakening her. He walked the still, empty streets of Columbia until the first gray light began in the east; then he made his way to the University campus. He sat on the stone steps in front of Jesse Hall and watched the light from the east creep upon the great stone columns in the center of the quad. He thought of the fire that, before he was born, had gutted and ruined the old building; and he was distantly saddened by the view of what remained. When it was light he let himself into the hall and went to his office, where he waited until his first class began.

He didn't see Katherine Driscoll again. After he left her, during the night, she got up, packed all her belongings, cartoned her books, and left word with the manager of the apartment house where to send them. She mailed the English office her grades, her instructions to dismiss her classes for the week and a half that remained of the semester, and her resignation. And she was on the train, on her way out of Columbia, by two o'clock that afternoon.

She must have been planning her departure for some time, Stoner realized; and he was grateful that he had not known and that she left him no final note to say what could not be said.

XIV

THAT SUMMER he did not teach; and he had the first illness of his life. It was a fever of high intensity and obscure origin, which lasted only a week; but it drained him of his strength, he became very gaunt, and suffered in its aftermath a partial loss of hearing. For the entire summer he was so weak and listless that he could walk only a few steps without becoming exhausted; he spent nearly all that time in the small enclosed porch at the back of the house, lying on the day bed or sitting in the old easy chair he had had brought up from the basement. He stared out the windows or at the slatted ceiling, and stirred himself now and then to go into the kitchen to get a bite of food.

He had hardly the energy to converse with Edith or even with Grace—though sometimes Edith came into the back room, spoke to him distractedly for a few minutes, and then left him alone as abruptly as she had intruded upon him.

Once, in the middle of summer, she spoke of Katherine.

"I just heard, a day or so ago," she said. "So your little coed has gone, has she?"

With an effort he brought his attention away from the window and turned to Edith. "Yes," he said mildly.

"What was her name?" Edith asked. "I never can remember her name."

"Katherine," he said. "Katherine Driscoll."

"Oh, yes," Edith said. "Katherine Driscoll. Well, you see? I told you, didn't I? I told you these things weren't important."

He nodded absently. Outside, in the old elm that crowded the back-yard fence, a large black-and-white bird—a magpie —had started to chatter. He listened to the sound of its calling and watched with remote fascination the open beak as it strained out its lonely cry.

He aged rapidly that summer, so that when he went back to his classes in the fall there were few who did not recognize him with a start of surprise. His face, gone gaunt and bony, was deeply lined; heavy patches of gray ran through his hair; and he was heavily stooped, as if he carried an invisible burden.

His voice had grown a little grating and abrupt, and he had a tendency to stare at one with his head lowered, so that his clear gray eyes were sharp and querulous beneath his tangled eyebrows. He seldom spoke to anyone except his students, and he responded to questions and greetings always impatiently and sometimes harshly.

He did his work with a doggedness and resolve that amused his older colleagues and enraged the younger instructors, who, like himself, taught only freshman composition; he spent hours marking and correcting freshman themes, he had student conferences every day, and he attended faithfully all departmental meetings. He did not speak often at these meetings, but when he did he spoke without tact or diplomacy, so that among his colleagues he developed a reputation for crustiness and ill temper. But with his young students he was gentle and patient, though he demanded of them more work than they were willing to give, with an impersonal firmness that was hard for many of them to understand.

It was a commonplace among his colleagues—especially the younger ones—that he was a "dedicated" teacher, a term they used half in envy and half in contempt, one whose dedication blinded him to anything that went on outside the classroom or, at the most, outside the halls of the University. There were mild jokes: after a departmental meeting at which Stoner had spoken bluntly about some recent experiments in the teaching of grammar, a young instructor remarked that "To Stoner, copulation is restricted to verbs," and was surprised at the quality of laughter and meaningful looks exchanged by some of the older men. Someone else once said, "Old Stoner thinks that WPA stands for Wrong Pronoun Antecedent," and was gratified to learn that his witticism gained some currency.

But William Stoner knew of the world in a way that few of his younger colleagues could understand. Deep in him, beneath his memory, was the knowledge of hardship and hunger and endurance and pain. Though he seldom thought of his early years on the Booneville farm, there was always near his consciousness the blood knowledge of his inheritance, given him by forefathers whose lives were obscure and hard and stoical and whose common ethic was to present to an oppressive world faces that were expressionless and hard and bleak.

And though he looked upon them with apparent impassivity, he was aware of the times in which he lived. During that decade when many men's faces found a permanent hardness and bleakness, as if they looked upon an abyss, William Stoner, to whom that expression was as familiar as the air he walked in, saw the signs of a general despair he had known since he was a boy. He saw good men go down into a slow decline of hopelessness, broken as their vision of a decent life was broken; he saw them walking aimlessly upon the streets, their eyes empty like shards of broken glass; he saw them walk up to back doors, with the bitter pride of men who go to their executions, and beg for the bread that would allow them to beg again; and he saw men, who had once walked erect in their own identities, look at him with envy and hatred for the poor security he enjoyed as a tenured employee of an institution that somehow could not fail. He did not give voice to this awareness; but the knowledge of common misery touched him and changed him in ways that were hidden deep from the public view, and a quiet sadness for the common plight was never far beneath any moment of his living.

He was aware, too, of the stirrings in Europe like a distant nightmare; and in July 1936, when Franco rebelled against the Spanish government and Hitler fanned that rebellion into a major war, Stoner, like many others, was sickened by the vision of the nightmare breaking out of the dream into the world. When the fall semester began that year the younger instructors could talk of little else; several of them proclaimed their intention of joining a volunteer unit and fighting for the loyalists or driving ambulances. By the close of the first semester a few of them had actually taken the step and submitted hasty resignations. Stoner thought of Dave Masters, and the old loss was brought back to him with a renewed intensity; he thought, too, of Archer Sloane and remembered, from nearly twenty years before, the slow anguish that had grown upon that ironic face and the erosive despair that had dissipated that hard self —and he thought that he knew now, in a small way, something of the sense of waste that Sloane had apprehended. He foresaw the years that stretched ahead, and knew that the worst was to come.

As Archer Sloane had done, he realized the futility and waste of committing one's self wholly to the irrational and dark forces that impelled the world toward its unknown end; as Archer Sloane had not done, Stoner withdrew a little distance to pity and love, so that he was not caught in the rushing that he observed. And as in other moments of crisis and despair, he looked again to the cautious faith that was embodied in the institution of the University. He told himself that it was not much; but he knew that it was all he had.

In the summer of 1937 he felt a renewal of the old passion for study and learning; and with the curious and disembodied vigor of the scholar that is the condition of neither youth nor age, he returned to the only life that had not betrayed him. He discovered that he had not gone far from that life even in his despair.

His schedule that fall was particularly bad. His four classes of freshman composition were spaced at widely separated hours six days a week. During all his years as chairman, Lomax had not once failed to give Stoner a teaching schedule that even the newest instructor would have accepted with bad grace.

On the first class day of that academic year, in the early morning, Stoner sat in his office and looked again at his neatly typed schedule. He had been up late the night before reading a new study of the survival of the medieval tradition into the Renaissance, and the excitement he had felt carried over to the morning. He looked at his schedule, and a dull anger rose within him. He stared at the wall in front of him for several moments, glanced at his schedule again, and nodded to himself. He dropped the schedule and the attached syllabus into a wastebasket and went to his filing cabinet in a corner of the room. He pulled out the top drawer, looked absently at the brown folders there, and withdrew one. He flipped through the papers in the folder, whistling silently as he did so. Then he closed the drawer and with the folder under one arm went out of his office and across the campus to his first class.

The building was an old one, with wooden floors, and it was used as a classroom only in emergencies; the room to which he had been assigned was too small for the number of students enrolled, so that several of the boys had to sit on the windowsills or stand. When Stoner came in they looked at him with the discomfort of uncertainty; he might be friend or foe, and they did not know which was worse.

He apologized to the students for the room, made a small joke at the expense of the registrar, and assured those who were standing that there would be chairs for them tomorrow. Then he put his folder on the battered lectern that rested unevenly on the desk and surveyed the faces before him.

He hesitated for a moment. Then he said, "Those of you who have purchased your texts for this course may return them to the bookstore and get a refund. We shall not be using the text described in the syllabus—which, I take it, you all received when you signed up for the course. Neither will we be using the syllabus. I intend in this course to take a different approach to the subject, an approach which will necessitate your buying two new texts."

He turned his back to the students and picked up a piece of chalk from the trough beneath the scuffed blackboard; he held the chalk poised for a moment and listened to the muted sigh and rustle of the students as they settled at their desks, enduring the routine that suddenly became familiar to them.

Stoner said, "Our texts will be"—and he enunciated the words slowly as he wrote them down—"*Medieval English Verse and Prose*, edited by Loomis and Willard; and *English Literary Criticism: The Medieval Phase*, by J. W. H. Atkins." He turned to the class. "You will find that the bookstore has not yet received these books—it may be as much as two weeks before they are in. In the meantime I will give you some background information upon the matter and purpose of this course, and I shall make a few library assignments to keep you occupied."

He paused. Many of the students were bent over their desks, assiduously noting what he said; a few were looking at him steadily, with small smiles that wanted to be intelligent and understanding; and a few were staring at him in open amazement.

"The primary matter of this course," Stoner said, "will be found in the Loomis and Willard anthology; we shall study examples of medieval verse and prose for three purposes—first, as literary works significant in themselves; second, as a demonstration of the beginnings of literary style and method in the English tradition; and third, as rhetorical and grammatical solutions to problems of discourse that even today may be of some practical value and application."

By this time nearly all the students had stopped taking notes and had raised their heads; even the intelligent smiles had become a trifle strained; and a few hands were waving in the air. Stoner pointed to one whose hand remained steady and high, a tall young man with dark hair and glasses.

"Sir, is this General English One, Section Four?"

Stoner smiled at the young man. "What is your name, please?"

The boy swallowed. "Jessup, sir. Frank Jessup."

Stoner nodded. "Mr. Jessup. Yes, Mr. Jessup, this is General English One, Section Four; and my name is Stoner—facts which, no doubt, I should have mentioned at the beginning of the period. Did you have another question?"

The boy swallowed again. "No, sir."

Stoner nodded and looked benevolently around the room. "Does anyone else have a question?"

The faces stared back at him; there were no smiles, and a few mouths hung open.

"Very well," Stoner said. "I shall continue. As I said at the beginning of this hour, one purpose of this course is to study certain works of the period roughly between twelve and fifteen hundred. Certain accidents of history will stand in our way; there will be linguistic difficulties as well as philosophical, social as well as religious, theoretical as well as practical. Indeed, all of our past education will in some ways hinder us; for our habits of thinking about the nature of experience have determined our own expectations as radically as the habits of medieval man determined his. As a preliminary, let us examine some of those habits of mind under which medieval man lived and thought and wrote . . ."

That first meeting he did not keep the students for the entire hour. After less than half the period he brought his preliminary discussion to a close and gave them a weekend assignment.

"I should like for each of you to write a brief essay, no more than three pages, upon Aristotle's conception of the *topoi* —or, in its rather crude English translation, topic. You will find an extended discussion of the 'topic' in Book Two of *The Rhetoric* of Aristotle, and in Lane Cooper's edition there is an introductory essay that you will find most helpful. The essay will be due on—Monday. And that, I think, will be all for today."

For a moment after he dismissed the class he gazed at the students, who did not move, with some concern. Then he nodded briefly to them and walked out of the classroom, the brown folder under his arm.

On Monday fewer than half the students had finished their papers; he dismissed those who handed their essays in and spent the rest of the hour with the remaining students, rehearsing the subject he had assigned, going over it again and again, until he was sure they had it and could complete the assigned essay by Wednesday.

On Tuesday he noticed in the corridors of Jesse Hall, outside Lomax's office, a group of students; he recognized them as members of his first class. As he passed, the students turned away from him and looked at the floor or the ceiling or at the door of Lomax's office. He smiled to himself and went to his office and waited for the telephone call that he knew would come.

It came at two o'clock that afternoon. He picked up the phone, answered, and heard the voice of Lomax's secretary, icy and polite. "Professor Stoner? Professor Lomax would like you to see Professor Ehrhardt this afternoon, as soon as possible. Professor Ehrhardt will be expecting you."

"Will Lomax be there?" Stoner asked.

There was a shocked pause. The voice said uncertainly, "I—believe not—a previous appointment. But Professor Ehrhardt is empowered to—"

"You tell Lomax he ought to be there. You tell him I'll be in Ehrhardt's office in ten minutes."

Joel Ehrhardt was a balding young man in his early thirties. He had been brought into the department three years before by Lomax; and when it was discovered that he was a pleasant and serious young man with no special talent and no gift for teaching, he had been put in charge of the freshman English program. His office was in a small enclosure at the far end of the large common room where twenty-odd young instructors had their desks, and Stoner had to walk the length of the room to get there. As he made his way among the desks, some of the instructors looked up at him, grinned openly, and watched his progress across the room. Stoner opened the door without knocking, went into the office, and sat down in the chair opposite Ehrhardt's desk. Lomax was not there.

"You wanted to see me?" Stoner asked.

Ehrhardt, who had a very fair skin, blushed slightly. He fixed a smile on his face, said enthusiastically, "It's good of you to drop by, Bill," and fumbled for a moment with a match, trying to light his pipe. It wouldn't draw properly. "This damned humidity," he said morosely. "It keeps the tobacco too wet."

"Lomax won't be here, I take it," Stoner said.

"No," Ehrhardt said, putting the pipe on his desk. "Actually, though, it was Professor Lomax who asked me to talk to you, so in a way"—he laughed nervously—"I'm really sort of a messenger boy."

"What message were you asked to deliver?" Stoner asked dryly.

"Well, as I understand it, there have been a few complaints. Students—*you* know." He shook his head commiseratingly. "Some of them seem to think—well, they don't really seem to understand what's going on in your eight o'clock class. Professor Lomax thought—well, actually, I suppose he's questioning the wisdom of approaching the problems of freshman composition through the—the study of—"

"Medieval language and literature," Stoner said.

"Yes," Ehrhardt said. "Actually, I think I understand what you're trying to do—shock them a bit, shake them up, try a new approach, get them to thinking. Right?"

Stoner nodded gravely. "There has been a great deal of talk in our freshman comp meetings lately about new methods, experimentation."

"Exactly," Ehrhardt said. "No one has more sympathy than I for experimentation, for—but perhaps sometimes, out of the very best motives, we go too far." He laughed and shook his head. "I certainly know I do; I'd be the first to confess it. But I—or Professor Lomax—well, perhaps some sort of compromise, some partial return to the syllabus, a use of the assigned texts—you understand."

Stoner pursed his lips and looked at the ceiling; resting his elbows on the arms of the chair, he placed the tips of his fingers together and let his chin rest on his thumb-tips. Finally, but decisively, he said, "No, I don't believe the—experiment—has had a fair chance. Tell Lomax I intend to carry it through to the end of the semester. Would you do that for me?"

Ehrhardt's face was red. He said tightly, "I will. But I imagine —I'm sure Professor Lomax will be most—disappointed. Most disappointed indeed."

Stoner said, "Oh, at first he may be. But he'll get over it. I'm sure Professor Lomax wouldn't want to interfere with the way a senior professor sees fit to teach one of his classes. He may disagree with the judgment of that professor, but it would be most unethical for him to attempt to impose his own judgment —and, incidentally, a little dangerous. Don't you agree?"

Ehrhardt picked up his pipe, gripped its bowl tightly, and contemplated it fiercely. "I'll—tell Professor Lomax of your decision."

"I'd be grateful if you would," Stoner said. He rose from his chair, walked to the door, paused as if reminded of something, and turned to Ehrhardt. He said casually, "Oh, another thing. I've been doing a little thinking about next semester. If my experiment works out, next semester I might try something else. I've been considering the possibility of getting at some of the problems of composition by examining the survival of the classical and medieval Latin tradition in some of Shakespeare's plays. It may sound a little specialized, but I think I can bring it down to a workable level. You might pass my little idea along to Lomax—ask him to turn it over in his mind. Maybe in a few weeks, you and I can—"

Ehrhardt slumped in his chair. He dropped his pipe on the table and said wearily, "All right, Bill. I'll tell him. I'll—thanks for dropping by."

Stoner nodded. He opened the door, went out, closed it carefully behind him, and walked across the long room. When one of the young instructors looked up at him inquiringly, he winked broadly, nodded, and—finally—let the smile come over his face.

He went to his office, sat at his desk, and waited, looking out the open doorway. After a few minutes he heard a door slam down the hall, heard the uneven sound of footsteps, and saw Lomax go past his office as swiftly as his limp would carry him.

Stoner did not move from his watch. Within half an hour he heard Lomax's slow, shuffling ascent of the stairway and saw him go once more past his office. He waited until he heard the door down the hall close; then he nodded to himself, got up, and went home.

It was some weeks later that Stoner learned from Finch himself what happened that afternoon when Lomax stormed into his office. Lomax complained bitterly about Stoner's behavior, described how he was teaching what amounted to his senior course in Middle English to his freshman class, and demanded that Finch take disciplinary measures. There was a moment of silence. Finch started to say something, and then he burst out laughing. He laughed for a long time, every now and then trying to say something that was pushed back by laughter. Finally he quieted, apologized to Lomax for his outburst, and said, "He's got you, Holly; don't you see that? He's not about to let go, and there's not a damn thing you can do. You want *me* to do the job for you? How do you think that would look—a dean meddling in how a senior member of the department teaches his classes, *and* meddling at the instigation of the department chairman himself? No, sir. You take care of it yourself, the best way you can. But you really don't have much choice, do you?"

Two weeks after that conversation Stoner received a memo from Lomax's office which informed him that his schedule for the next semester was changed, that he would teach his old graduate seminar on the Latin Tradition and Renaissance Literature, a senior and graduate course in Middle English language and literature, a sophomore literature survey, and one section of freshman composition.

It was a triumph in a way, but one of which he always remained amusedly contemptuous, as if it were a victory won by boredom and indifference.

XV

And that was one of the legends that began to attach to his name, legends that grew more detailed and elaborate year by year, progressing like myth from personal fact to ritual truth.

In his late forties, he looked years older. His hair, thick and unruly as it had been in his youth, was almost entirely white; his face was deeply lined and his eyes were sunken in their sockets; and the deafness that had come upon him the summer after the end of his affair with Katherine Driscoll had worsened slightly year by year, so that when he listened to someone, his head cocked to one side and his eyes intent, he appeared to be remotely contemplating a puzzling species that he could not quite identify.

That deafness was of a curious nature. Though he sometimes had difficulty understanding one who spoke directly to him, he was often able to hear with perfect clarity a murmured conversation held across a noisy room. It was by this trick of deafness that he gradually began to know that he was considered, in the phrase current in his own youth, a "campus character."

Thus he overheard, again and again, the embellished tale of his teaching Middle English to a group of new freshmen and of the capitulation of Hollis Lomax. "And when the freshman class of thirty-seven took their junior English exams, you know what class had the highest score?" a reluctant young instructor of freshman English asked. "Sure. Old Stoner's Middle English bunch. And we keep on using exercises and handbooks!"

Stoner had to admit that he had become, in the regard of the young instructors and the older students, who seemed to come and go before he could firmly attach names to their faces, an almost mythic figure, however shifting and various the function of that figure was.

Sometimes he was villain. In one version that attempted to explain the long feud between himself and Lomax, he had seduced and then cast aside a young graduate student for whom Lomax had had a pure and honorable passion. Sometimes he was the fool: in another version of the same feud, he refused to speak to Lomax because once Lomax had been unwilling to write a letter of recommendation for one of Stoner's graduate students. And sometimes he was hero: in a final and not often accepted version he was hated by Lomax and frozen in his rank because he had once caught Lomax giving to a favored student a copy of a final examination in one of Stoner's courses.

The legend was defined, however, by his manner in class. Over the years it had grown more and more absent and yet more and more intense. He began his lectures and discussions fumblingly and awkwardly, yet very quickly became so immersed in his subject that he seemed unaware of anything or anyone around him. Once a meeting of several members of the board of trustees and the president of the University was scheduled in the conference room where Stoner held his seminar in the Latin Tradition; he had been informed of the meeting but had forgotten about it and held his seminar at the usual time and place. Halfway through the period a timid knock sounded at the door; Stoner, engrossed in translating extemporaneously a pertinent Latin passage, did not notice. After a few moments the door opened and a small plump middle-aged man with rimless glasses tiptoed in and lightly tapped Stoner on the shoulder. Without looking up, Stoner waved him away. The man retreated; there was a whispered conference with several others outside the open door. Stoner continued the translation. Then four men, led by the president of the University, a tall heavy man with an imposing chest and florid face, strode in and halted like a squad beside Stoner's desk. The president frowned and cleared his throat loudly. Without a break or a pause in his extemporaneous translation, Stoner looked up and spoke the next line of the poem mildly to the president and his entourage: "'Begone, begone, you bloody whoreson Gauls!'" And still without a break returned his eyes to his book and continued to speak, while the group gasped and stumbled backward, turned, and fled from the room.

Fed by such events, the legend grew until there were anecdotes to give substance to nearly all of Stoner's more typical activities, and grew until it reached his life outside the University. It finally included even Edith, who was seen with him so rarely at University functions that she was a faintly mysterious figure who flitted across the collective imagination like a ghost: she drank secretly, out of some obscure and distant sorrow; she was dying slowly of a rare and always fatal disease; she was a brilliantly talented artist who had given up her career to devote herself to Stoner. At public functions her smile flashed out of her narrow face so quickly and nervously, her eyes glinted so brightly, and she spoke so shrilly and disconnectedly that everyone was sure that her appearance masked a reality, that a self hid behind the façade that no one could believe.

After his illness, and out of an indifference that became a way of living, William Stoner began to spend more and more of his time in the house that he and Edith had bought many years ago. At first Edith was so disconcerted by his presence that she was silent, as if puzzled about something. Then, when she was convinced that his presence, afternoon after afternoon, night after night, weekend after weekend, was to be a permanent condition, she waged an old battle with new intensity. Upon the most trivial provocation she wept forlornly and wandered through the rooms; Stoner looked at her impassively and murmured a few absent words of sympathy. She locked herself in her room and did not emerge for hours at a time; Stoner prepared the meals that she would otherwise have prepared and didn't seem to have noticed her absence when she finally emerged from her room, pale and hollow of cheek and eye. She derided him upon the slightest occasion, and he hardly seemed to hear her; she screamed imprecations upon him, and he listened with polite interest. When he was immersed in a book, she chose that moment to go into the living room and pound with frenzy upon the piano that she seldom otherwise played; and when he spoke quietly to his daughter, Edith would burst into anger at either or both of them. And Stoner looked upon it all—the rage, the woe, the screams, and the hateful silences—as if it were happening to two other people, in whom, by an effort of the will, he could summon only the most perfunctory interest.

And at last—wearily, almost gratefully—Edith accepted her defeat. The rages decreased in intensity until they became as perfunctory as Stoner's interest in them; and the long silences became withdrawals into a privacy at which Stoner no longer wondered, rather than offenses upon an indifferent position.

In her fortieth year, Edith Stoner was as thin as she had been as a girl, but with a hardness, a brittleness, that came from an unbending carriage, that made every movement seem reluctant and grudging. The bones of her face had sharpened, and the thin pale skin was stretched upon them as upon a framework, so that the lines upon the skin were taut and sharp. She was very pale, and she used a great deal of powder and paint in such a way that it appeared she daily composed her own features upon a blank mask. Beneath the dry hard skin, her hands seemed all bone; and they moved ceaselessly, twisting and plucking and clenching even in her quietest moments.

Always withdrawn, she grew in these middle years increasingly remote and absent. After the brief period of her last assault upon Stoner, which flared with a final, desperate intensity, she wandered like a ghost into the privacy of herself, a place from which she never fully emerged. She began to speak to herself, with the kind of soft reasonableness that one uses with a child; she did so openly and without self-consciousness, as if it were the most natural thing she could do. Of the scattered artistic endeavors with which she had occupied herself intermittently during her marriage, she finally settled upon sculpture as the most "satisfying." She modeled clay mostly, though she occasionally worked with the softer stones; busts and figures and compositions of all sorts were scattered about the house. She was very modern: the busts she modeled were minimally featured spheres, the figures were blobs of clay with elongated appendages, and the compositions were random geometric gatherings of cubes and spheres and rods. Sometimes, passing her studio—the room that had once been his study—Stoner would pause and listen to her work. She gave herself directions, as if to a child: "Now, you must put that here —not too much—here, right beside the little gouge. Oh, look, it's falling off. It wasn't wet enough, was it? Well, we can fix that, can't we? Just a little more water, and—there. You see?"

She got in the habit of talking to her husband and daughter in the third person, as if they were someone other than those to whom she spoke. She would say to Stoner: "Willy had better finish his coffee; it's almost nine o'clock, and he wouldn't want to be late to class." Or she would say to her daughter: "Grace really isn't practicing her piano enough. An hour a day at least, it ought to be two. What's going to happen to that talent? A shame, a shame."

What this withdrawal meant to Grace, Stoner did not know; for in her own way she had become as remote and withdrawn as her mother. She had got the habit of silence; and though she reserved a shy, soft smile for her father, she would not talk to him. During the summer of his illness she had, when she could do so unobserved, slipped into his little room and sat beside him and looked with him out the window, apparently content only to be with him; but even then she had been silent and had become restless when he attempted to draw her out of herself.

That summer of his illness she was twelve years old, a tall, thin girl with a delicate face and hair that was more blond than red. In the fall, during Edith's last violent assault upon her husband, her marriage, herself, and what she thought she had become, Grace had become almost motionless, as if she felt that any movement might throw her into an abyss from which she would not be able to clamber. In an aftermath of the violence, Edith decided, with the kind of sure recklessness of which she was capable, that Grace was quiet because she was unhappy and that she was unhappy because she was not popular with her schoolmates. She transferred the fading violence of her assault upon Stoner to an assault upon what she called Grace's "social life." Once again she took an "interest"; she dressed her daughter brightly and fashionably in clothes whose frilliness intensified her thinness, she had parties and played the piano and insisted brightly that everyone dance, she nagged at Grace to smile at everyone, to talk, to make jokes, to laugh.

This assault lasted for less than a month; then Edith dropped her campaign and began the long slow journey to where she obscurely was going. But the effects of the assault upon Grace were out of proportion to its duration.

After the assault, she spent nearly all her free time alone in her room, listening to the small radio her father had given her on her twelfth birthday. She lay motionless on her unmade bed, or sat motionless at her desk, and listened to the sounds that blared thinly from the scrollwork of the squat, ugly instrument on her bedside table, as if the voices, music, and laughter she heard were all that remained of her identity and as if even that were fading distantly into silence, beyond her recall.

And she grew fat. Between that winter and her thirteenth birthday she gained nearly fifty pounds; her face grew puffy and dry like rising dough, and her limbs became soft and slow and clumsy. She ate little more than she had eaten before, though she became very fond of sweets and kept a box of candy always in her room; it was as if something inside her had gone loose and soft and hopeless, as if at last a shapelessness within her had struggled and burst loose and now persuaded her flesh to specify that dark and secret existence.

Stoner looked upon the transformation with a sadness that belied the indifferent face he presented to the world. He did not allow himself the easy luxury of guilt; given his own nature and the circumstance of his life with Edith, there was nothing that he could have done. And that knowledge intensified his sadness as no guilt could have, and made his love for his daughter more searching and more deep.

She was, he knew—and had known very early, he supposed —one of those rare and always lovely humans whose moral nature was so delicate that it must be nourished and cared for that it might be fulfilled. Alien to the world, it had to live where it could not be at home; avid for tenderness and quiet, it had to feed upon indifference and callousness and noise. It was a nature that, even in the strange and inimical place where it had to live, had not the savagery to fight off the brutal forces that opposed it and could only withdraw to a quietness where it was forlorn and small and gently still.

When she was seventeen years old, during the first part of her senior year in high school, another transformation came upon her. It was as if her nature had found its hiding place and she was able at last to present an appearance to the world. As rapidly as she had gained it, she lost the weight she had put on three years before; and to those who had known her she seemed one whose transformation partook of magic, as if she had emerged from a chrysalis into an air for which she had been designed. She was almost beautiful; her body, which had been very thin and then suddenly very fat, was delicately limbed and soft, and it walked with a light grace. It was a passive beauty that she had, almost a placid one; her face was nearly without expression, like a mask; her light blue eyes looked directly at one, without curiosity and without any apprehension that one might see beyond them; her voice was very soft, a little flat, and she spoke rarely.

Quite suddenly she became, in Edith's word, "popular." The telephone rang frequently for her, and she sat in the living room, nodding now and then, responding softly and briefly to the voice; cars drove up in the dusky afternoons and carried her away, anonymous in the shouting and laughter. Sometimes Stoner stood at the front window and watched the automobiles screech away in clouds of dust, and he felt a small concern and a little awe; he had never owned a car and had never learned to drive one.

And Edith was pleased. "You see?" she said in absent triumph, as if more than three years had not passed since her frenzied attack upon the problem of Grace's "popularity." "You see? I was right. All she needed was a little push. And Willy didn't approve. Oh, I could tell. Willy never approves."

For a number of years, Stoner had, every month, put aside a few dollars so that Grace could, when the time came, go away from Columbia to a college, perhaps an eastern one, some distance away. Edith had known of these plans, and she had seemed to approve; but when the time came, she would not hear of it.

"Oh, no!" she said. "I couldn't bear it! My baby! And she *has* done so well here this last year. So popular, and so happy. She would have to adjust, and—baby, Gracie, baby"—she turned to her daughter—"Gracie doesn't *really* want to go away from her mommy. Does she? Leave her all alone?"

Grace looked at her mother silently for a moment. She turned very briefly to her father and shook her head. She said to her mother, "If you want me to stay, of course I will."

"Grace," Stoner said. "Listen to me. If you want to go— please, if you really want to go—"

She would not look at him again. "It doesn't matter," she said.

Before Stoner could say anything else, Edith began talking about how they could spend the money her father had saved on a new wardrobe, a really nice one, perhaps even a little car so that she and her friends could . . . And Grace smiled her slow small smile and nodded and every now and then said a word, as if it were expected of her.

It was settled; and Stoner never knew what Grace felt, whether she stayed because she wanted to, or because her mother wanted her to, or out of a vast indifference to her own fate. She would enter the University of Missouri as a freshman that fall, go there for at least two years, after which, if she wanted, she would be allowed to go away, out of the state, to finish her college work. Stoner told himself that it was better this way, better for Grace to endure the prison she hardly knew she was in for two more years, than to be torn again upon the rack of Edith's helpless will.

So nothing changed. Grace got her wardrobe, refused her mother's offer of a little car, and entered the University of Missouri as a freshman student. The telephone continued to ring, the same faces (or ones much like them) continued to appear laughing and shouting at the front door, and the same automobiles roared away in the dusk. Grace was away from home even more frequently than she had been in high school, and Edith was pleased at what she thought to be her daughter's growing popularity. "She's like her mother," she said. "Before she was married she was *very* popular. All the boys . . . Papa used to get so mad at them, but he was secretly very proud, I could tell."

"Yes, Edith," Stoner said gently, and he felt his heart contract.

It was a difficult semester for Stoner; it had come his turn to administer the university-wide junior English examination, and he was at the same time engaged in directing two particularly difficult doctoral dissertations, both of which required a great deal of extra reading on his part. So he was away from home more frequently than had been his habit for the last few years.

One evening, near the end of November, he came home even later than usual. The lights were off in the living room, and the house was quiet; he supposed that Grace and Edith were in bed. He took some papers he had brought with him to his little back room, intending to read a few of them after he got into bed. He went into the kitchen to get a sandwich and a glass of milk; he had sliced the bread and opened the refrigerator door when suddenly he heard, sharp and clean as a knife, a prolonged scream from somewhere downstairs. He ran into the living room; the scream came again, now short and somehow angry in its intensity, from Edith's studio. Swiftly he went across the room and opened the door.

Edith was sitting sprawled on the floor, as if she had fallen there; her eyes were wild, and her mouth was open, ready to emit another scream. Grace sat across the room from her on an upholstered chair, her knees crossed, and looked almost calmly at her mother. A single desk lamp, on Edith's work table, was burning, so that the room was filled with harsh brightness and deep shadows.

"What is it?" Stoner asked. "What's happened?"

Edith's head swung around to face him as if it were on a loose pivot; her eyes were vacant. She said with a curious petulance, "Oh, Willy. Oh, Willy." She continued to look at him, her head shaking weakly.

He turned to Grace, whose look of calm did not change.

She said conversationally, "I'm pregnant, Father."

And the scream came again, piercing and inexpressibly angry; they both turned to Edith, who looked back and forth, from one to the other, the eyes absent and cool above the screaming mouth. Stoner went across the room, stooped behind her, and lifted her upright; she was loose in his arms, and he had to support her weight.

"Edith!" he said sharply. "Be quiet."

She stiffened and pulled away from him. On trembling legs she stalked across the room and stood above Grace, who had not moved.

"You!" she spat. "Oh, my God. Oh, Gracie. How could you —oh, my God. Like your father. Your father's blood. Oh, yes. Filth. Filth—"

"Edith!" Stoner spoke more sharply and strode over to her. He placed his hands firmly on her upper arms and turned her away from Grace. "Go to the bathroom and throw some cold water on your face. Then go up to your room and lie down."

"Oh, Willy," Edith said pleadingly. "My own little baby. My very own. How could this happen? How could she—"

"Go on," Stoner said. "I'll call you after a while."

She tottered out of the room. Stoner looked after her without moving until he heard the tap water start in the bathroom. Then he turned to Grace, who remained looking up at him from the easy chair. He smiled at her briefly, walked across to Edith's work table, got a straight chair, brought it back, and placed it in front of Grace's chair, so that he could talk to her without looking down upon her upturned face.

"Now," he said, "why don't you tell me about it?"

She gave him her small soft smile. "There isn't much to tell," she said. "I'm pregnant."

"Are you sure?"

She nodded. "I've been to a doctor. I just got the report this afternoon."

"Well," he said and awkwardly touched her hand. "You aren't to worry. Everything will be all right."

"Yes," she said.

He asked gently, "Do you want to tell me who the father is?"

"A student," she said. "At the University."

"Had you rather not tell me?"

"Oh, no," she said. "It doesn't make any difference. His name is Frye. Ed Frye. He's a sophomore. I believe he was in your freshman comp class last year."

"I don't remember him," Stoner said. "I don't remember him at all."

"I'm sorry, Father," Grace said. "It was stupid. He was a little drunk, and we didn't take—precautions."

Stoner looked away from her, at the floor.

"I'm sorry, Father. I've shocked you, haven't I?"

"No," Stoner said. "Surprised me, perhaps. We really haven't known each other very well these last few years, have we?"

She looked away and said uncomfortably, "Well—I suppose not."

"Do you—love this boy, Grace?"

"Oh, no," she said. "I really don't know him very well."

He nodded. "What do you want to do?"

"I don't know," she said. "It really doesn't matter. I don't want to be a bother."

They sat without speaking for a long time. Finally Stoner said, "Well, you aren't to worry. It will be all right. Whatever you decide—whatever you want to do, it will be all right."

"Yes," Grace said. She rose from the chair. Then she looked down at her father and said, "You and I, we can talk now."

"Yes," Stoner said. "We can talk."

She went out of the studio, and Stoner waited until he heard her bedroom door close upstairs. Then, before he went to his own room, he went softly upstairs and opened the door to Edith's bedroom. Edith was fast asleep, sprawled fully clothed on her bed, the bedside light harsh upon her face. Stoner turned the light out and went downstairs.

The next morning at breakfast Edith was almost cheerful; she gave no sign of her hysteria of the night before, and she spoke as if the future were a hypothetical problem to be solved. After she learned the name of the boy she said brightly, "Well, now. Do you think we ought to get in touch with the parents or should we talk to the boy first? Let's see—this is the last week in November. Let's say two weeks. We can make all the arrangements by then, maybe even a small church wedding. Gracie, what does your friend, what's his name—?"

"Edith," Stoner said. "Wait. You're taking too much for granted. Perhaps Grace and this young man don't want to get married. We need to talk it out with Grace."

"What's there to talk about? Of course they'll want to get married. After all, they—they— Gracie, *tell* your father. Explain to him."

Grace said to him, "It doesn't matter, Father. It doesn't matter at all."

And it didn't matter, Stoner realized; Grace's eyes were fixed beyond him, into a distance she could not see and which she contemplated without curiosity. He remained silent and let his wife and daughter make their plans.

It was decided that Grace's "young man," as Edith called him, as if his name were somehow forbidden, would be invited to the house and that he and Edith would "talk." She arranged the afternoon as if it were a scene in a drama, with exits and entrances and even a line or two of dialogue. Stoner was to excuse himself, Grace was to remain for a few moments more and then excuse herself, leaving Edith and the young man alone to talk. In half an hour Stoner was to return, then Grace was to return, by which time all arrangements were to be completed.

And it all worked out exactly as Edith planned. Later Stoner wondered, with amusement, what young Edward Frye thought when he knocked timidly on the door and was admitted to a room that seemed filled with mortal enemies. He was a tall, rather heavy young man, with blurred and faintly sullen features; he was caught in a numbing embarrassment and fear, and he would look at no one. When Stoner left the room he saw the young man sitting slumped in a chair, his forearms on his knees, staring at the floor; when, half an hour later, he came back into the room, the young man was in the same position, as if he had not moved before the barrage of Edith's birdlike cheerfulness.

But everything was settled. In a high, artificial, but genuinely cheerful voice Edith informed him that "Grace's young man" came from a very good St. Louis family, his father was a broker and had probably at one time had dealings with her *own* father, or at least her father's bank, that the "young people" had decided on a wedding, "as soon as possible, very informal," that both were dropping out of school, at least for a year or two, that they would live in St. Louis, "a change of scenery, a new start," that though they wouldn't be able to finish the semester they would go to school until the semester break, and they would be married on the afternoon of that day, which was a Friday. And wasn't it all sweet, really—no matter what.

The wedding took place in the cluttered study of a justice of the peace. Only William and Edith witnessed the ceremony; the justice's wife, a rumpled gray woman with a permanent frown, worked in the kitchen while the ceremony was performed and came out when it was over only to sign the papers as a witness. It was a cold, bleak afternoon; the date was December 12, 1941.

Five days before the marriage took place the Japanese had bombed Pearl Harbor; and William Stoner watched the ceremony with a mixture of feeling that he had not had before. Like many others who went through that time, he was gripped by what he could think of only as a numbness, though he knew it was a feeling compounded of emotions so deep and intense that they could not be acknowledged because they could not be lived with. It was the force of a public tragedy he felt, a horror and a woe so all-pervasive that private tragedies and personal misfortunes were removed to another state of being, yet were intensified by the very vastness in which they took place, as the poignancy of a lone grave might be intensified by a great desert surrounding it. With a pity that was almost impersonal he watched the sad little ritual of the marriage and was oddly moved by the passive, indifferent beauty of his daughter's face and by the sullen desperation on the face of the young man.

After the ceremony the two young people climbed joylessly into Frye's little roadster and left for St. Louis, where they still had to face another set of parents and where they were to live. Stoner watched them drive away from the house, and he could think of his daughter only as a very small girl who had once sat beside him in a distant room and looked at him with solemn delight, as a lovely child who long ago had died.

Two months after the marriage Edward Frye enlisted in the Army; it was Grace's decision to remain in St. Louis until the birth of her child. Within six months Frye was dead upon the beach of a small Pacific island, one of a number of raw recruits that had been sent out in a desperate effort to halt the Japanese advance. In June of 1942 Grace's child was born; it was a boy, and she named it after the father it had never seen and would not love.

Though Edith, when she went to St. Louis that June to "help out," tried to persuade her daughter to return to Columbia, Grace would not do so; she had a small apartment, a small income from Frye's insurance, and her new parents-in-law, and she seemed happy.

"Changed somehow," Edith said distractedly to Stoner. "Not our little Gracie at all. She's been through a lot, and I guess she doesn't want to be reminded . . . She sent you her love."

XVI

THE YEARS of the war blurred together, and Stoner went through them as he might have gone through a driving and nearly unendurable storm, his head down, his jaw locked, his mind fixed upon the next step and the next and the next. Yet for all his stoical endurance and his stolid movement through the days and weeks, he was an intensely divided man. One part of him recoiled in instinctive horror at the daily waste, the inundation of destruction and death that inexorably assaulted the mind and heart; once again he saw the faculty depleted, he saw the classrooms emptied of their young men, he saw the haunted looks upon those who remained behind, and saw in those looks the slow death of the heart, the bitter attrition of feeling and care.

Yet another part of him was drawn intensely toward that very holocaust from which he recoiled. He found within himself a capacity for violence he did not know he had: he yearned for involvement, he wished for the taste of death, the bitter joy of destruction, the feel of blood. He felt both shame and pride, and over it all a bitter disappointment, in himself and in the time and circumstance that made him possible.

Week by week, month by month, the names of the dead rolled out before him. Sometimes they were only names that he remembered as if from a distant past; sometimes he could evoke a face to go with a name; sometimes he could recall a voice, a word.

Through it all he continued to teach and study, though he sometimes felt that he hunched his back futilely against the driving storm and cupped his hands uselessly around the dim flicker of his last poor match.

Occasionally Grace returned to Columbia for a visit with her parents. The first time she brought her son, barely a year old; but his presence seemed obscurely to bother Edith, so thereafter she left him in St. Louis with his paternal grandparents when she visited. Stoner would have liked to see more of his grandson, but he did not mention that wish; he had come to realize that Grace's removal from Columbia—perhaps even

459

her pregnancy—was in reality a flight from a prison to which she now returned out of an ineradicable kindness and a gentle good will.

Though Edith did not suspect it or would not admit it, Grace had, Stoner knew, begun to drink with a quiet seriousness. He first knew it during the summer of the year after the war had ended. Grace had come to visit them for a few days; she seemed particularly worn; her eyes were shadowed, and her face was tense and pale. One evening after dinner Edith went to bed early, and Grace and Stoner sat together in the kitchen, drinking coffee. Stoner tried to talk to her, but she was restless and distraught. They sat in silence for many minutes; finally Grace looked at him intently, shrugged her shoulders, and sighed abruptly.

"Look," she said, "do you have any liquor in the house?"

"No," he said, "I'm afraid not. There may be a bottle of sherry in the cupboard, but—"

"I've got most desperately to have a drink. Do you mind if I call the drugstore and have them send a bottle over?"

"Of course not," Stoner said. "It's just that your mother and I don't usually—"

But she had got up and gone into the living room. She riffled through the pages of the phone book and dialed savagely. When she came back to the kitchen she passed the table, went to the cupboard, and pulled out the half-full bottle of sherry. She got a glass from the drainboard and filled it nearly to the brim with the light brown wine. Still standing, she drained the glass and wiped her lips, shuddering a little. "It's gone sour," she said. "And I hate sherry."

She brought the bottle and the glass back to the table, sat down, and placed them precisely in front of her. She half-filled the glass and looked at her father with an odd little smile.

"I drink a little more than I ought to," she said. "Poor Father. You didn't know that, did you?"

"No," he said.

"Every week I tell myself, next week I won't drink quite so much; but I always drink a little more. I don't know why."

"Are you unhappy?" Stoner asked.

"No," she said. "I believe I'm happy. Or almost happy anyway. It isn't that. It's—" She did not finish.

By the time she had drunk the last of the sherry the delivery boy from the drugstore had come with her whisky. She brought the bottle into the kitchen, opened it with a practiced gesture, and poured a stiff portion of it into the sherry glass.

They sat up very late, until the first gray crept upon the windows. Grace drank steadily, in small sips; and as the night wore on, the lines in her face eased, she grew calm and younger, and the two of them talked as they had not been able to talk for years.

"I suppose," she said, "I suppose I got pregnant deliberately, though I didn't know it at the time; I suppose I didn't even know how badly I wanted, how badly I *had* to get away from here. I knew enough not to get pregnant unless I wanted to, Lord knows. All those boys in high school, and"—she smiled crookedly at her father—"you and mamma, you didn't know, did you?"

"I suppose not," he said.

"Mamma wanted me to be popular, and—well, I was popular, all right. It didn't mean anything, not anything at all."

"I knew you were unhappy," Stoner said with difficulty. "But I never realized—I never knew—"

"I suppose I didn't either," she said. "I couldn't have. Poor Ed. He's the one that got the rotten deal. I used him, you know; oh, he was the father all right—but I used him. He was a nice boy, and always so ashamed—he couldn't stand it. He joined up six months before he had to, just to get away from it. I killed him, I suppose; he was such a nice boy, and we couldn't even like each other very much."

They talked late into the night, as if they were old friends. And Stoner came to realize that she was, as she had said, almost happy with her despair; she would live her days out quietly, drinking a little more, year by year, numbing herself against the nothingness her life had become. He was glad she had that, at least; he was grateful that she could drink.

The years immediately following the end of the Second World War were the best years of his teaching; and they were in some ways the happiest years of his life. Veterans of that war descended upon the campus and transformed it, bringing to it a quality of life it had not had before, an intensity and turbulence that amounted to a transformation. He worked harder than he had ever worked; the students, strange in their maturity, were intensely serious and contemptuous of triviality. Innocent of fashion or custom, they came to their studies as Stoner had dreamed that a student might—as if those studies were life itself and not specific means to specific ends. He knew that never, after these few years, would teaching be quite the same; and he committed himself to a happy state of exhaustion which he hoped might never end. He seldom thought of the past or the future, or of the disappointments and joys of either; he concentrated all the energies of which he was capable upon the moment of his work and hoped that he was at last defined by what he did.

Rarely during these years was he removed from this dedication to the moment of his work. Sometimes when his daughter came back to Columbia for a visit, as if wandering aimlessly from one room to another, he had a sense of loss that he could scarcely bear. At the age of twenty-five she looked ten years older; she drank with the steady diffidence of one utterly without hope; and it became clear that she was relinquishing more and more control of her child to the grandparents in St. Louis.

Only once did he have news of Katherine Driscoll. In the early spring of 1949 he received a circular from the press of a large eastern university; it announced the publication of Katherine's book, and gave a few words about the author. She was teaching at a good liberal arts college in Massachusetts; she was unmarried. He got a copy of the book as soon as he could. When he held it in his hands his fingers seemed to come alive; they trembled so that he could scarcely open it. He turned the first few pages and saw the dedication: "To W.S."

His eyes blurred, and for a long time he sat without moving. Then he shook his head, returned to the book, and did not put it down until he had read it through.

It was as good as he had thought it would be. The prose was graceful, and its passion was masked by a coolness and clarity of intelligence. It was herself he saw in what he read, he realized; and he marveled at how truly he could see her even now. Suddenly it was as if she were in the next room, and he had only moments before left her; his hands tingled, as if they had touched her. And the sense of his loss, that he had for so long dammed within him, flooded out, engulfed him, and he let himself be carried outward, beyond the control of his will; he did not wish to save himself. Then he smiled fondly, as if at a memory; it occurred to him that he was nearly sixty years old and that he ought to be beyond the force of such passion, of such love.

But he was not beyond it, he knew, and would never be. Beneath the numbness, the indifference, the removal, it was there, intense and steady; it had always been there. In his youth he had given it freely, without thought; he had given it to the knowledge that had been revealed to him—how many years ago?—by Archer Sloane; he had given it to Edith, in those first blind foolish days of his courtship and marriage; and he had given it to Katherine, as if it had never been given before. He had, in odd ways, given it to every moment of his life, and had perhaps given it most fully when he was unaware of his giving. It was a passion neither of the mind nor of the flesh; rather, it was a force that comprehended them both, as if they were but the matter of love, its specific substance. To a woman or to a poem, it said simply: Look! I am alive.

He could not think of himself as old. Sometimes, in the morning when he shaved, he looked at his image in the glass and felt no identity with the face that stared back at him in surprise, the eyes clear in a grotesque mask; it was as if he wore, for an obscure reason, an outrageous disguise, as if he could, if he wished, strip away the bushy white eyebrows, the rumpled white hair, the flesh that sagged around the sharp bones, the deep lines that pretended age.

Yet his age, he knew, was not pretense. He saw the sickness of the world and of his own country during the years after the great war; he saw hatred and suspicion become a kind of madness that swept across the land like a swift plague; he saw young men go again to war, marching eagerly to a senseless doom, as if in the echo of a nightmare. And the pity and sadness he felt were so old, so much a part of his age, that he seemed to himself nearly untouched.

The years went swiftly, and he was hardly aware of their passing. In the spring of 1954 he was sixty-three years old; and he suddenly realized that he had at the most four years of teaching left to him. He tried to see beyond that time; he could not see, and had no wish to do so.

That fall he received a note from Gordon Finch's secretary, asking him to drop by to see the dean whenever it was convenient. He was busy, and it was several days before he found a free afternoon.

Every time he saw Gordon Finch, Stoner was conscious of a small surprise at how little he had aged. A year younger than Stoner, he looked no more than fifty. He was wholly bald, his face was heavy and unlined, and it glowed with an almost cherubic health; his step was springy, and in these later years he had begun to affect a casualness of dress; he wore colorful shirts and odd jackets.

He seemed embarrassed that afternoon when Stoner came in to see him. They talked casually for a few moments; Finch asked him about Edith's health and mentioned that his own wife, Caroline, had been talking just the other day about how they all ought to get together again. Then he said, "Time. My God, how it flies!"

Stoner nodded.

Finch sighed abruptly. "Well," he said, "I guess we've got to talk about it. You'll be—sixty-five next year. I suppose we ought to be making some plans."

Stoner shook his head. "Not right away. I intend to take advantage of the two-year option, of course."

"I figured you would," Finch said and leaned back in his chair. "Not me. I have three years to go and I'm getting out. I think sometimes about what I've missed, the places I haven't been to, and—hell, Bill, life's too short. Why don't you get out too? Think of all the time—"

"I wouldn't know what to do with it," Stoner said. "I've never learned."

"Well, hell," Finch said. "This day and age, sixty-five's pretty young. There's time to learn things that—"

"It's Lomax, isn't it? He's putting the squeeze on you."

Finch grinned. "Sure. What did you expect?"

Stoner was silent for a moment. Then he said, "You tell Lomax that I wouldn't talk to you about it. Tell him that I've become so cantankerous and ornery in my old age that you can't do a thing with me. That he's going to have to do it himself."

Finch laughed and shook his head. "By God, I will. After all these years, maybe you two old bastards will unbend a little."

But the confrontation did not take place at once, and when it did—in the middle of the second semester, in March—it did not take the form that Stoner expected. Once again he was requested to appear at the dean's office; a time was specified, and urgency was hinted.

Stoner came in a few minutes late. Lomax was already there; he sat stiffly in front of Finch's desk; there was an empty chair beside him. Stoner walked slowly across the room and sat down. He turned his head and looked at Lomax; Lomax stared imperturbably in front of him, one eyebrow lifted in a general disdain.

Finch stared at both of them for several moments, a little smile of amusement on his face.

"Well," he said, "we all know the matter before us. It is that of Professor Stoner's retirement." He sketched the regulations—voluntary retirement was possible at sixty-five; under this option, Stoner could if he wished retire either at the end of the current academic year, or at the end of either semester of the following year. Or he could, if it were agreed upon by the chairman of the department, the dean of the college, and the professor concerned, extend his retirement age to sixty-seven, at which time retirement was mandatory. Unless, of course, the person concerned were given a Distinguished Professorship and awarded a Chair, in which event—

"A most remote likelihood, I believe we can agree," Lomax said dryly.

Stoner nodded to Finch. "Most remote."

"I frankly believe," Lomax said to Finch, "it would be in the best interests of the department and college if Professor Stoner would take advantage of his opportunity to retire. There are certain curricular and personnel changes that I have long contemplated, which this retirement would make possible."

Stoner said to Finch, "I have no wish to retire before I have to, merely to accommodate a whim of Professor Lomax."

Finch turned to Lomax. Lomax said, "I'm sure that there is a great deal that Professor Stoner has not considered. He would have the leisure to do some of the writing that his"—he paused delicately—"his dedication to teaching has prevented him from doing. Surely the academic community would be edified if the fruit of his long experience were—"

Stoner interrupted, "I have no desire to begin a literary career at this stage in my life."

Lomax, without moving from his chair, seemed to bow to Finch. "I'm sure our colleague is too modest. Within two years I myself will be forced by regulations to vacate the chairmanship of the department. I certainly intend to put my declining years to good use; indeed, I look forward to the leisure of my retirement."

Stoner said, "I hope to remain a member of the department, at least until that auspicious occasion."

Lomax was silent for a moment. Then he said contemplatively to Finch, "It has occurred to me several times during the past few years that Professor Stoner's efforts on behalf of the University have perhaps not been fully appreciated. It has occurred to me that a promotion to full professor might be a fitting climax to his retirement year. A dinner in honor of the occasion—a fitting ceremony. It should be most gratifying. Though it is late in the year, and though most of the promotions have already been declared, I am sure that, if I insisted, a promotion might be arranged for next year, in commemoration of an auspicious retirement."

Suddenly the game that he had been playing with Lomax —and, in a curious way, enjoying—seemed trivial and mean. A tiredness came over him. He looked directly at Lomax and said wearily, "Holly, after all these years, I thought you knew me better than that. I've never cared a damn for what you thought you could 'give' me, or what you thought you could 'do' to me, or whatever." He paused; he was, indeed, more tired than he had thought. He continued with an effort, "That isn't the point; it has never been the point. You're a good man, I suppose; certainly you're a good teacher. But in some ways you're an ignorant son-of-a-bitch." He paused again. "I don't know what you hoped for. But I won't retire—not at the end of this year, nor the end of the next." He got up slowly and stood for a moment, gathering his strength. "If you gentlemen will excuse me, I'm a little tired. I'll leave you to discuss whatever it is you have to discuss."

He knew that it would not end there, but he did not care. When, at the last general faculty meeting of the year, Lomax, in his departmental report to the faculty, announced the retirement at the end of the next year of Professor William Stoner, Stoner got to his feet and informed the faculty that Professor Lomax was in error, that the retirement would not be effective until two years after the time that Lomax had announced. At the beginning of the fall semester the new president of the University invited Stoner to his home for afternoon tea and spoke expansively of the years of his service, of the well-earned rest, of the gratitude they all felt; Stoner put on his most crotchety manner, called the president "young man," and pretended not to hear, so that at last the young man ended by shouting in the most placatory tone he could manage.

But his efforts, meager as they were, tired him more than he had expected, so that by Christmas vacation he was nearly exhausted. He told himself that he was, indeed, getting old, and that he would have to let up if he were to do a good job the rest of the year. During the ten days of Christmas vacation he rested, as if he might hoard his strength; and when he returned for the last weeks of the semester he worked with a vigor and energy that surprised him. The issue of his retirement seemed settled, and he did not bother to think of it again.

Late in February the tiredness came over him again, and he could not seem to shake it off; he spent a great deal of his time at home and did much of his paper work propped on the day bed in his little back room. In March he became aware of a dull general pain in his legs and arms; he told himself that he was tired, that he would be better when the warm spring days came, that he needed rest. By April the pain had become localized in the lower part of his body; occasionally he missed a class, and he found that it took most of his strength merely to walk from class to class. In early May the pain became intense, and he could no longer think of it as a minor nuisance. He made an appointment with a doctor at the University infirmary.

There were tests and examinations and questions, the import of which Stoner only vaguely understood. He was given a special diet, some pills for the pain, and was told to come back at the beginning of the next week for consultation, when the results of the tests would be completed and put together. He felt better, though the tiredness remained.

His doctor was a young man named Jamison, who had explained to Stoner that he was working for the University for a few years before he went into private practice. He had a pink, round face, wore rimless glasses, and had a kind of nervous awkwardness of manner that Stoner trusted.

Stoner was a few minutes early for his appointment, but the receptionist told him to go right in. He went down the long narrow hall of the infirmary to the little cubicle where Jamison had his office.

Jamison was waiting for him, and it was clear to Stoner that he had been waiting for some time; folders and X-rays and notes were laid out neatly on his desk. Jamison stood up, smiled abruptly and nervously, and extended his hand toward a chair in front of his desk.

"Professor Stoner," he said. "Sit down, sit down."

Stoner sat.

Jamison frowned at the display on his desk, smoothed a sheet of paper, and let himself down on his chair. "Well," he said, "there's some sort of obstruction in the lower intestinal tract, that's clear. Not much shows up on the X-rays, but that isn't unusual. Oh, a little cloudiness; but that doesn't necessarily mean anything." He turned his chair, set an X-ray in a frame, switched on a light, and pointed vaguely. Stoner looked, but he could see nothing. Jamison switched off the light and turned back to his desk. He became very businesslike. "Your blood count's down pretty low, but there doesn't seem to be any infection there; your sedimentation is subnormal and your blood pressure's down. There is some internal swelling that doesn't seem quite right, you've lost quite a bit of weight, and—well, with the symptoms you've shown and from what I can tell from these"—he waved at his desk—"I'd say there's only one thing to do." He smiled fixedly and said with strained jocularity, "We've just got to go in there and see what we can find out."

Stoner nodded. "It's cancer then."

"Well," Jamison said, "that's a pretty big word. It can mean a lot of things. I'm pretty sure there's a tumor there, but—well, we can't be absolutely sure of anything until we go in there and look around."

"How long have I had it?"

"Oh, there's no way of telling that. But it feels like—well, it's pretty large; it's been there some time."

Stoner was silent for a moment. Then he said, "How long would you estimate I have?"

Jamison said distractedly, "Oh, now, look, Mr. Stoner." He attempted a laugh. "We mustn't jump to conclusions. Why, there's always a chance—there's a chance it's only a tumor, non-malignant, you know. Or—or it could be a lot of things. We just can't know for sure until we—"

"Yes," Stoner said. "When would you want to operate?"

"As soon as possible," Jamison said relievedly. "Within the next two or three days."

"That soon," Stoner said, almost absently. Then he looked at Jamison steadily. "Let me ask you a few questions, Doctor. I must tell you that I want you to answer them frankly."

Jamison nodded.

"If it is only a tumor—non-malignant, as you say—would a couple of weeks make any great difference?"

"Well," Jamison said reluctantly, "there would be the pain; and—no, not a *great* deal of difference, I suppose."

"Good," Stoner said. "And if it is as bad as you think it is—would a couple of weeks make a great difference *then*?"

After a long while Jamison said, almost bitterly, "No, I suppose not."

"Then," Stoner said reasonably, "I'll wait for a couple of weeks. There are a few things I need to clear up—some work I need to do."

"I don't advise it, you understand," Jamison said. "I don't advise it at all."

"Of course," Stoner said. "And, Doctor—you won't mention this to anyone, will you?"

"No," Jamison said and added with a little warmth, "of course not." He suggested a few revisions of the diet he had earlier given him, prescribed more pills, and set a date for his entrance into the hospital.

Stoner felt nothing at all; it was as if what the doctor told him were a minor annoyance, an obstacle he would have somehow to work around in order to get done what he had to do. It occurred to him that it was rather late in the year for this to be happening; Lomax might have some difficulty in finding a replacement.

The pill he had taken in the doctor's office made him a little light-headed, and he found the sensation oddly pleasurable. His sense of time was displaced; he found himself standing in the long parqueted first-floor corridor of Jesse Hall. A low hum, like the distant thrumming of birds' wings, was in his ears; in the shadowed corridor a sourceless light seemed to glow and dim, pulsating like the beat of his heart; and his flesh, intimately aware of every move he made, tingled as he stepped forward with deliberate care into the mingled light and dark.

He stood at the stairs that led up to the second floor; the steps were marble, and in their precise centers were gentle troughs worn smooth by decades of footsteps going up and down. They had been almost new when—how many years ago?—he had first stood here and looked up, as he looked now, and wondered where they would lead him. He thought of time and of its gentle flowing. He put one foot carefully in the first smooth depression and lifted himself up.

Then he was in Gordon Finch's outer office. The girl said, "Dean Finch was about to leave . . ." He nodded absently, smiled at her, and went into Finch's office.

"Gordon," he said cordially, the smile still on his face. "I won't keep you long."

Finch returned the smile reflexively; his eyes were tired. "Sure, Bill, sit down."

"I won't keep you long," he said again; he felt a curious power come into his voice. "The fact is, I've changed my mind —about retiring, I mean. I know it's awkward; sorry to be so late letting you know, but—well, I think it's best all around. I'm quitting at the end of this semester."

Finch's face floated before him, round in its amazement. "What the hell," he said. "Has anyone been putting the screws on you?"

"Nothing like that," Stoner said. "It's my own decision. It's

just that—I've discovered there *are* some things I'd like to do."
He added reasonably, "And I do need a little rest."

Finch was annoyed, and Stoner knew that he had cause to
be. He thought he heard himself murmur another apology; he
felt the smile remain foolishly on his face.

"Well," Finch said, "I guess it's not too late. I can start the
papers through tomorrow. I suppose you know all you need to
know about your annuity income, insurance, and things like
that?"

"Oh, yes," Stoner said. "I've thought of all that. It's all
right."

Finch looked at his watch. "I'm kind of late, Bill. Drop by
in a day or so and we'll clear up the details. In the meantime
—well, I suppose Lomax ought to know. I'll call him tonight."
He grinned. "I'm afraid you've succeeded in pleasing him."

"Yes," Stoner said. "I'm afraid I have."

There was much to do in the two weeks that remained before he was to go into the hospital, but he decided that he
would be able to do it. He canceled his classes for the next two
days and called into conference all those students for whom
he had the responsibility of directing independent research,
theses, and dissertations. He wrote detailed instructions that
would guide them to the completion of the work they had
begun and left carbon copies of these instructions in Lomax's
mailbox. He soothed those who were thrown into a panic by
what they considered his desertion of them and reassured those
who were fearful of committing themselves to a new adviser.
He found that the pills he had been taking reduced the clarity
of his intelligence as they relieved the pain; so in the daytime,
when he talked to students, and in the evening, when he read
the deluge of half-completed papers, theses, and dissertations,
he took them only when the pain became so intense that it
forced his attention away from his work.

Two days after his declaration of retirement, in the middle of
a busy afternoon, he got a telephone call from Gordon Finch.

"Bill? Gordon. Look—there's a small problem I think I
ought to talk to you about."

"Yes?" he said impatiently.

"It's Lomax. He can't get it through his head that you aren't
doing this on his account."

"It doesn't matter," Stoner said. "Let him think what he wants."

"Wait—that isn't all. He's making plans to go through with the dinner and everything. He says he gave his word."

"Look, Gordon, I'm very busy just now. Can't you just put a stop to it somehow?"

"I tried to, but he's doing it through the department. If you want me to call him in I will; but you'll have to be here too. When he's like this I can't talk to him."

"All right. When is this foolishness supposed to come off?"

There was a pause. "A week from Friday. The last day of classes, just before exam week."

"All right," Stoner said wearily. "I should have things cleared up by then, and it'll be easier than arguing it now. Just let it ride."

"You ought to know this too; he wants me to announce your retirement as professor emeritus, though it can't be really official until next year."

Stoner felt a laugh come up in his throat. "What the hell," he said. "That's all right too."

All that week he worked without consciousness of time. He worked straight through Friday, from eight o'clock in the morning until ten that night. He read a last page and made a last note, and leaned back in his chair; the light on his desk filled his eyes, and for a moment he did not know where he was. He looked around him and saw that he was in his office. The bookshelves were bulging with books haphazardly placed; there were stacks of papers in the corners; and his filing cabinets were open and disarranged. I ought to straighten things up, he thought; I ought to get my things in order.

"Next week," he said to himself. "Next week."

He wondered if he could make it home. It seemed an effort to breathe. He narrowed his mind, forced it upon his arms and legs, made them respond. He got to his feet, and would not let himself sway. He turned the desk light off and stood until his eyes could see by the moonlight that came through his windows. Then he put one foot before the other and walked through the dark halls to the out-of-doors and through the quiet streets to his home.

The lights were on; Edith was still up. He gathered the last of his strength and made it up the front steps and into the living room. Then he knew he could go no farther; he was able to reach the couch and to sit down. After a moment he found the strength to reach into his vest pocket and take out his tube of pills. He put one in his mouth and swallowed it without water; then he took another. They were bitter, but the bitterness seemed almost pleasant.

He became aware that Edith had been walking about the room, going from one place to another; he hoped that she had not spoken to him. As the pain eased and as some of his strength returned, he realized that she had not; her face was set, her nostrils and mouth pinched, and she walked stiffly, angrily. He started to speak to her, but he decided that he could not trust his voice. He let himself wonder why she was angry; she had not been angry for a long time.

Finally she stopped moving about and faced him; her hands were fists and they hung at her sides. "Well? Aren't you going to say anything?"

He cleared his throat and made his eyes focus. "I'm sorry, Edith." He heard his voice quiet but steady. "I'm a little tired, I guess."

"You weren't going to say anything at all, were you? Thoughtless. Didn't you think I had a right to know?"

For a moment he was puzzled. Then he nodded. If he had had more strength he would have been angry. "How did you find out?"

"Never mind that. I suppose everyone knows except me. Oh, Willy, honestly."

"I'm sorry, Edith, really, I am. I didn't want to worry you. I was going to tell you next week, just before I went in. It's nothing; you aren't to trouble yourself."

"Nothing!" She laughed bitterly. "They say it might be cancer. Don't you know what that means?"

He felt suddenly weightless, and he had to force himself not to clutch at something. "Edith," he said in a distant voice, "let's talk about it tomorrow. Please. I'm tired now."

She looked at him for a moment. "Do you want me to help you to your room?" she asked crossly. "You don't look like you'll make it by yourself."

"I'm all right," he said.

But before he got to his room he wished he had let her help him—and not only because he found himself weaker than he had expected.

He rested Saturday and Sunday, and Monday he was able to meet his classes. He went home early, and he was lying on the living-room couch gazing interestedly at the ceiling when the doorbell rang. He sat upright and started to rise, but the door opened. It was Gordon Finch. His face was pale, and his hands were unsteady.

"Come in, Gordon," Stoner said.

"My God, Bill," Finch said. "Why didn't you tell me?"

Stoner laughed shortly. "I might as well have advertised it in the newspapers," he said. "I thought I could do it quietly, without upsetting anyone."

"I know, but—Jesus, if I had known."

"There's nothing to get upset about. There's nothing definite yet—it's just an operation. Exploratory, I believe they call it. How did you find out anyway?"

"Jamison," Finch said. "He's my doctor too. He said he knew it wasn't ethical, but that I ought to know. He was right, Bill."

"I know," Stoner said. "It doesn't matter. Has the word got around?"

Finch shook his head. "Not yet."

"Then keep your mouth shut about it. Please."

"Sure, Bill," Finch said. "Now about this dinner party Friday—you don't have to go through with it, you know."

"But I will," Stoner said. He grinned. "I figure I owe Lomax something."

The ghost of a smile came upon Finch's face. "You *have* turned into an ornery old son-of-a-bitch, haven't you?"

"I guess I have," Stoner said.

The dinner was held in a small banquet room of the Student Union. At the last minute Edith decided that she wouldn't be able to sit through it, so he went alone. He went early and walked slowly across the campus, as if ambling casually on a spring afternoon. As he had anticipated, there was no one in the room; he got a waiter to remove his wife's name card and to reset the main table, so that there would not be an empty space. Then he sat down and waited for the guests to arrive.

He was seated between Gordon Finch and the president of the University; Lomax, who was to act as the master of cere-monies, was seated three chairs away. Lomax was smiling and chatting with those sitting around him; he did not look at Stoner.

The room filled quickly; members of the department who had not really spoken to him for years waved across the room to him; Stoner nodded. Finch said little, though he watched Stoner carefully; the youngish new president, whose name Stoner could never remember, spoke to him with an easy def-erence.

The food was served by young students in white coats; Stoner recognized several of them; he nodded and spoke to them. The guests looked sadly at their food and began to eat. A relaxed hum of conversation, broken by the cheery clatter of silverware and china, throbbed in the room; Stoner knew that his own presence was almost forgotten, so he was able to poke at his food, take a few ritual bites, and look around him. If he narrowed his eyes he could not see the faces; he saw colors and vague shapes moving before him, as in a frame, constructing moment by moment new patterns of contained flux. It was a pleasant sight, and if he held his attention upon it in a particu-lar way, he was not aware of the pain.

Suddenly there was silence; he shook his head, as if coming out of a dream. Near the end of the narrow table Lomax was standing, tapping on a water glass with his knife. A handsome face, Stoner thought absently; still handsome. The years had made the long thin face even thinner, and the lines seemed marks of an increased sensitivity rather than of age. The smile was still intimately sardonic, and the voice as resonant and steady as it had ever been.

He was speaking; the words came to Stoner in snatches, as if the voice that made them boomed from the silence and then diminished into its source. ". . . the long years of dedicated service . . . richly deserved rest from the pressures . . . es-teemed by his colleagues. . . ." He heard the irony and knew that, in his own way, after all these years, Lomax was speaking to him.

A short determined burst of applause startled his reverie. Beside him, Gordon Finch was standing, speaking. Though he looked up and strained his ears, he could not hear what Finch said; Gordon's lips moved, he looked fixedly in front of him, there was applause, he sat down. On the other side of him, the president got to his feet and spoke in a voice that scurried from cajolery to threat, from humor to sadness, from regret to joy. He said that he hoped Stoner's retirement would be a beginning not an ending; he knew that the University would be the poorer for his absence; there was the importance of tradition, the necessity for change; and the gratitude, for years to come, in the hearts of all his students. Stoner could not make sense of what he said; but when the president finished, the room burst into loud applause and the faces smiled. As the applause dwindled someone in the audience shouted in a thin voice: "Speech!" Someone else took up the call, and the word was murmured here and there.

Finch whispered in his ear, "Do you want me to get you out of it?"

"No," Stoner said. "It's all right."

He got to his feet, and realized that he had nothing to say. He was silent for a long time as he looked from face to face. He heard his voice issue flatly. "I have taught . . ." he said. He began again. "I have taught at this University for nearly forty years. I do not know what I would have done if I had not been a teacher. If I had not taught, I might have—" He paused, as if distracted. Then he said, with a finality, "I want to thank you all for letting me teach."

He sat down. There was applause, friendly laughter. The room broke up and people milled about. Stoner felt his hand being shaken; he was aware that he smiled and that he nodded at whatever was said to him. The president pressed his hand, smiled heartily, told him that he must drop around, any afternoon, looked at his wrist watch, and hurried out. The room began to empty, and Stoner stood alone where he had risen and gathered his strength for the walk across the room. He waited until he felt something harden inside him, and then he walked around the table and out of the room, passing little knots of people who glanced at him curiously, as if he were already a stranger. Lomax was in one of the groups, but he did not turn as Stoner passed; and Stoner found that he was grateful that they had not had to speak to each other, after all this time.

*

The next day he entered the hospital and rested until Monday morning, when the operation was to be performed. He slept much of that time and had no particular interest in what was to happen to him. On Monday morning someone stuck a needle in his arm; he was only half conscious of being rolled through halls to a strange room that seemed to be all ceiling and light. He saw something descend toward his face and he closed his eyes.

He awoke to nausea; his head ached; there was a new sharp pain, not unpleasant, in his lower body. He retched, and felt better. He let his hand move over the heavy bandages that covered the middle part of his body. He slept, wakened during the night and took a glass of water, and slept again until morning.

When he awoke, Jamison was standing beside his bed, his fingers on his left wrist.

"Well," Jamison said, "how are we feeling this morning?"

"All right, I think." His throat was dry; he reached out, and Jamison handed him the glass of water. He drank and looked at Jamison, waiting.

"Well," Jamison said at last, uncomfortably, "we got the tumor. Big feller. In a day or two you'll be feeling much better."

"I'll be able to leave here?" Stoner asked.

"You'll be up and around in two or three days," Jamison said. "The only thing is, it might be more convenient if you did stay around for a while. We couldn't get—all of it. We'll be using X-ray treatment, things like that. Of course, you could go back and forth, but—"

"No," Stoner said and let his head fall back on the pillow. He was tired again. "As soon as possible," he said, "I think I want to go home."

XVII

"OH, WILLY," she said. "You're all eaten up inside."

He was lying on the day bed in the little back room, gazing out the open window; it was late afternoon, and the sun, dipping beneath the horizon, sent a red glow upon the underside of a long rippling cloud that hung in the west above the treetops and the houses. A fly buzzed against the window screen; and the pungent aroma of trash burning in the neighbors' yards was caught in the still air.

"What?" Stoner said absently and turned to his wife.

"Inside," Edith said. "The doctor said it has spread all over. Oh, Willy, poor Willy."

"Yes," Stoner said. He could not make himself become very interested. "Well, you aren't to worry. It's best not to think about it."

She did not answer, and he turned again to the open window and watched the sky darken, until there was only a dull purplish streak upon the cloud in the distance.

He had been home for a little more than a week and had just that afternoon returned from a visit to the hospital where he had undergone what Jamison, with his strained smile, called a "treatment." Jamison had admired the speed with which his incision had healed, had said something about his having the constitution of a man of forty, and then had abruptly grown silent. Stoner had allowed himself to be poked and prodded, had let them strap him on a table, and had remained still while a huge machine hovered silently about him. It was foolishness, he knew, but he did not protest; it would have been unkind to do so. It was little enough to undergo, if it would distract them all from the knowledge they could not evade.

Gradually, he knew, this little room where he now lay and looked out the window would become his world; already he could feel the first vague beginnings of the pain that returned like the distant call of an old friend. He doubted that he would be asked to return to the hospital; he had heard in Jamison's voice this afternoon a finality, and Jamison had given him some pills to take in the event that there was "discomfort."

"You might write Grace," he heard himself saying to Edith. "She hasn't visited us in a long time."

And he turned to see Edith nodding absently; her eyes had been, with his, gazing tranquilly upon the growing darkness outside the window.

During the next two weeks he felt himself weaken, at first gradually and then rapidly. The pain returned, with an intensity that he had not expected; he took his pills and felt the pain recede into a darkness, as if it were a cautious animal.

Grace came; and he found that, after all, he had little to say to her. She had been away from St. Louis and had returned to find Edith's letter only the day before. She was worn and tense and there were dark shadows under her eyes; he wished that he could do something to ease her pain and knew that he could not.

"You look just fine, Daddy," she said. "Just fine. You're going to be all right."

"Of course," he said and smiled at her. "How is young Ed? And how have you been?"

She said that she had been fine and that young Ed was fine, that he would be entering junior high school the coming fall. He looked at her with some bewilderment. "Junior high?" he asked. Then he realized that it must be true. "Of course," he said. "I forgot how big he must be by now."

"He stays with his—with Mr. and Mrs. Frye a lot of the time," she said. "It's best for him that way." She said something else, but his attention wandered. More and more frequently he found it difficult to keep his mind focused upon any one thing; it wandered where he could not predict, and he sometimes found himself speaking words whose source he did not understand.

"Poor Daddy," he heard Grace say, and he brought his attention back to where he was. "Poor Daddy, things haven't been easy for you, have they?"

He thought for a moment and then he said, "No. But I suppose I didn't want them to be."

"Mamma and I—we've both been disappointments to you, haven't we?"

He moved his hand upward, as if to touch her. "Oh, no," he said with a dim passion. "You mustn't . . ." He wanted to say more, to explain; but he could not go on. He closed his eyes and felt his mind loosen. Images crowded there, and changed, as if upon a screen. He saw Edith as she had been that first evening they had met at old Claremont's house—the blue gown and the slender fingers and the fair, delicate face that smiled softly, the pale eyes that looked eagerly upon each moment as if it were a sweet surprise. "Your mother . . ." he said. "She was not always . . ." She was not always as she had been; and he thought now that he could perceive beneath the woman she had become the girl that she had been; he thought that he had always perceived it.

"You were a beautiful child," he heard himself saying, and for a moment he did not know to whom he spoke. Light swam before his eyes, found shape, and became the face of his daughter, lined and somber and worn with care. He closed his eyes again. "In the study. Remember? You used to sit with me when I worked. You were so still, and the light . . . the light . . ." The light of the desk lamp (he could see it now) had been absorbed by her studious small face that bent in childish absorption over a book or a picture, so that the smooth flesh glowed against the shadows of the room. He heard the small laughter echo in the distance. "Of course," he said and looked upon the present face of that child. "Of course," he said again, "you were always there."

"Hush," she said softly, "you must rest."

And that was their farewell. The next day she came down to him and said she had to get back to St. Louis for a few days and said something else he did not hear in a flat, controlled voice; her face was drawn, and her eyes were red and moist. Their gazes locked; she looked at him for a long moment, almost in disbelief; then she turned away. He knew that he would not see her again.

He had no wish to die; but there were moments, after Grace left, when he looked forward impatiently, as one might look to the moment of a journey that one does not particularly wish to take. And like any traveler, he felt that there were many things he had to do before he left; yet he could not think what they were.

He had become so weak that he could not walk; he spent his days and nights in the tiny back room. Edith brought him the books he wanted and arranged them on a table beside his narrow bed, so that he would not have to exert himself to reach them.

But he read little, though the presence of his books comforted him. He had Edith open the curtains on all the windows and would not let her close them, even when the afternoon sun, intensely hot, slanted into the room.

Sometimes Edith came into the room and sat on the bed beside him and they talked. They talked of trivial things—of people they knew casually, of a new building going up on the campus, of an old one torn down; but what they said did not seem to matter. A new tranquillity had come between them. It was a quietness that was like the beginning of love; and almost without thinking, Stoner knew why it had come. They had forgiven themselves for the harm they had done each other, and they were rapt in a regard of what their life together might have been.

Almost without regret he looked at her now; in the soft light of late afternoon her face seemed young and unlined. If I had been stronger, he thought; if I had known more; if I could have understood. And finally, mercilessly, he thought: if I had loved her more. As if it were a long distance it had to go, his hand moved across the sheet that covered him and touched her hand. She did not move; and after a while he drifted into a kind of sleep.

Despite the sedatives he took, his mind, it seemed to him, remained clear; and he was grateful for that. But it was as if some will other than his own had taken possession of that mind, moving it in directions he could not understand; time passed, and he did not see its passing.

Gordon Finch visited him nearly every day, but he could not keep the sequence of these visits clear in his memory; sometimes he spoke to Gordon when he was not there, and was surprised at his voice in the empty room; sometimes in the middle of a conversation with him he paused and blinked, as if suddenly aware of Gordon's presence. Once, when Gordon tiptoed into the room, he turned to him with a kind of surprise and asked, "Where's Dave?" And when he saw the shock of fear come over Gordon's face he shook his head weakly and said, "I'm sorry, Gordon. I was nearly asleep; I'd been thinking about Dave Masters and—sometimes I say things I'm thinking without knowing it. It's these pills I have to take."

Gordon smiled and nodded and made a joke; but Stoner knew that in that instant Gordon Finch had withdrawn from him in such a way that he could never return. He felt a keen regret that he had spoken so of Dave Masters, the defiant boy they both had loved, whose ghost had held them, all these years, in a friendship whose depth they had never quite realized.

Gordon told him of the regards that his colleagues sent him and spoke disconnectedly of University affairs that might interest him; but his eyes were restless, and the nervous smile flickered on his face.

Edith came into the room, and Gordon Finch lumbered to his feet, effusive and cordial in his relief at being interrupted.

"Edith," he said, "you sit down here."

Edith shook her head and blinked at Stoner.

"Old Bill's looking better," Finch said. "By God, I think he's looking much better than he did last week."

Edith turned to him as if noticing his presence for the first time.

"Oh, Gordon," she said. "He looks awful. Poor Willy. He won't be with us much longer."

Gordon paled and took a step backward, as if he had been struck. "My God, Edith!"

"Not much longer," Edith said again, looking broodingly at her husband, who was smiling a little. "What am I going to do, Gordon? What will I do without him?"

He closed his eyes and they disappeared; he heard Gordon whisper something and heard their footsteps as they drew away from him.

What was so remarkable was that it was so easy. He had wanted to tell Gordon how easy it was, he had wanted to tell him that it did not bother him to talk about it or to think about it; but he had been unable to do so. Now it did not seem really to matter; he heard their voices in the kitchen, Gordon's low and urgent, Edith's grudging and clipped. What were they talking about?

. . . The pain came upon him with a suddenness and an urgency that took him unprepared, so that he almost cried out. He made his hands loosen upon the bedclothes and willed them to move steadily to the night table. He took several of the pills and put them in his mouth and swallowed some water. A cold sweat broke upon his forehead and he lay very still until the pain lessened.

He heard the voices again; he did not open his eyes. Was it Gordon? His hearing seemed to go outside his body and hover like a cloud above him, transmitting to him every delicacy of sound. But his mind could not exactly distinguish the words.

The voice—was it Gordon's?—was saying something about his life. And though he could not make out the words, could not even be sure that they were being said, his own mind, with the fierceness of a wounded animal, pounced upon that question. Mercilessly he saw his life as it must appear to another.

Dispassionately, reasonably, he contemplated the failure that his life must appear to be. He had wanted friendship and the closeness of friendship that might hold him in the race of mankind; he had had two friends, one of whom had died senselessly before he was known, the other of whom had now withdrawn so distantly into the ranks of the living that . . . He had wanted the singleness and the still connective passion of marriage; he had had that, too, and he had not known what to do with it, and it had died. He had wanted love; and he had had love, and had relinquished it, had let it go into the chaos of potentiality. Katherine, he thought. "Katherine."

And he had wanted to be a teacher, and he had become one; yet he knew, he had always known, that for most of his life he had been an indifferent one. He had dreamed of a kind of integrity, of a kind of purity that was entire; he had found compromise and the assaulting diversion of triviality. He had conceived wisdom, and at the end of the long years he had found ignorance. And what else? he thought. What else?

What did you expect? he asked himself.

He opened his eyes. It was dark. Then he saw the sky outside, the deep blue-black of space, and the thin glow of moonlight through a cloud. It must be very late, he thought; it seemed only an instant ago that Gordon and Edith had stood beside him, in the bright afternoon. Or was it long ago? He could not tell.

He had known that his mind must weaken as his body wasted, but he had been unprepared for the suddenness. The flesh is strong, he thought; stronger than we imagine. It wants always to go on.

He heard voices and saw lights and felt the pain come and go. Edith's face hovered above him; he felt his face smile. Sometimes he heard his own voice speak, and he thought that it spoke rationally, though he could not be sure. He felt Edith's hands on him, moving him, bathing him. She has her child again, he thought; at last she has her child that she can care for. He wished that he could speak to her; he felt that he had something to say.

What did you expect? he thought.

Something heavy was pressing upon his eyelids. He felt them tremble and then he managed to get them open. It was light that he felt, the bright sunlight of an afternoon. He blinked and considered impassively the blue sky and the brilliant edge of the sun that he could see through his window. He decided that they were real. He moved a hand, and with the movement he felt a curious strength flow within him, as if from the air. He breathed deeply; there was no pain.

With each breath he took, it seemed to him that his strength increased; his flesh tingled, and he could feel the delicate weight of light and shade upon his face. He raised himself up from the bed, so that he was half sitting, his back supported by the wall against which the bed rested. Now he could see the out-of-doors.

He felt that he had awakened from a long sleep and was refreshed. It was late spring or early summer—more likely early summer, from the look of things. There was a richness and a sheen upon the leaves of the huge elm tree in his back yard; and the shade it cast had a deep coolness that he had known before. A thickness was in the air, a heaviness that crowded the sweet odors of grass and leaf and flower, mingling and holding them suspended. He breathed again, deeply; he heard the rasping of his breath and felt the sweetness of the summer gather in his lungs.

And he felt also, with that breath he took, a shifting some-where deep inside him, a shifting that stopped something and fixed his head so that it would not move. Then it passed, and he thought, So this is what it is like.

It occurred to him that he ought to call Edith; and then he knew that he would not call her. The dying are selfish, he thought; they want their moments to themselves, like children.

He was breathing again, but there was a difference within him that he could not name. He felt that he was waiting for something, for some knowledge; but it seemed to him that he had all the time in the world.

He heard the distant sound of laughter, and he turned his head toward its source. A group of students had cut across his back-yard lawn; they were hurrying somewhere. He saw them distinctly; there were three couples. The girls were long-limbed and graceful in their light summer dresses, and the boys were looking at them with a joyous and bemused wonder. They walked lightly upon the grass, hardly touching it, leaving no trace of where they had been. He watched them as they went out of his sight, where he could not see; and for a long time after they had vanished the sound of their laughter came to him, far and unknowing in the quiet of the summer afternoon.

What did you expect? he thought again.

A kind of joy came upon him, as if borne in on a summer breeze. He dimly recalled that he had been thinking of failure —as if it mattered. It seemed to him now that such thoughts were mean, unworthy of what his life had been. Dim presences gathered at the edge of his consciousness; he could not see them, but he knew that they were there, gathering their forces toward a kind of palpability he could not see or hear. He was approaching them, he knew; but there was no need to hurry. He could ignore them if he wished; he had all the time there was.

There was a softness around him, and a languor crept upon his limbs. A sense of his own identity came upon him with a sudden force, and he felt the power of it. He was himself, and he knew what he had been.

His head turned. His bedside table was piled with books that he had not touched for a long time. He let his hand play over

them for a moment; he marveled at the thinness of the fingers, at the intricate articulation of the joints as he flexed them.
He felt the strength within them, and let them pull a book
from the jumble on the tabletop. It was his own book that he
sought, and when the hand held it he smiled at the familiar red
cover that had for a long time been faded and scuffed.

It hardly mattered to him that the book was forgotten and
that it served no use; and the question of its worth at any
time seemed almost trivial. He did not have the illusion that
he would find himself there, in that fading print; and yet, he
knew, a small part of him that he could not deny *was* there, and
would be there.

He opened the book; and as he did so it became not his
own. He let his fingers riffle through the pages and felt a tingling, as if those pages were alive. The tingling came through
his fingers and coursed through his flesh and bone; he was minutely aware of it, and he waited until it contained him, until
the old excitement that was like terror fixed him where he lay.
The sunlight, passing his window, shone upon the page, and he
could not see what was written there.

The fingers loosened, and the book they had held moved
slowly and then swiftly across the still body and fell into the
silence of the room.

AUGUSTUS

For Nancy

AUTHOR'S NOTE

It is recorded that a famous Latin historian declared he would have made Pompey win the battle of Pharsalia had the effective turn of a sentence required it. Though I have not allowed myself such a liberty, some of the errors of fact in this book are deliberate. I have changed the order of several events; I have invented where the record is incomplete or uncertain; and I have given identities to a few characters whom history has failed to mention. I have sometimes modernized place names and Roman nomenclature, but I have not done so in all instances, preferring certain resonances to a mechanical consistency. With a few exceptions, the documents that constitute this novel are of my own invention—I have paraphrased several sentences from the letters of Cicero, I have stolen brief passages from *The Acts of Augustus*, and I have lifted a fragment from a lost book of Livy's *History* preserved by Seneca the Elder.

But if there are truths in this work, they are the truths of fiction rather than of history. I shall be grateful to those readers who will take it as it is intended—a work of the imagination.

I should like to thank The Rockefeller Foundation for a grant that enabled me to travel and begin this novel; Smith College in Northampton, Massachusetts, for affording me a period of leisure in which to continue it; and the University of Denver for a sometimes bemused but kind understanding which allowed me to complete it.

489

Prologue

Send the boy to Apollonia.

I begin abruptly, my dear niece, so that you will at once be disarmed, and so that whatever resistance you might raise will be too quick and flimsy for the force of my persuasions.

Your son left my camp at Carthage in good health; you will see him in Rome within the week. I have instructed my men to give him a leisurely journey, so that you might have this letter before his arrival.

Even now, you will have started to raise objections that seem to you to have some weight—you are a mother and a Julian, and thus doubly stubborn. I suspect I know what your objections will be; we have spoken of these matters before. You would raise the issue of his uncertain health—though you will know shortly that Gaius Octavius returns from his campaign with me in Spain more healthy than when he began it. You would question the care he might receive abroad—though a little thought should persuade you that the doctors in Apollonia are more capable of attending his ills than are the perfumed quacks in Rome. I have six legions of soldiers in and around Macedonia; and soldiers must be in good health, though senators may die and the world shall have lost little. And the Macedonian coastal weather is at least as mild as the Roman.

You are a good mother, Atia, but you have that affliction of hard morality and strictness which has sometimes disturbed our line. You must loosen your reins a little and let your son become in fact the man that he is in law. He is nearly eighteen, and you remember the portents at his birth—portents which, as you are aware, I have taken pains to augment.

You must understand the importance of the command with which I began this letter. His Greek is atrocious, and his rhetoric is weak; his philosophy is fair, but his knowledge of literature is eccentric, to say the least. Are the tutors of Rome as slothful and careless as the citizens? In Apollonia he will read philosophy and improve his Greek with Athenodorus; he will enlarge his knowledge of literature and perfect his rhetoric with Apollodorus. I have already made the necessary arrangements.

Moreover, at his age he needs to be away from Rome; he is a youth of wealth, high station, and great beauty. If the admiration of the boys and girls does not corrupt him, the ambitions of the flatterers will. (You will notice how skillfully I touch that country morality of yours.) In an atmosphere that is Spartan and disciplined, he will spend his mornings with the most learned scholars of our day, perfecting the humane art of the mind; and he will spend his afternoons with the officers of my legions, perfecting that other art without which no man is complete.

You know something of my feeling for the boy and of my plans for him; he would be my son in the fact of the law, as he is in my heart, had not the adoption been blocked by that Marcus Antonius who dreams that he will succeed me and who maneuvers among my enemies as slyly as an elephant might lumber through the Temple of the Vestal Virgins. Your Gaius stands at my right hand; but if he is to remain safely there, and take on my powers, he must have the chance to learn my strengths. He cannot do this in Rome, for I have left the most important of those strengths in Macedonia—my legions, which next summer Gaius and I will lead against the Parthians or the Germans, and which we may also need against the treasons that rise out of Rome. . . . By the way, how *is* Marcius Philippus, whom you are pleased to call your husband? He is so much a fool that I almost cherish him. Certainly I am grateful to him, for were he not so busily engaged in playing the fop in Rome and so amateurishly plotting against me with his friend Cicero, he might play at being stepfather to your son. At least your late husband, however undistinguished his own family, had the good sense to father a son and to find advancement in the Julian name; now your present husband plots against me, and would destroy that name which is the only advantage over the world that he possesses. Yet I wish all my enemies were so inept. I should admire them less, but I would be safer.

I have asked Gaius to take with him to Apollonia two friends who fought with us in Spain and who return with him now to Rome—Marcus Vipsanius Agrippa and Quintus Salvidienus Rufus, both of whom you know—and another whom you do not know, one Gaius Cilnius Maecenas. Your husband will know at once that the latter is of an old Etruscan line with some tinge of royalty; that should please him, if nothing else about this does.

You will observe, my dear Atia, that at the beginning of this letter your uncle made it appear that you had a choice about the future of your son. Now Caesar must make it clear that you do not. I shall return to Rome within the month; and, as you may have heard rumored, I shall return as dictator for life, by a decree of the Senate that has not yet been made. I have, therefore, the power to appoint a commander of cavalry, who will be second in power only to me. This I have done; and as you may have surmised, it is your son whom I have appointed. The fact is accomplished, and it will not be changed. Thus, if either you or your husband should intervene, there will be upon your house a public wrath of such weight that beside it my private scandals will seem no heavier than a mouse.

I trust that your summer at Puteoli was a pleasant one, and that you are now back in the city for the season. Restless as I am, I long for Italy now. Perhaps when I return, and after my business is done in Rome, we may spend a few quiet days at Tivoli. You may even bring your husband, and Cicero, if he will come. Despite what I say, I am really very fond of them both. As I am, of course, of you.

BOOK I

Chapter One

. . . I was with him at Actium, when the sword struck fire from metal, and the blood of soldiers was awash on deck and stained the blue Ionian Sea, and the javelin whistled in the air, and the burning hulls hissed upon the water, and the day was loud with the screams of men whose flesh roasted in the armor they could not fling off; and earlier I was with him at Mutina, where that same Marcus Antonius overran our camp and the sword was thrust into the empty bed where Caesar Augustus had lain, and where we persevered and earned the first power that was to give us the world; and at Philippi, where he traveled so ill he could not stand and yet made himself to be carried among his troops in a litter, and came near death again by the murderer of his father, and where he fought until the murderers of the mortal Julius, who became a god, were destroyed by their own hands.

I am Marcus Agrippa, sometimes called Vipsanius, tribune to the people and consul to the Senate, soldier and general to the Empire of Rome, and friend of Gaius Octavius Caesar, now Augustus. I write these memories in the fiftieth year of my life so that posterity may record the time when Octavius discovered Rome bleeding in the jaws of faction, when Octavius Caesar slew the factious beast and removed the almost lifeless body, and when Augustus healed the wounds of Rome and made it whole again, to walk with vigor upon the boundaries of the world. Of this triumph I have, within my abilities, been a part; and of that part these memories will be a record, so that the historians of the ages may understand their wonder at Augustus and Rome.

Under the command of Caesar Augustus I performed several functions for the restoration of Rome, for which duty Rome amply rewarded me. I was three times consul, once aedile and tribune, and twice governor of Syria; and twice I received the seal of the Sphinx from Augustus himself during his grave illnesses. Against Lucius Antonius at Perusia I led the victorious Roman legions, and against the Aquitanians at Gaul, and against the German tribes at the Rhine, for which service I refused a Triumph in Rome; and in Spain and Pannonia, too, were rebellious tribes and factions put down. By Augustus I was given title as commander in chief of our navy, and we saved our ships from the pirate Sextus Pompeius by our construction of the harbor west of the Bay of Naples, which ships later defeated and destroyed Pompeius at Mylae and Naulochus on the coast of Sicily; and for that action the Senate awarded me the naval crown. At Actium we defeated the traitor Marcus Antonius, and so restored life to the body of Rome.

In celebration of Rome's delivery from the Egyptian treason, I had erected the Temple now called the Pantheon and other public buildings. As chief administrator of the city under Augustus and the Senate, I had repaired the old aqueducts of the city and installed new ones, so that the citizens and populace of Rome might have water and be free of disease; and when peace came to Rome, I assisted in the survey and mapping of the world, begun during the dictatorship of Julius Caesar and made at last possible by his adopted son.

Of these things, I shall write more at length as these memories progress. But I must now tell of the time when these events were set into motion, the year after Julius Caesar's triumphant return from Spain, of which campaign Gaius Octavius and Salvidienus Rufus and I were members.

For I was with him at Apollonia when the news came of Caesar's death. . . .

II. LETTER: GAIUS CILNIUS MAECENAS
TO TITUS LIVIUS (13 B.C.)

You must forgive me, my dear Livy, for having so long delayed my reply. The usual complaints: retirement seems not to have improved the state of my health at all. The doctors shake their heads wisely, mutter mysteriously, and collect their fees. Nothing seems to help—not the vile medicines I am fed, nor even the abstinence from those pleasures which (as you know) I once enjoyed. The gout has made it impossible for me to hold my pen in hand these last few days, though I know how diligently you pursue your work and what need you have of my assistance in the matter of which you have written me. And along with my other infirmities, I have for the past few weeks been afflicted by an insomnia, so that my days are spent in weariness and lassitude. But my friends do not desert me, and life stays; for those two things I must be grateful.

You ask me about the early days of my association with our Emperor. You ought to know that only three days ago he was good enough to visit my house, inquiring after my illnesses, and I felt it politic to inform him of your request. He smiled and asked me whether or not I felt it proper to aid such an unregenerate Republican as yourself; and then we fell to talking about the old days, as men who feel the encroachment of age will do. He remembers things—little things—even more vividly than I, whose profession it has been to forget nothing. At last I asked him if he would prefer to have sent to you his own account of that time. He looked away into the distance for a moment and smiled again and said, "No—Emperors may let their memories lie even more readily than poets and historians." He asked me to send you his warm regards, and gave me permission to write to you with whatever freedom I could find.

But what freedom can I find to speak to you of those days? We were young; and though Gaius Octavius, as he was called then, knew that he was favored by his destiny and that Julius Caesar intended his adoption, neither he nor I nor Marcus Agrippa nor Salvidienus Rufus, who were his friends, could truly imagine where we would be led. I do not have the freedom of the historian, my friend; you may recount the movements of men and armies, trace the intricate course of state intrigues, balance victories and defeats, relate births and deaths —and yet still be free, in the wise simplicity of your task, from the awful weight of a kind of knowledge that I cannot name but that I more and more nearly apprehend as the years draw on. I know what you want; and you are no doubt impatient with me because I do not get on with it and give you the facts that you need. But you must remember that despite my services to the state, I am a poet, and incapable of approaching anything very directly.

It may surprise you to learn that I had not known Octavius until I met him at Brindisi, where I had been sent to join him and his group of friends on the way to Apollonia. The reasons

for my being there remain obscure to me; it was through the
intercession of Julius Caesar, I am sure. My father, Lucius, had
once done Julius some service; and a few years before, he had
visited us at our villa in Arezzo. I argued with him about something (I was, I believe, asserting the superiority of Callimachus's poems to Catullus's), and I became arrogant, abusive,
and (I thought) witty. I was very young. At any rate, he seemed
amused by me, and we talked for some time. Two years later, he
ordered my father to send me to Apollonia in the company
of his nephew.

My friend, I must confess to you (though you may not use
it) that I was in no profound way impressed with Octavius
upon that occasion of our first meeting. I had just come down
to Brindisi from Arezzo and after more than ten days of traveling, I was weary to the bone, filthy with the dust of the road,
and irritable. I came upon them at the pier from which we were
to embark. Agrippa and Salvidienus were talking together, and
Octavius stood somewhat apart from them, gazing at a small
ship that was anchored nearby. They had given no sign of noticing my approach. I said, somewhat too loudly, I imagine: "I
am the Maecenas who was to meet you here. Which of you is
which?"

Agrippa and Salvidienus looked at me amusedly and gave
me their names; Octavius did not turn; and thinking that I saw
arrogance and disdain in his back, I said: "And you must be the
other, whom they call Octavius."

Then he turned, and I knew that I was foolish; for there was
an almost desperate shyness on his face. He said: "Yes, I am
Gaius Octavius. My uncle has spoken of you." Then he smiled
and offered me his hand and raised his eyes and looked at me
for the first time.

As you know, much has been said about those eyes, more
often than not in bad meter and worse prose; I think by now he
must be sick of hearing the metaphors and whatnot describing
them, though he may have been vain about them at one time.
But they were, even then, extraordinarily clear and piercing
and sharp—more blue than gray, perhaps, though one thought
of light, not color. . . . There, you see? I have started doing
it myself; I have been reading too many of my friends' poems.

I may have stepped back a pace; I do not know. At any rate, I was startled, and so I looked away, and my eyes fell upon the ship at which Octavius had been gazing.

"Is that the scow that's going to take us across?" I asked. I was feeling a little more cheerful. It was a small merchant ship, not more than fifty feet in length, with rotting timbers at the prow and patched sails. A stench rose from it.

Agrippa spoke to me. "We are told that it is the only one available." He was smiling at me a little; I imagine that he thought me fastidious, for I was wearing my toga and had on several rings, while they wore only tunics and carried no ornaments.

"The stench will be unendurable," I said.

Octavius said gravely, "I believe it is going to Apollonia for a load of pickled fish."

I was silent for a moment; and then I laughed, and we all laughed, and we were friends.

Perhaps we are wiser when we are young, though the philosopher would dispute with me. But I swear to you, we were friends from that moment onward; and that moment of foolish laughter was a bond stronger than anything that came between us later—victories or defeats, loyalties or betrayals, griefs or joys. But the days of youth go, and part of us goes with them, not to return.

Thus it was that we crossed to Apollonia, in a stinking fish-boat that groaned with the gentlest wave, that listed so perilously to its side that we had to brace ourselves so that we would not tumble across the deck, and that carried us to a destiny we could not then imagine. . . .

I resume the writing of this letter after an interruption of two days; I shall not trouble you with a detailing of the maladies that occasioned that interruption; it is all too depressing.

In any event, I have seen that I do not give you the kind of thing that will be of much use to you, so I have had my secretary go through some of my papers in search of matters more helpful to your task. You may remember that some ten years ago I spoke at the dedication of our friend Marcus Agrippa's Temple of Venus and Mars, now popularly called the Pantheon. In the beginning I had the idea, later discarded, of doing a rather fanciful oration, almost a poem, if I may say so, which made some odd connections between the state of Rome as we had found it as young men and the state of Rome as this temple now represents it. At any rate, as an aid to my own solution to the problem that the form of this projected oration raised, I made some notes about those early days, which I now draw upon in an effort to aid you in the completion of your history of our world.

Picture, if you can, four youths (they are strangers to me now), ignorant of their future and of themselves, ignorant indeed of that very world in which they are beginning to live. One (that is Marcus Agrippa) is tall and heavy-muscled, with the face almost of a peasant—strong nose, big bones, and a skin like new leather; dry, brownish hair, and a coarse red stubble of beard; he is nineteen. He walks heavily, like a bullock, but there is an odd grace about him. He speaks plainly, slowly, and calmly, and does not show what he feels. Except for his beard, one would not know that he is so young.

Another (this is Salvidienus Rufus) is as thin and agile as Agrippa is heavy and stalwart, as quick and volatile as Agrippa is slow and reserved. His face is lean, his skin fair, his eyes dark; he laughs readily, and lightens the gravity which the rest of us affect. He is older than any of us, but we love him as if he were our younger brother.

And a third (is it myself?) whom I see even more dimly than the others. No man may know himself, nor how he must appear even to his friends; but I imagine they must have thought me a bit of a fool, that day, and even for some time afterward. I *was* a bit luxuriant then, and fancied that a poet must play the part. I dressed richly, my manner was affected, and I had brought along with me from Arezzo a servant whose sole duty it was to care for my hair—until my friends derided me so mercilessly that I had him returned to Italy.

And at last he who was then Gaius Octavius. How may I tell you of him? I do not know the truth; only my memories. I can say again that he seemed to me a boy, though I was a scant two years older. You know his appearance now; it has not changed much. But now he is Emperor of the world, and I must look beyond that to see him as he was then; and I swear to you that I, whose service to him has been my knowledge of the hearts of both his friends and enemies, could not have foreseen what he was to become. I thought him a pleasant stripling, no more, with a face too delicate to receive the blows of fate, with a manner too diffident to achieve purpose, and with a voice too gentle to utter the ruthless words that a leader of men must utter. I thought that he might become a scholar of leisure, or a man of letters; I did not think that he had the energy to become even a senator, to which his name and wealth entitled him.

And these were those who came to land that day in early autumn, in the year of the fifth consulship of Julius Caesar, at Apollonia on the Adriatic coast of Macedonia. Fishing boats bobbed in the harbor, and the people waved; nets were stretched upon rocks to dry; and wooden shacks lined the road up to the city, which was set upon high ground before a plain that stretched and abruptly rose to the mountains.

Our mornings were spent in study. We rose before dawn, and heard our first lecture by lamplight; we breakfasted on coarse food when the sun shone above the eastern mountains; we discoursed in Greek on all things (a practice which, I fear, is dying now), and spoke aloud those passages from Homer we had learned the night before, accounted for them, and finally offered brief declamations that we had prepared according to the stipulations of Apollodorus (who was ancient even then, but of even temper and great wisdom).

In the afternoons, we were driven a little beyond the city to the camp where Julius Caesar's legions were training; and there, for a good part of the rest of the day, we shared their exercises. I must say that it was during this time that I first began to suspect that I might have been wrong about Octavius's abilities. As you know, his health has always been poor, though his frailness has been more apparent than mine, whose fate it is, dear Livy, to appear the model of health even in my most extreme illness. I, myself, then, took little part in the actual drills and maneuvers; but Octavius always did, preferring, like his uncle, to spend his time with the centurions, rather than with the more nominal officers of the legion. Once, I remember, in a mock battle his horse stumbled and he was thrown heavily to the ground. Agrippa and Salvidienus were standing nearby, and Salvidienus started at once to run to his aid; but Agrippa held him by the arm and would not let him move. After a few

moments Octavius arose, stood stiffly upright, and called for
another horse. One was brought him, and he mounted and
rode the rest of the afternoon, completing his part in the exercise. That evening in our tent, we heard him breathing heavily,
and we called the doctor of the legion to look at him. Two of
his ribs were broken. He had the doctor bind his chest tightly,
and the next morning he attended classes with us and took an
equally active part in a quick-march that afternoon.

Thus it was during those first days and weeks that I came to
know the Augustus who now rules the Roman world. Perhaps
you will transform this into a few sentences of that marvelous history which I have been privileged to admire. But there
is much that cannot go into books, and that is the loss with
which I become increasingly concerned.

III. LETTER: JULIUS CAESAR TO GAIUS OCTAVIUS
AT APOLLONIA, FROM ROME (44 B.C.)

I was remembering this morning, my dear Octavius, the day
last winter in Spain when you found me at Munda in the midst
of our siege of that fortress where Gnaeus Pompeius had fled
with his legions. We were disheartened and fatigued with battle; our food was gone; and we were besieging an enemy who
could rest and eat while we pretended to starve them out. In
my anger at what seemed certain defeat, I ordered you to return to Rome, whence you had traveled in what seemed to me
then such ease and comfort; and said that I could not bother
with a boy who wanted to play at war and death. I was angry
only at myself, as I am sure you knew even then; for you did
not speak, but looked at me out of a great calm. Then I quieted a little, and spoke to you from my heart (as I have spoken
to you since), and told you that this Spanish campaign against
Pompeius was to settle at last and forever the civil strife and
faction that had oppressed our Republic, in one way or another, ever since my youth; and that what I had thought to be
victory was now almost certain defeat.

"Then," you said, "we are not fighting for victory; we are
fighting for our lives."

And it seemed to me that a great burden was lifted from
my shoulders, and I felt myself to be almost young again; for
I remembered having said the same thing to myself more than

thirty years before when six of Sulla's troops surprised me alone
in the mountains, and I fought my way through them to their
commander, whom I bribed to take me alive back to Rome.
It was then that I knew that I might be what I have become.

Remembering that old time and seeing you before me, I saw
myself when I was young; and I took some of your youth into
myself and gave you some of my age, and so we had together
that odd exhilaration of power against whatever might happen;
and we piled the bodies of our fallen comrades and advanced
behind them so that our shields would not be weighted with
the enemy's hurled javelins, and we advanced upon the walls
and took the fortress of Cordova, there on the Mundian plain.

And I remembered too, this morning, our pursuit of Gnaeus
Pompeius across Spain, our bellies full and our muscles tired
and the campfires at night and the talk that soldiers make when
victory is certain. How all the pain and anguish and joy merge
together, and even the ugly dead seem beautiful, and even the
fear of death and defeat are like the steps of a game! Here in
Rome, I long for summer to come, when we will march against
the Parthians and the Germans to secure the last of our important borders. . . . You will understand better my nostalgia
for past campaigns and my anticipation of campaigns to come
if I let you know a little about the morning that occasioned
those memories.

At seven o'clock this morning, the Fool (that is, Marcus
Aemilius Lepidus—whom, you will be amused to know, I
have had to make your nominal coequal in power under my
command) was waiting at my door with a complaint about
Marcus Antonius. It seems that one of Antonius's treasurers
was collecting taxes from those who, according to an ancient
law cited at tedious length by Lepidus, ought to have their
taxes collected by Lepidus's *own* treasurer. Then for another
hour, apparently thinking that allusive loquacity is subtlety, he
suggested that Antonius was ambitious—an observation that
surprised me as much as if I had been informed that the Vestal
Virgins were chaste. I thanked him, and we exchanged platitudes upon the nature of loyalty, and he left me (I am sure)
to report to Antonius that he perceived in me some excessive
suspicion of even my closest friends. At eight o'clock, three
senators came in, one after another, each accusing the other
of accepting an identical bribe; I understood at once that all

were guilty, that they had been unable to perform the service for which they were bribed, and that the briber was ready to make a public issue of the matter, which would necessitate a trial before the assembly—a trial that they wished to avoid, since it might conceivably lead to exile if they were unable to bribe enough of the jury to insure their safety. I judged that they would be successful in their effort to buy off justice, and so I trebled the reported amount of the bribe and fined each of them that amount, and resolved that I would deal similarly with the briber. They were well-pleased, and I have no fear of them; I know that they are corrupt, and they think that I am. . . . And so the morning went.

How long have we been living the Roman lie? Ever since I can remember, certainly; perhaps for many years before. And from what source does that lie suck its energy, so that it grows stronger than the truth? We have seen murder, theft, and pillage in the name of the Republic—and call it the necessary price we pay for freedom. Cicero deplores the depraved Roman morality that worships wealth—and, himself a millionaire many times over, travels with a hundred slaves from one of his villas to another. A consul speaks of peace and tranquillity— and raises armies that will murder the colleague whose power threatens his self-interest. The Senate speaks of freedom—and thrusts upon me powers that I do not want but must accept and use if Rome is to endure. Is there no answer to the lie?

I have conquered the world, and none of it is secure; I have shown liberty to the people, and they flee it as if it were a disease; I despise those whom I can trust, and love those best who would most quickly betray me. And I do not know where we are going, though I lead a nation to its destiny.

Such, my dear nephew, whom I would call my son, are the doubts that beset the man whom they would make a king. I envy you your winter in Apollonia; I am pleased with the reports of your studies; and I am happy that you get along so well with the officers of my legions there. But I do miss our talks in the evenings. I comfort myself with the thought that we shall resume them this summer on our Eastern campaign. We shall march across the country, feed upon the land, and kill whom we must kill. It is the only life for a man. And things shall be as they will be.

IV. QUINTUS SALVIDIENUS RUFUS: NOTES FOR A
JOURNAL, AT APOLLONIA (MARCH, 44 B.C.)

Afternoon. The sun is bright, hot; ten or twelve officers and
ourselves on a hill, looking down at the maneuvers of the cavalry on the field. Dust rises in billows as the horses gallop and
turn; shouts, laughter, curses come up to us from the distance,
through the thud of hoofbeats. All of us, except Maecenas,
have come up from the field and are resting. I have removed
my armor and am lying with my head on it; Maecenas, his tunic unspotted and his hair unruffled, sits with his back against
the trunk of a small tree; Agrippa stands beside me, sweat
drenching his body, his legs like stone pillars; Octavius beside
him, his slender body trembling from its recent exertion—one
never realizes how slight he is until he stands near someone like
Agrippa—his face pale, hair lank and darkened by sweat, plas-
tered to his forehead; Octavius smiling, pointing to something
below us; Agrippa nodding. We all have a sense of well-being;
it has not rained for a week, the weather has warmed, we are
pleased with our skills and with the skills of the soldiers.

I write these words quickly, not knowing what I shall have
occasion to use in my leisure. I must get everything down.

The horsemen below us rest; their horses mill around; Octavius sits beside me, pushes my head playfully off the armor; we
laugh at nothing in our feeling for the moment. Agrippa smiles
at us and stretches his great arms; the leather of his cuirass
creaks in the stillness.

From behind us comes Maecenas's voice—high, thin, a little
affected, almost effeminate. "Boys who play at being soldier,"
he says. "How unutterably boring."

Agrippa—his voice deep, slow, deliberate, with that gravity
that conceals so much: "If you had it in your power to remove
that ample posterior from whatever convenient resting place it
might encounter, you would discover that there are pleasures
beyond the luxuries you affect."

Octavius: "Perhaps we could persuade the Parthians to accept him as their general. That would make our task easier this
summer."

Maecenas sighs heavily, gets up, and walks over to where we
are lying. For one so heavy, he is very light on his feet. He says:

"While you have been indulging yourselves in your vulgar displays, I have been projecting a poem that examines the active versus the contemplative life. The wisdom of the one I know; I have been observing the foolishness of the other."

Octavius, gravely: "My uncle once told me to read the poets, to love them, and to use them—but never to trust them."

"Your uncle," says Maecenas, "is a wise man."

More banter. We grow quiet. The field below us is almost empty; the horses have been led away to the stables at the edge of the field. Below the field, from the direction of the city, a horseman, galloping at full speed. We watch him idly. He comes to the field, does not pause there, but crosses it wildly, careening in his saddle. I start to say something, but Octavius has stiffened. There is something in his face. We can see the foam flying from the horse's mouth. Octavius says: "I know that man. He is from my mother's household."

He is almost upon us now; the horse slows; he slides from his saddle, stumbles, staggers toward us with something in his hand. Some of the soldiers around us have noticed; they run toward us with their swords half-drawn, but they see that the man is helpless with exhaustion and moves only by his will. He thrusts something toward Octavius and croaks, "This—this—" It is a letter. Octavius takes it and holds it and does not move for several moments. The messenger collapses, then sits and puts his head between his knees. All we can hear is the hoarse rasp of his breathing. I look at the horse and think absently that it is so broken in its wind that it will die before morning. Octavius has not moved. Everyone is still. Slowly he unrolls the letter; he reads; there is no expression on his face. Still he does not speak. After a long while he raises his head and turns to us. His face is like white marble. He puts the letter in my hand; I do not look at it. He says in a dull, flat voice: "My uncle is dead."

We cannot take in his words; we look at him stupidly. His expression does not change, but he speaks again, and the voice that comes out of him is grating and loud and filled with uncomprehending pain, like the bellow of a bullock whose throat has been cut at a sacrifice: "Julius Caesar is dead."

"No," says Agrippa. "No."

Maecenas's face has tightened; he looks at Octavius like a falcon.

My hand is shaking so that I cannot read what is written. I steady myself. My voice is strange to me. I read aloud: "On this Ides of March Julius Caesar is murdered by his enemies in the Senate House. There are no details. The people run wildly through the streets. No one can know what will happen next. You may be in great danger. I can write no more. Your mother beseeches you to care for your person." The letter has been written in great haste; there are blots of ink, and the letters are ill-formed.

I look around me, not knowing what I feel. An emptiness? The officers stand around us in a ring; I look into the eyes of one; his face crumples, I hear a sob: and I remember that this is one of Caesar's prime legions, and that the veterans look upon him as a father.

After a long time Octavius moves; he walks to the messenger who remains seated on the ground, his face slack with exhaustion. Octavius kneels beside him; his voice is gentle. "Do you know anything that is not in this letter?"

The messenger says, "No, sir," and starts to get up but Octavius puts his hand on his shoulder and says, "Rest"; and he rises and speaks to one of the officers. "See that this man is cared for and given comfortable quarters." Then he turns to the three of us, who have moved closer together. "We will talk later. Now I must think of what this will mean." He reaches his hand out toward me, and I understand that he wants the letter. I hand it to him, and he turns away from us. The ring of officers breaks for him, and he walks down the hill. For a long time we watch him, a slight boyish figure walking on the deserted field, moving slowly, this way and that, as if trying to discover a way to go.

Later. Great consternation in camp as word of Caesar's death spreads. Rumors so wild that one can believe none of them. Arguments arise, subside; a few fist fights, quickly broken up. Some of the old professionals, whose lives have been spent in fighting from legion to legion, sometimes against the men who are now their comrades, look with contempt upon the fuss, and go about their business. Still Octavius has not returned from his lonely watch upon the field. The day darkens.

Night. A guard has been placed around our tents by Lugdunius himself, commander of the legion; for no one knows what enemies we have, or what may ensue. The four of us together in Octavius's tent; we sit or recline on pallets around the lanterns flickering in the center of the floor. Sometimes Octavius rises and sits on a campstool, away from the light, so that his face is in shadow. Many have come in from Apollonia, asking for more news, giving advice, offering aid; Lugdunius has put the legion at our disposal, should we want it. Now Octavius has asked that we not be disturbed, and speaks of those who have come to him.

"They know even less than we, and they speak only to their own fortunes. Yesterday—" he pauses and looks at something in the darkness—"yesterday, it seemed they were my friends. Now I may not trust them." He pauses again, comes close to us, and puts his hand on my shoulder. "I shall speak of these matters only with you three, who are truly my friends."

Maecenas speaks; his voice has deepened, and no longer shrills with the effeminacy that he sometimes affects: "Do not trust even us, who love you. From this moment on, put only that faith in us that you have to."

Octavius turns abruptly away from us, his back to the light, and says in a strangled voice: "I know. I know even that."

And so we talk of what we must do.

Agrippa says that we must do nothing, since we know nothing upon which we can reasonably act. In the unsteady light of the lanterns, he might be an old man, with his voice and his gravity. "We are safe here, at least for the time being; this legion will be loyal to us—Lugdunius has given his word. For all we know, this may be a general rebellion, and armies may already have been dispatched for our capture, as Sulla sent troops for the descendants of Marius—among whom was Julius Caesar himself. We may not be as lucky now as he was then. We have behind us the mountains of Macedonia, where they will not follow against this legion. In any event, we shall have time to receive more news; and we shall have made no move to compromise our position, one way or the other. We must wait in the safety of the moment."

Octavius, softly: "My uncle once told me that too much caution may lead to death as certainly as too much rashness."

I suddenly find myself on my feet; a power has come upon me; I speak in a voice that seems not my own: "I call you Caesar, for I know that he would have had you as his son."

Octavius looks at me; the thought had not occurred to him, I believe. "It is too early for that," he says slowly, "but I will remember that it was Salvidienus who first called me by that name."

I say: "And if he would have you as his son, he would have you act as he would have done. Agrippa has said that we have the loyalty of one legion here; the other five in Macedonia will respond as Lugdunius has, if we do not delay in asking their allegiance. For if we know nothing of what will ensue, they know even less. I say that we march on Rome with the legions we have and assume the power that lies there."

Octavius: "And then? We do not know what that power is; we do not know who will oppose us. We do not even know who murdered him."

Myself: "The power shall become what we make it to be. As for who will oppose us, we cannot know. But if Antonius's legions will join with ours, then—"

Octavius, slowly: "We do not even know who murdered him. We do not know his enemies, thus we cannot know our own."

Maecenas sighs, rises, shakes his head. "We have spoken of action, of what we shall do; but we have not spoken of the end to which that action is aimed." He gazes at Octavius. "My friend, what is it that you wish to accomplish, by whatever action we take?"

For a moment Octavius does not speak. Then he looks at each of us in turn, intently. "I swear to you all now, and to the gods, that if it is my destiny to live, I shall have vengeance upon the murderers of my uncle, whoever they may be."

Maecenas, nodding: "Then our first purpose is to ensure that destiny, so that you may fulfill the vow. We must stay alive. To that end we must move with caution—but we must move." He is walking about the room, addressing us as if we were schoolchildren. "Our friend Agrippa recommends that we remain here safely until we can know which way to move. But to remain here is to remain in ignorance. News will come from Rome—but it will be rumor confounded with fact, fact confounded with self-interest, until self-interest and faction become the source of all we shall know." He turns to me. "Our impetuous friend Salvidienus advises that we strike at once, finding advantage in the confusion that the world may now be in. To run in the dark against a timid opponent may win you the race; but it is as likely to plunge you over a cliff you cannot see, or lead you to a mark you do not wish to find. No. . . . All of Rome will know that Octavius has received word of his uncle's death. He shall return quietly, with his friends and his grief—but without the soldiers that both his friends and enemies might welcome. No army will attack four boys and a few servants, who return to grieve a relative; and no force will gather around them to warn and stiffen the will of the enemy. And if it is to be murder, four can run more swiftly than a legion."

We have had our say; Octavius is silent; and it occurs to me how odd it is that we will so suddenly defer to his decision, as we have not done before. Is it a power in him we sense and have not known earlier? Is it the moment? Is it some lack in ourselves? I will consider this later.

At last Octavius speaks: "We shall do as Maecenas says. We'll leave most of our possessions here, as if we intend to return; and tomorrow we make as much haste as we can to cross to Italy. But not to Brindisi—there's a legion there, and we cannot know its disposition."

"Otranto," Agrippa says. "It's nearer anyway."

Octavius nods. "And now you must choose. Whoever returns with me commits his fortune to my own. There is no other way, and there can be no turning back. And I can promise you nothing, except my own chance."

Maecenas yawns; he is his old self again. "We came across on that stinking fish-boat with you; if we could endure that, we can endure anything."

Octavius smiles, a little sadly. "That was a long time ago," he says, "that day."

We say nothing more, except our good nights.

*

I am alone in my tent; the lamp sputters on my table where I write these words, and through the tent door I can see in the east, above the mountains, the first pale light of dawn. I have not been able to sleep.

In this early morning stillness, the events of the day seem far away and unreal. I know that the course of my life—of all our lives—has been changed. How do the others feel? Do they know?

Do they know that before us lies a road at the end of which is either death or greatness? The two words go around in my head, around and around, until it seems they are the same.

Chapter Two

By the time you receive this letter, my son, you will have arrived at Brindisi and heard the news. It is as I feared: the will is now public, and you have been named Caesar's son and heir. I know that your first impulse will be to accept both the name and the fortune; but your mother implores you to wait, to consider, and to judge the world into which this will of your uncle invites you. It is not the simple country world of Velletri, where you spent your childhood; nor is it the household world of tutors and nurses where you spent your boyhood; nor is it the world of books and philosophy where you spent your youth, nor even the simple world of the battlefield to which Caesar (against my will) introduced you. It is the world of Rome, where no man knows his enemy or his friend, where license is more admired than virtue, and where principle has become servant to self.

Your mother begs you to renounce the terms of the will; you may do so without traducing the name of your uncle, and no one will think the worse of you. For if you accept the name and the fortune, you accept the enmity of both those who killed Caesar and those who now support his memory. You will have only the love of the rabble, as did Caesar; and that was not enough to protect him from his fate.

I pray that you receive this before you have acted rashly. We have removed ourselves from the danger in Rome, and will stay here at your stepfather's place in Puteoli until the chaos has settled into some kind of order. If you do not accept the will, you may travel safely across the country and join us here. It still is possible to lead a decent life in the privacy of one's own heart and mind. Your stepfather wishes to add some words to this.

Your mother speaks to you from the love that is in her heart; I speak to you from my affection, too, but also from my practical knowledge of the world and of the events of the past days.

You know my politics, and you know that there have been occasions in the past when I could not approve of the course that your late uncle pursued. Indeed, I have from time to time found it necessary, as has our friend Cicero, to assert this disapproval on the floor of the Senate. I mention this only to assure you that it is not from political considerations that I urge you upon the course that your mother has advised, but from practical ones.

I do not approve of the assassination, and had I been consulted about it I would most certainly have recoiled with such aversion that I myself might have been in danger. But you must understand that among the tyrannicides (as they call themselves) are some of the most responsible and respected citizens of Rome. They have the support of most of the Senate, and they are in danger only from the rabble; some of them are my friends, and however ill-advised were their actions, they are good men and patriots. Even Marcus Antonius, who has roused the rabble, does not move against them, and will not; for he, too, is a practical man.

Whatever his virtues, your uncle left Rome in a state from which it is not likely soon to recover. All is in doubt: his enemies are powerful but confused in their resolve, and his friends are corrupt and to be trusted by no one. If you accept the name and the inheritance, you will be abandoned by those who matter; you will have a name that is an empty honor, and a fortune that you do not need; and you will be alone.

Come to us at Puteoli. Do not involve yourself in issues whose resolution cannot improve your interest. Keep yourself aloof from all. You will be safe in our affections.

II. THE MEMOIRS OF MARCUS AGRIPPA: FRAGMENTS (13 B.C.)

. . . and at that news and in our grief we acted. We made haste to sail and had a stormy crossing to Otranto, where we landed in the dark of night and did not let our persons be known to any. We slept at a common inn and made our servants absent themselves, so that no one might suspect us; and before dawn we set out on foot toward Brindisi, as if we were country folk. At Lecce we were halted by two soldiers who watched the approach to Brindisi; and though we did not give our names, we were recognized by one who had been in the Spanish campaign. From him we learned that the garrison at Brindisi would welcome us, and that we might go there without danger. One walked with us while the other went ahead to tell of our coming, and we came to Brindisi with the full honor of a guard and the soldiers ranked on either side of us as we came into the city.

There we were shown a copy of Caesar's will which named Octavius his son and legatee, and gave his gardens to the people for their recreation and to every citizen of Rome three hundred pieces of silver from his fortune.

We had what news there was of Rome, which writhed in disorder; we had the names of those who murdered Caesar, and knew the lawlessness of the Senate that sanctioned the murder and set the murderers free; and we knew the grief and rage of the people under that lawless rule.

A messenger from the household of Octavius awaited us, and gave him letters from his mother and her husband which, out of their affection and regard, urged upon him that renunciation of the legacy which he could not make. The uncertainty of the world and the difficulty of his task strengthened his resolve, and we called him Caesar then and gave him our allegiance.

Out of their veneration for his murdered father and their love for his son, the legion at Brindisi and veterans from miles around thronged about him, urging him to lead them in vengeance against the murderers; but he put them off with many words of gratitude, and we went quietly in our mourning across the land, from Brindisi along the Appian Way to Puteoli, whence we purposed to enter Rome at a propitious time.

III. QUINTUS SALVIDIENUS RUFUS: NOTES FOR A JOURNAL, AT BRINDISI (44 B.C.)

We have learned much; we understand little. It is said that there were more than sixty conspirators. Chief among them were Marcus Junius Brutus, Gaius Cassius Longinus, Decimus Brutus Albinus, Gaius Trebonius—all supposed friends of Julius Caesar, some of whose names we have known since childhood.

And there are others whom we do not yet know. Marcus Antonius speaks against the murderers, and then entertains them at dinner; Dolabella, who approved the assassination, is made consul for the year by that same Antonius who has denounced the enemies of Julius Caesar.

What game does Antonius play? Where do we go?

IV. LETTER: MARCUS TULLIUS CICERO TO MARCIUS PHILIPPUS (44 B.C.)

I have just learned that your stepson, with three of his young friends, is even now on his way from Brindisi, where he landed only a few days ago; I am hastening this letter to you, so that you might have it before his arrival.

It is rumored that despite your letter of advice (a copy of which you were most kind to send to me, and which I acknowledge with much gratitude) he intends now to accept the terms of Caesar's will. I hope that this is not true, but I fear the rashness of youth. I entreat you to use what influence you have to dissuade him from this course, or, if the step has been taken, to persuade him to renounce it. To this end, I shall be glad to lend whatever assistance I can; I shall make preparations to leave my lodge here at Astura in the next few days, so that I may be with you at Puteoli when he arrives. I have been kind to him in the past, and I believe that he admires me.

I know that you bear some affection for the boy, but you must understand that he is, however remotely, a Caesar, and that the enemies of our cause may make use of him if he is allowed to go his own way. In times such as these, loyalty to our Party must take precedence over our natural inclinations; and none of us wants harm to come to the boy. You must speak to your wife about this (I remember that she has great power over her son) as persuasively as you can.

I have had news from Rome. The situation is not good, but neither is it hopeless. Our friends still do not dare show their faces there, and even my dear Brutus must do what he can in the countryside, rather than remain in Rome and repair the Republic. I had hoped that the assassination would at once restore our freedom, return us to the glory of our past, and rid us of the upstarts that now presume to disturb the order that we both love. But the Republic is not repaired; those who should act with fortitude seem incapable of resolution, and Antonius prowls like a beast from one spoil to another, pillaging the treasury and gathering power wherever he can. Had we to endure Antonius, I could almost regret the death of Caesar. But we will not have to endure him long—of that I am convinced. He moves so recklessly that he must destroy himself.

I am too much the idealist, I know—even my dearest friends do not deny that. Yet I most reasonably have faith in the eventual justice of our cause. The wound will heal, the thrashing will cease, the Senate will find that ancient purpose and dignity which Caesar almost extinguished—and you and I, my dear Marcius, will live to see that old virtue of which we have so often spoken once again settle like a wreath upon the brow of Rome.

The events of the past few weeks press upon me. These matters have taken so much of my time that my own affairs suffer. One of the managers of my property, Chrysippus, came to me yesterday and remonstrated seriously with me; two of my shops have fallen down and others are deteriorating so badly that not only the tenants, but even the mice have threatened to migrate! How fortunate I am to have followed Socrates—others would call this a calamity, but I do not even count it a nuisance. How insignificant are such things! In any event, as a result of a long discussion with Chrysippus, I have come up with a plan whereby I can sell a few buildings and repair others, so that I will make my loss a profit.

V. LETTER: MARCUS TULLIUS CICERO
TO MARCUS JUNIUS BRUTUS (44 B.C.)

I have seen Octavius. He is at his stepfather's villa at Puteoli, which is just next to mine; and since Marcius Philippus and I are friends, I have free access to see him when I wish. And I must tell you at once that he has, indeed, accepted the inheritance and the name of our dead enemy.

But before you despair, let me hasten to assure you that this acceptance is of less moment than either of us might have dreamed. The boy is nothing, and we need have no fear.

With him are three of his young friends: one Marcus Agrippa, a huge bumpkin who would appear more at ease tramping a

furrow, either before or after the plough, than walking in a
drawing room; one Gaius Cilnius Maecenas, a harsh-featured
but oddly effeminate youth who flounces rather than walks,
and who flutters his eyelashes in a most repulsive way; and
one Salvidienus Rufus, a thin intense boy who laughs a bit too
much, but who seems the most tolerable of the lot. So far as
I can gather, they are nobodies, with neither families of any
import nor fortunes of any account. (If it comes to that, of
course, neither is young Octavius's pedigree immaculate; his
grandfather, on his father's side, was a mere country moneylender, and beyond that only the gods know where he comes
from.)

In any event, the four of them wander about the house as if
they had nothing to do, talking to visitors and generally making nuisances of themselves. They seem to know nothing, for
you can hardly get an intelligent response from any of them;
they ask stupid questions, and then seem not to understand the
answers, for they nod vacantly and look somewhere else.

But I do not let either my contempt or my elation become
apparent. I put on a grave show with the boy. When he first
came, I clucked with sympathy and uttered platitudes about
the loss of close relatives. From his response, I became persuaded that his grief was personal rather than political. Then I
equivocated a bit, and suggested that however unfortunate the
assassination (you will forgive me that hypocrisy, dear Brutus),
there were many who thought that the act sprang from unselfish and patriotic motives. At no time did I detect in him any
sign that he was distressed by these advances. I believe that he
is in some awe of me, and that he may be persuaded to come
to our side, if I handle this with sufficient delicacy.

He is a boy, and a rather foolish boy at that; he has no idea
of politics, nor is he likely to have. He is activated neither by
honor nor ambition but by a rather gentle affection for the
memory of one he would had been his father. And his friends
look only for the advantage that they can have in his favor.
Thus he does not, I believe, constitute a danger for us.

On the other hand, we may be able to put this circumstance
to our benefit. For he does have claim to the name of Caesar,
and (if he can collect it) the inheritance. There are certain to
be some who will follow him merely because of the name he
has assumed; others, the veterans and retainers, will follow him

because of their memory of the man who gave him that name; and still others will follow out of confusion and whim. But the important thing to remember is that we shall have lost none of our own, for those who might follow him are those who otherwise would have followed Antonius! If we can persuade him to our cause, we shall have doubled our victory; for at the worst, we shall have weakened Antonius's side, and that alone would have been victory enough. We shall use the boy, and then we will cast him aside; and the tyrant's line shall have come to an end.

As you can easily understand, I cannot speak freely of these matters with Marcius Philippus; though he is our friend, he is in an awkward position. After all, he is married to the boy's mother; and no man is wholly free of the weaknesses that marital obligations occasionally raise. Besides, he is not of sufficient importance to entrust with everything.

You may keep this letter for less perilous times, but please do not send a copy to our friend Atticus. Out of admiration for me and out of pride in our friendship, he shows my letters to everyone, even if he does not publish them. And the information here should not be known at large, until the future has proved my observations to be true.

A postscript: Caesar's Egyptian whore, Cleopatra, has fled Rome, whether in fear of her life or in despair at the outcome of her ambitions, I do not know; we are well rid of her. Octavius goes to Rome to claim his inheritance, and he goes in utter safety. I could hardly hide my anger and sorrow when I heard this from him; for this stripling and his loutish friends can go there without risk to their persons, while you, my hero of the Ides of March, and our Cassius, must lurk like hunted animals beyond the precincts of the city you freed.

VI. LETTER: MARCUS TULLIUS CICERO TO MARCUS JUNIUS BRUTUS (44 B.C.)

The briefest of notes. He is ours—I am sure of it. He has gone to Rome, and he has spoken to the people, but only to claim his inheritance. I am told that he does not speak ill of you, or of Cassius, or of any of the others. He praises Caesar in the gentlest of terms, and lets it be known that he takes the inheritance out of duty and the name out of reverence, and that he intends to retire to private life once he has done with the matter at hand. Can we believe him? We must, we must! I shall court him when I return to Rome; for his name may still have value to us.

VII. LETTER: MARCUS ANTONIUS TO GAIUS SENTIUS TAVUS, MILITARY COMMANDER OF MACEDONIA (44 B.C.)

Sentius, you gamesome old cock, Antonius sends you greetings, and a report upon the latest triviality—an example of the kind of thing I am daily faced with, now that the burden of administration is upon me. I don't know how Caesar could endure it, day after day; he was a strange man.

That whey-faced little bastard, Octavius, came around to see me yesterday morning. He has been in Rome for the past week or so, acting like a bereaved widow, calling himself Caesar, all manner of nonsense. It seems that Gnaeus and Lucius, my idiot brothers, without consulting me, gave him permission to address the crowd in the Forum, if he would assure them that the speech would not be political. Did you ever hear of a speech that was not political? Well, at least he didn't try to stir them up; so he's not altogether a fool. He got some sympathy from the crowd, I'm sure, but that's about all.

But if not altogether, he certainly is *something* of a fool; for he gives himself airs that are damned presumptuous in a boy, especially in a boy whose grandfather was a thief and whose only name of any account is a borrowed one. He came to my house late in the morning, without an appointment, while half-a-dozen other people were waiting, and he had three of his retinue with him, as if he were a bloody magistrate and they were his lictors. I guess he supposed I would drop everything and come running out to him, which of course I did not do. I told my secretary to inform him that he had to await his turn; I half-expected and half-wanted him to walk out on me. But he didn't, so I kept him waiting for most of the rest of the morning, and finally let him come in.

I must confess that, despite the game I played with him, I was a little curious. I had only seen him a couple of times before—once, six or seven years ago, when he was about twelve, and Caesar let him give the panegyric at his grandmother Julia's funeral; and again, two years ago, at Caesar's Triumphal March after Africa, when I rode in the carriage with Caesar and the boy rode behind us. At one time, Caesar had talked to me a great deal about him; and I wondered if I had missed something.

Well, I hadn't. I shall never understand how the "great" Caesar could have made this boy the inheritor of his name, his power, and his fortune. I swear to the gods, if the will hadn't first been received and recorded in the Temple of the Vestal Virgins, I would have taken a chance on altering it myself.

I don't think I would have been so annoyed if he had left his airs in the reception room and had come into my office like anybody else. But he didn't. He came in flanked by his three friends, whom he presented to me as if I gave a damn about any of them. He addressed me with the proper amount of civility, and then waited for me to say something. I looked at him for a long time and didn't speak. I'll say this for him: he's a cool one. He didn't break and didn't say anything, and I couldn't even tell whether or not he was angry at having been made to wait. So finally I said:

"Well? What do you want?"

And even then he didn't blink. He said: "I have come to pay my respects to you, who were my father's friend, and to inquire about the steps that may be taken to settle his will."

"Your *uncle*," I said, "left his affairs in a mess. I would advise you not to wait around in Rome until they're straightened out."

He didn't say anything. I tell you, Sentius, there's something about that boy that rubs me the wrong way. I can't keep my temper around him. I said: "I would also advise you not to use his name quite so freely, as if it were your own. It's not your own, as you well know, and it won't be until the adoption is confirmed by the Senate."

He nodded. "I am grateful for the advice. I use the name as a sign of my reverence, not my ambition. But leaving the question of my name aside, and even my share of the inheritance, there is the matter of the bequest that Caesar made to the citizens. I judge that their temper is such that—"

I laughed at him. "Boy," I said, "this is the *last* bit of advice I'll give you this morning. Why don't you go back to Apollonia and read your books? It's much safer there. I'll take care of your uncle's affairs in my own way and in my own time."

You can't insult the fellow. He smiled that cold little smile at me and said, "I am pleased to know that my uncle's affairs are in such hands."

I got up from my table and patted him on the shoulder. "That's the boy," I said. "Now you fellows had better get running. I have a busy afternoon ahead of me."

And that was the end of that. I think he knows where he stands, and I don't think he's going to make any very large plans. He's a pompous, unimpressive little fellow, and he would be of no account at all—if only he didn't have some right to the use of that *name*. That alone won't get him very far, but it has proved annoying.

Enough of that. Come to Rome, Sentius, and I promise you that I'll not give you a word of politics. We'll see a mime at Aemelia's house (where, by special permission of a consul who will not be named here, the actresses are allowed to perform without the encumbrance of clothing), and we'll drink as much wine as we can, and contest among the girls which is the better man.

But I do wish the little bastard would leave Rome and take his friends with him.

VIII. QUINTUS SALVIDIENUS RUFUS:
NOTES FOR A JOURNAL (44 B.C.)

We have seen Antonius. Apprehensive; enormity of our task. He's against us, clearly; will use whatever means he has to stop us. Clever. Made us feel our youth.

But a most impressive man. Vain, yet boldly so. Cloud-white toga (heavy-muscled brown arms gleaming against it) with bright purple band delicately edged with gold; as big as Agrippa but moves like a cat rather than a bull; big-boned, dark handsome face, tiny white slashes of scars here and there; thin southern nose broken at one time; full lips turned up at corners; large, soft brown eyes that can flash in anger; booming voice that would overwhelm one with affection or force.

Maecenas and Agrippa, each in his way, furious. Maecenas deadly, cold (when he is serious, drops all mannerisms and even his body seems to harden); sees no possibility of conciliation, wants none. Agrippa, usually so stolid, trembles with rage, face flushed, huge fists clenched. But Octavius (we must now call him Caesar in public) seems oddly cheerful, not angry at all. He smiles, talks animatedly, even laughs. (It is the first time he has laughed since Caesar's death.) In his most difficult moment, he seems to have no cares at all. Was his uncle like this in danger? We have heard stories.

Octavius will not talk about our morning. We usually take our baths at one of the public places, but today we go to Octavius's home on the hill; he does not want to talk to strangers about our morning until we have discussed it, he says. We toss a ball among us for a while (note: Agrippa and Maecenas so angry they play badly, dropping the ball, throwing it carelessly, etc. Octavius plays coolly, laughing, with great skill and grace; I catch his mood; we dance around the other two, until they do not know whether they are angry at Antonius or us). Maecenas flings the ball away and shouts at Octavius:

"Fool! Don't you know what we have to face?"

Octavius stops dancing about, tries to look contrite, laughs again, goes to him and Agrippa, puts his arms around their shoulders. He says: "I'm sorry; but I can't stop thinking of that game we played this morning with Antonius."

Agrippa says: "It was no game. The man was deadly serious."

Octavius, still smiling: "Of course he was serious; but don't you see? He was afraid of us. He was more afraid of us than we are of him, and he doesn't know it. He doesn't even know it. That's the joke."

I start to shake my head, but Agrippa and Maecenas are looking strangely at Octavius. Long silence. Maecenas nods, face softens; shrugs with his old affectation, says negligently, pretending to be cross: "Oh, well, if you're going to be *priestly* about it, divining the hearts of men—" He shrugs again.

We go to bathe. We shall have dinner and talk later.

We are in accord; no precipitate action. We speak of Antonius, knowing that he is our obstacle. Agrippa sees him as the source of power. But how to get at it? We have no force of our own to wrest it from him, even if we dared to do so. We must somehow make him recognize us; that will be the first tiny advantage we have. Too dangerous to raise an army now, even to avenge the murder; Antonius's position in the matter too ambiguous. Does he want to avenge the murder as we do? Does he want only power? It is even possible that he was one of the conspirators. In the Senate, he supported an act that forgave the murderers, and gave Brutus a province.

Maecenas sees him as man of great force and action but unable to conceive the end to which action is directed. "He plots; he doesn't plan," Maecenas says. Unless he has discernible enemy, he will not move. But he must be made to move, otherwise we are at stalemate. Problem: How to make him move without his discovering his own fear of us.

I speak with some hesitation. Will they think me too timid? I say that I see Antonius as committed to same ends as ourselves. Powerful, support of legions, etc. Friend of Caesar. Brusqueness toward us not forgivable but understandable. Wait. Convince him of our loyalty. Offer our services. Work with him, persuade him to use his power to ends we have discussed.

Octavius says slowly: "I do not trust him, because there is a part of him that does not trust himself. Going to him would fix us too firmly in his course, and neither Antonius nor we know surely enough where that course leads him. If we are to be free to do what we must do, he must be made to come to us."

There is more talk; a plan emerges. Octavius is to speak to the people—here and there, small groups, nothing official. Octavius says: "Antonius has persuaded himself that we are innocents, and it is to our advantage that he continue that self-deception." So we will say nothing inflammatory—but we will wonder aloud why murderers have not been punished, why Caesar's bequest to the people has not been made, why Rome has forgotten so quickly.

And then an official speech to the populace in which Octavius announces that Antonius is unable (unwilling?) to release the monies to pay them, and that Octavius himself, out of his own pocket, will give them that which Caesar promised.

More discussion. Agrippa says that Octavius will have depleted his own fortune if Antonius does not release the funds then, and that if an army is needed we shall be helpless. Octavius replies that without the good will of the people, an army will be useless in any event; that we will buy power without seeming to want power; and that Antonius will be forced to move, one way or another.

It is settled. Maecenas will draft the speech, Octavius will finish it, we begin tomorrow. Octavius says to Maecenas: "And remember, my friend, that this is to be a simple speech, not a poem. In any event, I'm sure I'll have to untangle your inimitably labyrinthine prose."

They are wrong. Marcus Antonius has no fear of us or anyone.

IX. LETTER: GAIUS CILNIUS MAECENAS TO TITUS LIVIUS (13 B.C.)

Some years ago my friend Horace described to me the way he made a poem. We had had some wine and were talking seriously, and I believe that his description then was a more accurate one than that contained more recently in the so-called *Letter to the Pisos*—a poem upon the art of poetry of which, I must confess, I am not particularly fond. He said: "I decide to make a poem when I am compelled by some strong feeling to do so—but I wait until the feeling hardens into a resolve; then I conceive an end, as simple as I can make it, toward which that feeling might progress, though often I cannot see how it will do so. And then I compose my poem, using whatever means are at my command. I borrow from others if I have to—no matter. I invent if I have to—no matter. I use the language that I know, and I work within its limits. But the point is this: the end that I discover at last is not the end that I conceived at first. For every solution entails new choices, and every choice made poses new problems to which solutions must be found, and so on and on. Deep in his heart, the poet is always surprised at where his poem has gone."

I thought of that conversation this morning when I sat down to write you once again of those early days; and it occurred to me that Horace's description of the making of a poem had certain striking parallels to our own working out of our destinies in the world itself (though if Horace heard this, and recalled what he said, he would no doubt scowl dourly and say that it was all nonsense, that you made a poem by discovering a topic, disposing the topic properly, by playing this figure against that, by this disposition of the meter against that sense of the language, and so forth and so on).

For our feeling—or, rather, Octavius's feeling, in which we were caught up as the reader is caught in a poem—was occasioned by the incredible murder of Julius Caesar, an event which seemed more and more to have simply destroyed the world; and the end that we conceived was to have revenge upon the murderers, for the sake of our honor and the state's. It was as simple as that, or it appeared to be. But the gods of the world and the gods of poetry are wise, indeed; for how often they save us from the ends toward which we think we strive!

My dear Livy, I do not wish to play the father with you; but you did not even come to Rome until our Emperor had fulfilled his destiny and was master of the world. Let me tell you a little of those days, so that you might reconstruct, these many years later, the chaos that we confronted in Rome.

Caesar was dead—by the "will of the people," the murderers said; yet the murderers had to barricade themselves in the Capitol against those very people who had "commanded" the act. Two days later, the Senate gave its thanks to the assassins; and in the next breath approved and made law those very acts of Caesar for the proposal of which he had been killed. However terrible the deed, the conspirators had acted with bravery and force; and then they scattered like frightened women after they had taken their first step. Antonius, as Caesar's friend, roused the people against the assassins; yet the night before the Ides of March he had entertained the murderers at dinner, was seen speaking intimately with one of them (Trebonius) at the instant of the murder, and dined again with those same men two nights later! He aroused the populace again to burn and loot in protest against the murder; and then approved their arrest and execution for that lawlessness. He made Caesar's will to be read publicly; and then opposed its enactment with all his power.

Above all, we knew that we could not trust Antonius, and we knew him to be a formidable foe—not because of his shrewdness and skill, but because of his thoughtlessness and reckless force. For despite the sentimental regard in which some of the young now hold him, he was not a very intelligent man; he had no real purpose beyond the moment of his will; and he was not exceptionally brave. He did not even perform his own suicide well, and he did it long after his situation was hopeless, so that it was too late for it to be done with dignity.

How do you oppose a foe who is wholly irrational and unpredictable—and yet who, out of animal energy and the accident of circumstance, has attained a most frightening power? (Looking back on it, it is odd to remember that at once we construed Antonius to be our foe rather than the Senate, though our most obvious enemies were there; I suppose instinctively we felt that if such a bungler as Antonius could manage them, we should not have that much trouble with him either, when the time came.) I do not know how you oppose him; I only know what we did. Let me tell you of that.

We had seen Antonius and had been brusquely dismissed by him. He was the most powerful personage in Rome; we had nothing except a name. We determined that our first necessity was to get recognition from him. We had not been able to get that by overtures of friendship; thus we had to try the overtures of enmity.

First, we talked—among Antonius's enemies and among his friends. Or, rather, we questioned, innocently, as if we were trying to understand the events of the day. When did they suppose Antonius would give attention to Caesar's will? Where were the tyrannicides—Brutus, Cassius, the others? Had Antonius gone over to the Republicans, or was he still faithful to Caesar's Party of the People? That sort of thing. And we were careful to insure that reports of these conversations got back to Antonius.

At first there was no response from him. We persisted. And then at last we heard descriptions of his annoyance; retellings of insults he gave to Octavius began making the rounds; rumors and accusations against Octavius passed from lip to lip. And then we made the move that had to bring him into the open.

Octavius had, with some small assistance from me, composed a speech (I may have a copy of it somewhere among my papers; if my secretary can discover it, I will send it on to you), in which he sorrowfully announced to the people that despite the will, Antonius would not release Caesar's fortune to him, but that he (Octavius), having taken Caesar's name, would fulfill Caesar's obligations—that the bequest would be paid them out of his own pocket. The speech was made. There was nothing really inflammatory in it; the tone was one of sorrow, regret, and innocent bewilderment.

But Antonius acted precipitately, as we had hoped he would. He at once introduced legislation into the Senate which would prevent the legal adoption of Octavius; he allied himself with Dolabella, who at that time was co-consul with him and who had been close to the conspirators; he enlisted the support of Marcus Aemilius Lepidus, who immediately after the assassination had fled Rome and gone to his legion in Gaul; and he made open threats against Octavius's life.

Now you must understand that the position of many of the soldiers and citizens was extremely difficult—or at least so it seemed to them. The rich and powerful were almost without exception against Julius Caesar, and thus against Octavius; the soldiers and the middle citizenry almost without exception loved Julius Caesar, and hence favored Octavius; yet they knew that Marcus Antonius had been Caesar's friend. And now they were witnessing what they took to be a destructive battle between the only two persons who might take their part against the rich and aristocratic.

Thus it happened that Agrippa, who better than any of us knew the soldiers' life and language and habits of thought, went among those minor officers and centurions and common soldiers whom we knew to be veterans of the campaigns and friends to Caesar, and supplicated them to use their offices and common loyalty to quiet the dispute that had grown needlessly between Marcus Antonius and Octavius (whom he called Caesar to them). Assured of Octavius's love and convinced that Antonius could not look upon their efforts as rebellion or disloyalty, they acted.

They were persuaded (there were several hundred of them, I believe) to march first to Octavius's house on the hill. It was important that they go there first, you will understand. Octavius pretended surprise, listened to their pleas for friendship with Antonius, and made a brief speech to them in which he forgave Antonius the insults and agreed to repair the breach that had grown between them. You may be certain that we made sure Antonius was informed of this deputation; if they had marched upon his house without warning, he might easily have mistaken their intention and thought they were led against him in retaliation for his threats upon Octavius's life.

But he knew of their coming; and I have often tried to imagine his anger as he awaited them alone in that huge mansion where Pompeius once lived and that Antonius had appropriated after Caesar's murder. For Antonius knew that he had no choice but to wait, and he might have had an intimation then of the course his life was to run.

At Agrippa's prompting, the veterans insisted that Octavius come with them—which he did, though he would not walk in a position of honor, but was escorted at the rear of the line of march. I must say that Antonius behaved reasonably well when we marched into his courtyard. One of the veterans hailed him, he came out and saluted them, and listened to the speech that had already been given to Octavius—though he was a little curt and sullen when he agreed to the conciliation. Then Octavius was brought forward; he greeted Antonius, the salutation was returned, and the veterans cheered. We did not linger; but I was standing very near the two of them when they came together, and I shall always believe that there was a small, grudging, but appreciative smile on Antonius's face when they clasped hands.

That, then, was the first small power we had. And it was that upon which we built.

I tire, my dear Livy. I shall write again soon, when my health permits it. For there is more that may be said.

Postscript: I trust that you will be discreet in the use of what I tell you.

X. LETTER: MARCUS TULLIUS CICERO TO MARCUS JUNIUS BRUTUS (SEPTEMBER, 44 B.C.)

The events of the past few months have put me in despair. Octavius quarrels with Antonius; I have hope. Their differences are reconciled, they are seen together; I am fearful. They quarrel again, rumors of plots are in the air; I am puzzled. Once again they mend their disputes; and I am without joy. What does it all mean? Does either of them know where he is going? Meanwhile, their disputes and reconciliations keep all of Rome in a turmoil, and keep the assassination of the tyrant alive in the minds of everyone; and through it all, Octavius's strength and popularity steadily increase. I sometimes almost believe that we may have misjudged the boy—and then I am persuaded that it is the accident of event which makes him appear more capable than he is. I do not know. It is too dark.

I have found it necessary to speak against Antonius in the Senate, though it may have put me in some danger. Octavius gives me his support in private conversation, but he does not speak in public. In any event, Antonius now knows that I am his implacable enemy. He threatened such harm that I dared not give my second address to the Senate; but it will be published, and the world will know it.

XI. LETTER: MARCUS TULLIUS CICERO TO MARCUS JUNIUS BRUTUS (OCTOBER, 44 B.C.)

Recklessness, recklessness! Antonius has mobilized the Macedonian legions and goes to meet them at Brindisi; Octavius is enlisting the discharged veterans of Caesar's legions in Campania. Antonius intends to march to Gaul against our friend Decimus, ostensibly to avenge the assassination but in fact to augment his power by gaining the Gallic legions. It is rumored that he will march through Rome, showing his strength against Octavius. Shall we have war again in Italy? Can we trust so young a boy and with such a name as Caesar (as he calls himself) with our cause? Oh, Brutus! Where are you now, when Rome has need of you?

XII. CONSULAR ORDER TO GAIUS SENTIUS TAVUS, MILITARY COMMANDER OF MACEDONIA AT APOLLONIA, WITH LETTER (AUGUST, 44 B.C.)

By authority of Marcus Antonius, Consul to the Senate of Rome, Governor of Macedonia, Pontifex of the Lupercalian College, and Commander in Chief of the Macedonian Legions, Gaius Sentius Tavus is hereby ordered to command the chief officers of the Macedonian Legions to mobilize their forces in preparation for a crossing to Brindisi, to make this crossing at the earliest moment in his power, and to hold the legions in that place against the arrival of their supreme commander.

Sentius: this is important. He spent part of last year at Apollonia. He may have made friends with some of the officers. *Investigate this most carefully.* If there are those who seem inclined toward him, transfer them out of the legion at once, or get rid of them in some other way. But get rid of them.

XIII. A LIBEL: DISTRIBUTED TO THE MACEDONIAN LEGIONS, AT BRINDISI (44 B.C.)

To the followers of the murdered Caesar:

Do you march against Decimus Brutus Albinus in Gaul, or against the son of Caesar in Rome?

Ask Marcus Antonius.

Are you mobilized to destroy the enemies of your dead leader, or to protect his assassins?

Ask Marcus Antonius.

Where is the will of the dead Caesar which bequeathed to every citizen of Rome three hundred pieces of silver coin?

Ask Marcus Antonius.

The murderers and conspirators against Caesar are free by an act of the Senate sanctioned by Marcus Antonius.

The murderer Gaius Cassius Longinus has been given the governorship of Syria by Marcus Antonius.

The murderer Marcus Junius Brutus has been given the governorship of Crete by Marcus Antonius.

Where are the friends of the murdered Caesar among his enemies?

The son of Caesar calls to you.

XIV. ORDER OF EXECUTION, AT BRINDISI (44 B.C.)

To: Gaius Sentius Tavus, Military Commander of Macedonia
From: Marcus Antonius, Commander in Chief of the Legions
Subject: Treasonable actions in the Legions IV and Martian

*

The following officers will be presented at the headquarters of the Commander in Chief of the Legions, at the hour of dawn on the twelfth day of November.

P. Lucius	Cn. Servius
Sex. Portius	M. Flavius
C. Titius	A. Marius

At that hour on that day, these men shall suffer execution by beheading. In addition, there will be selected by lot fifteen soldiers from each of the twenty cohorts of the IV and Martian, who shall be executed with their officers in the same manner.

All the officers and men of all the Macedonian Legions are commanded to be present and witness this execution.

XV. THE ACTS OF CAESAR AUGUSTUS (A.D. 14)

At the age of nineteen, on my own initiative and at my own expense, I raised an army by means of which I restored liberty to the Republic, which had been oppressed by the tyranny of a faction.

Chapter Three

My dear old friend, these letters that you require of me—
I could not have suspected how they would take me back to
the days that are gone, and through what a strange tangle of
emotions I must go on that journey! Now in these uneventful
years of my retirement, as my time on earth draws to an end,
the days seem to hasten with unseemly speed; and only the past
is real, so that I go there as if I were reborn, as Pythagoras says
we are, into another time and another body.

So many things whirl around in my head—the disorder of
those days! Can I make sense of them, even to you, who know
more of the history of our world than any mortal? I comfort
myself with the certainty that you will make sense of what I tell
you, even if I cannot.

Marcus Antonius went to Brindisi to meet the Macedonian
legions that he had called up, and we knew that we must act.
We had no money: Octavius had stripped his fortune and sold
much of his property to discharge Julius's bequests to the people. We had no authority: according to the law, not for ten
years would Octavius be eligible to become even a member of
the Senate, and of course Antonius had blocked every special
privilege that the Senate would have given him. We had no
power: only a few hundred of the veterans of Caesar's army in
Rome had unequivocally declared for us. We had a name, and
the force of our determination.

So Octavius and Agrippa went immediately to the south, to
the Campanian coastal farms where Caesar had settled many
of his veterans. We knew what Antonius was offering recruits
as an enlistment bounty; we offered five times that amount.
We offered money that we did not have; it was a desperate
gamble, but it was a necessary one. I remained in Rome and
composed letters for distribution among the Macedonian legions that were nominally under Antonius's command. We had
had promises from them earlier, and had reason to believe that

some would defect to us, if the circumstances were right. As you know, the letters had their effect—though it was not precisely what we had anticipated.

For Antonius then made the first of his many serious blunders. Because of some wavering on the part of two of the legions—the Macedonian IV and the Martian, I believe—he had some three hundred officers and men put to death. More than the letters, I am sure, this action worked to our advantage. During the march to Rome, these two legions simply diverged to Alba Longa, and sent word to Octavius that they would cast their fortunes with his. It was not the cruelty of Antonius's act that outraged them, I think; soldiers are used to cruelty and death. But they could not trust themselves to a man who would act so rashly and unnecessarily.

In the meantime, Octavius and Agrippa had had a small success in raising the beginnings of an army to meet the Antonian threat. Some three thousand men with arms (though we let it be thought that it was double that number) assigned themselves to his command; and the same number without arms pledged themselves to our future. With a sizable portion of this three thousand, Octavius marched toward Rome, leaving Agrippa in command of the rest and charging him to march with them toward Arezzo (the place of my birth, as you will remember), and to raise whatever other troops he could on the way. It was a pitiful force to range against the power of our enemies; but it was more than we had had in the beginning.

Octavius encamped the army a few miles outside of Rome and entered the city with only a small body of men to guard his person, and offered his services to the Senate and the people against Antonius; it was known that Antonius was marching toward Rome, and no one could be sure of his purpose. But in their division and impotence, the Senate refused; and in their confusion and fear, the people did not speak as one. As a result, most of the army that we had raised at so much cost to ourselves dispersed, and we were left with fewer than a thousand men at Rome, and a few hundred more who marched (futilely, we thought) with Agrippa toward Arezzo.

Octavius had sworn to himself, to his friends, and to the people that he would have vengeance upon the murderers of his father. And now Antonius was marching through Rome on his way to Gaul—to punish (he said) Decimus Albinus, one of the conspirators. But we knew (and Rome feared) his real purpose, which was to gain for himself the Gallic legions under Decimus's command. With those legions, he would be invincible; and the world would lie like an unguarded treasure house before his plundering ambition. We simply faced the death of the Rome for which Caesar had given his life.

Do you see the position we were in? We had to prevent the punishment of one of those very criminals we had ourselves sworn to punish. And it became clear to us that, unexpectedly, another end had discovered us—an end larger than revenge and larger than our own ambitions. The world and our task enlarged themselves before us, and we felt that we peered into a bottomless chasm.

Without money, without the support of the people, without the authority of the Senate—we could only wait for what would ensue. Octavius withdrew the remnants of his army from the outskirts of Rome, and began slowly to follow Agrippa's little band to Arezzo—though it seemed now that there was no hope of diverting or even delaying Antonius's progress to Gaul.

And then Antonius made his second serious blunder.

In his vanity and recklessness, he marched into the city of Rome with his legions; and they were fully armed.

Not for forty years—since the butcheries of Marius and Sulla —had Roman citizens seen armed soldiers inside the city walls; and there were people still alive then who could remember the cobbles dark with blood, and there were senators then in the House who as young men had seen the rostrum piled with the heads of the senators of that day, and could remember the bodies left in the Forum to be devoured by dogs.

So Antonius swaggered and drank and whored through the city, and his soldiers plundered the houses of his enemies; and the Senate cowered, and did not dare oppose him.

Then the news came to Antonius from Alba that the Martian legion had deserted him and had declared for us. It is said that he was drunk at the time he got the news; in any event, he acted as if he were. For he precipitately called the Senate to meet (he was still consul, remember), and in a long irrational harangue demanded that Octavius be branded a public enemy. But before the speech was over, another piece of news came into the city, and was whispered among the senators even as Antonius was speaking. The Macedonian IV legion, following the Martian, had declared its allegiance to Octavius and the party of the Caesars.

In his rage, Antonius lost control of what little good sense he had. He had defied the constitution once by entering the city with his armed forces; now he defied law and custom by convening the Senate at night and by threatening his opponents with harm if they attended the meeting. In this illegal assemblage, he accomplished the following: he had Macedonia given to his brother, Gaius; and the provinces of Africa, Crete, Libya, and Asia to his own supporters. And then he hastened to the rest of his army at Tivoli, whence he began his march to Rimini, where he was to prepare his siege of Decimus in Gaul.

Thus, what Octavius could not accomplish by his caution, Antonius accomplished for us by his recklessness. Where there had been despair, I could see hope.

Now, my old friend, I will tell you something that no one knows; and you may use it in your history, if you wish. It is known that during the midst of these events, Octavius was on his slow march with the raggle of his troops to Arezzo; what is not known is that, at the moment of Antonius's open display of contempt toward the Senate and the law, and at the moment I judged the temper of the Senate and the people to be what they were, I sent an urgent message to Octavius to return, in dead secret, to Rome, so that we could make our plans. As Antonius swaggered boisterously out of the city, Octavius came secretly in.

And we laid the plan that would give us the world.

II. LETTER: MARCUS TULLIUS CICERO TO MARCUS JUNIUS BRUTUS, AT DYRRACHIUM (JANUARY, 43 B.C.)

My dear Brutus, the news we have in Rome from Athens fills all of us who honor the Republic with joy and hope. Had the others who are our heroes acted so boldly and with such decision as you have, our nation would not now be in such a state of turmoil. To think that, so shortly after the illegal assignment that Marcus Antonius made of Macedonia to his half-witted brother Gaius, now that same Gaius cowers in fear in Apollonia, while your armies grow and gather the strength that will one day be our salvation! Would that your cousin Decimus had had that same resolution and skill nine months ago, after our banquet of the Ides of March!

I am sure that the disturbing news of Antonius's new madness has reached you even in Dyrrachium. Disregarding all law and custom, he has terrorized the city; and now he marches into Gaul against Decimus. And until a few weeks ago, it was clear to all of us that he would be successful in that endeavor.

But young Caesar (I call him that now, despite my aversion to the name) and his young friend, Maecenas, came to me in secret with a plan. The boy has asked my advice before, and has courted me; but only recently have I become persuaded that he may be of serious consequence and help to us. Despite his incredible youth, and his much too diffident manner, he has accomplished remarkable things during these last few months.

Quite correctly, he pointed out to me that he maintains the only force capable of deterring Antonius: one army, under Marcus Agrippa, now marches to Arezzo, which is in the path of Antonius's intended entry into Gaul; and another, which has been discreetly encamped several miles from Rome, follows that; and the gods know how many other veterans and recruits they will pick up on the way. But (and this is what makes me begin to trust the young leader) he will not move illegally; he must have the sanction of the Senate and the people. And he proposes that I use my offices (which are still not inconsiderable, I imagine) to effect this sanction.

This I have consented to do, under conditions that are mutually agreeable. For his part, young Octavius Caesar asked that the Senate sanction his actions in raising the army; that the veterans who had joined him, as well as the IV Macedonian and the Martian legions, be formally given honor and the thanks of the people; that he himself be legally given command of the forces that he had raised and that no man be put in military authority over him; that the state defray the expenses of his army and supply them with the bounty he had promised them for their enlistment; that lands be allotted to the troops after their service; and that the Senate waive the law of age (as it has done before) and upon his successful alleviation of the siege of Decimus at Mutina, that he return to Rome as a senator and be allowed to stand for consul.

In another time and in other circumstances, these might have seemed excessive demands; but if Decimus falls, then we are ruined. I confess to you, my dear Brutus, I would have promised nearly anything; but I put a grave face on, and made some demands of my own.

I stipulated that in no way would he or his men take that revenge upon Decimus which he had earlier threatened; that he not oppose as a senator the decrees that I might pass in behalf of the legality of Decimus's position in Gaul; and that he not use the armies sanctioned by the Senate for an adventure against either you in Macedonia or our friend Cassius in Syria.

To all these conditions he agreed, and said, that so long as the Senate adhered to its part of the bargain, he would take no action on his own authority nor allow those under his command to do so.

Thus our cause advances. I have given the speech which put these proposals before the Senate; but as you know, the real work came before I dared to speak, and still I cannot rest in my labors.

III. QUINTUS SALVIDIENUS RUFUS: NOTES FOR A JOURNAL, AT ROME (DECEMBER, 44 B.C.)

Restless, I await my fate. Gaius Octavius is secretly in Rome; Agrippa marches to the north; Maecenas intrigues with everyone, our friends and enemies alike. Yesterday he returned from an afternoon spent with Fulvia herself, that red-faced harridan who is the wife of that same Antonius against whom we are to march. The Senate has given Octavius Caesar powers that a month ago we could not have dreamed: the legions of the next consuls, Hirtius and Pansa, are ours; Octavius has military powers second to none, he will be allowed into the senatorial ranks upon our return from the Gallic campaign—and I have been given the command of a legion, by Octavius himself with the sanction of the Senate. It is an honor that I could not reasonably have expected for many years.

Yet I am restless, and filled with a foreboding. For the first time I become unsure of the rightness of our course. Every success uncovers difficulties that we have not foreseen, and every victory enlarges the magnitude of our possible defeat.

Octavius has changed; he is no longer the friend we had in Apollonia. He seldom laughs, he takes almost no wine, and he seems to disdain even the harmless, distracting pleasures that we took with the girls once. So far as I know, he has not even had a woman since our return to Rome.

"So far as I know," I realize I have said. Once we knew all about each other; now he has become contained, withdrawn, almost secretive. I, to whom he once talked with open friendship; from whom he had no secret of his heart; with whom he shared the closest dreams—I no longer know him. Is it grief for his uncle that will not leave him? Is it that grief which has hardened into ambition? Or is it something else that I cannot name? A cold sadness has come over him and draws him apart from us.

In my leisure now in Rome, as I wait for the consular armies to be raised, I can think of these things, and wonder. Perhaps when I am older and wiser I shall understand them.

Gaius Octavius on Cicero: "Cicero is a hopeless conspirator. What he does not write to his friends, he tells to his slaves."

When did the distrust begin?—if it is distrust.

The morning that Octavius and Maecenas announced the plan to me?

I said: "We would aid that Decimus who was one of the murderers of Julius Caesar?"

Octavius said: "We would aid ourselves, so that we might survive."

I did not speak. Maecenas had not spoken.

Octavius said: "Do you remember the oath we made—you and I and Agrippa and Maecenas—that night in Apollonia?"

I said: "I have not forgotten."

Octavius smiled. "Nor have I. . . . We shall save Decimus, though we hate him. We shall save Decimus for that oath, and we shall save him for the law." For an instant his eyes were cold upon me, though I think he did not see me. Then he smiled again, as if remembering himself.

Did it begin with that?

Facts: Decimus was one of the murderers; Octavius goes to his aid. Casca was one of the murderers; Octavius has agreed not to oppose his election as tribune of the people. Marcus Antonius was a friend of Caesar; Octavius now opposes him. Cicero rejoices publicly in the murder; Octavius has made an alliance with him.

Marcus Brutus and Gaius Cassius raise armies in the East, plunder the treasuries of the provinces, and daily augment their strength; Marcus Aemilius Lepidus is secure in the West and waits with his legions—to what purpose no one knows; and in the south, Sextus Pompeius roams the seas at will, raising barbarian armies that may destroy us all. The legion that I command—all the legions in Italy—is the task too large?

But Gaius Octavius is my friend.

IV. LETTER: MARCUS TULLIUS CICERO
TO MARCUS AEMILIUS LEPIDUS AT
NARBONNE, FROM ROME (43 B.C.)

My dear Lepidus, Cicero sends you greetings, and begs you to remember your duty to the Senate and the Republic. I would not mention now the many honors I have been privileged to do you, were I not filled with gratitude for the many kindnesses you have done me. As we have assured each other in the past, our differences have always been honorable ones, and have rested upon our mutual love for the Republic.

Though I put little faith in such, the rumors in Rome are that you will join forces with Marcus Antonius against Decimus. I do not seriously entertain such a possibility, and I see the rumor only as a symptom of that disease of instability that now afflicts our poor Republic. But I think you should know that the rumor does persist, so that for your own safety and honor you might take the most urgent measures to prove it baseless.

The young Caesar, with the blessing of the Senate and the Republic, marches toward Mutina against the outlaw,

Antonius, who besieges Decimus. It may be that he will need
your aid. I know that you will now, as you have in the past, observe the order of the law and refuse the chaos of lawlessness,
for the sake of your position and the security of Rome.

V. LETTER: MARCUS ANTONIUS TO MARCUS AEMILIUS
   LEPIDUS AT NARBONNE, FROM MUTINA (43 B.C.)

Lepidus: I am at Mutina against the hired armies of the murderers of Caesar. Decimus is surrounded; he cannot break out.

I am informed that Cicero and others of his odor have been
writing you, urging treason against the memory of our slain
Julius. The reports of your intentions are ambiguous.

I am not a subtle man; I am not a flatterer; and you are not
a fool.

There are three courses open to you: you can march from
your camp to join me in the destruction of Decimus and the
enemies of Caesar, and thereby gain my eternal friendship and
the power that will come to you from the love of the people;
you can remain unconcerned and neutral in the comfort of
your encampment, and thereby receive neither my blame nor
the hatred of the people—nor their love; you can come to the
aid of the traitor Decimus and his "savior," the false son of our
leader, and thereby receive my enmity and the lasting despite
of the people.

I hope that you have the wisdom to choose the first course;
I fear that you will have the caution to choose the second; I
implore you, for your own safety, not to choose the third.

VI. THE MEMOIRS OF MARCUS
   AGRIPPA: FRAGMENTS (13 B.C.)

We found the Rome we entered torn by strife and ambition.
Marcus Antonius, the pretended friend of the slain Julius Caesar, consorted with the murderers, and would not allow him
whom we now called Octavius Caesar to receive the honors
and powers bequeathed him by his father. Upon ascertaining
the ambition of the usurper Antonius, Octavius Caesar took
himself into the countryside where his father's veterans tilled
the soil, and we raised those troops loyal to the memory of

their dead leader who would oppose with us the plunderers of our nation's dream.

Unlawfully, Marcus Antonius levied the Macedonian troops and marched with them into Rome, and thence to Mutina, where he laid siege to Decimus Brutus Albinus. And though Decimus had been among the murderers of Caesar, for the sake of order and the state, Octavius Caesar agreed to defend his lawful governorship of Gaul against the force of the outlaw Antonius; and with the thanks and sanction of the Senate, we gathered our forces and marched toward Mutina, where Antonius had encamped around the legions of Decimus.

Now I must tell of that campaign at Mutina, which was the first responsibility of war I had under Octavius Caesar and Rome.

The senatorial legions were under the command of the two consuls of the year, Gaius Vibius Pansa and Aulus Hirtius, the latter of whom had been the trusted general of our late Julius Caesar. Octavius Caesar commanded the Martian and Macedonian IV legions, though of the latter I had military leadership. Quintus Salvidienus Rufus had been given the military command of the new legion of recruits we had levied in the countryside of Campania.

Antonius had made his siege of Decimus complete, and he proposed to lie in wait until Decimus's legions, weakened by hunger, must attempt to break through his encampment. We determined that Decimus had put away enough food within the walls of Mutina to endure, so we made winter quarters at Imola, only a two-hour march from Mutina, so that we might quickly go to the aid of Decimus if he made a sally against the Antonian forces. But he cowered within the safety of the city walls, and would not fight; so that when spring came, we faced the prospect of breaking through Antonius's lines ourselves, to save that Decimus who would not save himself. Early in April we determined to move.

Around Mutina the ground is marshy and uneven, cut by gullies and streams; beyond this marsh Antonius was encamped. In secret we searched the land for a way to cross, and discovered a ravine that was unguarded; and in the dead of night, joined by Pansa and five cohorts of his legion, Octavius Caesar and Salvidienus and I led our Martian legion and other soldiers into this ravine, having wrapped our swords and spears with cloth so that the enemy would not be aware of our approach. The moon was full, but a heavy fog clung to the earth, so that we could not see before us; and in single file, each man's hand upon another's shoulder, we inched blindly through the glowing mist, never sure of where we went or whom we might encounter.

Through the night we crept, and in the morning came up on a high road in the marshes; we waited for the fog to lift, and saw no enemy ahead of us. But a sudden gleam came from the brush, and we heard a muffled voice, and we knew we were surrounded. The horn sounded the order for battle, and the soldiers came to their formation on the high ground. The young recruits were ordered by Pansa to stand aside, so as not to hinder the fighting of the veterans, but to stand in readiness if they were needed.

For these were veterans of the Martian legion, and they remembered the slaughter of their comrades at Brindisi by the Antonius they now opposed.

The space upon which we fought was so small that one side could not flank another; therefore, man fought man like gladiators in an arena, and the dust rose thick as the fog of the night before, and swords rang in the air, and no one shouted. We heard only the cries of the wounded and the deep groans of those who were dying.

We fought through the morning and through the afternoon, one line relieving another as it became exhausted. Once Octavius Caesar himself came near death when he seized the standard that our eagle-bearer, wounded, had let fall; and the consul, Pansa, in this engagement suffered a mortal wound. Antonius ordered fresh troops into the battle, and step by step we gave ground; but under the command of Salvidienus the recruits fought as bravely as the veterans, and we were able to enter again into our camp whence we had come the night before. Antonius did not continue the attack after nightfall, so we went into the marsh that was littered with the bodies of our comrades, and carried back the wounded. That night we saw the campfires of Antonius's army beyond the marsh, and heard the singing of his soldiers in their victory.

We feared the slaughter that the next day might bring, for we were weary and our numbers were reduced by half; and we knew that Antonius had troops that he had not used. But during that night, the legions of the consul Hirtius had been marching to our relief; and joining us, made an attack upon Antonius's camp, which was complacent and disordered in its false certainty of success. And the battles raged for many days, during which time the Antonian legions were reduced to half their number; our losses were very slight. Salvidienus was given the legions of the dying Pansa, and he led them with bravery and skill. At last, our armies broke into the very camp of Antonius; and the brave Hirtius was killed by one of Antonius's guards, outside the tent where Antonius had lately rested and whence he had fled.

Upon this defeat, Antonius lost heart; and gathering what remained of his troops, marched northward toward the Alps, which he crossed at further cost to his strength, and joined the forces of Marcus Aemilius Lepidus, who had remained safely at Narbonne.

After the flight of Antonius, Decimus, delivered from the siege, ventured outside the city walls. He sent messengers to Octavius Caesar, thanking him for his aid, and declaring that his own part in the murder of Julius Caesar had been caused by the deceptions of the other conspirators; and he asked that Octavius Caesar converse with him, in the presence of witnesses, so that he might be convinced of the sincerity of his gratitude. But Octavius Caesar declined his thanks, saying: "I did not come to save Decimus; therefore I will not accept his gratitude. I came to save the state; and I will accept its thanks. Nor will I speak to the murderer of my father, nor look upon his face. He may go in safety by the authority of the Senate, not by my own."

Six months later, Decimus was surprised and killed by a chieftain of one of the Gallic tribes. He had the head of Decimus severed, and sent it to Marcus Antonius, who gave him a small reward.

VII. SENATORIAL PROCEEDINGS (APRIL, 43 B.C.)

The third day of this month: the reading to the Senate of the dispatches from the Gallic campaign against the insurgent Marcus Antonius: by Marcus Tullius Cicero.

That the siege of Decimus Brutus Albinus is lifted; that the troops of Marcus Antonius are so reduced that they offer no immediate danger to the Republic; that the remnants of Antonius's army flee northward in disorder; that the consuls Aulus Hirtius and Gaius Vibius Pansa are dead, and that their legions are temporarily under the command of C. Octavius, who waits outside Mutina.

The sixth day of this month: resolutions of Marcus Tullius Cicero.

That fifty days of thanksgiving be declared, in which the citizens of Rome will offer their gratitude to the gods and the senatorial armies for the defeat of Marcus Antonius and the deliverance of Decimus Brutus Albinus.

That the dead consuls Hirtius and Pansa be accorded public funerals, with full honors.

That a public monument be erected to memorialize the glorious deed of the legions of Hirtius and Pansa.

That Decimus Brutus Albinus be given a senatorial triumph for his heroic defeat of the outlaw Marcus Antonius.

That the following directive be sent to Gaius Octavius at Mutina (copy appended):

"The Praetors, Tribunes of the Plebeians, the Senate, the People and Commoners of Rome, send greetings to Gaius Octavius, temporary commander of the Consular Legions:

"You are given the thanks of the Senate for the aid you have rendered Decimus Brutus Albinus in his heroic defeat of the insurgent armies of Marcus Antonius, and you are to know that, by edict of the Senate, Decimus Brutus has been made sole commander of the legions in the furtherance of the pursuit of the Antonian forces. You are therefore ordered to turn over the consular legions of Hirtius and Pansa to Decimus Brutus without delay. You are further ordered to disband those legions that you raised on your own authority, giving them the thanks of the Senate, which has formed a commission to study the advisability of offering them some reward for their services. An envoy from the Senate has been sent to Mutina to deal with these matters; you are to leave the transfer of powers to his offices."

All resolutions of Marcus Tullius Cicero passed by the Senate.

VIII. LETTER: GAIUS CILNIUS MAECENAS
TO TITUS LIVIUS (13 B.C.)

We had heard the witticism that Cicero made: "We shall do
the boy honor, we shall do him praise, and we shall do him
in." But I think that even Octavius did not expect the Senate
and Cicero to offer so blatant and contemptuous a dismissal.
Poor Cicero. . . . Despite the trouble he caused us and the
harm that he intended, we were always rather fond of him.
Such a foolish man, though; he acted out of enthusiasm, vanity, and conviction. We had learned early that we could not
afford those luxuries; we moved, when we had to move, out of
calculation, policy, and necessity.

I was, of course, in Rome during the whole of this affair
at Mutina; as you know I have led armies in my time (and
not altogether badly, if I may say so), but I have always found
the task rather boring—to say nothing of the discomfort. So
if you need details about the actual fighting, you will have to
go elsewhere. If our friend Marcus Agrippa would complete
that autobiography with which he has been threatening us, you
might find some helpful information there. But poor fellow, he
has such problems now (I am sure you know what I mean) that
it is unlikely he will.

Octavius needed someone in Rome a good deal more than
he needed an indifferent general—someone whom he could
trust to keep him informed of the latest shifts in the senatorial
whim, the latest intrigues, marriages, and so forth. And for this
task I was admirably suited, I believe. At that time (this was
nearly thirty years ago, remember) I fancied myself perfectly
cynical, I thought ambition of any kind terribly vulgar, I was
an inveterate gossip, and no one took me at all seriously. I
posted him a daily newsletter, and he kept me informed of the
situation in Gaul.

So the action of Cicero and the Senate did not catch him
unprepared.

My dear Livy, I chide you often for your Republican and
Pompeian sympathies; and though I tease you out of affection, I am sure that you have understood that there is an edge
of seriousness in my scolding. You came to manhood in the
northern tranquillity of Padua, which had for generations been

untouched by strife; and you did not even set foot in Rome until after Actium and the reform of the Senate. Had the chance occurred, it is most likely that you would even have joined with Marcus Brutus to fight against us, as our friend Horace did in fact do, at Philippi, those many years ago.

What you seem so unwilling to accept, even now, is this: that the ideals which supported the old Republic had no correspondence to the fact of the old Republic; that the glorious word concealed the deed of horror; that the appearance of tradition and order cloaked the reality of corruption and chaos; that the call to liberty and freedom closed the minds, even of those who called, to the facts of privation, suppression, and sanctioned murder. We had learned that we had to do what we did, and we would not be deterred by the forms that deceived the world.

To put it briefly, Octavius defied the Senate. He did not disband the legions he had raised; he did not relinquish the armies of Hirtius and Pansa to Decimus; he did not allow the envoys from Rome access to Decimus. He waited into the summer, and the Senate trembled.

Decimus hesitated to do anything at all; and his own soldiers, revulsed by his weakness, deserted by the thousands to us.

Cicero, fearful of our defiance, caused the Senate to order Marcus Brutus to return from Macedonia to Italy with his armies.

We waited, and learned that Antonius had entered Gaul, and had joined the remnants of his forces with those of Lepidus.

We had eight legions, with sufficient cavalry to support them, and several thousand lightly armed auxiliaries. Octavius left three of these legions and the auxiliaries under the command of Salvidienus at Mutina. He had messages sent to Atia and Octavia, his mother and sister, ordering them to take refuge in the Temple of the Vestal Virgins, where they would be safe from reprisals. And we marched on Rome.

It was a necessary action, you must understand; even had Octavius been willing to relinquish the power we had won and to retire from the public scene, he would have done so at the almost certain expense of his life. For it was clear that the Senate was now embarked upon the inevitable, though delayed, consequence of the assassination: the Caesareans had to be exterminated. Antonius would be crushed by the consular armies that had been augmented by those even larger ones of Brutus and Cassius, which were now (by invitation of the Senate) poised in the East, across the Adriatic Sea, waiting to invade Italy; and Octavius would be destroyed in one way or another, by edict of the Senate, or more likely by private murder. Thus it was that suddenly Antonius's cause became our own. The cause was survival; survival depended upon alliance; and alliance depended upon our strength.

We marched on Rome with our legions armed as if for battle, and the news of our approach raced before us like the wind. Octavius encamped his army outside the city upon the Esquiline hill, so that the people and the senators had but to raise their eyes to the east to know our strength.

It was over in two days, and not a drop of Roman blood was spilled.

Our soldiers had the bounty promised them before the campaign at Mutina; the adoption of Octavius by Julius Caesar was made into law; Octavius was given the vacant consulship of Hirtius; and we had eleven legions under our command.

On the fourth day after the Ides of August (though as you know the month then was called Sextilis), Octavius came into Rome to perform the ritual sacrifice attendant upon his accession to the consulship.

A month later he celebrated his twentieth birthday.

IX. LETTER: MARCUS TULLIUS CICERO TO OCTAVIUS CAESAR (AUGUST, 43 B.C.)

You are quite right, my dear Caesar; my labors for the state deserve the reward of tranquillity and rest. I shall therefore quit Rome and retire to my beloved Tusculum and devote my remaining years to those studies which I have loved second only to my country. If I have misjudged you in the past, I have done so out of that love which too often imposes on us both the cruel necessity of going against our more humane and natural inclinations.

In any event, I doubly rejoice that you grant leave of absence to Philippus and myself; for it means pardon for the past and indulgence for the future.

X. LETTER: MARCUS ANTONIUS TO OCTAVIUS CAESAR, FROM THE CAMP OF MARCUS AEMILIUS LEPIDUS NEAR AVIGNON (SEPTEMBER, 43 B.C.)

Octavius: My friend and lieutenant, Decius, whom you released at Mutina to return to me, tells me that you have treated those soldiers of mine that you captured with kindness and respect. For that, you have my gratitude. He further tells me that you made it apparent to him that you bear me no ill will, that you refused to surrender your troops to Decimus, and so forth.

I see no reason why we should not talk, if you think it might be helpful. Certainly you have more in common with my cause than you have with the cause of those time-servers in the Senate. By the way, is it true (as I fear) that they have now also made a public enemy of our friend Lepidus, whom a few months ago they honored with a statue in the Forum? Nothing surprises me any more.

You may have heard that Decimus is dead. A silly business: a little band of Gallic barbarians surprised him. I should have preferred to have dealt with him myself, at a later date.

We could meet at Bononia next month; I have some business there, mostly with the remnants of Decimus's troops, who have decided to come in with me. I would suggest that we not meet with our forces behind us—just a few cohorts, perhaps, for our personal safety. If we came together in full force, our soldiers might get out of hand. Lepidus will have to figure in this, too; so you can expect him. But our men can work out these details.

XI. SENATORIAL PROCEEDINGS: THE CONSULSHIPS OF QUINTUS PEDIUS AND OCTAVIUS CAESAR (SEPTEMBER, 43 B.C.)

That the sentence of outlawry against Marcus Aemilius Lepidus and Marcus Antonius be annulled and that letters of conciliation and apology be sent to them and the officers of their armies.

Passed by the Senate.

Senatorial Trial: against the murderers and conspirators in the murder of Julius Caesar. Prosecutors: Lucius Cornificius and Marcus Agrippa.

That the absent murderer Marcus Junius Brutus be forbidden the bounties of Rome and be condemned in his exile.

That the absent murderer Gaius Cassius Longinus be forbidden the bounties of Rome and be condemned in his exile.

That the Tribune of the People, P. Servilius Casca, having absented himself from the Senate in his guilty fear, be forbidden the bounties of Rome and condemned.

That the absent conspirator and pirate Sextus Pompeius be forbidden the bounties of Rome and be condemned in his exile.

All conspirators and murderers found guilty by Senatorial Jury and condemned to their fates.

XII. LETTER: GAIUS CILNIUS MAECENAS TO TITUS LIVIUS (12 B.C.)

Of all the memories you have dredged from my soul by your questioning, my dear Livy, now you have found the saddest. I have for several days delayed writing you, knowing that I must confront again that old pain.

We were to meet with Antonius at Bologna, and we marched from Rome with five legions of soldiers at our backs, it having been agreed that Antonius and Lepidus would bring no more troops than we did. The conference was to be held on that little island in the Lavinius, where the river widens toward the sea. Narrow bridges connected the island to both banks, and the country was perfectly flat, so that the armies could halt at some distance from the river, and yet keep each other in view at all times. Each side stationed a guard of perhaps a hundred men at either entrance of the bridge, and the three of us—myself, Agrippa, and Octavius—advanced slowly, while across from us Lepidus and Antonius, each with two attendants, came from the other bank at an equal pace.

It was raining, I remember—a gray day. There was a small hut of unhewn stone a few yards away from the bridge, and we made our way toward that, meeting Antonius and Lepidus at the door. Before we entered, Lepidus looked at us for weapons, and Octavius smiled, saying to him:

"We shall not harm each other. We have come here to destroy the assassins; we have not come to mimic them."

We stooped to enter the low door, and Octavius sat at the rough table in the center of the room, with Antonius and Lepidus on either side of him. You realize, of course, that a general agreement had been made even before we met: Octavius, Antonius, and Lepidus were to form a triumvirate modeled upon that of Julius Caesar, Gnaeus Pompeius, and Crassus, made nearly twenty years before; this triumviral power was to last for five years. This power would give them the rule of Rome, with the right to appoint urban magistrates and command the provincial armies. The provinces of the West (Cassius and Brutus held those of the East) were to be divided among the triumvirs. We had already accepted what was by far the most modest portion—the two Africas, and the islands of Sicily, Sardinia, and Corsica—and the possession of even those was in serious doubt since Sextus Pompeius illegally held Sicily and controlled nearly the whole of the Mediterranean; but land was not what we wanted from the compact. Lepidus retained what he had previously commanded: Narbonensis and the two Spains. And Antonius had the two Gauls, by far the richest and most important of the divisions. Behind it all, of course, was the necessity of our combining forces so that we might conquer Brutus and Cassius in the east and thus punish the murderers of Julius Caesar and bring order to Italy.

It became quickly clear that Lepidus was Antonius's creature. He was a pompous and fatuous man, though if he did not speak he made quite an imposing figure. You know the type —he looked like a senator. Antonius let him drone on for a few minutes, and then he made an impatient gesture.

"We can get to the details later," he said. "We have more important business now." He looked at Octavius. "You know that we have enemies."

"Yes," Octavius said.

"Even though the whole Senate was bowing and scraping when you left, you can be sure they're plotting against you now."

"I know," Octavius said. He was waiting for Antonius to continue.

"And not only in the Senate," Antonius said. He got up and walked restlessly about the room. "All over Rome. I keep remembering your Uncle Julius." He shook his head. "You can't trust anybody."

"No," Octavius said. He smiled softly.

"I keep thinking of them—soft, fat, rich, and getting richer." He pounded his fist on the table, so that some of the papers there were jarred to the clay floor. "And our soldiers are hungry, and will get hungrier before the year's out. Soldiers don't fight on empty stomachs and without something to look forward to after it's all over."

Octavius was watching him.

Antonius said: "I keep remembering Julius. If he had just had a little more resolve in dealing with his enemies." He shook his head again.

There was a long silence.

"How many?" Octavius asked quietly.

Antonius grinned and sat down at the table again. "I have thirty or forty names," he said negligently. "I imagine Lepidus has a few of his own."

"You've discussed this with Lepidus."

"Lepidus agrees," Antonius said.

Lepidus cleared his throat, stretched his arm out so that his hand rested on the table, and leaned back. "It is with much regret that I have come to the conclusion that this is the only course open to us, unpleasant though it may be. I assure you, my dear boy, that—"

"Do not call me your dear boy." Octavius did not raise his voice; like his face, it was totally without expression. "I am the son of Julius Caesar, and I am consul of Rome. You will not call me boy again."

"I assure you—" Lepidus said, and looked at Antonius. Antonius laughed. Lepidus fluttered his hands. "I assure you, I intended no—no—"

Octavius turned away from him and said to Antonius: "So it will be a proscription, as it was with Sulla."

Antonius shrugged. "Call it what you want to. But it's necessary. You know it's necessary."

"I know it," Octavius said slowly. "But I do not like it."

"You'll get used to it," Antonius said cheerfully, "in time."

Octavius nodded absently. He drew his cloak more tightly about his body, and got up from the table and walked to the window. It was raining. I could see his face. The raindrops hit the window casement and splashed on his face. He did not move. It was as if his face were stone. He did not move for a long time. Then he turned to Antonius and said:

"Give me your names."

"You will support this," Antonius said slowly. "Even though you don't like it, you will support it."

"I will support it," Octavius said. "Give me your names."

Antonius snapped his fingers, and one of his attendants handed him a paper. He glanced at it, and then looked up at Octavius, grinning.

"Cicero," Antonius said.

Octavius nodded. He said slowly: "I know that he has caused us some trouble and that he has offended you. But he has given me his word that he will retire."

"Cicero's word," Antonius said, and spat on the floor.

"He is an old man," Octavius said. "He can't have many more years."

"One more year—six months—a month is too long. He has too much power, even in his defeat."

"He has done me harm," Octavius said, as if to himself, "yet I am fond of him."

"We're wasting time," Antonius said. "Any other name—" he tapped the roll of paper "—I'll discuss with you. But Cicero is not negotiable."

Octavius almost smiled, I think. "No," he said, "Cicero is not negotiable."

He seemed to lose interest, then, in what they said. Antonius and Lepidus wrangled over names, and occasionally asked for his assent. He would nod absently. Once Antonius asked him if he did not want to add his own names to the list, and Octavius replied: "I am young. I have not yet lived so long as to acquire that many enemies."

And so, late that night, in the lamplight that flickered with every movement of the air, the list was drawn up. Seventeen of

the richest and most powerful senators were to be at once condemned to death and their fortunes confiscated; and a hundred
and thirty more were to be proscribed immediately thereafter,
and their names published, so that Rome might find limits in
which to contain its fear.

Octavius said: "If it is to be done at all, it must be done
without delay."

And then we slept, like common soldiers, wrapped in our
blankets, on the clay floor of the hut—it having been agreed
that none of us would speak to our armies until all the details
of the compact were settled.

As you know, my dear Livy, much has been said and written
of that proscription, both in blame and praise; and it is true
that the prosecution of the affair did get rather badly out of
hand. Antonius and Lepidus kept adding names to the list,
and a few of the soldiers used the confusion to settle their
own enmities and to enrich themselves; but such is to be expected. In the matter of passion, whether of love or war, excess
is inevitable.

Yet I have always been bewildered when, in the ease of
peace, men raise the questions of praise or blame. It seems to
me now that both judgments are inappropriate, and equally so.
For those who thus judge do not judge so much out of a concern for right or wrong as out of a protest against the pitiless
demands of necessity, or an approval of them. And necessity is
simply what has happened; it is the past.

We slept the night, and rose before dawn—and now, my
friend, I approach that sorrow of which I spoke at the beginning of this letter. It was dread of that approach, perhaps,
which invited me to this easy philosophizing, for which I trust
you will forgive me.

The proscriptions made, it now remained for the triumvirs
to settle the affairs of Rome for the next five years. It had already been agreed that Octavius would relinquish the consulship that he had so recently received from the Senate; by virtue
of their position, each of the triumvirs already had consular
powers, and it was felt that it was wiser to make use of lieu-
tenants to perform those senatorial duties, thus enlarging the
senatorial base of power and freeing the triumvirs to carry out

their military tasks unimpeded. The second day's business was to choose the ten consuls who would have authority over the city for the next five years, and to divide the available legions among the triumvirs.

We breakfasted on coarse bread and dates; Antonius complained of the simplicity of the fare; it was still raining. By noon the armies had been disposed, and in the transaction Octavius gained three legions that we had not had before, in addition to the eleven that we already commanded. The afternoon we were to devote to the choice of consuls.

It was an important negotiation, you understand; it was clear, though unspoken, that beyond the agreements we had made, there remained significant differences between the purposes of Marcus Antonius and Octavius Caesar. The consuls were the men who would represent the interests of the triumvirs, individually and collectively, in Rome; it was essential that we choose those whom we could trust, and yet those who were acceptable to the other parties. It was a rather delicate matter, as you can imagine; and it was not until late in the afternoon that we had proceeded to the fourth year.

And Octavius offered the name of Salvidienus Rufus.

I am sure that you have had, as we all have, that mysterious experience of prescience—a moment when, beyond reason and cause, at a word, or at the flicker of an eyelid, or at anything at all, one has a sudden foreboding—of what, one does not know. I am not a religious man; but I am sometimes nearly tempted to believe that the gods do speak to us, and that only in unguarded moments will we listen.

"Salvidienus Rufus," Octavius said; and I had within me that sudden sickening rise, as if I were falling from a great height.

For an instant Antonius did not move; then he yawned, and said sleepily: "Salvidienus Rufus. . . . Are you sure he's your choice?"

"He is my choice," Octavius said. "You should have no objection to him. He would be with me now, as are Agrippa and Maecenas, were he not commanding the legions I left behind before I came here." Octavius added dryly, "You will remember, I believe, how well he fought against you at Mutina."

Antonius grinned. "I remember. Four years. . . . Don't you think he might grow impatient in that time?"

"We will need him against Cassius and Brutus," Octavius said patiently. "We will need him against Sextus Pompeius. If we survive those battles, he shall have earned the office."

Antonius looked at him quizzically for a long moment; then he nodded, as if he had decided something. "All right," he said. "You can have him—either for the consulship or the proscription. Take your choice."

Octavius said: "I do not understand your joke."

"It's no joke." Antonius snapped his fingers; one of his attendants handed him a sheet of paper. Antonius dropped it negligently in front of Octavius. "I give him to you."

Octavius picked up the paper, unrolled it, and read. His face did not change expression. He read for a long time. He handed the paper to me.

"Is this Salvidienus's handwriting?" he asked quietly.

I read. I heard myself say, "It is Salvidienus's handwriting."

He took the letter from my fingers. He sat for a long time looking in front of him. I watched his face and heard the dull hiss of the rain as it fell on the thatched roof.

"It's not a great gift," Antonius said. "I have no use for him, now that we have our agreement. Now that you and I are together, I wouldn't be able to trust him. This kind of secret would do neither of us any good." He pointed to the letter. "He sent it to me just after I had joined Lepidus at Avignon. I must say I was tempted, but I decided to wait until I saw what came out of this meeting."

Octavius nodded.

"Shall we put his name on the list?" Antonius asked.

Octavius shook his head. "No," he said in a low voice.

"You have to get used to these things," Antonius said impatiently. "He's a danger to us now, or will be. His name goes on the list."

"No," Octavius said. He did not raise his voice, but the word filled the room. His eyes turned to Antonius, and they were like blue fire. "He is not to be proscribed." Then he turned away from Antonius, and his eyes dulled. He said in a whisper: "The matter is not negotiable." He was silent. Then he said to me: "You will write to Salvidienus and inform him that he is no longer a general of my armies, that he is no longer in my service, and—" he paused, "—that he is no longer my friend."

I did not look at the letter again; I did not have to. The words were in my mind, and they still are, after these more than twenty-five years, like an old scar. I give the words to you, as they were written:

"Quintus Salvidienus Rufus sends greetings to Marcus Antonius. I command three legions of Roman soldiers, and am constrained to remain inactive as Decimus Brutus Albinus organizes his forces for a probable pursuit of your army and yourself. Octavius Caesar has been betrayed by the Senate, and returns to Rome on a vain mission. I despair of his resolution, and I despair of our future. Only in you do I discern that purpose and will which may punish the murderers of Julius Caesar and rid Rome of the tyranny of an aristocracy. I will, therefore, put my legions at your disposal, if you will consent to honor me with a command equal to your own, and if you will agree to pursue the cause to which I committed myself with Octavius Caesar and which has been betrayed by ambition and compromise. I am ready to march to you at Avignon."

And so in my sorrow I sent the letter to him who had been our brother, using as messenger that Decimus Carfulenus who had jointly commanded at Mutina with Salvidienus. It was Carfulenus himself who told me of what ensued.

Salvidienus had had rumors of Carfulenus's mission, and waited for him alone in his tent. He was pale, Carfulenus said, but composed. He had been newly shaved, and in accordance with the necessity of the ritual his beard was deposited in the little silver box that lay open on his table.

"I have put away my boyhood," Salvidienus said, pointing to the box. "And now I may receive your message."

Carfulenus, so moved that he could not speak, gave him the letter. Salvidienus read it standing, nodded, and then sat down at his table, still facing Carfulenus.

"Do you wish to reply?" asked Carfulenus at last.

"No," Salvidienus said, and then he said: "Yes. I will reply." Slowly but without hesitation he removed a dagger from the folds of his toga, and with his strength and in Carfulenus's sight, he plunged it into his breast. Carfulenus leaped toward him, but Salvidienus raised his left hand to stay his advance.

And in a low voice, only a little breathless, he said: "Tell Octavius that if I cannot remain his friend in life, I may do so in death."

He remained seated at his table until his eyes dulled, and he toppled to the dust.

XIII. LETTER: ANONYMOUS TO MARCUS TULLIUS CICERO, AT ROME (NOVEMBER, 43 B.C.)

One who cherishes for you the tranquillity and rest that you might have in your retirement, urges you to quit the country that you love. You are in mortal and immediate danger, so long as you stay in Italy. A cruel necessity has forced one to go against his more humane and natural inclinations. You must act at once.

XIV. THE HISTORY OF ROME. TITUS LIVIUS: FRAGMENT (A.D. 13)

Marcus Cicero, shortly before the arrival of the triumvirs, had left the city, rightly convinced that he could no more escape Antonius than Cassius and Brutus could escape Octavius Caesar: at first he had fled to his Tusculan villa, then he set out by cross-country roads to his villa at Formia, intending to take ship from Gaeta. He put out to sea several times, but was driven back by contrary winds: and since there was a heavy ground swell and he could no longer endure the tossing of the ship, he at last became weary of flight and of life, and returned to his villa on the high ground, which was little more than a mile from the sea.

"Let me die," he said, "in my own country, which I have often saved."

It is known that his slaves were ready to fight for him with bravery and loyalty: but he ordered them to set down the litter, and to suffer quietly the hard necessity of fate. As he leaned from the litter and kept his neck still for the purpose, his head was struck off. But that did not satisfy the brutality of the soldiers: they cut off his hands, too, reviling them for having written against Antonius. So the head was brought to

Antonius and by his order set between the two hands on the rostrum where he had been heard as consul and as consular, where in that very year his eloquent invectives against Antonius had commanded unprecedented admiration. Men were scarcely able to raise their tearful eyes and look upon the mangled remains of their countryman.

Chapter Four

My dear Nicolaus, I send you greetings, as does our old friend and tutor, Tyrannion. I send you greetings from Rome, where I arrived only last week, after a long and most wearying journey—from Alexandria, by way of Corinth; by sail and by oar; by cart, wagon, and horseback; and sometimes even on foot, staggering beneath the weight of my books. One looks at maps, and does not truly apprehend the extent and variety of the world. It is a new sort of education, the gaining of which does not require a master. Indeed, if one travels enough, the pupil may become the master; our Tyrannion, so learned in all things, has been at some pains to question me about what I have seen during my travels.

I am staying with Tyrannion in one of a little group of cottages on a hill overlooking the city. It is a sort of colony, I suppose; several established teachers (one does not call them philosophers in Rome, where philosophy is somewhat suspect) live here, and a few younger scholars who, like myself, have been invited to live and study with their former masters.

I was surprised when Tyrannion brought me here, so far away from the city; and I was even more surprised when he explained the reason. It seems that the public library in Rome is worse than useless; an incredibly small collection, often badly copied, and as many books in this dreadful Latin tongue as in our own Greek! But Tyrannion assures me that whatever texts I may need are available, though in private collections. One of his friends, who lives here with us, is that Athenodorus of Tarsus of whom we heard so much at Alexandria; he has, Tyrannion assures me, access to the best private collections in the city, to which we wandering scholars always are welcome.

Of this Athenodorus I must say a few words. He is a most impressive man. He is only a few years older than Tyrannion —perhaps in his middle fifties—but he gives one the impression that he has the wisdom of all the ages somehow within his power. He is aloof and hard, but not unkind; he speaks seldom, and never engages in those playful debates with which the rest of us amuse ourselves; and we seem to follow him, though he does not lead. It is said that he has powerful friends, though he never drops a name; and his personage is such that we hardly dare to discuss such matters, even out of his presence. Yet for all his power in the world and of the mind, there is a sadness within him, the source of which I cannot discover. I have resolved to talk to him, despite my trepidation, and to learn what I may.

Indeed, you will be getting these letters through his auspices; he has access to the diplomatic pouch that goes weekly to Damascus, and he has let me know that he will have these letters included.

Thus, my dear Nicolaus, begins my adventure in the world. According to my promise, I shall write you regularly, sharing whatever new learning I get. I regret that you could not come with me, and I hope that the family affairs that keep you in Damascus soon are solved, and that you can join me in this strange new world.

You must think me a bad friend and a worse philosopher; I am not the former, but I may be on my way to becoming the latter. I had resolved to write you every week—and it is nearly a month since I have put pen to paper.

But this is the most extraordinary of cities, and it threatens to engulf even the strongest of minds. Days tumble after each other in a frenzy such as neither of us could have imagined during our quiet years of study together in the calm of Alexandria. I wonder if, in the balm and somnolence of your beloved Damascus, you can even conceive the quality that I am trying to convey to you.

With some frequency I am struck by the suspicion (perhaps it is only a feeling) that we are too complacent in our Greek pride of history and language, and that we too easily assume a superiority to the "barbarians" of the West who are pleased to call themselves our masters. (I am, you see, becoming somewhat less the philosopher and somewhat more the man of the world.) Our provinces have their charm and culture, no doubt; but there is a kind of vitality here in Rome that a year ago I could not have been persuaded was even remotely attractive. A year ago, I had only heard of Rome; now I have seen it; and at this moment I am not sure that I will ever return to the East, or to my native Pontus.

Imagine, if you will, a city which occupies perhaps half the area of that Alexandria where we studied as boys—and then think of that same city containing within its precincts more than twice the number of people that crowded Alexandria. That is the Rome that I live in now—a city of nearly a million people, I have been told. It is unlike anything I have ever seen. They come here from all over the world—black men from the burning sands of Africa, pale blonds from the frozen north, and every shade between. And such a polyglot of tongues! Yet everyone speaks a little Latin or a little Greek, so that no one need feel a stranger.

And how they crowd themselves together, these Romans. Beyond the walls of the city lies some of the most beautiful countryside that you can imagine; yet the people huddle together here like fish trapped in a net and struggle through narrow, winding little streets that run senselessly, mile after mile, through the city. During the daylight hours, these streets—all of them—are literally choked with people; and the noise and stench are incredible. A few months before his death, the great Julius Caesar decreed that only in the dark hours between dusk and dawn might wagons and carts and beasts of burden be allowed in the city; one wonders what it must have been like before that decree, when horses and oxen and goods-wagons of all descriptions mingled with the people on these impossible streets.

Thus the ordinary Roman who lives in the city proper must never have any sleep. For the noise of the day becomes the din of the night, as drovers curse their horses and oxen, and the great wooden carts groan and clatter over the cobblestones.

No one ventures out alone after dark, except those tradespeople who must and the very rich who can afford a bodyguard; even on moonlit nights the streets are pitch dark, since the rickety tenements are built so high that it is impossible for even a vagrant ray of moonlight to find its way down into the streets. And the streets are filled with the desperate poor who would rob you and cut your throat for the clothes you wear and the little silver you might carry with you.

Yet those who live in these towering ramshackle buildings are little safer than those who would wander the streets at night; for they live in constant danger of fire. At night, in the safety of my hillside cottage, I can see in the distance the fires break out like flowers blooming in the darkness, and hear the distant shouts of fear or agony. There are fire brigades, to be sure; but they are uniformly corrupt and too few to accomplish much good.

And yet in the center of this chaos, this city, there is, as if it were another world, the great Forum. It is like the fora that we have seen in the provincial cities, but much grander—great columns of marble support the official buildings; there are dozens of statues, and as many temples to their borrowed Roman gods; and many more smaller buildings that house the various offices of government. There is a good deal of open space, and somehow the noise and stench and smoke from the surrounding city seem not to penetrate here at all. Here people walk in sunlight in open space, converse easily, exchange rumors, and read the news posted at the various rostra around the Senate House. I come here to the Forum nearly every day, and feel that I am at the center of the world.

I begin to understand this Roman disdain for philosophy. Their world is an immediate one—of cause and consequence, of rumor and fact, of advantage and deprivation. Even I, who have devoted my life to the pursuit of knowledge and truth, can have some sympathy for the state of the world which has occasioned this disdain. They look at learning as if it were a means to an end; at truth as if it were only a thing to be used. Even their gods serve the state, rather than the other way around.

Here is a copy of a poem found this morning on every gate of importance that leads into the city. I shall not attempt a translation; I transcribe it in its Latin:

> Stop, traveler, before you enter this farmhouse,
> and look to yourself. There is a boy lives here
> with the name of a man. You will dine with him
> at your peril. Oh, he'll ask you, never fear;

he asks everyone. Last month his father died;
now the boy carouses on the stinking wine
of his freedom and lets the livestock run wild
beyond the broken fences—except for one,
the farrow of a pet pig he has taken
into his household. Do you have a daughter?
Look to her, also. This boy once had a taste
for girls lovely as she. He may change again.

I offer a gloss, in the manner of our old teachers. The "boy with the name of a man" is, of course, Gaius Octavius Caesar; the "father" who gave him the name is Julius Caesar; the "farrow" is one Clodia, daughter of the "pig" (that is the nickname given her by enemies), Fulvia, wife of Marcus Antonius, with whom Octavius alternately battles and reconciles. The "girl" alluded to in the last line is one Servilia, daughter of an ex-consul to whom Octavius was engaged, before (as it is said) under pressure from his own and Antonius's troops, he accepted a marriage agreement with Antonius's stepdaughter. There is, of course, more form than substance to the contract; the girl, I understand, is only thirteen years old. But it apparently has placated those forces that want to see Octavius and Antonius on amicable terms. The poem itself, no doubt, has other local allusions that I do not understand; it was almost certainly commissioned by one of the senatorial party who does not want a conciliation of Octavius and Antonius; it is a vulgar thing. . . . But it does have something of a ring to it, does it not?

I am forever surprised. The name of Octavius Caesar is on everyone's lips. He is in Rome; he is out of Rome. He is the savior of the nation; he will destroy it. He will punish the murderers of Julius Caesar; he will reward them. Whatever the truth, this mysterious youth has captured the imagination of Rome; and I, myself, have not been immune.

So, knowing that our Athenodorus has long lived in and around Rome, I took the occasion yesterday evening, after we had dined, to ask him a few questions. (Gradually, he has unbent toward me, and now we may exchange as many as half a dozen words at a time.)

I asked him what manner of man this was, this Octavius Caesar, as he calls himself. And I showed him a copy of the poem that I sent you earlier.

Athenodorus looked at it, his thin, hooked nose almost touching the paper, his thin cheeks drawn inward, his thin lips pursed. Then he handed it back to me, with the same gesture that he has when he returns a paper I have given him for his emendations.

"The meter is uncertain," he said. "The matter is trivial."

I have learned patience with Athenodorus. Again, I questioned him about this Octavius.

"He is a man like any other," he said. "He will become what he will become, out of the force of his person and the accident of his fate."

I asked Athenodorus if he had ever seen this youth, or talked to him. Athenodorus frowned and growled:

"I was his teacher. I was with him at Apollonia when his uncle was killed and he took the path that has led him where he is today."

For a moment I thought that Athenodorus was speaking in metaphor; and then I saw his eyes and knew he was speaking the truth. I stammered: "You—you know him?"

Athenodorus almost smiled. "I dined with him last week."

But he would not speak more of him, nor answer my questions; he seemed to think them unimportant. He said only that his former student could have become a good scholar, had he chosen to do so.

So I am even more nearly at the center of the world than I imagined.

I have attended a funeral.

Atia, the mother of Octavius Caesar, is dead. A herald came through the streets, announcing that the services would be held the next morning in the Forum. So I have at last set eyes upon that man whose person now is the most powerful in Rome, and hence (I suppose) in the world.

I got to the Forum early, so that I would have a good place to see, and waited at the rostrum where Octavius Caesar was to deliver the oration. By the fifth hour of the morning, the Forum was nearly filled.

And then the procession came—the ushers with their flaming torches, the oboists and the buglers and the clarionists playing the slow march, the bier with the body propped upon it, the mourners—and behind the procession, walking alone, a slight figure, whom I took at first to be a youth, since his toga was bordered with purple; it did not occur to me that he might be a senator. But it soon became clear that it was Octavius himself, for the crowd stirred as he passed, trying to get a better view of him. The bearers set the bier before the rostrum, the chief mourners seated themselves on little chairs in front, and Octavius Caesar walked slowly to the bier and looked for a moment at the body of his mother. Then he mounted the rostrum and looked at the people—a thousand, or more—who had gathered for the occasion.

I was standing very close—not more than fifteen yards away. He seemed very pale, very still, almost as if he himself were the corpse. Only his eyes were alive—they are a most startling blue. The crowd became very quiet; from the distance, I could hear the faint careless rumble of the city that went its way like a dumb beast.

Then he began to speak. He spoke very quietly, but in a voice so clear and distinct that he could be heard by everyone who had gathered.

I send you his words; the scribes with their tablets were there, and the next day copies of the oration were in every bookstall in the city.

He said: "Rome will not again see you, Atia, you who were Rome. It is a loss that only the example of your virtue makes endurable, which tells us that our grief, if held too deeply and too long, offends the very purpose of your living.

"You were a faithful wife to the father of my blood, that Gaius Octavius who was praetor and governor of Macedonia, and whose untimely death intervened between his person and the consulship of Rome. You were a stern and loving mother to your daughter, Octavia, who weeps now before your bier, and to your son, who stands before you for the last time and speaks these poor words. You were the dutiful and proper niece of that man who gave at last to your son the father of whom he had been cheated by fate, that Julius Caesar who was villainously murdered within earshot of this very spot where you so nobly lie.

"Of an honored Roman name, you had in full degree those old virtues of the earth which have nurtured and sustained our nation throughout its history. You spun and wove the cloth that furnished your household its clothing; your servants were as your own children; you honored the gods of your house and of your city. Through your gentleness you had no enemy but time, who takes you now.

"Oh Rome, look upon the one who lies here now, and see the best of your nature and your heritage. Soon we shall take these remains beyond the city walls, and there the funeral pyre will consume the receptacle of all that Atia was. But I charge you, citizens, do not let her virtues be entombed with her ashes. Rather let that virtue become your Roman lives, so that, though Atia's person be but ash, yet the better part of her will live on, entombed in the living souls of all Romans who come after her.

"Atia, may the spirits of the dead keep your rest."

A long silence stayed upon the crowd. Octavius stood for a moment on the rostrum. Then he descended, and they bore the body outside the Forum, and beyond the city walls.

I cannot bring myself to believe what I have seen, or to give credence to what I have heard. In this chaos, there is no official news; nothing is posted on the walls of the Senate House; one cannot even be sure that there is a Senate any more. Octavius Caesar has joined with Antonius and Lepidus in what amounts to a military dictatorship; and the enemies of Julius Caesar are proscribed. More than a hundred senators—*senators*—have been executed, their property and wealth confiscated; and many times that number of wealthy Roman citizens, often of noble name, are either murdered or fled from the city, their property and wealth in the hands of the triumvirs. Merciless. Among those proscribed: Paullus, the blood brother of Lepidus. Lucius Caesar, the uncle of Antonius. And even the famous Cicero is on the published list. These three, and others, I imagine, have fled the city, and may escape with their lives.

The bloodiest of the work seems to be in the hands of Antonius's soldiers. With my own eyes I have seen the headless bodies of Roman senators littering the very Forum which a week ago was their chief glory; and I have heard, from the safety of my hill, the screams of the rich who have waited too long to flee Rome and their riches. All except the poor, those with moderate wealth, and the friends of Caesar, walk in apprehension of what the morrow might bring, whether their names have been posted or not.

It is said that Octavius Caesar sits in his home and will not show his face nor view the dead bodies of his former colleagues. It is also said that it is Octavius himself who insists that the proscriptions be carried out ruthlessly, at once, and to the letter. One does not know what one may with safety believe.

Is this the Rome that I thought I was beginning to know, after these crowded months? Have I understood these people at all? Athenodorus will not discuss the matter with me; Tyrannion shakes his head sadly.

Perhaps I am less the man and more the youth than I had believed.

Cicero did not escape.

Yesterday, on a cool, bright December afternoon, wandering among the bookstalls in the shop area behind the Forum (it is safe to be on the streets now), I heard a great commotion; and against my better judgment, out of that curiosity that will someday lead me either to fame or death, I made my way inside the Forum gates. A great crush of people was milling around the rostrum near the Senate House.

"It's Cicero," someone said, and the name went like a whispering sigh among the people. "Cicero. . . ."

Not knowing what to expect, but dreading what I would see, I pushed my way through the crowd.

There on the Senate rostrum, placed neatly between two severed hands, was the withered and shrunken head of Marcus Tullius Cicero. Someone said that it had been placed there by order of Antonius himself.

It was the same rostrum from which, only three weeks before, Octavius Caesar had spoken so gently of his mother, who had died. Now another death sat upon it; and I could not help, at that moment, being somehow pleased that the mother had died before she had been made witness to what her son had wrought.

II. LETTER: MARCUS JUNIUS BRUTUS TO
OCTAVIUS CAESAR, FROM SMYRNA (42 B.C.)

I cannot believe that you truly apprehend the gravity of your
position. I know that you bear me no love, and I would be
foolish if I pretended that I bore you much more; I do not
write you out of regard for your person, but out of regard for
our nation. I cannot write to Antonius, for he is a madman; I
cannot write to Lepidus, for he is a fool. I hope that I may be
heard by you, who are neither.

I know that it is through your influence that Cassius and
I have been declared outlaws and condemned to exile; but
let neither of us believe that such a condemnation has more
permanent force of law than can be sustained by a flustered
and demoralized Senate. Let neither of us pretend that such
an edict has any kind of permanence or validity. Let us speak
practically.

All of Syria, all of Macedonia, all of Epirus, all of Greece, all
of Asia are ours. All of the East is against you, and the power
and wealth of the East is not inconsiderable. We control absolutely the eastern Mediterranean; therefore you can expect no
aid from your late uncle's Egyptian mistress, who might otherwise furnish wealth and manpower to your cause. And though
I bear him no love, I know that the pirate, Sextus Pompeius,
is nipping at your heels from the west. Thus I do not fear for
myself or my forces the war that now seems imminent.

But I do fear for Rome, and for the future of the state. The
proscriptions that you and your friends have instituted in Rome
bear witness to that fear, to which my personal grief must be
subordinate.

So let us forget proscriptions and assassinations; if you can
forgive me the death of Caesar, perhaps I can forgive you the
death of Cicero. We cannot be friends to each other; neither of
us needs that. But perhaps we can be friends to Rome.

I implore you, do not march with Marcus Antonius. Another battle between Romans would, I fear, destroy what little
virtue remains in our state. And Antonius will not march without you.

If you do not march, I assure you that you will have my
respect and my thanks; and your future will be assured. If we

cannot work together out of friendship to each other, yet we may work together for the good of Rome.

But let me hasten to add this. If you reject this offer of amity, I shall resist with all my strength; and you will be destroyed. I say this with sadness; but I say it.

III. THE MEMOIRS OF MARCUS AGRIPPA: FRAGMENTS (13 B.C.)

And after the triumvirate was formed and the Roman enemies of Julius Caesar and Caesar Augustus were put down, there yet remained in the West the forces of the pirate Sextus Pompeius, and in the East the exiled murderers of the divine Julius, that Brutus and Cassius who threatened the safety and order of Rome. True to his oath, Caesar Augustus resolved to punish the murderers of his father and restore order to the state, and deferred the matter of Sextus Pompeius to another time, taking only those actions against Pompeius that were necessary for the safety of the moment.

My energies at this time were devoted to enrolling and equipping in Italy those legions that were to lay siege to Brutus and Cassius in the East, and to organizing the lines of supply that would allow us to do battle on that distant soil. Antonius was to send eight legions to Amphipolis, on the Aegean coast of Macedonia, to harass the troops of Brutus and Cassius, so that they might not find an advantage of terrain in which to fight. But Antonius delayed the departure of his legions, so that they were forced to find an inferior position on the low ground west of Philippi, where the army of Brutus rested in security. It became necessary for Antonius to send other legions in support of those in Macedonia, but the fleets of Brutus and Cassius hovered around the harbor at Brindisi; so Augustus commanded me to insure safe passage for Antonius. And with the ships and legions that I had raised in Italy, we drove through the navy of Marcus Junius Brutus and landed twelve legions of troops upon the Macedonian shore at Dyrrachium.

But at Dyrrachium, Augustus fell gravely ill, and we would have waited in fear of his life; but he bade us continue, knowing that all would be lost if we delayed our attack upon the armies of the outlaws. And eight of our legions marched across the country to join the beleaguered advance troops of Marcus Antonius at Amphipolis.

Our way was hindered by the cavalry of Brutus and Cassius, and we suffered severe losses on our journey, arriving at Amphipolis with our troops weary and demoralized. When it became clear that the armies of Brutus and Cassius were securely entrenched upon the high ground at Philippi, protected on the north by mountains and on the south by a marsh that stretched from the camp to the sea, I resolved to send an urgent message to Caesar Augustus; for our task seemed hopeless to our soldiers, and I knew that their failing spirits must be revived.

And so, though gravely ill, Augustus forced his way across the country to reinforce us, and went among his men on a litter, being too weak to walk; and though his face was that of a corpse, his eyes were fierce and hard, and his voice was strong, so that the men took heart and resolve from his presence.

We determined to strike boldly and at once, for each day of waiting cost us supplies, while Brutus and Cassius had all the lanes of the sea for their support. So while three of the legions of Augustus, under my command, pretended to be intent upon constructing a causeway across the great marsh that protected the enemy's southern flank, thus diverting a large number of Republican troops to attack us, the legions of Marcus Antonius struck boldly and broke through the weakened line of Cassius, and pillaged the camp before Cassius could recover from his surprise. And Cassius, on a slight hill with a few of his officers, looked (it is said) to the north, and there saw the troops of Brutus in what he took to be full flight; knowing that his own army was defeated, and thinking that all was lost, he despaired; and fell upon his sword, ending his life there in the dust and blood at Philippi, taking revenge upon himself, it seemed, for the murder of the divine Julius, two years and seven months before.

What Cassius did not know was that the army of Brutus was not in flight. Divining our plan, and knowing that the army of Augustus was dispersed in its diversionary tactic, he made haste to invest our camp, and overran it, capturing many soldiers and killing many more. Augustus himself, half-conscious in his illness and unable to move, was carried from his tent by his doctor and hidden in the marsh until the battle was over and night fell, and he could be carried stealthily to where the remnants of the army had retreated and had joined with the troops of Marcus Antonius. The doctor swore that he had had a dream telling him to remove the ill Augustus, so that his life might be spared. . . .

IV. LETTER: QUINTUS HORATIUS FLACCUS TO HIS FATHER, FROM WEST OF PHILIPPI (42 B.C.)

My dear father, if you receive this letter, you will know that your Horace, a day ago a proud soldier in the army of Marcus Junius Brutus, at this moment, on this cold autumn night, sits in his tent, writing these words by the flickering light of a lantern, in disgrace with himself, if not with his friends. Yet he feels curiously free from the obsession that has gripped him these last several months; and if he is not happy, he is at least beginning to know who he is. . . . Today I was in my first battle; and I must tell you at once that at the first moment of serious danger to myself I dropped my shield and sword, and I ran.

Why I ever embarked upon this venture, I do not know; and surely you are too intelligent to know either. When, out of that kindness of yours to which I have grown so used that I sometimes do not think of it, you sent me to study in Athens year before last, I had no thought of engaging myself in anything so foolish as politics. Did I align myself with Brutus and accept a tribuneship in his army in a contemptible effort to rise above my station into the aristocracy? Was Horace ashamed of being the son of a mere freedman? I cannot believe that that is true; even in my youth and arrogance, I have known that you are the best of men, and I could not wish for a more noble and generous and loving father.

It was, I believe, because in my studies I had forgotten the world, and had begun almost to believe that philosophy was true. Liberty. I joined the cause of Brutus for a word; and I do not know what the word means. A man may live like a fool for a year, and become wise in a day.

I must tell you now that I did not drop my shield and run from the battle out of mere cowardice—though that was no doubt part of it. But when I suddenly saw one of Octavius

Caesar's soldiers (or maybe Antonius's, I do not know) advancing toward me with naked steel flashing in his hands and in his eyes, it was as if time suddenly stood still; and I remembered you, and all the hopes you had of my future. I remembered that you had been born a slave, and had managed to buy your freedom; that your labor and your life were early turned to your son, so that he might live in an ease and comfort and security that you never had. And I saw that son uselessly slaughtered on an earth he had no love for, for a cause he did not understand—and I had a sense of what your years might have been with the knowledge of your son's discarded life—and I ran. I ran over bodies of fallen soldiers, and saw their empty eyes staring at the sky which they would never see again; and it did not matter to me whether they were friend or foe. I ran.

If the fates are kind to me, I shall return to you in Italy. I shall fight no more. Tomorrow, I shall post this letter to you and make my preparations. If we are not attacked, I shall be in no danger; if we are, I shall run again. In any event, I shall not linger at this massacre that leads to an end I cannot see.

I do not know who will be victorious—the Party of Caesar or the Party of the Republic. I do not know the future of our country, or my own future. Perhaps I shall have to disappoint you, and become a tax collector like yourself. It is a position, however lowly in your eyes, to which you lend dignity and honor by your presence. I am your son, Horace, and proud to be so.

V. THE MEMOIRS OF MARCUS AGRIPPA: FRAGMENTS (13 B.C.)

And Brutus withdrew once more to the high ground and entrenchments at Philippi, whence, it became clear, he did not propose to retreat. We knew, perhaps better than Brutus, that each day of waiting cost us dearly, for our supplies were running low; nothing could be transported over the sea controlled by Brutus's navy; behind us were the flat and barren plains of Macedonia, and before us the hostile and barren hills of Greece. Thus we made to be copied sheets of reproaches to the officers of Brutus's army, taunting them with their timidity and cowardice; and at night we shouted challenges across the campfires, so that the soldiers could not even sleep in honor, but dozed fitfully in their shame.

For three weeks Brutus waited, until at last his men, chafing beneath the burden of their inaction, would wait no longer; and Brutus, fearful that his army would be depleted by desertions, ordered his men to descend from the entrenchments that might have saved them, and to attack our camp.

In the late afternoon they came down from the hill like a northern storm; no cries or shouts escaped their lips, and we heard only the clump of hooves and the pad of feet in the dust that came with them like a cloud. I ordered our line to give way before the initial attack; and as the enemy streamed into us, we closed the lines on either side, so that he had to fight on two flanks at once. And we broke the army in two, and each of those parts into two again, so that he could not re-form himself to withstand our attacks. By nightfall, the battle was over; and the stars heard the moans of the wounded, and watched impassively the bodies that did not move.

Brutus escaped with what remained of his legions, and made his way to the wilderness beyond the entrenchments at Philippi, which we had invested. He would have attacked again with what remained of his army, but his officers refused to risk themselves; and in the early dawn, the day after the Ides of November, on a lonely hillock overlooking the carnage of his will and resolve, with a few of his faithful officers, he fell upon his sword; and the army of the Republic was no more.

Thus was the murder of Julius Caesar avenged, and thus did the chaos of treason and faction give way to the years of order and peace, under the Emperor of our state, Gaius Octavius Caesar, now the August.

VI. LETTER: GAIUS CILNIUS MAECENAS TO TITUS LIVIUS (13 B.C.)

After Philippi, slowly, with many stops along the way, more dead than alive, he came back to Rome; he had saved Italy from its enemies abroad, and it remained for him to heal the nation that was shattered within.

My dear Livy, I cannot tell you the shock I had upon seeing him for the first time after those many months, when they carried him in secret to his house on the Palatine. I, of course, had remained in Rome during the fighting, according to Octavius's orders, so that I could keep an eye on things and do what I could to prevent Lepidus, either out of conspiracy or incompetence, from wholly disrupting the internal government of Italy.

He was not quite twenty-two years old that winter when he returned from the fighting, but I swear to you he looked double—treble—that age. His face was waxen, and, slight though he always was, he had lost so much weight that his skin sagged upon his bones. He had the strength to speak only in a hoarse whisper. I looked at him, and I despaired of his life.

"Do not let them know," he said, and paused a long time, as if the uttering of that phrase had exhausted him. "Do not let them know of my illness. Neither the people nor Lepidus."

"I will not, my friend," I told him.

The illness had, in fact, begun the year before, during the time of the proscriptions, and had grown steadily worse; and though the physicians who attended him had been paid handsomely and threatened with their livelihood, if not their lives, for any breach of secrecy, rumors of the illness had crept out. The doctors (a dreadful lot, then as now) might as well not have been called in; they were able to do nothing except prescribe noxious herbs and treatments of heat and cold. He was able to eat almost nothing, and upon more than one occasion he had vomited blood. Yet as his body had weakened, it seemed that his will had hardened, so that he drove himself even more fiercely in his illness than he had in his health.

"Antonius," he said in that terrible voice, "will not return yet to Rome. He has gone into the East to gather booty and to strengthen his position. I agreed to it—I would prefer to have him steal from the Asians and the Egyptians than from the Romans. . . . I believe he expects me to die; and though he hopes for it, I suspect he doesn't want to be in Italy when it happens."

He lay back on his bed, breathing shallowly, his eyes closed. At length he regained his strength, and said:

"Give me the news of the city."

"Rest," I said. "We shall have time when you are stronger."

"The news," he said. "Though my body cannot move, my mind can."

There were bitter things I had to tell him, but I knew that he would not have forgiven me had I sweetened them. I said:

"Lepidus negotiates secretly with the pirate, Sextus Pompeius; he has some notion, I believe, of allying himself with Pompeius against either you or Antonius, whichever proves weaker. I have the evidence; but if we confront him with it, he will swear that he negotiates only to bring peace to Rome. . . . Out of Philippi, Antonius is the hero and you are the coward. Antonius's pig of a wife and his vulture of a brother have spread the stories—while you cowered and quaked in fear in the salt marsh, Antonius bravely punished the enemies of Caesar. Fulvia makes speeches to the soldiers, warning that you will not pay them the bounties that Antonius promised; while Lucius goes about the countryside stirring up the landowner and the farmer with rumors that you will confiscate their properties to settle the veterans. Do you want to hear more?"

He even smiled a little. "If I must," he said.

"The state is very near to being bankrupt. Of the few taxes that Lepidus can collect, a trickle goes into the treasury; the rest goes to Lepidus himself and, it is said, to Fulvia, who, it is also said, is preparing to raise independent legions, in addition to those that rightfully belong to Antonius. I have no proof of this, but I imagine it is true. . . . So it would seem that you got the lesser bargain in Rome."

"I would prefer the weakness of Rome to all the power of the East," he said, "though I am sure this is not what Antonius had in mind. He expects that if I do not die, I will go under with the problems here. But I will not die, and we will not go under." He raised himself a little. "We have much to do."

And the next day, in his weakness, he arose from his bed, and put his illness aside as if it were of no moment and no account.

We had much to do, he said. . . . My dear Livy, that admirable history of yours—how might it evoke the bustles and delays, the triumphs and defeats, the joys and despairs of the years following Philippi? It cannot do so, and no doubt it should not. But I must not digress, even to praise you; for you will scold me again.

You have asked me to be more particular about the duties I performed for our Emperor, as if I were worthy of a place in your history. You honor me beyond my merits. Yet I am pleased that I am remembered, even in my retirement from public affairs.

The duties that I performed for our Emperor . . . I must confess that some of them seem to me now ludicrous, though of course they did not seem so then. The marriages, for example. Through the influence and by the edicts of our Emperor, it is now possible for a man of substance and ambition to contract a marriage on grounds that are rational—if "rational" is not too contradictory a word to describe such an odd and (I sometimes think) unnatural relationship. Such was not possible in the days of which I speak—in Rome, at least, and to those of public involvement. One married for advantage and political necessity—as, indeed, I myself did, though my Terentia was on occasion an amusing companion.

I must say, I was rather good at such arrangements—and I must also confess that as it turned out none were advantageous or even necessary. I have always suspected that it was that knowledge which led Octavius, some years later, to institute those not altogether successful marriage laws, rather than the kind of "morality" imputed to them. He has often chided me about my advice in those early days. For it was invariably wrong.

For example: The first marriage I contracted for him was in the very early days, before the formation of the triumvirate. The girl was Servilia, the daughter of that P. Servilius Isauricus who, when Cicero opposed Octavius after Mutina, agreed to stand for senior consul with Octavius against Cicero—and the marriage to his daughter was to be our surety that he would be supported by the power of our arms, if that became necessary. As it turned out, Servilius was impotent in his dealings with Cicero and was of no help to us; the marriage never took place.

The second was even more ludicrous than the first. It was to Clodia, daughter of Fulvia and stepdaughter to Marcus Antonius, and it was a part of the compact that formed the triumvirate; the soldiers wanted it, and we saw no reason to deny them their whim, however meaningless it was. The girl was thirteen years old, and as ugly as her mother. Octavius saw her twice, I believe, and she never set foot in his house. As you know, the marriage did nothing to quiet Fulvia or Antonius; they continued their plotting and their treason, so that after Philippi, when Antonius was in the East and Fulvia was openly threatening another civil war against Octavius, we had to make our position clear by effecting a divorce.

It was, however, my responsibility for the third contract which Octavius most nearly resented, I think; it was with Scribonia, and it was accomplished within the year after his divorce from Clodia, during our most desperate months, when it seemed that we would either be crushed by the Antonian uprisings in Italy, or by the encroachment of Sextus Pompeius from the south. In what seems now a too desperate effort at conciliation, I went to Sicily to negotiate with Sextus Pompeius—an impossible task, for Pompeius was an impossible man. He was a bit mad, I think—more like an animal than a human. He *was* an outlaw, and that in more than the legal sense; he is one of the few men with whom I have had converse who so repelled me that I had difficulty in dealing with him. I know, my dear Livy, that you admired his father; but you never met either of them, and you certainly did not know his son. . . . In any event, I talked to Pompeius, and extracted what I thought was an agreement—and sealed the compact with an arrangement of marriage with that Scribonia, who was the younger sister of Pompeius's father-in-law. Scribonia, Scribonia. . . . She has always seemed to me the epitome of womankind: coldly suspicious, politely ill-tempered, and narrowly selfish. It is a wonder that my friend ever *did* forgive me for that arrangement. Perhaps it was because from that marriage came the one thing that my friend loves as much as he loves Rome—his daughter, his Julia. He divorced Scribonia on the day of his daughter's birth, and it is a wonder that he ever married again. But he did marry again, and it was an arrangement in which I had no part. . . . As it turned out, the marriage to Scribonia was fraudulent to begin with; for as I was negotiating with Pompeius, he himself was already deep in negotiations with Antonius, and the marriage contract was a mere ruse to lull our suspicions. Such, my dear Livy, was the nature of politics in those days. But I must say (though I would not repeat it to our Emperor), looking back on it all, these affairs did have their humorous side.

For my responsibility in arranging only one marriage have I ever felt any shame; even now, I cannot take it as lightly as I ought to be able to do—though I suppose no great harm was done.

At about the time I was negotiating with Pompeius and arranging the marriage with Scribonia, the barbarian Moors, aroused by Fulvia and Lucius Antonius, rose up against our governor in Outer Spain; our generals in Africa, again at the instigation of Fulvia and Lucius, began to war with each other; Lucius pretended that his life had been threatened, and marched with his (and Fulvia's) legions on Rome. They were repulsed there by our friend Agrippa, and surrounded in the town of Perusia, whose inhabitants (Pompeians and Republicans, mostly) aided them with vigor and enthusiasm. We really didn't know how much a part in all this Marcus Antonius had, though we suspected; therefore we did not dare destroy his brother, for fear that if he were guilty, Marcus Antonius would use this as a pretext to attack us from the east; and that if he were innocent, he would misunderstand our action, and take revenge upon us. We did not punish Lucius, but we showed little mercy to those who had aided him, putting the most treacherous to death and exiling the less dangerous—though we let the ordinary citizens go free, and even recompensed them for the property we destroyed. Among those exiled (and this, my dear Livy, will appeal to your perhaps overdeveloped sense of irony) was one Tiberius Claudius Nero, who was allowed to make his way to Sicily with his newborn son, Tiberius, and his very young wife, Livia.

During all the months of the turmoil in Italy, we had written often to Antonius, trying to describe the activities of his wife and brother and trying to ascertain his part in the disturbances; and though we received letters from Antonius, none of them replied to those we had sent, as if he had not received them. It was winter, of course, when we wrote most urgently; and few of the sea lanes were open; it is possible that he did not receive them. In any event, the spring and part of the summer passed without clear word from him; and then we got an urgent message from Brindisi that Antonius's fleet was sailing toward the harbor, and that the navy of Pompeius was coming up from the north to join him. And we learned that some months earlier, Fulvia had sailed to Athens to meet her husband.

We did not know what to expect, and yet we had no choice. Weak as we were, with our legions scattered against the various troubles on our borders and in our nation, we marched toward Brindisi, fearful that Antonius had landed and was leading his soldiers to meet us. But we learned that the city of Brindisi had refused to let Antonius through the harbor gates, and so we encamped and awaited what would happen. Had Antonius attacked in full force, we no doubt could not have survived.

But he did not attack, nor did we. Our own soldiers were famished and ill-equipped; the soldiers of Antonius were weary with their travels and wanted only to see their families in Italy. Had either side been foolish enough to press the issue, we probably would have had a mutiny.

And then an agent that we slipped among the Antonian forces returned with some startling news. Antonius and Fulvia had quarreled bitterly at Athens; Antonius had left in a rage; and now Fulvia, suddenly and inexplicably, was dead.

We encouraged some of our trusted soldiers to fraternize with the troops of Antonius; and soon deputations from both sides approached their respective leaders and demanded that Antonius and Octavius once more reconcile their differences, so that not again would Roman be pitted against Roman.

And thus the two leaders met, and another war was averted. Antonius protested that Fulvia and his brother had acted without his authority, and Octavius pointed out that he had taken no revenge on either of them for their actions, out of regard for their relationship to Antonius. A pact was signed; a general amnesty for all previous enemies of Rome was declared; and a marriage was arranged.

The marriage was negotiated by me; and it was between Antonius and Octavia, the older sister of our Emperor, who had been widowed only a few months ago, and left with her infant son, Marcellus.

My dear Livy, you know my tastes—but I almost believe I could have loved women, had many of them been like Octavia. I admired her then as I do now—she was very gentle and without guile, she was quite beautiful, and she was one of the two women I have ever known who had both an extensive knowledge and deep understanding of philosophy and poetry, the other being Octavius's own daughter, Julia. Octavia was not a plaything, you understand. My old friend Athenodorus used to say that had she been a man, and less intelligent, she could have become a great philosopher.

I was with Octavius when he explained the necessity to his sister—of whom he was very fond, as you know. He could not look her in the eye when he spoke. But Octavia merely smiled at him and said: "If it must be done, my brother, it must be done; I shall try to be a good wife to Antonius and remain a good sister to you."

"It is for Rome," Octavius said.

"It is for us all," his sister said.

It was necessary, I suppose; we hoped that such a marriage might lead us to a lasting peace; we knew that it would give us a few years. But I must say, I still feel that twinge of regret and sorrow; Octavia must have had some rather bad times.

Though, as it turned out, Antonius was a rather intermittent husband. That might have made it more endurable for her. Yet she never spoke harshly of Marcus Antonius, even in later years.

Chapter Five

Antonius to Octavius, greetings. I do not know what you expect of me. I renounced my late wife and ruined my brother's career, because their actions had displeased you. To cement our joint rule, I married your sister, who, though a good woman, is not to my taste. To assure you of my good faith, I sent Sextus Pompeius and his navy back to his Sicily, though (as you well know) he would have joined me against you. To augment your power, I agreed to strip Lepidus of all the provinces he held, save Africa. I agreed, even, after my marriage to your sister, to be designated Priest to the deified Julius—though it seemed odd to be priest to an old friend, a man with whom I have whored and drunk, and though my acceptance of the priesthood was more advantageous to your name than to mine. Finally, I have absented myself from my homeland, so that I may raise the money in the East that will insure our future authority, and to make some order out of the chaos into which our Eastern provinces have fallen. As I said, I do not know what you expect of me.

If I have allowed the Greeks to pretend to themselves that I am the revived Bacchus (or do you prefer Dionysus?), it is so that their love for me will give me some control over them. You criticize me for "playing the Greek" and for assuming the role of the Incarnate Bacchus at the Festival of Athena; and yet you must know that when I agreed to do so, I insisted that the Celestial Athena bring me a dowry—and that by that insistence, I have enriched our treasury by more than I could have done by levying taxes, and have also escaped the resentment that would have inevitably resulted from such a levy.

As for the Egyptian matters that you so delicately raise: first, it is true that I have accepted certain of the Queen's subjects as my aides. This is both helpful to my task, and necessary to my diplomacy. But even if all this were merely for my own pleasure, I see no reason why you should object: Ammonius

583

you know yourself, for he was a friend of your late uncle (or "father," as you now may call him)—and he serves me as faithfully as he served Julius and as he served his Queen. As for Epimachos, whom you call a mere "soothsayer," such a designation reveals (if you will forgive me) a profound ignorance about these Eastern matters. This "mere soothsayer" is an extraordinarily important man: he is the High Priest of Heliopolis, the Incarnation of Thoth, and the Keeper of the *Book of Magic*. He is a good deal more important than any of our own "priests," and he is useful to me; and besides, he is an amusing fellow.

Second, there was never any secret about my connection with the Queen two years ago in Alexandria. But I recall to you that that was two years ago, before either of us had any notion that I might one day become your brother-in-law. And you need not bring up the matter of the twins with which Cleopatra has presented me; they may or may not be my own; whether they are or not is no matter. I have not made secret, either, that I have left children all over the world; these new ones would mean neither more nor less to me than the others. When I have time from my duties, I take my pleasure, and I take it where I can find it. I shall continue to do so. At least, my dear brother, I do not hide my propensities; I am no hypocrite; and your own affairs, I should point out, are not so well hidden as you imagine.

You should know me better than to think (if, indeed, you do think it, as you pretend) that my liaison with Cleopatra had anything to do with my confirmation of her sovereignty in Egypt. For if this confirmation is to my advantage, so it is to yours. Egypt is the richest of the Eastern nations, and its treasury will be open to us, if we need it. And it is the only Eastern nation that has any semblance of an army, and at least a part of this army will be at our disposal. Finally, it is easier to deal with a single strong monarch who feels some security in his (or her) position than with half a dozen weak ones who feel none.

These things, and many others, should be clear to you, who are no fool.

I will not accept the terms of whatever game it is you think you are playing.

II. LETTER: MARCUS ANTONIUS TO
GAIUS SENTIUS TAVUS (38 B.C.)

That bloody and outrageous little hypocrite! I am stretched between laughter and anger—laughter at the hypocrisy, and anger at what his hypocrisy might conceal.

Does he imagine that I am without my sources of information here in Athens? I am not shocked by anything he does, and I do not take that high moral tone that he loves to affect. He may divorce as many a Scribonia as he likes, even on the day that she gives birth to a daughter that (given Scribonia) must be his; he may even take within the week another wife, who is already pregnant by her former husband. He may perform this public scandal (and even the more private ones that you report to me), and he will get no remonstrances from me; he may be as bizarre as he likes in his private preferences.

But I know my recent "brother"; and I know that he does nothing from passion or whim. He is such a cold-blooded fish that I must almost admire him.

It must be clear to everyone that his divorce of Scribonia signifies that we no longer have an understanding with her kinsman, Sextus Pompeius. What can I make of this? Why was I not consulted? Does it mean that we are to make war on Sextus? Or will Octavius go it alone?

And what of his new wife, this Livia? You tell me that Octavius once exiled her husband from Italy, because he was a Republican and opposed him at Perusia. Does the new marriage mean that he is again trying to find favor with the remnants of the Republican Party? I do not know what all of this means. . . . You must write often, Sentius; I must be kept informed, and I can trust few, nowadays. I wish I were in Rome; but I cannot leave my task here.

I have been trying to persuade myself that the kind of life I am now leading is worth the trouble. My present wife is as cold and proper in fact as her brother is in pretense. And though I can find my pleasure here and there, I have to be so discreet that the pleasure is reduced almost to nothing. Daily, I am tempted to send her packing; but I have no cause, she is with child, and to divorce her now would cause a breach with her brother that I cannot afford.

III. EXTRACTS FROM REPORTS: EPIMACHOS,
HIGH PRIEST OF HELIOPOLIS, TO CLEOPATRA,
THE INCARNATE ISIS AND QUEEN OF THE
WORLDS OF EGYPT (40–37 B.C.)

Greetings, Revered Queen. This day, at first for amusement and then from desperation, Marcus Antonius diced with Octavius Caesar. For nearly three hours they played, and Antonius lost consistently, winning perhaps one out of four throws. Octavius is well pleased, Antonius annoyed. I cast the sands, and went into a trance, from which I told the story of Eurystheus and that Heracles who became his servant because of the perfidy of the gods. Suggest that in your next letter to him, you refer to some demeaning task you dreamed he had to perform for someone weaker and less worthy than himself. I was grave and portentous; you must be humorous and light.

My auguries have been to no avail; he is married to Octavia, the sister of his enemy. It is the pledge that will satisfy the populace and the soldiers.

I send you two waxen effigies. You are to find in your palace a remote room which has but one door. You are to place the effigy of Antonius on the side of the room where there is a door, the effigy of Octavia on the side where there is none. You are to do this with your own hands; let no one assist you. Then you are to have built between the figures a heavy wall, extending from the floor to the ceiling; there must be no fissure between the two. Each day, at sun's rising and sun's setting, you are to have my priest, Epiktetas, perform the spell outside the room. He will know what to do.

We go to Athens with Octavia, who is now with child and will deliver within three months. I have presented to Antonius a pair of identical greyhounds, which he has raced and of which he has become inordinately fond. On the day that Octavia's child is born, I shall cause the dogs to disappear. You must write him within the next few weeks of a dream that you had about the twins.

*

The child that Octavia has delivered is a daughter; thus there is no potential heir to his name. The God of the Sun has bowed to our will and has heeded our demands.

He quarrels with Octavius; they are reconciled by Octavia, who takes the part of her husband against her brother. Antonius's suspicions of her are almost gone, and he seems grudgingly fond of her, though he is still made impatient by her quietness and calm. Does Epiktetas perform faithfully the spell, as you instructed him?

He has had a dream of being bound to a couch while his tent burned around him. The soldiers of his army walked past the burning tent, and did not heed his calls, as if they did not hear him. Finally he burst his bonds, but the fire was around him so fiercely that he could not see which way to turn to escape. He awoke in fear, and called for me.

I fasted for three days, and gave him the portents of the dream. I told him that the fire was the intrigue in Rome, heaped and kindled by Octavius Caesar. That he was in a tent, I said, revealed two things: his position (he has no secure and permanent place in the Roman world), and his nature (that he is a soldier). That he was bound to his couch, I said, signified that by his inactivity he had betrayed his nature and allowed himself to become weak and hence impotent to the intrigues against him and to the circumstance of fate. That his soldiers did not heed his calls revealed that by his betrayal of his nature, he had lost control of his men; that he is properly a man of action, not of words; that men would bend to his deeds, not his talk.

He has become thoughtful, and he studies maps. I say nothing to him, but I believe he is again considering taking up arms against the Parthians. For this, he will come to know that he needs your aid. Discreetly, let him know that it is at his disposal. Thus, you may draw him again to our cause, and insure the future glory of Egypt.

IV. LETTER: CLEOPATRA TO MARCUS
ANTONIUS, FROM ALEXANDRIA (37 B.C.)

My dear Marcus, you must forgive my long silence, as I have forgiven yours. And you must forgive me, too, if I write you now as a woman, rather than as the Queen who is your faithful ally and whose strength is ever at your disposal. For I have been most gravely ill these last few months, and have not wished to cause you concern for my infirmities; indeed, I should not write you now, had not my frailty and my heart overcome my Queenhood.

Sleep is reluctant to cover my eyes; my strength is stolen by fevers that even the skills of my physician, Olympus, cannot allay; I take little food; and despair is like a serpent that creeps into the emptiness of my spirit.

Oh, Marcus, how weary all this must make you! Yet I know your kindness, and know that you will indulge the weakness of an old friend, who thinks of you often and remembers many things.

Perhaps it is that remembering, rather than the advice of Olympus, which has persuaded me to take the journey from Alexandria to Thebes. Olympus says that in the temple there, the Supreme God, Amen-Ra, will take away my illness and return my strength. You used to tease me about my regard for these Egyptian gods; perhaps you were right in that, as you were in so many things. For I almost refused him; and then I remembered (it seems so long ago) another spring, when you and I floated down the Nile and side by side lay on our couch and watched the fertile banks slip by and felt upon our bodies the cool river breeze; and the farmers and herdsmen knelt, and even the goats and cattle seemed to pause in obeisance to us, raising their heads to watch our passing. And Memphis, where they held the bullfights in our honor, and Hermopolis and Akhetaton, where we were God and Goddess, Osiris and Isis. And then the Thebes of the Hundred Gates, and the drowsy days and gay nights . . .

Remembering this, I felt the beginnings of strength return to me; and I told Olympus that I would make the journey and enter the temple of Amen-Ra. But if I am returned to health, it will be from the nourishment I take from these memories along the way, which I hold as dear as my life.

V. LETTER: MARCUS ANTONIUS TO
OCTAVIUS CAESAR (37 B.C.)

You have broken our treaty with Sextus Pompeius, a treaty to which I pledged my word; it is rumored that you intend war upon him, though you have not consulted me in the matter; you intrigue against my reputation, though I have done neither you nor your sister any harm; you seek to subvert from me the little strength I have in Italy, though I have given you, out of my loyalty, much of the power you now have; in short, you have repaid my loyalty with betrayal, my honor with your treachery, my generosity with your self-interest.

You may do what you want in Rome; I will no longer be concerned. When we agreed to extend the triumvirate earlier this year, I hoped that we might, at last, work together. We cannot.

I send your sister and her children to you. You may inform her upon her arrival that she is not to return to me. Though she is a good woman, I want no tie with your house. As for divorce, that I will leave entirely to your discretion. I know that you will decide that matter in terms of your own interest. I do not care.

I shall not dissemble with you; I have no need to; I fear neither you nor your intrigues.

I shall begin my Parthian campaign this spring, without the legions you promised and did not deliver to me. I have summoned Cleopatra to Antioch. She will supply the troops that I need.

If Rome is dying in the web that you weave around her, Egypt will thrive in the power that I will give her. I bequeath the corpse to you; for myself, I prefer the living body.

VI. LETTER: MARCUS ANTONIUS
TO CLEOPATRA (37 B.C.)

Empress of the Nile, Queen of the Living Suns, and my beloved friend—take this letter from Fonteius Capito; I have asked him to deliver it into your hands alone. You may trust him as you have trusted me, and question him about all those matters upon which this letter does not touch. I am—as you have so often and wisely observed—a man of action, not of words.

Thus my words cannot tell you of the despair I felt when I learned you were ill, nor of the joy that overwhelmed sorrow when I learned that on the journey back from the Thebes that we both remember, your health was returning, like a bird returning home. You wonder how I know this? I must confess—I have had my benevolent spies in your midst, who, out of love for us both and out of respect for my deep solicitude, have kept me informed of your welfare. For despite the circumstances that have kept us apart, my concern for you has never wavered; and if sometimes I have not written, it is for the reason that such a reminder of our past happiness would give me a pain of loss I could not bear.

But as Fonteius will tell you, I have awakened as if from a dream. Oh, my little kitten, who are a Queen, do you know the bitter cost to me of our long separation? Of course you do —and I know you understand. I remember your telling me of your unhappiness when, as a young girl, for reasons of dynasty, your father would have wed you to your young brother so that you might have begotten children to continue the line of the Ptolemies. Yet your womanhood prevailed; and even as an Isis must become a woman, so must a Hercules become a man. It is too burdensome always to remain God and Goddess, King and Queen.

Will you let Fonteius bring you to Antioch, where I will be awaiting you? Even if your love for me has gone, I must see you again, so that I may see for myself that you are well. And there are matters of state that we may discuss, even if you are to refuse the matters of the heart. Come to me, if only out of respect for what we both must remember.

VII. THE MEMOIRS OF MARCUS AGRIPPA: FRAGMENTS (13 B.C.)

After the battle of Philippi, the triumvir Antonius being occupied with his adventures in the Eastern world, it remained for Caesar Augustus to repair the harms of the civil wars, and to bring order into the Italy of Rome. He walked among the treasons of his colleague, Antonius, and did not falter; at Perusia, the armies under my command quieted the insurrection raised by Antonius's brother Lucius; and Caesar Augustus, in his mercy, spared his life, though his crime had been grave.

But of all the impediments that lay between Caesar Augustus and the order that was necessary for the salvation of Rome, the gravest was that raised by the traitor and pirate, Sextus Pompeius, who unlawfully governed the islands of Sicily and Sardinia, and whose ships roamed the seas at will, plundering and destroying those merchant vessels that supplied the grain for Rome's survival. So serious were the depredations of Sextus Pompeius that the city came to be in danger of famine; and in their desperation and fear, the people rioted in the streets, to no end save to relieve themselves of a creeping despair. Caesar Augustus, in his pity for the people, offered Pompeius terms; for we had not the strength to meet him in battle. A treaty was signed, and for a period grain flowed back into Rome; and I was sent by Caesar Augustus to Transalpine Gaul as governor, where I was to organize the Gallic legions against the growing hostility of the barbarian tribes before returning to Rome the following year as consul.

But hardly had the treaty been signed before Sextus Pompeius began conspiring with Antonius, and soon the treaty was broken, and Sextus resumed his piracy and plunder. Caesar Augustus recalled me to Rome before the year was out; for the sake of starving Rome, we had no choice but to prepare for war.

The genius of Rome is in its land, its soil; it has never felt at home upon the sea. And yet we knew that if we were to overcome Sextus Pompeius, we must do so upon the sea; for like all unnatural creatures, that was his habitat, and there he would lurk, even if we drove him off the land he held. Caesar Augustus and the Senate appointed me admiral of the Roman navy, and gave to me the charge of establishing for the first time in our history a formidable Roman fleet. I commissioned to be built some three hundred vessels, to augment those few already under the command of Caesar Augustus; and to man these vessels, Augustus gave freedom to twenty thousand slaves in exchange for their faithful service. And since we could not train upon the open sea—for sometimes the vessels of the pirate Pompeius sailed within easy sight of the Italian shore—I made to be cut a deep channel between the lakes of Lucrine and Avernus at Naples, so that they became one body of water; and by reinforcing the Via Herculeana (said to have been built by Hercules himself) with concrete, and opening it at either end to the sea, I caused to be formed that which is now called the Bay of Julius, in honor of my commander and my friend.

And in that bay, protected by land on all sides from the weather and from unfriendly ships, for the year of my consulship, and into the year beyond, I trained the navy that was to confront the seasoned veterans of the pirate Pompeius. And in the summer we were ready.

On the first day of that month which had recently been named in honor of the Divine Julius, we set sail southward for Sicily, where we were to be joined by the auxiliary fleets of Antonius from the east and those of Lepidus from the north. Unseasonable and violent storms met us, and we suffered losses; and though the fleets of Antonius and Lepidus sought shelter, the Roman fleets of Augustus, under his command and my own, sailed through the storms; and though we were delayed, we met the enemy ships at Mylae, on the northern shore of Sicily, and so severely punished them that they were forced to withdraw to the shallow waters where we could not follow; and we invested the town of Mylae, whence the pirate forces had drawn many of their supplies.

Unprepared for our strength, the ships of Pompeius broke before our assault; with the aid of a grappling hook that I had devised, we were able to board many of the ships, and we captured more than we sank, adding them to our growing fleet. And we captured the coastal fortresses of Hiera and Tyndarus, and it seemed to Pompeius that unless he could conclude a decisive victory, and destroy our ships, all the coastal strongholds from which he drew his supplies would fall into our hands; and he would be lost.

Thus he hazarded his fleet in all its strength, in waters favorable to his own ships, to defend the port city of Naulochus, which we would have to take before we could secure Mylae, a few miles to the south, the first stronghold we had captured.

Skilled as he was, Pompeius was unable to prevail against our heavier ships; though he could outmaneuver us, he was reduced at last to attempting to sweep away the banks of oars by which we were moved, though by this effort he lost more ships than he disabled. Twenty-eight Pompeian vessels were sunk with all their crews; the rest were captured, or suffered such damage as to make them inoperable. Only seventeen ships of the entire fleet escaped our assault, and they sailed eastward, with Sextus Pompeius aboard and in pitiful command.

It is said by some that Pompeius sailed eastward in the hope of joining the absent triumvir Antonius, whom he wished to incite anew against Caesar Augustus; it is said by others that he wished to join with Phraates, the barbarian king of Parthia, who warred against our Eastern provinces. In any event, he made his way to the province of Asia, and resumed his occupation of robbery and pillage. There he was captured by the centurion Titius, whose life Pompeius himself once had spared, and was put to death like a common bandit. Thus was the devastation of piracy at last put down in the seas that surrounded the Italy of Rome.

Weary from battle, our forces yet had to invest the other coastal cities of Sicily which had supplied Pompeius, the chief of which was Messina, where most of Pompeius's land armies were stationed. According to the orders of Caesar Augustus, we were to blockade this city, and await his arrival to meet the battle, if there were to be one. But at this time, and at last, the vessels commanded by the triumvir Lepidus, who had joined in none of the battles at sea, met our ships at Messina; and despite my deliverance to him of the orders of Caesar Augustus, he entered into negotiations with the local commander; and refreshed by his peaceful cruise from Africa, he informed me that by his own authority he relieved me of my command; and he received the surrender of all the Pompeian legions in Messina, requiring pledges of fealty to his own authority, and added those legions to those that he already commanded. In our weariness and pain, we awaited the arrival of Caesar Augustus.

VIII. MILITARY ORDER (SEPTEMBER, 36 B.C.)

To: L. Plinius Rufus, Military Commander of the Pompeian Legions at Messina
From: Marcus Aemilius Lepidus, Imperator and Triumvir of Rome, Ruler of Africa and Commander in Chief of the African

Legions, Consular and Pontifex Maximus of the Senate of Rome
Subject: The Surrender of the Pompeian Legions in Sicily

Having this day surrendered to my sole authority the legions of the defeated Sextus Pompeius, you are to inform the officers and soldiers formerly under your command of the following:

(1) That they are granted amnesty for all crimes committed before this day against the legitimate authority of Rome, and will suffer no punishment either from my hands or from the hands of any other.

(2) That they are to have neither negotiation nor converse with the officers or men of any legion not under my command.

(3) That their safety and well-being is assured under my responsibility, and that they are to obey no commands from any other than myself or my appointed officers.

(4) That they are to mingle freely with the legions under my command, and are to consider themselves as brothers-in-arms, not as enemies.

(5) That the city of Messina, as a conquered city, is open to them for their enrichment as equally as it is to my own soldiers.

IX. LETTER: GAIUS CILNIUS MAECENAS TO TITUS LIVIUS (13 B.C.)

My dear Livy, I got the news just this morning—Marcus Aemilius Lepidus is dead at Circeii, where he has been living in his retirement and, I suppose, shame, for the past twenty-four years. He was our enemy—yet after so long, the death of an old enemy is curiously like the death of an old friend. I am saddened, as was our Emperor, who informed me of the death and told me that he will allow a public funeral in Rome, a funeral in the old style, if his descendants wish it. And so, after all these years, Lepidus returns to Rome and to the honor that he forsook that day in Sicily, nearly a quarter of a century ago. . . .

It occurs to me that that is one of the things that I have not written to you about. Had I done so a week ago, I would no doubt have gone about it rather lightly; it would have seemed to me one of those half-humorous memories out of the past.

But this death has cast a different light upon that memory, and it seems to me now oddly sad.

After a long and disheartening and bloody struggle, the pirate Sextus Pompeius was defeated—by the fleet and legions under the command of Marcus Agrippa and Octavius, and supposedly with the aid of Lepidus. Lepidus and Agrippa were to blockade the city of Messina on the Sicilian coast, so that the scattered fleet of Sextus Pompeius would have no safe harbor to repair the damages done by Agrippa and Octavius. But the commander of the city, one Plinius, having heard of the defeat suffered by Sextus, and at the behest of Lepidus, surrendered the city and eight Pompeian legions without a fight. Lepidus accepted the surrender, and, despite Agrippa's remonstrances, put the legions under his own command; and he allowed the Pompeian as well as his own fourteen legions to plunder and sack the city which, by its surrender, had put itself under his protection.

You understand, my dear Livy, that war is never pretty, and that one must expect a certain brutality from soldiers. But Agrippa came with Octavius into the city after the night of the plunder; and Agrippa has told me a little, though our Emperor would never speak of it.

The houses of the rich and poor were burned without discrimination or reason; hundreds of innocent townspeople, who had been guilty of nothing save the misfortune of having their town occupied by the Pompeian legions—old men, and women, and even children—were slaughtered and tortured by the troops. Agrippa told me that even in the late morning after the carnage, when he and our Emperor rode into the city, they could hear like a single sound the moan and cry of the wounded and dying.

And when our Emperor confronted Lepidus at last, after having dispatched many of his men to care for the suffering townspeople, he was so moved by sorrow that he could not speak; and poor, ignorant Lepidus, mistaking that silence for weakness and in the hysteria of what he must have conceived to be an invincible power afforded him by his sudden acquisition of the twenty-two rested and well-fed legions under his command, peremptorily ordered his colleague, to whom he spoke in contemptuous and threatening tones, to quit Sicily; and said that if he wished to remain a triumvir, he must be content with only Africa, which he (Lepidus) was willing to relinquish to him. It was an extraordinary speech. . . .

Poor Lepidus, I have said. It was a strange delusion he had. Our Emperor did not speak in reply to Lepidus's preposterous claim.

The next day, accompanied only by Agrippa and six body-guards, he came into the city, and went to the small Forum, and spoke to the soldiers of Lepidus and the surrendered troops of Sextus Pompeius, and told them that the promises of Lepidus were empty without his assent, and that they were in danger of putting themselves beyond the protection of Rome if they persisted in following a false leader. He had the name of Caesar, and that probably would have been enough to lead the soldiers to reason, even without Lepidus's fatal error. For Lepidus's own guard, in Lepidus's presence, made to attack the person of our Emperor, who might indeed have been gravely wounded or even killed, had not one of his guards interposed himself between the Emperor and a hurled javelin, giving his life.

Agrippa told me that as the guard fell at our Emperor's feet, a strange hush fell upon the crowd, and that even the body-guards of Lepidus remained still and did not pursue their advantage. Octavius looked with sorrow upon the body of his fallen guard, and then lifted his eyes to the multitude before him.

He said quietly, but in a voice that carried to all the soldiers: "Thus by leave of Marcus Aemilius Lepidus, another brave and loyal Roman soldier, who offered harm to none of his comrades, is dead in a foreign land."

He had his other guards pick up the body and bear it aloft; and in front of the guard, unprotected, as if at a funeral, he walked through the crowd; and the soldiers parted before him like stalks of grain before the wind.

And one by one the legions of Sextus Pompeius deserted Lepidus, and joined our forces outside the city; and then the legions of Lepidus, despising the sluggishness and ineptness of their leader, came to our side; until Lepidus, with only a few who remained loyal to him, was helpless inside the city walls.

Lepidus must have expected to be captured and executed, yet Octavius did not move. One would have thought that in such a position he would have chosen suicide, but Lepidus did not. Rather, he sent a messenger to Octavius, and asked pardon, and asked that his life be spared. Octavius agreed, and set a condition.

Thus, on a bright chill morning in the early fall, Octavius ordered an assembly of all the officers and centurions of the legions of Marcus Aemilius Lepidus and Sextus Pompeius, and the officers and centurions of his own legions, in the Forum of Messina. And Lepidus made a public plea for mercy.

With his sparse gray hair blowing in the wind, in a plain toga with none of the colors of office, without attendants, he walked slowly the length of the Forum and mounted the platform where Octavius stood. There he knelt and asked forgiveness for his crimes, and made public relinquishment of all his powers. Agrippa has said that his face was without color or expression, and that his voice was like the voice of one in a trance.

Octavius said: "This man is pardoned, and he will walk with safety among you. No harm is to come to him. He will be exiled from Rome, but he is under the protection of Rome; and he is stripped of all his titles save that of Pontifex Maximus, which is a title that only the gods can take from him."

Without saying more, Lepidus rose and went to his quarters. And Agrippa told me a curious thing. As he was walking away, Agrippa said to Octavius: "You have given him worse than death."

And Octavius smiled. "Perhaps," he said. "But perhaps I have given him a kind of happiness."

. . . I wonder what his last years were like, in his exile at Circeii. Was he happy? When one has had power in his grasp, and has failed to hold it, and has remained alive—what does one become?

X. THE MEMOIRS OF MARCUS AGRIPPA:
FRAGMENTS (13 B.C.)

And we returned to Rome and the gratitude of the Roman people, whom we had saved from starvation. In the temples of the cities of Italy, from Arezzo in the north to Vibo in the south, statues of Octavius Caesar were raised, and he was worshiped by the people as a god of the hearth. And the Senate and the people of Rome made to be erected in the Forum a statue of gold, in commemoration of the order that had been restored to sea and land.

To celebrate the occasion, Octavius Caesar remitted the debts and taxes of all the people, and gave them assurance of final peace and freedom when Marcus Antonius had subdued the Parthians in the East. And upon my own head, after giving thanks to Rome for its steadfastness, he placed the crown of gold adorned with images of our ships. It was an honor given to no one before and to no one since.

Thus while Antonius in the distant East hunted the barbarian Parthian tribes, in Italy Caesar Augustus devoted himself to securing the borders of his homeland, neglected by the many years of dissension in which it had suffered. We conquered the Pannonian tribes and drove the tribal invaders from the coast of Dalmatia, so that Italy was secure from any threat from the north. In these campaigns, Octavius Caesar himself led his troops, and received honorable wounds in the battles.

Chapter Six

My dear Strabo, I have witnessed an event, the significance of
which only you, the dearest of all my friends, will apprehend.
For on this day Marcus Antonius, triumvir of Rome, has become Imperator of Egypt—a king in fact, though he does not
call himself such. He has taken in marriage that Cleopatra who
is the Incarnate Isis, Queen of Egypt, and Empress of all the
lands of the Nile.

I give you news that, I suspect, none of Rome has heard
yet, possibly not even that young ruler of the Roman world
of whom you have so often written and whom you so admire;
for the marriage was sudden, and known even to this Eastern
world only a few days before the actual event. Oh, my old
friend, I would almost relinquish some part of that wisdom
toward which we both have so laboriously striven, if I could
but see the look upon your face at this moment! It must be
one of surprise—and a little chagrin? You will forgive one who
chides and teases you; I cannot resist provoking what I hope
is a friendly envy in one whose good fortune in the world has
provoked the same in me. For you must have known that your
letters from Rome have raised that envy in me. How often in
Damascus did I wish that I was with you there, in the "center
of the world," as you have called it, conversing with the great
men you mention with such frequency and such intimacy. Now
I, too, have come into the world; and by a stroke of good fortune, which I still cannot quite believe, I have secured a most
remarkable position. I am tutor to the children of Cleopatra,
master of the Royal library, and principal of the schools of the
Royal household.

All of this has happened so quickly that I can hardly believe it, and I still do not fully understand the reasons for the
appointment. Perhaps it is because I am nominally a Jew yet
a philosopher and no fanatic, and because my father has had
some small business connection with the court of King Herod,
whom Marcus Antonius has recently legitimatized as King of

all Judaea and with whom he wants to live in peace. Could politics touch one so unpolitical as myself? I hope that I am being too modest; I would like to think that my reputation as a scholar has had the final weight in the matter.

In any event, I was approached by an emissary of the Queen at Alexandria, where I had gone on some business for my father, in the course of which I took the time to make use of the Royal library; I was approached, and I accepted at once. Aside from the material advantages of the position (which are considerable), the Royal library is the most remarkable I have ever seen; and I will have continual access to books that few men have used or even seen before.

And now that I am a member of the Royal household, I travel wherever the Queen goes; thus, I arrived in Antioch three days ago, though her children remain in the palace at Alexandria. I do not fully understand why the ceremonies were held here, rather than in the Royal palace at Alexandria; perhaps Antonius does not wish to flout Roman law too openly, even though he seems to have cast his fortunes in the East (what *is* the Roman legality of this matter, I wonder, since, it is said, he has not bothered to obtain a legal divorce from his former wife?); or perhaps he merely wants to make clear to the Egyptians that he does not usurp the authority of their Queen. Perhaps there is no meaning.

However that may be, the ceremonies have been held; and to all the Eastern world, the Queen and Marcus Antonius are man and wife; and whatever Rome may think, they are the joint rulers of this world. Marcus Antonius has announced publicly that Caesarion (known to be the child of his one-time friend, Julius Caesar) is heir to the throne of Cleopatra, and that the twins that the Queen has borne are to be considered his legitimate offspring. He has, moreover, increased the extent of Egypt's possessions many-fold; the Queen now has under her authority all of Arabia, including Petra and the Sinai Peninsula; that part of Jordan which lies between the Dead Sea and Jericho; parts of Galilee and Samaria; the whole of the Phoenician coast; the richest parts of Lebanon, Syria, and Cilicia; the whole of the Island of Cyprus, and a part of Crete. Thus I, who was once a Syrian Roman, might now consider myself a Syrian Egyptian; but I am neither. Like you, my old friend, I am a scholar, who would be a philosopher; and I am no more Roman or Egyptian than was our Aristotle a Greek, who never lost his love and pride for his native Ionia. I shall emulate that greatest of all men, and remain content to be a Damascene.

Yet as you yourself have so often said, the world of affairs is an extraordinarily interesting one; and perhaps neither of us, even in the arrogance of our youth, ought to have so removed ourselves from it in our studies. The way to knowledge is a long journey, and the goal is distant; and one must visit many places along the way, if he is to know that goal when he arrives at it.

Though I have seen her at a distance, I have not yet had an audience with the Queen by whom I am employed. Marcus Antonius is everywhere—jovial, familiar, and not at all forbidding. He is a little like a child, I think—though his hair is graying, and he is getting a bit fat.

I think I shall again be happy in Alexandria, as I was during our student days.

As I believe I mentioned in my last letter to you, I had seen the Queen only at a distance—at the wedding ceremony which united her to Marcus Antonius and the power of Rome, a ceremony which only those attached to the Royal household were allowed to attend.

The palace at Antioch is not so imposing as that in Alexandria, but it is grand enough; and at the wedding, I was crowded to the rear of the long hall, from which vantage I could make out very little, though an ebony dais had been raised, upon which Cleopatra and Antonius stood. All I could see of the Queen was her jeweled gown, which sparkled in the torchlight, and the great disk of gold representing the sun, which was set above her crown of state. She moved in a slow and grave manner, as if she were indeed the goddess that her title proclaims her to be. It was an extraordinarily elaborate ceremony (though described by some of my new friends as really rather simple), the significance of which I do not understand; priests marched about and chanted various incantations in that ancient form of the language which only they can speak;

anointings with various oils were made; wands were waved. It was all very mystifying and (I must confess I thought) rather uncivilized, almost barbaric.

And so I went to my first audience with the Queen with an odd feeling, as if I were going into the presence of some Medea or Circe, neither quite goddess nor quite woman, but something more unnatural than either.

My dear Strabo, I cannot tell you how fortunately I was surprised, and how happy I was at my surprise. I expected to encounter a swarthy and rather hefty woman, such as one sees in the market place; I met a slender woman of fair skin and soft brown hair, with enormous eyes, who had poise and dignity and an extraordinary charm, who put me at ease at once and bade me sit near her on a couch no less luxurious than her own, as if I were a guest in a simple and friendly household. And we spoke at length upon those ordinary topics which constitute any civilized conversation. She laughs easily and quietly, and seems totally attentive to her audience. Her Greek is impeccable; her Latin is at least as good as mine; and she speaks casually to her servants in a dialect I cannot understand. She is widely and intelligently read—she even shares my admiration for our Aristotle, and assures me that she knows my own work upon his philosophy, and that her understanding has been enhanced by that knowledge.

I am not, as you know, a vain man; and even if I were, I believe my vanity would have been overwhelmed by my gratitude and my admiration for this most extraordinary of women. That one so charming could also rule one of the richest lands in the world is almost beyond belief.

I have been back in Alexandria for three weeks now, and I have begun my duties; Marcus Antonius and the Queen remain in Antioch, where Antonius is making preparations for his march, later in the year, against the Parthians. My duties are not heavy; I have as many slaves as I need for the management of the Queen's library, and the children take up little of my time.

The twins—Alexander of the Sun and Cleopatra of the Moon—are only a few months more than three years old, and therefore not capable of taking any instruction; but I have been directed to speak to them each day, for a few moments at least, in Greek and (at the Queen's insistence) even in Latin, so that when they grow older the sounds of the language will not be unfamiliar to their ears.

But Ptolemy Caesar—called Caesarion by the people—who is almost twelve years old, is another matter. I believe I would have guessed that he might be the son of the great Julius Caesar, even had I not known it. He recognizes his destiny, and he is prepared for it; he swears that he remembers his father from his mother's residence in Rome, just before the assassination —though he could hardly have been four years old at the time of that event. He is serious, utterly without humor, and oddly intent on whatever he does. It is as if he never had a childhood, and did not want one; he speaks of the Queen as if she were not his mother at all, but only the powerful sovereign that she is; and he awaits the day of his assumption of the Queen's throne, not impatiently, but with the same certainty that he waits the morning sunrise. He would frighten me a little, I believe, if he were to hold the vast power that his mother now has.

But he is a good student, and it is a pleasure to teach him.

For those who put stock in such things, it has been an ominous winter—almost no rainfall, so that the crops will be sparse this year; and a series of cyclones has swept across the lands of Syria and Egypt from the east, laying waste whole villages before spending themselves in the sea. And Antonius has marched from Antioch against the Parthians with what is said to be the greatest expeditionary army since the time of the Macedonian, Alexander the Great (whose blood, it is said, flows in the veins of Cleopatra)—more than sixty thousand seasoned veterans, ten thousand troops of horse from Gaul and Spain, and thirty thousand auxiliary forces recruited from the kingdoms of the Eastern provinces to support the regulars. My young Caesarion, with the innocent ruthlessness of youth (he has recently become interested in the art of warfare), has said that such an army is wasted against the Eastern barbarians; were he king, he says—as if war were truly the game that it seems to him now —he would turn the army toward the west where there is more than plunder to be gained.

The Queen has returned from Antioch, by way of Damascus, and will remain in Alexandria until Antonius concludes his campaign against the Parthians. Knowing that Damascus was my birthplace, she was kind enough to call me into her chambers and give me the news. It is extraordinary how thoughtful and human the great can be. For in Damascus, she had a meeting with King Herod on some business regarding the rents from some balsam fields; and remembering an earlier conversation with me, she inquired after the health of my father, and asked Herod to have conveyed to him greetings from his son and from the Queen.

I have not heard from him since those greetings were conveyed, but I am sure he is pleased. He is growing old, and is becoming feeble in his age. I suspect that at such a time one looks back upon one's life and wonders at its worth, and needs the kindness of some assurance.

II. LETTER: MARCUS ANTONIUS TO CLEOPATRA, FROM ARMENIA (NOVEMBER, 36 B.C.)

My dear wife, I now thank my Roman gods and your Egyptian ones that I did not succumb to my own desires and to your determination, and allow you to accompany me on this campaign. It has been even more difficult than I anticipated; and it is clear that what I had hoped would be concluded this fall will now have to wait until spring.

The Parthians have proved to be a wily and resourceful foe, and they have made more intelligent use of their terrain than I might have foreseen. The maps made by Crassus and Ventidius on their campaigns here have proved worse than useless; treasons among some of the provincial legions have harmed our cause; and this abominable countryside does not furnish sufficient food to keep my legions in health through the winter.

Thus I have withdrawn from my siege of Phraaspa, where we could not have endured the cold; and for twenty-seven days we have made our way across the country, nearly all the way from the Caspian Sea, and now rest in the comparative safety of Armenia, though we are tired, and illness pervades the camp.

Yet all in all, the campaign has, I believe, been a successful one, though I fear that many of my weary soldiers would not agree with me. I know the Parthian tricks now; and we have mapped the territory with sufficient accuracy to serve us next year. I have sent to Rome the news of our victory.

But you must understand that, despite the tactical success of the campaign, I am now in most desperate straits. We cannot stay in Armenia; I do not fully trust my host, King Artavasdes, who deserted me at a crucial moment in Parthia—though I cannot now upbraid him, since we are his guests. Therefore I shall march with a few legions to Syria, and the rest of the army will join me after it has recovered from its exhaustion.

To endure the winter, even in Syria, we shall need provisions; for we are like beggars now. We shall need food, and clothing, and the materials necessary to repair our damaged war machines. We shall also need horses to replenish those lost in battle and to the weather, so that we might continue training for the campaign next spring. And I must have money. My soldiers have not been paid for months, and some are threatening revolt. And we shall need these things quickly. I attach to this letter a detailed list of those things that I absolutely require, and a supplementary list of things that may be needed later in the winter. I cannot exaggerate our need.

We shall winter in the little village of Leuke Kome, just south of Beirut. You may not have heard of it. There is sufficient dockage there for the ships that you will send. Be careful. For all I know, the mad Parthians may be roaming the coast lines by the time you receive this. But there should be no danger of blockage at Leuke Kome. I trust that this letter will reach you soon, however rough the winter seas are; we shall not be able to endure for many more weeks without provisions.

Outside my tent the snow is falling, so that the plain on which we are encamped is invisible. I can see no other tent; I can hear no sound. I am cold, and in the silence more aware of my loneliness than you can imagine. I long for the warmth of your arms and for the intimacy of your voice. Come to me in Syria with your ships. I must stay there with my troops, else they will scatter before spring comes, and our sacrifices will have been for naught; and yet I cannot suffer another month without your presence. Come to me, and we shall make of Beirut another Antioch, or Thebes, or Alexandria.

Revered Queen: No man is more courageous than that Marcus
Antonius whom you have honored by your presence and raised
at your side to overlook the world. He fights more bravely than
prudence should allow, and endures privations and hardships
which would destroy the most seasoned common soldier. But
he is no general, and the campaign has been a disaster.

If what I report to you contradicts what you may have heard
from other sources, you must know that I write nevertheless
in friendship for your husband, in reverence for you, and in
anxiety for Egypt and her future.

In the spring we marched from Antioch to Zeugma on the
River Euphrates, and thence northward along that river, where
food was plentiful, to the watershed between the Euphrates
and the River Araxes, and then southward toward the Parthian
citadel of Phraaspa. But before Phraaspa, to save time, Marcus
Antonius divided his army, sending our supply train, with our
food and baggage, and our battering rams and siege wagons
by a more level passage, while the bulk of the army advanced
rapidly to its goal.

But while that army advanced in safety, the Parthians descended from the mountain upon the more slowly moving
force that we had divided from us. News reached us of the attack, but when we arrived it was too late to save anything. The
escort was slain, our supplies were burned, our siege wagons
and engines of war were all destroyed; and only a few soldiers
remained unharmed behind hastily thrown up fortifications.
We then dispersed the attacking Parthians, who, having done
their damage, prudently withdrew to the mountains that they
knew, and where we dared not follow.

That was the "victory" that Marcus Antonius reported to
Rome. We counted eighty Parthian dead.

Despite the destruction of all our instruments of siege, all
our replacement supplies, our food—Marcus Antonius persisted in his siege of the Parthian city of Phraaspa. Even if the
city had not been prepared for us, the task would have been

nearly impossible, since we had only the arms that we bore at our sides. We could not lure them into open battle; when we foraged for food, the detachments were set upon by the Parthian archers who appeared from nowhere to kill, and who disappeared again; and winter drew on. For two months we persisted; and at last Antonius exacted from King Phraates a pledge that we would be allowed to retreat from his country without hindrance. And so in mid-October, hungry and exhausted, we began our return whence we had begun, five months before.

For twenty-seven days, in bitter cold, through drifts of snow and in swirling winds, we struggled over mountains and unprotected plains; and upon eighteen separate occasions we were attacked by the mounted archers of the perfidious Phraates. They swooped from everywhere—upon our rear, our flanks, our fronts; let fly their arrows before we could prepare ourselves; and then were gone back into their barbaric darkness, while the poor blind animal that was their victim lumbered on.

It was in these awful days of retreat that your Marcus Antonius showed himself to be the man that he is. He endured all the hardships of his men; he would take no food other than that taken by his comrades, who were reduced to gnawing roots and foraging for insects in rotting wood; nor would he wear clothing warmer than they wore themselves.

We are in Armenia now, where we cannot stay; the King of this country, nominally our ally but no more trustworthy than our foe, has furnished us with a little food. We leave for Syria soon. But I have made an accounting of our losses, and I give them to you.

In these five months, we have lost nearly forty thousand men, many to Parthian arrows, but more to the cold and disease; of these, twenty-two thousand were Antonius's Roman veterans, the best warriors in the world, it is said; and these cannot be replaced, unless Octavius Caesar consents to replace them—and that is not likely. Virtually all the horse is gone. We have no reserve of supplies. We have no clothing, except the rags we wear. We have no food, save that which is in our bellies.

Thus, Revered Queen, if you wish to save even a remnant of this army, you must accede to your husband's request for supplies. Out of his pride, he may not, I fear, wish you to know how desperate his plight is.

IV. MEMORANDUM: CLEOPATRA TO THE
MINISTER OF SUPPLIES (36 B.C.)

You are hereby authorized to procure and prepare for shipment to the Imperator Marcus Antonius at the port of Leuke Kome in Syria the following items:

Garlic: 3 tons
Wheat or spelt, according to supply: 30 tons
Salt fish: 10 tons
Cheese (of goat): 45 tons
Honey: 600 casks
Salt: 7 tons
Sheep, ready for slaughter: 600
Sour wine: 600 barrels

In addition to above items: if there is significant surplus of dried vegetables in the silos, you are to include that surplus in your shipment. If there is no surplus, you are to allow the foregoing to suffice.

You are also to procure a sufficient quantity of heavy woolen cloth, of the second quality (240,000 yards of the broad width) to manufacture 60,000 winter cloaks; sufficient coarse linen (120,000 yards of the middle width) for the manufacture of a like number of military tunics; and sufficient cured leather (soft) of horse or bullock (2000 skins) to manufacture a like number of pairs of shoes.

Speed is crucial in this matter. You are to assign a sufficient number of tailors and bootmakers to the appropriate ships so that the manufacture of these items may take place there and be completed in a voyage of eight to ten days.

The ships (twelve in number, waiting in the Royal harbor) will be made ready to sail within three days, at which time all procurement and loading must have been completed. The displeasure of your Queen would attend your failure.

V. MEMORANDUM: CLEOPATRA TO THE MINISTER OF FINANCE (36 B.C.)

Despite whatever orders or requests you may receive, either from his representative or from Marcus Antonius himself, you are to disburse no monies from the Royal treasury without the explicit approval and authorization of your Queen. Such approval and authorization is to be honored only if it is delivered by hand by a known representative of the Queen herself, and only if it bears the Royal seal.

VI. MEMORANDA: CLEOPATRA TO THE GENERALS OF THE EGYPTIAN ARMY (36 B.C.)

Despite whatever orders or requests you may receive, either from his representatives or from Marcus Antonius himself, you are neither to allocate nor promise any troops from the Egyptian army without the explicit approval and authorization of your Queen. Such approval and authorization is to be honored only if it is delivered by hand by a known representative of the Queen herself, and only if it bears the Royal seal.

VII. LETTER: CLEOPATRA TO MARCUS ANTONIUS, FROM ALEXANDRIA (WINTER, 35 B.C.)

My dear husband, the Queen has ordered that the needs of your brave army be filled; and your wife like a trembling girl flies to meet you, as rapidly as the uncertain winter sea will carry her. Indeed, even as you read this letter, she is no doubt at the prow of the ship that leads the line of supply, straining her eyes in vain for the Syrian coast where her lover waits, cold in the weather, but warm in the anticipation of her lover's arms.

As a Queen, I rejoice at your success; as a woman, I bewail the necessity that has kept us apart. And yet during these hurried days since I received your letter, I have concluded (can I be wrong?) that at last woman and Queen may become one.

I shall persuade you to return with me to the warmth and comfort of Alexandria, and to leave the completion of your success in Parthia for another day. It will be my pleasure to persuade you as a woman; it is my duty to persuade you as a Queen.

The treasons that you have seen in the East have had their birth in the West. Octavius plots against you still, and libels you to those whose salvation is to love you. I know that he has tried to subvert Herod; and I am persuaded by all the intelligence that I can gather that he is responsible for the defections of the provincial legions that hampered your success in Parthia. I must convince you that there are barbarians in Rome as well as in Parthia; and their use of your loyalty and good nature is more dangerous than any Parthian arrow. In the East there is only plunder; but in the West there is the world, and such power as only the great can imagine.

But even now my mind wanders from what I say. I think of you, the mightiest of men—and I am woman again, and care nothing for kingdoms, for wars, for power. I come to you at last, and count the hours as if they were days.

VIII. LETTER: GAIUS CILNIUS MAECENAS TO TITUS LIVIUS (12 B.C.)

How delicately you put things, my dear Livy; and yet, beneath that delicacy, how clear are your brutal alternatives! Were we "deceived" (and therefore fools), or did we "withhold" some information (and were therefore liars)? I shall reply somewhat less delicately than you question.

No, my old friend, we were not deceived about the matter of Parthia; how could we have been deceived? Even before we got Antonius's account of the campaign, we knew the truth of it. We lied to the Roman people.

I must say that I am a good deal less offended by your question than by what I perceive to lie behind it. You forget that I am an artist myself, and know the necessity of asking what to ordinary people would seem the most insulting and presumptuous things. How could I take offense at that which I myself would do, without the slightest hesitation, for the sake of my art? No, it is what I perceive in the tenor of your question that begins to give me offense; for I think (I hope I am wrong) I detect the odor of a moralist. And it seems to me that the moralist is the most useless and contemptible of creatures. He is useless in that he would expend his energies upon making judgments rather than upon gaining knowledge, for the reason that judgment is easy and knowledge is difficult. He is contemptible in that his judgments reflect a vision of himself which in his ignorance and pride he would impose upon the world. I implore you, do not become a moralist; you will destroy your art and your mind. And it would be a heavy burden for even the deepest friendship to bear.

As I have said, we lied; and if I give the reasons for the lie, I do not explain in order to defend. I explain to enlarge your understanding and your knowledge of the world.

After the Parthian debacle, Antonius sent to the Senate a dispatch describing his "victory" in the most glowing and general terms; and demanded, though in absentia, the ceremony of a triumph. We accepted the lie, allowed it currency, and gave him his triumph.

Italy had been racked by two generations of civil wars; the immediate history of a strong and proud people was a history of defeat, for none is victor in a civil strife; after the defeat of Sextus Pompeius, peace seemed possible; the news of such an overwhelming defeat might have been simply catastrophic, both to the stability of our government and to the soul of the people. For a people may endure an almost incredible series of the darkest failures without breaking; but give them respite and some hope for the future, and they may not endure an unexpected denial of that hope.

And there were more particular reasons for the lie. The defeat of Sextus Pompeius had been accomplished only shortly before we got the news from Parthia; the auxiliary legions had been disbanded and settled on the lands promised them; the prospect that they might be called again would have wholly disrupted all land values outside of Rome, and would have proved disastrous to an already precarious economy.

Finally, and most obviously, we still had some hope that Antonius might be deflected from his Eastern dream of Empire and become once again a Roman. It was a vain hope, but at that time it seemed a reasonable one. To have refused him his triumph—to have told your "truth" to all of Rome—would have made it impossible for him ever to have returned in honor or in peace.

In my account of these events, I have been saying "we"; but you must understand that for nearly three years after the defeat of Sextus Pompeius, Octavius and Agrippa were only occasionally in Rome; most of their time was spent in Illyria, securing our borders and subduing the barbarian tribes that theretofore had ranged freely up and down the Dalmatian shore-lands, and had even pillaged villages on the Adriatic coast of Italy itself. During this time I was entrusted with the official seal of Octavius. These decisions were mine, though in every instance, I am proud to say, they were approved by the Emperor, though often after the fact. I remember once he returned to Rome, briefly, to recuperate from a wound received in a battle against one of the Illyrian tribes; and he said to me, only half-jokingly, I think, that with Agrippa at the head of his army and with me, however unofficially, at the head of his government, he felt that the security of the nation demanded that he relinquish any pretense to either position, and for his own pleasure become the head of my stable of poets.

Marcus Antonius. . . . The charges and countercharges that have come down through the years! But beneath them, the truth was there, though the world may never fully apprehend it. We played no game; we had no need to. Though many senators in Rome, being of the old Party and somehow irrationally reversing allegiances and seeing Antonius as the only hope of recapturing the past, we knew to be against us and for Antonius, yet the people were for us; we had the army; and we had sufficient senatorial power to carry at least the most important of our edicts.

We could have endured Marcus Antonius in the East as an independent satrap or Imperator or whatever he chose to call himself, so long as he remained a Roman, even a plundering Roman; we could have endured him in Rome, even with his recklessness and ambition. But it was being forced upon us that he had caught the dream of the Greek Alexander, and that he was sick from that dream.

We gave him his triumph; it strengthened his senatorial support, but it did not draw him back to Rome. We offered him the consulship; he refused it, and did not return to Rome. And in what was really a last desperate effort to avert what we knew was coming, we returned to him the seventy ships of his fleet that had helped us defeat Sextus Pompeius, and we sent two thousand troops to augment his depleted Roman legions. And Octavia sailed with the fleet and soldiers to Athens, in the hope that Antonius might be dissuaded from his awful ambition and return to his duty as husband, Roman, and triumvir.

He accepted the ships; he enlisted the troops; and he refused to see Octavia, nor even gave her dwelling in Athens, but sent her forthwith back to Rome. And as if to leave no doubt in the minds of any of his contempt, he staged a triumph in Alexandria—in *Alexandria*—and presented a few token captives, not to a Senate, but to Cleopatra, a foreign monarch, who sat above even Antonius himself and upon a golden throne. It is said that a most barbaric ceremony followed the triumph —Antonius robed himself as Osiris, and sat beside Cleopatra, who was gowned as Isis, that most peculiar goddess. He proclaimed his mistress to be Queen of Kings, and proclaimed that her Caesarion was joint monarch over Egypt and Cyprus. He even had struck coins on one side of which was a likeness of himself and on the other a likeness of Cleopatra.

As if it were an afterthought, he had sent to Octavia letters of divorce, and had her evicted without ceremony or warning from his Roman dwelling.

We could not then evade what must ensue. Octavius returned from Illyria, and we began to prepare for whatever madness might come from the East.

IX. SENATORIAL PROCEEDINGS, ROME (33 B.C.)

On this day Marcus Agrippa, Consular and Admiral of the Roman Fleet, Aedile of the Roman Senate, does declare, for the health and welfare of the Roman people, and for the glory of Rome, the following:

I. From his own funds, and without recourse to the public treasury, Marcus Agrippa will have repaired and restored all public buildings that have fallen into neglect, and will have cleaned and repaired the public sewers that carry the waste of Rome into the Tiber.

II. From his own funds Marcus Agrippa will make available to all free-born inhabitants of Rome sufficient olive oil and salt to suffice their needs for one year.

III. For both men and women, free-born and slave, the public baths will for the period of one year be open for use without fee.

IV. To protect the gullible and ignorant and poor, and to halt the spread of alien superstition, all astrologers and Eastern soothsayers and magicians are forbidden within the city walls, and those who now practice their vicious trades are ordered to quit the city of Rome, upon pain of death and forfeiture of all monies and properties.

V. In that Temple known as Serapis and Isis, the trinkets of Egyptian superstition shall no longer be sold or purchased, upon pain of exile for both purchaser and seller; and the Temple itself, built to commemorate the conquest of Egypt by Julius Caesar, is declared to be a monument of history, and not a recognition of the false gods of the East by the Roman people and the Roman Senate.

X. PETITION: THE CENTURION QUINTUS APPIUS
TO MUNATIUS PLANCUS, COMMANDER OF THE
ASIAN LEGIONS OF THE IMPERATOR MARCUS
ANTONIUS, FROM EPHESUS (32 B.C.)

I, Appius, son of Lucius Appius, am of the Cornelian tribe and of Campanian origin. My father was a farmer, who left me a few acres of land near Velletri, which from the age of eighteen to twenty-three I tilled for a humble livelihood. My cottage is there yet, overseen by the wife I married in my youth, who, though a freedwoman, is chaste and faithful; and the land is tended by the three of my sons who remain alive. Two sons I lost—one to disease, and the eldest to the Spanish campaign against Sextus Pompeius, under Julius Caesar, these many years ago.

For the sake of Italy and my posterity, I became a soldier in the twenty-third year of my life, in the consulship of Tullius Cicero and Gaius Antonius, who was uncle to the Marcus Antonius who is now my master. For two years I was a common soldier in that army under Gaius Antonius which defeated in honorable battle the conspirator Catiline; in my third year as a soldier I was with Julius Caesar in his first Spanish campaign, and though I was a young man, in reward for my bravery in battle, Julius Caesar made me a lesser centurion of the IV Macedonian legion. I have been a soldier for thirty years; I have fought in eighteen campaigns, in fourteen of which I was centurion and in one of which I was acting military tribune; I have fought under the command of six duly elected consuls of the Senate; I have served in Spain, Gaul, Africa, Greece, Egypt, Macedonia, Britain, and Germany; I have marched in three triumphs, I have five times received the laurel crown for saving the life of a fellow soldier; and I have twenty times been decorated for bravery in battle.

The oath I took as a young soldier bound me to the authority of the magistrates, the consuls, and the Senate for the defense of my country. To that oath I have been faithful, and have served Rome with that honor of which I am capable. I am now in my fifty-third year, and I ask release from military service, so that I may return to Velletri and spend my remaining years in privacy and peace.

I know that, in the law, you may refuse this release, despite my age and service, since I volunteered freely for another campaign; and I know, too, that what I shall now say may put me in jeopardy. If it is to do so, I shall accept my fate.

When I was detached from the army of Marcus Agrippa and sent to Athens and thence to Alexandria and finally here to Ephesus and the army of Marcus Antonius, I did not protest; that is the soldier's lot, and I have grown accustomed to it. I had fought the Parthians before, and had no fear of them. But the events of the past few weeks have put me into a deep doubt; and I must turn to you, with whom I fought in Gaul under Julius Caesar, and whose honorable behavior toward me gives me some hope that you may hear me before you judge me too harshly.

It is clear that we shall not fight the Parthians, or the Medians, or anyone else to the East. And yet we arm, and we train, and we build the engines of war.

I have given my oath to the consuls and the Senate of the Roman people; it is an oath that I have not broken.

And yet where is the Senate now? And where is my oath to find its fulfillment?

We know that three hundred senators and the two consuls of the year have quit Rome, and are now here in Ephesus, where the Imperator Marcus Antonius has convened them against the seven hundred senators who have remained in Rome; and new consuls in Rome have replaced those who have come here.

To whom do I owe my oath? Where is the Roman people, whom the Senate must represent?

I do not hate Octavius Caesar, though I would fight him, were that my duty; I do not love Marcus Antonius, though I would die for him were that my duty. It is not the place of the soldier to think of politics, and it is not the business of the soldier to hate or love. It is his duty to fulfill his oath.

A Roman, I have fought against Romans before, though I have done so with sorrow. But I have not fought against Romans under the banner of a foreign queen, and I have not marched against my nation and my countrymen as if they were the painted barbarians of a foreign province, to be plundered and subdued.

I am an old man, and tired, and I ask release to return quietly to my home. But you are my commander, and I shall not move against your authority. If it is your decision that I may not be released, I shall acquit myself with that honor in which I trust I have lived.

XI. LETTER: MUNATIUS PLANCUS, COMMANDER
OF THE ASIAN LEGIONS, TO OCTAVIUS
CAESAR, FROM EPHESUS (32 B.C.)

Though we have differed, I have not been your enemy so much as I have been friend to Marcus Antonius, whom I have known since those days when we were both the trusted generals of your late and divine father, Julius Caesar. Through all the years, I have tried to be loyal to Rome, and yet be loyal to the man whom I have had for friend.

It is no longer possible for me to remain loyal to both. As if in an enchantment, Marcus Antonius follows blindly wherever Cleopatra will lead; and she will lead where her ambition takes her, and that is simply the conquest of the world, the succession of her progeny in kingship over that world, and the establishment of Alexandria as the capital of that world. I have been unable to dissuade Marcus Antonius from this disastrous course. Even now, troops from all the Asian provinces gather at Ephesus to join the sad Roman legions which Antonius will hurl against Rome; the doors of Cleopatra's treasury are open to prosecute the war against Italy; and she will not leave Marcus Antonius's side, but goads him bitterly toward your destruction and the fulfillment of her ambition. It is said that henceforward she will march at his side and command, even in battle. Not only myself, but all of his friends have urged him to send Cleopatra back to Alexandria, where her presence might not provoke the hatred of the Roman troops, but he will not, or cannot, move.

Thus I have been forced to choose between a waning friendship for a man and a steady love for my country. I return to Italy, and I renounce the Eastern adventure. And I will not be alone. I have spent my life with the Roman soldier, and I think I know his heart; many will not fight under the banner of a foreign queen, and those who in their confusion will fight, will do so with sorrow and reluctance, so that their strength and soldierly determination will be lessened.

I come to you in friendship, and I offer you my services; if you cannot accept the former, perhaps you will find use for the latter.

XII. THE MEMOIRS OF MARCUS AGRIPPA: FRAGMENTS (13 B.C.)

I come now to the account of those events which led to the battle of Actium and at last to the peace of which Rome had long despaired.

Marcus Antonius and the Queen Cleopatra gathered their strength in the East, and moved their armies from Ephesus to the Island of Samos, and thence to Athens, where they poised in threat to Italy and peace. In the second consulship of Caesar Augustus, I was aedile of Rome; and when the year of those duties was over, we turned ourselves to the task of rebuilding the armies of Italy that would repel the threat of Eastern treason, a task which necessitated our absence from

Rome for many months. We returned to discover the Senate subverted by the friends of Antonius who were the enemies of the Roman people; we opposed those enemies, and when it became clear to them that they would not prevail in their designs against the order of Italy, the two consuls of the year, and behind them three hundred senators without faith or love for their homeland, quit Rome and made their way out of Italy to join Antonius; and went without hindrance or threat from Caesar Augustus, who saw them depart with sorrow, but without anger.

And in the East, loyal Roman troops, at first by tens and then by hundreds, refusing the yoke of a foreign queen, made their way to Italy; and from them we knew that there would be no escape from war; and knew also that that war would come soon, for Antonius was weakening from the desertions, and would, if he delayed too long, be wholly dependent upon the caprice and inexperience of his barbarian legions and their Asian commanders.

Thus in the late autumn of the year after his second consulship, Caesar Augustus, with the consent of the Senate and the Roman people, did declare that a state of war existed between the Roman people and Cleopatra, Queen of Egypt; and led by Caesar Augustus, the Senate in solemn march took themselves to the Campus Martius, and at the Temple of Bellona, the herald read the words of war, and the priests made sacrifice of a white heifer to the goddess, and prayed that the army of Rome be made safe in all the battles that were to come.

After the defeat of Sextus Pompeius, Augustus had vowed to the Roman people that the civil wars were ended, and that not again would the soil of Italy suffer to receive the blood of her sons. Throughout the winter we trained our soldiers on land, repaired and augmented our fleet, exercising upon the sea when weather allowed us; and in the spring, learning that Marcus Antonius had gathered his fleet and his army at the seaward opening of the Bay of Corinth, whence he purposed to strike swiftly across the Ionian Sea at the Eastern coast of Italy, we moved against him, to save Italy from the wounds of war.

Against us was arrayed the might of the Eastern world—one hundred thousand troops, of which thirty thousand were Roman, and five hundred ships of war, deployed along the coastal lands of Greece; and eighty thousand reserves of troops that remained in Egypt and Syria. Against this force we brought fifty thousand Roman soldiers, a number of which were veterans of the sea campaign against Pompeius, two hundred fifty ships of war, the latter under my command, and one hundred fifty vessels of supply.

The coast of Greece boasts few harbors that may be defended, and thus we had no trouble landing the troops that would fight Antonius on the land; and the ships under my command blockaded the sea routes of supply from Syria and Egypt, so that the forces of Cleopatra and Marcus Antonius would have to depend upon the land that they had invaded for food and supplies.

Loath to take Roman lives, throughout the spring we skirmished, hoping to accomplish our ends by blockade rather than warfare; and in the summer, we moved in strength to the Bay of Actium, where the largest enemy force was concentrated, hoping to lure there those who would prevent our pretended invasion, in which effort we succeeded. For Antonius and Cleopatra sailed in full complement to rescue the ships and men we did not intend to attack, and we fell back before the advance of their ships, and let them enter into the bay, whence we knew eventually they would have to emerge. We would force them to do battle upon sea, though their strength was upon the land.

The mouth of the Bay of Actium is less than one half a mile in width, though the bay itself widens considerably within, so that the enemy ships had sufficient room to harbor; and while they rested inside with the soldiers encamped ashore, Caesar Augustus sent troops of infantry and cavalry around them, and fortified the encirclement, so that they would have retreated overland at great cost. And we waited; for we knew that the armies of the East suffered from hunger and disease, and could not muster the strength for a retreat by land. They would fight by sea.

The ships of war that we had returned to Antonius after the defeat of Sextus Pompeius were the largest of the fleet, and I had learned that those which Antonius had built to war against us were even larger, some carrying as many as ten banks of oars and girded by bands of iron against ramming; such ships are nearly invincible against smaller ships in direct combat, when there is no room for maneuvering. Therefore I had much earlier resolved to rely upon a preponderance of lighter and more maneuverable craft, with as few as two and as many as six banks of oars, and none larger; and resolved to be so patient as to lure the Eastern fleets into the open sea. For at Naulochus, against Pompeius, we had had to engage the enemy ships at shore, where swiftness meant nothing.

We waited; and on the first day of September we saw the lines of vessels draw up for battle, and saw those burned for which there were no rowers; and we made ready for what must ensue on the morrow.

The morning came bright and clear; the harbor and the sea beyond were smooth like a table of translucent stone. The Eastern fleet raised sail, as if hoping to pursue us when a wind came up; the oarsmen dipped their oars; and the fleet, like a solid wall, moved slowly across the water. Antonius himself commanded the starboard squadron of the three groups, which were so close that often the opposing oars clashed together, and the fleet of Cleopatra followed behind the center squadron at some distance.

My own squadron opposed that of Antonius; and those ships commanded by Caesar Augustus were at the port. We were beyond the mouth of the bay, and spread thinly out in a curving line, so that we had no ships behind us.

As the enemy advanced toward us, we did not move; he paused at the mouth, and no oar was dipped for several hours. He wished us to move upon him; we did not move; we waited.

And at last, out of impatience or an excess of boldness, the commander of the port squadron moved forward; Caesar Augustus made as if to withdraw from danger; the squadron pursued him without thought, and the rest of the Eastern fleet followed. Our center squadron fell back, we lengthened our line, and the enemy fleet rode in like fish into a net, and we surrounded them.

Until nearly dusk the battle raged, though the issue was at no time in serious doubt. We had not raised sail, and we could move swiftly about the heavier ships; and having hoisted sail, the enemy's decks did not afford room for slingers and archers to work effectively; and the sails offered easy targets for the fireballs that we catapulted. Our own decks were clear so that when we grappled a ship, our soldiers in superior numbers could board the enemy and overcome him with some ease.

He would attempt to form a wedge so that he could break our line; we darted upon him and broke his formation, so that he had to fight singly; he tried to form again, and we broke him again, so that at last each ship fought for its own survival, as best it could. And the sea blazed with ships that we fired, and we heard above the roar of the flames the screams of men who burned with their ships, and the sea darkened with blood and was awash with bodies that had thrown off armor and struggled weakly to escape the fire and the sword and the javelin and the arrow. Though they opposed us, they were Roman soldiers; and we were sickened at the waste.

During all the fighting, the ships of Cleopatra had hung back in the harbor; and when at last a breeze sprang up, she had her sails set into the wind, and swung around the ships that were locked in battle and made toward the open sea where we could not follow.

It was one of those curious moments in the confusion of warfare with which all soldiers are familiar. The vessel which carried Caesar Augustus and my own ship had come so close together that we could look into each other's eyes and could even shout to be heard above the furor; not thirty yards away, where it had been pursued and then left, was the ship of Marcus Antonius. I believe that all three of us saw the purple sail of Cleopatra's departing flagship at the same time. None of us moved; Antonius stood at the prow of his ship as if he were a carven figurehead, looking after his departing Queen. And then he turned to us, though whether he recognized either of us I do not know. His face was without expression, as if it were that of a corpse. Then his arm lifted stiffly, and dropped; and the sails were thrust into the wind, and the great ship turned slowly and gathered speed, and Marcus Antonius followed after his Queen. We watched the pitiful remains of his own ships that escaped the slaughter, and we did not attempt to pursue. I did not see Marcus Antonius again.

Deserted by their leaders, the remaining ships surrendered; we cared for our wounded enemies, who were also our brothers, and we burned those ships that remained of the Antonian force; and Caesar Augustus said that no Roman soldier who had been our enemy should suffer for his bravery, but should be returned to honor and the safety of Rome.

We knew that we had won the world; but there were no songs of victory that night, nor joy among any of us. Late into the night the only sound that could be heard was the lap and hiss of water against the burning hulls and the low moans of the wounded; a glow of burning hung over the harbor, and Caesar Augustus, his face stark and reddened in that glow, stood at the prow of his ship and looked upon the sea that held the bodies of those brave men, both comrade and foe, as if there were no difference between them.

XIII. LETTER: GAIUS CILNIUS MAECENAS TO TITUS LIVIUS (12 B.C.)

In reply to your questions:

Did Marcus Antonius plead for his life? Yes. It is a matter best forgotten. I had a copy of the letter once. I have destroyed it. Octavius did not reply to the letter. Antonius was not murdered; he did commit suicide, though he bungled the job and died slowly. Let him remain in peace; do not pursue these matters too far.

The matter of Cleopatra: (1) No, Octavius did not arrange her murder. (2) Yes, he did speak to her in Alexandria before she took her life. (3) Yes, he would have spared her life; he did not want her dead. She was an excellent administrator, and could have retained titular control of Egypt. (4) No, I do not know what went on in the interview at Alexandria; he has never chosen to speak of it.

The matter of Caesarion: (1) Yes, he was only seventeen years old. (2) Yes, it was our decision that he be put to death. (3) Yes, it is my judgment that he was the son of Julius. (4) No, he was not put to death because of his name, but because of his ambition, which was inarguable. I spoke to Octavius about his youth, and Octavius reminded me that he himself had been seventeen once, and ambitious.

The matter of Antyllus, the son of Marcus Antonius. Octavius had him put to death. He also was seventeen years of age. He was much like his father.

The matter of Octavius's return to Rome: (1) He was thirty-three years of age. (2) Yes, he received the triple triumph then, at the beginning of his fifth consulship. (3) Yes, that was the same year he fell ill, and we despaired again of his life.

You must, my dear Livy, forgive the curtness of my replies. I am not offended; I am only tired. I look back upon those days as if they happened to someone else, almost as if they were not real. If the truth were known, I am bored with remembering. Perhaps I shall feel better tomorrow.

BOOK II

Chapter One

I am Hirtia. My mother, Crispia, was once a slave in the house-hold of Atia, wife to Gaius Octavius the Elder, niece to Julius Caesar the God, and mother to that Octavius whom the world knows now as Augustus. I cannot write, so I speak these words to my son Quintus, who manages the estates of Atius Sabinus in Velletri. He writes these words so that our posterity may know of the time before them, and of the part their ancestors had in that time. I am in my seventy-second year, and the end of my life comes toward me; I wish to say these words before the gods close my eyes forever.

Three days ago my son took me into Rome, so that before my eyes dimmed beyond sight I might look again upon the city that I remembered from my youth; and there an event befell me which raised memories of a past so distant that I thought I could never return to it. After more than fifty years, I saw again that one who is now master of the world and who has more titles than my poor mind can remember. But once I called him "my Tavius," and held him in my arms as if he were my own. I shall speak later of that; now I must say my memories of an earlier time.

My mother was born a slave in the Julian household. She was given to Atia first as a playmate, and then as a servant. But even when she was young, she was granted her freedom for faithful service, so that she might, in the law, marry the freed-man Hirtius, who became my father. My father was overseer of all the olive groves on the Octavian estate at Velletri; and it was in a cottage near the villa, on the hill above the groves, that I was born, and where I lived in the kindness of that household for the first nineteen years of my life. Now I have returned to Velletri; and if the gods are willing, I shall die in that cottage in the contentment of my childhood.

My mistress and her husband did not stay often at the villa; they lived in Rome, for Gaius Octavius the Elder was a man of importance in the government of those days. When I was ten years old, my mother informed me that Atia had given birth to a son; and because he was sickly, she decided that he would spend his infancy in the country air, away from the stench and smoke of the city. My mother had recently given birth to a stillborn child, and could nurse her mistress's son. And as my mother took a child to her breast as if it were her own, so did my young heart, which was beginning to stir toward the dream of motherhood.

As young as I was, I washed his body; swaddled him; held his tiny hand when he took his first steps; saw him grow. In my childhood game of motherhood, he was my Tavius.

When that one whom I then called Tavius was five years old, his father returned from a long stay in the land of Macedonia and visited with his family for a few days; he planned to move southward to another of his residences in Nola, where we were to join him for the winter season. But he became suddenly ill, and died before we could take the journey; and my Tavius lost the father whom he had never known. I held him in my arms to comfort him. I remember that his little body quivered; he did not cry.

For four more years he remained in our care, though a teacher was sent from Rome to attend him; and occasionally his mother visited. When I was in my nineteenth year, my mother died; and my mistress Atia—who after her time of mourning and in her duty had married again—decided that her son must return to Rome so that he might begin to prepare himself for manhood. And in her kindness and for the safety of my future, Atia gave into my keeping a portion of land sufficient to keep me from ever living in want; and for the well-being of my person, she gave me in marriage to a freedman of her family, who had a modest but safe prosperity in a flock of sheep that grazed in the mountain country near Mutina, north of Rome.

Thus I went from my youth and became a woman, and in the way of things had to say good-by to the child I had pretended was mine. The days of play were over for me; yet it was I who wept when I had to take leave of Tavius. As if I were the child who needed comfort, he embraced me, and told me he would not forget me. We vowed that we would see each other again; we did not believe that we would. And so the child that had been my Tavius went his way to become the ruler of the world, and I found the happiness and purpose for which the gods had destined me.

How might an ignorant old woman understand greatness in one whom she has known as an infant, as a toddling child, as a boy who ran and shouted with his playmates? Now everywhere outside of Rome, in the villages and towns of the countryside, he is a god; there is a temple in his name in my own town of Mutina, and I have heard that there are others elsewhere. His image is on the hearths of the country folk throughout the land.

I do not know the ways of the world or of the gods; I remember a child who was almost my own, though not born of my body; and I must say what I remember. He was a child with hair paler than the autumn grain; a fair skin that would not take the sun. At times he was quick and gay; at other times quiet and withdrawn. He could be made quickly angry, and as easily removed from that anger. Though I loved him, he was a child like any other.

It must be that even then the gods had given him the greatness that all the world has learned; but if they had, I swear he did not know it. His playmates were his equals, even the children of the lowest slaves; he gave as he received in his tasks or his play. Yes, the gods must have touched him, and yet in their wisdom prevented him from knowing; for I heard in later years that there were many portents at his birth. It is said that his mother dreamed that a god in the form of a serpent entered her, and that she conceived; that his father dreamed that the sun rose from the loins of his wife; and that miracles beyond understanding took place all over Italy at the moment of his birth. I say only what I have heard, and speak of the memories of those days.

And now I must tell of that meeting which raised these thoughts in my head.

My son Quintus wanted me to see the great Forum where he often went to take care of business matters for his employer; and so he aroused me at the first hour of the day, so that we could walk the streets before they were crowded. We had seen the new Senate House, and were walking up the Via Sacra toward the Temple of Julius Caesar, which was white as mountain snow in the morning sunlight. I remembered that once when I was a child I had seen this man who has become a god; and I wondered at the greatness of that world of which I had been a part.

We paused for a moment to rest beside the temple. In my age I tire easily. And as we rested, I saw walking up the street toward us a group of men whom I knew to be senators; they wore the togas with the purple stripes. In their midst was a slight figure, bowed as I am bowed, wearing a broad-brimmed hat and with a staff in one hand. The others seemed to be directing their words toward him. My eyes are weak; I could not make out his features; but some power of knowledge came upon me, and I said to Quintus:

"It is he."

Quintus smiled at me, and asked: "It is who, Mother?"

"It is he," I said, and my voice trembled. "It is that master of whom I have spoken, who once was in my care."

Quintus looked at him again, and took my arm, and we went closer to the street so that we could watch his passing. Other citizens had noticed his approach, and we crowded among them.

I did not intend to speak; but as he passed, those memories of my childhood came up within me, and the word was spoken.

"Tavius," I said.

The word was hardly more than a whisper, but it was said as he passed me; and the one whom I had not intended to address paused and looked at me as if he were puzzled. Then he gestured to the men around him to remain where they were, and he came up to me.

"Did you speak, old mother?" he asked.

"Yes, Master," I said. "Forgive me."

"You said a name by which I was known as a child."

"I am Hirtia," I said. "My mother was your foster nurse when you were a child in Velletri. Perhaps you do not remember."

"Hirtia," he said, and he smiled. He came a step nearer, and looked at me; his face was lined and his cheeks sunken, but I could see that boy I had known. "Hirtia," he said again, and touched my hand. "I remember. How many years . . ."

"More than fifty," I said.

Some of his friends approached him; he waved them away.

"Fifty," he said. "Have they been kind to you?"

"I have raised five children, of whom three live and prosper. My husband was a good man, and we lived in comfort. The gods have taken my husband, and now I am content that my own life draws to an end."

He looked at me. "Among your children," he said, "were there daughters?"

I thought it a strange question. I said: "I was blessed only with sons."

"And they have honored you?"

"They have honored me," I said.

"Then your life has been a good one," he said. "Perhaps it has been better than you know."

"I am content to go when the gods call me," I said.

He nodded, and a somberness came upon his face. He said with a bitterness I could not understand: "Then you are more fortunate than I, my sister."

"But you—" I said, "—you are not like other men. In the countryside your image protects the hearth. And at the crossroads, and in the temples. Are you not happy in the honor of the world?"

He looked at me for a moment, and did not answer. Then he turned to Quintus, who stood beside me. "This is your son," he said. "He has your features."

"It is Quintus," I said. "He is manager of all the estates of Atius Sabinus at Velletri. Since I was widowed, I have been living with Quintus and his family there. They are good people."

He looked at Quintus for a long time without speaking. "I did not have a son," he said. "I had only a daughter, and Rome."

I said, "All the people are your children."

He smiled. "I think now I would have preferred to have had three sons, and to have lived in their honor."

I did not know what to say; I did not speak.

"Sir," my son said; his voice was unsteady. "We are humble people. Our lives are what they have been. I have heard that today you speak to the Senate, and thus give to the world your wisdom and your counsel. Beside yours, our fortune is nothing."

"Is it Quintus?" he said. My son nodded. He said: "Quintus, today in my wisdom, I must counsel—I must order the Senate

to take from me that which I have loved most in this life."
For a moment his eyes blazed, and then his face softened, and
he said: "I have given to Rome a freedom that only I cannot
enjoy."

"You have not found happiness," I said, "though you have
given it."

"It is the way my life has been," he said.

"I hope that you become happy," I said.

"I thank you, my sister," he said. "There is nothing that I
can do for you?"

"I am content," I said. "My sons are content."

He nodded. "I must perform this duty now," he said; but for
a long while he was silent, and did not turn away. "We did see
each other again, as we promised long ago."

"Yes, Master," I said.

He smiled. "Once you called me Tavius."

"Tavius," I said.

"Good-by, Hirtia," he said. "This time, perhaps we shall—"

"We shall not meet again," I said. "I go to Velletri, and I
shall not return to Rome."

He nodded, and he put his lips to my cheek, and he turned
away. He walked slowly down the Via Sacra to join those who
waited for him.

These words I have spoken to my son, Quintus, on the third
day before the Ides of September. I have spoken them for my
sons and for their children, now and to come, so that for as
long as this family endures it might know something of its
place in the world that was Rome, in the days that are gone.

II. THE JOURNAL OF JULIA, PANDATERIA (A.D. 4)

Outside my window, the rocks, gray and somber in the brilliance of the afternoon sun, descend in a huge profusion
toward the sea. This rock, like all the rock on this island of Pandateria, is volcanic in origin, rather porous and light in weight,
upon which one must walk with some caution, lest one's feet
be slashed by hidden sharpnesses. There are others on this island, but I am not allowed to see them. Unaccompanied and
unwatched, I am permitted to walk a distance of one hundred
yards to the sea, as far as the thin strip of black-sand beach; and

to walk a like distance in any direction from this small stone hut that has been my abode for five years. I know the body of this barren earth more intimately than I have known the contours of any other, even that of my native Rome, upon which I lavished an intimacy of almost forty years. It is likely that I shall never know another place.

On clear days, when the sun or the wind has dispersed the mists that often rise from the sea, I look to the east; and I think that I can sometimes see the mainland of Italy, perhaps even the city of Naples that nestles in the safety of her gentle bay; but I cannot be sure. It may be only a dark cloud that upon occasion smudges the horizon. It does not matter. Cloud or land, I shall not approach closer to it than I am now.

Below me, in the kitchen, my mother shouts at the one servant we are allowed. I hear the banging of pots and pans, and the shouting again; it is a futile repetition of every afternoon of these years. Our servant is mute; and though not deaf, it is unlikely that she even understands our Latin tongue. Yet indefatigably my mother shouts at her, in the unflagging optimism that her displeasure will be felt and will somehow matter. My mother, Scribonia, is a remarkable woman; she is nearly seventy-five, yet she has the energy and the will of a young woman, as she goes about setting in some peculiar order a world that has never pleased her, and berating it for not arranging itself according to some principle that has evaded them both. She came with me here to Pandateria, not, I am sure, out of any maternal regard, but out of a desperate pursuit of a condition that would confirm once again her displeasure with existence. And I allowed her to accompany me out of what I believe was an appropriate indifference.

I scarcely know my mother. I saw her upon few occasions when I was a child, even less frequently when I was a girl, and we met only at more or less formal social gatherings when I was a woman. I was never fond of her; and it gives me now some assurance to know, after these five years of enforced intimacy, that my feeling for her has not changed.

I am Julia, daughter of Octavius Caesar, the August; and I write these words in the forty-third year of my life. I write them for a purpose of which the friend of my father and my old tutor, Athenodorus, would never have approved; I write them for myself and my own perusal. Even if I wished it otherwise, it is unlikely that any eyes save my own shall see them. But I do not wish it otherwise. I would not explain myself to the world, and I would not have the world understand me; I have become indifferent to us both. For however long I may live in this body, which I have served with much care and art for so many years, that part of my life which matters is over; thus I may view it with the detached interest of the scholar that Athenodorus once said I might have become, had I been born a man and not the daughter of an Emperor and god.

—Yet how strong is the force of old habit! For even now, as I write these first words in this journal, and as I know that they are written to be read only by that strangest of all readers, myself, I find myself pausing in deliberation as I seek the proper topic upon which to found my argument, the appropriate argument itself, the constitution of the argument, the effective arrangement of its parts, and even the style in which those parts are to be delivered. It is myself whom I would persuade to truth by the force of my discourse, and myself whom I would dissuade. It is a foolishness, yet I believe not a harmful one. It occupies my day at least as fully as does the counting of the waves that break over the sand upon the rocky coast of this island where I must remain.

Yes: it is likely that my life is over, though I believe I did not fully apprehend the extent to which I knew the truth of that until yesterday, when I was allowed to receive for the first time in nearly two years a letter from Rome. My sons Gaius and Lucius are dead, the former of a wound received in Armenia and the latter of an illness whose nature no one knows on his way to Spain, in the city of Marseilles. When I read the letter, a numbness came upon me, which in a removed way I judged to have resulted from the shock of the news; and I waited for the grief which I imagined would ensue. But no grief came; and I began to look upon my life, and to remember the moments that had spaced it out, as if I were not concerned. And I knew that it was over. To care not for one's self is of little moment, but to care not for those whom one has loved is another matter. All has become the object of an indifferent curiosity, and nothing is of consequence. Perhaps I write these words and employ the devices that I have learned so that I may discover whether I may rouse myself from this great indifference into which I have descended. I doubt that I shall be able to do so, any more than I should be able to push these massive rocks down the slope into the dark concern of the sea. I am indifferent even to my doubt.

I am Julia, daughter of Gaius Octavius Caesar, the August, and I was born on the third day of September in the year of the consulship of Lucius Marcius and Gaius Sabinus, in the city of Rome. My mother was that Scribonia whose brother was father-in-law to Sextus Pompeius, the pirate whom my father destroyed for the safety of Rome two years after my birth. . . .

That is a beginning of which even Athenodorus, my poor Athenodorus, would have approved.

III. LETTER: LUCIUS VARIUS RUFUS TO PUBLIUS VERGILIUS MARO, FROM ROME (39 B.C.)

My dear Vergil, I trust that your illness does not progress, and that the warmth of the Neapolitan sun has indeed bettered the state of your health. Your friends send their best wishes, and have charged me to assure you that our well-being depends upon your own; if you are well, so are we. Your friends also have charged me to convey to you our regrets that you could not attend the banquet at the home of Claudius Nero last night, a celebration from whose effects I am just this afternoon beginning to recover. It was an extraordinary evening, and it may beguile you from your discomfort if I give you some account of it.

Do you know Claudius Nero, your would-be host? He speaks of you with some familiarity, so I suspect that you have at least met him. If you do know him, you may remember that only two years ago he was in exile in Sicily for having opposed our Octavius Caesar at Perusia; now he has apparently renounced politics, and he and Octavius seem to be the best of friends. He is quite old, and his wife, Livia, seems more nearly his daughter than his spouse—a fortunate circumstance, as you shall shortly understand.

It turned out to be a literary evening, though I doubt that Claudius planned it that way. He is a good fellow, but he has little learning. It soon became clear that Octavius was really behind it all, and that Claudius was, as it were, the pseudo-host. The occasion was designed to honor our friend Pollio, who will at last give to the Roman people that library he has been promising, so that learning may flourish even among the common people.

It was a mixed gathering, but, as it turned out, a rather fortunate one. Most were our friends—Pollio, Octavius and (alas!) Scribonia, Maecenas, Agrippa, myself, Aemilius Macer; your "admirer" Mevius, who no doubt wangled the invitation from Claudius, who knew no better than to invite him; one whom none of us knew, an odd little Pontene from Amasia called Strabo, a sort of philosopher, I believe; for embellishment, several ladies of quality, whose names I cannot recall; and to my surprise (and I suspect to your pleasure) that rather blunt but appealing young man whose work you have been kind enough to admire, your Horace. I believe that Maecenas was responsible for his invitation, despite the rudeness he suffered at Horace's hands several months ago.

I must say that Octavius was in extraordinary good spirits, almost loquacious, despite the usual long face that Scribonia wore. He has just returned from Gaul, you know, and perhaps the rather severe months there have made him hungry for civilized company; moreover, it seems now that the difficulties with both Marcus Antonius and Sextus Pompeius are in abeyance, if not finally settled. Or perhaps his gaiety had its source in the presence of Claudius's wife, Livia, to whom he seems to have taken a strong fancy.

In any event, Octavius insisted upon playing the part of the wine-master, and mixed the wine much more strongly than he usually does, with nearly equal parts of water, so that even before the first course arrived most of us were a little tipsy. He insisted that Pollio, rather than himself, be placed at the position of honor beside Claudius; while he chose to recline at the inferior position at the table, with Livia beside him.

I must say that Octavius and Claudius were exceedingly civilized toward each other, given the circumstances; one would almost think that they had reached an understanding. Scribonia sat at the other table, gossiping with the ladies and glowering at the table where we sat—though the gods know why she should glower. She dislikes the marriage as much as Octavius does, and there is no secret about the fact that a divorce will be effected as soon as Octavius's child is born. . . . What games they must play, those who have power in the world! And how ludicrous must they seem to the Muses! It must be that those who are nearest to the gods are most at their mercy. We are most fortunate, my dear Vergil, that we need not marry to ensure our posterity, but can make the children of our souls march beautifully into the future, where they will not change or die.

Claudius serves a good table, I must say—a very decent Campanian wine before the meal, and a good Falernian afterwards. The meal was neither ostentatiously elaborate nor affectedly simple: oysters, eggs, and tiny onions to begin; roast kid, broiled chicken, and grilled bream; and a variety of fresh fruits.

After the meal, Octavius proposed that we toast the Muses, and that we converse upon their separate functions; and argued briefly with himself as to whether we should drink individual toasts to the ancient three or to the more recent nine; and finally, after pretending a great struggle, decided upon the latter.

"But," he said, and glanced, smiling, at Claudius, "we must honor the Muses to this extent; we must not allow them to be soiled by any mention of politics. It is a subject that might embarrass us all."

There was general, if nervous, laughter; and I suddenly realized how many enemies, past and potential, were in the room. Claudius, whom Octavius had exiled from Italy less than two years before; Pollio himself, our guest of honor, who was an old friend of Marcus Antonius; our young Horace, who only three years ago had fought on the side of the traitor Brutus; and Mevius, poor Mevius, whose envy ran so deep that no man might be spared from the treachery of his flattery, or vice versa.

Pollio, being the guest of honor, began. With an apologetic bow to Octavius, he chose to extol the ancient Muse of Memory, Mneme; and likening all mankind to a single body, he went on to compare the collective experience of mankind to the mind of that body; and thence rather neatly (though obviously) he spoke of the library which he was establishing in

Rome as if it were the most important quality of the mind, memory; and concluded that the Muse of Memory presided over all the others in a beneficent reign.

Mevius gave a tremulous sigh and said to someone in a loud whisper: "Beautiful. Oh, how beautiful!" Horace glanced at him, and raised a dubious eyebrow.

Agrippa addressed himself to Clio, the Muse of History; Mevius whispered loudly something about manliness and bravery; and Horace glowered at Mevius. Upon my turn, I spoke of Calliope—rather badly, I fear, since I could not allude to my own work upon the slain Julius Caesar, even though it is a poem, without trespassing upon Octavius's interdiction against politics.

It was all rather dull, I fear, though Octavius, reclining with Livia seated beside him in the torchlight, seemed pleased; it was his animation and gaiety that made possible what otherwise would have been impossible.

He assigned to Mevius (rather obviously, I thought, though Mevius was too full of himself to notice) that Thalia who is the Muse of Comedy; and Mevius, delighted to be singled out, launched into a long, farcical account (stolen, I believe, from Antiphanes of Athens) about the upstarts of old Athens —slaves, freedmen, and tradespeople—who presumed to set themselves upon a level with their social betters; who wangled invitations to the homes of the great, and gorged themselves at their tables, abusing the kindness and generosity of their noble hosts; and how Thalia, the goddess of the comic spirit, to punish such interlopers, called down upon them certain afflictions, so that their class might be distinguished, and so that the nobility might be protected. Some, Mevius said, she made dwarfs, and gave thatches of hair like the hay in which they were born, and afflicted with the manners of the stable. And so on, and so on.

It became quickly clear that Mevius was attacking your young friend Horace, though for what reason none was quite sure. And no one knew precisely how to behave; we looked at Octavius, but his face was impassive; we looked at Maecenas, who seemed unconcerned. None would look at Horace, except myself, who was seated next to him. His face was pale in the flickering light.

Mevius finished and sat back, satisfied that he had flattered a patron and destroyed a possible rival. There was a murmur. Octavius thanked him, and said:

"Now who shall speak for that Erato who is the Muse of Poetry?"

And Mevius, raised by what he thought was his success, said: "Oh, Maecenas, of course; for he has courted the Muse and won her. It must be Maecenas."

Maecenas waved languidly. "I must decline," he said. "These last months, she has wandered from my gardens. . . . Perhaps my young friend Horace will speak for her."

Octavius laughed, and turned toward Horace with perfect civility. "I have met our guest only this evening, but I will presume upon that slight acquaintance. Will you speak, Horace?"

"I will speak," Horace said; but for a long time he was silent. Without waiting for a servant, he poured himself a measure of unmixed wine, and drank it at once. And he spoke. I give you his words as I remember them.

"You all know the story of the Greek Orpheus of whom our absent Vergil has written so beautifully—son of Apollo and the Muse Calliope, whom the god honored by the presence of his manhood, and inheritor of the golden lyre which sent forth light into the world, making even the stones and trees glimmer in a beauty not apprehended before by man. And you know of his love for Eurydice, of which he sang with such purity and grace that Eurydice thought herself to be part of the singer's own soul and came to him in marriage, at which Hymen wept, as if at a fate no one could imagine. And you know, too, how Eurydice at last, wandering foolishly beyond the precincts of her husband's magic, was touched by a serpent that came out of the bowels of the earth, and dragged from the light of life into the darkness of the underground—where Orpheus in his despair followed, having bound his eyes against a dark that no man can imagine. And there he sang so beautifully and gave such light to the darkness, that the very ghosts shed tears, the wheel upon which Ixion whirled in terror stilled; and the demons of the night relented, and said that Eurydice might return with her husband to the world of light, upon the condition that Orpheus remain blindfolded and not look back upon the wife who followed him. . . .

"The legend does not tell us why Orpheus broke the vow; it tells us only that he did, that he saw where he had been, and saw Eurydice drawn back into the earth, and saw the earth close around her so that he could not follow. And legend tells of how thereafter Orpheus sang his sorrow, and how the maidens who had lived in light only and could not imagine where he had been, came to him and offered themselves to beguile him from his knowledge; and how he refused them, and how in their anger then they shouted down his song, so that its magic could not stay them, and in their mania tore his body apart, and cast it in the River Hebrus, where his severed head continued to sing its wordless song; and the very shores parted and widened so that the singing head might be borne in safety out to the landless sea. . . . This is the story of the Greek Orpheus which Vergil has told us, and to which we have listened."

A silence had come upon the room; Horace dipped his cup into the jar of wine and drank again.

"The gods in their wisdom," he said, "tell us all of our lives, if we will but listen. I speak to you now of another Orpheus—not the son of a god and goddess, but an Italian Orpheus whose father was a slave, and whose mother had no name. Some, no doubt, would scoff at such an Orpheus; but they would scoff who have forgotten that all Romans are descended from a god, and bear the name of his son; and from a mortal woman, and wear her humanity. Thus even a dwarf who wears upon his head a thatch of hay may have been touched by a god, if he springs from the earth that Mars loved. . . . This Orpheus of whom I speak received no golden lyre, but only a poor torch from a humble father who would have given his life that his son might be worthy of his dream. Thus was this young Orpheus in his childhood shown the light of Rome, equally with the sons of the rich and mighty; and in his young manhood, at the cost of his father's substance was shown too the source of what was said to be the light of all mankind that came from the mother city of all knowledge, Athens. Thus his love was no woman; his Eurydice was knowledge, a dream of the world, to which he sang his song. But the world of light that was his dream of knowledge became eclipsed by a civil war; and forsaking the light, this young Orpheus went into the darkness to retrieve his dream; and at Philippi, almost forgetting his song, he fought against one whom he thought to represent the powers of darkness. And then the gods, or the demons—he knows not which, even now—granted him the gift of cowardice, and bade him flee the field with the power of his dream and knowledge intact, and bade him not to look back upon what he fled. But like the other Orpheus, just as he was safely escaped, he did look back; and his dream vanished, as if a vapor, into the darkness of time and circumstance. He saw the world, and knew he was alone—without father, without property, without hope, without dreams. . . . It was only then that the gods gave to him their golden lyre, and bade him play not as they but as he wished. The gods are wise in their cruelty; for now he sings, who would not have sung before. No Thracian maidens blandish him, nor offer him their charms; he makes do with the honest whore, and for a fair price. It is the dogs of the world that yap at him as he sings, trying to drown his voice. They grow in number as more he sings; and no doubt he, too, will suffer to have his limbs torn from his body, even though he sing against the yapping, and sing as he is carried to that sea of oblivion which will receive us all. . . . Thus, my masters and my betters, I have told you a tedious story of a local Orpheus; and I wish you well with his remains."

My dear Vergil, I cannot tell you how long the silence lasted; and I cannot tell you the source of that silence, whether it was shock or fear, or whether all (like myself) had been entranced as if by a true Orphic lyre. The torches, burning low, flickered; and for a moment I had the odd feeling that we all, had, indeed, been in that underground of which Horace had been speaking, and were emerging from it, and dared not look back. Mevius stirred, and whispered fiercely, knowing that he would be heard by whom he intended:

"Philippi," he said. "Power of darkness, indeed! Is this not treason against the triumvir? Is this not treason?"

Octavius had not moved during Horace's recital. He raised himself on his couch and sat beside Livia. "Treason?" he said gently. "It is not treason, Mevius. You will not speak so again in my presence." He rose from his couch and crossed over to where Horace sat. "Horace, will you permit me to join you?" he asked.

Our young friend nodded dumbly. Octavius sat beside him, and they spoke quietly. Mevius said no more that night.

Thus, my dear Vergil, did our Horace, who has already endeared himself to us, find the friendship of Octavius Caesar. All in all, it was a successful evening.

IV. LETTER: MEVIUS TO FURIUS BIBACULUS, FROM ROME (JANUARY, 38 B.C.)

My dear Furius, I really have not the heart to write you at any length about that disastrous evening at the home of Claudius Nero last September, the only pleasant aspect of which was the absence of our "friend" Vergil. But perhaps it is just as well; for certain events have transpired since that evening that make the whole affair even more ludicrous than it seemed then.

I don't really remember all who were there—Octavius, of course, and those odd friends of his: the Etruscan Maecenas, bejeweled and perfumed, and Agrippa, smelling of sweat and leather. It was ostensibly a literary evening, but my dear, to what low state have our letters fallen! Beside these, even that whining little fraud, Catullus, would have seemed almost a poet. There was Pollio, the pompous ass, to whom one must be pleasant because of his wealth and political power, and to whose works one must listen endlessly if one is foolish enough to attend his parties, stifling laughter at his tragedies and feigning emotion at his verses; Maecenas again, who writes lugubrious poems in a Latin that seems almost like a foreign tongue; Macer, who has discovered a Tenth Muse, that of Dullness; and that extraordinary little upstart, Horace, whom, you will be happy to hear, I rather effectively disposed of during the course of the evening. Garrulous politicians, luxuriant magpies, and illiterate peasants deface the garden of the Muses. It's a wonder that you and I can find the courage to persist!

But the social intrigues that evening were a good deal more interesting than the literary ones, and it is about that which I really want to write you.

We all have heard of Octavius's proclivities toward women. I really had not given the reports so much credence before that evening—he is such a pallid little fellow that one might think a glass of unmixed wine and a fervent embrace would send him lifeless to join his ancestors (whoever *they* might be)—but now I begin to suspect that there may be truth in them.

The wife of our host was one Livia, of an old and conservative Republican family (I have heard that her own father was slain by the Octavian army at Philippi). An extraordinarily beautiful girl, if you like the type—a modest and proper figure, blonde, perfectly regular features, rather thin lips, softly spoken, and so forth; very much the "patrician ideal," as they say. She is quite young—perhaps eighteen—yet she has already given her husband, who must be thrice her age, one son; and she was again rather visibly pregnant.

I must say, we all *had* had a great deal to drink; nevertheless, Octavius's conduct was really extraordinary. He mooned over her like a love-sick Catullus, stroking her hand, whispering in her ear, laughing like a boy (though of course he is really little more, despite the importance he has assigned to himself), all manner of nonsense; and all this wholly in view of his own wife (not that *that* really mattered, though she too is pregnant), and of Livia's husband, who seemed either not to notice or to smile benignly, like an ambitious father rather than a husband whose honor ought to have been offended. At any rate, at the time I thought little of it; I considered it rather vulgar behavior, but what (I asked myself) might one expect from the grandson of an ordinary small-town moneylender. If having filled one cart he wanted to ride in another that was full too, that was his business.

But now, four months after that evening, such an extraordinary scandal is buzzing over Rome that I am sure you would not forgive me if I failed to inform you of it.

Less than two weeks ago, his erstwhile wife, Scribonia, gave birth to a girl child—though it would seem that even the *adoptive* son of a god should have been able to manage a boy. On the same day of the birth, Octavius delivered to Scribonia a letter of divorce—which in itself was not surprising, the whole affair having been negotiated in advance, it is said.

But—and here is the scandal—in the week following, Tiberius Claudius Nero gave Livia a divorce; and the next day gave her (though pregnant still), and with a substantial dowry, to Octavius as wife; the whole affair was sanctioned by the Senate, priests made sacrifices, the whole foolish business.

How *can* anyone take such a man seriously? And yet they do.

V. THE JOURNAL OF JULIA, PANDATERIA (A.D. 4)

The circumstances of my birth were known to all the world long before they were known to me; and when at last I had the age to comprehend them, my father was the ruler of the world, and a god; and the world has long understood that the behavior of a god, however odd to mortals, is natural to himself, and comes at last to seem inevitable to those who must worship him.

Thus it was not strange to me that Livia should be my mother, and Scribonia merely an infrequent visitor to my home —a distant but necessary relative whom everyone endured out of an obscure sense of obligation. My memories of that time are dim, and I do not fully trust them; but it seems to me now that those years were ordinarily pleasant. Livia was firm, majestic, and coldly affectionate; it was what I grew to expect.

Unlike most men of his station, my father insisted that I be brought up in the old way, in his own household, in the care of Livia rather than a nurse; that I learn the ways of the household —to weave and sew and cook—in the ancient manner; and yet that I be educated in the degree that would befit the daughter of an Emperor. So in my early years I wove with the slaves of the household, and I learned my letters, Latin and Greek, from my father's slave Phaedrus; and later I studied at wisdom under his old friend and tutor Athenodorus. Though I did not know it at the time, the most significant circumstance of my life was the fact that my father had no other children of his own. It was a fault of the Julian line.

Though I must have seen him seldom in those years, his presence was the strongest of any in my life. I learned my geography from his letters, which were read to me daily; they were sent in packets from wherever he had to be—in Gaul, or Sicily, or Spain; Dalmatia, Greece, Asia, or Egypt.

As I said, I must have seen him seldom; yet even now it seems that he was always there. I can close my eyes, and almost feel myself thrown into the air, and hear the ecstatic laughter of a child's safe terror, and feel the hands catch me from the nothingness into which I had been tossed. I can hear the deep voice, comforting and warm; I can feel the caresses upon my head; I can remember the games of handball and pebbles; and I can feel my legs strain up the little hills in the garden behind our house on the Palatine, as we walked to a point where we could see the city spread out like a gigantic toy beneath us. Yet I cannot remember the face, then. He called me Rome, his "Little Rome."

My first clear visual memory of my father came when I was nine years old; it was in his fifth consulship, and upon the occasion of his triple triumph for his victories in Dalmatia, Actium, and Egypt.

Since that time, there have been no such celebrations of military exploits in Rome; later my father explained to me that he had thought even the one in which he took part was vulgar and barbaric, but that it was politically necessary at the time. Thus, I do not now know whether the grandeur I saw then has been enhanced by its uniquity and its subsequent absence, or whether it was the true grandeur of my memory.

I had not seen my father for more than a year, and he had no chance to visit Rome before the ceremonial march into the city. It was arranged that Livia and I and the other children of the household should meet him at the city gates, where we were escorted by the senatorial procession and placed in chairs of honor to await his coming. It was a game to me; Livia had told me that we were going to be in a parade, and that I must remain calm. But I could not restrain myself from jumping from my chair, and straining my eyes to find the approach of my father down the winding road. And when at last I saw him, I laughed and clapped my hands, and would have run toward him; but I was restrained by Livia. And when he came near enough to recognize us, he spurred his horse ahead of the soldiers he was leading, and caught me in his arms, laughing, and then embraced Livia; and he was my father. It was, perhaps, the last time that I was able to think of him as if he were a father like any other.

For quickly he was moved away by the praetors of the Senate, who fastened about him a cloak of purple and gold and led him into the turreted chariot, and led Livia and me to stand beside him there; and the slow procession toward the Forum began. I remember my fear and disappointment; my father beside me, though he steadied me gently with his hand upon my shoulder, was a stranger. The horns and trumpets at the head of the procession sounded their battle calls; the lictors with their laureled axes moved slowly ahead; and we went into the city. The people crowded the squares where we passed and shouted so loudly that even the sound of the horns was muted; and the Forum where we halted at last swarmed with Romans, so that not a stone upon the ground could be seen.

For three days the ceremonies lasted. I spoke to my father when I could; and though Livia and I were at his side nearly all the time, during his speeches and the sacrifices and the presentations, I felt him drawn away from me into the world that I was beginning to see for the first time.

Yet he was gentle toward me all the time, and answered me when I spoke as if I mattered to him as much as I ever had. I remember once I saw drawn in one of the processions, on a cart gleaming with gold and bronze, the carven figure of a woman, larger than life, upon a couch of ebony and ivory, with two children lying on either side of her; their eyes were closed, as if in sleep. I asked my father who the lady was supposed to be, and he looked at me a long time before he answered.

"That was Cleopatra," he said. "She was Queen of a great country. She was an enemy to Rome; but she was a brave woman, and she loved her country as much as any Roman might love his; she gave her life so that she might not have to look upon its defeat."

Even now, after all these years, I remember the strange feeling that came over me upon hearing that name in those circumstances. It was, of course, a familiar name; I had heard it often before. I thought then of my Aunt Octavia, who in fact shared the responsibility of the household with Livia, and whom I knew had once been married to this dead Queen's husband, that Marcus Antonius who was also dead. And I thought of the children for whom Octavia cared and with whom I daily played and worked and studied: Marcellus and his two sisters, the fruit of her first marriage; the two Antonias who were the issue of her marriage to Marcus Antonius; Jullus, who was the son of Marcus Antonius by an earlier marriage; and at last of that little girl who was the new pet of the household, the little Cleopatra, daughter of Marcus Antonius and his Queen.

But it was not the strangeness of that knowledge that caused my heart to come up in my throat. Though I did not have the words to say it then, I believe it occurred to me for the first time that even a woman might be caught up in the world of events, and be destroyed by that world.

Chapter Two

To her husband, Livia sends greetings and prayers for his safety; and according to his instructions, an account of those matters for which he has evidenced concern.

The works which you set into motion before your departure northward proceed as you ordered. The repairs upon the Via Flaminia are completed, two weeks before the scheduled date that you gave to Marcus Agrippa, who will send you a full accounting of the work in the next packet of mail. Both Maecenas and Agrippa, who confer with me daily, ask me to assure you that the census will be completed before your return; and Maecenas projects that the increase in revenue from this revised tax base will be even more considerable than he had anticipated.

Maecenas also has asked me to convey to you his pleasure in your decision not to invade Britain; he is confident that negotiation will accomplish as much; and even if the negotiation does not, the possible cost of the conquest would outweigh the recovery of the defaulted tribute. I, too, am happy at your decision; but for the more affectionate reason of regard for your safety.

I slight these reports, knowing that you will get fuller accounts from those who have the details more firmly in hand, and knowing that your interest in hearing from me lies elsewhere. Your daughter is in good health, and she sends you her love. Yes: your letters are read to her daily, and she speaks of you often.

You will be pleased to learn that the last week has seen a decided improvement in her behavior toward the household servants; I am sure that your letter upon the subject had a great effect. This morning she spent nearly two hours at the spinning wheel, and not once did she complain or speak disrespectfully to any who worked with her. She is at last, I believe, beginning to accustom herself to the notion that she may be both a woman and the daughter of an Emperor. Her health is excellent; and she will have grown so that upon your return, you may hardly know her.

The account of that other part of her education, upon which you have insisted and to which with some reluctance I have acquiesced, I shall leave to others, whose reports you will find included in these packets.

There is a bit of gossip that will both please and amuse you. Maecenas has asked me to convey to you the information that he is at last acceding to your wishes and taking a wife; he asked me to give you the news because (he said) the subject was too painful for him to broach himself. As you might expect, he is making a great show of his misery; but I think he is rather enjoying the idea. His wife to be is one Terentia, of a family of no particular importance; Maecenas sniffs, and says that he has nobility enough for them both. She is a pretty little thing, and seems content with the marriage; it appears that she perfectly understands Maecenas's propensities, and is willing to accept them. I believe that she will please you.

Your sister sends you her affectionate greetings, and asks you to give the same to her Marcellus, whom she trusts has been a pleasant companion to his uncle. And I send you my love, and ask you to give to my Tiberius the same. Your family in Rome awaits your return.

Gaius Octavius Caesar, at Narbonne in Gaul, from his servant and devoted friend, Phaedrus. I address you Gaius, for I speak on a household matter.

Your daughter Julia is fast approaching that point in her education at which I can no longer adequately perform as you would wish. I say this with reluctance, for you know my fatherly fondness of her. You have proved me wrong. I doubted that any girl might progress in her studies as rapidly and as ably as might a boy of the same station, equally capable of diligence and understanding. Indeed, of the many of your relatives' children of like age whom you have been kind enough to put under my tutelage, both boys and girls, she has made the most rapid progress, so that even at the age of eleven, she is rapidly approaching the point at which she should be put in another's care. She composes easily in Greek; she has mastered those more fundamental elements of rhetoric which I have exposed her to, though my teaching her such an unladylike subject has occasioned a minor scandal among her fellow pupils; and your friend Horace intermittently aids her with that poetry in his own tongue, a literature of which my command is adequate but not sufficient for your daughter. I gather that the more feminine parts of her curriculum are not so much to her liking —her musicianship is barely adequate, and though she has a natural physical grace, she does not really take to the more formal elements of her dancing lessons; but I also gather that such fashionable accomplishments lie outside your own interest as well. Were I so foolish to think that you might be pleased by flattery, I should pretend no surprise and affect some such nonsense as expecting so much from the daughter of the son of a god, Emperor of all the world, and so forth. But we both know that her character is her own, and that it is a strong one.

I propose, therefore, that in the near future her education be turned over to one more wise and learned than myself, that Athenodorus who was once your own teacher and who is now your friend. He knows her mind, they get on well, and he has consented to the task which I have had the presumption to suggest. I understand that he is to write you regarding another matter, and that in that letter he will also give you his thoughts upon this.

I trust that your journey in Gaul will not keep you away from your daughter longer than is necessary. The only serious distraction in her studies with me is her longing for your presence. I am, Gaius, your faithful servant and, I trust, your friend, Phaedrus of Corinth.

Athenodorus to Octavius, greetings. As you knew I would, I applaud your decision to establish a system of schools in Gaul. You are quite right; if the people there are to become a part of Rome, they must have the Roman tongue, whereby they may know that history and that culture in which they are to thrive. I would to the gods that the fashionable riffraff here in Rome, some of whom you are pleased to call your friends, had so much concern for the education of their own children as you have for your subjects in distant lands. It may be that those in other lands shall become more Roman than we who remain in the heart of our country.

There will be no difficulty in finding teachers to staff the schools; I shall, if you wish, make specific recommendations. Since you have brought peace and some measure of prosperity to our nation, learning has begun to flourish among those classes from whom you must draw your teachers, though perhaps flourish is too strong a word. In general, I would suggest: (1) that you not depend upon the easy idealism of the well-to-do young, whose enthusiasm is almost certain to disappear in the isolation of the provinces; (2) that so far as possible you choose your teachers from native stock and not depend upon the Greeks or Egyptians or whatever, since their students must at least know what a Roman looks like if he is to really apprehend Roman culture; and (3) that you *not* depend upon slaves or even too heavily upon freedmen to fill those pedagogic ranks of which you speak. I think you must understand my reasons for this advice. I know that it has been the tradition in Rome to raise even a slave above a gentleman, if he is learned enough. In Rome he is content to remain a slave, if he can become rich; but in Gaul there will not be the opportunity for the kind of fiscal corruption that he can find in Rome, and he will be discontented. You know yourself that many slaves, especially the learned and rich (our friend Phaedrus excepted, of course), are contemptuous of Rome and its ways, and resentful even of that condition out of which they have not chosen to purchase themselves. In short, in Gaul there will not be the complex of forces that operate here to subject them to some kind of order. I assure you that there are sufficient Italians, from both the countryside and the city, who for a decent wage and some honor, would be happy to fulfill your purposes.

As for the matter of your daughter: Phaedrus has spoken to me, and I have consented. I assume that you will approve. I have now educated so many of the Octavian clan that it would seem inappropriate to me for you to look elsewhere. You may call yourself Emperor of the world; that is not my concern. In this matter, I insist that I remain your master; and I should not like to see the final education of Julia in the hands of anyone other than myself.

II. THE JOURNAL OF JULIA, PANDATERIA (A.D. 4)

For the past several years, since shortly after my arrival upon this island of Pandateria, it has been my habit to arise before dawn and to observe the first glimmer of light in the east. It has become nearly a ritual, this early vigil; I sit without moving at an eastern window, and measure the light as it grows from gray to yellow to orange and red, and becomes at last no color but an unimaginable illumination upon the world. After the light has filled my room, I spend the morning hours reading one or another of those books from the library that I was allowed to bring with me here from Rome. The indulgence of my library was one of the few allowed me; yet of all that might have been, it is the one that has made this exile the most nearly endurable. For I have returned to that learning which I abandoned many years ago, and it is likely that I should not have done so had not I been condemned to this loneliness; I sometimes can almost believe that the world in seeking to punish me has done me a service it cannot imagine.

It has occurred to me that this early vigil and this study is a regimen that I became used to many years ago, when I was little more than a child.

When I was twelve years old, my father decided that it was time for me to forgo my childhood studies, and put myself in the care of his old teacher, Athenodorus. Before that, I had, in addition to the kind of education imposed upon my sex by Livia, merely been exercised in the reading and composition of Greek and Latin, which I found remarkably easy, and in arithmetic, which I found easy but dull. It was a leisurely kind of learning, and my tutor was at my disposal at any hour of the day, with no very rigid schedule that I had to follow.

But Athenodorus, who gave me my first vision of a world outside myself, my family, and even of Rome, was a stern and unrelenting master. His students were few—the sons of Octavia, both adopted and natural; Livia's sons, Drusus and Tiberius; and the sons of various relatives of my father. I was the only girl among them, and I was the youngest. It was made clear to all of us by my father that Athenodorus was the master; and despite whatever name and power the parents of his students might have, Athenodorus's word in all matters was final, and that there was no recourse beyond him.

We were made to arise before dawn and to assemble at the first hour at Athenodorus's home, where we recited the lines from Homer or Hesiod or Aeschylus that we had been assigned the day before; we attempted compositions of our own in the styles of those poets; and at noon we had a light lunch. In the afternoon, the boys devoted themselves to exercises in rhetoric and declamation, and to the study of law; such subjects being deemed inappropriate for me, I was allowed to use my time otherwise, in the study of philosophy, and in the elucidation of whatever poems, Latin or Greek, that I chose, and in composition upon whatever matters struck my fancy. Late in the afternoon, I was allowed to return to my home, so that I might perform my household duties under the tutelage of Livia. It was a release that became increasingly irksome to me.

For as within my body there had begun to work the changes that led me to womanhood, there began to work also in my mind the beginnings of a vision that I had not suspected before. Later, when we became friends, Athenodorus and I used to talk about the Roman distaste for any learning that did not lead to a practical end; and he told me that once, more than a hundred years before my birth, all teachers of literature and philosophy were, by a decree of the Senate, expelled from Rome, though it was a decree that could not be enforced.

It seems to me that I was happy, then, perhaps as happy as I have been in my life; but within three years that life was over, and it became necessary for me to become a woman. It was an exile from a world that I had just begun to see.

III. LETTER: QUINTUS HORATIUS FLACCUS TO ALBIUS TIBULLUS (25 B.C.)

My dear Tibullus, you are a good poet and my friend, but you are a fool.

I will say it as plainly as possible: you are *not* to write a poem celebrating the marriage of young Marcellus and the Emperor's daughter. You have asked me for my advice, I have given it as strongly as I might give a command, and for the several reasons that I shall proceed to enumerate.

First: Octavius Caesar has made it clear, even to me and Vergil, who are among his closest friends, that he would be most unhappy if we ever alluded, directly or indirectly, to the personal affairs of any member of his family in one of our own poems. It is a principle upon which he stands firm, and it is a principle which I understand. Despite your hints to the contrary, he is deeply attached both to his wife and his daughter; he does not wish to condemn the bad poem which offers them praise, nor does he wish to praise the good poem which might offer them offense. Moreover, his life with his family is nearly his only respite from the burdensome and difficult task he has in attempting to run this chaotic world that he has inherited. He does not wish that respite endangered.

Second: your natural talent does not lie in the direction that you describe, and you are unlikely to write a good poem upon this subject. I have admired your poems upon your lady friends; I have not admired your poems upon your friend and commander in chief, Messalla. To write an indifferent poem upon a dangerous topic is to choose to behave foolishly.

And third: even if you were able to somehow turn the natural bent of your talent in another direction, the few attitudes you hint at in your letter convince me that you had better not try what you propose. For no man may write a good poem the worth of whose subject he doubts; and no poet can will away his misgivings. I say this not in recrimination of your uncertainties, my friend; I say it merely as a fact. Were I to engage myself in the composition of such a poem as you propose, I might discover that I had the same ones.

And yet I believe that I would not. You hint that you suspect a coldness in the Emperor's feelings toward his daughter, and that in the marriage he is "using" her for purposes of state. The latter may be true; the former is not.

I have known Octavius Caesar for more than ten years; he is my friend, and we are on truly equal terms. As any friend might do, I have praised him when in my judgment he deserved praise, I have doubted him when I judged he merited doubt, and I have criticized him when I believed that he deserved criticism. I have done these publicly, and with utter freedom. Our friendship has not suffered.

Thus, when I speak to you now of this matter, you will understand that I speak as freely as I ever have, and as I ever will.

Octavius Caesar loves his daughter more than you understand; if he has a fault, it is that his feeling for her is too deep. He has overseen her education with more care than many a less busy father has given to that of a son; nor has he been content to limit her learning to the weaving and sewing and singing and lute-playing and the usual smattering of letters that most women get in school. Julia's Greek is now better than her father's; her knowledge of literature is impressive; and she has studied both rhetoric and philosophy with Athenodorus, a man whose wisdom and learning could augment even our own, my dear Tibullus.

During these years when he so often has had to be absent from Rome, not a week has gone by that his daughter has not received in the mail a packet of letters from her father; I have seen some of them, and they display a concern and kindness that is indeed touching.

And upon those welcome occasions when his duties allowed him the freedom of his family and his home, he spent what might seem to some an inordinate amount of time with his daughter, behaving with the utmost simplicity and joy in her presence. I have seen him roll hoops with her as if he, too, were a child, and let her ride upon his shoulders as if he were a horse, and play blindman's buff; I have seen them fish together from the banks of the Tiber, laughing in delight when their hooks snagged a tiny sunfish; and I have seen them walk in perfect companionship in the fields beyond their home, picking wild flowers for the dinner table.

But if you have doubts in that part of your soul which is the poet's, I know that I cannot allay them, though I might erase them from that part of your mind that is a man's. You know that if another father chose for his daughter a husband as rich and promising as young Marcellus, you would applaud his foresight and his concern. You know, too, that the "youth" of Julia in this matter would, in another instance, be cause for another kind of concern. How old was that lady (whom you have chosen to disguise as Delia) when first *you* began your campaign against her virtue? Sixteen? Seventeen? Younger?

No, my dear Tibullus, you are well advised not to write this poem. There are many other subjects, and many other places to find them. If you wish to retain the admiration of your Emperor, stick to those poems about your Delias, which you do so well. I assure you that Octavius reads them and admires them; hard as it may be for you to believe, when he reads a poem he admires good writing more than praise.

IV. THE JOURNAL OF JULIA, PANDATERIA (A.D. 4)

In my life, I had three husbands, none of whom I loved. . . .

Yesterday morning, not knowing what I wished to say, I wrote those words; and I have been pondering what they might mean. I do not know what they mean. I only know that the question occurred to me late in my life, at a time when it no longer mattered.

The poets say that youth is the day of the fevered blood, the hour of love, the moment of passion; and that with age come the cooling baths of wisdom, whereby the fever is cured. The poets are wrong. I did not know love until late in my life, when I could no longer grasp it. Youth is ignorant, and its passion is abstract.

I was betrothed first when I was fourteen years of age to my cousin, Marcellus, who was the son of my father's sister Octavia. It was perhaps a measure of my ignorance, and the ignorance of all women, that such a marriage seemed to me perfectly ordinary at the time. Ever since I could remember, Marcellus had been a familiar part of our household, along with the other children of Octavia and Livia; I had grown up with him, but I did not know him. Now, after nearly thirty years, I have hardly a memory of what he was like or even of his physical appearance. He was tall, I believe, and blond in the Octavian way.

But I remember the letter my father sent informing me of the betrothal. I remember the tone of it. It was almost as if he were writing to a stranger; his tone was pompous and stiff, and that was unlike him. He wrote from Spain, where for nearly a

year he had been engaged in putting down the border insur-
rections, a mission upon which Marcellus, though only seventeen years of age, had accompanied him. Persuaded (he said)
by Marcellus's fortitude and loyalty, and concerned that his
daughter be placed in the care of one whose worth was beyond
dispute, he had determined that this marriage was in the best
interests of myself and of our family. He wished me happiness,
regretted that he would not be in Rome to take his proper part
in the ceremony, and said that he was asking his friend Marcus
Agrippa to take his place; and told me that Livia would inform
me further upon what was expected of me.

At the age of fourteen, I believed myself to be a woman; I
had been taught to believe so. I had studied with Athenodorus;
I was the daughter of an Emperor; and I was to be married. I
believe I behaved in a most urbane and languid fashion, until
the urbanity and languidness became almost real; I had no apprehension of the world that I was beginning to enter.

And Marcellus remained a stranger. He returned from
Spain, and we spoke distantly, as we always had done. The arrangements for the wedding proceeded as if neither of us was
involved in our fates. I know now, of course, that we were not.

It was a ceremony in the old fashion. Marcellus gave me a
gift, before witnesses, of an ivory box inlaid with pearls from
Spain, and I received it with the ritual words; the night before
the wedding, in the presence of Livia and Octavia and Marcus
Agrippa, I bade farewell to the toys of my childhood, and gave
those that would burn to the household gods; and late that
night Livia, acting as my mother, braided my hair into the six
plaits that signified my womanhood, and fastened them with
the bands of white wool.

I went through the ceremony as if through a dream. The
guests and relatives gathered in the courtyard; the priests said
the things that priests say; the documents were signed, witnessed, and exchanged; and I spoke the words that bound me
to my husband. And in the evening, after the banquet, Livia
and Octavia, according to ceremony, dressed me in the bridal
tunic and led me to Marcellus's chamber. I do not know what
I expected.

Marcellus sat upon the edge of the bed, yawning; the bridal
flowers were strewn carelessly upon the floor.

"It is late," Marcellus said, and added in the voice he had used toward me as a child; "get to bed."

I lay beside him; I imagine I must have been trembling. He yawned once more, turned upon his side away from me, and in a few moments was asleep.

Thus did my wifehood begin; and it did not change substantially during the two years of my marriage to Marcellus. As I wrote earlier, I hardly remember him now; there is little reason why I should.

V. LETTER: LIVIA TO OCTAVIUS CAESAR IN SPAIN (25 B.C.)

To her husband, Livia sends affectionate greetings. I have followed your instructions; your daughter is married; she is well. I hasten over this bare information so that I might write of the matter that is of more immediate concern to me: the state of your health. For I have heard (do not ask the source of my information) that it is more precarious than you have let me know; and thus I begin to apprehend the urgency you have felt in seeing your daughter safely married, and am therefore more ashamed than I might have been of my opposition to the marriage, and I sorrow at the unhappiness that that opposition must have caused you. Please be assured now that my resentment is gone, and that at last my pride in our marriage and our duty has laid to rest my maternal ambitions for my own son. You are right; Marcellus carries the name of the Claudian, the Julian, and the Octavian tribes, whereas my Tiberius carries the name only of the Claudian. Your decision is, as usual, the intelligent one. I forget sometimes that our authority is more precarious than it seems.

I implore you to return from Spain. It is clear that the climate there encourages those fevers to which you are subject, and that in such a barbaric place you cannot receive proper care. In this your physician agrees with me, and adds his professional supplication to my affectionate one.

Marcellus returns to you within the week. Octavia sends her love, and asks that you guard the safety of her son; your wife also sends her love, and her prayers for your recovery, and for the well-being of her son Tiberius. Please return to Rome.

VI. LETTER: QUINTUS HORATIUS FLACCUS TO PUBLIUS VERGILIUS MARO, AT NAPLES (23 B.C.)

My dear Vergil, I urge you to come to Rome with all possible speed. Ever since his return from Spain, our friend's health has declined; and now his condition is exceedingly grave. The fever is constant; he cannot rise from his bed; and his body has shrunken so that his skin seems like cloth upon frail sticks. Though we all put on cheerful countenances, we have come to despair of his life. We do not deceive him; he, too, feels that his life draws to a close; he has given to his co-consul his records of the army and of revenue, and has given to Marcus Agrippa his seal, so that there might be an adequate succession of his authority. Only his physician, his intimate friends, and his immediate family are allowed in his presence. A great calm has come upon him; it is as if he wishes to savor for the last time all that he has held dearest to his heart.

Both Maecenas and I have been staying here at his private house on the Palatine, so that we might be near him when he wishes aid or comfort. Livia attends him meticulously and with the dutifulness that he so admires in her; Julia laughs and teases him, as he so enjoys, when she is in his presence, and weeps most pitifully when she is out of his sight; he and Maecenas speak fondly of the days of their youth; and Agrippa, strong as he is, can hardly keep his composure when he speaks to him.

Though he would not impose himself and though he does not say so, I know that he wants you here. Sometimes, when he is too weary to converse with his family, he asks me to read to him some of those poems of ours that he has most admired; and yesterday he recalled that happy and triumphant autumn, only a few years ago, when he returned from Samos, after the defeat of the Egyptian armies, and we were all together, and you read to him the completed *Georgics*. And he said to me, quite calmly and without pity of self: "If I should die, one of the things that I shall most regret is not having been able to attend the completion of our old friend's poem upon the founding of our city. Do you think it would please him to know this?"

Though I was hardly able to speak, I said, "I am sure it would, my friend."

He said, "Then you must tell him so when you see him."

"I shall tell him when you have recovered," I said.

He smiled. I could not endure it longer. I made some apology, and went from his room.

As you can see, the time may be short. He is in no pain; he retains his faculties; but his will is dying with his body.

Within the week, if his condition does not improve, his physician (one Antonius Musa, whose abilities, despite his fame, I do not trust) is prepared to put into effect a final and drastic remedy. I urge you to attend him before that desperation is performed.

VII. MEDICAL DIRECTIVE OF ANTONIUS MUSA,
THE PHYSICIAN, TO HIS ASSISTANTS (23 B.C.)

The Preparation of the Baths. Three hundred pounds of ice, to be delivered to the residence of the Emperor Octavius Caesar, at the designated hour. This may be obtained from the storehouse of Asinius Pollio on the Via Campana. The ice is to be broken into pieces of the size of a tightly closed fist, and only those pieces that can be seen to be free of sediment are to be used. Twenty-five of these pieces are to be put into the bath, which will contain water to the depth of eight inches, where they shall be let to remain until all are melted.

The Preparation of the Ointment. One pint of my own powder, to which has been added two spoonfuls of finely ground mustard seed; which mixture is to be added to two quarts of the finest olive oil, which is to be heated just below the point of boiling, and then allowed to cool to the exact degree of body warmth.

The Treatment of the Patient. The patient is to be immersed fully, with the water covering every part of his body except the head, into the cold bath, where he is to remain for the length of time required to count slowly to one hundred. He is then to be removed and wrapped in the undyed blankets of wool, which have been heated over hot stones. He is to remain wrapped until he sweats freely, at which point the entirety of his body is to be anointed with the prepared oil. He is then to be returned to the cold bath, to which has been added sufficient ice to return it to its original coldness.

This treatment is to be repeated four times; then the patient will be allowed to rest for two hours. This routine of treatment shall be continued until the patient's fever subsides.

VIII. THE JOURNAL OF JULIA, PANDATERIA (A.D. 4)

When my father returned home from Spain, I knew at once the reason for my marriage. He had not expected to survive even the journey to his family, so grave had been his illness in Spain; to insure my future, he gave me to Marcellus; and to insure the future of what he often called his "other daughter," he gave Rome to Marcus Agrippa. My marriage to Marcellus was largely a ritual affair; technically I became nonvirginal; but I was hardly touched by the union and I remained a girl, or nearly so. It was during the illness of my father that I became a woman, for I saw the inevitability of death and knew its smell and felt its presence.

I remember that I wept, knowing that my father would die, whom I had known only as a child; and I came to know that loss was the condition of our living. It is a knowledge that one cannot give to another.

Yet I tried to give it to Marcellus, since he was my husband and I had been taught my proper behavior. He looked at me in bewilderment, and then said that however unfortunate, Rome would endure the loss, since our Emperor had had the foresight to leave his affairs in order. I was angry then, for I felt that my husband was cold and I knew that he thought himself to be the heir to my father's power, and foresaw the day when he too would be an Emperor; now I know that if he were cold and ambitious, it was the only way he knew; it was the life to which he had been reared.

My father's recovery from the illness that should have led to his death was regarded by the world as a miracle emanating from his divinity, and thus in the normal order of things. When the physician Antonius Musa at last performed his desperate treatment, which in later years came to bear his name, the arrangements for my father's funeral were already being made. Yet he survived the treatment, and slowly began to recover, so that by late summer he had regained some of his weight and was able to stroll for a few minutes each day in the garden behind our house. Marcus Agrippa returned the seal of the Sphinx that had been entrusted to him, and the Senate decreed a week of thanksgiving and prayer in Rome, and the people in the countryside all over Italy erected images of him on the crossroads, in celebration of his health and to protect travelers on their journeys.

When it was clear that my father would regain his health, my husband, Marcellus, fell ill with the same fever. For two weeks the fever worsened, and at last the physician Antonius Musa prescribed the same treatment that had saved my father. In another week, in the midst of the rejoicing over the recovery of the Emperor, Marcellus was dead; and I was a widow in my seventeenth year.

IX. LETTER: PUBLIUS VERGILIUS MARO TO QUINTUS HORATIUS FLACCUS (22 B.C.)

The sister of our friend Octavius still grieves for her son; time does not bring her that gradual diminution of pain, which is time's only gift; and I fear that my poor efforts to give her heart some solace may have had an effect I did not intend.

Last week, Octavius, knowing that I had been moved to compose a poem upon the death of his nephew, urged me to come again to Rome so that he might hear what I had done; and when I informed him that the poem I had written I intended to incorporate in that long work upon Aeneas, the completed parts of which he has rather extravagantly admired, he suggested that it might give some comfort to his sister to know that her son was so admired by the Roman people that he would live in their memories for so long as they had them. Thus he invited her to be present at the reading, informing her of the nature of the occasion.

Only a few were present at Octavius's house—Octavius himself, of course, and Livia; his daughter Julia (it is difficult to think of one so young and beautiful as a widow); Maecenas and Terentia; and Octavia, who came into the room as if she were a walking corpse, dreadfully pale, with deep shadows under her eyes. Yet she seemed composed, as always, and behaved with graciousness and consideration to those who could comfort her.

We talked quietly for a while, remembering Marcellus; once or twice, Octavia almost smiled, as if charmed by a pleasant memory of her son. And then Octavius asked me to read to them what I had written.

You know the poem and its place in my book; I shall not repeat it. But whatever faults the poem may have in its present state, it was a moving occasion; for a moment we saw Marcellus walking once more among the living, vital in the memories of his friends and his countrymen.

When I finished, there was a quietness in the room, and then a gentle murmuring. I looked at Octavia, hoping that I might see in her face, beyond the sadness, some comfort in the knowledge of our concern and pride. But I saw no comfort there. What I saw I cannot truly describe; her eyes blazed darkly, as if they burned deep in her skull, and her lips were drawn in the awful semblance of a grin that bared her teeth. It was a look, it seemed to me, almost of pure hatred. Then she gave a high toneless little scream, swayed sideways, and fell upon her couch in a dead faint.

We rushed to her; Octavius massaged her hands; she gradually revived, and the ladies took her away.

"I am sorry," I said at last. "If I had known— I only intended her some comfort."

"Do not reproach yourself, my friend," Octavius said quietly. "Perhaps you have given her a comfort, after all—one that none of us can see. We cannot know at last the effects of what we do, whether for good or ill."

I have returned to Naples; tomorrow I shall resume my labors. But I am troubled by what I have done, and I cannot but fear for the future happiness of that great lady who has given so much to her country.

X. LETTER: OCTAVIA TO OCTAVIUS CAESAR, FROM VELLETRI (22 B.C.)

My dear brother, I arrived, safe but weary, in Velletri yesterday afternoon, and have been resting since. Below my window is the garden where we used to play as children. It is somewhat overgrown now, or at least it seems so to me; most of the shrubs have succumbed to the winter weather, the beeches need pruning, and one of the old chestnut trees has died. Nevertheless, it is pleasant to gaze upon this spot and recall those days when we were free from the cares and sorrows of the world, so many years ago.

I write you upon two matters: first, to extend my long over-due apologies for my behavior on that awful night when our friend Vergil read to us of my late son; and second, to make a request.

When next you have occasion to write or speak to Vergil, will you explicitly ask his forgiveness for me? I did not intend my action, and I would be regretful if he took it as an unkindness. He is a good and gentle man, and I would not have him be-lieve that I thought otherwise.

But it is the request that I make to you with which I am more concerned.

I wish to have your permission to retire from that world of affairs in which I have lived for as long as I can remember, so that I may spend the years that remain to me in the quiet and solitude of the country.

All my life I have done the duty required of me by my fam-ily and my country. I have performed this duty willingly, even when it went against the inclinations of my person.

In my childhood and early youth, under the tutelage of our mother, I performed the duties of the household with willing pleasure; and after her death, I more fully performed them for you. When it became necessary to our cause to conciliate the enemies of Julius Caesar, I gave myself in marriage to Gaius Claudius Marcellus, and upon his death I became wife to Mar-cus Antonius. To the best of my abilities, I was a good wife to Marcus, while remaining your sister and dutiful to our family. After Marcus Antonius divorced me and cast his fortunes in the East, I raised the children of his other marriages as if they were my own, indeed, even that Jullus Antonius of whom you now are so fond; after his death, I took under my protection those children of his by Cleopatra that survived the war.

Both of your wives I have treated as my sisters, though the first was too ill-tempered to receive my kindness and the sec-ond too ambitious for herself to trust my duty to our common cause. And from my own body I have given five children to our family and to the future of Rome.

Now my first-born and only son, my Marcellus, is dead in your service; and the happiness of his sister, Marcella, my beloved second-born, is threatened by the necessity of your policy. Fifteen years ago—perhaps even ten years ago—I should have been proud that you had chosen one of my children to shape in the succession of your destiny. But now I believe that my pride is vain, and I do not persuade myself that the possession of fame and power is worth the price of it. My daughter is happy in her marriage to Marcus Agrippa; I believe she loves him; I trust that he is fond of her. The divorce that you propose between them will not make her unhappy because she shall have lost the power and prestige that have accreted to her by the marriage; she shall be unhappy because she shall have lost a man for whom she feels respect and affection.

You must understand me, my dear brother; I do not quarrel with your decision; you are right. It is both fitting and necessary that your successor be one with your daughter, either through marriage or parentage. And Marcus Agrippa is the most able man of all your friends and associates. He is my friend, as well as my son-in-law; despite whatever may happen I trust that he shall remain the former.

And thus without resentment let me ask that the permission that I must give for this divorce be the last public act that I shall have to commit. I grant the permission. Now I wish to remove myself from the household in Rome, and remain with my books here in Velletri for as long as I may. I do not renounce your love; I do not renounce my children; I do not renounce my friends.

But the feeling that I had that awful evening, when Vergil read to us of Marcellus, remains with me, and shall remain for as long as I live; it was as if suddenly, and for the first time, I truly saw that world in which you must live, and saw the world in which I had lived without seeing for so long. There are other ways and other worlds in which one might live, humbler and more obscure, perhaps—though what is that in the eyes of the indifferent gods?

I have not done so yet, but within a few years I shall have reached the age when it will no longer be seemly for me to marry again. Give me these few years; for I do not wish to marry, and I shall not regret not having done so, even when

I am old. That which we call our world of marriage is, as you know, a world of necessary bondage; and I sometimes think that the meanest slave has had more freedom than we women have known. I wish to spend the remainder of my life here; I shall welcome my children and grandchildren to visit me. There may be a kind of wisdom somewhere in myself, or in my books, that I shall find in the quiet years that lie ahead.

Chapter Three

Of all the women I have known, I have admired Livia the most. I was never fond of her, nor she of me; yet she behaved toward me always with honesty and civility; we got along well, despite the fact that my mere existence thwarted her ambitions, and despite the fact that she made no secret of her impersonal animosity toward me. Livia knew herself thoroughly, and had no illusions about her own nature; she was beautiful, and used her beauty without vanity; she was cold, and thus could feign warmth with utter success; she was ambitious, and employed her considerable intelligence exclusively to further her ambition's end. Had she been a man, I do not doubt that she would have been more ruthless than my father, and would have been troubled by fewer compunctions. Within her nature she was an altogether admirable woman.

Though I was only fourteen years of age at the time and could not understand the reason for it, I knew that Livia opposed my marriage to Marcellus, seeing it as a nearly absolute impediment to her son Tiberius's succession to power. And when Marcellus died so quickly after our marriage, she must have felt the possibility of her ambition urgently renewed. For even before the obligatory months of mourning had elapsed, Livia approached me. My father, having been offered the dictatorship of Italy in the wake of a famine, and having refused, had some weeks before prudently removed himself from Rome upon the pretext of business in Syria, so that he might not have further to exacerbate the frustrations of the Senate and the people by the presence of his refusal. It was a tactic that he employed often in his life.

As was her habit, Livia came at once to the point.

"Your time of mourning will be ended soon," she said.

"Yes," I replied.

"And you will be free to marry again."

"Yes."

666

"It is not appropriate that a young widow should remain long unmarried," she said. "It is not the custom."

I believe I did not reply. I must have thought even then that my widowhood was as much a matter of form as my marriage had been.

Livia continued. "Is your grief such that the prospect of marriage offends you?"

I remembered that I was my father's daughter. "I shall do my duty," I said.

Livia nodded as if she had expected the answer. "Of course," she said. "It is the way. . . . Did your father speak to you of this matter? Or has he written?"

"No," I said.

"I am sure that he has been considering it." She paused. "You must understand that I speak now for myself, not your father. But were he here, I would have his permission."

"Yes," I said.

"I have behaved toward you as if you were my daughter," Livia said. "Insofar as it has been possible, I have not acted against your interests."

I waited.

She said slowly, "Do you find my son at all to your liking?"

I still did not understand. "Your son?"

She made a little impatient gesture. "Tiberius, of course."

I did not find Tiberius to my liking, and I never had; I did not know why. Later I came to understand that it was because he discovered in all others those vices he would not recognize in himself. I said: "He has never been fond of me. He thinks me flighty and unstable."

"That is no matter, even if it is true," Livia said.

"And he is betrothed to Vipsania," I said. Vipsania was the daughter of Marcus Agrippa; and though younger than I, she was almost my friend.

"Nor does that matter," Livia said, still impatiently. "You understand such things."

"Yes," I said, and did not speak further. I did not know what to say.

"You know that your father is fond of you," Livia said. "Some have thought him too fond of you, but that is of no substance here. At issue is the fact, which you know, that he will listen to you more attentively than most fathers will listen to their daughters, and that he would hesitate to go against your wishes. Your wishes carry great weight with him. Therefore, if you find the idea of marriage to Tiberius not disagreeable to you, it would be appropriate for you to let your father know that."

I did not speak.

"On the other hand," Livia said, "if you find the idea wholly disagreeable, you would do me a service now to let me know. I have never dissembled with you."

My head was whirling. I did not know what to say. I said: "I must obey my father. I do not wish to displease you. I do not know."

Livia nodded. "I understand your position. I am grateful to you. I shall not trouble you more with this."

. . . Poor Livia. I believe that she thought then that everything was arranged, and that her will would prevail. But it did not, on that occasion. It was perhaps the bitterest blow of her life.

II. LETTER: LIVIA TO OCTAVIUS CAESAR, AT SAMOS (21 B.C.)

I have been in all things obedient to your will. I have been your wife, and faithful to my duty; I have been your friend, and faithful to your interests. So far as I can determine, I have failed you in only one regard, and I grant that that is an important one: I have not been able to give you a son, or even a child. If that is a fault, it is one which is beyond my control; I have offered divorce, which, out of what I believed to be affection for my person, you have often refused. Now I cannot be sure of that affection, and I am bitterly troubled.

Though I had reasonable cause to believe that you should have thought my Tiberius to be more nearly your own son than was Marcellus, who was only your nephew, I forgave your choice upon the grounds of your illness and upon the grounds of your plea that Marcellus carried the blood of the Claudian, the Octavian, and the Julian lines, while Tiberius carried only the Claudian. I even forgave what I must see now as your insults to my son; if in the extreme youth in which you judged him he displayed what appeared to be some instability of character and excess of behavior, I might suggest that the character of a boy is not the character of a man.

But now your course is clear, and I cannot conceal from you my bitterness. You have refused my son, and thus you have refused a part of me. And you have given your daughter a father rather than a husband.

Marcus Agrippa is a good man, and I know that he has been your friend; I bear no ill will for his person. But he bears no name, and whatever virtues he may possess are merely his own. It may have been amusing to the world that a man with such a lack of breeding might hold so much power as a subordinate of the Emperor; it will not be amusing to the world that now he is the designated successor, and thus nearly equal to the Emperor himself.

I trust you understand that my position has become nearly impossible; all Rome expected that Tiberius should become betrothed to your daughter, and that in the normal course of affairs he should have had some part in your life. Now you have refused him that.

And you remain abroad upon the occasion of this marriage of your daughter, as you did upon the first—whether out of necessity or choice, I do not know. And I do not care.

I shall continue in my duty toward you. My house will remain your house, and open to you and your friends. We have been too close in our common endeavors for it to be otherwise. I shall, indeed, attempt to continue to remain your friend; I have not been false to you, in thought or word or deed; and I shall not be in the future. But you must know the distance that this has put between us; it is farther than even the Samos where you now sojourn. It shall remain so.

Your daughter is married to Marcus Agrippa, and has removed herself to his house; she is now mother to that Vipsania Agrippa, who once was her playmate. Your niece, Marcella, bereft of a husband, is with your sister at Velletri. Your daughter seems content with her marriage. I trust that you are the same.

III. BROADSHEET: TIMAGENES OF ATHENS (21 B.C.)

Now who is mightier in the house of Caesar—
the one whom all call Emperor and the August,
or that one who, by all custom, should have been
his loving helpmate, dutiful to both bed
and banquet hall? See now how ruler is ruled:
the torches flicker, the company is gay,
and laughter flows more quickly than wine. He speaks
to his Livia, and will not be heard by her;
he speaks again, and is frozen by a smile.
It is said that he refused her a bauble;
you'd think the *Tiber* was *agrip* in winter ice!

But, ruled or ruler, it is no great matter.
There, from a corner, some Lesbia gives a glance
that darkens the torches; bright Delias languish
on couches, their shoulders bare in the dim light;
but he disdains them all. For boldly there comes
to him the wife of a friend (who does not see,
his eyes being filled with the vision of a boy
dancing to the torchlight). Why not? he thinks,
this ruler of men. Of his time, Maecenas
has given freely; this other little thing
he never uses, surely he'd not begrudge.

IV. LETTER: QUINTUS HORATIUS FLACCUS TO GAIUS CILNIUS MAECENAS, AT AREZZO (21 B.C.)

The author of the libel is, indeed, as you suspected, that same
Timagenes whom you have encouraged and aided, to whom
you unwisely gave your friendship, and whom you introduced
into the household of our friend. Besides being an ungrateful
guest and uncertain in his meter, he is most foolishly indis-
creet; he has bragged about his accomplishment to those who
he imagines will admire him, while attempting secrecy among
those who will not. He would have at once the responsibility
of fame and the pleasure of anonymity, a condition which is
clearly impossible.

Octavius knows his identity. He will take no action, though

(needless to say) Timagenes is no longer welcome in his house. He has asked me to assure you that he holds you in no way responsible for the betrayal; indeed, he is as much concerned for your feelings in the matter as he is for his own, and hopes that you have not suffered an undue embarrassment. His regard for you is as warm as ever; he regrets your absence from Rome, and is affectionately jealous of the time you have decided to spend at the feet of the Muses.

I, too, regret not seeing you more often; but I believe that I understand even more fully than our friend the contentment you must feel in the quiet and beauty of your Arezzo, away from the bustle and stench of this most extraordinary city. Tomorrow I return to my little place above the Digentia, whose murmur will soothe my ears and at length return me from noise to language. How trivial all these matters will seem there, as they must seem to you in your retreat.

V. LETTER: NICOLAUS OF DAMASCUS TO STRABO OF AMASIA, FROM ROME (21 B.C.)

My dear old friend, you have been eminently correct in your descriptions and enthusiasms over the years—this is the most extraordinary of cities in the most extraordinary of times. Being here now, I think that this is where my destiny has aimed me all my life, though I cannot bewail the long chain of circumstances that has delayed my discovery.

As you may know, I have in recent years become of increasing use to Herod, who knows that he rules Judaea only by the protection of Octavius Caesar; now I am in Rome upon another service to Herod, the extraordinary nature of which I shall reveal to you in due course. At the moment I shall content myself with saying that necessary to that service was the somewhat intimidating duty of presenting myself to Octavius Caesar himself. For despite the fact that you have written me so often of your familiarity with him, his fame and power are such as to overwhelm even your assurances. And I had, after all, once been tutor to the children of his enemy, Cleopatra of Egypt.

But again you were, as you are in all things, right; he put me at my ease at once, greeting me with even more warmth than

I might have expected as an envoy from Herod, and recalled his friendship with you, remarking upon how often you had mentioned my name. I did not wish, upon such slight acquaintance, to bring up to him the matter which I had been sent to accomplish; and thus I was particularly pleased when he invited me the next evening to dine with him at his private residence —I had, of course, presented myself to him at the Imperial Palace, which I understand he uses only during his official day.

I must not really have believed you when you wrote me of the modesty of his home. The simple luxury of my own quarters in Jerusalem would put this house to shame; I have seen moderately successful tradespeople live in more elegance! And it is not, I believe, merely an affectation of that austerity toward which he urges others; in this charming and comfortable little house, he seems a friendly host eager to please his guests, rather than the ruler of the world.

Let me set the scene for you and recapture the essence of that evening, in the manner of our master, Aristotle, in those marvelous *Conversations* that we used to study.

The meal—three excellent courses, served in a comfortable style between the austere and elegant—is over. The wine is mixed and poured, the servants moving noiselessly among the guests. It is a small gathering, of Octavius Caesar's relatives and friends. Reclining beside Octavius is Terentia, the wife of Maecenas, who (to my regret, for I should have liked to meet him) is out of the city for the season, devoting himself to his literary studies in the north; upon another couch are Julia, the Emperor's young and beautiful and vivacious daughter, and her new husband, Marcus Agrippa, a large and solid man, who, despite his distinction and importance, seems oddly out of place in this company; the great Horace, short and somewhat stout with graying hair around a young face, has pulled down beside him the Syrian dancing girl who earlier entertained us, and (to her nervous yet exultant delight) is teasing her to laughter; the young Tibullus (who languishes in the absence of his mistress) sits with his wine and observes the company with benevolent sadness; nearby sits his patron Messalla (who once, it is said, was proscribed by the triumvirs, who fought with Marcus Antonius against Octavius Caesar, and who now sits in easy friendship with his host and one-time enemy!) and that Livy, whom you have mentioned so often, and whose first books of that long history of Rome which he has projected, have begun to appear regularly in the book-stalls. Messalla proposes a toast to Octavius Caesar, who in turn proposes a toast to Terentia, whom he attends with courtesy and regard. We drink, and the conversation begins. Our host speaks first.

OCTAVIUS CAESAR: My dear and old friends, I take this occasion to present our guest. From our friend and ally in the East, that Herod who governs Judaea, comes the emissary Nicolaus of Damascus, who also is a scholar and philosopher of much distinction, and therefore doubly welcome in the company which graces my home upon this happy occasion. I am sure that he would wish to give you the greetings of Herod himself.

NICOLAUS: Great Caesar, I am humbled by your hospitality and honored beyond my merits to be included in the company of your renowned and intimate friends. Herod does, indeed, wish me to convey to you and your colleagues in the destiny of Rome his respectful greetings. The kindness and mutual affection which I have observed this evening persuade me that I shall be allowed to speak to you openly of that mission I have come to fulfill from the ancient land of Judaea. As a token of the boundless respect in which he holds Octavius Caesar, my friend and master Herod has given me leave to travel to Rome in order to speak to that man who has led Rome into the light of order and prosperity, and who has united the world. In honor of that Caesar, who is my host, I propose to write a Life, which will celebrate his fame to all the world.

OCTAVIUS CAESAR: As flattered as I am by this gesture of my good friend Herod, I must protest that my accomplishments do not merit such attention. I cannot persuade myself that the considerable talents which you, our new friend Nicolaus, possess should be put to so unimportant a purpose. Therefore, for the sake of those more significant tasks of learning which you might perform, and for the sake of my own sense of propriety and yet with all my gratitude and friendship, I must attempt to dissuade you from this unworthy task.

NICOLAUS: Your modesty, great Caesar, does honor to your person. But my master Herod would have me protest that modesty, and remind you that, great as your fame is, yet there are those in distant lands who have heard of your great accomplishments only by word of mouth. Even in Judaea, where the Latin tongue is used only by the educated few, there are those who do not know of your greatness. Thus were a record of your deeds put into that Greek language which all know, then would Judaea and much of the Eastern world be cognizant even more deeply of their dependence upon your beneficent power; and therefore might Herod more firmly rule, under your auspices and wisdom.

AGRIPPA: Great Caesar and dear friend, you have heeded my counsel before; I beseech you to do so again. Be persuaded by Nicolaus's eloquent request, and forsake your modesty in the interest of that which you must love more than your own person—that Rome, and the order which you have bequeathed her. The admiration which men in distant lands will give to you, will become love for the Rome that you have built.

LIVY: I shall make bold to add my voice to the persuasions you have heard. I know the reputation of this Nicolaus who stands before us now, and you could not put your fame in more trustworthy hands. Let mankind repay in some small measure that which you have given in such abundance.

OCTAVIUS CAESAR: I am at last persuaded. Nicolaus, you have the freedom of my house and you have my friendship. But I would beg you to confine your labors to those matters which have to do only with my acts in regard to Rome, and do not trouble your readers with those unimportant things that might have to do with my person.

NICOLAUS: I accede to your wishes, great Caesar, and shall endeavor by my poor efforts to do justice to your leadership of the Roman world.

. . . And thus, my dear Strabo, was the matter accomplished; Herod will be pleased, and I flatter myself by imagining that Octavius (he insists that I use the familiar address to him, in the intimacy of his house) has full confidence in my abilities to perform this work. You understand, of course, that the foregoing account has been submitted to the formal necessities of the dialogue in which I have cast it; the actual conversation was a good deal more informal and more lengthy; there was much bantering, all quite good-natured; Horace made jokes about Greeks who bore gifts, and asked if I intended to compose my work in prose or in verses; the vivacious Julia, who teases her father constantly, informed me that I could write anything I wanted, since her father's Greek was such that he could easily take an insult as a compliment. But I have, I believe, captured in my account the essence of the matter; for however these people make jokes with each other, there is a kind of serious-ness going on—or at least, so it seems to me.

Besides, in order to take further advantage of my stay here (which promises to be a lengthy one), I have projected a new work beyond the *Life of Octavius Caesar*, which Herod has commissioned. It shall be called "Conversations with Notable Romans," and I expect that what you have read will be a part of it. Does it strike you as a feasible idea? Do you think that the dialogue is a suitable form in which to cast it? I shall await your advice, which I treasure as much as always.

VI. LETTER: TERENTIA TO OCTAVIUS CAESAR, IN ASIA (20 B.C.)

Tavius, dear Tavius—I say our name for you, but you do not appear. Can you know how cruel your absence is? I rail against your greatness, which calls you away and keeps you in a country that is strange and detestable to me, because it holds you as I cannot. I know that you have told me that rage against necessity is the rage of a child; but your wisdom has fled from me with your body, and I am a restless child until you return.

How could I have been persuaded to let you go from me, who could not be happy for even a day outside your presence, once you had loved me? The scandal, you said, if I followed you—but there can be no scandal where there is common knowledge. Your enemies whisper; your friends are silent; and both know you are above the customs that others find neces-sary to lead orderly lives. Nor would there have been harm to anyone. My husband, who is my friend as well as yours, does not have that pride of possession that a lesser man might have; from the beginning it was known between us that I would have lovers, and that Maecenas would go where his tastes led him. He was not a hypocrite then, nor is he now. And Livia seems content with things as they are; I see her at readings, and she speaks to me civilly; we are not friends, but we are pleasant to each other. On my part, I am almost fond of her; for she chose to relinquish you, and thus you became mine.

Are you mine? I know that you are when you are with me, but when you are so far away—where is your touch, that tells me more than I have known before? Does my unhappiness please you? I hope it does. Lovers are cruel; I would almost be happy, if I could know that you are as unhappy as I am. Tell me that you are unhappy, so that I may have some comfort.

For I find no comfort in Rome; all things seem trivial to me now. I attend those festivals required of me by my position, the rituals seem empty; I go to the Circus, I cannot care who wins the races; I go to readings, my mind wanders from the poems read—even those of our friend Horace. And I have been faithful to you, all these weeks—I would tell you so, even if it were not true. But it is true; I have been. Does that matter to you?

Your daughter is well and is pleased with her new life. I visit with her and Marcus Agrippa once or twice a week. Julia seems pleased to see me; we have become friends, I believe. She is very heavy with child now, and seems proud of her impending motherhood. Would I want a child by you? I do not know. What would Maecenas say? It would be another scandal, but such an amusing one! . . . You see how I chatter on to your memory, as I used to do to your presence.

There is no gossip amusing enough to pass on to you. The marriages that you encouraged before you left Rome have at last taken place. Tiberius, it seems, has given up his ambitions, and is wed to Vipsania; and Jullus Antonius is wed to Marcella. Jullus seems happy that he is now officially your nephew and a member of the Octavian family, and even Tiberius seems grumpily content—even though he knows that Jullus's union with your niece is more advantageous than his own marriage to one of Agrippa's daughters.

Will you return to me this autumn, before the winter storms make your voyage impossible? Or will you wait until spring? It seems to me that I shall not be able to endure your absence for so long. You must tell me how I may endure.

VII. LETTER: QUINTUS HORATIUS FLACCUS TO
GAIUS CILNIUS MAECENAS, AT AREZZO (19 B.C.)

Our Vergil is dead.

I have just received the news, and I write you of it before grief overwhelms the numbness that I feel now, a numbness that must be a foretaste of that inexorable fate that has overtaken our friend, and which pursues us all. His remains are in Brindisi, attended by Octavius. The details are sketchy; I shall pass on to you what I have learned, for I have no doubt that Octavius's grief will delay his writing to you for some time.

Apparently the work of revision upon his poem, for the sake of which he had absented himself from Italy, had been going badly. Thus when Octavius, returning to Rome from Asia, stopped off at Athens, he had little difficulty persuading Vergil to accompany him back to Italy, for which he was already homesick, though he had been away for less than six months. Or perhaps he had some intimation of his death, and did not want his body to waste in a foreign soil. In any event, before setting out on the final journey, he persuaded Octavius to visit Megara with him; perhaps he wished to see that valley of rocks where the young Theseus is said to have slain the murderer Sciron. Whatever the reason, Vergil remained too long in the sun, and became ill. However, he insisted upon continuing the voyage; aboard ship, his condition worsened, and an old malaria returned upon him. Three days after landing at Brindisi, he died. Octavius was at his bedside, and accompanied him as far as any can on that journey from which there is no return.

I understand that he was delirious much of the time during his last days—though I have no doubt that Vergil delirious was more reasonable than most men lucid. At the end he spoke your name, and mine, and that of Varius. And he elicited from Octavius the promise that the unperfected manuscript of his *Aeneid* be destroyed. I trust that the promise will not be kept.

I wrote once that Vergil was half my soul. I feel now that I understated what I thought then was an exaggeration. For at Brindisi lies half the soul of Rome; we are diminished more than we know. —And yet my mind returns to smaller things, to things that only you and I, perhaps, can ever understand. At Brindisi, he lies. When was it that the three of us traveled so

happily across Italy, from Rome to Brindisi? Twenty years. . . .
It seems yesterday. I can still feel my eyes smart from the smoke
of the green wood that the innkeepers burned in their fire-
places, and hear our laughter like that of boys released from
school. And the farm girl we picked up at Trivicus, who promised to come to my room, and did not; I hear Vergil mocking
me, and remember the horseplay. And the quiet talk. And the
luxuriant comfort of Brindisi, after the countryside.

I shall not return to Brindisi again. Grief comes upon me
now, and I cannot write more.

VIII. THE JOURNAL OF JULIA, PANDATERIA (A.D. 4)

In my youth, when I first knew her, I thought Terentia to be
a trivial, foolish, and amusing woman, and I could not understand my father's fondness for her. She chattered like a magpie, flirted outrageously with everyone, and it seemed to me
that her mind had never been violated by a serious thought.
Though he was my father's friend, I did not like her husband,
Gaius Maecenas; and I was never able to understand Terentia's
agreement to that union with him. Looking back upon it, I can
see that my marriage to Marcus Agrippa was nearly as strange;
but then I was young and ignorant, and so filled with myself
that I could see nothing.

I have come to understand Terentia, I believe. In her own
way, she may have been wiser than any of us. I do not know
what has become of her. What does become of people who slip
quietly out of your life?

I believe now that she loved my father, perhaps in a way
that even he did not understand. Or perhaps he did. She was
reasonably faithful to him, taking casual lovers only during his
protracted absences. And perhaps, too, his fondness for her
was more serious than his appearance of amused toleration
led me then to believe. They were together for more than ten
years, and seemed happy to be so. I see now—perhaps I dimly
saw even then—that my judgments were those of youth and
position. My husband, who could have been my father, was
the most important man in Rome and its provinces during my
father's absence; and I imagined myself to be another Livia, as
proud and grave as she, at the side of one who might as well
have been the true Emperor. Thus it did not seem appropriate

to me that my father should love one so unlike Livia (and, as I foolishly thought, myself) as Terentia. But I remember things now that I did not recognize then.

I remember when my father returned alone from Asia, having only a few days before, at Brindisi, held in his arms his dying friend Vergil, and watched the breath go out of his body. Terentia was the only one who gave him comfort. Livia did not; I did not. I knew the idea of loss, but not its self. Livia spoke to him the ritual words that were meant to be comfort: Vergil had done his duty to his country, he would live in the memories of his countrymen, and the gods would receive him as one of their favored sons. And she hinted that too much grief was unseemly from the person of the Emperor.

My father looked at her gravely, and said: "Then the Emperor will show that grief that befits an Emperor. But how shall the man show the grief that befits him?"

It was Terentia who gave him comfort. She wept at the loss of their friend, recalled old memories, until my father became the man and wept too, at last had to comfort Terentia, and thus was comforted himself.

. . . I do not know why I thought of Terentia today, or of the death of Vergil. The morning is bright; the sky is clear; and far beyond my window, to the east, I see that point of land that juts into the sea above Naples. Perhaps I remembered that Vergil lived there when he was not in Rome, and remembered that he had been fond of Terentia in that dour way of his that concealed so much sentiment. And Terentia is a woman, even as I once was.

Even as I once was. . . . Was Terentia content to be a woman, as I was not? When I lived in the world, I believed that she was content, and had a secret contempt for her. Now I do not know. I do not know the human heart of another; I do not even know my own.

IX. LETTER: NICOLAUS OF DAMASCUS
TO STRABO OF AMASIA (18 B.C.)

Herod is in Rome. He is well pleased with my life of Octavius Caesar, which has been published abroad, and wishes me to remain here in the city for an indefinite period, so that he might have a trustworthy liaison with the Emperor. It is rather a delicate position, as you might imagine; but I feel confident that I can acquit my duties. Herod knows that I have the confidence and friendship of the Emperor, and I believe he has the wisdom to understand that I will betray neither; he is practical enough, at least, to know that if I do so, I should be of no further use to either of them.

Despite your kind praise, I have at last come to the conclusion that I would be wise to abandon the projected work that was to be called "Conversations with Notable Romans." As I have come to know these people, I have been forced to acknowledge that the Aristotelian mode in which we have both been schooled simply is not one in whose terms they may be defined. It is a difficult decision for me to make, for it must signify one of two things: either those modes in which we were schooled are incomplete, or I am not so finished a scholar of the master as I had led myself to believe. The former is too nearly inconceivable and the latter too humiliating to contemplate; and I would make this admission to none save you, who are the friend of my youth.

Let me try to demonstrate what I mean by an example.

All Rome is aflutter with the news of the latest law enacted by the Senate, which by a recent edict of Octavius Caesar has been reduced to some six hundred members. It is, in short, an effort to codify the marriage customs of this odd country, customs which have in recent times been more nearly acknowledged by abandonment than adherence. Among other things it gives to freed slaves more rights of marriage and property than they have had before, and that has caused some grumbling in certain quarters; but such grumblings are drowned by the cries of outrage at the more startling parts of the law, of which there are two. The first forbids any man who is or will be eligible by reason of his wealth to become a senator, to marry a freedwoman, an actress, or the daughter of an actor or actress. Nor shall the daughter or granddaughter of one of senatorial rank marry a freedman, an actor, or the son of one of those in the acting profession. No freeborn man, regardless of rank, shall marry a prostitute, a procuress, anyone convicted of a criminal act, one who has been an actress—or any woman who has been apprehended and convicted of adultery, regardless of her rank.

But the second part of the law is even more drastic than the first; for it provides that any father who apprehends an adulterer of his daughter in his own home, or the home of his son-in-law, is permitted (though not required) to kill the adulterer without fear of reprisal, and is permitted to do the same to his daughter. A husband is permitted to kill the offending man, but not his wife; in any event, he is required to denounce the offending wife and divorce her, else he may be prosecuted himself as a procurer.

As I say, all Rome is aflutter. Lampoons are circulated wildly; rumors abound; and each citizen has his own notion of what the whole thing means. Some take it seriously; some do not. Some say that it ought to be called the Livian rather than the Julian Law, and suspect that somehow Livia managed to insinuate it behind Octavius Caesar's back, in revenge for his own liaison with a certain lady who is also the wife of his friend. Others attribute it to Octavius himself; and of those, his enemies pretend outrage at his hypocrisy, others are heartened by what they see as the re-establishment of the "old virtues," and yet others see it as some obscure plot on the part of either Octavius Caesar or his enemies.

Through all the uproar, the Emperor himself walks calmly, as if he had no notion of what anyone was saying or thinking. But he does know. He always knows.

That is one side of the man.

Yet there is another. It is one that I, and a few of his friends know. It is unlike the one that I have shown you.

Upon formal occasions, I have been guest in his home on the Palatine, where Livia reigns. These occasions have been pleasant and not at all strained; Octavius and Livia behave toward each other with perfect civility, if not warmth. Upon other occasions I have been guest at the home of Marcus Agrippa and Julia while Octavius was present, usually in the company of Terentia, the wife of Gaius Maecenas. And upon several intimate and casual occasions I have been guest at the home of Maecenas himself, also in the presence of Octavius and Terentia. The three of them behave toward each other with the ease of old friendship.

Yet his liaison with Terentia is known to all, and has been for several years.

And there is more. Almost like a philosopher, he is with-out faith in the old gods of his countrymen; yet almost like a peasant, he is extraordinarily superstitious. He will use the auguries of his priests to any purpose that seems convenient to him, and be convinced of their truth because of his successful use of them; he will scoff (in a friendly fashion) at what he calls the "transcendent pomposity" of the God of my countrymen, and wonder at the sloth of a race that can invent only one god. "It is more fitting," he said once, "for the gods to be many, and to strive among themselves, as men do. . . . No. I do not believe that the strange God of your Jews would do for us Romans." And once I chided him (we have become that friendly) for his faith in portents and dreams, and he replied: "Upon more than one occasion my life has been saved by my believing what my dreams told me. Once it is not saved, I shall cease believing in them."

In all things, he is the most prudent and cautious man, and will leave nothing to chance that may be gained by careful planning; yet he loves nothing more than to play at dice, and will willingly do so for hours upon end. Several times he has sent a messenger to me, inquiring of my leisure; and I have played with him, though I take more pleasure in observing my friend than I do in the silly game of chance we play. He is utterly serious when he plays, as if his Empire depended upon the turn of the pieces of bone; and when, after two or three hours of play, he has won a few pieces of silver, he is as pleased as if he had conquered Germany.

He confessed to me once that in his youth he had aspired to be a man of letters, and had written poems in competition with his friend Maecenas.

"Where are the poems now?" I asked him.

"Lost," he said. "I lost them at Philippi." He seemed almost sad. Then he smiled. "I even wrote a play, once, in the Greek fashion."

I chided him a little. "Upon one of your strange gods?"

He laughed. "A man," he said, "only a foolish man who was too proud, that Ajax who took his life with his sword."

"And is that, too, lost?"

He nodded. "In my modesty, I took his life again—with my

eraser. . . . It wasn't a very good play. My friend Vergil assured me that it was not."

We were both silent for a moment. A sadness had come over Octavius's face. Then he said almost roughly: "Come. Let's have another game." And he shook the dice and threw them on the table.

Do you see what I mean, my dear Strabo? There is so much that is not said. I almost believe that the form has not been devised that will let me say what I need to say.

X. LETTER: QUINTUS HORATIUS FLACCUS TO OCTAVIUS CAESAR (17 B.C.)

You must forgive me for returning your messenger without reply to your invitation. He made it clear that you had bidden him wait upon me; I returned him to you upon my own responsibility.

You ask me to compose the choral hymn for the centennial festival that you have decreed this May. You know that I am flattered that you should think me worthy; we both know that the man who should have had the honor is dead; and I know how deeply important you consider this celebration to be.

Thus, you are no doubt puzzled at my uncertainty about accepting the commission, an uncertainty that has given me a sleepless night. I have at last concluded that it is my duty and my pleasure to accede to your wish; but I think you ought to know the considerations which occasioned my hesitation.

Please know that I understand the difficulty of your task in running this extraordinary nation that I love and hate, and this more extraordinary Empire at which I am horrified and filled with pride. I know, better than most, how much of your own happiness you have exchanged for the survival of our country; and I know the contempt you have had for that power which has been thrust upon you—only one with contempt for power could have used it so well. I know all these things, and more. Thus, when I venture a disagreement with you, I do so in the full knowledge of the wisdom which I confront.

Yet I cannot persuade myself that your new laws will bring anything but grief to yourself and your country.

I know the corruption of our city which you would stem, and I know the intent of the laws, I believe. In the circles in which you move, and which I observe, copulation has become an act designed to obtain power, either social or political; an adulterer may be more dangerous than a conspirator, both to your person and his country; and that act whose natural end is affectionate pleasure has become a dangerous means toward ambition. The slave may gain power over a senator, thus over the ordinary citizen, and at last justice is subverted. I know these things, which your laws would hope to prevent.

Yet you, yourself, could not wish to have these laws enforced universally, with the rigor that law must be enforced. Such an enforcement would be disastrous to yourself, and to many of your most loyal friends. And though those who know your purpose understand that you intend to define a spirit and an ideal, the mass of your enemies will not understand this; and you may discover that your laws against adultery may be put to even more corrupt use than that which they were designed against.

For no law may adequately determine a spirit, nor fulfill a desire for virtue. That is the function of the poet or the philosopher, who may persuade because he has no power; the power you have (which, as I have said, you have used so wisely in the past) cannot legislate against the passions of the human heart, however disruptive to order those passions may be.

Nevertheless, I shall write the choral hymn for the celebration, and I shall take pride in the task. I share your concern and your hope, though I fear the means you have taken to fulfill them. I have been wrong in the past; I hope that I am wrong now.

XI. THE JOURNAL OF JULIA, PANDATERIA (A.D. 4)

In this island prison, my life over, I wonder without caring at things I might not have wondered at, had that life not come to an end.

Downstairs in her little bedroom, my mother is asleep; our servant does not stir; even the ocean, which usually whispers against the sand, is still. The midday sun burns upon the rocks, which absorb the heat and throw it back into the air, so that

nothing—not even a vagrant gull—will move in its heaviness.
It is a powerless world, and I wait in it.

It is odd to wait in a powerless world, where nothing matters. In the world from which I came, all was power; and everything mattered. One even loved for power; and the end of love
became not its own joy, but the myriad joys of power.

I was married to Marcus Vipsanius Agrippa for nine years;
and according to the world's understanding of such matters, I
was a good wife. During his lifetime I gave four children into
his hands, and gave one more after his death. They were all
his children, and three of them—since they were male—might
have mattered to the world. As it turned out, none of them
did.

It was, I believe, the birth of my two sons, Gaius and Lucius,
that gave me the first real taste of that most irresistible of all
passions, the passion for power. For Gaius and Lucius were
immediately adopted by my father, it being understood that in
the event of his death, first my husband and then one or the
other of my sons would succeed as Emperor and First Citizen
of the Empire of Rome. At the age of twenty-one I discovered
that I was, except for Livia herself, the most powerful woman
in the world.

It is empty, the philosophers say; but they have not known
power, as a eunuch has not known a woman, and thus can look
upon her unmoved. In my life I could never understand my
father not apprehending that joy of power by which I learned
to live, and which made me happy with Marcus Agrippa, who
(as Livia often said in her bitterness) might as well have been
my father.

I have often wondered how I might have managed the power
I had, had I not been a woman. It was the custom for even the
most powerful of women, such as Livia, to efface themselves
and to assume a docility that in many instances went against
their natures. I knew early that such a course was not possible
for me.

I remember once that my father upbraided me for speaking
in what he thought to be an unwomanly and arrogant tone
to one of his friends, and I replied that though he might forget that he was the Emperor, I would not forget that I was
the Emperor's daughter. It was a retort that gathered some

currency in Rome. My father seemed amused by it, for he repeated it often. I do not believe he understood what I meant.

I was the Emperor's daughter. I was wife to Marcus Agrippa, who was my father's friend; but before and after that, I was the Emperor's daughter. It was accepted by all that my duty was to Rome.

Yet there was a part of me which, as year followed year, I came to know with increasing intimacy; it was a part that refused that duty, knowing it was a duty without reward. . . .

A moment ago I wrote of power, and of the joy of power. I think now of the devious ways in which a woman must discover power, exert it, and enjoy it. Unlike a man, she cannot seize it by force of strength or mind or desire; nor can she glory in it with a man's open pride, which is the reward and sustenance of power. She must contain within her such personages that will disguise her seizure and her glory. Thus I conceived within myself, and let forth upon the world, a series of personages that would deceive whoever might look too closely; the innocent girl who did not know the world, upon whom a doting father lavished a love he could not give elsewhere; the virtuous wife, whose only pleasure was in her duty toward her husband; the imperious young matron, whose whim became the public's wish; the idle scholar, who dreamed of a virtue beyond Roman duty, and fondly pretended that philosophy might be true; the woman who, late in life, discovered pleasure, and used men's bodies as if they were the luxurious ointments of the gods; and who herself at last was used, to the intensest pleasure she had ever known. . . .

I was twenty-one years of age when my father decreed the centennial festival to commemorate the founding of Rome, and I had given birth to my second son. My father and my husband were the chief worshipers at the festival, and made many sacrifices to those gods whose descendants are said to have established our city. It fell to me and Livia to preside equally at the banquet of the hundred matrons; I sat on the throne of Diana, and Livia across from me on the throne of Juno; and we received the ritual worship. I saw the faces of the richest and most influential women in Rome look up at me; I knew that many of them were married to enemies of my father who would have murdered him, were they not afraid. They looked at me with that odd expression that goes with the recognition of power; it was not love, nor respect, nor hatred, nor even fear. It was something that I had not seen before, and I felt for a moment that I had just been born.

Within a few weeks after the festival, my husband was to travel upon a variety of missions to the East—to the provinces of Asia Minor; to Macedonia, where my own father had spent his boyhood; to Greece; to Pontus and Syria, and wherever necessity might take him. It was, of course, contrary to all custom that I should accompany him; and until the festival, it had not occurred to me that I might do so, in defiance of custom.

But I did accompany him, despite the anger and persuasions of my father. I remember that my father said: "No wife has ever followed a proconsul and his soldiers into foreign lands; that is a task for freedwomen and prostitutes."

And I replied: "I would know, then, if you prefer me to appear a prostitute before my husband, or be a prostitute in Rome."

I intended the remark flippantly, and my father received it so; but I remember that it occurred to me afterward that it might not have been a joke; and I wondered if I had not been more serious than I had thought. In any event, my father relented; I joined my husband's retinue, and for the first time in my life, with my children and my servants, I crossed the borders of my native land.

From Brindisi to Apollonia, we crossed that little stretch of sea where the Adriatic empties into the Mediterranean; landing at Apollonia, we visited the sites where my husband and my father had companioned when they were boys. It was an easy and pleasant time, but I was eager to go onward, to places more strange and untrodden by Roman feet. From Apollonia we traveled northward through Macedonia to the new territories of Moesia, as far as the River Danube; and I saw strange people, who upon the approach of our carriages and horses, dodged like animals back into the forest, and would not be enticed into the open; they spoke in strange tongues, and many were dressed in the furs of wild animals. And I saw the bleak lives of the soldiers who had the misfortune to be stationed at this outpost of the Empire. They seemed strangely contented, and my husband spoke to them as if theirs were the most natural way of life that he could imagine. I had difficulty remembering that much of his life had been spent thus, in the days before I was born.

After the inspection of the Danube stations, we turned southward, somewhat hurriedly; for the autumn was upon us, and we wished to escape the rigors of a northern winter. I was beginning to regret my decision to accompany Marcus Agrippa, and to long for the comforts of Rome.

But we rested at Philippi, and my spirits raised. My husband showed me the places where he had done battle with the forces of Brutus and Cassius, and told me the tales of those days; and then we made our way leisurely to the shores of the Aegean, and sailed upon that blue water among the islands; and the weather warmed as we went southward.

And I began to know why the gods had sent me upon this journey, far from the city of my birth.

Chapter Four

For the past three years, I have, in my letters to you, wondered why our friend Octavius Caesar insisted that I accompany Marcus Agrippa and his wife on this long Eastern tour; for it is clear that my connection with Herod is, in itself, not sufficient to justify my long absence from Rome. I now begin to understand his reasons; and before you know them, you shall wonder at my writing to you, in your retirement, rather than to Octavius Caesar himself. But if you will attend me, you will gradually begin to understand.

I write you from Jerusalem, where a few months ago Marcus Agrippa and Julia came with me, upon the invitation of Herod, who offered us a rest from our travels. Agrippa's stay in Jerusalem was limited, however; for no sooner had he arrived than word came of serious disturbances in the Bosporus. The old King, faithful to Rome, is dead; and his young wife, Dynamis, imagining herself no doubt a northern Cleopatra, but perhaps unmindful of that unhappy lady's fate, has allied herself with a barbarian named Scribonius; and in defiance of Roman policy, has declared herself, with her lover, to be the ruler of her husband's kingdom. Indeed, it is rumored that she, at the instigation of her lover, had a hand in her own husband's death. In any event, Marcus Agrippa, knowing that this kingdom is the last bulwark against the northern barbarians, determined to go there and put down the revolt; this he is now in the process of doing, with ships and men provided by Herod.

It was, of course, impossible for Julia to accompany him. She showed no real desire to do so; but neither would she accept Herod's plea that she remain in Jerusalem until her husband rejoined her, nor did she show any inclination to return to Rome. Rather, despite our entreaties, she gathered her retinue, and upon departure of her husband northward, she herself departed for Greece, and for those islands to the north from which she and her husband were recently returned. I have received some alarming news from that part of the world, where she now is; and that news, my dear Maecenas, is the occasion for this letter.

For the past two years, during their leisurely journey southward among the Aegean islands and the coastal cities of Greece and Asia, both Marcus Agrippa and Julia have been received with the honors due the representatives of the Emperor Octavius Caesar and Rome. But in especial Julia, since she is the daughter of the Emperor, has been the recipient of that sort of adulation of which only the island and Eastern Greeks are capable.

The adulation began in an ordinary enough way. At Andros, in honor of her visit, a statue in her likeness was erected; the inhabitants of Mytilene, on the Island of Lesbos, hearing of the homage given by the inhabitants of Andros, constructed a larger statue, in the twin likeness of Julia and the goddess Aphrodite; and thereafter, as island and city learned of the approach of Julia and Agrippa, the ceremonies became more and more extravagant, until at last Julia came to be regarded as the goddess Aphrodite herself, returned to earth, and came to be worshiped (at least ritually) by the people.

I am sure that you will agree that in all this extravagancy, ludicrous as it may appear to civilized men, there is nothing really very harmful; for in these public demonstrations, the Greeks were witty enough to have modified these odd ceremonies so that they might offend no one, and so that they might appear almost Romanized.

But in the midst of all this, something rather extraordinary has begun to happen to the person of Julia, of whom I have been (as you know) rather fond. It is almost as if she has begun to take on some of the attributes of that personage to whom she has been ritually likened; she has become imperious and indifferently arrogant, as if she indeed were not truly mortal.

This has for some time been my impression of her character; but I have just received news from Asia which sadly confirms what had been uncertain.

The report is that Julia, having spent the day in Ilium wandering among the ruins of the ancient site of Troy, attempted to cross the Scamander River by night. By some circumstance that is not clear, the raft bearing Julia and her attendants was overturned, and all were swept downstream. It was, no doubt,

a near thing for all of them. In any event, she was finally rescued (by whom, it is not clear); but in her anger at the villagers
who, she charges, did not attempt to rescue her, and in the
name of her husband, Marcus Agrippa, she imposed upon the
village a fine of one hundred thousand drachmas, which would
amount to nearly a thousand drachmas for each of them. It is a
heavy fine, indeed, for poor people, many of whom would not
see a thousand drachmas in a lifetime of labor.

It is said that these villagers, though they heard the cries for
help, came to the bank of the river, and watched, and would
not attempt the rescue. I believe that this is probably a true account of the incident. Nevertheless, despite what might seem
the obvious guilt of the villagers, I shall intercede. I shall ask
a favor of Herod (who owes me several), and request that he
persuade Marcus Agrippa to remit the fine. I shall do so, not
out of pity for the villagers, but out of apprehension for the
safety of the house of Octavius Caesar.

For Julia had not spent the day as an innocent tourist at
Ilium; and her crossing the Scamander was not an innocent
return to her quarters.

I spoke earlier of those public ceremonies—part religious,
part political, and part social—in which Julia was elevated upon
the throne of Aphrodite. By dwelling upon them, I suppose I
have been putting off speaking of another kind of ceremony
that is not public, but which is secret and unknown and somewhat frightening to this age of enlightenment.

There is a secret cult among these island and Eastern Greeks
which worships a goddess whose name (at least to all those
who are not initiates) is unknown. She is said to be the goddess
of all gods and goddesses; her power is beyond the power of all
the other gods conceived by mankind. Upon certain occasions,
the power of this goddess is celebrated by rituals—though what
they are no one knows, since the cult is shrouded in the secrecy
of its fervor or its shame. But no secret is absolute; and in my
travels I have heard enough of this cult to fill me with a revulsion at its nature and an apprehension of its consequences.

It is a female cult; and though there are priests, they are
castrates who at one time allowed themselves to be used as
sacrificial victims to the goddess. These victims are chosen
by the priestesses—it is said that sometimes the priestesses

choose their own sons as victims, since within their peculiar doctrine such a victim is the most honored and fortunate of men. He must be under the age of twenty; he must be virginal; and he must be a willing victim.

I do not know the precise nature of the rite; but I have heard, myself, from afar, the flute music and the chants in the sacred groves where the rites are performed. It is said that for three days the initiates and the members of the cult "purify" themselves by abstinence from all fleshly things; it is said, further, that when the rites begin the celebrants intoxicate themselves by dancing, by singing, and the drinking of certain libations —whether of wine or some more mysterious substance, no one knows. Then, when the celebrants are in a frenzy induced by their music and dancing and strange drink, the ceremony begins. One of several sacrificial victims is brought before the woman who has been chosen as the ritual incarnation of the Great Goddess. Save for the fur of some wild animal tied loosely about his waist, he is naked; he is bound to a cross made of some sacred wood from the trees by the grove, by wrist and foot, with lengths of laurel wreath. After he has been placed before the goddess, the celebrants dance about him; it is said that they fling their own clothing from their bodies in their frenzy as they dance. Then the goddess approaches the boy and with the sacred knife loosens the fur that hides his nakedness; and when she finds a victim that pleases her, she cuts the laurel that constrains him, and leads him to a cave in the sacred grove, which has been prepared for the "marriage" of the goddess and the mortal.

The marriage is supposed to be a ritual marriage; but it is a female cult, and secret, and sanctioned neither by law nor public custom. The goddess and her victim remain unseen in the cave for three days; it is said that the goddess uses her victim in whatever way pleases her; food and drink are put at the entrance of the cave, and those celebrants on the outside indulge in whatever lust or perversity that their frenzy leads them to.

After three days, the goddess and her mortal lover emerge from the cave, and cross a body of water to another sacred grove, which becomes the Island of the Blessed; and there the mortal lover becomes immortal, at least in the barbaric minds of the celebrants.

It is known to all that from Ilium to Lesbos this cult prevails, and that it numbers among its members those who belong to the richest and most cultivated families in that part of the world. When Julia's raft was upset, she was returning from such a rite as I have described, completing the prescribed ritual, crossing to the Island of the Blessed. She had been the incarnation of the goddess. And the villagers, in their abhorrence of such dark practices, could not overcome their fear of these strange beings, who (they thought) lived in a world beyond their comprehension and experience. I cannot allow the fine levied upon them to stand; for if I do, the secrecy (which now protects Julia, the unknowing Marcus Agrippa, Octavius Caesar, and even Rome itself) may be broken.

And beyond the vile practices which are rumored, there is another that is even more serious; the members of the cult are required to abjure all authority beyond the dictates of their own desires, and have no allegiance to any man, or law, or mortal custom. Thus, not only is the license of immorality encouraged—but murder, treason, and all other conceivable unlawful acts.

My dear Maecenas, I trust that now you understand why I could not write the Emperor; why I cannot speak to Marcus Agrippa; why I must burden you with this problem, even in your retirement from public affairs. You must find a way to persuade your friend and master to force Julia to return to Rome. If she is not now corrupted beyond retrieval, she will be soon, if she remains in this strange land that she has discovered.

II. THE JOURNAL OF JULIA, PANDATERIA (A.D. 4)

I have never known why my father ordered me, in terms that I could not disobey, to return to Rome. He never gave me a reason sufficient to justify the strength of his command; he merely said that it was unseemly that the wife of the Second Citizen be so long absent from the people who loved her, and that there were certain social and religious duties that only I and Livia could perform. I did not believe that that was the true reason for my recall, but he did not allow me to question him further. But he could not fail to know that I had resented my return; it seemed to me then that I was being exiled from the only life in which I had ever been myself, and that I was to spend my days performing a kind of duty in which I no longer could see any meaning.

In any event, it was Nicolaus—that odd little Syrian Jew, of whom my father was unaccountably fond and whom he trusted —who delivered the message to me, traveling all the way from Jerusalem to find me at Mytilene on Lesbos.

I was angry, and I said to him: "I will not go. He cannot force me to return."

Nicolaus shrugged. "He is your father," he said.

"My husband," I said. "I am with my husband."

"Your husband," Nicolaus said; "your husband is in the Bosporus. Your husband is your father's friend. Your father is the Emperor. He misses you, I suspect. And Rome—it will be spring when we return."

And so we set sail from Lesbos, and I watched the islands slip by, like clouds in a dream. It was my life, I thought, that slipped behind me; it was the life in which I had been a queen, and more than a queen. And as the days passed, and as we drew nearer to Rome, I knew that she who returned was not the same woman who had left, three years before.

And I knew that the life to which I returned would be different. I did not know how it would be so, but I knew that it would be. Not even Rome could awe me now, I thought. And I remember that I wondered if I would still feel like a child when I saw my father.

I returned to Rome in the year of the consulship of Tiberius Claudius Nero, the son of Livia and the husband of my husband's daughter, Vipsania. I was twenty-five years of age. Who had been a goddess returned to Rome a mere woman, and in bitterness.

III. LETTER: PUBLIUS OVIDIUS NASO TO SEXTUS PROPERTIUS, IN ASSISI (13 B.C.)

Dear Sextus, my friend and my master—how do you thrive in that melancholy exile you have imposed upon yourself? Your Ovid beseeches you to return to Rome, where you are sorely missed. Things here are not nearly so gloomy as you may have been led to believe; a new star is in the Roman sky, and once again those who have the wit to do so may live in gaiety and pleasure. Indeed, during the past few months, I have concluded that I would be in no other time and in no other place.

You are the master of my art, and older than I—yet can you be sure that you are wiser? Your melancholy may be of your own constitution, rather than Rome's making. Do return to us; there is pleasure yet, before the night comes down upon us.

But forgive me; you know that I am not suited for weighty talk, and once having begun cannot sustain it. I intended at the outset of this letter merely to tell you of a delightful day, hoping that I could persuade you by that to return to us.

Yesterday was the anniversary of the Emperor Octavius Caesar's birth, and thus a Roman holiday; yet it began for me unpropitiously enough. I was in my office disgracefully early—at the first hour, no less, just as the sun was beginning to struggle up from the east through the forest of buildings that is Rome, bringing the city to its feet—for though one may not plead a case on such a holiday as this, one may have to do so the next day; and I had a particularly difficult brief to prepare. It seems that Cornelius Apronius, who has retained me, is suing Fabius Creticus for nonpayment for some lands, while Creticus is countersuing, claiming that the title to the lands is faulty. Both are thieves; neither has a case; thus the skill of the brief and the persuasion of the pleading are most important—as, of course, is the chance of magistrate.

In any event, I had been working all morning; marvelous lines kept popping into my head, as they always do when I am laboring at something that bores me; my secretary was particularly slow and fumbling; and the noise that came from the Forum grated against my ears much more fiercely than it should have done. I was becoming increasingly irritable, and for the hundredth time swore that I should give up this foolish career that in the long run will only give me riches I do not need and the dull distinction of senatorial office.

Then, in the midst of my boredom, a remarkable thing happened. I heard a clatter outside my door, and laughter; and though I heard no knock, my door burst open, and there stood before me the most remarkable eunuch I have ever seen —coiffed and perfumed, dressed in elegant silks, with emeralds and rubies on his fingers, he stood before me as if he were better than a freedman, better even than a citizen.

"This is not the Saturnalia," I said angrily. "Who has given you leave to burst in upon me?"

"My mistress," he said in a shrill, effeminate voice; "my mistress bids you attend me."

"Your mistress," I said, "may rot, for all I care. . . . Who is she?"

He smiled as if I were a slug at his feet. "My mistress is Julia, daughter of Octavius Caesar, the August, Emperor of Rome and First Citizen. Do you wish to know more, lawyer?"

I suppose I gaped at him; I did not speak.

"You will attend me, I presume?" he said haughtily.

In an instant my irritation was gone. I laughed, and tossed the sheaf of papers I had been clutching toward my secretary. "Do the best you can with these," I said. Then I turned to the slave who waited for me. "I will attend you," I said, "wherever your mistress would have you lead me." And I followed him out the door.

As is my wont, dear Sextus, I shall digress for a moment. In a casual way, I had met the lady in question a few weeks before, at a huge party given by that Sempronius Gracchus whom we both know. The Emperor's daughter had returned only a month or so before from a long journey in the East, where she had accompanied her husband, Marcus Agrippa, on some business of his, and where Agrippa remains yet. I was anxious to meet her, of course; since her return, the fashionable people of Rome have been talking of nothing else. So when Gracchus, who seems to be on rather friendly terms with her, invited me, I of course quickly accepted.

There were literally hundreds of people at the party at Sempronius Gracchus's villa—really too large a gathering to be very amusing, I suppose, but it was pleasurable in its own way. Despite the numbers of people, I had the chance to meet Julia, and we bantered for a few moments. She is an utterly charming woman, exquisitely beautiful, and really quite intelligent and well-read. She was kind enough to indicate that she had read some of my poems. Knowing her father's reputation for rectitude (as do you, my poor Sextus), I tried to make a sort of rueful apology for the "naughtiness" of my verse. But she smiled at me in that devastating way she has, and said: "My dear Ovid, if you try to convince me that though your verse is naughty, your life is chaste, I shall not speak to you again."

And I said, "My dear lady, if that is the condition, I shall attempt to convince you otherwise."

And she laughed and moved away from me. Though it was a pleasant interlude, it did not occur to me that she would give me another thought, let alone remember my existence for two whole weeks. And yet she did; and yesterday I found myself in her company once more, following the circumstance which I have described.

Outside my door, attended by bearers, there were perhaps half a dozen litters, canopied with silk of purple and gold; they teemed with the movements of their occupants, and laughter shook the street. I stood, not knowing where to turn; my castrate chaperon had wandered away and was haranguing some of the lesser slaves. Then someone stepped from a litter, and I saw at once that it was she, the Julia who had so kindly interrupted my tedious morning. Then another stepped from the litter and joined her. It was Sempronius Gracchus. He smiled at me. I went toward them.

"You have saved me from a death by boredom," I said to Julia. "What now will you do with that life which belongs to you?"

"I shall use it frivolously," she said. "Today is my father's birthday, and he has given me permission to invite some of my friends to sit with him in his box at the Circus. We shall watch the games, and gamble away our money."

"The games," I said. "How charming." I intended my remark to be neutral, but Julia took it as irony. She laughed.

"One does not have that much concern for the games," she said. "One goes to see, and to be seen, and to discover less common amusements." She glanced at Sempronius. "You will learn, perhaps." She turned from me then, and called to the others, some of whom had stepped out of their litters to stretch their legs. "Who would share his seat with Ovid, the poet of love, who writes of those things to which you have dedicated your lives?"

Arms waved from litters, my name was shouted: "Here, Ovid, ride with us—my girl needs your advice!" "No, *I* need your advice!" And there was much laughter. I finally chose a litter in which there was room for me, the bearers hoisted their burdens, and we made our way slowly through the crowded streets toward the Circus Maximus.

We arrived at noon, just as the hordes of people were streaming out of the stands for a hasty lunch before the resumption of the games. I must say, it gave me an odd feeling to see those masses, recognizing the colors of our litters, part before our advance, as the earth parts before the advance of a plow. Yet they were gay, and waved to us and shouted in the most friendly manner.

We debarked from our litters; and with Julia, Sempronius Gracchus, and another whom I did not know leading our band, we made our way among those arcades that honeycomb the Circus toward the stairs. Occasionally from the doorway of one of these arcades, an astrologer would beckon and call to us, whereupon someone in our party would shout: "We know our future, old man!" and throw him a coin. Or a prostitute would show herself and beckon enticingly to one who seemed unattached, whereupon one of the ladies might call to her in mock terror, "Oh, no! Don't steal him from us. He might never return!"

We mounted the stairs; and as we approached the Imperial box there were shushings and calls for quiet, out of deference for the presence of Octavius Caesar. But he was not in the box when we arrived; and I must say that, despite the pleasure I was having in the company of this most delightful troop, I found myself a little disappointed.

For as you know, Sextus, unlike you—not being an intimate of Maecenas, as you are, nor needing that intimacy— I have never met Octavius Caesar. I have seen him from afar, of course, as has everyone in Rome: but I know of him only that which you have told me.

"The Emperor is not here?" I asked.

Julia said, "There are certain kinds of bloodshed that my father does not enjoy." She pointed down at the open space of the course. "He usually comes late, after the animal hunt is over."

I looked to where she was pointing; the attendants were dragging away the slain animals and raking over the earth that was spotted with blood. I saw several tigers, a lion, and even an elephant being dragged across the ground. I had attended one of these hunts before, when I first came to Rome, and had found it extremely dull and common. I suggested as much to Julia.

She smiled, "My father says that either a fool is killed, or a dumb beast, and he cannot bring himself to care which. And besides, there are no wagers to be made on these contests between hunters and beasts. My father enjoys the wagering."

"It's late," I said. "He will be here, won't he?"

"He must," she said. "The games honor his birthday; and he would not be discourteous to anyone who so honors him."

I nodded, and recalled that the games were being presented to him by one of the new praetors, Jullus Antonius. I started to say something to Julia; but I remembered who Jullus Antonius was, and I checked my speech.

But Julia must have noticed my intention, for she smiled. "Yes," she said. "In particular, my father would not be discourteous to the son of an old enemy, whom he has forgiven, and whose son he has preferred to some who are his own kin."

Wisely (I think), I nodded, and did not speak more of the matter. But I wondered about this son of Marcus Antonius, whose name, even these many years after his death, still is honored by many of the citizens of Rome.

Yet there is little time to wonder about things of that sort in such gay company. The servants brought tidbits of food on golden plates, and poured wine into golden cups; and we ate, and drank, and chattered as we watched the crowd straggle back to their seats for the afternoon races.

By the sixth hour, the stands were filled, and it seemed to me overflowing with a good part of the population of Rome. Then suddenly, above the natural noise of the crowd, a great roar went up; many of the populace were standing, and were pointing toward the box where we reclined. I turned around, glancing over my shoulder. At the rear of the box, in the shadows, stood two figures, one rather tall, the other short. The tall one was dressed in the richly embroidered tunic and the purple-bordered toga of a consul; the shorter wore the plain white tunic and toga of the common citizen.

The taller of the two was Tiberius, stepson of the Emperor

and consul of Rome; and the shorter was, of course, the Emperor Octavius Caesar himself.

They came into the box; we rose; the Emperor smiled and nodded to us, and indicated that we should seat ourselves. He sat beside his daughter, while Tiberius (a dour-faced young man, who seemed not to want to be where he was) found a seat somewhat removed from the rest of the party, and spoke to no one. For several moments the Emperor and Julia talked together, their heads close; the Emperor glanced at me, and said something to Julia, who smiled, nodded, and then beckoned me to join them.

I approached, and Julia presented me to her father.

"I am pleased to meet you," the Emperor said; his face was lined and weary, his light hair shot with white—but his eyes were bright and piercing and alert. "My friend Horace has spoken of your work."

"I hope kindly," I said, "but I cannot pretend to compete with him. My Muse is smaller and more trivial, I fear."

He nodded. "We all obey whatever Muse chooses us. . . . Do you have any favorites today?"

"What?" I said blankly.

"The races," he said. "Do you have any favorite drivers?"

"Sir," I said, "I must confess that I come to the races more nearly for the society than for the horses. I really know very little about them."

"Then you don't wager," he said. He seemed a little disappointed.

"On everything but the races," I said. He nodded and smiled a little, and turned to someone behind him.

"Which do you pick in the first?"

But whoever it was to whom he spoke did not have time to answer. At the far end of the race course, gates opened, trumpets sounded, and the procession entered. It was led by Jullus Antonius, the praetor who had financed the games; he was dressed in a scarlet tunic, over which he wore the purple-bordered toga, and carried in his right hand the golden eagle, which seemed almost ready to take flight from the ivory rod which supported it; and upon his head was the golden wreath of laurel. In his chariot drawn by his magnificent white horse, I must say he was an impressive figure, even at the distance from which I saw him.

Slowly the procession went round the track. Behind Jullus Antonius walked the priests of the rites, who attended the statues, thought by the ignorant to be the literal embodiments of the gods; then came the drivers who were to race, resplendent in their whites and reds, and greens and blues; and at last a crew of dancers and mimes and clowns, who cavorted and tumbled upon the track while the priests relinquished their effigies to the platform around which the racers would drive their chariots.

And then the procession made its way to the Emperor's box. Jullus Antonius halted, saluted the Emperor, and gave him the games in dedication of his birthday. I must say, I looked at Jullus with some curiosity. He is an extraordinarily handsome man—his muscular arms brown from the sun, his face dark and slightly heavy, with very white teeth and curling black hair. It is said that he closely resembles his father, though he is less inclined to fat.

The dedication over, Jullus Antonius came closer to the box and called up to the Emperor:

"I'll join you later, when I get them started."

The Emperor nodded; he seemed pleased. He turned to me. "Antonius knows the horses, and the riders. Listen to him. You'll learn a bit about racing."

I must confess, Sextus, that the ways of the great are beyond me. The Emperor Octavius Caesar, master of the world, seemed concerned only with the impending races; to the son of a father whom he had defeated in battle and whom he forced to commit suicide, he was warm and friendly and natural; and he spoke to me as if we both were the most common of citizens. I remember that I thought briefly of the possibility of a poem upon the subject; but just as quickly I rejected the idea. I am sure that Horace could have done one, but that is not my (or our) sort of thing.

Jullus Antonius disappeared into a gate at the far end of the course, and a few moments later reappeared in his enclosure above the starting gate. A roar went up from the crowd; Jullus Antonius waved, and looked down at the racers lined up beneath him. Then he threw down the white flag, the barriers dropped, and in a cloud of dust the chariots set off.

I stole a glance at the Emperor, and was surprised to see that he seemed hardly interested in the race, now that it had begun. He discerned my glance, and said to me: "One does not bet on the first race, if one is wise. The horses are made so nervous by the procession that they seldom run according to their natures."

I nodded, as if what he said made sense to me.

Before the chariots had completed four of their seven laps, Jullus Antonius joined us. He seemed to know most of the people in the box, for he nodded to them in a friendly manner, and spoke a few of their names. He sat between the Emperor and Julia, and soon the three of them were exchanging wagers and laughing among themselves.

And so the afternoon went. Servants came with more food and wine, and with damp towels so that we could wipe the dust of the track from our faces. The Emperor wagered on every race, sometimes betting with several persons at once; he lost carelessly, and won with great glee. Just before the beginning of the last race, Jullus Antonius rose to leave, saying that he had some last duties at the starting gate. He bade me good-by, and expressed the hope that we might meet again; he bade good-by to the Emperor; and then bowed with what I took to be an elaborate and private irony to Julia, who threw back her head and laughed.

The Emperor frowned, but said nothing. Shortly thereafter, when the crowd had streamed out of the Circus, we took our leave. A few of us gathered at Sempronius Gracchus's home for a while in the evening; and I learned what may have been the source of the little byplay between Jullus Antonius and the Emperor's daughter. It was Julia herself who told me.

Julia's husband, Marcus Agrippa, had once been married to the younger Marcella, daughter of the Emperor's sister, Octavia; early in Julia's widowhood, he had been persuaded by the Emperor to divorce Marcella and marry Julia. And only recently had Jullus Antonius married that Marcella who had been Agrippa's wife.

"It's rather confusing," I said lamely.

"Not really," said Julia. And then she laughed. "My father has it all written down, so that one might always know to whom one is married."

And that, my dear Sextus, was my afternoon and evening. I saw the new, and I saw the old; and Rome is again becoming a place where one can live.

IV. THE JOURNAL OF JULIA, PANDATERIA (A.D. 4)

I am allowed no wine, and my food is the coarse fare of the peasant—black bread, dried vegetables, and pickled fish. I have even taken on the habits of the poor; at the end of my day, I bathe and take a frugal meal. Sometimes I take this meal with my mother, but I prefer to dine alone at the table before my window, where I can watch the sea roll in on the evening tide.

I have learned to savor the simple taste of this coarse bread, indifferently baked by my mute servant. There is a grainy taste of earth to it, enhanced by the cold spring water that serves as my wine. Eating it, I think of the hundreds upon hundreds of thousands of the poor and the enslaved who have lived before me—did they learn to savor their simple fare, as I have? Or was the taste of their food spoiled in their mouths by their dreams of the foods they might have eaten? Perhaps one must come to taste as I have done—from the richest and most exotic viands to those of the utmost simplicity. Yesterday evening, sitting at this table where I now write these words, I tried to recall the taste and texture of those foods, and I could not. And in that general effort to recall what I shall never experience again, I remembered an evening at the villa of Sempronius Gracchus.

I do not know why I remembered that particular evening; but suddenly, in this Pandaterian twilight, the scene sprang before me, as if it were being re-enacted upon the stage of a theater, and the remembering caught me before I could fend it off.

Marcus Agrippa had returned from the East and joined me in Rome, where he stayed for three months; and I became pregnant with my fourth child. Shortly thereafter, at the beginning of the year, my father sent Agrippa north to Pannonia, where the barbarian tribes were again threatening the Danube frontier. And Sempronius Gracchus, to celebrate my freedom and to herald the arrival of spring, gave a party, the like of which (he promised everyone) Rome had not seen before; all of my friends, from whom I had been separated while my husband was in Rome, would be there.

Despite the libels that were circulated later, Sempronius Gracchus was not my lover then. He was a libertine, and he treated me (as he treated many women) with an easy familiarity that might give rise to rumors, however false. At that time I was still conscious of the position which my father imagined I ought to occupy; and the time that I had been a goddess at Ilium was like a dream that waited to be fulfilled. I had, for a while, become someone other than myself.

Early in March, my father assumed the office of pontifex maximus, which had been vacated by the death of Lepidus; and he decreed a day of games to celebrate the event. Sempronius Gracchus said that if the old Rome must have a high priest, the new Rome demanded a high priestess; so Sempronius had his party at the end of March, and the city chattered with reports of what the guests were to expect. Some said that the guests would be transported from place to place on tamed elephants; some said that a thousand musicians had been brought from the East, and as many dancers; fancy fed upon expectation, and expectation nourished fancy.

But a week before the date of the party, news reached Rome that Agrippa, having more quickly settled the border uprising than anyone expected, had returned to Italy by way of Brindisi. He proposed to travel across country to our villa near Puteoli, where I was to meet him.

I did not meet him. Despite the annoyance of my father, I proposed that I join my husband the following week, after he had rested from his journey.

When I made this proposal, my father looked at me coldly. "I take it that you wish instead to attend that party which Gracchus is giving."

"Yes," I said. "I am to be the guest of honor. It would be rude to refuse, so late."

"Your duty is to your husband," he said.

"And to you, and to your cause, and to Rome," I said.

"These young people that you spend your time with," he said. "Has it occurred to you to compare their behavior with that of your husband and his friends?"

"These young people," I said, "are friends of mine. You may be assured that when I grow old, they will be old, too."

He smiled a little then. "You are right," he said. "One forgets. We all grow old, and we once were young. . . . I will explain to your husband that you have duties that keep you in Rome. But you will join him the week after."

"Yes," I said. "I will join him then."

Thus it was that I did not join my husband in the South, and thus it was that I attended Sempronius Gracchus's party. It became, indeed, the most famous party in Rome for many years, but for reasons that no one could have foreseen.

There were no tame elephants to transport the guests from place to place, or any of the other wonders that had been rumored; it was simply a gathering of a few more than a hundred guests, attended by nearly as many servants and musicians and dancers. We ate, we drank, we laughed. We watched the dancers dance, and joined them, to their delight and confusion; and to the sound of tambourines and harps and oboes we wandered through the gardens where fountains augmented the music and the torchlight played upon the water in another dance beyond the skill of human bodies.

Toward the end of the evening there was to be a special performance of the musicians and dancers, and the poet Ovid was to read a new poem, composed in my honor. Sempronius Gracchus had constructed for me a special chair of ebony, and secured it on a slight rise of the earth in the garden, so that all the guests could (as Gracchus said, with that irony he always had) pay me homage. . . .

I sat upon the chair, and saw them beneath me; a breeze came up, and I could hear it rustle among the cypresses and plane trees as it touched my silken tunic like a caress. The dancers danced, and the oiled flesh of the men rippled in the torchlight; and I remembered Ilium and Lesbos, where once I had been more than a mortal. Sempronius reclined beside my throne, on the grass; and for a moment I was as happy as I had been, and was myself.

But in this happiness, I became aware of someone standing beside me, bowing, attempting to get my attention; I recognized him as a servant from my father's household, and motioned for him to wait until the dance was over.

When the dancers had finished, and after the languorous applause of the guests, I allowed the servant to approach me.

"What does my father require of me?" I asked him.

"I am Priscus," he said. "It is your husband. He is ill. Your father leaves within the hour for Puteoli, and asks you to follow."

"Is it a serious matter, do you think?"

Priscus nodded. "Your father leaves this night. He is concerned."

I turned away from him, and looked at my friends who lounged in their ease and gaiety on the grassy slopes of Sempronius Gracchus's garden. The sound of their laughter, more charming and delicate than the music that had moved the dancers, floated up to me on the warm spring breeze. I said to Priscus:

"Return to my father. Tell him that I shall join my husband. Tell him not to wait for me. Tell him that I will leave here shortly, and will join my husband by my own means."

Priscus hesitated. I said:

"You may speak."

"Your father wishes you to return with me."

"Tell my father that I have always done my duty to my husband. I cannot leave now. I will see my husband later."

Priscus left then, and I started to speak to Sempronius Gracchus about the news I had received; but Ovid had taken his place before me, and had begun to speak the poem that he had written in my honor; I could not interrupt him.

At one time I knew that poem by memory; now I cannot recall a word of it. It is strange that I cannot, for it was a remarkable poem. I believe he never included it in one of his books; he said that it was my own, and should belong to no one else.

I did not see my husband again. He was dead by the time my father reached Puteoli; the illness, which the doctors never really discovered, was rapid and, I hope, merciful. He was a good man, and kind to me; I'm afraid he never realized I knew that. And I believe my father never forgave me for not joining him that night.

. . . It was the truffles. We had a delicacy of truffles that evening at the villa of Sempronius Gracchus. The earthy taste of those truffles was brought back by the earthy taste of this black bread, and that reminded me of the evening when I became a widow for the second time.

V. POEM TO JULIA:
ATTRIBUTED TO OVID (CIRCA 13 B.C.)

Restless, and wandering aimlessly, I pass temples and groves
  where
Gods live—Gods who invite passers to worship as they
Pause in the ancient groves where no ax has, in our memory's
  Mortal endurance, bit hungrily branches or shrubs.
Where might I pause? Janus watches unmoving as I approach
  him,
  And as I pass him by—quicker than any discerns
Save he. Now: here is Vesta—reliable, nice in her own way,
  I think; so I call out. She does not answer me, though.
Vesta is tending her flame—no doubt she is cooking for
  someone.
  She waves carelessly, still bending above her hot stove.
Sadly, I shake my head and move on. And now Jupiter
  thunders,
  Eyes crackling light at me. What? Does he insist that I
  swear
Something that might change my ways? "Ovid," he thunders,
  "is there no
  End to this love-making life? trivial versing? your vain
Posturing?" I try answering; no pause comes in the thunder.
  "Look to the years, poor poet; put on the senator's robes,
Think of the state—or at least try to." Deafened by thunder,
  I cannot
  Hear more. Sadly, I pass. Now at the Temple of Mars,
Weary, I halt; and I see, more fearsome than any—his left
  hand
  Sowing a field and his right slashing a sword through the
  air—
Ultimate Mars! old father of living and dying! I call him
  Joyfully, hoping at last I will be welcomed. But no.

He who protects and gives name to this March, to this month
    of my own birth,
  Will not receive me. I sigh; is there no place for me, Gods?

Now in despair, and ignored by the most ancient Gods of my
    ancient
Country, I wander beyond all of their precincts, and let
Various breezes carry me where they will. And at last—soft,
  Distant, and sweet—sounds come: oboe and tambour and
    flute;
Music of laughter; the wind; bird songs; leaves rustling in
    twilight.
  Now it's my hearing that leads; I have to follow, so that
Eyes may glimpse what the music has promised. And
    suddenly,
  Open before me, a stream, gushing with springs that invade
Cavern and grotto, and idly meander through lilies that
    tremble
  As if suspended in air; surely, I say to myself,
Surely there dwells here divinity—one that I haven't before
    known.
  Nymphs in their gossamer gowns celebrate spring and the
    night;
Yet, above all, high, radiant in beauty, a Goddess, to whom
    turn
  All eyes. Worshiped in joy, prayed to by gaiety, she smiles,
Brightening the twilight, more gently than does our Aurora;
    her beauty
  Outshines that of the high Juno. I think: It's a new
Venus come down from her high place; no one has seen her
    before, yet all
  Know they must worship her. Hail, Goddess! we leave the
    old Gods
Safe in their groves. Let them scowl at the world, let them
    scold who will listen;
  Here a new season is born; here a new country is found,
Deep in the soul of that Rome we loved of old. We must
    welcome the new, and
  Live in its joy, and be gay; soon will the night come on;
    soon,

Soon we will rest. But for now we are granted this beauty
    around us,
Granted this Goddess who gives life to this sacred grove.

VI. THE JOURNAL OF JULIA, PANDATERIA (A.D. 4)

My husband died on the evening of Sempronius Gracchus's
party; I would not have seen him, even if I had left as my father wanted. My father traveled all night without pausing, and
arrived at Puteoli the next day to find his oldest friend dead. It
is said that he looked at the body of my husband almost coldly,
and did not speak for a long time. And then with that cold
efficiency of his he spoke to Marcus Agrippa's aides, who were
putting on their shows of grief. He ordered the body prepared
for the procession that would return to Rome; he had word
sent back to the Senate to direct the procession; and—still
without rest—he accompanied the body of Marcus Agrippa
on its slow and solemn journey back to Rome. Those who saw
him enter the city said that his face was like stone as he limped
at the head of the procession.

I was, of course, present at the ceremonies in the Forum,
where my father delivered the funeral oration; and I can attest
to his coldness there. He spoke before the body of Marcus
Agrippa as if it were a monument, rather than what remained
of a friend.

But I can also attest to what the world did not know. After
the ceremony was over, my father retired to his room in his
private house on the Palatine, and he saw no one for three
days, during which time he took no food. When he emerged,
he appeared to be years older; and he spoke with an indifferent
gentleness that he had never had before. With the death of
Marcus Agrippa, there was a death within him. He was never
quite the same again.

To the citizens of Rome, my husband left in perpetuity the
gardens he had acquired during the years of his power, the
baths he had built, and a sufficient amount of capital to maintain them; in addition, he left to every citizen one hundred
pieces of silver; to my father he left the rest of his fortune, with
the understanding that it was to be used for the benefit of his
countrymen.

I thought myself cold, for I did not grieve for my husband. Beneath the ritual show of grief demanded by custom, I felt —I felt almost nothing. Marcus Agrippa was a good man; I never disliked him; I was, I suppose, fond of him. But I did not grieve.

I was in my twenty-seventh year. I had given birth to four children, and was pregnant with a fifth. I was a widow for the second time. I had been a wife, a goddess, and the second woman of Rome.

If I felt anything upon the occasion of my husband's death, it was relief.

Four months after the death of Marcus Agrippa, I gave birth to my fifth child. It was a boy. My father named the child Agrippa, after its father. He would, he said, adopt the child when it came of an age. It was a matter of indifference to me. I was happy to be free of a life that I had found to be a prison.

I was not to be free. One year and four months after the death of Marcus Agrippa, my father betrothed me to Tiberius Claudius Nero. He was the only one of my husbands whom I ever hated.

VII. LETTER: LIVIA TO TIBERIUS CLAUDIUS NERO, IN PANNONIA (12 B.C.)

You are, my dear son, to follow my advice in this matter.

You are to divorce Vipsania, as my husband has ordered; and you are to marry Julia. It has been arranged, and I have had no small part in the arrangement. If you wish to be angry at any for this turn of events, I must receive a part of that anger.

It is true that my husband has not honored you by adoption; it is true that he does not like you; it is true that he has sent you to replace Agrippa in Pannonia only because there is no one else readily available whom he can trust with the power; it is true that he has no intention of allowing you to succeed him; it is true that you are, as you have said, being used.

It does not matter. For if you refuse to allow yourself to be used, you will have no future; and all my years of dreaming of your eventual greatness will have been wasted. You will live out your life obscurely, in disfavor and contempt.

I know that my husband wishes only for you to act as nominal father to his grandsons, and that he hopes that one or the other of them may be made ready to succeed him, when they are old enough. But my husband's health has never been robust; one cannot know how much longer the gods will allow him to live. It is possible that you may succeed him, beyond his wishes. You have the name; you are my son; and I shall inevitably inherit some power, in the unhappy event of my husband's death.

You dislike Julia; it does not matter. Julia dislikes you; it does not matter. You have a duty to yourself, to your country, and to our name.

You will know in time that I am correct in this; and in time your anger will abate. Do not put yourself in the danger that your impetuosity might invite. Our futures are more important than our selves.

Chapter Five

I knew Livia's strength, and I knew the necessity of my father's policy. Livia's ambition for her son was the most steadfast and remarkable one that I have ever known; I have never understood it, and I suspect that I never shall. She was a Claudian; her husband before my father, whose name Tiberius retained, had been a Claudian. Perhaps it was the pride in that ancient name that persuaded her of Tiberius's destiny. I have thought, even, that she might have been more fond of her former husband than she pretended, and saw the memory of him in her son. She was a proud woman; and I have suspected from time to time that she felt that in some indefinable way she had been demeaned by taking to her bed my father, whose name at that time certainly was not so distinguished as her own.

My father had dreamed that Marcellus, his sister's son, would succeed him; thus, he betrothed me to him. Marcellus died. And then he dreamed that Agrippa would succeed him, or at least would bring one of my sons (whom my father had adopted) to a point of sufficient maturity to adequately carry on his duties. Agrippa died, and my sons were still children. No male of the Octavian line remained, and there was no one else whom he could trust or over whom he had sufficient power. There was only Tiberius, whom he detested, though he was his stepson.

Shortly after the death of Marcus Agrippa, the inevitability of what I had to do began to work inside me like an infected wound whose existence I would not admit. Livia smiled at me complacently, as if we shared a secret. And it was not until I was near the end of my year of mourning that my father summoned me to tell me what I already knew.

He met me himself at the door, and dismissed the servants who had accompanied me. I remember the quietness of the house; it was late in the afternoon, but no one seemed about, except my father.

He led me across the courtyard to the little cubicle off his bedroom that he used as an office. It was very sparsely furnished, with a table and a stool and a single couch. We sat and talked for a while. He asked about the health of my sons, and complained that I did not bring them to visit him often enough. We talked of Marcus Agrippa; he asked me if I still grieved for him. I did not answer. There was a silence. I asked:

"It is to be Tiberius, isn't it?"

He looked at me. He breathed deeply, and let his breath out, and looked at the floor. He nodded.

"It is to be Tiberius."

I knew it was to be, and had known; yet a shock like fear went through me. I said:

"I have obeyed you in all things since I can remember. It has been my duty. But in this I find myself near to disobedience."

My father was silent. I said:

"You once made me compare Marcus Agrippa to some of my friends of whom you disapproved. I joked, but I did compare; and you must know the outcome of that comparison. I ask you now to compare Tiberius to my late husband, and ask yourself how I might endure such a marriage."

He lifted his hands, as if to fend off a blow; still he did not speak. I said:

"My life has been at the service of your policy, of our family, and of Rome. I do not know what I might have become. Perhaps I might have become nothing. Perhaps I might—" I did not know what to say. "Must I go on? Will you not give me rest? Must I give my life?"

"Yes," my father said. He still did not look at me. "You must."

"Then it is to be Tiberius."

"It is to be Tiberius."

"You know his cruelty," I said.

"I know," my father said. "But I know too that you are my daughter, and that Tiberius would not dare to harm you. You will find a life beyond your marriage. In time, you will grow used to it. We all grow used to our lives."

"There is no other way?"

My father rose from the stool upon which he had been seated and paced restlessly across the floor. I noticed that his limp had grown more pronounced.

"If there was another way," he said at last, "I would take it. There have been three plots against my life since the death of Marcus Agrippa. They were foolishly conceived and ill managed, and therefore easy to discover and deal with. I have been able to keep them secret. But there will be others." His clenched fist struck his open palm softly, three times. "There will be others. The old ones will not forget that an upstart rules them. They will forgive neither his name nor his power. And Tiberius—"

"Tiberius is a Claudian," I said.

"Yes. Your marriage will not guarantee the safety of my authority, but it will help it. The nobility will be a little less dangerous if they believe that one of their own, one who has the Claudian blood, might succeed me. At least it will give them the possibility of patience."

"Will they believe that you would make Tiberius your successor?"

"No," my father said in a low voice. "But they would believe that I might make a Claudian grandson my successor."

Until that moment, although I had accepted the idea of the marriage as inevitable, I had not accepted its actuality.

I said: "So I am once again to be the brood sow for the pleasure of Rome."

"If it were only myself," my father said. He turned his back to me. I could not see his face. "If it were only myself, I would not ask this of you. I would not allow you to marry such a man. But it is not only myself. You have known that from the beginning."

"Yes," I said. "I have known that."

My father spoke as if he were talking to himself. "You have your children by a good man. That will comfort you. You will remember your husband through the children that you have."

We talked longer that afternoon, but I cannot remember what was said. I believe that a numbness must have come over me, for I remember feeling nothing after the first rush of bitterness. Yet I did not dislike my father for doing what he had to do; I should no doubt have done the same thing, had I been in his position.

Nevertheless, when the time came for me to leave, I asked my father a question. I did not ask it angrily, or in bitterness, or even in what might have seemed pity for myself.

"Father," I asked, "has it been worth it? Your authority, this Rome that you have saved, this Rome that you have built? Has it been worth all that you have had to do?"

My father looked at me for a long time, and then he looked away. "I must believe that it has," he said. "We both must believe that it has."

I was in my twenty-eighth year when I was married to Tiberius Claudius Nero. Within the year I had performed my duty, and delivered a child that bore the Claudian and Julian blood. It was a duty that both Tiberius and I found difficult to fulfill; and even that difficulty, it turned out, was in vain. For the child, a boy, died within a week after its birth. Thereafter, Tiberius and I lived apart; he was abroad much of the time, and I discovered again a way of life in Rome.

II. LETTER: PUBLIUS OVIDIUS NASO TO SEXTUS PROPERTIUS (10 B.C.)

Why do I write you the news of this place to which, you have made clear, you intend never to return? In which, you assure me, you no longer have the slightest interest? Is it that I distrust your resolve? Or do I hope merely (and in vain, no doubt) to shake it? In the five or six years that you have absented yourself from our city, you have written exactly nothing; and though you profess to be content with the rural charms of Assisi, and with your books, I cannot easily believe that you have forsaken the Muse whom once you served so well. She waits for you in Rome, I am sure; and I hope that you will return to her.

It has been a quiet season. A lovely lady (whose name you know, but which I shall not mention) has been absent from our circles for more than a year now, which absence has diminished our joy and our humanity. Widowed young, she was persuaded to remarry; and we all know that her new marriage has caused her great unhappiness. Though an important man, her husband is the dourest and least affable man you can imagine; he has no taste for happiness, and cannot endure it in another. He is relatively young—perhaps thirty-two or three—yet except for his appearance, one might take him for a graybeard, he is so irascible and disapproving. He is, I suppose, the kind of man that was common in Rome some fifty or sixty years ago; and he is admired by many of the "older families" simply because of that. No doubt he is a man of principle; yet I have observed that strong principle, coupled with a sour disposition, can be a cruel and inhuman virtue. For with that one can justify nearly anything to which the disposition leads him.

But we hope for the future. The lady of whom I have spoken, recently gave birth to a son who died within the week of his birth; the husband, it is understood, will absent himself from Rome on some business on the northern frontiers; and perhaps once again we shall have in our midst her whose wit, gaiety, and humanity may lead Rome out of the dull hypocrisy of its past.

I shall not subject you, my dear Sextus, to one of my disquisitions; but it seems to me more nearly true, as the years pass, that those old "virtues," of which the Roman professes himself to be so proud, and upon which, he insists, the greatness of the Empire is founded—it seems to me more and more that those "virtues" of rank, prestige, honor, duty, and piety have simply denuded man of his humanity. Through the labors of the great Octavius Caesar, Rome is now the most beautiful city in the world. May not its citizens now have the leisure to indulge their souls, and thus lead themselves, like the city in which they live, toward a kind of beauty and grace they have not known before?

III. LETTER: GNAEUS CALPURNIUS PISO TO TIBERIUS CLAUDIUS NERO, IN PANNONIA (9 B.C.)

My dear friend, I include herewith those reports you have asked me to gather. They come from a variety of sources, which for the time being I shall not name, in the unlikely event that eyes other than your own might see this. In some cases I have transcribed the reports verbatim; in others I have summarized. But the pertinent information is here; and you may be assured that the original documents are safe in my possession, in the event that you might, at a later time, wish to use them.

These reports cover the period of one month, November.

On the third day of this month, between the tenth and eleventh hours of the day, a litter borne by the slaves of Sempronius

Gracchus arrived at the lady's residence. The litter was evidently expected, for the lady emerged quickly from her house, and was borne across the city to the villa of Sempronius Gracchus, where a large party was assembled. During the banquet, the lady shared Gracchus's couch; they were observed to carry on a long and intimate conversation. No report of the substance of this conversation is available. A good deal of wine was consumed, so that by the end of the banquet many of the guests were inordinately gay. The poet Ovid read for their entertainment a poem of his that fit the occasion, which is to say one that was suggestive and improper. After this reading, a troupe of mimes performed *The Adulterous Wife*, but more brazenly than is usual. There was music afterward. At some time during the musical performance, people began to drift out of the hall; among these were the lady in question and Sempronius Gracchus. The lady was not seen again until near dawn, when she was observed entering the litter that had waited for her outside Sempronius Gracchus's residence. Thence she was transported to her home.

Two days before the Ides of this month, the lady entertained a group of her friends on her own responsibility. Among the male visitors were Sempronius Gracchus, Quinctius Crispinus, Appius Claudius Pulcher, and Cornelius Scipio; among the lesser guests were the poet Ovid and the Greek Demosthenes, the son of the actor and recently a citizen of Rome. The drinking of wine began early, shortly before the tenth hour, and continued late into the night. Though some of the guests left after the first watch, a larger number remained; and these late stayers, led by the lady, quit the rooms and the gardens, and made their way into the city, coming to a halt in their litters among the walks and buildings of the Forum. Though the Forum was nearly deserted at that hour, yet a small number of townspeople and tradesmen and police observed the party, and may be persuaded to testify, if the need arises. The drinking of wine continued, and that Demosthenes, the son of the actor, for the entertainment of the partygoers, delivered a mock oration from the rostrum beside the Senate House. It was extempore, and no copy could be made; but it seemed to burlesque the kind of speech that the Emperor has often delivered from the same spot. After the speech, the party disbanded; and the

lady returned to her home, accompanied by Sempronius Gracchus. It was nearing dawn.

For the next six days nothing untoward occurred in the lady's activities. She attended an official banquet at the home
of her parents; with her mother, she sat with the four elder
Vestal Virgins at the theater; she attended the Plebeian Games,
and remained circumspectly in the box with her father and his
friends, among whom were the consul of the year, Quinctius
Crispinus, and the proconsul Jullus Antonius.

On the fourth day after the Ides, she was guest of honor at
the villa of Quinctius Crispinus at Tivoli. She was accompanied
on her journey to Tivoli by Sempronius Gracchus and Appius
Claudius Pulcher and a retinue of servants. The weather being
mild, the entertainment was held out-of-doors; and it continued far into the night. There was much wine, there were male
and female dancers (who did not confine their performances to
the theater on the grounds, but danced, nearly naked, among
the guests, who wandered about the grounds), and musicians
who played Greek and Eastern music. At one time, a number of guests (the lady in question among them), both male
and female, plunged into the swimming pool; and though the
torchlight was dim, it could be seen that they had divested
themselves of their clothing, and were swimming freely together. After the swimming, the lady was seen to retreat into
the wooded part of the garden with the Greekling Demosthenes; they did not return for several hours. The lady stayed at
the villa of Quinctius Crispinus for three days, and each evening was much the same as the other.

I trust, my dear Tiberius, that these reports will be of use
to you. I shall continue to gather the information that you
require, in as discreet a manner as I can. And you may depend
upon me in any eventuality.

IV. LETTER: LIVIA TO TIBERIUS CLAUDIUS NERO, IN PANNONIA (9 B.C.)

You are to obey me in this, and you are to obey me at once. You
are to destroy all the "evidence" that you have so painstakingly

gathered, and you are to inform your friend Calpurnius that he is to do nothing more of this nature in your behalf.

What, may I ask, did you propose to do with this "evidence" you think you have? Do you propose to use it for a divorce? And if so, is the cause that your "honor" has been sullied? or do you dream that you will advance our cause by means of this divorce? In any of these fancies you are in error, and seriously so. Your "honor" will not be sullied as long as you remain abroad, for it will be clear to everyone that your wife is not under your control in such a circumstance, especially since you are serving your country and your Emperor; if on the other hand it comes to light that you have been gathering "evidence" and withholding it until a propitious time, then you will seem a fool, and all the honor that you may have gained shall have been lost. And if you dream that you advance yourself by insisting upon a divorce, you shall be mistaken again. Once such a step is taken, you will have no connection to that power we both have dreamed of; your wife may be "disgraced," but you will have gained nothing from that; you shall have lost the beginning that we have made.

It is true that at the moment it seems you have no chance to fulfill our mutual ambition; at the moment, even Jullus Antonius, the son of my husband's old enemy, has been advanced beyond you, and is as close to the accession of power as you are. Except for your name. My husband is old, and we cannot be sure of what the future will bring. Our weapon must be patience.

I know that your wife is adulterous; it is likely that my husband knows it also. Yet if you invoke those laws which he has made, and force him to punish his daughter by them, he will never forgive you; you might as well never have sacrificed your personal life in the first place.

We must bide our time. If Julia is to bring disgrace upon herself, she must do it herself; you must not be involved in any way, and you will be able to remain uninvolved only if you are careful to stay abroad. I urge you to lengthen your business in Pannonia as long as you reasonably can. So long as you remain away from your household, and away from Rome, our cause remains alive.

V. LETTER: MARCELLA TO JULIA (8 B.C.)

Julia, dear, please come to our house next Wednesday for
dinner, and a simple entertainment afterward. Some of your
friends (who are also *our* friends, I might add) will be there
—certainly Quinctius Crispinus, perhaps others. And of course
you are to bring anyone you wish.

I'm so *glad* that we've become friends again, after all these
years. I often remember our childhoods, with such fondness
—all those children! And the games we played! You, and poor
Marcellus, and Drusus, and Tiberius (sorry!) and my sisters—
I can't even *remember* them all now. . . . Do you remember
that even Jullus Antonius lived with us for a while, after his father's death? My mother cared for him when he was little, even
though he was not her own. And now Jullus is my husband. It's
a strange world. We have so many things to reminisce about.

Oh, my dear, I know it was I who caused the estrangement
between us. But I did feel awkward when my uncle (your father!) forced Marcus Agrippa to divorce me so that he could
marry you. I *know* you had nothing to do with it—but I was
young, and felt that *never* would I have a husband so important as Marcus was. And I *did* resent you, though I knew that
you were not at fault. But things work out for the best, I've
always believed; and perhaps Uncle Octavius is wiser than we
know. I am well pleased with Jullus. Oh, to tell the truth, Julia,
I am more pleased with him than I was with Marcus Agrippa.
He is younger and more handsome, and nearly as important
as Marcus was. Or he will be, I'm sure. My uncle seems very
fond of him.

Oh, I do chatter on, don't I? I'm still the chatterbox. We
don't change very much, do we, over the years? I *do* hope I
haven't offended you by anything I've said. I may not be any
wiser than I used to be, but I'm older; and I *have* learned that
it's foolish for women to hold their marriages against each
other. They have nothing to do with us, really, have they? At
least, so it seems to me.

Oh, you *must* come to our party. Everyone will be devas-
tated if you do not. Shall I have some of my servants call for
you? Or had you rather come by your own means? Do let me
know.

And bring *whomever* you like—though there will be some very interesting people here. We understand your situation perfectly.

VI. LETTER: GNAEUS CALPURNIUS PISO TO TIBERIUS CLAUDIUS NERO, IN GERMANY (8 B.C.)

I hasten to write you, my friend, before you get the news elsewhere and move without the knowledge that ought to determine any action. I have spoken to your mother; and despite our recent disagreement about the "reports" I have been sending you, we are, I believe, in full agreement about what you should do now. You must understand that she cannot speak directly; she will in no way betray the trust of her husband, nor will she recommend in secret what she could not do openly.

Within a few days you will receive a message from your stepfather in which you will be offered the consulship for next year. You may be pleased to know that I will be offered the co-consulship. In ordinary times, and under ordinary circumstances, this might have been thought of as a triumph; but neither the times nor the circumstances are ordinary, and it is essential that you act with the utmost caution.

You must, of course, accept the consulship; it would be unthinkable to refuse it, and disastrous to any future ambition you might have.

But you must not stay in Rome. Your stepfather's aim, of course, is to see that you do. But you must not. Before you leave Germany for the inauguration here, you must arrange your affairs so that it will become absolutely necessary for you to return there as soon as you possibly can. If you have no one you can trust, you must deliberately put your armies in a dangerous position, so that you must return to remedy the danger. I am sure you will be able to arrange something.

I shall now attempt to explain the reasons to justify this seemingly strange course that you must take.

Your wife continues to live as she has done for more than a year. She is openly contemptuous of your marriage contract, and careless of your reputation. Her father must know something of her conduct, yet he does nothing to prevent it—whether out of policy, or affection, or blindness, I do not know.

Despite the marriage laws (or perhaps because the Emperor himself inaugurated them), no one quite dares to be the public informer. Everyone knows that the laws are not enforced, and knows it would be inexpedient to insist upon their enforcement now, especially when they would be enforced against one so powerful and popular as your wife.

For she is powerful; and she is popular. Whether by design or accident (and I suspect the former), she has gathered into her circle some of the most powerful younger people in Rome. And it is here that the danger lies.

Those with whom she now regularly and most intimately consorts are your most dangerous enemies, and that they may also oppose the Emperor does not diminish the threat to your position. It does, in fact, enhance that threat.

As you well know, the power that you have is in your following, which is largely made up of families such as mine, who are (in your stepfather's words) the "old Republicans." We are rich, we are ancient, and we are closely knit; but it has been the policy for nearly thirty years to see to it that our public power is limited.

I fear that the Emperor wants you to return as a kind of buffer between the factions—his own, and that of the younger people, of whom Julia is an especial favorite.

If you return and allow yourself to be placed between them, you will, quite simply, be chewed up. And then you will be spit out. And your stepfather will have eliminated a dangerous rival, without having appeared to have lifted a hand. More importantly, he will have discredited an entire faction, without having elevated another. For as long as the faction of the young is fond of his daughter, he trusts that the danger that confronts him is negligible.

But you will be destroyed.

Consider the possibilities.

First: The Claudians and their followers may, under our leadership, gain enough power to turn the Empire back to the course it once followed, and to reinstitute the values and ideals of the old days. This is highly unlikely, but I grant that it is possible. But even if we are able to do so, then we will in all likelihood have united against us both the New People of your stepfather, and the New Young. I think we both would shudder at the consequences of such a unification.

Second: If you remain in Rome, your wife will continue to work against your interests—whether out of design or whim does not matter. She will do so. It is clear that she considers that her power comes from the Emperor, not from your name or station. She is the Emperor's daughter. You would be powerless against her will, and would be made to seem foolish if you set yourself against that will and did not prevail.

Third: Her continued life of dissipation and self-indulgence will, among both your friends and your enemies, offer continued occasion for gossip. Were you to act against this life of hers and insist upon a divorce, it would bring a scandal upon the Octavian house, it is true; it would also gain you the eternal despite of the Emperor and those who support him. If you do *not* act against her behavior, you will seem a weakling; you may even be accused of complicity in her law-breaking.

No, my dear Tiberius, you must not return to Rome with any intention of remaining here, while things are as they are. It is fortunate that I have been made co-consul with you. While you are away, you may be sure that I will protect your interests. It is ironic that I, unworthy as I am, shall be able to do so with more safety and more effectiveness than you might be able to do. It is a most depressing commentary upon the course that our lives have taken us.

Your mother sends her love to you. She will not write until you have received the message from the Emperor. Though she does not say so, I have good reason to believe that she supports me in this most urgent advice that I have given you.

VII. LETTER: NICOLAUS OF DAMASCUS TO STRABO OF AMASIA (7 B.C.)

For the past fourteen years, I have been content to live in Rome, first in the service of Herod and Octavius Caesar, and then in the service and friendship of Octavius Caesar alone; as you may have inferred from my letters, I had begun to think of this city as my home. I have broken most of my ties abroad; and since the deaths of my parents, I have felt no desire or necessity to return to the land of my birth.

But in a few days I shall be entering my fifty-seventh year; and during the last few months—perhaps it is longer—I have come to feel less and less that this is my homeland. I have come to feel that I am a stranger in this city that has been so kind to me, and in which I have been on the most intimate terms with some of the greatest men of our time.

Perhaps I am mistaken, but there seems to me an air of ugly unrest in Rome; it is not that uncertain restlessness that you must have known in the early days of Octavius Caesar's power, nor the restless excitement that infected me when I first came here fourteen years ago.

Octavius Caesar has brought peace to this land; not since Actium has Roman raised sword against Roman. He has brought prosperity to the city and the countryside; not even the poorest of the people wants for food in the city, and those in the provinces prosper from the beneficences of Rome and Octavius Caesar. Octavius Caesar has brought liberty to the people; no longer need the slave live in fear of the arbitrary cruelty of his master, nor the poor man fear the venality of the rich, nor the responsible speaker fear the consequences of his words.

And yet there is an ugliness in the air which, I fear, bodes ill for the future of the city, the Empire, and the reign of Octavius Caesar himself. Faction is ranged against faction; rumors abound; and no one seems content to live in the comfort and dignity which their Emperor has made possible. These are extraordinary people. . . . It is as if they cannot endure safety and peace and comfort.

So I shall leave Rome, this city that has been my home for so many rich years. I shall return to Damascus, and live out the days that remain to me among my books and whatever words I may write. I shall leave Rome in sorrow and love—without anger or recrimination or disappointment. And I realize as I write these words that I really am saying that I shall leave my friend, Octavius Caesar, with these feelings within me. For Octavius Caesar is Rome; and that, perhaps, is the tragedy of his life.

Oh, Strabo, if the truth were known, I feel that his life is over; in these past few years he has endured more than any man ought to endure. His face has upon it the inhuman composure of one who knows his life is over, and who waits only upon the decay of the flesh which signifies that end.

I have never known a man to whom friendship meant so much; and I mean a friendship of a particular kind. His true friends were those whom he knew when he was young, before he gained the power that he now has. I suppose that one with power can trust only those whom he knew and could trust before he had power; or it may be something else. . . . And now he is alone. He has no one.

Five years ago his friend, Marcus Agrippa, whom he had made his son-in-law, died in the loneliness of his return to Italy from a foreign land; and Octavius Caesar could not even bid him farewell. The year following, that good lady, his sister Octavia, died in the bitter isolation she had chosen away from the city and her brother, on a simple farm at Velletri. And now the last of his old friends, Maecenas, is dead; and Octavius Caesar is alone. No one from his youth remains alive, and therefore there is no one whom he feels that he can trust, no one to whom he can talk about those things that are nearest to him.

I saw the Emperor the week after Maecenas died; I had been in the country during the unhappy event, and I hurried back as soon as I learned of it. I tried to offer him my condolences.

He looked at me with those clear blue eyes that are so startlingly young in his lined face. There was a little smile on his lips.

"Well, our comedy is almost over," he said. "But there can be much sadness in a comedy."

I did not know what to say. "Maecenas," I began. "Maecenas—"

"Did you know him well?" Octavius asked.

"I knew him," I said, "but I do not think I knew him well."

"Few people knew him well," he said. "Not many liked him. But there was a time when we were young—Marcus Agrippa was young, too—there was a time when we were friends, and knew that we would be friends for as long as we lived. Agrippa; Maecenas; myself; Salvidienus Rufus. Salvidienus is dead too, but he died long ago. Perhaps we all died then, when we were young."

I became alarmed, for I had never heard my friend talk disconnectedly before. I said: "You are distraught. It is a heavy loss."

He said: "I was with him when he died. And our friend Horace was there. He died very quietly; he was conscious until the end. We talked about the old times together. He asked me to look out for Horace's welfare; he said that poets had more important things to do than to care for themselves. I believe

Horace sobbed and turned away. Then Maecenas said that he was tired. And he died."

"Perhaps he was tired."

He said: "Yes, he was tired."

There was a silence between us. And then Octavius said:

"And there will be another soon. Another who is tired."

"My friend—" I said.

He shook his head, still smiling. "I do not mean myself; the gods will not be so kind. It is Horace. I saw the look on his face afterward. Vergil, and then Maecenas, Horace said. He reminded me later that once, many years ago, in a poem—he was making a little fun of one of Maecenas's illnesses—and in the poem he said to Maecenas—can I remember it?—'On the same day shall the earth be heaped upon us both. I make the soldier's vow—you lead, and we shall go together, both ready to slog the road that ends all roads, inseparable friends.' . . . I don't think that Horace will outlive him by many months. He does not wish to."

"Horace," I said.

"Maecenas wrote badly," Octavius said. "I always told him that he wrote badly."

. . . I could not comfort him. Two months later Horace was dead. He was discovered one morning by his servant, in his little house above the Digentia. His face was quiet, as if he were simply asleep. Octavius had his ashes interred beside those of Maecenas, at the farther end of the Esquiline hill.

The only one alive now whom he loves is his daughter. And I fear for that love; I fear most desperately. For his daughter seems to grow more careless of her position month by month; her husband will not live with her, but remains abroad, though he is consul for the year.

I do not believe that Rome can endure the death of Octavius Caesar, and I do not believe that Octavius Caesar can endure the death of his soul.

VIII. THE JOURNAL OF JULIA, PANDATERIA (A.D. 4)

The way of life that I had in Rome, then, was a way of almost utter freedom. Tiberius was abroad, spending even the year of his consulship in Germany, organizing the outposts there against the encroachments of the barbarian tribes. Upon the few occasions that he had to return to Rome, he made a ritual visit, and quickly found business elsewhere.

The year after his consulship, my father, upon his own initiative, ordered a replacement for him on the German frontier, and ordered my husband to return to his duties in Rome. And Tiberius refused. It was, I thought, the most admirable thing he had ever done; and I almost respected him for his courage.

He wrote to my father indicating his refusal to pursue a public life, and expressing a desire to retire to the Island of Rhodes, where his family had extensive holdings, to devote the rest of his years to his private studies of literature and philosophy. My father pretended anger; I think that he was pleased. He imagined that Tiberius Claudius Nero had served his purpose.

I have often wondered what my life would have been like, had my husband meant what he wrote to my father.

Chapter Six

I. LETTER: GNAEUS CALPURNIUS PISO TO
TIBERIUS CLAUDIUS NERO, ON RHODES (4 B.C.)

My dear Tiberius, your absence is regretted by your friends in
Rome, which seems content in its own stagnation. Yet for the
present, perhaps that stagnation is fortunate. There is no news
of the past year that might profoundly affect our futures—and
that, I suppose, in these days, is the best we can hope for.

Herod the Jew is dead at last, and that is perhaps best for
all of us. During the last few years of his life, he was no doubt
mad, and growing madder; I know the Emperor had become
profoundly distrustful of him, and perhaps was considering to
effect his overthrow; and that, of course, if it came to war,
would have united the people behind the Emperor as nothing
else might have done. Just a few days before he died, Herod
had put to death one of his sons, whom he suspected of having
plotted against him—which gave the Emperor occasion for another of his witticisms. "I had rather," he said, "be Herod's pig
than his son." In any event, he is succeeded by another of his
sons, who has made sincere overtures to Rome; so the possibility of an armed excursion seems remote at this time.

Incidental to Herod's death, and preceding it by some time
was the departure from Rome of the unpleasant little Nicolaus
of Damascus, of whom the Emperor has always been so fond.
This may seem a trivial thing to record, yet it has some bearing
on our futures, I believe; for this departure has saddened the
Emperor more than one might reasonably expect. For now
none of his old close friends remain—and he seems to grow
more bitter and more private as the months succeed one another. And of course as one grows so, one's grasp upon power
and authority progressively must weaken.

And that grasp does seem to be weakening, though in ways
that are not yet significant enough to raise uncautious hopes.
For example: this year, he refused the clamor of the Senate
to accept his thirteenth consulship, pleading age and weariness. When it became clear that he was firm in his decision,
the Senate demanded to know whom he would have to serve

in his place—and he named Gaius Calvisius Sabinus! Do you remember the name? He is an old Caesarean, older even than the Emperor himself, and was consul once under the triumvirate, some thirty-five years ago, and served under the Emperor and Marcus Agrippa in the naval battles against Sextus Pompeius! The other consul is one Lucius Passienus Rufus (if you can imagine one of such an undistinguished name serving as consul), of whom you may or may not have heard. He is one of the new men, and I really have no idea of his allegiance to the family of the Emperor. I suspect that he will support the government, no matter who might be in power. So the consulship of this year promises no real consolidation that might be ranged against your eventual assumption of power. One who is senile, and one who has no name!

Somewhat more depressing (though we knew it had to come, eventually) were the rites of manhood conferred by the Emperor upon your stepsons. Gaius and Lucius (though neither is sixteen yet) are now citizens of Rome, they wear the togas of manhood, and no doubt as soon as he dares, the Emperor will give each of them at least nominal command of an army. Fortunately, he would not dare do more than that at the moment; and none of us knows what the future may bring. He will see that his old friend, Marcus Agrippa, though dead, is somehow in the center of things, even if it is only through his sons.

None of this, my dear Tiberius, need disturb us, I think; we have expected much of it, and that which we did not expect certainly has done us no harm.

But I fear that my concluding observations, tentative though they may be, offer some cause for apprehension. As you may have suspected, these observations have to do with the recent activities of your wife.

The scandals surrounding your wife have to some degree subsided, and they have done so for several reasons. First, the public is growing used to her behavior; second, what is often described as her infectious charm and gaiety have gone a long way toward softening opinion about her; third, her popularity among the young seems to be growing rather than diminishing; and last (and this is, for reasons that I shall shortly explain, the most ominous) her more blatant disregard of the proprieties seems to have diminished, and to have diminished substantially. It is to this last that I shall address myself.

Her rather indiscriminate and promiscuous choice of lovers seems to be a thing of the past. Sempronius Gracchus, as far as I can gather, is no longer her lover, but remains a friend; the same may be said for Appius Claudius Pulcher, and several others of note. The rather despicable toys with which she once amused herself (such as that Demosthenes, who was little better than a freedman, though technically a citizen) have been discarded; she seems, in a curious way, to have become more serious, though she retains sufficient wit and humor and abandon to still be a favorite of the frivolous young.

This is not to say that she is no longer adulterous; she is. But she seems to have chosen a lover of somewhat more substance than the riffraff she once favored, and one of more danger. It is Jullus Antonius, whose wife (once the intimate of Julia) has conveniently begun to travel abroad a good deal more than she is accustomed to doing.

There still are gatherings of her old friends, of course; but Jullus is always with her, and the discussions are reported to be of a much less frivolous nature than they had been before —though they remain, in my eyes, frivolous enough. At least, I trust that my reports are accurate in this respect. They discuss philosophy, literature, politics, and the theater—all such matters.

I do not know what to make of it, nor does Rome. I do not know whether her father is aware of this new affair, or not; if he is, he condones it; if he is not, he is a fool; for he therefore knows less than any of his fellow citizens. I do not know whether her recent behavior will help us or harm us. But you may be assured that I shall make it my business to keep myself fully informed upon this new development, and that I shall impart what I learn to you. I do have certain sources of information in the household of Jullus Antonius, and I shall develop more—discreetly, you may be sure. I shall not develop these sources in your wife's household. That would be altogether too dangerous to me, to you, and to our cause.

I trust that you will destroy this letter—or if you do not, be sure that it is secreted so that it cannot fall into unfriendly hands.

II. THE JOURNAL OF JULIA, PANDATERIA (A.D. 4)

My old friend and tutor Athenodorus once told me that our ancient Roman ancestors thought it unhealthy to bathe more than once or twice a month, that their daily ablutions consisted only of washing from their arms and legs the dirt that had been gathered in the day's labor. It was the Greeks, he said (with a kind of ironic pride), who had introduced to Rome the habit of the daily bath, and who had taught their barbaric conquerors the elaborate possibilities to be discovered in this ritual. . . . Though I have discovered the excellent simplicity of peasant food, and hence, no doubt, in that respect returned to the ways of my ancestors, I have not yet persuaded myself to adopt their habits of the bath. I bathe nearly every day, though I have no retinue to serve me with oils and perfumes, and my bath has but one wall—the rock cliff that rises above the shore of this island that is my home.

In the second year of my marriage to Marcus Agrippa, he opened in Rome, for the comfort of the people, what was said to be the most opulent bathhouse in the history of our city. Before that, I had not often attended the public baths; I believe that when I was young, Livia, fancying herself the model of the ancient virtues, disapproved of the luxuries offered at such places; and I must have caught the infection of her virtue. But my husband had read in a work by a Greek physician that bathing ought not to be looked upon merely as a luxury, that it might indeed contribute toward the prevention of mysterious illnesses that periodically swept through any crowded city; he wished to encourage as many of the common people as he might to avail themselves of such hygienic measures, and he persuaded me to occasionally forsake the privacy of my own bath and go among the people, so that all would see that it was fashionable to frequent the public baths. I went as if it were a duty; but I had to admit to myself that it became a joy.

I had never known the people before. I had seen them in the city, of course; they had waited on me in the shops; I had spoken to them, and they had spoken to me. But they had known always who I was: I was the Emperor's daughter. And I had known (or thought I had known) that their lives were so distant from my life that they might as well belong to another species. But naked in the bath, surrounded by hundreds of women who shout and scream and laugh, an Emperor's daughter is indistinguishable from the sausagemaker's wife. And an Emperor's daughter, vain though she might be, discovered an odd pleasure in such an indistinguishability. So I became a connoisseur of baths, and remained one for the rest of my life; and after the death of Marcus Agrippa, I discovered baths in Rome whose existence I had never dreamed of, which offered pleasures that it seemed I had known once, but in a dream. . . .

And now, still, I bathe nearly every day, as I imagine the soldier does, or the peasant, after his work is done, if there is a stream nearby. My bathhouse is the sea, and the marble of the pool is the black volcanic sand that gleams in the afternoon sun. There is a guard who attends me—I suspect that he has been ordered to prevent me from drowning myself—and stands impassively away from me, watching me incuriously as I let my body into the water. He is a castrate. His presence does not disturb me.

On quiet afternoons, when the sea is calm, the water is like a mirror; and I can see my face reflected there. It amazes me that my hair is nearly white now, and that my face is becoming lined. I was always vain about my hair, which began to go gray when I was very young. I remember that my father came upon me once when one of my maidservants was plucking out these gray hairs, and he asked me: "Do you look forward to becoming bald?" I replied that I did not. "Then," he said, "why do you allow your servant to hasten that condition?"

. . . The hair is nearly white, the face is lined—and as I lie in this shallow water, the body that I see seems to have nothing to do with that face. The flesh is as firm as it was twenty years ago, the stomach flat, the breasts full. In the chill water, the nipples harden, as once they did beneath the caress of a man; and in the buoyancy of the water, the body undulates, as once it did when it took its pleasure. It has served me well, this body, over the years—though it began its service later than it might have done. It began its service late, for it was told that it had no rights, and must by the nature of things be subservient to dictates other than its own. When I learned that the body had its rights, I had been twice married, and was the mother of three children. . . .

And yet that first knowledge was like a dream, and for many years I did not believe it. It was at Ilium, and I was worshiped as a goddess. Even now, it is like a dream; but I remember that at first I thought it all an amusing foolishness, a barbaric and charming foolishness.

I came to see that it was not. . . . That youth I chose that day in the sacred grove could not have been more than nineteen; he was virginal; and he was the most beautiful boy I have ever seen. I can close my eyes, and see his face, and almost feel the firm softness of his body. I believe that when I took him into the cave, I did not intend to fulfill the ritual. I did not have to; I was the Mother Goddess, and my power was absolute. But I did fulfill the ritual, and discovered the power of my body and the power of its needs. It was a power that I had been led to believe did not exist. . . . He was a sweet boy. I wonder what became of him, after he had entered the goddess and lain with her.

I believe that I must have lived in a kind of dream until the death of Marcus Agrippa. I could not believe what I had discovered, and yet its presence was with me always. I was faithful to Marcus Agrippa—I could not feel that the goddess who took her lover then at Ilium was wife to Agrippa; I was not faithful to Tiberius Claudius Nero.

It was after the death of that good man, Marcus Agrippa, that Julia, daughter of Octavius Caesar, the August, discovered the power that had been hidden within her, and discovered the pleasure that she could take. And the pleasure she could take became her power, and it seemed to her that it was a power beyond that of her name and of her father. She became herself.

Yes, it has served me well, this body that is blurred by the water, that I can see as I lie supine in my pelagic bath. It has served me, while seeming to serve others. It has always served me. The hands that roamed upon these thighs roamed there for me, and the lover to whom I gave pleasure was a victim of my own desire.

Sometimes, bathing, I think of those who have given this body pleasure—Sempronius Gracchus, Demosthenes, Appius Pulcher, Cornelius Scipio—I cannot remember their names now, many of them. I think of them, and their faces and their bodies merge together, so that they are as one face and one body. It has been six years since I have known the touch of a man, six years since beneath my hand or my lips I have caressed the flesh of a man. I am forty-four years old; four years ago I entered my old age. And yet still at the thought of that flesh, I can feel my heartbeat quicken; I can almost feel myself to be alive, though I know that I am not.

For a while, I was the goddess to the mystery of all my pleasure; and then I became a priestess, and my lovers were the adepts. I served us well, I think.

And I think at last of the one from whom I had ultimate pleasure, one for whom all the others had been prelude, so that I might be prepared. I knew the taste and heft of his flesh more intimately than I have known anything else. I cannot believe that six years have gone. I think of Jullus. The tide rises gently, and the water moves over my body. If I do not move, I may think of him. I think of Jullus Antonius.

III. LETTER: GNAEUS CALPURNIUS PISO TO TIBERIUS CLAUDIUS NERO, IN RHODES (3 B.C.)

I must say at the outset, my friend, that I am filled with apprehension; and I do not know whether it is justified or not. Let me give you a few causes, so that you may judge the soundness of my feeling.

Your wife, so far as I can determine, has been faithful to one man for more than a year. That man is, as you know, Jullus Antonius. She is seen constantly in his company; indeed, the liaison has become so widely recognized that no longer does either of them try to dissemble it. Julia receives guests in his home, and directs the activities of his servants. Her father *must* know of the affair by now, and yet he remains on friendly terms with his daughter, and with Jullus Antonius. Indeed, it is rumored that Julia intends to divorce you, and to take Jullus as her husband. In this rumor, however, I think we can put very little credence. Octavius Caesar would never allow it. Such an official alliance would simply destroy the delicate balance of power that he maintains, and he knows it. I mention the rumor only to indicate to you the extent to which the affair has grown.

Despite the scandal of his relationship with the Emperor's daughter—or perhaps because of it, for who can know the mind of the people?—Jullus Antonius's popularity continues to grow. He is at the moment, I should imagine, the second or third most powerful man in Rome; he has a very large following in the Senate, a following which, I must say, he uses most discreetly. Yet despite this discretion, I do not trust him. He has made no move to court those senators who have some influence with the military; he smiles upon all; he even conciliates his enemies. Yet I suspect that like his father he has ambitions; and unlike his father, he is able successfully to hide them from the world.

And, alas, your popularity among the masses seems to be suffering. It is in part because of your necessary absence; but that is not all. Libels and lampoons about you are being circulated widely; this, of course, is usual. Any distinguished figure is at the mercy of versifiers and hacks. But the distribution of these libels is far greater than any that I can remember in years; and they are particularly vicious. It seems almost that there is a campaign of sorts under way to discredit you. It does not do so, of course; no one who was your friend will become your enemy because of these libels, but it does seem to me symptomatic of something.

And the Emperor, I am sad to say, does not unbend in his dislike of you, despite the entreaties of your mother and your friends. So we can expect no comfort from that quarter.

Despite all this, you are well advised to remain in Rhodes. Let the lampooners invent their salacious poems; so long as you remain abroad, you will not be forced to act. The memories of men are short.

Jullus Antonius has gathered around him a band of poets —nothing so distinguished as those who were friends to the Emperor, of course; and I suspect that some of the libels and lampoons have been coming (anonymously, of course) from their pens. Some write poems in praise of Jullus himself; and he has let it be known that his maternal grandmother was a Julian. The man is ambitious; I am sure of that.

Do not forget that you have friends in Rome; and the absence of your self does not mean that you are not present in all our minds. It is a depressing strategy, but a necessary one, this waiting; do not become too impatient. I shall, as I have done, keep you informed of all that is pertinent here in the city.

IV. THE JOURNAL OF JULIA, PANDATERIA (A.D. 4)

Before Jullus Antonius and I became lovers, he used to tell me about his early years, and about his father, Marcus Antonius. Jullus had not been a favorite of his father—that distinction had fallen to his elder brother, Antyllus—and he remembered him as if he were almost a stranger. In his early years, Jullus had been raised by my Aunt Octavia, who, though a stepmother, was closer to him than had been his natural mother, Fulvia. Often, as I sat quietly with Jullus Antonius and Marcella and talked, it occurred to me that it was the most amazing thing that once, as small children, we had all played together at my Aunt Octavia's house. I could not then, and cannot now, re-call those days with any precision; and when we tried to talk about childhoods and dredge up memories of them, it was as if we were inventing the characters and the events of a play, out of the conventions and necessities of an occasion in the past.

I remember one late evening, when the three of us lingered after the other few dinner guests had departed. It was a hot night, so we removed ourselves from the dining room and lounged in the courtyard. The stars glimmered through the soft air; the servants had gone; and our music was the myste-rious chirp and whisper of the innumerable insects hidden in the darkness. We had been talking quietly, toward no particular end, of the accidents that befall us in our living.

"I have often wondered," Jullus said, "what would have hap-pened to our country had my father been less impetuous and had managed to prevail over my friend Octavius Caesar."

"Octavius," I said, "is my father."

"Yes," Jullus said. "And he is my friend."

"There are those," I said, "who would have preferred such a victory over him."

Jullus turned to me and smiled. In the starlight, I could see the heavy head and the delicate features. He did not resemble the busts of his father that I had seen.

"They are wrong," he said. "Marcus Antonius had the inherent weakness of trusting too much the mere presence of himself. He would have erred, and he would have fallen, sooner or later. He did not have the tenacity that the Emperor has."

"You seem to admire my father," I said.

"I admire him more than I do Marcus Antonius," he said.

"Even though—" I said, and paused.

He smiled again. "Yes. Even though Octavius had my father and my elder brother put to death. . . . Antyllus was very much like Marcus Antonius. I believe Octavius saw that, and he did what was necessary. I was never fond of Antyllus, you know."

I believed I shivered, though the night was not cool.

"If you had been a few years older . . ." I said.

"It is quite likely that he would have put me to death also," Jullus said quietly. "It would have been the necessary thing to do."

And then Marcella said petulantly and somewhat sleepily, "Oh, let's not talk of unpleasant things."

Jullus turned to her. "We are not, my dear wife. We are talking of the world, and of the things that have happened in it."

Two weeks later, we became lovers.

We became lovers in a way that I could not have foreseen. I believe I determined that evening that we should become lovers, and I foresaw nothing in my conquest of Jullus Antonius that I had not seen before. Though I was fond of his wife, who was also my cousin, I knew her to be a trivial woman, as tiresome as I have found most women to be; and Jullus I took to be a man like all men—as eager for the power of conquest as for the pleasure of love.

To one who has not become adept at the game, the steps of a seduction may appear ludicrous; but they are no more so than the steps of a dance. The dancers dance, and their skill is their pleasure. All is ordained, from the first exchange of glances until the final coupling. And the mutual pretense of both participants is an important part of the elaborate game —each pretends helplessness beneath the weight of passion, and each advance and withdrawal, each consent and refusal, is necessary to the successful consummation of the game. And yet the woman in such a game is always the victor; and I believe she must have a little contempt for her antagonist; for he is conquered and used, as he believes that he is conqueror and user. There have been times in my life when, out of boredom, I have abandoned the game, and have attacked frontally, as a conquering soldier might attack a villager; and always the man, however sophisticated, and however he might dissemble, was extraordinarily shocked. The end was the same, but the victory was, for me, never quite complete; for I had no secret to hide from him and, therefore, no power over his person.

And so I planned the seduction of Jullus Antonius as carefully as a centurion might plan an advance upon the flank of an enemy, though in the ritual of this encounter, I thought, the enemy always wishes to be conquered. I gave him glances, and looked away hurriedly; I brushed against him, and drew away as if in confusion; and at last, one evening, I managed to arrange for us to be alone together at my house.

I languished on my couch; I said words that invited the hearer to offer comfort; I let my dress fall away from my legs a little, as if in distracted carelessness. Jullus Antonius moved across the room and sat beside me. I pretended confusion, and let my breath come a little faster. I waited for the touch, and prepared a little speech about how fond I was of Marcella.

"My dear Julia," Jullus said, "however attractive I find you, I must tell you at once that I do not intend to become another stallion in your stable of horses."

I believe that I was so startled that I sat upright on my couch. I must have been startled, for I said the most banal thing I can imagine: "What do you mean?"

Jullus smiled. "Sempronius Gracchus. Quinctius Crispinus. Appius Pulcher. Cornelius Scipio. Your stable."

"They are my friends," I said.

"They are my associates," Jullus said, "and they have been of service to me from time to time. But they are horses I would not run with. And they are unworthy of you."

"You are as disapproving," I said, "as my father."

"Do you hate your father so much, then, that you will not attend him?"

"No," I said quickly. "No. I do not hate him."

Then Jullus looked at me intently. His eyes were dark, almost black; my father's were a pale blue; but Jullus's eyes had that same intense and searching light, as if something were burning behind them.

He said: "If we become lovers, we shall do so in my own time and at terms more advantageous to us both."

And he touched me on the cheek, and he rose, and he left my room.

I sat where he left me for a long while, and I did not move.

I cannot remember my emotions at being so refused; it had not happened to me before. I must have been angry; and yet I believe that there must have been a part of me that was relieved, and grateful. I had, I suppose, begun to be bored.

For the next several days, I saw none of my friends. I refused invitations to parties, and once when Sempronius Gracchus called upon me unexpectedly, I had my maidservant, Phoebe, tell him that I was ill, and was receiving no visitors. And I did not see Jullus Antonius—whether out of shame or anger, I did not know.

I did not see him for nearly two weeks. Then, late one afternoon, after a leisurely bath, I called for Phoebe to bring my oils and fresh clothing. She did not answer. I drew a large towel about me, and stepped into the courtyard. It was deserted. I called again. After a moment, I crossed the courtyard and entered my bedroom.

Jullus Antonius stood in the room, his tunic bright in the shaft of late afternoon sunlight that slanted through the window, his face dark in the dimness above that light. For several moments neither of us moved. I shut the door behind me, and came a little into the room. Still Jullus did not speak.

Then, very slowly, he came toward me. He took the large towel that I had wrapped around me and slowly unwound it from my body. Very gently he toweled my body dry, as if he were a slave of the bath. Still I did not move, or speak.

Then he moved back from me, and looked at me where I stood, as if I were a statue. I believe I was trembling. Then he stepped forward, and touched me with his hands.

Before that afternoon, I had not known the pleasures of love, though I thought I had. And in the months that came that pleasure fed upon itself, and multiplied; and I came to know the flesh of Jullus Antonius as I had known nothing else in my life.

Even now, after these many years, I can taste the bitter sweetness of that body, and feel beneath me the firm warmth. It is odd that I can do so, for I know that the flesh of Jullus Antonius now is smoke, and is dispersed into the air. That body is no more, and my body remains upon this earth. It is odd to know that.

No other man has touched me since that afternoon. No man shall touch me for as long as I shall live.

V. LETTER: PAULLUS FABIUS MAXIMUS TO OCTAVIUS CAESAR (2 B.C.)

I do not know whether I write you now as a consular of Rome who is your friend, or as your friend who is consular. But write you I must, though we see each other almost daily; for I cannot bring myself to speak to you of this matter, and I cannot put what I have to say in one of the official reports that I give you regularly.

For what I must reveal to you touches upon both your public and your private self, and in such a way that I fear they cannot be separated, one from the other.

When at first you commissioned me to investigate those rumors which you judged to be so persistent as to be disturbing, I must confess that I thought you overly concerned; rumor has become a way of life in Rome, and if one spent his time investigating all that he hears, he would have not a moment for any other business that ought to occupy him.

So, as you know, I began the investigation with a great deal of skepticism. Now I am grieved to tell you that your apprehensions were right, and that my skepticism was mistaken. The matter is even more alarming than you initially suspected, or could imagine.

There is a conspiracy; it is a serious one; and it has gone a long way toward its completion.

I shall report my findings as impersonally as I can, though you must understand that my feelings protest against the coldness of my words.

Some seven or eight years ago—the year that he was consul —I relinquished to the service of Jullus Antonius, as a librarian, a slave whom I had some time earlier freed, one Alexas Athenaeus. Alexas was and is an intelligent man, and he has remained loyal to me through the years; he is, I am sure, a friend. When he learned of the investigation that I was conducting, he came to me in a highly distraught state, bringing with him certain documents removed from the secret files of Jullus Antonius, and a most disturbing series of revelations.

There is, incontrovertibly, a plot against the life of Tiberius. The conspirators have enlisted the support of certain factions around Tiberius in his retirement on Rhodes. He is to be murdered in the manner that Julius Caesar was murdered, and it is to be made to appear that it is an authentic uprising against the authority of Rome. Upon this pretext of danger it is planned that an army will be raised under the auspices of the senator and ex-consul Quinctius Crispinus, an army whose ostensible purpose is to protect Rome, but whose actual purpose is to assume power for that faction of conspirators. If you oppose the raising of this army, you will be made to seem either cowardly or indifferent; if you do not oppose it, your position and your person may be in danger, to say nothing of the orderly future of Rome.

For there is strong evidence that a direct attempt will be made upon your life at the same time that the plan against Tiberius is carried out.

The conspirators are: Sempronius Gracchus, Quinctius Crispinus, Appius Pulcher, Cornelius Scipio—and Jullus Antonius. I know that the last name will cause you particular pain. I thought that Jullus was my friend, and I thought that he was yours. He is not.

But this is not the end of my report.

Alexas Athenaeus also informs me that, unknown to Jullus Antonius, there has been insinuated into his household a slave who is in actuality an agent of Tiberius. This agent is privy to the conspiracy; indeed, it was something that Tiberius's agent let drop that first aroused Alexas's suspicions. And the agent has been reporting directly to Tiberius about this affair. And from all that I can gather, Tiberius has a plan, too.

He apparently has as much proof of the conspiracy as I have;

and he intends to use that proof. He intends to expose the plot in the Senate, using as his spokesman the senator and his former co-consul, Gnaeus Calpurnius Piso. Calpurnius will insist upon a trial for high treason; the Senate will be forced to accede; and Tiberius will then raise an army in Rhodes and return to Rome, ostensibly to protect you and the Republic. He will be a popular hero; and you will be made to seem a fool. Your power will be lessened; Tiberius's will be increased.

And there is yet one other thing—and this is the most painful —that I must report.

I am sure that for the past several years, since the absence of Tiberius Claudius Nero, you have not been wholly unaware of the activities of your daughter. I am sure that, out of pity for her condition and affection for her person, you have, as it were, looked the other way—as have most of your friends and even some of your enemies. But it becomes clear from the documents that I have in my possession that Julia has been intimate with each of the conspirators; and her lover of the past year has been Jullus Antonius.

If this matter becomes public, it will almost certainly be made to seem that Julia herself is a part of the conspiracy; and Tiberius may well have in his possession papers more damaging even than we imagine.

In any public disclosure of the plot, she will inevitably be implicated; and she is likely to be implicated so deeply that she will be found as guilty of treason as any of the conspirators. It is no secret that she hates Tiberius, and it is no secret that she loves Jullus Antonius.

The documents to which I have referred are safe in my possession. No eyes have seen them save mine and Alexas Athenaeus (and, of course, the conspirators), and no other eyes shall. They remain for you to use, however you may judge best.

Alexas Athenaeus is in hiding; the documents that he has taken from the household of Jullus Antonius are sure to be missed, and he is in fear of his life. He is a most remarkable man; I trust him. He has assured me that, despite his loyalty to Jullus Antonius, he reveres the Emperor and Rome more. He will testify, if need be. But I make a personal plea. If it is necessary to put him to torture to validate his testimony, please arrange it so that it is a ritual torture rather than an actual one.

I trust the man implicitly, and he has lost nearly everything by his revelation.

My dear friend, I should have preferred to take my life than to be the one to impart this information. But I could not do so. The safety of your person and the safety of Rome must take precedence over what now seems would be the comfort of my own death.

I await whatever orders you may give me.

VI. THE JOURNAL OF JULIA, PANDATERIA (A.D. 4)

It is autumn in Pandateria. Soon the winds from the north will sweep down upon this bare place. They will whistle and moan among the rocks, and the house in which I live, though of this native stone, will tremble a little in the blast; and the sea will beat with a seasonal violence against the shores. . . . Nothing changes here except the seasons. My mother still shouts at our servant and directs her indefatigably—though it seems to me that in the last month or so she has become a bit more feeble. I wonder if she, too, will die upon this island. If so, it will be her choice; I have none.

I have not written in this journal for nearly two months; I had thought that I had no more to tell myself. But today I was allowed to receive another letter from Rome, and it contained news that reawakened memories of the days when I lived; and so I speak once more to the wind, which will carry my words away in the mindless force of its blowing.

When I wrote of Jullus Antonius, it occurred to me that it was an appropriate moment to cease these entries into a journal that sprawls itself out to no end. For if for a year or so Jullus Antonius brought me alive into the world, he also thrust me into this slow death of Pandateria, where I may observe my own decay. I wonder if he foresaw what might happen. It does not matter. I cannot hate him.

Even at the moment when I knew that he had destroyed us both, I could not hate him.

And so I must write of one more thing.

In the consulships of Octavius Caesar, the August, and Marcus Plautius Silvanus, I, Julia, daughter of the Emperor, was accused before the Senate convening in Rome of adultery, and hence of the abrogation of the marriage and adultery laws that my father had passed by edict some fifteen years before. My accuser was my father. He went into great detail about my transgressions; he named my lovers, my places of assignation, the dates. In the main, the details were correct, though there were a few unimportant names that he omitted. He named Sempronius Gracchus, Quinctius Crispinus, Appius Pulcher, Cornelius Scipio, and Jullus Antonius. He described drunken revels in the Forum and debaucheries upon the very rostrum from which he had first delivered his laws; he spoke of my fre- quentation of various houses of prostitution, implying that out of perversity I sold myself to anyone who would have me; and he described my visits to those unsavory bath establishments which permitted mixed bathing and encouraged all manner of licentiousness. These were exaggerated, but there was enough truth in them to make them persuasive. And at last he de- manded that, in accordance with his Julian Laws, I be exiled forever from the precincts of Rome, and requested the Senate to order me placed on this Island of Pandateria, to live out the rest of my life in contemplation of my vices.

If history remembers me at all, history will remember me so.

But history will not know the truth, if history ever can.

My father knew of my affairs. They may have pained him, but he knew of them, and understood the reasons, and did not upbraid me unduly. He knew of my love for Jullus Antonius; and I think, almost, he was happy for me.

In the consulships of Gaius Octavius Caesar and Marcus Plautius Silvanus, I was condemned to exile so that I would not be executed for high treason to the state of Rome.

It is autumn in Pandateria, and it was autumn that afternoon in Rome, six years ago, when my life ended. I had not heard from Jullus Antonius in three days. Messages that I sent to his house were returned unopened; servants that I sent were refused admittance, and came back to me puzzled. I tried to imagine those things that one in love is wont to imagine, but I could not; I knew that something else was amiss, something more serious than what a jealous lover can raise to beguile and torture one's lover.

But I swear I did not know what it was. I did not suspect; or perhaps I refused to suspect. I did not even suspect when, on the afternoon of the third day of silence, a messenger and four guards appeared at my door to take me to my father. I did not even recognize the significance of the guards; I imagined that they were there as a ritual protection of my safety.

I was carried by litter through the Forum and up the Via Sacra and past the Imperial Palace and up the little hill to my father's house on the Palatine. The house was almost deserted, and when the guards escorted me across the courtyard toward my father's study, the few servants who were around turned away from me, as if in fear. It was only then, I believe, that I began to suspect the seriousness of the matter.

When I was led into the room, my father was standing, as if awaiting me. He motioned the guards to leave; and he looked at me for a long while before speaking.

For some reason, I observed him very closely for those moments. Perhaps, after all, I did know. His face was lined, and there were wrinkles of weariness around those pale eyes; but in the dimness of the room, the face might have been that of him whom I remembered from my childhood. At last I said:

"What strangeness is this? Why have you brought me here?"

Then he came forward and very gently kissed me on the cheek.

"You must remember," he said, "that you are my daughter and that I have loved you."

I did not speak.

My father went to the little desk in the corner of the room and leaned on it for a moment, his back toward me. Then he straightened, and without turning said to me:

"You know one Sempronius Gracchus."

"You know that I do," I said. "You know him also."

"You have been intimate with him?"

"Father—" I said.

Then he turned to me. In his face there was such pain that I could not bear to look. He said: "You must answer me. Please, you must answer."

"Yes," I said.

"And Appius Pulcher."

"Yes."

"And Quinctius Crispinus and Cornelius Scipio?"

"Yes," I said.

"And Jullus Antonius."

"And Jullus Antonius," I said. "The others—" I said, "the others do not matter. That was a foolishness. But you know that I love Jullus Antonius."

My father sighed. "My child," he said, "this is a matter that has nothing to do with love." He turned away from me once again and picked up some papers from his desk. He handed them to me. I looked at them. My hands were shaking. I had not seen the papers before—some letters, some diagrams, some that appeared to be timetables—but now I saw names that I knew. My own. Tiberius's. Jullus Antonius's. Sempronius, Cornelius, Appius. And I knew then why I had been summoned before my father.

"Had you read those documents carefully," my father said, "you would know that there is a conspiracy against the government of Rome, and that the first step of that conspiracy is the murder of your husband, Tiberius Claudius Nero."

I did not speak.

"Did you know of this conspiracy?"

"Not a conspiracy," I said. "No. There was no conspiracy."

"Did you speak to any of these—friends of yours about Tiberius?"

"No," I said. "Perhaps in passing. It was no secret that—"

"That you hated him?"

I was silent for a moment. "That I hated him," I said.

"Did you speak of his death?"

"No," I said. "Not in the way you mean. Perhaps I said—"

"To Jullus Antonius?" my father asked. "What did you say to Jullus Antonius?"

I heard my voice tremble. I stiffened my body, and said as clearly as I could: "Jullus Antonius and I wish to marry. We have talked of marriage. It is possible that in talking of that I spoke wishfully of Tiberius's death. You would not have given your consent for a divorce."

"No," he said sadly, "I would not."

"Only that," I said. "I said only that."

"You are the Emperor's daughter," my father said; and he was silent for a moment. Then he said: "Sit down, my child," and motioned me toward the couch beside his desk.

"There is a conspiracy," he said. "There is no doubt of that.

Your friends, whom I have named; and others. And you are involved. I do not know the extent and nature of your guilt, but you are involved."

"Jullus Antonius," I said. "Where is Jullus Antonius?"

"That will wait," he said. And then he said: "Did you know that there was also an attempt to be made on my life, after the death of Tiberius?"

"No," I said. "That cannot be true. It cannot be."

"It is true," my father said. "I should hope that they would not have let you know, that they would have made it appear an accident, or illness, or something of that sort. But it would have happened."

"I did not know," I said. "You must believe that I did not know."

He touched my hand. "I hope you never knew of that. You are my daughter."

"Jullus—" I said.

He raised his hand. "Wait. . . . If I were the only one who had this knowledge, the matter would be simple. I could suppress it, and take my own measures. But I am not the only one. Your husband—" He said the word as if it were an obscenity. "Your husband knows as much as I do—perhaps more. He has had a spy in the household of Jullus Antonius, and he has been kept informed. It is Tiberius's plan to expose the plot in the Senate, and to have his representatives there press for a trial. It will be a trial for high treason. And he plans to raise an army and return to Rome, to protect my person and the Roman government against its enemies. And you know what that would mean."

"It would mean the danger of your losing your authority," I said. "It would mean civil war again."

"Yes," my father said. "And it would mean more than that. It would mean your death. Almost certainly, it would mean your death. And I am not sure that even I would have the power to prevent that. It would be a matter for the Senate, and I could not interfere."

"Then I am lost," I said.

"Yes," my father said, "but you are not dead. I could not endure knowing that I had allowed you to die before your time. You will not be tried for treason. I have composed a letter which I shall read to the Senate. You will be charged under my law of the crime of adultery, and you will be exiled from the city and provinces of Rome. It is the only way. It is the only way to save you and Rome." He smiled a little, though I could see that his eyes were moist. "Do you remember, I used to call you my Little Rome?"

"Yes," I said.

"And now it seems that I was right. The fate of one may be the fate of the other."

"Jullus Antonius," I said. "What will become of Jullus Antonius?"

He touched my hand again. "My child," he said, "Jullus Antonius is dead. He took his life this morning, when he learned beyond doubt that the plot was discovered."

I could not speak. At last I said, "I had hoped . . . I had hoped . . ."

"I shall not see you again," my father said. "I shall not see you again."

"It does not matter," I said.

He looked at me once more. Tears came into his eyes, and he turned away. In a few moments the guards entered the room and took me away.

I have not seen my father since. I understand that he will not speak my name.

In the news that I received from Rome this morning was the information that after all these years Tiberius has returned from Rhodes and is now in Rome. He has been adopted by my father. If he does not die, he will succeed my father, and become the Emperor.

Tiberius has won.

I shall write no more.

BOOK III

August 9

My dear Nicolaus, I send you affectionate greetings and my thanks for the recent shipment of those dates of which I am so fond, and which you have been kind enough to furnish me over the years. They have become one of the most important of the Palestinian imports, and they are known throughout Rome and the Italian provinces by your name, which I have given them. The *nicolai*, I call them; and the designation has persisted among those who can afford their cost. I hope it amuses you to learn that your name is known better to the world through this affectionate eponym than through your many books. We both must have reached the age when we can take some ironic pleasure in the knowledge of the triviality into which our lives have finally descended.

I write you from aboard my yacht, the one upon which so many years ago you and I used to float leisurely among the little islands that dot our western coastline. I sit where we used to sit—slightly forward of midship upon that canopied platform which is raised so that the constant and slow movement of the sea might be observed without hindrance. We set sail from Ostia this morning, in an unseasonably chill hour before dawn; and now we are drifting southward toward the Campanian coast. I have determined that this shall be a leisurely journey. We shall depend upon the wind to carry us; and if the wind refuses, we shall wait upon it, suspended by the vast buoyancy of the sea.

Our destination is Capri. Some months ago one of my Greek neighbors there asked me to be guest of honor at the yearly gymnastic competitions of the island youths; I demurred at the time, pleading the burden of my duties. But a short while ago, it became necessary for me to travel southward upon another mission, and I determined to give myself the pleasure of this holiday.

Last week my wife approached me with that rather stiff formality she has never lost, and requested that I accompany her and her son on a journey to Benevento, where Tiberius had to go on some business connected with his new authority. Livia explained to me what I already knew—that the people are not persuaded that I am fond of my adopted son, and that any display of affection or concern I might show will make more secure Tiberius's eventual succession to my power.

Livia did not put the matter so directly as she might have; despite her strength of character, she has always been a diplomatic woman. Like one of those Asian diplomats with whom I have dealt for much of my life, she wished to suggest to me without brutally stating the case that the days of my life are limited in number, and that I must prepare the world for that moment of chaos which will inevitably follow my death.

Of course Livia was in this matter, as she has been in most, quite reasonable and correct. I am in my seventy-sixth year; I have lived longer than I have wished to do, and such mortal boredom does not augment longevity. My teeth are nearly gone; my hand shakes with an occasional palsy that always surprises me; and the lassitude of age pulls at my limbs. When I walk I sometimes have the odd sensation that the earth is shifting under my feet, that the stone or brick or patch of earth upon which I step may suddenly move beneath me, and that I shall fall free of the earth to wherever one goes when time has done with one.

And so I acceded to her request, upon the condition that my accompaniment be a ceremonial one. I suggested that since sea travel makes Tiberius ill, he and his mother take the land route to Benevento, while I traveled in the same direction by sea; and that if either of them wished to make public the news that the husband or adoptive father traveled with them, I would not dispute it. It is a satisfactory arrangement, and I imagine that we all are more pleased by this subterfuge than we would have been by public honesty.

Yes, my wife is a remarkable woman; I suppose I have been more fortunate than most husbands. She was quite beautiful when she was a young woman, and she has remained handsome in her age. We loved each other for only a few years after our marriage, but we remained civil; and I believe that at last we have become something like friends. We understand each other. I know that deep within her Republican heart she has always felt that she married beneath her station, that she traded the dignity of an ancient title for the brute power of one whose authority was undeserved by his more humble name. I have come to believe that she did so for the sake of her first-born son, Tiberius, of whom she has always been inexplicably fond and for whom she has had the most tenacious ambition. It was this ambition that caused the first estrangement between us, an estrangement that grew so deep that at one period of our lives I spoke to my wife only of topics upon which I had made careful notes, so that we might not have to undergo the additional burden of misunderstanding, real or imagined.

And yet in the long run, despite the difficulties it caused between Livia and me, that ambition has worked for the benefit of my authority and Rome. Livia was always intelligent enough to know that her son's succession depended upon my undisputed retention of power, and that he would be crushed if he were not bequeathed a stable Empire. And if Livia is capable of contemplating my death with equanimity, I am sure that she will contemplate her own in a like manner; her real concern is for that order of which we both are mere instruments.

So in deference to that concern for order which I share, and in preparation for this voyage, three days ago I deposited at the Temple of the Vestal Virgins four documents, which are to be opened and read to the Senate only upon the occasion of my death.

The first of these was my will, which bequeaths to Tiberius two-thirds of my personal property and wealth. Though Tiberius does not need it, such a bequest is a necessary gesture to an adequate succession. The remaining portion—except for minor provisions for the citizens and various relatives and friends—goes to Livia, who will also by this document be adopted into the Julian family and be allowed to assume my titles. The name will not please her, but the titles will; for she will understand that her son will gain stature by her possession of the titles, and that her ambition will be that much more easily fulfilled.

The second was a set of directions for my funeral. Those who must put themselves in charge of that matter will no doubt exceed my instructions, which are lavish and vulgar enough to begin with; but such excesses invariably please the people, and thus are necessary. I comfort myself with the knowledge that I shall not have to be witness to this last display.

The third document was an account of the state of the Empire; the number of soldiers on active duty, the amount of money that is (or should be) in the treasury, the financial obligations of the government to provincial leaders and private citizens, the names of those administrators who are fiscally and otherwise responsible—all such matters that must be made public for the safety of order and the prevention of corruption. In addition, I appended to this account some rather strong suggestions to my successor. I advised against extending Roman citizenship so capriciously or widely as to weaken the center of the Empire; I advised that all men in high administrative positions be employed by the government at a fixed salary, so that temptation to undue power and corruption might be lessened; and at last I charged that under no circumstances should the frontiers of the Empire be extended, but that the military be employed solely to defend the established borders, especially against the German barbarians, who seem never to tire of their senseless adventures. I do not doubt that this advice will in the long run be ignored; but it will not be ignored for a few years, and I shall at least have left my country that poor legacy.

And finally I gave into the keeping of those estimable ladies in their temple a statement setting forth an account of all my acts and services to Rome and its Empire, with directions that this statement be engraved upon bronze tablets and attached to the columns that so ostentatiously rear themselves outside that even more ostentatious mausoleum that I have decreed will hold my ashes.

I have a copy of this document before me now, and from time to time I glance at it, as if it were written by someone else. During its composition, I found it necessary upon occasion to refer to a number of other works, so distant in time were some of the events that I had to record. It is remarkable to have grown so old that one must depend upon the work of others to search into one's own life.

Among the books that I consulted were that *Life* of me which you wrote when you first came to Rome, those portions of our friend Livy's history of the *Founding of the City* which concerns itself with my early activities, and my own *Notes for an Autobiography*—which, after all these years, seems also to be the work of someone other than myself.

If you will forgive me for saying so, my dear Nicolaus, all these works seem to me now to have one thing in common: they are lies. I trust that you will not too literally apply this remark to your own work; I believe you know what I mean. There are no untruths in any of them, and there are few errors of fact; but they are lies. I wonder if during your recent years of study and contemplation in the quiet of your far Damascus you have come to understand this also.

For it seems to me now that when I read those books and wrote my words, I read and wrote of a man who bore my name but a man whom I hardly know. Strain as I might, I can hardly see him now; and when I glimpse him, he recedes as in a mist, eluding my most searching gaze. I wonder, if he saw me, would he recognize what he has become? Would he recognize the caricature that all men become of themselves? I do not believe that he would.

In any event, my dear Nicolaus, the completion of these four documents and their deposition in the Temple of the Vestal Virgins may be the last official acts that I shall have to perform; I have in effect relinquished my power and my world, as I drift now southward toward Capri, and drift more slowly toward that place where so many of my friends have gone before me; and at last I may have a holiday that will not be disturbed by a sense of anything left undone. For the next few days at least, no messenger will rush to me with news of a new crisis or a new conspiracy; no senator will importune my support for a foolish and self-serving law; no lawyers will plead before me the cases of equally corrupt clients. My only duties are to this letter that I write, to the great sea that so effortlessly supports our frail craft, and to the blue Italian sky.

For I travel nearly alone. Only a few oarsmen are aboard, and I have given orders that they shall not work at their stations except in the event of a sudden squall; a few servants lounge at the stern of our craft and laugh lazily; and near the prow, always observing me carefully, is a new young physician that I have employed, one Philippus of Athens.

I have outlived all my physicians; it is some comfort to me to know that I shall not outlive Philippus. Moreover, I trust the boy. He seems to know very little; and he has not yet been a doctor long enough to have learned the easy hypocrisy that deludes his patients and at the same time fills his own purse. He offers no remedy for my disease of age, and does not subject me to those tortures for which so many so eagerly pay. He is a little nervous, I think, knowing himself to be in the presence of one whom he too solemnly considers the Emperor of the world; yet he is not obsequious, and he looks after my comfort rather than what another might think of as my health.

I tire, my dear Nicolaus. It is my age. The vision in my left eye is nearly gone; yet if I close it, I can see, to the east, the soft rise of the Italian coast that I have loved so well; and I can discern, even in the distance, the shapes of particular cottages and even make out the movement of figures upon the land. In my leisure I wonder at the mysterious lives that these simple folk must lead. All lives are mysterious, I suppose, even my own.

Philippus is stirring and looking at me apprehensively; it is clear that he wants me to cease what he takes to be work rather than pleasure. I shall forestall his ministrations, desist for a while, and pretend to rest.

At the age of nineteen, on my own initiative and at my own expense, I raised an army by means of which I restored liberty to the Republic, which had been oppressed by the tyranny of faction. For this service the Senate, with complementary resolutions, enrolled me in its order, in the consulship of Gaius Pansa and Aulus Hirtius, and gave me at the same time consular precedence in voting and the authority to command soldiers. As propraetor it ordered me, along with the consuls, "to see that the Republic suffered no harm." In the same year, moreover, as both consuls had fallen in war, the people elected me consul and a triumvir for settling the constitution.

Those who slew my father I drove into exile, punishing their deed by due process of law; and afterward when they waged war upon the Republic I twice defeated them in battle. . . .

Thus begins that account of my acts and services to Rome of which I wrote you earlier this morning. During the hour or so that I lay on my couch and pretended to doze, thus affording

Philippus some respite from his concern, I thought again of this account, and of the circumstances under which it was composed. It shall be engraved upon bronze tablets and attached to those columns that mark the entrance to my mausoleum. Upon those columns there will be sufficient space for six of these tablets, and each of the tablets may contain fifty lines of about sixty characters each. Thus the statement of my acts must be limited to about eighteen thousand characters.

It seems to me wholly appropriate that I should have been forced to write of myself under these conditions, arbitrary as they might be; for just as my words must be accommodated to such a public necessity, so has my life been. And just as the acts of my life have done, so these words must conceal at least as much truth as they display; the truth will lie somewhere beneath these graven words, in the dense stone which they will encircle. And this too is appropriate; for much of my life has been lived in such secrecy. It has never been politic for me to let another know my heart.

It is fortunate that youth never recognizes its ignorance, for if it did it would not find the courage to get the habit of endurance. It is perhaps an instinct of the blood and flesh which prevents this knowledge and allows the boy to become the man who will live to see the folly of his existence.

Certainly I was ignorant that spring when I was eighteen years of age, a student at Apollonia, and got the news of Julius Caesar's death. . . . Much has been made of my loyalty to Julius Caesar; but Nicolaus, I swear to you, I do not know whether I loved the man or not. The year before he was killed, I had been with him on his Spanish campaign; he was my uncle, and the most important man I had ever known; I was flattered at his trust in me; and I knew that he planned to adopt me and make me his heir.

Though it was nearly sixty years ago, I remember that afternoon on the training field when I got the news of my Uncle Julius's death. Maecenas was there, and Agrippa, and Salvidienus. One of my mother's servants brought me the message, and I remember that I cried out as if in pain after I read it.

But at that first moment, Nicolaus, I felt nothing; it was as if the cry of pain issued from another throat. Then a coldness came over me, and I walked away from my friends so that they could not see what I felt, and what I did not feel. And as I walked on that field alone, trying to rouse in myself the appropriate sense of grief and loss, I was suddenly elated, as one might be when riding a horse he feels the horse tense and bolt beneath him, knowing that he has the skill to control the poor spirited beast who in an excess of energy wishes to test his master. When I returned to my friends, I knew that I had changed, that I was someone other than I had been; I knew my destiny, and I could not speak to them of it. And yet they were my friends.

Though I probably could not have articulated it then, I knew that my destiny was simply this: to change the world. Julius Caesar had come to power in a world that was corrupt beyond your understanding. No more than six families ruled the world; towns, regions, and provinces under Roman authority were the currencies of bribery and reward; in the name of the Republic and in the guise of tradition, murder and civil war and merciless repression were the means toward the accepted ends of power, wealth, and glory. Any man who had sufficient money could raise an army, and thus augment that wealth, thereby gaining more power, and hence glory. So Roman killed Roman, and authority became simply the force of arms and riches. And in this strife and faction the ordinary citizen writhed as helplessly as the hare in the trap of the hunter.

Do not mistake me. I have never had that sentimental and rhetorical love for the common people that was in my youth (and is even now) so fashionable. Mankind in the aggregate I have found to be brutish, ignorant, and unkind, whether those qualities were covered by the coarse tunic of the peasant or the white and purple toga of a senator. And yet in the weakest of men, in moments when they are alone and themselves, I have found veins of strength like gold in decaying rock; in the cruelest of men flashes of tenderness and compassion; and in the vainest of men moments of simplicity and grace. I remember Marcus Aemilius Lepidus at Messina, an old man stripped of his titles, whom I made publicly to ask forgiveness for his crimes and beg for his life; after he had done so in front of the troops that he had once commanded, he looked at me for a long moment without shame or regret or fear, and smiled, and turned from me and strode erectly toward his obscurity.

And at Actium, I remember Marcus Antonius at the prow of his ship looking at Cleopatra as her own fleet departed leaving him to certain defeat, knowing at that moment that she had never loved him; and yet upon his face was an expression almost womanly in its wise affection and forgiveness. And I remember Cicero, when at last he knew that his foolish intrigues had failed, and when in secret I informed him that his life was in danger. He smiled as if there had been no strife between us and said, "Do not trouble yourself. I am an old man. Whatever mistakes I have made, I have loved my country." I am told that he offered his neck to his executioner with that same grace.

Thus I did not determine to change the world out of an easy idealism and selfish righteousness that are invariably the harbingers of failure, nor did I determine to change the world so that my wealth and power might be enhanced; wealth beyond one's comfort has always seemed to me the most boring of possessions, and power beyond its usefulness has seemed the most contemptible. It was destiny that seized me that afternoon at Apollonia nearly sixty years ago, and I chose not to avoid its embrace.

It was more nearly an instinct than knowledge, however, that made me understand that if it is one's destiny to change the world, it is his necessity first to change himself. If he is to obey his destiny, he must find or invent within himself some hard and secret part that is indifferent to himself, to others, and even to the world that he is destined to remake, not to his own desire, but to a nature that he will discover in the process of remaking.

And yet they were my friends, and dearest to me at the precise moment when in my heart I gave them up. How contrary an animal is man, who most treasures what he refuses or abandons! The soldier who has chosen war for his profession in the midst of battle longs for peace, and in the security of peace hungers for the clash of sword and the chaos of the bloody field; the slave who sets himself against his unchosen servitude and by his industry purchases his freedom, then binds himself to a patron more cruel and demanding than his master was; the lover who abandons his mistress lives thereafter in his dream of her imagined perfection.

Nor do I exempt myself from this contrariness. When I was young, I would have said that loneliness and secrecy were forced upon me. I would have been in error. As most men do, I chose my life then; I chose to enclose myself in the half-formed dream of a destiny no one could share, and thus abandoned the possibility of that kind of human friendship which is so ordinary that it is never spoken of, and thus is seldom cherished.

One does not deceive oneself about the consequences of one's acts; one deceives oneself about the ease with which one can live with those consequences. I knew the consequences of my decision to live within myself, but I could not have foreseen the heaviness of that loss. For my need of friendship increased to the degree that I refused it. And I believe that my friends—Maecenas, Agrippa, Salvidienus—never could fully understand that need.

Salvidienus Rufus, of course, died before he could have understood it; like myself, he was driven by energies of youth so remorseless that consequence itself became nothing, and the expense of energy became its own end.

The young man, who does not know the future, sees life as a kind of epic adventure, an Odyssey through strange seas and unknown islands, where he will test and prove his powers, and thereby discover his immortality. The man of middle years, who has lived the future that he once dreamed, sees life as a tragedy; for he has learned that his power, however great, will not prevail against those forces of accident and nature to which he gives the names of gods, and has learned that he is mortal. But the man of age, if he plays his assigned role properly, must see life as a comedy. For his triumphs and his failures merge, and one is no more the occasion for pride or shame than the other; and he is neither the hero who proves himself against those forces, nor the protagonist who is destroyed by them. Like any poor, pitiable shell of an actor, he comes to see that he has played so many parts that there no longer is himself.

I have played these roles in my life; and if now, when I come to the final one, I believe that I have escaped that awkward comedy by which I have been defined, it may be only the last illusion, the ironic device by which the play is ended.

When I was young, I played the role of scholar—which is to say, one who examines matters of which he has no knowledge.

With Plato and the Pythagoreans, I floated through the mists
where souls are supposed to wander in search of new bodies;
and for a while, convinced of the brotherhood of man and
beast, I refused to eat any flesh, and felt for my horse a kinship that I had not dreamed possible. At the same time, and
without discomfort, I as fully adopted the opposing doctrines
of Parmenides and Zeno, and felt at home in a world that was
absolutely solid and motionless, without meaning beyond itself, and hence infinitely manipulatable, at least to the contemplative mind.

Nor when the course of events around me altered did it
seem inappropriate that I assume the mask of a soldier and
play out that appointed role. *Wars, both civil and foreign, I
undertook throughout the world, on sea and land. . . . Twice I
triumphed with an ovation, thrice I celebrated curule triumphs,
and was saluted as Imperator twenty-one times.* Yet, as others
have suggested, perhaps with more tact than I deserved, I was
an indifferent soldier. Whatever successes I have claimed came
from those more skillful in the art of battle than I—Marcus
Agrippa first, and then those who inherited the skills of which
he was author. Contrary to the libels and rumors spread during
the early days of my military life, I was not more cowardly than
another, nor did I lack the will to endure the hardships of campaign. I believe that I was then even more nearly indifferent to
the fact of my existence than I am now, and the endurance of
the rigors of warfare afforded me a curious pleasure that I have
found elsewhere neither before nor since. But it always seemed
to me that there was a peculiar childishness about the fact of
war, however necessary it might have been.

It is said that in the ancient days of our history, human rather
than animal sacrifices were offered to the gods; today we are
proud to believe that such practices have so receded into the
past that they are recorded only in the uncertainty of myth and
legend. We shake our heads in wonderment at that time so far
removed (we say) from the enlightenment and humanity of the
Roman spirit, and we marvel at the brutality upon which our
civilization is founded. I, too, have felt a distant and abstract
pity for that ancient slave or peasant who suffered beneath the
sacrificial knife upon the altar of a savage god; and yet I have
always felt myself to be a little foolish to do so.

For sometimes in my sleep there parade before me the tens of thousands of bodies that will not walk again upon the earth, men no less innocent than those ancient victims whose deaths propitiated an earlier god; and it seems to me then, in the obscurity or clarity of the dream, that I am that priest who has emerged from the dark past of our race to speak the rite that causes the knife to fall. We tell ourselves that we have become a civilized race, and with a pious horror we speak of those times when a god of the crops demanded the body of a human being for his obscure function. But is not the god that so many Romans have served, in our memory and even in our time, as dark and fearsome as that ancient one? Even if to destroy him, I have been his priest; and even if to weaken his power, I have done his bidding. Yet I have not destroyed him, or weakened his power. He sleeps restlessly in the hearts of men, waiting to rouse himself or to be aroused. Between the brutality that would sacrifice a single innocent life to a fear without a name, and the enlightenment that would sacrifice thousands of lives to a fear we have named, I have found little to choose.

I determined early, however, that it was disruptive of order for men to give honor to those gods who spring from the darkness of instinct. Thus I encouraged the Senate to declare the divinity of Julius Caesar, and I erected a temple in his honor in Rome so that the presence of his genius might be felt by all the people. And I am sure that after my death, the Senate will in like manner see fit to declare my divinity also. As you know, I am already thought to be divine in many of the towns and provinces of Italy, though I have never allowed permission for this cult to be practiced in Rome. It is a foolishness, but it is no doubt necessary. Nevertheless, of all the roles that I have had to play in my lifetime, this one of being a mortal god has been the most uncomfortable. I am a man, and as foolish and weak as most men; if I have had an advantage over my fellows, it is that I have known this of myself, and have therefore known their weaknesses, and never presumed to find much more strength and wisdom in myself than I found in another. It was one of the sources of my power, that knowledge.

It is afternoon; the sun begins its slow descent to the west. A calm has come upon the sea, so that the purple sails above me hang slack against the pale sky; our boat sways gently upon the waves, yet does not move forward to any perceptible degree. The oarsmen, who all day have been taking their leisure, look at me with a bored apprehension, expecting me to rouse them from their ease and urge them to labor against the calm that has stilled us. I shall not do so. In half an hour, or an hour, or two hours, a breeze will rise; then we shall make for the coast and find safe harbor and drop anchor. Now I am content to drift where the sea will take me.

Of all the curses of age, this sleeplessness which increasingly I must endure is the most troublesome. As you know, I have always been subject to insomnias; but when I was younger, I was able to put that nocturnal restlessness of mind to purpose, and I almost enjoyed those moments when it seemed to me that all the world slept and I alone had leisure to observe its repose. Beyond the urgings of those who would advise my policy in the terms of their own vision of the world, which is to say in their visions of themselves, I had the freedom of contemplation and silence; many of my most important policies were determined as I lay awake on my bed in the early hours before dawn. But the sleeplessness that I have recently been undergoing is of a different kind. It is no longer that restlessness of a mind so intent upon its play that it is jealous of that slumber which would rob it of consciousness of itself; it is, rather, a sleeplessness of waiting, a long moment in which the soul prepares itself for a repose unlike any that mind or body has ever known before.

I have not slept this night. Near sunset, we harbored a hundred yards or so offshore in a little cove that protects the few fishing boats of some nameless village, the thatched huts of which are nestled on the slopes of a small hill perhaps half a mile inland. As evening came on, I watched the lamps and the fires glimmer against the dark, and watched until they flickered out. Now, once again, the world is asleep; a number of the crew has taken advantage of the night air, and chosen to sleep on deck; Philippus is below, next to the cabin in which he thinks I rest. Gently, invisibly, the little waves lap against the side of our ship; the night breeze whispers upon our furled sail; the lamp on my table glows fitfully, so that now and then I have to strain my eyes to see these words that I write to you.

During this long night, it has occurred to me that this letter does not serve the purpose for which it was intended. I wished at first, when I began writing to you, merely to thank you for the *nicolai*, to assure you of my friendship, and perhaps to give us both some comfort in our old age. But in the course of that friendly courtesy, I can see that it has become something else. It has become another journey, and one which I did not foresee. I go toward Capri for my holiday; but it seems to me now, in the quietness of this night, beneath the mysterious geometry of the stars, where nothing exists except this hand that forms the curious letters which by some other mysterious process you will understand, it seems to me that I go somewhere else, to a place as mysterious as any I have ever seen. I shall write further tomorrow. Perhaps we can discover that place toward which I travel.

August 10

There was a damp chill in the air when we embarked from Ostia yesterday, and rather foolishly I remained on deck so that I might see the Italian shore recede in the soft mist, and so that I could begin this letter to you—a letter which I intended at first simply to convey my thanks for the *nicolai*, and to assure you of my continuing affection, despite our long absence from each other. As you shall have understood by now, however, the letter has become more than that; and I beg the indulgence of an old friend to hear out what I shall discover to say. In any event, the chill brought on one of my colds, which has become a fever; and I became once again accustomed to an indisposition. I have not told Philippus of this new illness; I have, rather, reassured him of my well-being; for it appears that I am under some compulsion to complete the task of this letter, and I do not wish to be interrupted by Philippus's solicitudes.

The question of my health has always been less interesting to me than it has been to others. From my youth I have been frail, and subject to such a variety of maladies that more doctors than I like to imagine have been made wealthy. Their wealth has been largely unearned, I suspect; but I do not begrudge them what I have given them. So often has my body led me near death that, in my sixth consulship, when I was thirty-five years old, *the Senate decreed that every four years the consuls and the priests of the orders undertake vows and make sacrifices for the state of my health. To fulfill these vows, games were held* so that the people might be made to remember their prayers, *and all citizens, both individually and by municipalities, were encouraged to perform continued sacrifices for my health at the temples of the gods.* It was a foolishness, of course; but it did at least as much for my health as the various medications and treatments that my doctors subjected me to, and it let the people feel that they were participating in the fate of the Empire.

Six times during my life has this tomb of my soul led me to the brink of that eternal darkness into which all men sink at last, and six times it has stepped back, as if at the behest of a destiny it could not overmaster. And I have long outlived my friends, in whose lives I existed more fully than in my own. All are dead, those early friends. Julius Caesar died at fifty-eight, nearly twenty years younger than I am now; and I have always believed that his death came as much from that boredom which presages carelessness as from the assassins' daggers. Salvidienus Rufus died at the age of twenty-three, in his pride and by his own hand, because he thought he had betrayed our friendship. Poor Salvidienus. Of all my early friends, he was most like me. I wonder if he ever knew that the betrayal was my own, that he was the innocent victim of an infection that he caught from me. Vergil died at fifty-one, and I was at his bedside; in his delirium, he thought he died a failure, and made me promise to destroy his great poem on the founding of Rome. And then Marcus Agrippa, at the age of fifty, who had never had a day of illness in his life, died suddenly, at the height of his powers, before I could reach him to bid him farewell. And a few years later—in my memory, the years dissolve into one another, like the notes of tambour and lute and trumpet, to make a single sound—within a month of each other, Maecenas and Horace were dead. Except for you, my dear Nicolaus, they were the last of my old friends.

It seems to me now, as my own life is slowly trickling away, that there was a kind of symmetry in their lives that my own has not had. My friends died at the height of their powers, when they had accomplished their work and yet had further triumphs to look forward to; nor were they so unfortunate to come to believe that their lives had been lived for nothing. For nearly twenty years, it seems to me now, my life has been lived for nothing. Alexander was fortunate to have died so young, else he would have come to know that if to conquer a world is a small thing, to rule it is even less.

As you know, both my admirers and detractors have likened me to that ambitious young Macedonian; it is true that the Roman Empire is now constituted of many of the lands that Alexander first conquered, it is true that like him I came to my power as a young man, and it is true that I have traveled in many of the lands that he first subjugated to his rather barbaric will. But I have never wished to conquer the world, and I have been more nearly ruled than ruler.

The lands that I have added to our Empire, I have added to insure the safety of our frontiers; had Italy been safe without those additions, I should have been content to remain within our ancient borders. As it turned out, I have had to spend more of my life than I would have liked in foreign lands. From the mouth where the Bosporus spills into the Black Sea to the farthest shores of Spain I have traveled, and from the cold wastes of Pannonia where the German barbarians are contained to the burning deserts of Africa. Yet more often than not I did not go as conqueror, but as emissary, in peaceful negotiation with rulers that were more likely to resemble tribal chieftains than heads of state, and who often had neither Latin nor Greek. Unlike my uncle Julius Caesar, who found some odd renewal in such extended travels, I never felt at home in those distant lands, and always longed for the Italian countryside, and even Rome.

And yet I came to have respect and even some affection for these strange people, so unlike Romans, with whom I had to deal. The northern tribesman, his half-naked body swathed in the skins of animals he had killed with his own hands, staring at me through the smoke of a campfire, was not unlike the swarthy African who entertained me in a villa the opulence of which would dim that of many a Roman mansion; nor was the turbaned Persian chieftain with his carefully curled beard and his curious trousers and cloak embroidered with gold and silver thread, his eyes as watchful as those of a serpent, unlike the Numidian savage chieftain who stood before me with his javelin and his shield of elephant hide, his ebon body wrapped loosely with the skin of a leopard. At one time or another I have given power to such men; I have made them kings in their lands and given them the protection of Rome. I have even made them citizens, so that the stability of their kingdoms might have the name of Rome behind them. They were barbarians; I could not trust them; and yet more often than not I found as much to admire in them as I did to detest. And knowing them made me more fully understand my own countrymen, who have often seemed to me as strange as any people who inhabit the world.

Beneath the perfume and under the coiffure of the Roman dandy who minces about his carefully tended garden in his toga of forbidden silk, there is the rude peasant who walks behind his plough and is anointed by the dust of his labor; hidden by the marble façade of the most opulent Roman mansion there is the straw-thatched hut of the farmer; and within the priest who by solemn ritual dispatches the white heifer there is the laboring father who would provide meat for his family's table and clothing against the winter's chill.

At one time, when it was necessary for me to secure the favor and gratitude of the people, I was in the habit of arranging gladiatorial games. At that time, most of the contestants were criminals whose offenses would otherwise have been punishable by death or deportation. I gave them the choice of the arena or the legal consequences of their acts, and further stipulated that the defeated fighter might plead for mercy, and that he who survived three years, no matter what his offense might have been, would be set free. I had no surprise that the criminal condemned to death or relegated to the mines might choose the arena; but it always surprised me that a criminal who had been exiled from Rome more quickly chose the arena than the relatively safe hazards of a strange country. I never enjoyed these contests, yet I forced myself to attend them, so that the people might feel that I shared in their pleasure; and their pleasure in this carnage was extraordinary to behold. It was as if they took some strange sustenance into their lives by observing another less fortunate than they relinquish his own. More than once I have had to calm the lust of the mob by sparing the life of some poor wretch who had fought bravely;

and I have observed, as if upon a single face, the sullen disappointment of unconsummated lust. At one time I suspended those games in which one or another of the contestants was intended to lose his life, and substituted boxing matches, in which Italian was pitted against barbarian; but this did not please the mob, and others who wished to buy the admiration of the people produced spectacles of such carnage and abandon that I was forced to give up my substitution and once again be guided by the desires of my countrymen, so that I might control them.

I have seen gladiators return to their quarters from the arena, covered with sweat and dust and blood, and weep like women over some small thing—the death of a pet falcon, an unkind note from a lover, the loss of a favorite cloak. And in the stands I have seen the most respectable of matrons, her face distorted as she shouted for the blood of a hapless fighter, later in the quietness of her home care for her children and her servants with the utmost gentleness and affection.

Thus if there runs in the blood of the most worldly Roman the rustic blood of his peasant ancestor, there runs also the wild blood of the most untamed northern barbarian; and both are ill-concealed behind the façade he has erected not so much to disguise himself from another as to mask himself against his own recognition.

It occurs to me, as we drift slowly southward, that without my having to tell them to do so, the crew, since they are under no compulsion to make haste, have instinctively kept always in sight of land, though as the wind has changed we have had to go to some trouble to make corrections to follow the irregular line of the coast. There is something deep within the Italian heart that does not like the sea, a dislike that has seemed to some so intense as to be nearly abnormal. It is more than fear, and it is more than the natural propensity of the peasant to husband his land, and to avoid that which is so unlike it. Thus the eagerness of your friend Strabo to sail blithely upon unknown seas, in search of strangeness, would bewilder the ordinary Roman, who ventures beyond the sight of land only upon the occasion of such a necessity as war. And yet under Marcus Agrippa the Roman navy has become the most powerful in the history of the world, and the battles that saved Rome from its enemies were fought upon the sea. Nevertheless, the dislike remains. It is a part of the Italian character.

It is a dislike of which the poets have been aware. You know that little poem of Horace's addressed to the ship that was bearing his friend Vergil to Athens? He advanced the conceit that the gods had separated land from land by the unimaginable depths of ocean so that the peoples in those lands might be distinct, and man in his foolhardiness launches his frail bark upon an element that ought not to be touched. And Vergil himself, in his great poem upon the founding of Rome, never speaks of the sea except in the most ominous of terms: Aeolus sends his thunder and winds upon the deep, waves are lifted so high that they obscure the stars, timbers are broken, and men see nothing. And even now, after so many years and so many readings of the poem, I am still moved nearly to tears by the thought of Palinurus, the helmsman, betrayed by the god of sleep into the depths of the ocean, where he drowns, and for whom Aeneas mourns, thinking of him as too trustful in the calm of sea and sky, lying naked on an unknown shore.

Of the many services that Maecenas performed for me, the most important seems to me now to be this: He allowed me to know the poets to whom he gave his friendship. They were among the most remarkable men I have ever known; and if the Roman, as he often did, treated them with as much disdain as he dared, it was a disdain that masked a fear perhaps not wholly unlike that feeling he had about the sea. A few years ago it became necessary for me to banish the poet Ovid from Rome because of his involvement in an intrigue that threatened to disturb the order of the state; since his part in the intrigue was more nearly mischievous and social than malevolent and political, I made the banishment as light as possible; I shall lift the banishment soon, and allow him to return from the cold north to the more temperate and pleasing climate of Rome. Yet even in his place of banishment, that half-barbaric little town of Tomis that huddles near the mouth of the Danube, he continues to write his poems. We correspond occasionally, and are on friendly enough terms; and though he misses the pleasures of Rome, he does not despair of his condition. But of the several poets that I have known, Ovid is the only one whom I could not fully trust. And yet I was fond of him, and remain so.

I could trust the poets because I was unable to give them what they wanted. An Emperor may give to an ordinary man the means to a wealth that would confound the most extraordinary taste for luxury; he may bequeath such power that few men dare to oppose it; he may confer such honor and glory upon a freedman that even a consul might feel constrained to behave toward him with some deference. Once I offered to Horace the position of my private secretary; it would have made him one of the most influential men in Rome, and, had he been even discreetly corrupt, one of the richest. He replied that, alas, the state of his health precluded his acceptance of a post fraught with such responsibilities. We both knew that the post was more nearly ceremonial than laborious, and that his health was excellent. I could not be offended; he had the little farm that Maecenas had given him, a few servants, his grape arbors, and enough income to import an excellent wine.

I suspect that I have admired the poets because they seemed to me the freest and therefore the most affectionate of men, and I have felt a closeness to them because I have seen in the tasks that they set for themselves a certain similarity to the task that long ago I set for myself.

The poet contemplates the chaos of experience, the confusion of accident, and the incomprehensible realms of possibility —which is to say the world in which we all so intimately live that few of us take the trouble to examine it. The fruits of that contemplation are the discovery, or the invention, of some small principle of harmony and order that may be isolated from that disorder which obscures it, and the subjection of that discovery to those poetic laws which at last make it possible. No general ever more carefully exercises his troops in their intricate formations than does the poet dispose his words to the rigorous necessity of meter; no consul more shrewdly aligns this faction against that in order to achieve his end than the poet who balances one line with another in order to display his truth; and no Emperor ever so carefully organizes the disparate parts of the world that he rules so that they will constitute a whole than does the poet dispose the details of his poem so that another world, perhaps more real than the one that we so precariously inhabit, will spin in the universe of men's minds.

It was my destiny to change the world, I said earlier. Perhaps I should have said that the world was my poem, that I undertook the task of ordering its parts into a whole, subordinating this faction to that, and adorning it with those graces appropriate to its worth. And yet if it is a poem that I have fashioned, it is one that will not for very long outlive its time. When Vergil died, he earnestly beseeched me to destroy his great poem; it was not complete, he said, and imperfect. Like a general who sees a legion destroyed and does not know that two others have triumphed, he thought himself to be a failure; and yet his poem upon the founding of Rome will no doubt outlast Rome itself, and certainly it will outlast the poor thing that I have put together. I did not destroy the poem; I do not believe that Vergil thought I would. Time will destroy Rome.

My fever has not abated. An hour ago, I had a sudden attack of dizziness and a sharp pain in my left side, followed by a numbness. I discover that my left leg, always a little weak, is now hardly capable of movement. It will still support my weight, but it drags beneath me uselessly; and when I prick it with my stylus, there is the merest ghost of a pain.

I still have not informed Philippus of my condition; there is nothing that he can do to relieve my condition, and I should prefer not to humiliate him by forcing him to perform vain solicitudes upon a body whose deterioration is far beyond the reach of any ministrations he might attempt. After all these years, I cannot be angry at a body that fails; despite its weakness, it has served me well; and it is perhaps appropriate that I should attend its demise, as I might attend the death of an old friend, remembering as the soul slips away into whatever immortality it might find, the mortal soul which could not in life separate itself from the animal that was its guest. I am able now, and have been for some months, almost to detach myself from the body that contains me and observe this semblance of myself. It is not an ability altogether new, and yet it seems to me now that it is more natural than it has been before.

And so, detached from a failing body, almost oblivious to the pain that now is its habitation, I float above the unimaginable sea southward toward Capri. The high sun glints upon the water that parts before our prow, the white foam hisses as it spreads and disperses upon the waves. I shall rest from my task, and perhaps some of my strength will return. This evening we harbor at Puteoli. And tomorrow we shall land at Capri, where I shall perform what might be the last of my public functions.

We are at harbor. It is early afternoon, and the mists have not yet blurred the coastal lands from the sight of the sea voyager. I remain at my table, and occupy my leisure with this letter. I believe that Philippus, who continues to watch me from his station at the prow of our ship, has begun to suspect that the condition of my health has sharply worsened. A look of doubt has settled upon his fine young face, and his hazel eyes beneath the brows that are straight and delicate as a woman's glance at me from time to time. I do not know how much longer I shall be able to conceal my condition from him.

We have dropped anchor at a little cove just north of Puteoli; and farther north is Naples, where some years ago Marcus Agrippa constructed a causeway between the sea and the Lucrine Lake, so that the Roman fleet might conduct its maneuvers safe from the vicissitudes of weather and the pirate fleets of Sextus Pompeius. At one time, as many as two hundred war ships trained upon that inland harbor, and thus became capable of defeating Sextus Pompeius and saving Rome. But during these years of peace, silt has been allowed to clog the entrance to this training ground; and now I understand that it has been turned into an oyster bed so that the Roman rich might have the pleasures of their new existences enhanced. From where we are anchored, I cannot see this harbor, and I am just as pleased that I cannot.

In recent years the possibility has occurred to me that the proper condition of man, which is to say that condition in which he is most admirable, may not be that prosperity, peace, and harmony which I labored to give to Rome. In the early years of my authority, I found much to admire in my countryman; in the midst of privation he was uncomplaining and sometimes almost gay, in the midst of war he had more care for the life of a comrade than he did for his own, and in the midst of disorder he was resolute and loyal to the authority of Rome, wherever he thought that authority might lie. For more than forty years we have lived the Roman peace. No Roman has fought Roman, no barbarian foot has trod in unchallenged enmity upon Italian soil, no soldier has been forced to bear arms against his will. We have lived the Roman prosperity. No person in Rome, however lowly, has gone without his daily ration of grain; the provincial citizen is no longer at the mercy of famine or natural disaster, but may be sure of aid in any extremity; and any citizen, whatever his birth, may become as rich as his endeavor and the accidents of the world allow him. And we have lived the Roman harmony. I organized the courts of Rome so that each man might go before a magistrate with some assurance of receiving at least a modicum of justice; I codified the laws of the Empire, so that even the provincial might live in some security from the tyranny of power or the corruption of greed; and I made the state secure against the brutal force of ambitious power by instituting and enforcing those laws against treason that Julius Caesar had promulgated before his death.

And yet there is now upon the Roman face a look which I fear augurs badly for his future. Dissatisfied with honest comfort, he strains back toward the old corruption which nearly robbed the state of its existence. Though I gave the people freedom from tyranny and power and family, and freedom to speak without fear of punishment, nevertheless *the dictatorship of Rome was offered to me by both the people and the Roman Senate, first when I was absent in the East,* following the defeat of Marcus Antonius at Actium, *and later during the consulship of Marcus Marcellus and Lucius Arruntius, after I had saved Italy, at my own expense, from that famine which destroyed the grain supply of Italy. Upon neither occasion did I accept,* though I incurred the displeasure of the people. And now the sons of senators, who might be expected to serve their fellow men or even themselves with some honor, clamor to hazard their lives in the arena, pitting themselves against common gladiators, for what they imagine to be the sport of danger. So has Roman bravery descended into the common dust.

Marcus Agrippa's harbor now furnishes oysters for the Sybarite of Rome, the bodies of honest Roman soldiers fertilize his luxuriant garden of clipped box and cypress, and the tears of their widows make his artificial streams flow merrily in the Italian sunlight. And in the north the barbarian waits.

The barbarian waits. Five years ago, on that part of the German frontier that is marked by the Upper Rhine, a disaster befell Rome from which she has not yet recovered; it is perhaps a portent of her fate.

From the northern shore of the Black Sea to the lower coast of the German Ocean, from Moesia to Belgium, a distance of more than a thousand miles, Italy lies unprotected by any natural barrier from the Germanic tribes. They cannot be defeated, and they cannot be persuaded from their habits of pillage and murder. My uncle was not able to do so, nor could I during the years of my authority. Therefore it was necessary to fortify that frontier, to protect at once the northern provinces of Rome and at last to protect Rome itself. The most difficult part of that frontier, since it protected land that was particularly rich and fertile, was the area in the northwest, below the Rhine. Thus, of the twenty-five legions of some one hundred and fifty thousand soldiers that protected the Empire of Rome, five legions of the most experienced veterans I had assigned to that small region. They were under the command of Publius Quintilius Varus, who had successfully served as proconsul of Africa and governor of Syria.

I suppose that I must hold myself responsible for that disaster, for I allowed myself to be persuaded to give the German command to Varus. He was a distant relative of my wife, and he had been of some service to Tiberius in the past. It was one of the most serious mistakes I ever made, and the only time in my memory that I placed a man of whom I knew so little in such a high position.

For on the rude and primitive border of that northern province, Varus imagined that he might still live in the luxury and ease of Syria; he remained aloof from his own soldiers, and began to trust those German provincials who were adept at flattery and able to offer him some semblance of the sensual life to which he had become accustomed in Syria. Chief among these sycophants was one Arminius of the Cherusci, who had once served in the Roman army and had been rewarded by the gift of citizenship. Arminius, who spoke fluent Latin despite his barbaric origin, gained the confidence of Varus, so that he might further his own ambitions of power over the scattered

German tribes; and when he was sufficiently sure of Varus's credulity and vanity, he falsely informed him that the distant tribes of the Chauci and the Bructeri were in revolt and sweeping southward to threaten the security of the provincial border. Varus, in his arrogance and recklessness, would not listen to the counsel of others; and he withdrew three legions from the summer camp on the Weser and marched northward. Arminius had laid his plans well; for as Varus led his legions through the forest and marshland toward Lemgo, the barbarian tribes that had been forewarned and prepared by Arminius, fell upon the laboring legions. Confused by the suddenness of the attack, unable to maintain an orderly resistance, bewildered by the thick forest and rain and marshy ground, they were annihilated. Within three days, fifteen thousand soldiers were slain or captured; some of the captured were buried alive by the barbarians, some were crucified, and some were offered to the northern gods by the barbaric priests, who decapitated them and secured the heads to trees in the sacred groves. Fewer than a hundred soldiers managed to escape the ambush, and they reported the disaster. Varus was either slain or took his own life; no one could be sure which. In any event, his severed head was returned to me in Rome by a tribal chieftain named Maroboduus, whether out of an anxious piety or an exultant mockery I do not know. I gave the poor remnant of Varus a decent burial, not so much for the sake of his soul as for the sake of the soldiers who had been led to disaster by his authority. And still in the north the barbarian waits.

After his victory on the Rhine, Arminius did not have the wit to pursue his advantage; the north lay open to him—from the mouth of the Rhine nearly to its confluence with the Elbe —and yet he was content merely to plunder his neighbors. The following year, I put the German armies under the command of Tiberius, since it was he who had persuaded me to appoint Varus. He recognized his own part in the disaster, and knew that his future depended upon his success in subduing the Germans and restoring order in those troubled northern provinces. In this endeavor he was successful, largely because he relied upon the experience of the veteran centurions and tribunes of the legions rather than upon his own initiative. And so now there is an uneasy peace in the north, though Arminius remains free, somewhere in that wilderness beyond the border he disturbed.

Far to the east, beyond even India, in a part of that unknown world where no Roman has been known to set foot, there is said to be a land whose kings, over unnumbered successive reigns, have erected a great fortress wall that extends hundreds of miles across the entirety of their northern frontier, so that their kingdom might be protected against the encroachments of their barbaric neighbors. It may be that this tale is a fantasy of an adventurer; it may even be that there is no such land as this. Nevertheless, I will confess that the possibility of such a project has occurred to me when I have had to think of our northern neighbors who will be neither conquered nor appeased. And yet I know that it is useless. The winds and rains of time will at last crumble the most solid stone, and there is no wall that can be built to protect the human heart from its own weakness.

For it was not Arminius and his horde; it was Varus in his weakness who slaughtered fifteen thousand Roman soldiers, as it is the Roman Sybarite in his life of shade who invites the slaughter of thousands more. The barbarian waits, and we grow weaker in the security of our ease and pleasure.

Again it is night, the second night of this voyage which, it becomes clearer and clearer to me, may be my last. I do not believe that my mind fails with my body, but I must confess that the darkness came over me before I even noticed its encroachment; and I found myself staring sightlessly to the west. It was then that Philippus could no longer avoid his anxiety and approached me with that slightly rude manner of his that so transparently reveals his shyness and uncertainty. I allowed him to place his hand upon my forehead so that he could judge the extent of my fever, and I answered a few of his questions —untruthfully, I might add. But when he tried to insist that I retire to my room below deck, so that I might be protected from the night air, I assumed the role of the willful and crotchety old man and pretended to lose my temper. I did so with such energy that Philippus was convinced of my strength, and was content to send below for some blankets with which I promised to wrap myself. Philippus elected to stay on deck, so that he could keep an eye on me; but soon he nodded, and now, curled on the bare deck, his head cradled in his folded arms, with that touching faith and completeness of the young, he sleeps, certain that he will awake in the morning.

I cannot see it now, but earlier, before the late afternoon mists rose from the sea to shroud the western horizon, I thought I could make out its contours, a dark smudge against the vast circle of the sea. I believe that I saw the Island of Pandateria, where for so many years my daughter suffered to live in her exile. She is no longer on Pandateria. Ten years ago, I judged that it was possible to allow her to return in safety to the mainland of Italy; now she abides in the Calabrian village of Reggio, at the very toe of the Italian boot. For more than fifteen years, I have not seen her, or spoken her name, or allowed the fact of her existence to be mentioned in my presence. It was too painful for me. And that silence merely defined another of the many roles that contained me in my life.

My enemies have found an understandable pleasure in contemplating the ironic use to which I finally had to put those marriage laws that I promulgated and had enacted by the Senate some thirty years ago; and even my friends have found occasion to be displeased by their existence. Horace once told me that laws were powerless against the private passions of the human heart, and only he who has no power over it, such as the poet or the philosopher, may persuade the human spirit to virtue. Perhaps in this instance both my friends and enemies were right; the laws did not move the people toward virtue, and the political advantage I achieved by pleasing the older and more staid segments of the aristocracy was momentary.

I was never so foolish as to believe that my laws of marriage and adultery would be obeyed; I did not obey them, nor did my friends. Vergil, when he invoked the Muse to assist him in the writing of *The Aeneid*, did not in any substantial way believe in her whom he invoked; it was a way that he had learned to begin the poem, a way to announce his intention. Thus those laws which I initiated were not intended so much to be obeyed as to be followed; I believed that there was no possibility of virtue without the idea of virtue, and no effective idea of virtue that was not encoded in the law itself.

I was mistaken, of course; the world is not poem; and the laws did not accomplish the purpose for which they were intended. But in the end they were of use to me, though I could not have foreseen that use; and I have not been able to regret since then that I allowed them. For they saved the life of my daughter.

As one grows older, and as the world becomes less and less to him, one wonders increasingly about those forces that propelled him through time. Certainly the gods are indifferent to the poor creature who struggles toward his fate; and they speak to him so obliquely that at last he must determine for himself the meanings they portend. Thus in my role of priest, I have examined the entrails and livers of a hundred beasts, and with the aid of the augurs have discovered or invented whatever portents seemed to me appropriate to my intention; and concluded that the gods, if they do exist, do not matter. And if I encouraged the people to follow these ancient Roman gods, I did so out of necessity rather than any religious conviction that those forces rest very securely in their supposed persons. . . . Perhaps you were right after all, my dear Nicolaus; perhaps there is but one god. But if that is true, you have misnamed him. He is Accident, and his priest is man, and that priest's only victim must be at last himself, his poor divided self.

As they have known so many things, the poets have known this better than most, though they have put the knowledge in terms that may seem trivial to some. I agreed with you in the past that they spoke too much of love, and gave too much value to what at best was a pleasant pastime; but I am no longer sure that that agreement was well advised. *I hate and I love*, Catullus said, speaking of that Clodia Pulcher whose family caused so much difficulty in Rome, even in our time and long after her death. It is not enough; but what better way might we begin to discover that self which is never wholly pleased or displeased with what the world offers?

You must forgive me, Nicolaus; I know that you will disagree, and that you have no way to voice your disagreement; but I have in late years sometimes thought that it might be possible to construct a system of theology or even a religion around the idea of love, if that idea were extended somewhat beyond its usual application, and approached in a certain way.

Now that I am no longer capable of it, I have been examining that mysterious power that in its many varieties existed within me for so many years. Perhaps the name that we give to the power is inadequate; but if it is, so are the names, spoken and unspoken, that we give to all the simpler gods.

I have come to believe that in the life of every man, late or soon, there is a moment when he knows beyond whatever else he might understand, and whether he can articulate the knowledge or not, the terrifying fact that he is alone, and separate, and that he can be no other than the poor thing that is himself. I look now at my thin shanks, the withered skin upon my hand, the sagging flesh that is blotched with age; and it is difficult for me to realize that once this body sought release from itself in that of another; and that another sought the same from it. To that instant of pleasure some dedicate all their lives, and become embittered and empty when the body fails, as the body must. They are embittered and empty because they have known only the pleasure, and do not know what that pleasure has meant. For contrary to what we may believe, erotic love is the most unselfish of all the varieties; it seeks to become one with another, and hence to escape the self. This kind of love is the first to die, of course, failing as the body that carries it fails; and for that reason, no doubt, it has been thought by many to be the basest of the varieties. But the fact that it will die, and that we know it will die, makes it more precious; and once we have known it, we are no longer irretrievably trapped and exiled within the self.

Yet it alone is not enough. I have loved many men, but never as I have loved women; the love of a man for a boy is a fashion in Rome that you have observed with some wonder and I believe repulsion, and you have been puzzled by my tolerance of such practices, and more puzzled perhaps because despite my tolerance I have not engaged in them myself. But that kind of love which is friendship has seemed to me best disengaged from the pleasures of the flesh; for to caress that body which is of one's own sex is to caress one's self, and thus is not an escape of the self but an imprisonment within it. For if one loves a friend, he does not become that other; he remains himself, and contemplates the mystery of one that he can never be, of selves that he has never been. To love a child may be the purest form of this mystery; for within the child are potentialities that he can hardly imagine, that self which is at the furthest remove from the observer. My love for my adopted children and for my grandchildren has been the object of some amusement among those who have known me, and has been seen as an indulgence of an otherwise rational man, as a sentimentality of an otherwise responsible father. I have not seen it so.

One morning some years ago, as I walked down the Via Sacra toward the Senate House, where I was to give that address which would condemn my daughter to a life of exile, I met one whom I had known when I was a child. It was Hirtia, the daughter of my old nurse. Hirtia had cared for me as if I were her own child, and had been given her freedom for her faithful service. I had not seen her for fifty years, and would not have known her had not a name I once was known by slipped from her lips. We spoke of the times of our childhoods, and for a moment the years slipped away from me; and in my grief I almost told Hirtia of what I had to do. But as she spoke of her own children, and her life, and as I saw the serenity with which she had returned to the place of her birth so that she might meet her death in the pleasant memory of that lost youth, I could not speak. For the sake of Rome and my authority, I was to condemn my own daughter; and it occurred to me that had Hirtia had the power to make the choice, Rome would have fallen and the child would have survived. I could not speak, for I knew that Hirtia would not understand my necessity, and would be troubled for the little time that remained in her life. For a moment, I was a child again, and mute before what I took to be a wisdom that I could not fathom.

It has occurred to me since that meeting with Hirtia that there is a variety of love more powerful and lasting than that union with the other which beguiles us with its sensual pleasure, and more powerful and lasting than that platonic variety in which we contemplate the mystery of the other and thus become ourselves; mistresses grow old or pass beyond us; the flesh weakens; friends die; and children fulfill, and thus betray, that potentiality in which we first beheld them. It is a variety of love in which you, my dear Nicolaus, have found yourself for much of your life, and it is one in which our poets were happiest; it is the love of the scholar for his text, the philosopher for his idea, the poet for his word. Thus Ovid is not alone in his northern exile at Tomis, nor are you alone in your far Damascus, where you have chosen to devote your remaining years to your books. No living object is necessary for such pure love; and thus it is universally agreed that this is the highest form of love, since it is for an object that approaches the absolute.

And yet in some ways it may be the basest form of love. For if we strip away the high rhetoric that so often surrounds this notion, it is revealed simply as a love of power. (Forgive me, my dear Nicolaus; let us pretend that once again we are engaging in one of those quibbles with which we used to amuse ourselves.) It is the power that the philosopher has over the disembodied mind of his reader, the power that the poet has over the living mind and heart of his listener. And if the minds and hearts and spirits of those who come under the spell of that appointed power are lifted, that is an accident which is not essential to the love, or even its purpose.

I have begun to see that it is this kind of love that has impelled me through the years, though it has been necessary for me to conceal the fact from myself as well as from others. Forty years ago, when I was in my thirty-sixth year, the Senate and people of Rome accorded me the title of Augustus; twenty-five years later, when I was in my sixty-first year, and in the same year that I exiled my daughter from Rome, the Senate and people gave me the title of Father of my Country. It was quite simple and appropriate; I exchanged one daughter for another, and the adoptive daughter acknowledged that exchange.

To the west, in the darkness, lies the Island of Pandateria. The little villa where Julia lived for five years is uninhabited now and by my orders uncared for. It is open to the weather and the slow erosion of time; in a few years it will begin to crumble, and time will take it, as it takes all things. I hope that Julia has forgiven me my sparing her life, as I have forgiven her for having thought to take mine.

For the rumors that you must have heard are true. My daughter was a member of the conspiracy that had as its end the assassination of her husband, and the murder of myself. And I invoked those marriage laws that had so long lain unused and condemned her to a life of exile, so that she might not be condemned to death by the secret effort of her husband, Tiberius, who would have made her endure a trial for treason.

I have often wondered whether my daughter has ever admitted to herself the extent of her own guilt. I know that the last time I saw her, in her confusion and grief at the death of Jullus Antonius, she was not able to do so. I hope that she will never be able to do so, but will live out her life in the belief that she was the victim of a passion which led to her disgrace, rather than a participant in a conspiracy that would certainly have led to her father's death, and almost certainly would have destroyed Rome. The first I might have allowed; the second I could not.

I have relinquished whatever rancor I might have had against my daughter, for I have come to understand that despite her part in the conspiracy there was always a part of Julia that remained the child who loved the father who was perhaps too doting; a part of her that must have recoiled in horror from what she felt she was at last driven to do; a part of her that still, in the loneliness of Reggio, remembers the daughter that once she was. I have come to understand that one can wish for the death of another and yet love that victim without appreciable diminution. At one time I was in the habit of calling her my Little Rome, an appellation that has been widely misunderstood; it was that I wished my Rome to become the potentiality that I saw in her. In the end, they both betrayed me; but I cannot love them the less for that.

To the south of our anchorage, the Lucrine Lake, dredged once by honest Italian hands so that the Roman fleet might protect the people, furnishes oysters for the tables of the Roman rich; Julia languishes on the barren Calabrian coast at Reggio; and Tiberius will rule the world.

I have lived too long. All those who might have succeeded me and striven for the survival of Rome are dead. Marcellus, to whom I first betrothed my daughter, died at the age of nineteen; Marcus Agrippa died; and my grandsons, the sons of Agrippa and Julia, Gaius and Lucius, died in the service of Rome; and Tiberius's brother, Drusus, who was both more able and equable than his brother, and whom I raised as my own son, died in Germany. Now only Tiberius remains.

I have no doubt that more than any other Tiberius was responsible for the fate of my daughter. He would not have hesitated to implicate her in the conspiracy against his life and my own, and he would have been pleased to see the Senate pass the sentence of death upon her, while he assumed the demeanor of sorrow and regret. I cannot bring myself to do other than despise Tiberius. At the center of his soul there is a bitterness that no one has fathomed, and in his person there is an essential cruelty that has no particular object. Nevertheless he is not a weak man, and he is not a fool; and cruelty in an Emperor is a lesser fault than weakness or foolishness. Therefore I have relinquished Rome to the mercies of Tiberius and to the accidents of time. I could do no other.

August 11

During the night, I did not move from my couch but kept a vigil on the stars that move slowly in their eternal voyage across the great dome of the sky. Toward dawn, for the first time in days, I dozed a little; and I had a dream. I was in that curious state where one dreams and knows that one dreams, yet finds there a reality which mocks that of one's waking life; I wished to remember the contours of that other world; but when I was awakened, the memory of the dream fled into the brightness of the morning.

I was awakened by the stirring of the crew, and by the sound of a distant singing; for a moment, in my confusion, I thought of those Sirens of whom Homer wrote so beautifully, and imagined myself to be bound to the mast of my ship, helpless against the call of an unimaginable beauty. But it was not the Sirens; it was a grain-ship from Alexandria that sailed slowly toward us from the south, and the Egyptian crew, dressed in white robes with garlands on their heads, stood on deck singing in their native tongue as they approached us; and the musky odor of burning incense was borne to us on the morning breeze.

We watched their approach with some puzzlement, until at last the huge ship which dwarfed our own came so close that we could make out the smiling swarthy faces of the men; and then the captain stepped forward and hailed me by name.

With some difficulty, which I trust I concealed even from Philippus, I rose from my couch and went to the deck rail, upon which I leaned while I returned the greeting of this captain. It appeared that the ship had unloaded a cargo of goods at the harbor between Puteoli and Naples, and had been informed of my presence nearby; and the crew had wished, before they made their way back to their far Egyptian homeland, to greet me and to give me thanks. The ship was so close that I did not have to shout, and I could see clearly the dark face of the captain. I inquired his name; it was Pothelios. And as the crew continued its low singing, Pothelios said to me:

"You have given us the liberty to sail the seas and thus furnish Rome with the bountiful goods of Egypt; you have rid the seas of those pirates and brigands that in the past would have made that liberty empty. Thus the Egyptian Roman may prosper, and may return to his homeland secure in the knowledge that only the accidents of wind and wave threaten his safety. For all this we give thanks to you, and pray that the gods will allow you good fortune for the rest of your days."

For a moment I could not speak. Pothelios had addressed me in a stiff but passable Latin; and it occurred to me that thirty years ago he would have spoken in that demotic Egyptian Greek and that I would have been hard put to understand him. I returned the captain's thanks and said a few words to the crew, and directed Philippus to see that each member of that crew be given some coins of gold. Then I returned to my couch, from where I watched the huge freighter turn slowly away from us and move southward, its sails bulging in the wind, its crew waving and laughing, happy in their safety and homeward voyage.

And so now we too move southward, and our less bulky ship dances upon the waves. The sunlight catches the flecks of white foam that top the little waves, the waves slap gently and whisper against the sides of our ship, the blue-green depth of the sea seems almost playful; and I can persuade myself now that after all there has been some symmetry to my life, some point; and that my existence has been of more benefit than harm to this world that I am content to leave.

Now throughout this world the Roman order prevails. The German barbarian may wait in the North, the Parthian in the

East, and others beyond frontiers that we have not yet conceived; and if Rome does not fall to them, it will at last fall to that barbarian from which none escape—Time. Yet now, for a few years, the Roman order prevails. It prevails in every Italian town of consequence, in every colony, in every province—from the Rhine and the Danube to the border of Ethiopia; from the Atlantic shores of Spain and Gaul to the Arabian sands, and the Black Sea. Throughout the world I have established schools so that the Latin tongue and the Roman way may be known, and have seen to it that those schools will prosper; Roman law tempers the disordered cruelty of provincial custom, just as provincial custom modifies Roman law; and the world looks in awe upon that Rome that I found built of crumbling clay and that now is made of marble.

The despair that I have voiced seems to me now unworthy of what I have done. Rome is not eternal; it does not matter. Rome will fall; it does not matter. The barbarian will conquer; it does not matter. There was a moment of Rome, and it will not wholly die; the barbarian will become the Rome he conquers; the language will smooth his rough tongue; the vision of what he destroys will flow in his blood. And in time that is ceaseless as this salt sea upon which I am so frailly suspended, the cost is nothing, is less than nothing.

We approach the Island of Capri. It shines like a jewel in the morning sun, a dark emerald rising out of the blue sea. The wind has almost died, and we float as if upon the air toward that quiet and leisurely place where I have spent so many happy hours. Already the island inhabitants, who are my neighbors and my friends, have begun to gather at the harbor; they wave, and I can hear their voices calling. Gaily, gaily they call to me. In a moment I shall rise and answer them.

The dream, Nicolaus; I remember the dream I had last night. I dreamed I was again at Perusia, during the time of Lucius Antonius's uprising against the authority of Rome. All winter we had blockaded the town, hoping to effect Lucius's surrender and thus avoid the shedding of Roman blood. My men were weary and disheartened by the long waiting, and threatened revolt. To give them hope, I ordered that an altar be constructed outside the city walls and that sacrifice be offered to Jupiter. And this is the dream:

A white ox, never yoked to the plough, was led to the altar by the attendants; its horns were gilded, and its head was garlanded by a wreath of laurel. The rope was slack; the ox came forward willingly, its head raised. Its eyes were blue, and they seemed to be looking at me, as if the beast recognized who was to be its executioner. The attendant crumbled the salt cake on its head; it did not move; the attendant tasted the wine, and then poured the libation between its horns. Still the ox did not move. The attendant said: "Shall it be done?"

I raised my ax; the blue eyes were upon me; they did not waver. I struck, and said: "It is done." The ox quivered and sank slowly to its knees; still its head was upraised, and its eyes were upon me. The attendant drew his dagger and slit the throat, catching the blood in his goblet. And even as the blood flowed the blue eyes seemed to look into mine, until at last they glazed and the body toppled to one side.

That was more than fifty years ago; I was in my twenty-third year. It is curious that I should dream of that after so long a time.

Epilogue

I was surprised and pleased, my dear Seneca, to receive your letter; I trust that you will forgive my delay in replying. Your inquiry reached me in Rome on the very day that I was leaving the city, and I have only just begun to get settled in my new home. You will be pleased to learn that at last I have taken the advice you have given me, both to my face and in your writings, and have retired from the bustle and confusion of my practice, so that I might devote myself to the quiet dignity of learning, and pass on to others what little knowledge I have gained through the years. I write these words from my villa outside Naples; the sunlight, dispersed by the budding grapevines that arch over my terrace, dances over the paper upon which these words appear; and I am as happy as you promised I would be in my retirement. For that assurance and the truth of it, I wish to thank you.

Over the years our friendship has, indeed, been too sporadic; I am only grateful to you for remembering me, and for overlooking the fact that I did not speak out on your behalf during that unfortunate time that you were forced to spend on the barren waste of Corsica; you have understood better than most, I suspect, that a poor physician without worldly power, nor even a hundred like him, could have prevailed against the will of one so erratic as our late Emperor Claudius. All of us who have admired you, even in our silence, are elated that once again your genius may brighten the Rome that you have loved.

You ask me to write about that matter of which we have spoken upon those too infrequent occasions that we have had to converse—my brief acquaintance with the Emperor Caesar Augustus. I am happy to accede to your request, but you must know that I am consumed with a friendly curiosity: may we expect a new essay? an Epistle? or perhaps, even, a tragedy? I shall wait eagerly to learn the use to which you intend to put my few memories.

When we have spoken of the Emperor before, perhaps desiring a friendship which I imagined might be enhanced by your continued curiosity, I have been somewhat too mysterious and selfish with the information I would impart. But now I am in my sixty-sixth year—ten years younger than Octavius Caesar when he died. And I believe that I have at last gone beyond that vanity against which you have so often inveighed, yet have been kind enough to except me. I shall tell you what I remember.

As you know, I was physician to Octavius Caesar for only a few months; but in those few months, I was always near him, more often than not within a distance from which I could hear him call; and I was with him when he died. I do not know even now why he chose me to attend him during those months that he knew were to be his last; there were many others more famous and more experienced than I; and I was only in my twenty-sixth year at the time. Nevertheless, he did choose me; and though I could not conceive it in my youth, I suspect now that he was fond of me, in that curious detached way that he seemed to have. And though I was able to do nothing for him in his last days, he saw to it that I was a rich man after his death.

After a leisurely voyage of several days south from Ostia, we debarked at Capri; and though it was clear that his health was failing, he would not be so impolite as to ignore the throng that awaited him. He chatted with many of them, calling them by name, though upon occasion in his weakness he had to lean on my arm. Since most of the inhabitants of Capri are Greek, he spoke to them in that language, apologizing from time to time for his rather strange accent. At last he was content to bid his neighbors farewell, and we made our way to the Emperor's villa, which commanded a remarkable view of the Bay of Naples, not many miles away. I persuaded him to rest, and he seemed content to do so.

He had promised the island youths to observe the gymnastic competition that had been arranged to select those who would represent the island in the games at Naples the following week; and despite my protestations, he insisted upon fulfilling that promise; and again despite my wishes, he invited them all to his villa that evening for a banquet in their honor.

He was extraordinarily gay at the banquet. He invented licentious epigrams in Greek, and encouraged the young men to groan at their badness; he joined them in their boyish games of throwing crusts of bread at each other; and in the face of their strenuous activities of the afternoon, he jokingly insisted upon calling them the "Idle-landers" rather than the "Islanders," because of the leisurely life that they ordinarily led. He promised to attend the games in Naples, in which they were to compete; and insisted that he was gambling his entire fortune on their success.

We remained at Capri for four days. Most of the time the Emperor sat quietly, gazing at the sea, or at the Italian coast line to the east. There was a quiet smile on his face, and every once in a while he would nod slightly, as if he were remembering something.

On the fifth day we crossed to Naples. By this time the Emperor was so weak that he could not walk unassisted. Nevertheless, he insisted that he be taken to the games at which he had promised the young athletes he would be present; and I confess that, though I knew his end was near, I could not but assent to his going. It was clear that it would have made the difference of only a few days, at the most. He sat all afternoon in the blazing sun, cheering the Caprian Greeks to their victories; and when the contests were over, he found himself unable to rise from his chair.

We carried him from the stadium on a litter, and he let it be known that he wished to go at once to one of his childhood homes, at Nola. Since it was a journey of only eighteen miles, I consented; and we arrived at his old home in the early hours of the morning.

Knowing that the end was near, I had word sent to Benevento where Livia and her son Tiberius had been staying for several days. According to the Emperor's instructions, I made it clear that he did not wish to see Tiberius, though he would allow the information to be spread that Tiberius had indeed attended him during his last hours.

On the morning of the day he died, he said to me:

"Philippus, it is near, is it not?"

There was something in his manner that forbade me to dissemble with him.

"One cannot be sure," I said. "But it is near. Yes."

He nodded tranquilly. "Then I must fulfill the last of my obligations."

A number of his acquaintances—I believe he had no one then whom he would have called a friend—had heard of his illness in Rome, and had made haste to Nola. He received them, bade them farewell, and admonished them to assist in the orderly transference of his power, and obliged them to support Tiberius in his accession to authority. When one of them made a show of weeping, he became displeased, and said:

"It is unkind of you to weep upon the occasion of my contentment."

He wished to see Livia alone, then. But when I made a movement to leave the room, he beckoned me to stay.

When he spoke to Livia, I could tell that he was weakening rapidly. He made a gesture to her; she knelt and kissed him on the cheek.

"Your son—" he said. "Your son—"

He breathed hoarsely for a moment; his jaw went slack; and then, by an apparent effort of his will, he regained a little of his strength.

"We need not forgive ourselves," he said. "It has been a marriage. It has been better than most."

He fell back upon his bed; I rushed to his side; he still breathed. Livia touched his cheek. She lingered beside him for a moment, and left the room.

Some moments later, he opened his eyes suddenly and said to me:

"Philippus, my memories. . . . They are of no use to me now."

For a moment, then, it seemed that his mind wandered, for he suddenly cried out: "The young! The young will carry it before them!"

I put my hand upon his brow; he looked at me again, raised himself upon one elbow, and smiled; then those remarkable blue eyes glazed; his body twitched once; and he toppled on his side.

Thus died Gaius Octavius Caesar, the August; it was at three o'clock in the afternoon, on the nineteenth day of August, in the consulships of Sextus Pompeius and Sextus Appuleius. He died in the same room that his natural father, the elder Octavius, had died in seventy-two years before.

Of that long letter which Octavius wrote to his friend Nicolaus in Damascus, I must say one thing. It was entrusted to my care for delivery; but in Naples, I received word that Nicolaus himself had died two weeks before. I did not inform the Emperor of this, for it seemed to me at the time that he was happy in the thought that his old friend would read his last words.

Within a few weeks after his death, his daughter Julia died in her confinement at Reggio; it was whispered by some that her former husband, the Emperor Tiberius, allowed her to starve. Of that rumor I do not know the truth, nor I suspect does anyone who is now alive.

It is the fashion of the day, and it has been the fashion for more than thirty years, for many of the younger citizens to speak with some condescension of the long reign of Octavius Caesar. And he himself, toward the end of his life, thought that all of his work had been for nothing.

Yet the Empire of Rome that he created has endured the harshness of a Tiberius, the monstrous cruelty of a Caligula, and the ineptness of a Claudius. And now our new Emperor is one whom you tutored as a boy, and to whom you remain close in his new authority; let us be thankful for the fact that he will rule in the light of your wisdom and virtue, and let us pray to the gods that, under Nero, Rome will at last fulfill the dream of Octavius Caesar.

Rome, Northampton, Denver, 1967–1972

RELATED WRITINGS

The "Western": Definition of the Myth

G IVEN THE dense history of the American West, nearly unexplored in its most fundamental aspects and potentially
the richest of American myths, why has there not emerged a
modern novelist of the first rank to deal adequately with the
subject? Why has the West not produced its equivalent of New
England's Melville or Hawthorne—or, in modern times, of the
South's Faulkner or Warren?

The question has been asked before, but the answers usually
given are somewhat too easy. It is true that the Western subject
has had the curious fate to be exploited, cheapened and sen-
timentalized before it had a chance to enrich itself naturally,
through the slow accretion of history and change. It is true
that the subject of the West has undergone a process of mindless stereotyping by a line of literary racketeers that extends
from the hired hacks of a hundred years ago who composed
Erastus Beadle's Dime Novels to such contemporary pulp writers as Nelson Nye and Luke Short—men contemptuous of the
stories they have to tell, of the people who animate them and
of the settings upon which they are played. It is true that the
history of the West has been nearly taken over by the romantic
regionalist, almost always an amateur historian with an obsessive but sentimental concern for Western objects and history, a
concern which is consistently a means of escaping significance
rather than a means of confronting it.

But the real reason that the Western theme remains inade-
quately explored is more fundamental. It concerns a misunderstanding of the nature of the subject out of which the theme
emerges and hence a misunderstanding of its implications, literary and otherwise.

There are, broadly speaking, two kinds of uses to which the
Western myth has been put in modern fiction—the first and
more familiar is found in the conventional "Western"; the second is found in the serious treatment of the Western theme by
such novelists as Walter van Tilburg Clark, A. B. Guthrie and
Frederick Manfred. At first glance, it might seem that these

795

two uses have as little in common as have the two sets of authors who employ them. But I believe that if they are examined
with some care it will become clear that they do have failings
in common, and that an understanding of both the uses and
their failures will suggest an answer to the question with which
I began this note.

In its simplest form, the conventional Western involves an
elemental conflict between the personified forces of Good and
Evil, as these are variously represented by cowboy and rustler,
cowboy and Indian, the marshal and the bank robber, or (in
a later and more socially conscious version of the formula) by
the conflict between the squatter and the landowner. Com-
plications may enter—the marshal may be beset with worldly
temptations; the landowner, imperfectly evil, may enlist our
sympathies for a moment; and in curious neo-classic variations,
passion may set itself against honor.

It is tempting to dismiss such familiar manipulation of the
myth; but the formula persists, and with a disturbing vigor.
However cheaply it may be presented, however superficially
exploited, its persistence demonstrates the evocation of a deep
response in the consciousness of the people. The response is
real; but though it may have been widely identified as such,
it is not, I believe, really a response to the *Western* myth. It is,
rather, a response to another habit of mind, deeply rooted and
essentially American in its tone and application.

That is the New England Calvinist habit of mind, whose
influence upon American culture has been both pervasive
and profound. The early Calvinists saw experience as a never-
ending contest between Good and Evil. Though fundamentally corrupt, man might receive, through the grace of God, a
state of salvation. Of this inner state of Grace man can never
be fully sure, but he may suspect its presence by such outward
signs as wealth, power or worldly success. Since this state is
the choice of God, the elect tend to be absolutely good; and
the more numerous damned tend to be absolutely evil. This
affair is wholly predetermined; man's will avails him only the
illusion of choice; and the world is only a stage upon which
mankind acts out a drama in which Good will ultimately prevail and in which Evil will inevitably be destroyed. In the very
simplicity and inadequacy of this world view lies its essentially

dramatic nature. All experience is finally allegorical, and its meaning is determined by something outside itself.

The relationship between this habit of mind and the typically primitive Western is immediately apparent. The hero is inexplicably and essentially good. His virtue does not depend upon the "good deeds" he performs; rather, such deeds operate as outward signs of inward grace. Similarly, the villain is by his nature villainous, and not made so by choice, circumstances or environment; more often than not these are identical to those of the hero. And even in those instances, relatively infrequent today, when the villain is Indian or Mexican, the uses of racial origin are not so conventionally bigoted as they might appear. Racial backgrounds are not explanations of villainy; they are merely outward signs of inward damnation. In the curiously primitive nature of this drama, it is necessary that we know at every moment the figure in whom Evil is concentrated and that we be constantly assured that it is doomed to destruction. Beneath the gunplay, the pounding hooves and the crashing stagecoaches, there is a curious, slow, ritualistic movement that is essentially religious.

There are, to be sure, more sophisticated variations upon this allegorical formula, though even the variations have inescapable connections with the original Calvinistic base. For example, in Owen Wister's *The Virginian*, though the hidden base is Calvinistic, certain recognizable Emersonian revisions upon the doctrine emerge. In the Emersonian formula, the Natural Man (i.e., the man who places his faith in his instinct rather than in his reason) replaces the Elect of God. In either formula, the end is a state of Grace, but in the Emersonian version the reliance upon instinct may come about either accidentally out of ignorance or by an initial act of the will whereby one chooses to relinquish the will. The Virginian, the Natural Man, is good by virtue of his "naturalness"; Trampas is evil in the older, more purely Calvinistic sense; and the school-teacher, Mary Wood, is the figure of Emersonian compromise, the neither-good-nor-evil, code-produced human being whose salvation lies in the surrender of the intellect.

If, viewed in this manner, *The Virginian* seems a grotesque echo of Henry James's formula (the "natural," crude, innocent

American versus the "unnatural," sensitive, cultured European), we should not be surprised. Calvinism, as it manifests itself in literary art, is most likely to move toward allegory, as does the primitive Western; but when the more serious artist can no longer sustain the religious faith necessary for allegory, then the transformed Calvinist habit of mind is likely to move toward the novel of manners. Henry James, a Calvinist out of the Emersonian transformation, was a novelist of manners less from choice than from necessity; he perceived that "essences" of tremendous complexity lay in human character, and that these essences existed mysteriously, obscurely. The only way to get at them was by an examination of their outward manifestations, which were most precisely discoverable in the manners of individuals, classes, or even nations. To put it baldly, the novel of allegory depends upon a rigid and simple religious or philosophical system; the novel of manners depends upon a stable and numerous society, one in which the moral code can in some way be externalized in the more or less predictable details of daily life.

It seems obvious, then, that the Western landscape and subject, especially in their historic beginnings, are not really appropriate to the Calvinistic formula which has most frequently enclosed them. What has been widely accepted as the "Western" myth is really a habit of mind emerging from the geography and history of New England and applied uncritically to another place and time.

If the popular Western mechanically and irrelevantly furnishes forth perfunctory details, using stories so stereotyped and empty that they have become independent of human beings, and therefore contemptuous of them, what of the serious novel that would make use of the Western theme and subject?

Because of their integrity and talent, one might wish to exempt such novelists as Walter van Tilburg Clark, Frederick Manfred and even A. B. Guthrie from a charge even remotely similar to the one leveled against the legion of hacks who have done so much to cheapen the Western theme. But with the possible exception of Clark, each of these novelists is, in his own way, guilty of mistaking the real nature of his subject and of imprecisely adjusting his form to the demands of that subject.

It is not that they have hit upon the wrong myth, but that they have failed to recognize in the first place that their subject is mythic. Moment by moment, the good novelist is confronted by the necessities and implications of his matter; the worth of his novel will in many respects be dependent upon his success in adjusting form to subject.

Novelists have used, singly or in combination, four forms: the tragic, the comic, the epic and the mythic.

The details which formalize the tragic subject are most often historical and "true," either in fact or effect; thus tragedy has the advantage of seeming inevitable. So that they may have great powers of generalization, its characters are usually of high rank, most often functionaries of the state; the province of tragedy is public life, and hence the feeling that it evokes is public feeling. It is a requisite of tragedy that its outcome be unfortunate, because its theme is the cost of disorder in an ordered universe.

Comedy, on the other hand, is non-historical and invented; the characters are of low or moderate estate—or if they are not, the novelist's focus is upon the non-public aspects of their lives; the conflicts which turn the plot and impel the characters are relatively trivial; the field in which they exist is that of private experience. Thus, the subject of comedy is most often domestic or social; and the outcome, if not always joyful, is at least ironic and mixed. Comedy has been profoundly influential upon the development of the novel; from its near-beginnings in Madame de LaFayette, Defoe and Fielding, and through its development in Jane Austen, Henry James and Ford Madox Ford, it has achieved most of its distinction as a form by exploring the comic subject.

The epic was a form most meaningful to primitive cultures seeking unification of scattered strengths and cultural resources; it has been used imperfectly and with relative infrequency in the last two or three hundred years. Since its central character embodies the most primitive nationalistic aspirations of a people, its plot, though embedded in a kind of history, is really an accretion of fantastic and superhuman adventures. Because its intention is relatively simple, its structure is sequential and re-petitive. Unlike the tragic character, the epic character tends to be one-dimensional, flat and not particularly distinguished by intellectual or moral powers. His virtues are the simple ones of physical courage and strength, singleness of purpose and blind endurance. Again, unlike tragedy, the outcome of the epic is always fortunate for the real subject, the people—though the hero may sacrifice himself to make that outcome possible. Its tone is triumphant; its rhetoric is inflated, extreme; as a form that embodies an intention prior to that of tragedy, it is a movement through those conflicts that must be overcome to establish order in the first place. It does not move among the conflicts that threaten an order long established.

It is upon this epic subject, or more exactly upon the form and manner which is an outgrowth of the subject, that the novelist who would put to serious use the Western theme has most frequently and unfortunately stumbled.

Superficially, the Western adventure seems typically epic, compounded as it is of individual acts of bravery; of strength and endurance before dreadful hardships; of treks across un-known lands; of enemies subjugated and wild beasts slain; of heroes whose names have come down with legendary force. But despite its appearance, the adventure is not epical, and it is not so essentially.

What gives the epic its unique force and what finally justifies and sustains both its rhetoric and repetitive structure, is its fun-damentally nationalistic nature. The heroism, the bloodletting, the superhuman bravery, the terrible mutilations—these are given point and intensity only by the nationalistic impulse that lies behind them. Without that impulse, the adventure (han-dled epically) is empty, is bombast, is violence without rage.

Myth bears certain resemblances to the other forms and sub-jects I have mentioned; but these are in the main superficial. As in tragedy, the mythic subject rises from the enveloping action of history, but the events that detail that subject are invented. For example, in *Moby-Dick* we are at all times profoundly aware of the social, economic, religious and political forces that impel the *Pequod* and its crew upon their journey, and we believe in those forces as a matter of course. But the events and charac-ters which specify the quest are intensely symbolic and they compel belief on a level different from that of historical reality.

Like the tragic character, the mythic character is designed to generalize the subject; but whereas the tragic character gets his generalizing power from his high rank (ideally, as the functionary of the state, he is a perfect and inclusive type whose fate is inextricably tied to that of his subjects), the mythic character gets his generalizing power from his archetypal nature. The mythic subject typically involves a quest—one that is essentially inner, however externally it may disclose itself. Thus its feeling is neither public in the large and impersonal sense that tragic feeling must be, nor private in the small and domestic sense that comic feeling must be. It is that feeling which comes with an awareness of the cost of insight, the exaction of the human spirit by the terror of truth. The outcome of myth is always mixed; its quest is for an order of the self that is gained at the expense of knowing at last the essential chaos of the universe.

The pure critic or anthropologist might wish to separate myth from its historic base; but in the twentieth century the practicing novelist cannot do so. By his nature, he is not "pure"; and since in the main his imagination is historical, he cannot commit himself seriously to localities, times and subjects that he cannot feel in his bones; therefore the habitation of myth is of great importance to him. In the history of the Western landscape, and in its relation to human character, he may find that habitation, and I know of no other place from which the myth might so richly proceed.

But if the myth is to emerge with some meaning, the novelist must consider the implications of its history.

The history of the West is in some respects the record of its exploitation. Its early exploitation by the Spanish moving up from Mexico was clearly nationalistic, for the open purpose of strengthening an already powerful nation and church. But the American frontiersman, who came from the East through Kentucky and Tennessee and out of St. Louis, was a lone human being who went upon plain and mountain, who subjugated nature on his own terms, and who exploited the land for his own benefit. There was no precise ideological motive for his exploitation, and because of that lack of external motive the adventure became all the more private and intense. Removed from a social structure of some stability, imbued to some degree with a New England–Calvinist-Emersonian tradition that afforded him an abstract view of the nature of his experience, he suddenly found himself in the midst of a few desperate and concrete facts, primary among which was the necessity for survival in a universe whose brutality he had theretofore but dimly suspected. And whether he wished to or not, he was forced to reconsider those ideas he held about the nature of himself and the world in which he lived, ideas that had once, since they sprang from the very social and economic structure they explained, served him quite adequately.

The Western adventure, then, is not really epical; no national force stronger than himself pushed the American frontiersman beyond the bounds of his known experience into the chaos of a new land, into the unknown. His voyage into the wilderness was most meaningfully a voyage into the self, experimental, private and sometimes obscure.

We may now turn to those novelists, whom I mentioned earlier, who have chosen to deal with the Western adventure but who have mistaken the nature of their subject and who have, consciously or unconsciously, imposed epic strategies upon mythic subjects.

The first (and the best of them) is Walter van Tilburg Clark; the novels with which I am concerned are *The Oxbow Incident* and *The Track of the Cat*. I deal with Clark first in order to get him out of the way, since he has managed to escape the trap into which the others have fallen. He has managed to escape for reasons that may be technically described as accidental, though of course the escape is really a solution and in art there are no accidents. Both of these novels are essentially morality plays, but of a pronounced human subtlety and complexity; and though both make use of the Western landscape, it is not really necessary to either of them. Insofar as these matters can be pinned down, Clark seems to have gathered most of his technical resources from a study of the French novel, particularly the Flaubertian novel, with its concern for locked structure, restrained prose and physical detail raised to symbolic import. Thus, the precisely located scene of his novels is more nearly a necessity demanded by his technique than a genuine use of scene as an aspect of subject. Clark certainly has imposed no epic strategies upon his work, but neither has he availed himself of the Western myth. Which is to say that he is not an essentially *Western* novelist in the sense that I have been using that word. I hardly need to add that there is no reason why he should be.

The Big Sky was A. B. Guthrie's first serious novel, and it remains his best. Guthrie began as a writer of popular fiction, and even in his more serious work he is primarily concerned with the feelings that rise from his subjects rather than with their meanings. In this accidental respect, and on a less intense level, his intention is similar to that of the writer of epic. Moreover, the structure of *The Big Sky* is fundamentally epic; it is sequential, accretive and repetitive, and its primary purpose is to display the epical virtues of physical strength, courage and endurance in its chief characters. But no very vital purpose animates the adventures of the characters; they are flat and typical in the most limited sense of that word; and because of their purposelessness and flatness, the impact of experience upon them is curiously unreal and almost totally visual. We finally see that both plot and character are merely the means whereby we "experience" the landscape, which is the real subject of the novel. This suggests, perhaps, that Guthrie's novel has no true subject. It is an apparatus designed with some elaboration for the rather simple purpose of expressing a few vague and romantic feelings about the land itself. It is unsatisfactory as a work of art; its epical structure and character depiction are irrelevant, if not misleading, since they spring from an imprecise feeling about the subject rather than from an understanding of it. And though a wake of feeling ripples after it, the novel itself is curiously unmemorable.

Frederick Manfred in *Lord Grizzly* displays that ability without which no novelist can long endure—the instinct to choose a good subject. *Lord Grizzly* deals with one of the most potentially rich myths of the West, and one which has the advantage of being firmly embedded in historical fact. It is the story of Hugh Glass, the old hunter who, attacked and terribly wounded by a grizzly, and armed only with a hunting knife, yet manages to slay the bear. Left by his two companions to die, he survives. Without weapons or food, he crawls two hundred miles to take revenge upon the men who abandoned him. Out of history we know that he found them, yet took no revenge; out of myth we reconstruct the meaning he earned which made the exaction of revenge impossible.

But again, upon the mythic subject has been imposed those devices and techniques which derive from the epic intention. Although the structure of *Lord Grizzly* is not so loose and anecdotal as that of *The Big Sky*, it nevertheless has some of that expansiveness and irrelevance of detail endemic to the epic. In the primitive epic, the unused detail is present, we feel, because of a childlike wonder at its mere existence; but in the literary epic, the only kind possible today, the same detail seems ornamental, artificial and strangely jarring. Moreover, Manfred has chosen a rhetoric derived from the Homeric epic, the Old Testament and folk speech which tends to inflate the subject where it needs constriction and to deflate it where it needs elevation—a rhetoric, in short, which falsifies the subject. Only occasionally does the detail manage to emerge genuinely from the style; but when it does, we can measure the loss achieved by Manfred's choice of certain epical techniques which, imposed upon an unwilling detail, falsify the value of the subject rather than reveal and judge it for what it might be.

It is not surprising that the commercial exploiters of the Western theme have so mistaken the nature of their subject that, unaware, they have imposed upon it a fundamentally alien New England–Calvinistic world view; it is both surprising and disturbing that such talented novelists as Guthrie and Manfred have made a parallel mistake about the nature and implications of their subjects.

The nineteenth- and early twentieth-century adventure of the American West is essentially mythic. It is not tragic: there is no order to be disturbed, its heroes are not of high rank, and the feeling that emerges from the adventure is not public, in the tragic sense of the word. It is not comic: no elaborate social structure furnishes the details of manners, and the difficulties are neither slight nor trivial. Nor is it epic. Except in the Indian wars, its field of action is neither nationalistic nor political.

The mythic subject is one that has not yet found its proper form. I believe that the most usable and authentic myth available to us may be discovered in the adventure of the American West. Viewed in a certain way, the American frontiersman

—whether he was hunter, guide, scout, explorer or adventurer —becomes an archetypal figure, and begins to extend beyond his location in history. He is nineteenth-century man moving into the twentieth century; he is European man moving into a new continent; he is man moving into the unknown, into potentiality, and by that move profoundly changing his own nature. He and the land into which he moves may have their counterparts in both *Sir Gawaine and the Green Knight* and in *Moby-Dick*—which is to say that, though the myth which embodies him has its locality and time, it is confined by neither. He walks in his time and through his adventure, out of history and into myth. He is an adventurer in chaos, searching for meaning there. He is, in short, ourselves.

Fact in Fiction:
Problems for the Historical Novelist

"HISTORY, HISTORY! We fools, what do we know or care?" Nearly fifty years ago, in *In the American Grain*, William Carlos Williams thus expressed his ironic frustration at an aspect of an American heritage that he had discovered and that we have all come to know. A few years earlier, in 1919, on the witness stand in his libel suit against the *Chicago Tribune*, Henry Ford had declared: "History is bunk," a sentiment which many of his compatriots had expressed before and have echoed since with more elegance and less precision. It is a sentiment that we once thought peculiarly American; it has now become international. We avoid the past, and thus we fear the future; and so we pretend to ourselves that we find a sufficiency in that immediate present which precariously exists at the ends of our nerves.

We avoid the historical past, because a knowledge of it is humiliating to us. It is humiliating because it is a part of the truth about ourselves, and we will face anything before we will face that. We will observe it at a distance, as if it had nothing to do with us, as if it were a stage or screen upon which romantic figures that remotely resemble ourselves perform as if in a dream; or we will view it through the provincial lenses of the present, as if immediate prejudice might cure an accidental myopia.

But the questions that such comments raise are too large for me to handle, and more beguiling than definitive. My concerns are local. What is the relationship of the form of fiction to the content of the historical past? What kinds of historical fiction can we profitably distinguish? What are some of the special problems that the historical novelist must solve?

For nearly thirty years I have been trying to write novels, and increasingly during those years the accidents of my interests have led me to consider such questions as these, and other questions that they imply. These considerations have emerged gradually, and they are no doubt amateurish; but they have emerged from my experience as a novelist, and thus they may have a certain authenticity and interest, however limited.

During these thirty years, I have published four novels. The first of these, *Nothing But the Night*, was written during World War II, and was published in 1948. Since I had grown up in several small Texas towns, the setting of this novel was vaguely urban, and as sophisticated as I could make it—it was my own way of escaping history—in a city that might have been San Francisco, which I had seen for only a few hours before being sent across the Pacific in a troop ship. Its time was contemporary, though in the novel I resolutely refused to acknowledge the existence of that War of which I was a wholly unimportant and somewhat reluctant part. It was a short novel, and of a genre that was to some extent fashionable in those days; it was what was called a "psychological" novel, its real landscape was interior, and the time in which it was set seemed to be of no great significance. It was not a good novel, and I mention it only to establish a context and hint at a progression.

My second novel, *Butcher's Crossing*, written between the years 1954 and 1959 and published in 1960, was as different from the first as one can imagine. It was set in the American west—from Kansas to Colorado—of the 1880's. The characters were invented (the non-writer often calls them "imaginary" characters), as were the events which made up the novel; that is to say, they did not have their counterparts in recorded history. But the ideas which moved among the characters were real ideas: they were the ideas of Emerson and Thoreau, or more generally the transcendental ideas about the relation of man to his universe that animated the intellectual New England of the middle nineteenth century; and the dilemma that the novel posed was a real—that is to say, historical—dilemma. It was the conflict between preconceived abstract idea and immediate experience, and a possible result of that conflict, as specified in character and society. Likewise, the events themselves, though imagined, had their source in certain historical forces that were crucial in the latter half of the nineteenth century: in large, the movement from East to West and the expansion of the American Frontier; in small, the few years that saw the extinction of the great buffalo herds of the West and the concomitant impact upon economics, politics, and man's relation to the land he lived on and the culture he inhabited. It was, in short, a species of historical novel, in which specific detail and character were not minutely determined but influenced in a large sense by the forces of history.

In my third novel, *Stoner*, I returned, if that is the word, to a nearer time and closer scene; and for a while I even thought that I was writing what a reviewer or critic might call a "contemporary" novel. My hero was a man who was raised in the rural poverty of America in the early part of this century, who out of one of those mysterious accidents of character and fate, without which a writer would have nothing to write about, became a teacher; who married badly, who had a child, and who had a love affair that was doomed; whose lifelong dedication was to his work, which he thought to be important; and who died, a failure in the eyes of the world but not in his own nor (I would hope) those of the reader, in the year 1954. The novel was published in 1965, ten years after the fictional death of my main character. Contemporary enough, one would suppose, without being a headline or a *Time* magazine story.

And yet—was it really that contemporary? Many of the events in the novel took place before my birth; and I found that, if I wished to be accurate and specific, and therefore authentic, I had to do nearly as much research for this novel as I had for the one that had preceded it, one that could be called without dispute, a "historical" novel. What were the draft laws of World War I? How many automobiles might one have expected to see in a small middle western college town of 1916 or 1917? What salary was a young instructor paid at that time? What was the clothing like? What were the hair styles? What was the impact of prohibition? And so forth. Moreover, I discovered that I had chosen as the structural convention of the novel a form more closely associated with history than with fiction —the biography. And one critic suggested that this novel was, after all, a *kind* of historical novel; the man was dead, the time was gone, the nature of the institution had changed, and the subject of the novel was tradition, which is a special name for history.

I concluded then that I must not know what the historical novel was, and so I began to work on my fourth novel. For nearly unaccountable reasons, it was a novel about Caesar

Augustus, the founder of the Roman Empire, who flourished in the first centuries B.C. and A.D., some two thousand years ago.

What follows will be a few more or less random reflections upon the problems and necessities of the historical novel, as I see them, and as they have been defined and limited by my practice as a novelist. If I have discussed at too great length my own work, it is not altogether out of immodesty; I know my own work, and I know my intentions, and I know where I have been. And if I do not speak out of authority, I at least speak out of interest.

If I am unable to distinguish absolutely between the historical and contemporary novel, I have, I am relieved to say, distinguished company. I should like to begin these reflections of my own with a reflection by someone else, the French novelist Marguerite Yourcenar, the author of another novel about the later Roman Empire, the *Memoirs of Hadrian*, which, if not among the greatest novels, is among the wisest:

> Those who put the historical novel in a category apart are forgetting that what every novelist does is only to interpret, by means of the techniques which his period affords, a certain number of past events; his memories, whether personal or impersonal, are all woven of the same stuff as History itself. The work of Proust is a reconstruction of a lost past quite as much as is *War and Peace*. The historical novel in the 1830's, it is true, tends toward melodrama, and to cloak-and-dagger romance; but not more than does Balzac's magnificent Duchess of Langeais, or his startling Girl with the Golden Eyes, both of wholly contemporary setting. Flaubert painstakingly rebuilds a Carthaginian palace by charging his description with hundreds of minute details, thus employing essentially the same method as for his picture of Yonville, a village of his own time and of his own Normandy. In our day, when introspection tends to dominate literary forms, the historical novel, or what may for convenience's sake be called by that name, must take the plunge into time recaptured, and must fully establish itself within some inner world.

Thus Miss Yourcenar sees no essential difference between the novel of history and the novel of the near present. Nor, may I add, do I. Fashion may sternly decree at one moment that it is proper to devote our concerns to one cause or another, to adopt one attitude or another, to perceive value in one subject or another; yet as we have seen fashion will decree otherwise a moment thence.

And yet the matter is not quite so simple. There are special problems in the writing of historical novels, even if we discount the melodramatic pot-boilers that have amused or bored us for so many years.

There are at least two kinds of historical novels, both of which I have been guilty. First, there is the novel of invented incident and character, which tries to be faithful to the detail, idea, and quality of a historical period, yet not to the specific events of history or the fates of individual historical characters. This kind of novel may be either dull and trivial, or it may be interesting and serious. It is, alas, more frequently the former, though there are exceptions. The particular danger of the historical novel of invented incident is that the historical detail and background become mere decoration, a sort of cardboard set against which twentieth century men and women, dressed in quaint costumes, act out twentieth century dramas. Character, scene, and milieu exist, not as a realized whole, but as disparate and exotic elements in a fiction that we cannot, finally, believe, and thus cannot take seriously.

The second kind of historical novel is that in which the author has chosen to construct his fiction not only around the demands of a defined historical time, but has chosen also to use historical figures and hence some of the actual events of history. This is the older method of historical fiction—the method of Sophocles, of Seneca, of William Shakespeare; and when I speak of the historical novel hereafter, I shall in the main be speaking of this kind.

And yet this kind, too, has its dangers. The writer, if he is lazy or insecure—and what writer is not?—is faced with constant temptations. He may be tempted to allow the brute impact of past events to over-determine the structure of his novel—thus doing badly what time has done well, and what academic historians have done adequately. He may be tempted into a kind of antiquarianism, wherein his interest in the facts of history overwhelm his fictional imagination, to the distress of the reader. Tempted by the historical record, he may succumb to the illusion that history has created his characters, and that as a novelist he need do no more than accede to history, and to repeat and embellish the record, with whatever accuracy he chooses.

Or he may (as I fear Robert Graves too often does) impose upon that record and the characters who make it possible, certain theories, attitudes and even cosmologies that have their sources in areas remote from what he seems to be writing about. I do not mean to disparage Mr. Graves's historical novels: many of them are wonderfully informative and entertaining, though the entertainment springs largely from the knowledge we get rather than from that immersion in the mystery of other human beings, without which no novel can be wholly satisfactory.

Indeed, Mr. Graves, in a review of Rex Warner's *The Young Caesar* (a novel he did not particularly admire), put the matter more succinctly than I am able to do: "The only excuse I have ever found myself for writing a historical novel is that an obviously untrue or inadequate treatment has been given a real story by the original analysts. If I feel convinced that something very different happened, yet cannot prove it, a suggested restoration in fictional form is tempting. But the novelist needs to be two jumps ahead of the academic historian, know as much as he does, and invent nothing anachronistic or factually disproveable. It is hardly enough to retell accepted history with dramatic embellishments; there should be a ghost clamouring for justice to be done him."

I cannot disagree with what Mr. Graves has said; it seems to me that it is, on an apparent level, nearly indisputable—as far as it goes. But in one sense, Mr. Graves is speaking as a proud novelist who has been made aware of the inadequacies of the academic historian and would correct them, a sentiment with which I have considerable sympathy. But does it say all that needs to be said?

The very term, "historical novel," implies a double responsibility on the part of the writer foolish enough to commit himself to this form. It implies a respect for the record of experience, and yet implies an even firmer respect for the truth to be found in that form of knowledge—the novel—to which he has given the deepest energies of his being. Perhaps the dilemma was best suggested (apocryphally or not) by the great Latin historian of whom it is recorded that he said he would have made Pompey win the battle of Pharsalia had the effective turn of the sentence required it. The truth of form and the truth of fact—sometimes they seem irreconcilable. And yet is this conflict peculiar to the novel of history? I suspect that every novelist finds it in every novel he writes, and must discover his own solution.

In regard to this matter of fact and form, a question occurs that is curious to me. Why is it that many of the serious novelists who have had the most obsessive regard for the existence of history, whether they can properly be called historical novelists or not, are among those who have in this century performed the most interesting technical experiments in the form of the novel? I think of James Joyce and the grab-bag of history that affords him so much detail in *Ulysses* and especially *Finnegans Wake*; of William Faulkner, with that great myth of history that animates nearly every word that he has written; and among those who have written more or less explicitly historical novels, the Thornton Wilder of *The Ides of March*, the Robert Penn Warren of *All the King's Men*, the Marguerite Yourcenar of the *Memoirs of Hadrian*, and the Herman Broch of *The Death of Vergil*. On the other hand, why is it that those novelists who are most concerned with the immediacies of experience, who in some instances are even anti-historical—such as Hemingway, Fitzgerald, Lawrence, naturalists such as Dreiser and Farrell—why is it that those novelists make use of what may be called, for lack of a better word, conventional form, the novel constructed straightforwardly, for better or worse, of narrative and scene, in temporal sequence?

Perhaps it is because of the nature of the materials with which the writer of the historical novel works. His plot, as it were, is given; though he may manipulate it, he works within its terms. Moreover, the materials with which he works are public; everyone will know that Julius Caesar was assassinated on the fifteenth of March, sometime in the first century B.C., and that he was succeeded by his young nephew, Octavius, later named Caesar and Augustus. In the novel of invented incident, it is obvious that the form must be largely at the service of plot, or story, or the disposition of event, or whatever; that is to say, it is to some extent determined. But if the plot is, in its broad outlines given and public, form may to that extent be less determined; and thus it may range more freely over its materials, becoming more unexpected and unpredictable, revealing delicacies and nuances at unexpected moments.

This was not always the case, of course; Greek tragedy was historical, as (with one exception) were the histories and tragedies of Shakespeare; and both, in varying degrees, were written according to formulae. In our own time, an excellent novel by Janet Lewis—*The Wife of Martin Guerre*—is quite traditional, Miss Lewis subtly employing both the style and the chronological structure of the historian. But established convention made it necessary for both Greek and English Renaissance tragedy to be written in certain ways, and Miss Lewis in her novel was faced with the same practical problem that a novelist who invents his materials is faced with; though historically true (it is recorded in Samuel March Phillips's *Famous Cases of Circumstantial Evidence*, and elsewhere) Miss Lewis's matter would be unfamiliar to nearly any reader, however well-informed; thus the necessity to delineate the details in as straightforward a manner as possible. And necessity, in Miss Lewis's case, becomes a virtue.

But if there are dangers, there are advantages in the historical novel that justify the risks that one must take. A few years ago in an essay titled "The Donatan Tradition," in his book *Woe or Wonder*, J. V. Cunningham summarized some of the views of Donatus on tragedy and comedy: "the plot of tragedy is commonly historical and true, not feigned. . . . But if tragedy is historical, it is not merely realistic as distinguished from being fanciful; it has rather the compelling absoluteness of accomplished fact. Hence its effect will be accompanied by the recognition that things could not be otherwise, since this is how in fact they were." In comedy, of course, the story is invented, the characters tend to be of moderate estate, the difficulties that arise are relatively slight, and the outcome of it all tends to be joyful. Though Donatus and Cunningham are speaking of tragedy and comedy, I believe that we can, without being guilty of too severe a violation, transfer these observations to the two kinds of novels—historical and non-historical —that have been the pivots of these remarks.

Yet we are none of us, readers or writers, really either Hellenists or members of an English Renaissance audience; and though whether we know it or not we may all be the inheritors of the Donatan tradition, we are also inheritors of other traditions, by which the necessities of the older must be qualified. We avoid the past, and thus we fear the future, I said at the beginning of these notes: and yet that immersion in the immediacies of our experience with which we beguile ourselves is no doubt one of those circumstances of modern life that none of us can ignore, and within whose terms we must somehow work.

Thus it seems to me that the historical novelist, if he is to be a serious novelist, has a double responsibility—he must be faithful to the actuality and detail of the past, and he must be faithful to the reality in which he presently lives. And in his special task, one fidelity will not do without the other.

Some years ago the playwright Arthur Miller in *The Crucible* went to some trouble to misrepresent the nature and history of early New England witchcraft in order to make some comments and judgments (with which all of us would no doubt agree) about a phenomenon known as McCarthyism. Now the difficulty that such a performance raises is both moral and literary; to lie about the past for the sake of the true present is nevertheless to lie, and that sort of lie discovered in fiction is a destructive flaw in a literary work. It should be clear that I am not objecting to seacoasts in various Bohemias; I am objecting to a misrepresentation that permeates an entire work, and thus in the long run renders that work, as work, unbelievable.

Perhaps more common, especially in the more "popular" kinds of historical fictions, is the opposite misrepresentation, in which any sense of the present is abandoned for the supposed sake of the "authentic" past; it is the characteristic nineteenth century method which is best exemplified by Sir Walter Scott and his imitators in both the nineteenth and twentieth centuries. At best, this is a kind of antiquarianism, in which the past, however interesting, is seen as detached from the present, and thus from ourselves; at worst, it is a kind of sentimentalism, in which we see Old Souths and Wests and Ancient Greeces that never were.

Nor may that sense of the present be imposed by any of the theories (usually cyclical) derived from certain philosophies of history, anthropology, psychology, or whatever; however complicated they may appear to be, such theories are too neat to adequately contain what the novelist must know and tell of the people who will inhabit the world of his fiction. This is a kind of didacticism which would reduce a fiction, however complex or advanced or relevant it might appear, to the level of parable or Sunday School anecdote.

Near the end of "The Dead," James Joyce describes a moment of apprehension in which Gabriel Conroy finds himself: "His soul had approached that region where dwell the vast hosts of the dead. He was conscious of, but could not apprehend, their wayward and flickering existence. His own identity was fading out into a grey impalpable world: the solid world itself, which these dead had one time reared and lived in, was dissolving and dwindling."

It is from such a consciousness that the novelist of history must proceed, and it is such a consciousness that he must raise in his reader. He must know that in the long run the connection between past and present, and the significance of one to the other, is not to be found in those institutions that they seem to have in common, nor in the broad recurrences of events, nor even in the persistence of problems from one age to another. It is to be found in human beings, their oddnesses and similarities, their quirky persistences, their common humanity and inhumanity. Thus no Caesar Augustus is a Franklin Roosevelt, nor a John Kennedy, nor a Richard Nixon. Insofar as he existed, he was himself. Insofar as he exists, he is all of us.

The Future of the Novel

I TAKE MY title from an essay by Henry James, published first in the year 1900. It was written in response to doubts about the future of the novel voiced then, and echoed now, more than seventy years later. James concluded that the novel had a future, and I shall conclude the same. But there are some problems along the way to this conclusion, and I should like to consider them.

The novel is unfortunate in these respects: it has had its Longinus before it has had its Aristotle, and it has had to withstand a destructive revolution at a moment in its history when it was just beginning to know its own identity, before it had become a habit of our minds or of our culture. As a consequence, present-day novelistic theory is a shambles, and novelistic practice is forlorn. These two misfortunes are related, and I shall take them up in turn.

When Aristotle examined the art of poetry in *The Poetics* and the practical art of prose in *The Rhetoric*, both were viable literary forms; and he perceived his function to be to offer a kind of anatomy of those forms. To offer an anatomy presupposes the prior existence of a body, and the function of an anatomy is fundamental. For its purpose is to show how the brute mechanism works, how the thing gets from one place to another, and how the various parts fit together to allow it to get from one place to another, with a degree of efficiency. It is that which must be done before anything else ought to be attempted.

So, when Longinus, in *On the Sublime*, wanted to examine a particular kind of effect that poetic language made upon the reader, he could with some assurance rely upon a long critical tradition out of Aristotle. Because of this tradition, he could know what a poem was, anatomically; and he could be reasonably sure that his reader knew also. Thus, he could speak with some intelligence and assurance upon his subject.

The problem is this: largely because of this Aristotelian anatomical tradition, we have for the past two thousand years been able, with some confidence, to examine other aspects of the art of poetry, because we have been able to take its anatomy for granted. Indeed, we are in the curious position of being so sure of it that we can sometimes afford to forget that it exists. This is, perhaps, the function of any new tradition: to subsume and forget that which it incorporates from earlier traditions. And all modern critics are more nearly like Longinus than they are like Aristotle, because they have to be, and because they can afford to be. The modern critical tradition, which begins in the very early nineteenth century with Coleridge and which has not ended, is essentially a poetic tradition of a very special kind; its terms are designed to deal with a particular kind of poetry, in the context that I have indicated.

Upon this familiar tradition the novel has appeared, like an unexpected and eccentric stranger. And our response has been all too human and predictable: we cover the unexpectedness by the polite forms of social behaviour, pretending that we were simply waiting for him; we try to fit his eccentricities into the pigeon-holes of our expectations; and we insist that he is not a stranger at all. In short, we treat the novel as if it were the familiar poem; and we have known how to deal with *that* for more than two thousand years.

But the novel, as a form that we could recognize and call as such today, is less than three hundred years old; and as an *art* form, taken seriously by both the writer and his reader, it is less than that. Jane Austen's first published novel appeared in 1811, Balzac's first serious novel in 1829, Stendhal's in 1830; Flaubert's *Madame Bovary* was published in 1857, a little more than a hundred years ago.

Now on those rare occasions when a genre that is substantially new makes its appearance, it is likely to do so either independently or in defiance of an existing tradition; in every tradition there is what might be called a counter-tradition, one which takes an apparent delight in going in the opposite direction of the prevailing tendency. Thus the novel, in its self-conscious beginnings, very early in the nineteenth century, was a strong, overt, public vehicle; its concern was more with the body than the spirit, more with what people did than what they felt; and it carried one into the natural world rather than away from it. In other words, it deliberately proceeded in a direction away from the prevailing tradition.

This prevailing tradition is, of course, the Romantic tradition, which has its definition (for our purposes, at least) in the writings of Wordsworth and Coleridge. It has also been called the lyric-spasmodic tradition, since it receives its character from the following articles of belief: first, that the only serious literary performance is the poetic one, from which it follows, by circular logic, that any serious literary performance is by its nature poetic, however it may appear; second, that the poetic performance is essentially lyric and spasmodic; that is, controlled not so much by tradition as by inspiration, not so much by the grammatical and phonetic demands of poetic form as by the transcendental and emotive demands of the poet and his reader; third, that the ultimate aim of the poem is to escape the worldly limitations of time and circumstance, even though it must use worldly objects of the sense to perform this escape; and fourth, that the sensible objects which appear to constitute the poem really refer to something other than themselves, outside of time and space, hence the poem itself is a symbolic object which must be apprehended, if it is to perform its symbolic function, in an epiphanic moment, a frozen instant of time.

Two more things need to be said about this tradition. First, it was a remarkably energetic and serious one, to which a number of men of genius attached themselves, thus forcing it upon the consciousness of a civilization. Second, it was a revolutionary movement, which wished to destroy much that had gone before it. It is to this last point that I wish to address myself for a few moments.

It is the fate of revolution to fail only when it succeeds. For once it has succeeded in its aim—an aim nearly always suggested by some notion of a "new" freedom—it must institutionalize that aim in order to discover it and to preserve it. And an institution by its nature is stable, proscriptive, resistant to change, inimical to freedom; thus revolution invites stability, and stability invites revolution—and there is no rest for human kind.

Moreover, revolutions proceed by stages, so that in the long run, in a given culture, no single revolution can be seen as distinct from one that preceded it. Thus the literary revolution that began in the second decade of this century—the year 1914 is a convenient date—was only another phase of the one that preceded it by just about one hundred years; and like all revolutions, it took its sustenance from that very condition which it aimed to destroy.

The novel, then, as it came into the twentieth century, had just begun to be taken seriously, by critics, by readers, and indeed by the novelists themselves. It was, therefore, particularly vulnerable to the forces of critical fashion; it does not occur to us to behave properly unless we are expected to behave so, and unless we are told to do so.

Thus, the novel was beginning to be widely considered as a serious art form at the precise moment of literary history when the impulse toward experimentation and literary revolution was at its beginning and hence at its most energetic. Revolution is necessarily destructive; experimentation is not its end, it is its means. And thus, at the beginning of this century, the novelist found himself in an awkward position: he was persuaded to work toward the destruction of a tradition that had not yet been firmly established. This revolutionary movement is now more than fifty years old; it has become another tradition, of a special and limited kind; it is the establishment; it is, in other words, dead. And the writer who feeds upon a dead tradition is engaged in the performance of a gesture; he is merely fashionable, and he has forgotten why he does what he does.

I shall restate the problem: two generations of novelists have been educated by a set of critical theories that have been formed, not about the art of the novel, but about the art of the poem. As a consequence of this, the art of the novel has deteriorated seriously in our time, and especially during the last thirty years.

Now the obvious must be said. Novels are not poems. There are distinct differences, and I believe that these differences are important. Therefore I shall enumerate some of them, and discuss those that I enumerate.

First, the poem is written in metrical language, and the novel is written in the language of prose; moreover, the poem moves to its predetermined end by a primary concern with this language, whereas the novel moves to its end by a primary concern with structure. Second, the form of the poem is primary and it determines poetic content, whereas in the novel the content is primary and it determines novelistic form. And finally, the poem—the lyric poem, especially—because of the insistence of its form moves toward stasis and perfection, whereas the novel because of the insistence of its content moves toward flux and indeterminacy.

The language of poetry is metrical language, and that is what the poet begins with; in the long run, the language determines the specific form of the poem, and the form determines the content. Metrical language makes possible the poetic line, which is the most visible aspect of poetic form. And the function of the line is, among other things, to display in a particular way the details of the poem. And since these details are so visibly and deliberately displayed, they have a kind of importance and, hence, intensity, that they could not have in prose. Thus, the form of the poem suggests to us that there is something special, indeed something extraordinary about the details which that form has chosen; the language of poetry moves naturally toward the extraordinary—or, more exactly, the language of poetry suggests that its details are extraordinary, however they might have appeared, translated in prose. This point may be easily demonstrated by citing any one of dozens of poems by the late William Carlos Williams, whose chief stock-in-trade was the heightening of the most apparently ordinary things by strictly poetic and linear means:

> There were the roses, in the
>   rain.
> Don't cut them, I pleaded.
>   They won't last, she said
> But they're so beautiful
>   Where they are.
> Agh, we were all beautiful
>   once, she said,
> and cut them and gave them to
>   me in my hand.

Now, notice that a narrative is implied by this brief poem; but the force of the poem does not come from the narrative, it comes from the linear display of the ordinary details; its force is immediate, not cumulative; and we take it as an object, not as a structure of time. And the details are extraordinary not in themselves, but because the author has made them so by his use of the language and of the poetic line.

The language of the novel is prose, and moreover narrative prose. It is necessarily so because of the inherent structure of the novel, which discovers itself in the content of the novel; I shall have more to say of this later. And if the language of poetry moves toward the extraordinary, the language of prose moves toward the ordinary; if it wishes to rise above the ordinary, it must make an effort to do so by one or both of two means: by the means of rhetorical flourish (which ought to be used with great discretion), and more importantly by means of the structure, which is a nonlinguistic aspect of the novel form.

Despite the fact that it has been fairly effectively disguised by the experimental tradition, the language of the novel is, as I have said, narrative prose; that is, it is the kind of prose that, beyond the grammatical requirements of the language, depends upon temporal sequence for its configuration. This happens, and then this happens, and then this happens.

I must say, incidentally—and I say it with some reluctance —that beauty of style in the novel is not all-important. We can hardly conceive of a good poem being badly written—such a statement would, I believe, strike all of us as a contradiction in terms. But, alas, a novel may be indifferently or even badly written, and still be a good, or even a great novel: I once had a friend who declared that one could find better prose on a can of tomatoes than one could find in Balzac. And we have all read Dreiser. If we prefer a novel that is well-written—and I think that most of us do—we prefer it because we like adornment; and in the novel style is adornment—most pleasing and valuable and sometimes crucial, but an adornment nevertheless. A novel that depends solely, or almost solely, upon the beauties of style for its existence is a novel that we shall not read for very long.

We may as well face it—the novel depends upon its content, and from that content derives its form. This is the second difference between the form of the novel and the form of the poem which I mentioned earlier. I shall be specific. A given sonnet by William Shakespeare says what it has to say because

William Shakespeare decided to write a sonnet; he could have chosen to write something else, because there were other choices available to him. The *Paradise Lost* of John Milton says what it has to say because Milton chose to write an epic; and there were other choices available to him. And even the "Sunday Morning" of Wallace Stevens says what it has to say because Stevens chose to write in a form that he had learned from a wide reading in the English Romantics, especially the Wordsworth of the *Prelude*, and the French Symbolists, especially Mallarmé. It is a practical matter, as well as a theoretical one. When you sit down to write a poem, you know you are going to write a poem; you are not going to paint a picture, or write a novel, or compose a symphony. You may have your subject, or think you have your subject, in your head; but before you can do anything else, you must have, consciously or unconsciously, some notion of the shape that will contain what you think is in your head. And if you are any kind of poet at all, you will choose your particular form, and allow that form to determine your content. If you choose to write a sonnet, you cannot write a *Paradise Lost*, or even an *Essay on Man*.

We can, with a fair degree of accuracy, describe the forms of poetry, even of modern poetry; there are fewer of them than we are led to believe. But no one has tried to define the content of poetry, for the simple reason that it cannot be done; we must describe the specific contents of specific poems, precisely for the reason that the form is the distinguishing characteristic, and not the content. Neither has anyone tried to describe the content of the novel. But that task is, I believe, possible; and if it has not been done, it has not been for the reasons that I have indicated earlier; the critics of the novel, and many novelists themselves, in the modern tradition, have looked at the novel as if it were a species of poetry, and have persuaded themselves, by a kind of critical hypnosis, that what cannot be said of the poem also cannot be said of the novel.

But the content of the novel can be described, and I shall proceed to attempt to do so. The content of the novel—of any novel—is simply this: it is the realized and presented history of a person, or persons, moving through sensibly experienced space and time, between the recognized intervals of birth and death. This history and this movement may be interesting or dull, intelligent or stupid, vital or trivial; there are good novels, and there are bad. But, good or bad, with the proper qualifications, this will be true of every novel you have read; I do not speak of those you have not read, or those that have not been written. This is a simple description, but an accurate one; it is also a sufficient one, for it will allow us to say something about our immediate subject, which is the form of the novel.

You will have realized, I trust, that this general description of the content of the novel is also a general description of its form; and this is precisely my point. It is a description that will account for such diverse novels as Defoe's *Robinson Crusoe*, Flaubert's *Madame Bovary*, and Joyce's *Ulysses* and *Finnegans Wake*.

Let us look for a moment at *Ulysses*, which has become in the modern tradition a touchstone of novelistic practice. *Ulysses* is the history—partial in presentation but full in symbolic implication—of Stephen Daedalus and Leopold Bloom as they move through the places of Dublin, Ireland, for a twenty-two or twenty-three hour period, in the year 1900. The novel begins at a specific instant in time, and it ends at another. This is the implicit content, and this is the implicit structure.

But the point I want to make here is suggested by the word "implicit." For *Ulysses* is important historically, if not absolutely, because of Joyce's deliberate effort to destroy that very structure that made his novel possible in the first place. Temporal sequence is interrupted, so that from moment to moment we hardly know where we are; it is distorted, so that we feel that we have been transported to another world where time and space as we have known them do not pertain; we see place as nightmare, and nightmare as place. In one sense, it is as if a bomb has been thrown; and if we wish to have repaired the place of devastation, we must do it for ourselves, by fitting this piece here and that piece there, as we say, "This is what it *must* have looked like, before it was torn apart." It is a scene of destruction, with which we have become all too familiar in our time.

As I have said, in revolution experimentation is not the end, it is the means. It is only when the revolution is over that the means become the end, and are solidified by the old revolutionaries, now become the new establishment.

This destruction may or may not have been what Joyce intended, at least in the beginning. What Joyce may have intended seems not really very drastic at all. For reasons that I have indicated before, Joyce seems to have intended something so apparently harmless, and actually destructive, as this: he simply wanted the novel to do what he knew the poem did. He wanted to make of the novel a kind of poem; hence his effort to destroy the novel as a viable literary form.

This is not opinion; this is fact. It is precisely what Joyce announced in the novel that preceded *Ulysses, The Portrait of the Artist as a Young Man*, in a kind of latter-day *Essay of Dramatic Poesy* which becomes a key part of a modern novel. It is the famous dialog between Stephen and Lynch, and it suggests clearly the aesthetic of the novel that Joyce followed in both *Ulysses* and *Finnegans Wake*. Speaking of the aesthetic emotion, Stephen says:

> . . . The feelings excited by improper art are kinetic, desire or loathing. Desire urges us to abandon, to go from something. These are kinetic emotions. The arts which excite them, pornographical or didactic, are therefore improper arts. The esthetic emotion (I use the general term) is therefore static. The mind is arrested and raised above desire or loathing. . . . Beauty . . . awakens, or ought to awaken, or induces, or ought to induce, an esthetic stasis, an ideal pity or an ideal terror, a stasis called for, prolonged and at last dissolved by what I call the rhythm of beauty.

This is late Romantic doctrine given to us in the language of scholasticism, in the language of Saint Thomas Aquinas; and it would be unremarkable except for two things: first, Joyce deliberately and overtly applies this poetic doctrine to the dramatic form, by which he means the novel; and second, in his own novels he attempts to practice what he preaches. The implications of the passage are these: the novel is seen as a fixed, prior, undefined but not undefinable form, under the terms of which the content is organized for the evocation in the reader of a certain kind of emotion; form is first, content is second. It is significant that Joyce chose to contain the detail of his novel in a thematic—that is to say, static—abstraction taken from the *Odyssey* of Homer. Second, the temporal sequence, insofar as it is recognizably what it is, is improper to art, since it does not conduce to stasis or arrest, which are the proper functions of art. And finally, the form of the novel—nontemporal and nonkinetic—exists independently of what the novel wants to say; it is finally a kind of poem, and a very special poem at that —a lyric-spasmodic poem, or more locally, the kind of poem so admired by the late Romantics and symbolists such as Walter Pater and Algernon Charles Swinburne.

Now the kind of emotion toward which Joyce aspired to induce in his reader, and according to the terms of which he went about predetermining his form, may be found in three places: in an epiphanic religious experience of a particular sort, in the reading of such a lyric-spasmodic poem as I have described, and in the act of love. I shall speak of the last, because it is the most interesting.

Part of the charm of sexual intercourse lies in its form, which includes both ritual and relative brevity. The orgasmic moment could not be endured if it lasted for very long, and in the human culture at least it receives much of what we rather bloodlessly call its value from the form that contains it —from the ritual (or the parody of the ritual) which celebrates by largely formal means the human consciousness of love, of commitment, the consciousness of the other, and the impossible dream of a oneness with nature. And so, in such novels as *Ulysses* and *Finnegans Wake*, the sustained demands that their form makes upon us are finally unendurable, and we are forced to withdraw from it, to examine it in the cool and abstract light of modern scientific and philosophic literary inquiry, as if that form had nothing to do with ourselves, or our experience. We are, finally, bored.

And though there is always the genuine issue of the intrinsic interest that we may have in Joyce's mind—it was a remarkable one—there lurks within us still the suspicion that the novel form, even as Joyce altered and weakened it, was not the most appropriate way available to him to display that mind to us. At last perhaps we are intrigued by such novels because of their impossibility; one is reminded of the chess game, which was described as being so interesting that it was foolish.

I come to the last of those points that have to do with the differences between the poem and the novel.

The poem moves toward perfection, because that is where its form tells it that it must go. I use the term "perfection" here in its technical rather than its evaluative sense. The language of the poem is determined by the laws and principles of its meter, as are the lines of the poem, and the relations of the lines, and, in the last analysis, the grammatical units that make up the lines. Because of this determination, by meter, by rhyme, and by whatever pattern the poet has in his head before he writes the poem, it must move toward exclusion rather than inclusion: thus, it moves toward simplicity. And the rhythmical regularity of the language—that is, its meter—imposes upon the statement of the poem a kind of formality that will be found in no other literary form, and thus moves it toward a kind of finality, that is almost mathematical in the exactness of what is said: this much, and no more.

The novel, on the other hand, moves in a direction that is nearly opposite. As I have said, the content of the novel determines the form, rather than the other way around; and the content of the novel leads inevitably toward uncertainty, apprehensions of chaos, and the sense of the complexity that lies behind the biological fundamentals of our existence. Indeed, this very aspect of content is also the theme of much of the fiction in our tradition. The poem tells us: the apparent chaos of experience may be contained by the simplest external forms, if we will use the means at our disposal to do so—for if chaos is a reality, so is order. The novel tells us: the apparently simple, abstract biological forms within which our lives seem to move—the patterns of birth, growth, and death—contain chaoses and uncertainties and complexities that we could not have foretold, forces which constantly burst through the fundamental patterns that contain them, and make them possible.

In this connection, I should like for a moment to speak about life, with which both the poem and the novel have some connection. There are few things that we can know with any certainty about life, but one of them is this: we live within the terms of two opposing sets of principles, neither of which is finally reconcilable with the other. We live in order and chaos, in predictability and uncertainty, in determination and accident. We live in the order of our minds and the chaoses of our hearts, and sometimes the other way around; we live under the rule of law and in the disorder of human passions; we rise to see the sun and know that a certain number of hours and minutes later we may expect the darkness, but we cannot be sure of what will happen in those hours; we can conceive and determine nearly any course of action, and we discover that accident has intervened so that it cannot be fulfilled. I am aware that philosophy has solved these problems, and I am also aware that life has not.

Now perhaps it is not too fanciful to suppose that the form of the novel and the form of the poem are reflections of these opposing principles, indeed of this law that seems to govern our existence. And if it is not too fanciful to suggest that, perhaps neither is it too fanciful to suggest that, as in life, the very strength of the principles depends upon their being kept apart, that we may live with them only if they are kept distinct, that we risk our lives and our sanity if we confuse them. In simpler terms, a poem is a poem, a novel is a novel, and we had better not pretend to ourselves that the one is the other.

Let us see if we can gather some of the pieces together. I shall conclude these remarks by making a few comments upon some recent criticism of the novel. The criticism is not unique to our time, but it is characteristic of it.

Now it must be understood first of all that such criticism that I shall discuss has little to do with truth. From the time of Dr. Johnson until our own, the dominant trend in literary discussion has been toward the evaluative, no matter what such criticism may have pretended to itself and to its readers. Such criticism, then, as we have known for the past two hundred years characteristically says very little about what it pretends to deal with; what such criticism is really about is the age in which it exists, and it is most valuably interpreted as a record of what an age thinks of itself, or what it thinks it ought to think of itself.

I take as my text a passage from the famous Spanish philosopher and critic, José Ortega y Gasset. I have chosen this passage because Ortega is an able man, because his remarks are wholly characteristic of dominant modern novelistic criticism, and because he is wrong.

In an essay titled "Notes on the Novel," Ortega writes: "Anyone who gives a little thought to the conditions of a work of art must admit that a literary genre may wear out." He is, of course, speaking of the novel. Novels, he further states, have been written about nearly every conceivable subject, and we are no longer "fascinated by a novel . . . because of its subject," which "can be told in a few words and in this form holds no interest." Finally, he writes, "today the novel is, and must be, a sluggish form—the very opposite, therefore, of a story, a 'serial,' or a thriller" because our "interest has shifted from the plot to the figures, from actions to persons." And he asks, implying his own answer, "Should we, by any chance, now be again in the process of turning from action to the person, from function to substance? Such a transition would be indicative of an emerging classicism." And, he summarizes: "My thesis is that in the novel the so-called dramatic interest has no aesthetic value but forms a mechanical necessity. The reason for this necessity is to be found in a general law of the human soul." And he is kind enough to give us the general law of the human soul, and it turns out to be a philosophic shibboleth: he tells us that the highest function of the human soul is to aspire toward contemplation rather than action, though some minimal impulse toward action is necessary for the contemplative state. Again, I quote: "Hence it appears that those elements which seem to disturb pure contemplation—interests, sentiments, compulsions, affective preferences—are precisely its indispensable instruments." Thus the novel is seen as essentially static, though with a necessary (and regrettable) minimum of action.

I shall take up these points in the order that they occur in Ortega's text. First of all, anyone who has given a little thought to the conditions of a work of art probably has, like Ortega, at least flirted with the notion that a literary genre might wear out. But the fact is, very few, if any of them, have. The drama, in the western tradition alone, is something more than twenty centuries old; and though it has a bad hundred years now and then, it has not worn out. The genre of the epic poem is perhaps older, but it has managed to persist through Homer, and assorted Roman writers, and the unknown author of *Beowulf*, and Dante, and Milton, and only a few years ago the modern poet, William Carlos Williams, gave us a twentieth century version of the genre in his *Paterson*, a long poem which fulfills every important condition of the epic. Indeed, it may be worthwhile to attempt to retrieve the notion of genre from the aestheticians and critics, who have made a hash of it. Fundamentally, a genre is not a thing in itself; it is a set of ways that a thing has of becoming; and the notion of it springs from a set of literary presuppositions, among which are these: (1) that there are many differing intentions that a literary artist may legitimately have; (2) that these intentions are roughly classifiable; (3) that certain forms or strategies have been discovered, or are discoverable, which tend to lead toward the embodiment of certain intentions; (4) that certain strategies are more or less appropriate to certain intentions; and (5) that in literature at least procedures (or means) tend to influence the outcome of the literary work.

While appearing to defend the notion of genre, Ortega really is attempting to destroy it; and in this he is squarely in the midst of the modern tradition. What Ortega is suggesting is essentially what Coleridge suggested, a hundred and fifty years before him—that there is a virtual equivalence between the sensibility of the poet (and hence of his reader), and the form of the poem itself. In the Romantic view, form is seen as organic, and must change to accommodate new sensibilities.

But the fact is, form does not change to accommodate sensibility, new or old, any more than grammar does. In one literary era certain aspects of form may become more fashionable than others; we have seen this happen in the eighteenth century, and we have seen it happen in the twentieth. Perhaps my point will be clearer if I offer an example. I suppose we would all agree that the sensibility of the fourteenth century Englishman was profoundly different from the sensibility of his eighteenth century counterpart. And yet if we compare (let us say) Chaucer's *Nun's Priest's Tale* and (let us say) Alexander Pope's *Rape of the Lock*, we shall find many more similarities in form than we shall find dissimilarities. Both are written in decasyllabic, rhyming couplets; both are narrative in structure; in both poems the poetic line tends to display a complete grammatical unit; both are written in a language that proceeds from ordinary, cultivated English speech. The differences are nonformal, accidental, and historical; and it is through *these* differences—vocabulary, historical style, subject matter, and the linguistically revealed attitudes of the author—that the new sensibility of the poet and audience is accommodated. The form remains substantially the same, and it is adequate to its task.

Ortega's characterization of the novel as a sluggish form, and his insistence that its proper function is to appeal to the contemplative, nonactive, and essentially nontemporal state of the human soul, which is its highest state, is substantially the same view as Joyce's which posited the novel as a kind of epiphany, nonkinetic, absolute, nontemporal, both in effect and form. It is the novel become poem, and the poem seen as spasm.

One last thing might be said about Ortega's insistence upon new and fresh subject matter. It is an important insistence, for it reveals a bias that Ortega is apparently unaware that he has, and it reveals the same bias absorbed by many of his followers. Such an insistence upon fresh subject matter sounds very much like a fashionably modern search for novelty, the search for the sensation whose primary value is that it is new. The difficulty is, of course, that such a search is self-defeating; for once the new is apprehended and owned, it is no longer new, its primary value is destroyed, and frustration feeds upon the very end whereby frustration would be defeated.

What, then, may we say of the novel, as we find it in the debris of modern critical theory and modern fictional practice? Does anything remain?

It is a stubborn, recalcitrant, and pragmatic creature that we have been talking about. It is, one might almost say, the most unimaginative of all the literary forms. That is at once its limitation, and its strength. Despite what philosophy—new or old—or what theology—new or old—or psychology—new or old—would teach it, it goes on insisting in its maddening way that one day follows another between birth and death; that men recognize this sequence of days and months and years; that perceptible beings, men and women, displace perceptible space in perceptible time; and that what they recognizably do is of some significance, both to themselves and to others.

At the beginning of this article I suggested that one of the problems of the novel was that unlike the poem and the drama it had not had the kind of solidifying critical force such as that represented by Aristotle; and without an Aristotle, one can ill afford a Longinus. Needless to say, I do not offer myself as an Aristotle, nor do I offer this commentary as a *Poetics* of the novel. I am a novelist, and I am perhaps too close to the torrent to see the course of the river. So I shall conclude with several difficult questions and a few simple answers.

What is a novel? Does it have a nature, like an organism—an amoeba, a tse-tse fly, or a fieldmouse—or is it in the long run merely an idea, without the tough, minute limitations of specific and describable existence? Is it, in other words, an amusing invention, or does it perform a function in what might be called the ecology of the human spirit? My answer is that, metaphorically, at least, it is an organism, that it does perform a function in that ecology; thus it is a phenomenon that can be talked about, described, and to a certain extent understood. It is, in other words, available to an anatomy.

If it is available to this anatomy, what shall the anatomy be like? Where shall it begin? Can we distinguish the novel as simply as we can the poem, to which we can point and say with some certainty, "It begins with metrical language, and discovers its nature from that property." Can we say anything so definite about the novel? I believe that we can, though we must look to the structure of the novel and its content rather than to its language. The novel discovers its nature from its content, and becomes a form designed to deal with the inhabitants of a natural world; it is sequential in structure, and cumulative in effect. A poem can be nearly empty of content, and if it is short enough we can still read it with pleasure, for the simple beauties of its form; a novel cannot be empty of content, for that is its form. And if you object that the "modern" novel is modern precisely insofar as it tries to avoid naturalistic bases and the logic of temporal sequence, I can only reply that you do not try to avoid what is not there.

Does it not follow, then, that since the natural world is what it is, all novels will then begin to look alike, at least in form? My answer is, Yes, they will—in just the sense that one declarative sentence is in form very much like another. Predictable form is the primary condition of art. Within a given form, there can be good sentences and bad, good poems and bad, good novels and bad.

But behind all these questions, there is an insistent one; it is the one contained in the title of this article, and it cannot be answered. We ask questions for three reasons: because we do not know the answers, or because we have forgotten them, or because we want to express an attitude without taking the responsibility for it. I shall conclude by asking this third kind of question.

The novel, the novel . . . what is to become of it? we ask. For more than two hundred years we have spoken of it as if it were an uncertain child, bright with promise, erratic, recalcitrant, evasive of authority, holding darkly within it the seeds of its own destruction. We speak of it, in short, as if it were a kind of incipient juvenile delinquent—our own child, whom we have done the best we could by. And like all parents, we have expectations of it that are nearly impossible: we want it, at once, to be both what we have been, and what we have not, what we would like to be, and what we would not, what we dream of ourselves, and what we know ourselves to be.

And if its future does not exist—then neither does our own.

Remarks upon Accepting the National Book Award for Augustus, 1973

I AM PLEASED to be a recipient of this award in a year that has seen the publication of so much interesting and vital fiction, and more than somewhat intimidated to be among the distinguished company that this year's nominations represent. In the current issue of *The Massachusetts Review*, Shaun O'Connell speaks of the work of several members of this company and says, "Any year which can produce such fulfilled fictional designs cannot be all bad, and the novel, therefore, cannot be anything but living, thriving," a sentiment with which I must concur. Henry James called it "the great form" and suggested that it can "be made to stretch anywhere—it will take in absolutely anything. . . . for its subject, magnificently, it has the whole human consciousness." And most movingly, he added that, "til the world is an unpeopled void, there will be an image in the mirror."

Since the time that Henry James wrote these words—around 1900—the necessity of that image of humanity has been questioned and sometimes denied. After a rather worn remark by a popular journalist about the "death of the novel," my friend Brock Brower, whose novel THE LATE GREAT CREATURE was one of the nominees for this award, is said to have said: "Listen, there's only one stable institution in this country. It's not Princeton, it's not I.T. & T., it's not marriage, it's the novel." I hope Brock really said that; as a novelist, I may truthfully pretend that he did.

In any event, as I accept this award, I hope I may do so not so much for myself but for those others, named and nameless, who have given, give, and will give the deepest energies of their beings to the maintenance of that stable institution, and who against the odds of their own human limitations and the pressure of fashion try to perfect the image in that mirror of humanity at which we all must look.

CHRONOLOGY

NOTE ON THE TEXTS

NOTES

Chronology

1922   Born John Edward Jewell on August 29, in Clarksville, Texas, to J. E. Jewell and Amelia Walker (b. 1898), married January 21, 1921. Mother comes from a family of vegetable farmers. Father's birth year unknown and family background obscure. He is "a few years older" than his wife.

1923   J. E. moves wife and son 250 miles north to Wichita Falls, Texas, which has become a boomtown due to oil and land speculation. Williams's maternal grandparents follow. J. E. takes a job selling agricultural supplies in a local store, but tempted by the opportunity to make a quick killing in one of the many risky ventures the area is awash in, he buys and quickly flips a piece of land for a cash payment. According to Williams's mother, J. E. makes the mistake of talking about his success and flashing his new bankroll at stops on his drive back home. He is murdered by a hitchhiker who gets wind of his good fortune. Possibly fabricated, this version of his father's death, revealed to Williams at age nine, is the one that Williams carries for the rest of his life.

1924   Amelia meets George Williams, twelve years her senior, who does odd jobs and manual labor. His family has connections with banking, he says, but he prefers to live a less proper, less confining life. They soon marry.

1925   Williams's halfsister, George Rae, born in May.

1926–32   Until the story he hears at age nine of the death of J. E. Jewell, Williams believes that his stepfather is his biological father—he has been raised as John Ed Williams, despite the fact that George Williams never legally adopts him—and that he and George Rae are full siblings. Grows up reading adventure stories in *Flying Magazine*, *Blue Book of Fiction and Adventure*, and many Zane Grey Westerns.

1933–35   Attends Reagan Junior High in Wichita Falls. Becomes enamored with Ronald Colman's portrayal of Sidney Carton in the 1935 film version of *A Tale of Two Cities*. Will sport an ascot in later years and attempt to emulate the suave, dapper, melancholy composure of the actor and character.

Stepfather lands a civil service job as a custodian at the newly built U.S. post office in Wichita Falls, earning a salary large enough to allow the family of four to rent a whole house in the center of town.

1936   Enters Wichita Falls Senior High School, where he joins the school newspaper and submits poems to the school literary magazine. Also takes a part-time job at a local bookshop, The Lovelace Bookstore, which exposes him to a wide range of modern writers. It is a job he will keep throughout his high school years.

1938   Maternal grandparents move into the Williams house. Grandmother Walker dies.

1939   Graduates from high school, writing in a yearbook essay, "We linger for an instant in a morass of stupidity and conceit and then we graduate from high school." Enters Hardin Junior College in Wichita Falls in August. Pays little attention to course work, failing freshman English ("I deserved to flunk. I didn't do the work," he says in a later interview), preferring to spend his time at the student newspaper, literary club, and drama society. Also performs on the local radio station KWFT, writing a weekly original drama, playing parts, and hiring actors. This continues into the spring semester, even while he is in danger of flunking out altogether. "I'd already read most of what we were studying," he remarks.

1940   Decides not to reenroll for his sophomore year. Produces and stages a three-week run of Thornton Wilder's *Our Town* at a local theater.

1941   In the spring, appears onstage in Ibsen's *Pillars of Society*. His modest theatrical successes, coupled with his clear, deep speaking voice, convince him he has a future in radio. Takes a job as the morning news announcer on KRRV radio in Sherman, Texas. Calling himself "Jon Williams," he reports on matters of local and human interest, interviewing politicians and covering county fairs. Before the end of the year, moves to a station with a larger broadcast range and audience, KDNT in Denton, Texas. Hired as a newsman, he also takes on the role of engineer and assistant station manager, as well as writing advertising copy. While setting up equipment for a broadcast at North Texas State College, meets Alyeene Bryan, a music and drama student.

1942   Marries Alyeene on April 5. For the wedding announce-
        ment gives his name as "Jon Williams" and claims to have
        a bachelor's degree from the University of New Mexico
        and to have done graduate work in Chicago. To avoid be-
        ing drafted and assigned to an infantry unit, enlists in the
        Army Air Corps on October 6. The Air Corps is calling for
        men with radio or mechanical experience to fly transport
        and supply missions in both the European and Pacific the-
        aters of World War II. Sent to Greensboro, North Caro-
        lina, for training.

1943   In January, leaves San Francisco on a troopship bound for
        the Far East. Assigned to the 10th Air Force, 443 Troop
        Carrier Group. Final destination Sookerating Airfield on
        India's border with Tibet. Works as a radioman on trans-
        port aircraft, flying five-hundred-mile daily runs over the
        Himalayas to resupply Chiang Kai-shek's National Army,
        engaged in fighting the Japanese. Later, claims his C-45
        was shot down while flying a mission, killing most of the
        crew. Contracts malaria during his time at war. Promoted
        to sergeant. Will suffer from nightmares and recurrences of
        malaria for years afterward.

1944   Still in India, receives letter from Alyeene asking for a di-
        vorce. While on leave in Calcutta, begins, hesitantly, to
        write fiction—a novel—trying to find a style to probe the
        psychological—the interior—life of a single individual.
        In one extract from his notebooks, he writes: "Take any
        man, study him carefully. . . . Understand his likes and
        dislikes. . . . know a little about his background, his
        environment. . . . Season with a little imagination and
        sympathy—and you'll have a novel."

1945   Returns in the spring to the United States and civilian life.
        Finalizes his divorce from Alyeene. Heads to Key West,
        Florida, where—encouraged by an old college friend
        working in advertising there—he finds a job with a new
        radio station, WKWF. By June, he is at the control board
        of "the southernmost radio station in the U.S." In the fall
        completes, after six revisions, the novel begun in India
        the previous year, titling it *Nothing But the Night*. The
        typescript is read by a Key West acquaintance, Professor
        George "Ken" Smart of the University of Alabama, who
        recognizes Williams's budding talent and recommends
        that he apply to study English at Alabama and attend the
        creative writing seminar there.

1946   Defers a decision on enrolling at Alabama to visit his ail-
            ing tubercular mother, now living with his stepfather and
            halfsister George Rae in Pasadena, California. Takes a
            job reading meters for the Southern California Gas Com-
            pany. George Rae introduces him to Yvonne Stone, a ju-
            nior college student and fellow actress at the Pasadena
            Playhouse. On July 15, mother dies at the age of forty-
            eight. Harper & Brothers, to whom Williams sends *Noth-
            ing But the Night* on Smart's recommendation, rejects
            the novel as unsalvageable. It is impossible, according
            to editor Edward Aswell at Harper & Brothers, for the
            reader to care about what happens to so unsympathetic
            a main character. The poems Williams circulates to var-
            ious magazines are also rejected. Finally opting to apply
            for admission to Alabama for the fall term, he is rejected
            there as well. At a loss what to do with the novel, sends
            it to The Swallow Press in Denver, which has put out a
            call for works that might not be to the taste of the East
            Coast publishers. Alan Swallow, publisher and English
            professor at the University of Denver, contacts Williams,
            offering a serious critique of the novel and suggesting this
            might not be the book with which to attempt to break
            into print. Revises the book and continues to send it out
            without success.

1947   In April, Swallow reconsiders, deciding that *Nothing But
            the Night* might after all be suited to his new line, "The
            Short Fiction Club," and offers to publish it. Swallow,
            much as "Ken" Smart had done, also urges Williams to
            come to the University of Denver to study English and
            creative writing with an eye to completing a graduate de-
            gree as well. As at Alabama, Williams discovers the uni-
            versity is not inclined to accept any of his Hardin Junior
            College credits, but Swallow steps in and secures a place
            for him. On August 28, marries Yvonne in Pasadena. The
            two head immediately for Denver for the start of the fall
            semester.

1948   In addition to resuming his undergraduate studies, Wil-
            liams becomes poetry editor of the campus magazine *Foot-
            hills* and joins Swallow Press as its associate editor. Meets
            Avalon Smith (known as "Lonnie"); a contributor to *Foot-
            hills*, she is also pitching in at Swallow Press. *Nothing But
            the Night* printed in March by The Swallow Press. Distri-
            bution begins over the spring and summer. (Swallow Press

books are not widely distributed. Alan Swallow stores the books in his garage and ships orders himself—relying primarily on word of mouth, not advertising.) Sales of the novel are considered only "fair," even by the standards of a publisher facing substantial marketing limitations. There are no professional or trade reviews. Williams reads Yvor Winters's book of critical essays, *In Defense of Reason*, published the year before by Swallow. This encounter with Winters's anti-Romantic aesthetic, his championing of a restrained, stoical literary style, and his decidedly unorthodox view of the canon of English verse will have an enormous impact on Williams's career both as a writer and as an academic. In April, Alan Swallow introduces John and his wife, Yvonne, to a visiting friend, bohemian writer Douglas Woolf—an American cousin of Leonard Woolf. Within months Yvonne begins an affair with Woolf that leads to the dissolution of the marriage, after Yvonne runs off to join Woolf in Tucson, Arizona, in July.

1949 In January, Swallow publishes Williams's collection of poems, *The Broken Landscape*. The Williamses' divorce becomes final in February. On March 24, Williams and Lonnie marry in Provo, Utah. Receives his B.A. degree in English. Begins working on a second novel, "Splendid in Ashes," whose main character, a sort of Nietzschean hero, is dead when the novel opens.

1950 Earns his M.A. in English. His essay "J. V. Cunningham: The Major and the Minor," which had been rejected by *Poetry* magazine the year before, published in the Summer issue of the *Arizona Quarterly*; it is Williams's first significant publication as a literary critic. On Swallow's recommendation, applies to and is accepted into the doctoral program in English at the University of Missouri in Columbia, Missouri. The program allows for a creative writing component in working toward a Ph.D. The couple arrive in the fall of 1950, Lonnie to start courses in English in graduate school. Immediately, Williams joins The Tabard Inn, an all-male social club for students and teachers, devoted to banquets and literary conversation. At one of these gatherings Williams hears the story of the decades-long enmity between two University of Missouri English professors, which often played out through departmental maneuverings. It will become a source for his novel *Stoner*.

1951   Sends "Splendid in Ashes" to Alan Swallow, who is en-
            thusiastic but declines to publish it—it is an "experimen-
            tal" novel along the lines of *Nothing But the Night*, which
            Swallow admits didn't sell many copies. He recommends
            an agent of his acquaintance, who sends the book to every
            major publisher in New York—all quickly reject it, some-
            times praising the writing, but expressing puzzlement
            as to what exactly the protagonist's dilemma is and (like
            criticism of the first book) why anyone should care about
            what happens to "this uninteresting and irritating person."
            "Too long and too pretentious," sums up an editor at E. P.
            Dutton. The novel will not be published.

1952   First child, a daughter christened Katherine, born in Octo-
            ber. Spurred by Yvor Winters's and Alan Swallow's admi-
            ration for the poetry of the English Renaissance, decides
            to write his doctoral dissertation on the works of Fulke
            Greville, poet and friend of Sir Philip Sidney. Greville's
            poems have been singled out for high praise and quoted
            extensively in Winters's critical writings.

1954   In June, Williams's doctoral dissertation, "The World and
            God: The Poems and Dramas of Fulke Greville," is ac-
            cepted and he passes his oral exams. Alan Swallow secures
            him a teaching position at the University of Denver. Wil-
            liams and his wife, Lonnie, spend the summer visiting his
            sister, George Rae, down in Mexico, where she has been
            living a largely bohemian life with her husband, writer Wil-
            lard "Butch" Marsh. Returns to Denver for the fall term
            as an assistant professor and takes over from Swallow, now
            departed from the faculty, as director of the creative writing
            program. Second daughter, Pamela, born in November.

1955   Begins to collect regional maps and to research western
            history, making a yearlong study. Although he will lose all
            his research during a move to a new faculty building, he
            retains his primary insight: that the West was in many ways
            a dream created by the East, something the eastern pop-
            ular imagination made up, a West that never existed. He
            wants to write about an easterner confronting the actual
            West—a Harvard-educated pioneer testing his spiritual
            ideas about the West against the real thing. Starts to draft
            his new novel, calling it initially "The Naked World."

1956   Expands the creative writing program's scope to include
            summer writing courses, followed by a four-week writers'

conference that brings established authors to meet students. A son, Jonathan, is born in June.

1958   In the summer, sends the completed first draft of "The Naked World" to novelist Janet Lewis, wife of Yvor Winters. She recognizes its power, writing that the characters "exist only in the moment. They have no pasts and no futures. This makes the events very intense. . . . Congratulations. It is the most extraordinary reversal of procedure from your first novel." Williams secures an experienced New York agent, Marie Rodell, to handle the book. At almost the same time, on a tip from a friend of Williams, Macmillan editor Cecil Scott contacts him directly and asks to read the manuscript. Macmillan has just instituted a new fiction prize worth $7,500, and Scott thinks "The Naked World" should compete. If it wins, Macmillan will publish.

1959   "The Naked World" comes in second in Macmillan's contest, but Scott decides he wants to publish the book nonetheless. Begins to work on a new novel about a college professor, drawing partly on the story he heard in Missouri nine years before. Applies for a Guggenheim grant to work on the book. Approached by University of Missouri Press, who are considering publishing his dissertation on Fulke Greville, but they ultimately withdraw the offer.

1960   Now titled *Butcher's Crossing*, Williams's second novel is published on March 15 by Macmillan. The book receives a harshly negative review in *The New York Times* by Nelson Nye, a writer of popular Westerns. Viewing it as a failed attempt at a conventional Western, Nye calls it "practically plotless . . . [with] little excitement. . . . [It] moves as though hauled by a snail through a pond of molasses." Reviews in the midwestern and western papers are better, praising the book's unique take on the Old West. Sales of the book are small, a few thousand copies. Williams is turned down for a Guggenheim. Continues drafting his novel about a college professor, which now has "A Matter of Light" as its working title. Begins a relationship with Nancy Leavenworth, a twenty-five-year-old divorcée with four children, who enrolled as a student at Denver in the spring and is taking all the poetry classes Williams offers.

1961   Continues the development of the creative writing department at Denver, establishing a doctoral program requiring proficiency in two foreign languages, oral examinations, and the submission and acceptance of a novel, or a collection of short stories or poetry, to earn a degree. This makes Denver one of the first two such programs in America. Publishes "The 'Western': Definition of the Myth" in *The Nation* in November.

1962   Conceives the idea of editing an anthology of English Renaissance poetry, partly to buff up his academic resumé and partly hoping that significant course adoptions would provide a stream of continuing income that *Butcher's Crossing* never produced. Also sees this as a chance to put forward in classrooms the literary taste and viewpoint of his intellectual mentor, Yvor Winters, whose high estimation of some of the less canonical poets and poems of the sixteenth century was not, Williams felt, widely enough shared. Macmillan passes, but his editor there finds a willing publisher in Anchor Books, paperback division of Doubleday, which offers Williams a generous advance and plans a 10,000-copy first printing. Work on the anthology goes quickly; he also makes good progress with "A Matter of Light," telling his agent that he expects to have a finished typescript for her before the summer of 1963.

1963   Accepted into a six-week summer program on Elizabethan poetry at Oxford University. *English Renaissance Poetry* published in May. In mid-June sends the completed text of "A Matter of Light" to his agent, who thinks the book, with its understated prose and twilight moods, will have trouble finding an audience in the current market. Travels to Europe with Lonnie, but she returns to America after only three weeks in England. Williams decides to stick to his original plan and in August, when Oxford sessions end, heads to Rome. He is thinking about his next novel, perhaps to be set in Rome in classical times. Macmillan, with first option rights to "A Matter of Light," turns it down. Meanwhile, on July 19, Yvor Winters sends a bombshell letter to Anchor Books, angrily asserting that Williams's anthology is lifted almost entirely from Winters's work: 80 percent of the poems in the anthology are poems that Winters himself singled out for praise and discussion in his critical writings on the period; moreover, Williams's introduction simply repeats the same arguments about the period that Winters made two decades earlier, with Winters's fresh and original insights treated as if they were Williams's own—without attribution. "I don't want any communication with Williams," he writes, "unless it is to plead for mercy. I'll wreck this book, unless you provide proper acknowledgement." All future printings (the anthology was selling well) will contain this acknowledgment in the front of each book. Williams stays in Rome for six weeks, beginning to see the Roman emperor Augustus as the central figure in his next novel. In late September, sails back to the U.S. and heads to Denver for the beginning of the fall semester. Making the rounds, "A Matter of Light" is rejected by several of the major publishing houses.

1964   As publishers continue to pass on "A Matter of Light," Williams decides to try to change the book's luck with a new title: "A Matter of Love." At the same time, his effort to gain publication of "A Shape of Air," his second gathering of poems, fails. Finally, in June, "A Matter of Love" reaches the desk of Corlies "Cork" Smith, a respected editor at the Viking Press. Impressed by the quality of the writing, though unhappy with the title, Smith offers Williams a contract, which he signs in July. The novel is to be released simply as *Stoner*. On the academic side, things are also brighter: He is promoted to full professor for the fall of 1964. In addition, the university secures a $50,000 Rockefeller Grant to fund a literary quarterly with a national profile. The magazine is to be called *The University of Denver Quarterly* (later the *Denver Quarterly*), and Williams is chosen to be its editor, a responsibility he assumes the following year.

1965   Alan Swallow publishes Williams's second collection of poems, *The Necessary Lie*. *English Renaissance Poetry*, now with the acknowledgment of Winters's contribution included, goes into a second edition. *Stoner* is published by the Viking Press on April 23, 1965. Only lightly reviewed, the book sells what Viking considers a disappointing 1,700 copies in the first two months. Cork Smith tells Williams, "The book is moving slowly. But that in no way diminishes our feelings about the novel. You were right and we were right."

1966   In February, ten months after the publication of *Stoner*, Irving Howe's laudatory review appears in *The New Republic*. He calls the book "serious, beautiful and affecting. . . . [Williams] is devoted to the sentence as a form." The review comes too late to meaningfully improve the book's sales, but, according to Williams, "gave the book a kind of underground life." In July, visits his sister and brother-in-law in Mexico, for the first time in twelve years. In August, joins the faculty at the Bread Loaf Writers Conference in Vermont for their annual two-week summer session. He will teach there every summer through 1972. On November 24, Thanksgiving Day, Williams's mentor and publisher Alan Swallow dies of a heart attack at the age of fifty-one.

1967 In May, sails alone to Europe on a grant to do research and continue writing the novel that is already titled *Augustus*. Spends the better part of two months based in Rome, making briefer excursions to pertinent places around the Mediterranean: Greece, Turkey, Yugoslavia. On sabbatical in the States, alone in his mountain cabin in Pine, Colorado, for the fall semester, continues to work toward completion of the novel by the summer of 1968.

1968 In January, takes up a writer-in-residence appointment at Smith College in Northampton, Massachusetts, for the spring term. Finishes the first chapter of *Augustus* there. Returning to Denver in May, after being gone from home for the better part of a year, and with his marriage dissolving, moves in with Nancy Leavenworth, with whom he has been continuously involved since 1960.

1969 In January, the Williamses divorce. Williams sets up house with Nancy Leavenworth, who had been teaching high school English and is now an instructor at a nearby state college.

1970 On May 27, Willard Marsh, Williams's brother-in-law, author of the novel *Week with No Friday* and more than one hundred published short stories, dies of a heart attack in Mexico, age forty-eight. Around this time Williams discovers that *Stoner* had gone out of print four years before —only one year after publication. His editor, Cork Smith, had failed to notify the author or agent. In December, Williams and Nancy marry. Three of her children are living at home with them.

1972 In January, Pocket Books reissues *Stoner* in paperback. In April, Williams submits the completed *Augustus* to Viking. Refuses to allow two paperback publishers to reissue

Butcher's Crossing because they both want to market it as a Western. On October 31, Viking publishes *Augustus*. It is reviewed more widely and more favorably in both the U.S. and the U.K. than his two previous novels. Thomas Lask, in his October 29 *New York Times* book review, writes: "John Williams has fashioned an always engaging, psychologically convincing work of fiction. He has done so without employing the usual attention-catching devices. There are no sex-and-saber scenes, no examples of Hollywood pageantry, not much in the way of individual derring-do. In fact, in its restraint and literary severity, the novel suggests those qualities that the old schoolbooks told us were the proud possessions of the ancient Romans." The book will sell about 10,000 copies in hardcover.

1973   On April 10 *Augustus* shares the National Book Award for fiction—and the accompanying $1,000—with John Barth's *Chimera*. This is the first time in any category that the award has been split between two authors. On April 12, Williams accepts his award in a ceremony at Lincoln Center in New York. Despite telling an interviewer beforehand (vexed that Barth's more "experimental" work was granted equal honors) that he will speak "in defense of the goddamn novel," he is gracious to both Barth and his listeners, quoting his fellow finalist, novelist Brock Brower: "There's only one stable institution in this country. It isn't Princeton. It isn't I.T.&T. It isn't marriage. It's the novel." Two weeks after the award ceremony, accepts a visiting professorship at Brandeis University in Waltham, Massachusetts, for the academic year 1973–74. Back in Denver before his move east, he demands a raise and more time off from teaching so he can write. He is turned down. He is not popular with some other members of the faculty, who find him arrogant. Ruffled by the administration's refusal to grant him leeway for more writing time, he begins to disengage from some of his obligations, delegating several of his editorial duties at the *Denver Quarterly*. His teaching, however, still engages him, and his newly burnished reputation as a novelist draws students to the program. "Fact in Fiction: Problems for the Historical Novelist" published in the Winter issue of the *Denver Quarterly*.

1974   As a native son of Texas, receives the Texas Institute of Letters award for fiction. "The Future of the Novel" published by Salem Press in *Contemporary Literary Experience*.

1975   Steps down as director of the creative writing program,
            after neglecting to properly guide one of his doctoral stu-
            dents through the stages of his thesis. Marie Rodell, his
            agent, dies. Her assistant, Frances Collin, takes over. Wil-
            liams remains her client.

1976   Not willing to grant Williams the liberties he asked for ear-
            lier, the university appoints him Laurence Phipps Professor
            of Humanities, an endowed chair, which will require him
            to teach only two quarters a year. The Williamses take ad-
            vantage of this arrangement, spending time in Key West,
            where he had lived briefly and happily in 1945.

1978   Now on a reduced teaching schedule, the Williamses relo-
            cate to Key West for a good part of each year, finally buy-
            ing a house there. Begins work on a new novel, "The Sleep
            of Reason," about war and art forgery. The title comes
            from a painting by Francisco Goya, *The Sleep of Reason
            Brings Forth Monsters*.

1979   Sends a letter to his department chairman, furious that in
            his absence courses in literary theory have been added to
            the curriculum. While he feels his voice should be given
            special weight at the university, most colleagues view him
            as having had one foot out the door for a long time. His
            complaints are ignored. Plans to spend four months fol-
            lowing the 1980 spring semester at Yaddo, the artist colony
            in upstate New York.

1980   After X-rays reveal a spot on his right lung, undergoes
            surgery; the small nodule removed is non-cancerous. On
            medical leave from the university during the first half of the
            year. As a result of his operation and recuperation, spends
            only July and August at Yaddo. His new novel has reached
            about 100 pages in draft—it will never stretch much be-
            yond that, remaining incomplete.

1981   An excerpt from "The Sleep of Reason" published in Oc-
            tober in *Ploughshares*.

1984   In Key West, where the community of well-known writers
            is extensive, accepts poet John Ciardi's invitation to be a
            member of the faculty of The Key West Literary Seminar,
            an annual four-day event Ciardi founded in 1983. But the
            Williamses also chafe at the prospect of living full-time in
            the Keys with little to do. "I was just hanging out for a
            year. It was awful. The small island gets smaller," he writes.

They also both need the kind of access to doctors that is less available there.

1985   Inducted into The American Academy of Arts and Letters and awarded $5,000. On the invitation of his old Bread Loaf colleague, poet Miller Williams, moves with Nancy to Fayetteville, Arkansas, to deliver an autumn series of lectures at the University of Arkansas. They like the town and the feel of the place.

1986   A symposium, "A Celebration of John Williams," held in March at the Denver Public Library. Richard Yates is on the panel that evening discussing Williams's work and Williams reads Chapter 2 of "The Sleep of Reason," while taking breaths of oxygen from a portable tank, which he has been doing on occasion for a number of years. In the early spring, the couple move to Fayetteville permanently. Officially retires from University of Denver after thirty-two years on the faculty. A special Winter issue of the *Denver Quarterly* is devoted to the writing of John Williams and includes a long excerpt from "The Sleep of Reason," a selection of previously unpublished poems, and an interview with Williams as well as a gathering of essays about Williams.

1987   On Williams's urging, his sister, George Rae, twice widowed, alcoholic, moves to Fayetteville.

1988   The University of Arkansas Press reissues *Stoner* and *Butcher's Crossing* in paperback as part of the University of Arkansas Reprint Series. "So I seem to be returning to where I began, with a smallish press. I'm just as pleased; it has a nice symmetry," he writes to a friend.

1992   Has a bad fall and a long stay at the university hospital. Ill health brought on by decades of heavy drinking and smoking has been a routine part of his life for years.

1994   Dies on March 3 of respiratory failure.

1995   *Augustus* reissued by the University of Arkansas Press.

2006   New York Review Books reissues *Stoner* in paperback, followed by *Butcher's Crossing* (2007), *Augustus* (2014), and *Nothing But the Night* (2019).

2013   *Stoner* tops best-seller lists in Europe, spurring further sales in the U.S.

Note on the Texts

This volume contains three novels by John Williams—*Butcher's Crossing* (1960), *Stoner* (1965), and *Augustus* (1972)—as well as a selection of the author's related writings, comprising "The Western: Definition of the Myth" (1961), "Fact in Fiction: Problems for the Historical Novelist" (1973), "The Future of the Novel" (1974), and Williams's remarks upon accepting the National Book Award for *Augustus* (1973).

After joining the English Department at the University of Denver in 1954, Williams undertook extensive research for his second novel, *Butcher's Crossing*, set in the American West of the 1870s. In a temporary setback, he lost a year's worth of notes when he moved his office to a new building with the rest of the English Department. He later called it a "most fortunate accident," imagining the ways in which his research would have inhibited him. "I might have tried to force what I had learned into the novel," he recalled; "as it was, I simply wrote the novel, and I found that when I needed a fact it would come to me." Even so, the novel progressed slowly. In the summer of 1958, Williams completed a draft of "The Naked World," as his novel-in-progress was then called, and secured an experienced agent, Marie Rodell, to represent the book. Before Rodell was able to submit the typescript to publishers, Cecil Scott at Macmillan, acting on a tip, approached Williams directly, inquiring about the manuscript. "I made it quite clear to him that you were handling the book," Williams wrote to Rodell, "and that if he became seriously interested that he would have to work through you." With Williams's consent, Rodell submitted the novel to Macmillan after Scott promised to enter it in Macmillan's new fiction award contest, which carried a prize of $7,500. In May 1959, Williams's novel came in second in the contest, but Cecil Scott made an offer anyway—and then a counteroffer, when Rodell received a late competitive bid from Little, Brown & Co. Williams accepted Macmillan's counteroffer.

With publication of "The Naked World" scheduled for spring 1960, Williams began to have reservations about his title, despite reassurances from Cecil Scott, and proposed several alternatives, including "The Crossing," "The Hunt," "Hunt in the Valley," and "The Western Path." "I like best of any of your suggested titles, and better than any title I have come up with myself, *Butcher's Crossing*," Scott wrote in the summer of 1959; "it will give the reader a certain clue to the contents." The title was settled. Published on March 15, 1960, the novel received several positive notices, notably in the *Chicago Tribune* and the *St. Louis Post Dispatch*, but a damaging review appeared in the Book Review section of *The New York Times* on Sunday, April 3, 1960. "Brace yourself for a shock next Sunday," Williams's agent, Marie Rodell, warned her author. Writing in his column "Western Roundup," Nelson Nye condemned *Butcher's Crossing* as "plotless" and generating "little excitement." "The story . . . moves as though hauled by a snail through a pond of molasses," Nye wrote. "You can leave it anytime, a lot of people will." More than these harsh judgments, the treatment of his novel as a "Western" troubled Williams, especially when it was intended to call into question the conventions of the genre. *Butcher's Crossing* sold only modestly—a few thousand copies. The book was subsequently reprinted in paperback during Williams's lifetime, by Dolphin Books in 1962 and by the University of Arkansas Press in 1988. For the latter, part of the University of Arkansas Reprint Series, Williams substituted epigraphs from Emerson's *Nature* and Melville's *The Confidence Man* for the original epigraph from Yvor Winters's poem "The Journey" (more than two decades earlier his mentor, Winters, had accused Williams of plagiarizing him, and the two men never forgave each other—see pages 844–845 in this volume). *Butcher's Crossing* was published in London by Victor Gollancz Ltd. in 1960 in a setting identical to the Macmillan edition and subsequently in paperback by Panther Books. The text of *Butcher's Crossing* presented here is taken from the first American edition with the exception of the revision that Williams made to the epigraph for the University of Arkansas Press paperback (noted above).

Two years before the publication of *Butcher's Crossing*, Williams was already planning his third novel, *Stoner*, centered on the interior life of an "undistinguished" professor. It would be "a novel about a man who finds no meaning in the world or in himself," he explained to Marie Rodell in September 1958, "but who does find meaning and a kind of victory in the honest and dogged pursuit of his profession." In 1960, he reported making progress on the novel but did not send a completed draft to Rodell until June 1963, before departing for Oxford to attend a summer course on Elizabethan poetry. That summer and fall he made rapid progress revising the novel. Rodell was not sanguine about its prospects, but Williams assured her that he "had no illusions it would be a 'bestseller' or anything like that. . . . The only thing I'm sure of is that it's a good novel; in time it may even be thought of as a substantially good one." Titled "A Matter of Light" and then "A Matter of Love," the novel made the rounds to editors and was rejected by several publishing houses, including Macmillan, before Cork Smith, a senior editor at the Viking Press, finally made an offer in July 1964. Smith did not like the working title, but that was a detail. "On the basis of all I know about the books they publish and seem to like I probably could not have chosen a house that would have pleased me better," Williams wrote to Rodell.

Now titled *Stoner*, after its academic protagonist, Williams's third novel was published by the Viking Press on April 23, 1965. There was little review attention, and two months after its publication sales were under 2,000 copies. A belated, laudatory review by Irving Howe appeared in *The New Republic* on February 22, 1966, but came too late to boost sales of the novel. "Given the quantity of fiction published in this country each year, it seems unavoidable that most novels should be ignored and that among these a few should nonetheless be works of distinction," Howe wrote. "*Stoner*, a book that received very little notice . . . is, I think, such a work." The novel was reprinted during Williams's lifetime in paperback by Lancer Books (1966), Pocket Books (1972), and the University of Arkansas Press (1988). *Stoner* was not published in England until 1973, when Allen Lane published it simultaneously with *Augustus*, in a setting identical to the Viking Press edition. This volume presents the text of the first American edition published by the Viking Press.

In May 1967, Williams traveled to Europe for two months on a grant to undertake research for his epistolary novel, *Augustus*, set in the final days of the Roman Republic and the beginning of the Empire. By the end of July, he had finished an outline of his novel and made progress in the following year while on sabbatical from the University of Denver. "Since I plan carefully," he wrote, "I am not faced with the problem of major reorganization after a first draft is completed." When Williams resumed his teaching duties, he preferred to write in the morning on days he was not in the classroom, leaving the afternoons for sketching out the next day's work. Williams sent the novel to his supportive editor at the Viking Press, Cork Smith, in the spring of 1972. Before taking a forced leave of absence from the publishing house, Cork Smith made an important editorial suggestion that Williams implemented: the elimination of the novel's numbered chapters, and the grouping of its letters, journal entries, and memoranda instead into three "Books" and an "Epilogue."

Augustus was published by the Viking Press on October 31, 1972. The novel received far more notice than either of his other two major novels and shared the National Book Award in 1973 with John Barth's *Chimera*. "These books represent considerable variety of fictive methods and styles," Jonathan Yardley, one of the judges of the National Book Award, said, explaining the committee's unprecedented decision to split the fiction award between two novels; "that same variety is reflected in the tastes and interests of the five members of our panel. Because of this variety the panel has decided to give the award in fiction to two books, both of uncommon quality, which are similar in subject matter but which represent dissimilar approaches to the writing of fiction." *Augustus* sold a "respectable" 10,000 copies. It was reprinted in paperback by Dell Press and Penguin Books during Williams's lifetime, and in 1995, the year after Williams's death, by the University of Arkansas Press. In 1973, *Augustus* was published in London by Allen Lane in a setting identical to the Viking Press edition. This volume presents the text of the first American edition published by the Viking Press.

The section of this volume titled "Related Writings" presents three essays published by Williams from 1961 to 1974 as well as his remarks upon accepting the National Book Award for *Augustus* in 1973. "The Western: Definition of the Myth" was published in *The Nation* on November 18, 1961, and reprinted in *The Popular Arts: A Critical Reader*, ed. Irving Deer and Harriet A. Deer (New York: Charles Scribner's Sons, 1967). The text presented here is taken from its original printing in *The Nation*. "Fact in Fiction: Problems for the Historical Novelist" was published in the *Denver Quarterly* in 1973, and this volume prints the text from the *Denver Quarterly*. The text of "The Future of the Novel" presented here is that found in its original publication in *Contemporary Literary Criticism*, edited by David Madden (Pasadena, CA: Salem Press, 1974). Williams's remarks upon accepting the National Book Award were delivered at Lincoln Center's Alice Tully Hall, in New York City, on the evening of April 12, 1973. The text printed in this volume is taken from a photocopy of the typescript in the John Edward Williams Papers, in the Special Collections of the University of Arkansas Libraries.

This volume presents the texts of the original printings chosen for inclusion here, but it does not attempt to reproduce nontextual features of their typographic design. The texts are presented without change, except for the correction of typographical errors. Spelling, punctuation, and capitalization are often expressive features and are not altered, even when inconsistent or irregular. The following is a list of typographical errors corrected, cited by page and line number: 2.22, Will; 14.12, aimlesssly; 39.39, somewhat; 73.35, Andrew's; 177.3, raising.; 184.2, noncommitally; 265.39, on a; 368.25–26, hestitated; 382.37, Wr.; 467.15, crochety; 600.10, Library; 756.26, *complimentary*; 800.34 (and *passim*), *Moby Dick*; 807.35, century;; 807.38, concommitant; 812.17 (and *passim*), *Finnegan's*; 818.4, lyricspasmodic; 818.18, space hence; 820.6, indeterminancy; 822.10, Mallarme.; 830.35, time,.

Notes

In the notes below, the reference numbers denote page and line of this volume (the line count includes headings). Biblical quotations are keyed to the King James Version. Quotations from Shakespeare are keyed to *The Riverside Shakespeare*, ed. G. Blakemore Evans (Boston: Houghton Mifflin, 1974). For further biographical background than is provided in the Chronology, see Charles J. Shields, *The Man Who Wrote the Perfect Novel: John Williams, Stoner, and the Writing Life* (Austin: University of Texas Press, 2018) and interviews conducted by Bryan Woolley and Dan Wakefield in, respectively, the *Denver Quarterly* 20, no. 3 (Winter 1986) and *Ploughshares* 7, nos. 3–4 (Fall/Winter 1981).

BUTCHER'S CROSSING

2.19 yarb-doctors] Itinerant patent medicine salesmen who peddle folk cures containing herbs (of which the word "yarbs" is an Ozark dialect variant), roots, and other such ingredients.

2.22 Peter the Wild Boy] A boy discovered in 1725 in the woods near Hamelin, Germany, living a feral existence. Of unknown parentage, he was determined to be about twelve years old; he walked on all fours and could not be taught to speak a language.

5.3 dougherty] Four-wheeled covered wagon with side doors, two or three transverse seats for passengers, and canvas side curtains. Dougherty wagons were made for long-distance travel.

5.34 nankeen] A stout cotton material, usually of brownish yellow color, named after Nanking, China, where it was originally manufactured. Mainly used for making trousers, it was sometimes used for footwear as well.

7.14 doubletree] Crossbar on a wagon or carriage to which two whiffletrees (singletrees) are attached for harnessing two animals abreast.

10.18 linsey-woolsey] Coarse twill or plain-woven fabric woven with a linen warp and a woolen weft. Similar fabrics woven in colonial America and having a cotton warp and woolen weft were also called linsey-woolsey, or wincey.

34.33–34 Clarendon Street near Beacon and the river Charles.] Clarendon and Beacon Streets are located in the Back Bay section of Boston, which would become a prosperous neighborhood. However, the Back Bay area was still a tidal basin of the Charles River in the early 1850s, when Will Andrews

—who is in his early twenties when the novel takes place, in the mid-1870s—would have been born. Land reclamation and subsequent development only began in 1859.

39.31–34   I become a transparent eyeball. . . . through him.] Cf. Ralph Waldo Emerson, *Nature* (1836): "Standing on the bare ground, — my head bathed by the blithe air, and uplifted into infinite spaces, — all mean egotism vanishes. I become a transparent eye-ball; I am nothing; I see all; the currents of the Universal Being circulate through me; I am part or parcel of God."

74.14–15   Pawnee Fork . . . Smoky Hill.] Pawnee Fork, a tributary of the Arkansas River, in western Kansas. The Santa Fe Trail crossed the river in two places. Smoky Hill, a river flowing east from Colorado into Kansas.

102.19   off-ox] The ox on the right-hand side in a paired team, so called because the driver typically walks next to the left-hand ox of the pair, and thus becomes more familiar with its ways.

120.35   Sharps rifle] A large-bore (.52-caliber) single-shot rifle, designed by Christian Sharps and manufactured by his company from 1848 to 1881. The Sharps was renowned for its long-range accuracy.

138.31   "Jezebels,"] Jezebel, biblical wife of King Ahab of Israel. A wicked woman. See especially 1 Kings 16:31–32, 1 Kings 18:13–46, 1 Kings 19:1–3, and 1 Kings 21:5–16.

229.32–33   The bottom's dropped out . . . hide business is finished.] After the buffalo trade peaked in Kansas in the years from 1871 to 1874, it began to decline there earlier than it did in other territories. This was due in part to legislation that restricted hunting, and in part to strong competition from traders in the territories farther north.

253.10–11   Boylston Street . . . Clarendon] Streets in the Back Bay section of Boston. See also note 34.33–34.

STONER

261.1   College of Agriculture.] Although the University of Missouri College of Agriculture was established in 1870, the full four-year agricultural program began only in 1901.

270.10–12   Tristan, Iseult . . . bright Paris] Tristan and Iseult were adulterous lovers in a number of chivalric romances based on Celtic legend, according to which they fell in love as the result of drinking a magic potion. The most famous version of the legend is Gottfried von Strassburg's (c. 1211–1215), composed in Middle High German. Paolo and Francesca were illicit lovers in thirteenth-century Rimini, Italy. On discovering Francesca's adultery, her husband accidentally killed her after slaying Paolo. In Dante's *Inferno*, Canto V, the poet places the pair in Hell among the lustful. Helen and Paris are adulterous lovers of Greek myth. The Trojan War was triggered when Paris, a son of the Trojan king, Priam, absconded with Helen, wife of the Greek king Menelaus.

270.15   local habitation] See *Midsummer Night's Dream*, V.i.14–17: "And as imagination bodies forth / The forms of things unknown, the poet's pen / Turns them to shapes and gives to airy nothing / A local habitation and a name."

279.40   schooners] In the United States, large round drinking glasses with short stems, ordinarily used to serve beer.

280.35   sulphur-and-molasses] According to old wives' tales, forcing sulfur and molasses down the throats of young people in early spring provided a healthy thickening of the blood (supposedly made thin during winter). The preparation was also occasionally taken as a spring tonic because of the purgative properties of sulfur.

282.15   Poor Toms . . . a-cold."] In *King Lear*, III.vi, Tom is the character of a crazed pauper, enacted by Edgar, the legitimate son of the Duke of Gloucester, as he shelters in a hovel on the heath. Tom repeats the phrase "Tom's a-cold" several times during his encounter there with Lear.

288.5   lean and hungry look] See *Julius Caesar*, I.ii.193, where Julius Caesar voices his concerns about Cassius's ambitions and intentions.

288.33–34   Château-Thierry] During World War I, in early June 1918, American troops helped stop a major German offensive in heavy fighting around Château Thierry, a town on the Marne River fifty-five miles northeast of Paris.

290.16–17   a Catullus or a more gentle and lyrical Juvenal] Gaius Valerius Catullus (c. 84–54 B.C.E.) was a Roman poet celebrated for his lyric gift. His poems drew on personal life—family, friends, enemies, love, sexual matters— rather than public life and heroic deeds. Decimus Junius Juvenalis (c. 60–127 C.E.) was a Roman poet whose most well-known work, the *Satires*, targets the mores and values of his contemporaries.

290.26   the Argonne] Forest in northeastern France, 135 miles east of Paris, through which American troops pushed in the final offensive of World War I, known as the Meuse-Argonne Offensive, which lasted from September 26, 1918, until the Armistice on November 11, 1918. American troops sustained more than 110,000 casualties.

306.11   "If it's to be done . . . done quickly."] Cf. *Macbeth*, I.vii.1–2.

366.3   trivium] The three basic disciplines of the seven liberal arts as defined by the ancient Greeks and Romans: grammar, logic, and rhetoric. (The remaining four disciplines, known as the "quadrivium," were mathematics, astronomy, geometry, and music.)

370.13–16   "Donatus . . . the Middle Ages.] Aelius Donatus (fl. 354 C.E.) was the most famous Latin grammarian of late antiquity. His theory of tragedy and the fundamental differences between tragedy and comedy circulated widely in school texts through the medieval period and well into the sixteenth century and beyond. For a summary account of Donatus's views on tragedy and comedy, see p. 813 in this volume, where Williams quotes J. V. Cunningham's essay "The Donatan Tradition."

373.8   idolized Shakespeare this side of idolatry] Cf. Ben Jonson, *Timber: or, Discovers* (1640), where Jonson refers to his rival Shakespeare, the man and the playwright: "I loved the man, and do honour his memory on this side of idolatry as much as any."

373.13–14   blush unseen . . . desert air] See Thomas Gray, "Elegy Written in a Country Churchyard" (1751), lines 55–56.

384.28–30   Life, like a dome . . . to fragments.] Percy Bysshe Shelley, "Adonais" (1821), stanza 52, lines 3–5.

384.35–36   'Beauty is truth . . . to know.] Keats, "Ode on a Grecian Urn" (1820), lines 49–50.

387.5   *Everyman*] Fifteenth-century English morality play.

387.24–25   Marlowe—the mighty line—"] See line 30 in Ben Jonson's "To the Memory of My Beloved the Author, Mr. William Shakespeare," a dedicatory poem that appears as part of the front matter of the Shakespeare First Folio (1623). Jonson avows that Shakespeare's dramatic verse "outshone" even the strikingly forceful blank-verse lines of his contemporary, Christopher Marlowe.

437.30   WPA] Works Progress Administration, an agency created by executive order in 1935 as part of President Franklin D. Roosevelt's New Deal. It employed millions to carry out public works projects.

438.28   loyalists] Those who supported or fought in defense of the Republic against the forces of the fascist Generalissimo Francisco Franco during the Spanish Civil War (1936–39).

AUGUSTUS

488.1   *For Nancy*] Nancy Gardner Williams, Williams's fourth and last wife.

491.2   JULIUS CAESAR TO ATIA] Julius Caesar (100–44 B.C.E.), Roman general, triumvir, and dictator who was at the center of events leading to the end of the Roman Republic. After the death of his fellow triumvir Crassus, in 53 B.C.E., and the realignment of the other triumvir, Pompey, with the Senate, Caesar broke the law by leading his forces south across the Rubicon River into Italy in 49 B.C.E., triggering the Roman civil war. Caesar rapidly took control of Italy and then pursued Pompey into Greece, defeating him at the battle of Pharsalus (48 B.C.E.). Three years later, in 46–45 B.C.E., he vanquished the last of Pompey's supporters. On the Ides of March in the following year, 44 B.C.E., Caesar was assassinated on the Senate floor by a group of senators led by the conspirators Cassius and Brutus. Atia Balba (85–43 B.C.E.), a niece of Julius

Caesar (the daughter of his elder sister, Julia Minor), was the mother of Gaius Octavius (later Augustus) and of Octavia.

491.3   Apollonia] Roman city and a center of Greek learning in southern Illyria; its ruins are located near the eastern coast of the Adriatic Sea in Albania.

491.7   Carthage] Ancient city on the north coast of Africa (present-day Tunisia), a rich trading hub and the Roman Republic's greatest rival for power in the Mediterranean, destroyed by the Romans during the Third Punic War (149–146 B.C.E.) and refounded by Julius Caesar as a Roman colony. The ruins of Carthage are located near modern Tunis.

491.12   a Julian] The *gens Julia*, an ancient and powerful patrician family, which claimed descent from Julus, son of Aeneas and grandson of Venus.

491.16–17   Gaius Octavius . . . campaign with me in Spain] Gaius Octavius (63 B.C.E.–14 C.E.), later Augustus, was the adoptive son and heir of his great-uncle Julius Caesar. Pompey's popularity remained strong after his death in Hispania (modern-day Spain and Portugal), and his sons staged a reprisal against Julius Caesar there. They were defeated on March 17, 45 B.C.E., at Munda. Caesar's decisive victory over the Pompeian forces allowed him to return to Rome.

491.21   six legions of soldiers] A legion was the largest unit of the Roman army. Caesar's legions had approximately 3,500 men during his campaign in Gaul.

491.35–492.2   In Apollonia . . . Apollodorus.] Born in Canana near Tarsus, Athenodorus (74 B.C.E.–7 C.E.) was a Stoic, friend of Cicero and Strabo, and teacher of the young Gaius Octavius, and later court philosopher to his former pupil after he assumed the title of Augustus. Apollodorus (c. 104–22 B.C.E.), born in Pergamum, was a Greek rhetorician chosen by Julius Caesar to take charge of the education of Octavius.

492.14–16   he would be my son . . . Marcus Antonius] In a codicil to his will, Caesar adopted his grandnephew Octavius and made him his heir. Roman statesman and general Marcus Antonius, commonly known as Marc Antony (83–30 B.C.E.), helped his relative Julius Caesar drive the forces of Pompey from Italy.

492.17–18   as slyly . . . Temple of the Vestal Virgins] One of Rome's most important and visible temples, The Temple of the Vesta, also known as the Temple of the Vestal Virgins, was a small circular building located prominently on the east side of the Forum. It housed the sacred fire of the goddess Vesta, patroness of the domestic hearth and symbol of Roman prosperity, and was tended by six or seven priestesses, the Vestal Virgins, who were sworn to an oath of chastity. An inner sanctum of the Temple housed wills and other important legal documents as well as sacred objects, including the Palladium, a small wooden image of Athena said to have been rescued from the ruins of Troy by Rome's mythic founder, Aeneas.

492.25–30   Marcius Philippus . . . plotting against me with his friend Cicero] Lucius Marcius Philippus, a Roman statesman and consul (56 B.C.E.), was the second husband of Atia and hence stepfather to Octavius. He helped to pass legislation against Caesar in the Senate, although he avoided overt participation in the war between Caesar and Pompey. During the civil wars, Marcus Tullius Cicero (106–43 B.C.E.), Roman statesman, consul (63 B.C.E.), orator, lawyer, and writer, advocated a return to republican government. When Octavius, Marcus Aemilius Lepidus, and Marcus Antonius formed the Second Triumvirate, Cicero, who had particularly antagonized Marcus Antonius, was proscribed as an enemy of the state and executed. His head and hands were displayed in the Forum.

492.31–33   your late husband . . . advancement in the Julian name] Atia's first husband was Gaius Octavius (c. 100–59 B.C.E.), father of Octavius (later Augustus). From an equestrian family, he rose to praetorship and governed Macedonia.

492.37–39   two friends . . . Marcus Vipsanius Agrippa and Quintus Salvidienus Rufus] Agrippa (c. 63–12 B.C.E.), Roman general and statesman, helped his close friend Octavian take power after Julius Caesar's murder. In 23 B.C.E. Agrippa married Augustus's daughter, Julia, thus becoming the heir apparent to imperial rule. Salvidienus (d. 40 B.C.E.) was a Roman general, and a close friend and advisor of Augustus in the early years, notable for his rapid downfall when Augustus denounced him in the Senate for plotting with Antonius against him.

493.1–3   Gaius Cilnius Maecenas . . . tinge of royalty] Maecenas (c. 70–8 B.C.E.), perhaps descended from an Etruscan family, was a diplomat and, above all, a great literary patron of the Augustan age, fostering the careers of both Horace and Vergil, both of whom dedicated major works to him. A close friend and early supporter of Augustus, he governed Rome and Italy in Augustus's absences.

493.9   dictator for life] In 44 B.C.E., Julius Caesar was named *dictator perpetuus* (dictator for life); he had been named dictator by the Senate four times previously.

493.18   Puteoli] Modern-day Pozzuoli, Roman colony and important seaport north of Naples. In the late Republic many of Rome's elites owned villas there.

493.22   Tivoli] Named "Tibur" in antiquity, a town northeast of Rome, offering impressive views of the Campagna. Augustus, Maecenas, and Horace had villas there.

497.4–15   Actium . . . Mutina . . . Philippi . . . in a litter] The battle of Actium (September 2, 31 B.C.E.) was a naval engagement between the forces of Octavius and those of Marcus Antonius and Cleopatra; Octavius's decisive victory left him the undisputed ruler of the Roman world. A dozen years earlier, in the battle of Mutina (April 21, 43 B.C.E.), Republican forces led by Hirtius and Pansa and supported by the legions loyal to Octavius fought the Caesarean forces of Marcus Antonius in an inconclusive engagement, although Antonius was forced to retreat into Gaul after encircling Brutus at Mutina. The battle of Philippi (October 3 and 23, 42 B.C.E.) comprised two engagements on the plains of Philippi in Macedonia: the result of these was that Marcus Antonius and Octavius (though in ill health) defeated the Republicans. After their defeat, Caesar's murderers, Brutus and Cassius, both took their own lives.

497.11   Caesar Augustus] In 27 B.C.E., the Senate conferred on Octavius the new titles of *Augustus* and *princeps* (first citizen). Historians regard this moment as the beginning of the Roman Empire.

497.17   mortal Julius . . . a god] On January 1, 42 B.C.E., by decree of the Senate, Julius Caesar was deified and granted the title *Divus Julius.*

497.19–20   tribune to the people] The establishment of the *tribunus plebis* (tribune of the common people) in c. 500–450 B.C.E. was the first major check on senatorial power in the history of the Roman Republic. Elected by the plebeian assembly, tribunes had the power to assemble the plebeians and elicit resolutions. By the third century B.C.E., they had the power to lay proposals before the Senate.

497.20   consul] From 509 to 27 B.C.E., the year in which the Roman Senate gave Octavius Caesar the new titles of *Augustus* and *princeps*, the consuls were the chief military and civil magistrates. Two consuls were elected annually. The title was primarily symbolic after the establishment of the Empire.

497.33   the restoration of Rome] As aedile, Agrippa undertook the building or repair of many Roman buildings, sewers, aqueducts, and streets. See also note 613.29.

497.37–498.1   Against Lucius Antonius . . . Roman legions] Lucius Antonius (c. 78–c. 39 B.C.E.), younger brother and ally of Marcus Antonius. When Lucius Antonius spoke out against the distribution of lands to Octavius's veterans, Octavius moved against him. Besieged at Perusia in 40 B.C.E., he surrendered and was later pardoned.

498.1–3   Aquitanians in Gaul . . . Triumph in Rome] The Roman historian Cassius Dio (c. 155–c. 235 C.E.) reports that Agrippa turned down a triumph because it would be inappropriate to accept it when Octavius faced continuing challenges. A triumph was an extravagant procession of victory by a Roman general to the temple of Jupiter on the Capitol. Accompanied by gladiatorial combats, chariot races, theatrical performances, and other festivities, triumphal processions often featured the defeated monarchs of defeated nations walking in chains.

498.6–9   Sextus Pompeius . . . coast of Sicily.] After the death of their father, Pompey the Great, in 48 B.C.E., Sextus Pompeius (c. 67–35 B.C.E.) and his older brother Gnaeus Pompeius, together with Scipio, Cato the Younger, and others, continued the struggle against Octavius. Sextus Pompeius built a large naval force, enabling him to ravage the coast of Italy. He was eventually defeated by Agrippa in two naval encounters off the coast of Sicily—at Mylae in August 36 B.C.E. and, a month later, at Naulochus. He fled to Asia Minor where he was captured and executed.

498.12–13   In celebration . . . the Pantheon] Agrippa's Pantheon was constructed about 25 B.C.E., dedicated to all the gods. The present-day Pantheon, erected by the emperor Hadrian and dedicated about 126 C.E., was built on the site of the earlier structure.

498.29   TITUS LIVIUS] Roman historian (59 B.C.E.–17 C.E.), known as Livy. His *Ab Urbe Condita* (*From the Founding of the City*), known as *History of Rome* in English, was a monumental history of the Roman state from its mythical founding in 753 B.C.E. to the reign of Augustus; only 35 of its original 142 parts survive.

500.5–6   superiority of Callimachus's poems to Catullus's] Callimachus was a Hellenistic Greek poet and scholar (c. 305–240 B.C.E.), known for his witty, learned short poems and epigrams. Apart from six hymns and about sixty epigrams, only fragments of his work survive. The nakedly emotional love poetry of Catullus (c. 84–54 B.C.E.) is often contrasted with the lighthearted frivolity of Hellenistic epigrams such as those composed by Callimachus. Some of Catullus's poems are critical of Julius Caesar. See also note 290.16–17.

500.14   Brindisi to Arezzo] Brundisium (modern-day Brindisi), on the Adriatic coast of southern Italy, was a Roman city of strategic importance, serving as a launching point for armies and merchants. The Appian Way terminated in Brundisium. An ancient Etruscan city, Arezzo was fifty miles south of Florence.

503.35   the centurions] A centurion was a professional officer in the Roman army, the head of a *centuria*, literally a group of one hundred, the smallest unit in a legion.

505.1–3   when six of Sulla's troops . . . to Rome.] Lucius Cornelius Sulla (138–78 B.C.E.), Roman general and statesman, was victor in Rome's first major civil war (88–82 B.C.E.). The first leader of the Republic to seize political power by force, he was named dictator by the Senate in 82 B.C.E., with powers to "make laws and settle the constitution"; he resigned the position in 79 B.C.E., when he felt he had completed the tasks he had been set. One of his political targets was the young Julius Caesar, who fled Rome and took refuge in the Sabine territory; after being arrested by Sulla's troops, he bribed them to spare his life. In his memoirs Sulla noted that he regretted having spared Caesar's life.

505.25–26   Marcus Aemilius Lepidus—] Roman general and statesman (89–late 13 or early 12 B.C.E.). In 27 B.C.E., Lepidus, Octavius, and Marcus Antonius formed the Second Triumvirate. After helping defeat Pompey's son Sextus, in 36 B.C.E., Lepidus challenged Octavius for control of Sicily, but Lepidus's legions defected to Octavius, who chose to pardon him.

507.25   cuirass] Armor, the breastplate and backplate.

510.34–36   Sulla sent . . . Julius Caesar himself.] In 82 B.C.E., after Sulla had
been named dictator by the Senate, he drew up a list of those he considered
enemies of the state, initiating a period of terror in Rome. Proscription was
often a death sentence, since a proscribed person was stripped of citizenship
and protection under the law, and reward money was awarded for information
leading to the capture or death of any such enemy of the state. Among those
proscribed by Sulla were those with political or family connections to his former rival Gaius Marius (c. 157–86 B.C.E.). Julius Caesar was the nephew of
Marius and the son-in-law of Cinna, leader of the Marian party after the death
of Marius. See also note 505.1–3.

514.10–11   Velletri . . . your childhood] Velitrae (modern-day Velletri) was
an ancient town southeast of Rome in the Alban Hills, home of Augustus's
paternal family.

516.36–37   Marcus Junius Brutus, Gaius Cassius Longinus, Decimus Brutus
Albinus, Gaius Trebonius—] Marcus Junius Brutus (85–42 B.C.E.), more commonly known as Brutus; Gaius Cassius Longinus (c. 86–42 B.C.E.), or simply
Cassius, brother-in-law to Brutus; Decimus Brutus Albinus (81–43 B.C.E.), or
Decimus, an ardent supporter of Julius Caesar in the civil war between Caesar
and Pompey; and Gaius Trebonius (c. 92–43 B.C.E.) were among the most
prominent of the sixty or so Roman statesmen involved in the plot to assassi-
nate Julius Caesar in 44 B.C.E. All four were dead within two and a half years
after the assassination.

517.3–4   Dolabella . . . counsel for the year] After Caesar's death, Publius
Cornelius Dolabella (d. 43 B.C.E.), a patron of Caesar, assumed the consulship
(44 B.C.E.), becoming the colleague of Antonius.

517.21   my lodge . . . at Astura] Astura was a small island in Latium, now a
peninsula, forty-five miles south of Rome, where Cicero had a villa to which he
retired in 45 B.C.E. after the death of his daughter, Tullia.

520.18   Atticus] Titus Pomponius Atticus (110–32 B.C.E.), wealthy but non-
political Roman from an equestrian family, remembered for his friendship with
Cicero. Cicero's informal and often chatty letters to Atticus, comprising sixteen volumes, are a witness to Roman life and politics from 68 to 44 B.C.E.,
when Caesar was assassinated.

521.19   the Forum] The *forum Romanum*, located between the Palatine and
Capitoline Hills, the center of Roman religious, ceremonial, and commercial
life. Political activity often took place in the part of the Forum known as the
Comitium (Meeting-place), an open-air space for public assemblies. During
the imperial period, the Forum saw the construction of honorary monuments
and buildings, and a simultaneous shift away from entertainment.

522.3–4   Caesar's Triumphal March after Africa] In 46 B.C.E., after defeating Scipio and Cato in the African provinces, Julius Caesar celebrated four

triumphs—for his victories in Gaul, Egypt, Asia Minor, and Africa—each separated by short intervals. After his defeat of Pompey's sons at Munda in 45 B.C.E., he celebrated a fifth triumph.

526.14   my friend Horace] Quintus Horatius Flaccus (65–8 B.C.E.), known as Horace in English, a Latin lyric poet and satirist, was patronized by Maecenas.

526.17–18   than that . . . *Letter to the Pisos*—] Among the first published treatises on poetic craft (c. 13 B.C.E.), Horace's literary epistles have come to be known as *Ars Poetica* (*Poetic Art*). The phrase "in medias res"—part of a passage in which the poet advises his reader to begin a work "in the middle of things"—comes from the *Ars Poetica*.

531.29   GAIUS SENTIUS TAVUS] Fictional character, perhaps based on G. Sentius Saturninus, a Roman military commander who became governor of Syria (9 B.C.E.–7 C.E.) under Augustus.

534.10–11   reborn, as Pythagoras says we are . . . another body.] See Xenophanes's mocking reference to Pythagoras's belief in the transmigration of souls in a surviving fragment: "They say that once when a puppy was being whipped, [Pythagoras], who was passing by, took on it, saying, 'Stop! Do not beat it! It is the soul of a friend; I recognize the voice!'"

536.26–32   Not for forty years . . . by dogs.] In the civil war fought between Marius and Sulla (88–87 B.C.E.), Sulla crossed the city limits with his army, taking Rome by force. Marius resisted Sulla's forces with an ad hoc army composed of gladiators but was forced to flee the city. Returning from exile a year later in 87 B.C.E. when Sulla's troops were involved in the campaign against Mithradates of Pontus (present-day northern Turkey), Marius invaded Rome with his own legions, executing many of Sulla's supporters.

537.33   DYRRACHIUM] Ancient Greek and later Roman city on the Adriatic, known today as Durrës (Albania).

537.38–538.3   illegal assignment . . . in Apollonia] After the assassination of Julius Caesar, Marcus Antonius appointed his younger brother Gaius (82–42 B.C.E.) governor of Macedonia, in northern Greece, where Caesar's assassins had fled and where, ultimately, they would be defeated at the battle of Philippi. Brutus succeeded in ousting Gaius from office and eventually had him executed in 42 B.C.E.

538.4–6   Would that your cousin Decimus . . . Ides of March!] In a letter written to Brutus and Cassius two days after the assassination of Caesar, Decimus Brutus, a distant cousin of Brutus, suggested they flee Italy. "If the situation improves," he wrote, "we shall return to Rome; if there is no change we shall live in exile; if the worst happens, we shall make a last stand."

539.32–33   the next counsels Hirtius and Pansa] Roman statesmen and generals Aulus Hirtius and Gaius Vibius Pansa Caetronianus became consuls on January 1, 43 B.C.E. See also note 497.4–15.

541.12   Sextus Pompeius roams the seas at will] See note 498.6–9.

541.18   NARBONNE] The city of Narbo Martius (now Narbonne) was established in 118 B.C.E. and soon after became the capital of the Roman province of Transalpine Gaul (the part of current-day France situated on the Mediterranean, later known as Gallia Narbonensis).

544.29   eagle-bearer] Bearer of the legionary eagle standard, a symbol of Roman pride and a means of communication in battle. Some legions were identified by other totemic animals such as the boar, the horse, and the wolf.

546.20   "The Praetors] Praetors were elected magistrates under the Republic; sometimes the title could refer as well to certain military officials. In a book about Roman law, Cicero describes the praetorian power as having originated with the ancient kings of Rome; in the mid-300s B.C.E., the praetorship took over certain judicial duties from the consulship.

548.1–2   you did not . . . until after Actium] Until after Rome's civil wars had safely concluded. See note 497.4–15.

549.22   month then was called Sextilis] The eighth month of the year was renamed *Augustus* (August) in 8 B.C.E., in honor of the emperor.

551.2   Lucius Cornificius] Roman politician and consul (35 B.C.E.), friend and ally of Octavius. In 43 B.C.E., he prosecuted Brutus in absentia for the murder of Caesar. He later fought in Sicily against Pompey's son Sextus.

552.23–24   Narbonensis and the two Spains.] Gallia Narbonensis was the province occupying what is now southern France. Hispania Citerior (Hither Hispania) was the province corresponding to what is now the northeastern half of the Spanish peninsula; Hispania Ulterior (Outer Hispania) sat just below it, opposite the northern coast of Africa.

552.24   the two Gauls] Cisalpine Gaul was the province covering the area roughly corresponding to northwestern Italy today and Transalpine Gaul the province occupying what is now the southern part of France. See also note 541.18.

559.16–560.6   Marcus Cicero . . . their countryman.] Fragment of Livy in Seneca the Elder, *Suasoriae*, 6.17.

559.20   Formia] Formiae (Latin), a settlement of the Volsci people and later a fashionable Roman summer resort. Situated on the Gulf of Gaeta northwest of Rome, it was destroyed in 842 C.E. by the Saracens.

561.2–3   STRABO OF AMASIA TO NICOLAUS OF DAMASCUS] Strabo of Amasia, a contemporary of Augustus (c. 64 B.C.E.–c. 24 C.E.), was a Greek geographer and historian whose treatise *Geographica*, extant today, is an encyclopedic study of Mediterranean places and peoples. Nicolaus of Damascus (c. 64 B.C.E.–after 4 C.E.), versatile Greek or Syrian writer, was a friend and biographer of both Augustus and Herod, and a tutor to the twin children of Marcus Antonius and Cleopatra.

561.4–5   our old friend and tutor, Tyrannion] Tyrannio the Elder (Latin), a Greek grammarian born in the early first century B.C.E., was originally called Theophrastus but nicknamed Tyrannio by his teacher. Brought to Rome as a slave, he was soon emancipated and became a teacher and librarian. His most famous pupil was the geographer Strabo.

561.29–30   Athenodorus of Tarsus] See note 491.35–492.2.

565.12–13   Clodia, daughter of . . . Fulvia] Of noble birth, Fulvia (c. 83–40 B.C.E.) wielded considerable power through her successive marriages to three Roman statesmen—Publius Clodius Pulcher, Gaius Scribonius Curio, and Marcus Antonius. Her marriage to Clodius produced a son, also named Publius Clodius Pulcher, and a daughter, Claudia (born c. 56 B.C.E.). After the assassination of Caesar and the formation of the Second Triumvirate, Marcus Antonius married Claudia, his stepdaughter, to Octavius as a means of cementing the two triumvirs' relationship.

567.32–34   Gaius Octavius . . . consulship of Rome.] In 59 B.C.E., Gaius Octavius, father of the future Augustus, sailed to Rome to stand for election as consul but died before reaching the city. His son Octavius was four years old at the time.

567.35   your daughter, Octavia] Octavia the Younger (c. 69–11 B.C.E.), daughter of Gaius Octavius and Atia Balba, sister of the future Augustus, was the fourth wife of Marcus Antonius.

568.32–34   Among those proscribed . . . uncle of Antonius.] Even though Lucius Aemilius Paullus, consul in 50 B.C.E., supported Cicero in condemning the Second Triumvirate, the triumvir Lepidus allowed him to escape from Rome. Lucius Julius Caesar, consul in 64 B.C.E., fled to the safety of the home of his sister, Marcus Antonius's mother, after his proscription. He was eventually pardoned.

571.22   Amphipolis] Ancient Greek and later Roman city near the Aegean, on the east bank of the Strymon.

578.16   my Terentia] Maecenas's wife.

578.25–38   The girl . . . never took place.] At the time Octavius married Marcus Antonius's stepdaughter Claudia (see note 565.12–13), he was betrothed to Servilia, daughter of Publius Servilius Isauricus, who served as consul in 48 B.C.E. with Julius Caesar. Octavius compensated Servilius Isauricus by awarding him a second consulship, in 41 B.C.E.

578.36–579.7   The second . . . a divorce.] In *Augustus* 62, Suetonius reports that Octavius divorced Claudia, Marcus Antonius's stepdaughter, before the marriage was consummated. See also note 565.12–13.

579.8–10   third contract . . . with Scribonia] Octavius married Scribonia (c. 70 B.C.E.–16 C.E.) in 40 B.C.E. as a conciliatory gesture to Sextus Pompeius, who was the husband of Scribonia's niece or sister. Scribonia was the mother of Octavius's only child, Julia, and accompanied her daughter into exile in 2 B.C.E.

579.21   admired his father] In the Roman civil wars, Livy was sympathetic to Gnaeus Pompeius Magnus, or Pompey the Great (106–48 B.C.E.), and more generally to the Republican cause.

579.32   his Julia.] Julia the Elder (39 B.C.E.–14 C.E.), only daughter of Augustus. Her mother was Scribonia, the emperor's second wife. Julia was briefly married to Marcellus (25–23 B.C.E.) and then Agrippa (21 B.C.E.). After Agrippa's death (12 B.C.E.), Augustus forced her to marry his heir, Tiberius.

579.32–34   He divorced Scribonia . . . married again.] Octavius divorced Scribonia on the day of Julia's birth (October 30, 39 B.C.E.) in order to marry Livia Drusilla (56 B.C.E.–29 C.E.), also known as Julia Augusta after 14 C.E. She was Augustus's third and last wife.

580.26–30   Among those exiled . . . wife, Livia.] The suggestion is that Livy would be amused by the irony that Augustus had exiled both Livia, his future wife and eventual empress, and her son Tiberius, whom he would later adopt as his son and who eventually succeeded him.

583.13–16   Priest to the deified Julius . . . to mine.] In 40 B.C.E., the Senate confirmed Marcus Antonius as the *flamen Divi Julii*, a priest of the deified Julius Caesar, the first person to serve in that role. As the adopted son of the deified Julius, Octavius therefore shared a divine heritage with his great-uncle.

583.23   Bacchus . . . prefer Dionysus?] Dionysus (Bacchus in the Roman pantheon), the Greek god of wine, theater, and ecstatic inebriation, was the son of Zeus and Semele.

584.7–9   High Priest of Heliopolis, the Incarnation of Thoth . . . Keeper of the *Book of Magic*.] High Priest of Heliopolis, or the High Priest of Ra (*wr-m3w*), was an ancient Egyptian title, literally "Greatest of the Seers of Heliopolis." Thoth, Egyptian god of learning and the patron of scribes, was represented as having the head of either a baboon or an ibis. Among the Divine Books said to have been written by Thoth were books of magic.

586.3   CLEOPATRA, THE INCARNATE ISIS] Cleopatra (69–30 B.C.E.), last ruler of the Ptolemaic dynasty of Egypt, was considered in her lifetime the incarnation of Isis, the Egyptian mother-goddess to whom great magical powers were ascribed. Worship of Isis eventually spread throughout the Roman Empire.

586.11–12   Eurystheus and that Heracles . . . the gods.] In Greek myth, Heracles performed his famous Labors as an atonement for the murders of his wife and children. The twelve Labors were set for him by the cruel Eurystheus, king of Tiryns, one of the cities of Mycenae.

588.21   Supreme God, Amen-Ra] Egyptian god, in whom the deities Amen and Ra, the sun god, were merged; at the height of Egypt's power during the New Kingdom, Amen-Ra was the king of the Egyptian pantheon.

588.31–32   Hermopolis and Akhetaton] Hermopolis, ancient Egyptian city on the Nile between Upper and Middle Egypt, devoted to the cult of Hermes, who was thought by the Greeks to correspond to the Egyptian deity Thoth. Akhetaton (present-day Tell el-Amarna or Amarna) was an ancient Egyptian city on the Nile that was founded in 1336 B.C.E. by the pharaoh Akhenaton, who wanted to convert his country to the monotheistic worship of the Sun, represented as a disk known as Aton.

588.32   we were God and Goddess, Osiris and Isis.] Marcus Antonius and Cleopatra presented themselves both as the Greek gods Dionysus and Aphrodite and as the Egyptian deities Osiris and Isis, who were siblings and consorts. Osiris was the god of death and the underworld (see also note 586.3).

588.33   Thebes of the Hundred Gates] Ancient Egyptian city on the Nile, in Upper Egypt near the Valley of the Kings. Homer refers to the city as having a hundred gates (*Iliad*, Book IX, 381–84), in contradistinction to the Greek city of Thebes, which had seven gates.

589.24   my Parthian campaign] In 37 B.C.E., Marcus Antonius amassed a force of 100,000 against the Parthians but made only minor conquests, suffering heavy losses.

589.26   Antioch] The capital of the Hellenistic Greek kingdom of the Seleucid dynasty (current Syria), founded by one of Alexander the Great's generals. Syria was the most important Roman colony in Asia, and Antioch the third largest city in the Empire.

592.3   Via Herculeana] Ancient road on a mound, near Lake Lucrine in southern Italy, Campania.

592.20   Mylae] See note 498.6–9.

593.10–11   Phraates . . . eastern provinces.] Phraates IV (d. 2 B.C.E.), king of Parthia (c. 37–2 B.C.E.), who repulsed Marcus Antonius in 36 B.C.E. (see also note 589.24). Four years earlier, a large Parthian army had invaded eastern Roman territory in 40 B.C.E. In 20 B.C.E., Augustus and Phraates entered a long-term peace agreement, allowing both rulers to deploy resources and military forces to other frontiers.

594.1   Pontifex Maximus] Highest officer of the state religion of Rome during the Republic, and director of the college of *pontifices*. The college's duties included oversight of games, festivals, and sacrifices and advised magistrates on matters of sacred law. An increasingly political position, it was a title held by Julius Caesar, M. Aemilius Lepidus, and Augustus.

599.34   nominally a Jew] Nicolaus of Damascus may have been a Hellenized Jew. See also note 561.2–3.

599.36–600.1   King Herod . . . of all Judea] Herod I (c. 73–4 B.C.E.), also known as Herod the Great, was appointed king of the client state of Judea by Marcus Antonius and the Senate. Despite having backed Marcus Antonius in the civil wars, Herod was confirmed in his rule by Augustus and expanded the territories of Judea.

602.5–6　some Medea or Circe] In Greek mythology, Medea aided Jason in his quest to capture the Golden Fleece. Euripides's tragedy *Medea* adapts the aftermath of that tale: now returned to Greece, Jason deserts Medea in order to marry Creusa, the daughter of Creon, king of Corinth; in revenge, Medea murders the princess and later kills her own sons by Jason. In Homer's *Odyssey*, Circe is a powerful nymph whose magic turns Odysseus's men into swine; he spends a year with her as her lover before he resumes his voyage home.

603.4　Ptolemy Caesar—] Ptolemy XV Caesar (47–30 B.C.E.), nicknamed Caesarion (Little Caesar), was the son of Cleopatra by Julius Caesar. After Caesar's assassination, Caesarion was titular co-pharaoh of Egypt with his mother; he was murdered on Augustus's orders shortly after Cleopatra's suicide in August, 30 B.C.E.

604.25–26　Crassus and Ventidius on their campaigns] While governor of Syria (54 B.C.E.), Crassus, who together with Caesar and Pompey made up the First Triumvirate, invaded Parthia without the approval of the Senate; during the battle of Carrhae in the following year his legions were decisively defeated and Crassus mortally wounded. The battle of Carrhae marked the end of the First Triumvirate. Publius Ventidius partly avenged the Roman defeat at Carrhae with important victories in Asia and Syria in 39 and 38 B.C.E.

613.29　Aedile] Roman magistrate responsible for the maintenance of roads, the water supply, and the market as well as administration of the games.

614.13　Temple known as Serapis and Isis . . . Roman Senate.] Serapis was a god combining Egyptian and Greek characteristics whose worship was promoted by the Ptolemies. The Temple to Serapis and Isis was located in the Campus Martius, east of the Saepta Julia. Augustus and Agrippa took legal measures to repress Egyptian cults.

614.21　MUNATIUS PLANCUS] Lucius Munatius Plancus (c. 87–15 B.C.E.), Roman statesman and consul (42 B.C.E.) remembered for his shifting loyalties. He abandoned Brutus and Cicero to their fates when Lepidus, Octavius, and Marcus Antonius formed the Second Triumvirate, and switched his allegiance to Octavius after Marcus Antonius's campaign against the Parthians ended badly.

614.38–615.1　Gaius Antonius . . . the Conspirator Catiline] The aristocrat Lucius Sergius Catilina ("Catiline") plotted to overthrow the Republic during the consulship of Cicero and Gaius Antonius (63 B.C.E.); after the plot was discovered and denounced by Cicero, Catiline fled Rome. In 62 B.C.E., forces under Gaius Antonius engaged with Catiline's army near Pistoia, Italy, where Catiline was killed.

615.36–37　the Medians] The Medes, an ancient people whose language was akin to Old Persian. They occupied the mountainous areas southwest of the Caspian Sea, in modern-day Iran.

617.32–33   Ephesus . . . Island of Samos] Ephesus, an ancient Greek city on the Ionian coast. Like the Aegean island of Samos, part of the Roman province of Asia since 129 B.C.E.

618.24   the Campus Martius . . . Temple of Bellona] The Campus Martius was the level ground between the Tiber River and the Capitoline, Quirinal, and Pincian Hills, increasingly used during the Republic as a public space for numerous temples and monuments recording victories. During the imperial era, it also became a site for entertainment. Dedicated in 296 B.C.E., the Temple of Bellona (Roman goddess of war) stood in the Campus Martius and was a gathering place for the Senate when it had to deal with military matters.

629.38–40   Via Sacra . . . Temple of Julius Caesar . . . morning sunlight.] The Via Sacra (the "sacred way") was the most important and most heavily traveled thoroughfare in Rome, running from the top of the Velia to the Forum. The Temple of Julius Caesar (42–29 B.C.E.) stood prominently in the middle of the eastern edge of the Forum. See Suetonius, *Augustus* 28.3: "Augustus improved the city so greatly that he could rightly boast to have found it sun-baked brick and left it marble."

632.29   PANDATERIA] Small barren island of volcanic origin, located twenty-nine miles from the coastal city of Gaeta (Lazio) in the Tyrrhenian Sea, best known as the island to which Augustus banished his daughter, Julia, in 2 B.C.E.

635.14–15   LUCIUS VARIUS RUFUS . . . PUBLIUS VERGILIUS MARO] Lucius Varius Rufus (c. 74–14 B.C.E.), Latin poet of the Augustan age, friend and literary executor of Vergil. After Vergil's death in 19 B.C.E., Varus and Tucca prepared the still-unfinished manuscript *Aeneid* for publication (see also note 677.31–33). Publius Vergilius Maro (70–19 B.C.E.), commonly known as Vergil or Virgil, the greatest Latin poet of the Augustan age, author of the *Eclogues* (42–37 B.C.E.), the *Georgics* (37–30 B.C.E.), and the *Aeneid* (29–19 B.C.E.).

635.22   Claudius Nero] Tiberius Claudius Nero (85–33 B.C.E.), member of the *gens Claudia*, first husband of Livia, and biological father of the emperor Tiberius.

636.2   our friend Pollio] Gaius Asinius Pollio (76 B.C.E.–4 C.E.), Roman statesman, supporter of Marcus Antonius, historian, and patron of Vergil. While distributing lands to veterans in Cisalpine Gaul in 41 B.C.E., he saved Vergil's property from confiscation. Vergil's *Eclogues* may have been dedicated to Pollio.

636.8   Aemilius Macer] Latin poet (d. 16 B.C.E.), two of whose poems survive in fragments.

636.9   your "admirer" Mevius] Maevius, or Mevius, Latin poet whom Vergil dismisses as worthless in *Eclogue* III, lines 90–91.

637.35–36   Ancient Muse of Memory, Mneme] Classical Greek mythology identifies nine muses, but according to an earlier tradition there were only three: Mneme (Memory) and her sisters Aoide (Song) and Melete (Meditation). In his poem about the origins of the gods, *Theogony*, the Greek poet Hesiod (fl. c. 700 B.C.E.) describes the canonical nine muses, daughters of Zeus and Mnemosyne ("Memory").

638.10   Calliope—] Muse of epic poetry. Hesiod identifies Calliope as the noblest of the nine muses.

638.11–13   my own work upon . . . against politics.] A few surviving fragments of a poem by Varius entitled *De Morte* ("On Death") may have concerned the assassination of Julius Caesar.

638.21–22   stolen . . . from Antiphanes of Athens] None of the plays of the prolific Greek poet Antiphanes (c. 408–334 B.C.E.) survive.

639.19–20   story of the Greek Orpheus . . . Vergil has written so beautifully—] See Vergil's *Georgics*, Book IV, lines 464–527.

642.6   FURIUS BIBACULUS] Marcus Furius Bibaculus (b. 103 B.C.E.), Latin satirical poet of the Augustan age, mentioned together with Catullus by sources. His work survives only in small fragments.

642.26–27   a Tenth Muse, that of Dullness] There are nine canonical muses: see note 637.35–36.

647.8–9   repairs upon the Via Flaminia] Built in 220 B.C.E. by C. Flaminius and repaired by Augustus during his seventh consulship (27 B.C.E.), the Via Flaminia was the great northern road of Italy, leading from Rome through the Apennines to the Adriatic coast. The repairs to Via Flaminia were among numerous restoration projects undertaken by Augustus. See Augustus, *Res Gestae Divi Augusti* (*The Deeds of the Divine Augustus*), VI.20.

652.24–26   once, more than . . . expelled from Rome.] In 161 B.C.E., the praetor M. Pomponius, acting on a decree passed by the Senate, expelled teachers of rhetoric and philosophy. During this period, when the Roman state was conquering and absorbing the city-states of Greece, the Senate feared the corrosive influence of Greek learning on Roman moral and political life.

652.33   ALBIUS TIBULLUS] Latin elegiac poet (c. 55–19 B.C.E.) of the Augustan age.

653.19–21   poems upon your lady friends . . . commander in chief, Messalla.] Tibullus's surviving work comprises two books of love poetry, the first concerning his mistress, Delia, the second a subsequent mistress, Nemesis. In addition to the love poems, both books contain works in honor of his patron, Valerius Messalla Corvinus. In his *Amores*, Ovid writes: "So Nemesis and Delia will live on, one his new love, the other his first."

657.25–27   the Claudian, the Julian, and the Octavian tribes . . . the Claudian.] A central unit of Roman social organization was the clan or tribe, *gens* (plural *gentes*), from which Romans derived their names. The *gens Claudia* and *gens Julia* were distinguished patrician families in ancient Rome, the *gens Octavia* an established plebeian family. Through his father, Marcellus was related to the Claudian *gens*; through his mother, Octavia, to the Julian and Octavian *gentes*. Livia's son Tiberius, by her first husband, Tiberius Claudius, was related only to the Claudians.

658.32   the completed *Georgics*] Vergil's second major work, after the *Eclogues*, composed 37 to 30 B.C.E. at the request of his patron Maecenas. The *Georgics* ("farming") refers to the imminent composition of Vergil's great national epic, the *Aeneid*, which the poet had nearly completed at the time of his death, in 19 B.C.E.

658.35–36   poem upon the founding of our city.] The *Aeneid*, composed from 29 to 19 B.C.E., about the adventures of Aeneas, the refugee Trojan prince who was the legendary founder of Rome, explicitly connects Rome's mythic past to its golden Augustan present. Aeneas's son, Iulus, was the mythic ancestor of the *gens Julia*.

659.17   Via Campana] Major Roman road on the right bank of the Tiber.

660.33–35   Antonius Musa . . . already being made.] Antonius Musa, a celebrated botanist, was physician to Augustus and cured the emperor of a serious illness in 23 B.C.E., earning him considerable acclaim. The plant group Musa, which includes the banana and plantain, was named after him.

661.27–28   her son . . . had them.] See the *Aeneid*, Book VI, lines 854–86.

662.17–19   Then she gave . . . dead faint.] The fourth-century *Life* of Vergil by Aelius Donatus is the source of this anecdote. Book 6 of Vergil's *Aeneid* contains a laudatory reference to Octavia's son and Augustus's presumptive heir Marcellus, who died aged nineteen in 23 B.C.E. Donatus relates how Octavia fainted when Vergil read this passage to the imperial family. The French painter Jean-Joseph Taillasson's *Vergil Reading the* Aeneid *to Augustus and Octavia* (oil on canvas, 1787) is the best-known pictorial representation of this moving episode.

663.33   Jullus Antonius] Roman statesman and poet (43–2 B.C.E.), second son of Marcus Antonius and his third wife, Fulvia. Raised by Octavia, favored by Augustus, he became romantically involved with Augustus's daughter, Julia.

664.1–4   Now my first-born . . . necessity of your policy.] Marcellus died in 23 B.C.E. at nineteen in Baiae, Campania, while in the service of his uncle. Agrippa divorced Marcellus's sister, Marcella, in 21 B.C.E. to marry Julia, daughter of Augustus.

667.31   Vipsania,"] Vipsania Agrippina (36 B.C.E.–20 C.E.), daughter of Agrippa and Pomponia Caecilia Attica, and first wife of Tiberius.

670.1   TIMAGENES] Greek rhetorician and historian who came to Rome as a captive in 55 B.C.E. and was later freed. Timagenes wrote a work on the deeds of Augustus, which does not survive. He was initially favored by Augustus, but his candor put him at odds with the emperor.

671.13   my little place above the Digentia] Horace's country retreat, his Sabine villa (northeast of Rome), celebrated in his verse. The villa was beside the stream Digentia. The ruins of the villa have been located near present-day Licenza and suggest a structure on a grand scale.

672.18–19   Aristotle, in those marvelous *Conversations*] Except for small fragments, the dialogues of the Greek philosopher Aristotle (384–322 B.C.E.) do not survive.

672.35–38   the young Tibullus . . . his patron Messalla] See notes 652.33 and 653.19–21.

673.27   propose to write a Life] Nicolaus's *Life of Augustus* (*Bios Kaisaros*) was completed after the emperor's death in 14 C.E.

676.15   the Circus] A circus was a Roman stadium for chariot-racing and other entertainment. Here, the reference is to the Circus Maximus, the largest of the circuses, located in the valley between the Palatine and Aventine Hills. Founded in the sixth century B.C.E. and rebuilt by Julius Caesar, it accommodated about 150,000 spectators.

677.20–21   Megara . . . the murderer Sciron.] In Greek mythology, Sciron was a bandit who preyed on travelers on the cliff-hugging road from Athens to Megara; he would demand that his victims wash his feet, and as they knelt to do so he would kick them into the sea. Sciron was eventually killed by Theseus, the founder of Athens, who threw him over the same cliff.

677.31–33   elicited from Octavius . . . his *Aeneid* be destroyed.] At the time of Vergil's death in 19 B.C.E., the *Aeneid* remained unfinished: the text as we have it has incomplete verses as well as a number of inconsistencies. In the biography of Vergil that forms part of his *Lives of the Poets*, the historian Suetonius (69–c. 122 C.E.) describes how Vergil instructed his literary executors, Varius and Tucca, to destroy his manuscript, a request that Augustus himself countermanded.

680.21–23   latest law . . . reduced to six hundred members.] In 18 B.C.E., Augustus purged the Senate, reducing its members from 900 or 1,000 to 600. There were various reforms of the Senate throughout the Augustan period.

680.31–40   The first forbids . . . her rank.] In 18 or 17 B.C.E., the Senate passed the *Lex Julia de maritandis ordinibus*, intended to promote marriage and procreation while regulating marriage between people of different classes.

681.1–9   But the second part . . . as a procurer.] In 18 B.C.E., the Senate passed the *Lex Julia de adulteriis*, making adultery a crime against the family and the state.

681.13–14   Livian rather . . . Julian Law] Roman laws were typically named after the consuls presiding when the laws were passed; the suggestion here is that Livia, rather than Octavius, is behind the moral legislation.

683.16–17 to compose the choral hymn . . . this May.] Celebrated during the Republic and Empire, the secular games (*ludi saeculare*), involving sacrifices and theatrical performances taking place over three days and three nights, were intended to signal the arrival of a new age or *saeculum*. When Augustus revived the secular games in 17 B.C.E. as a celebration of the new world order, they had not been held since 146 B.C.E. He commissioned Horace to write the official hymn, the *Carmen saeculare* (*Secular Hymn*), which was sung by paired choruses of boys and girls.

689.17–23 The old King . . . husband's kingdom.] After the death of the Bosporan king Asander (110–17 B.C.E.), a certain Scribonius became the consort of Dynamis, the widowed queen, and ascended to the throne. Scribonius, who was anti-Roman, was killed by the people of Bosporus after Agrippa intervened.

690.38 Scamander River] See Book XXI of the *Iliad*: the Scamander is a river near Troy whose tutelary god is roused to anger by Achilles's killing spree, which, the god complains, has choked his waters with dead bodies.

691.5 drachmas] Drachma, ancient Greek silver coin.

694.32 PUBLIUS OVIDIUS NASO TO SEXTUS PROPER] Publius Ovidius Naso (43 B.C.E.–17 C.E.), commonly known as Ovid, Latin poet of the Augustan period best known at the time for his erotic poetry (*The Art of Love, Ars Amatoria*, and *The Cure for Love, Remedia Amoris*), who would go on to write his mythological epic, *Metamorphoses*. Sextus Propertius (c. 48–15 B.C.E.), Latin elegiac poet of the Augustan age, member of the circle of poets under the patronage of Maecenas.

695.13–14 Yesterday . . . Octavius Caesar's birth] Augustus (Gaius Octavius) was born on September 23, 63 B.C.E.

696.3–4 not the Saturnalia . . . upon me?"] Celebrated in mid-December in honor of Saturn, Saturnalia had a carnival-like atmosphere in which Roman social norms were upended. Slaves were permitted temporary liberty to do as they wished, and a mock-king, *Saturnalicius princeps*, presided over the festivities. Much of the spirit of the Saturnalia was preserved, as the holiday was adapted by Christians, in Christmas and Boxing Day.

696.22 Sempronius Gracchus] Alleged paramour of Julia, daughter of Augustus. Tacitus calls him *pervicax adulter* (persistent adulterer).

707.8–709.3 Restless . . . sacred grove.] Although invented by Williams, this poem, a pastiche of Ovidan themes and formal elements, strongly recalls the first poem of the collection of exile poetry known as *Tristia* ("Sorrows"), in which the poet imagines his new book of poems arriving in Rome but finding no welcome there.

712.6 Claudian] *Gens Claudia*, one of Rome's oldest and noblest families.

716.26 GNAEUS CALPURNIUS PISO] Roman statesman (c. 44 B.C.E.–20 C.E.) belonging to the distinguished *gens Calpurnia*. A friend of Tiberius, he held consulship with him in 7 B.C.E. and was appointed governor of Syria in 17 C.E. He took his life in 20 C.E. after the Senate prosecuted him for the death of Germanicus, heir apparent to Tiberius.

717.9–11   The poet Ovid . . . suggestive and improper.] The precise reasons for Ovid's exile from Rome in 8 C.E. remain unknown; however, in Book II of the autobiographical poem he wrote in exile, *Tristia*, Ovid writes that "two crimes, a poem and a blunder, have brought me ruin."

717.12   mimes performed *The Adulterous Wife*] A mime in Roman culture was a type of popular entertainment representing scenes from ordinary life often in a low or ridiculous manner; as such, it differed greatly from both tragedy and comedy. The adulterous wife was a stock character in such mimes.

717.22–25   Sempronius Gracchus . . . the Greek Demosthenes] With the exception of Ovid, all alleged lovers of Julia.

718.5–6   four elder Vestal Virgins.] Chosen between the ages of six and ten, the Vestal Virgins, *sacerdotes Vestales*, served a minimum of thirty years. See also note 492.17–18.

718.6   Plebeian Games] Roman festival established c. 220 B.C.E. in honor of Jupiter. Held in November, the *Ludi Plebeii* included theatrical performances, games, and other spectacles for the entertainment of the common people.

720.1   MARCELLA] See note 664.1–4.

724.9–10   not since Actium . . . against Roman.] See note 497.4–15.

729.1   Gaius Calvisius Sabinus!] Roman statesman and consul (39 B.C.E.). He attempted to protect Caesar on the Ides of March.

729.6–9   Lucius Passienus Rufus . . . one of the new men] Roman senator and consul in 4 B.C.E. with Gaius Calvisius Sabinus. The designation *novus homo* (new man) refers to the first person in a given family to serve in the Senate.

740.12   PAULLUS FABIUS MAXIMUS] Roman statesman (d. 14 C.E.), consul in 11 B.C.E., and an intimate friend of Augustus.

755.40   Philippus of Athens.] Williams's invention.

756.23–36   *At the age of nineteen . . . in battle. . . .*] See Augustus, *Res Gestae*, lines 1–2.

756.27–28   *Gaius Pansa and Aulus Hirtius*] See notes 497.4–15 and 539.32–33.

761.1–7   Plato and the Pythagoreans . . . opposing doctrines of Parmenides and Zeno] Both Plato and the Pythagoreans theorized about the relationship of the material to the eternal. Plato's dialogues present Socrates as arriving at a theory according to which objects and even certain concepts that are apprehensible to humans ("justice") were mere reflections or instantiations of absolute essences ("Forms"); members of the Pythagorean sect believed in "metempsychosis," i.e., that the human soul is immortal and migrates, after one body dies, into another. Plato's dialogue *Parmenides* imagines a confrontation between Socrates and his philosophical opponents, Parmenides, who argued that the cosmos is an unchanging "one," and his younger associate Zeno.

761.13–16   *Wars, both civil and foreign . . . twenty-one times.*] See *Res Gestae*, 3–4.

765.1–7   *the senate decreed . . . temples of the gods.*] See *Res Gestae*, 9.

766.3   Alexander . . . died so young] Alexander the Great (356–323 B.C.E.) was thirty-two when he died after a ten-day illness.

769.4–5   little poem of Horace's . . . Vergil to Athens?] See Horace, *Odes*, I.iii.

769.9–14   And Vergil . . . Aeolus . . . see nothing.] In the *Aeneid*, Book I, lines 50–80, Juno, who seeks to prevent Aeneas from reaching Italy, asks the god Aeolus, keeper of the winds, to unleash his winds in order to create a storm that will shipwreck the hero.

769.16–19   Palinurus, the helmsman . . . unknown shore.] In the *Aeneid*, Palinurus is the helmsman of Aeneas's ship who falls overboard; his death is viewed as a sacrifice that guarantees the hero's eventual arrival in Italy. See Book V, lines 779–871.

769.27–33   Banish the poet Ovid . . . climate of Rome.] Ovid languished in exile on the Black Sea until his death in 17 C.E. See also note 717.9–11.

773.23–29   *the dictatorship . . . did I accept*] See *Res Gestae*, 5.

774.19–20   Publius Quintilius Varus] Roman general (46 B.C.E.–9 C.E.) whose catastrophic loss of three legions to Germanic tribes in the battle of the Teutoburg Forest in 9 C.E. halted Roman expansion beyond the Rhine.

774.35–37   Arminius of the Cherusci . . . gift of citizenship.] Born a prince of the Germanic Cherusci tribe, Arminius (c. 19 B.C.E.–21 C.E.) served in the Roman auxiliary forces, attaining equestrian status. His knowledge of Roman military theory and tactics was crucial to his defeat of the Romans in the battle of the Teutoburg Forest.

775.23   Maroboduus] Chief of the Macromanni (d. 37 C.E.), a Germanic group of people.

778.29–30   *I hate and I love*, Catullus said] See Catullus 85: "I hate and I love. Why I do this, perhaps you ask. / I know not, but I feel it happening and I am tortured."

778.30–32   Clodia Pulcher . . . her death.] The scandalous love life of Clodia Pulcher, thought to be the addressee of Catullus's love poems, resulted in legal entanglements that eventually involved Cicero, who defended one of Clodia's lovers in a murder case that resulted from a charge of poisoning brought by Clodia. Her brother, Clodius, one of Cicero's political enemies, was married to Fulvia, eventually the mother of Julia's lover Jullus Antonius.

781.22–26   the Senate . . . Father of my Country.] See Augustus, *Res Gestae*, 35: "In my thirteenth consulship [2 B.C.E.] the Senate, the equestrian order, and the whole of people of Rome gave me the title of *Father of my Country* and resolved that this should be inscribed in the porch of my house and in the Curia Julia and in the Forum Augustum below the chariot which had been set there in my honor by decree of the Senate."

787.2–3   LUCIUS ANNAEUS SENECA] Commonly known as Seneca or Seneca the Younger (c. 4 B.C.E.–65 C.E.), Roman statesman, Stoic, and playwright whose works include *Thyestes*, *Hercules*, and *Medea*.

787.22–23   unfortunate time . . . waste of Corsica] Seneca was banished by Claudius to Corsica (41–49 C.E.) for alleged adultery with Julia Livilla, sister of the former emperor Caligula.

791.20–21   Tiberius . . . Caligula . . . Claudius] Tiberius Caesar Augustus (42 B.C.E.–37 C.E.), Augustus's heir, reigned from 14 to 37 C.E. and was portrayed by Suetonius and Tacitus as brutal and vengeful. Caligula, formally Gaius Caesar Augustus Germanicus (12–41 C.E.), third Roman emperor, was known as cruel, autocratic, and capricious ("for me anything is licit," Suetonius, *Caligula* 29), reigning from 37 C.E. until his assassination in 41 C.E. Tiberius Claudius Caesar Augustus Germanicus (10 B.C.E.–54 C.E.), known as Claudius, was the fourth Roman emperor (41–54 C.E.). Claudius conducted *in camera* trials that brought ruin on leading citizens and alienated the Senate by entrusting administration to Greek freedmen.

791.21–26   our new Emperor . . . Octavius Caesar.] Seneca was tutor to the young Nero and became an important political advisor after Nero became emperor, in 54 C.E.; at the beginning of the new reign he guided his former pupil, seeking to reverse the worst abuses of the Claudian regime. Nero's reign, which became a byword for grandiosity, lasted fourteen years; he was eventually condemned by the Senate and, in the face of a military coup by his generals, committed suicide, in 68 C.E., three years after he had condemned Seneca to death.

RELATED WRITINGS

795.18   Nelson Nye] Nelson C. Nye (1907–1993), a writer and reviewer of Western novels. Writing in his *New York Times Book Review* column, "Western Roundup" (April 3, 1960), Nye harshly reviewed *Butcher's Crossing*, dismissing it as a plotless and unreadable Western. See also pp. 1–255 in this volume.

807.19–20   set in the American West . . . of the 1880's.] In *Butcher's Crossing*, the hunter Miller tells Andrews that he saw the large herd of buffalo in Colorado in "the fall of sixty-three." Andrews asks, "Ten years . . . Why haven't you gone back?" See pp. 27–29 in this volume and note 34.33–34.

809.19–37   Those who put . . . inner World.] "Reflections on the Composition of *Memoirs of Hadrian*," in Marguerite Yourcenar, *Memoirs of Hadrian* (New York: Farrar, Straus & Co., 1963).

811.16–17   review of . . . *The Young Caesar*] Graves's review "Caesar and the Pirates" appeared in *The New Republic* on May 26, 1958, and was later reprinted as "The Pirates Who Captured Caesar," in Robert Graves, *Food for Centaurs* (Garden City, New York: Doubleday, 1960).

812.2–5   the great Latin historian . . . required it.] The great Latin historian is Livy. Cf. Lytton Strachey, *Spectatorial Essays* 13 (1964): "When Livy said that he would have made Pompey win the battle of Pharsalia, if the turn of the sentence had required it, he was not talking utter nonsense, but simply expressing an important truth in a highly paradoxical way,—that the first duty of a great historian is to be an artist."

816.2–3   essay by Henry James . . . year 1900.] In 1900, James's essay "Future of the Novel" appeared in the *Saturday Review of Books and Art*, a weekly supplement of *The New York Times*. In England, the essay had appeared previously in *The International Library of Famous Literature* (1899).

820.26–35   There were roses . . . my hand.] William Carlos Williams, "The Act," published in Williams's collection *The Clouds* (1948).

833.12–17   Henry James . . . the mirror."] Henry James, "Future of the Novel" (1899). See note 816.2–3.

*This book is set in 10 point ITC Galliard, a face designed
for digital composition by Matthew Carter and based
on the sixteenth-century face Granjon. The paper is acid-free
lightweight opaque that will not turn yellow or brittle with age.
The binding is sewn, which allows the book to open easily and lie flat.
The binding board is covered in Brillianta, a woven rayon cloth
made by Van Heek–Scholco Textielfabrieken, Holland.
Composition by Dianna Logan, Clearmont, MO.
Printing by Sheridan Grand Rapids, Grand Rapids, MI.
Binding by Dekker Bookbinding, Wyoming, MI.
Designed by Bruce Campbell.*

THE LIBRARY OF AMERICA SERIES

Library of America fosters appreciation of America's literary heritage by publishing, and keeping permanently in print, authoritative editions of America's best and most significant writing. An independent nonprofit organization, it was founded in 1979 with seed funding from the National Endowment for the Humanities and the Ford Foundation.

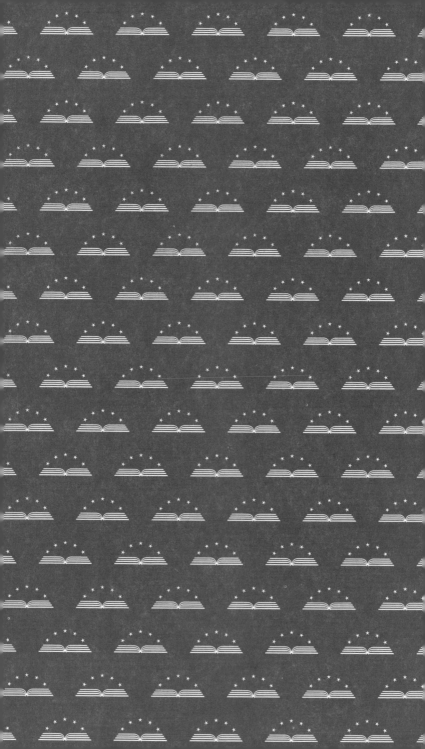